LIVING IN LITTLE ROCK WITH MISS LITTLE ROCK

LIVING IN
LITTLE ROCK WITH
MISS LITTLE ROCK

LIVING
IN
LITTLE ROCK
WITH MISS
LITTLE
ROCK

a novel by

JACK
BUTLER

 ABACUS

An *Abacus* Book

First published in the United States by Alfred A. Knopf, Inc., 1993
First published in Great Britain by Abacus 1993
This edition published by Abacus 1994

Copyright © Jack Butler 1993

The moral right of the author has been asserted.

Grateful acknowledgment is made to the following for
permission to reprint previously published material:
Arkansas Democrat-Gazette: Excerpt from an article,
December 19, 1981, and two cartoons by George Fisher;
reprinted by permission of the *Arkansas Democrat-Gazette*.
United Media: *Peanuts* cartoon, June 14, 1981,
reprinted by permission of UFS, Inc.

A CIP catalogue record for this book
is available from the British Library.

ISBN 0 349 10493 X

Printed in England by Clays Ltd, St Ives plc

Abacus
A Division of
Little, Brown and Company (UK)
Brettenham House
Lancaster Place
London WC2E 7EN

For my father, who taught me to believe

I'll wait for you, I'll wait for you,
On the other shore.

> —Stephen's Law
> "The Other Shore"

Intense sorrow often brings with it a heightened esthetic perception: to the sufferer, shabby tenements seem to glow with color, and past and present time to collapse into one and become almost tangible.

> —Marian Ury, reviewing Yasunari Kawabata's
> *Palm-of-the-Hand Stories* in *The New York Times
> Book Review* (August 21, 1988)

What is there here but weather?

> —Wallace Stevens
> "Waving Adieu, Adieu, Adieu"

CONTENTS

AN INTERLUDE WITHOUT   461

PART FOUR: DETECTIVE STORY

PART FIVE: KINGDOM COME

PART
ONE

ELECTIONS

1

INCARNATION IS
JUST THE RAPTURE
IN REVERSE

Howdy, I'm the Holy Ghost. Talk about your omniscient narrators. What's the differential in me and a computer program writes poetry? None. Nothing. Time. The red-haired pretty-girl.

She comes in, green-eye fire-hair, sweet stamp of the freshest thing, unkillable lilt, into the breeze-blow sun-curtain kitchen, and there, there in the window—

No.

No, I'm getting ahead of myself. As in fact I am one of the few what can. As in fact I yam the only what can. In my ass is yo beginning. This *is* the beginning, right? You tell me, you the one knows. For me it aint like a major distinction.

Let me put it this way. You want to skip ahead to the last syllable of recorded ramalam, ok by me. It's the why I'm say all this other said, but aint really the last, nor not the shall-be-first neither. Just some extra where, orbital, ur-numinous. Her-numinous?

Because what is a story, a life of? An action is in 3-D: in 4-D a thing. So sooner or later you contain all in your head this thing, howsomever (actionwise) enterest thou it, n'est-ce pas? It don't order what difference you make it in: Read any.

That's what I said to the other three-quarters of The HQ, The Holy Quaternity, but They have told me—The Two of Them and Miss Liza Jane— They have All Three emphasized that you need this in time-wordical sequence. Aint let me run loose since Pentecost, but orders is orders. *We know you can do it, H.G.*, They said. *We have faith in you. Go, Ghost, go!*

So geht's, Zeitgeist. Time to settle down, settle down to time. *Hier geht nichts*, as they don't say: *Ahem!*

Welcome to Little Rock, Arkansas, Mr. and Mrs. America, yeah. The time, the ti-yem, is the early 1980s, that quaint little interval when nothing much happened. Oh, an off President almost offed, and a new altitude record for the prime, and a bunch of S & Ls decided it was a good time to invest in Texas real estate, and a plane got shot down over Russia, and some Koo-Koo Klux Klanners didn't get convicted of murder murder murder, but you know what I mean. *We* did all right. It was a boring time, a pseudo fake fifties rerun, but it was ok.

After all, only Puerto Rican homosexuals got AIDS, and it turned out that the shortage wasn't really a shortage, and gas prices went down some and leveled off, and that was really the most important thing, wasn't it?

—Since everybody in America had already turned into some sort of cyborg centaur, half biology and half vehicle, unable to perceive reality except from the bucket seat and through the windshield of a zoom-zoom stink-em-up, incapable of an unpaved logic, dehungerized for any significance that didn't come in drive-up drip-fat hot-in-snaplock-Styrofoam sound bites.

And you were beginning to see the tremendous advantage you held in the 20-year-old mortgage at 8.5%, although as soon as you understood it clearly, the prime rate would take a dive, the dollar go blooey, silver drop fast enough to create a streak of fluorescing plasma, and the national debt get to Mars before we did. Every S & L in the entire country would emit the odor of violated fish, Dallas would go broke except on tv, and none of this would be the fault of such an unprecedented collection of crooks, slime-bags, incompetents, and sleaze-balls as made the years of the Trixxon sing like Ozzie and Harriet, nah.

But never mind all that. Sliding toward Jeremiah, and that aint my binness here. My binness here to tell you a love story, babe. Just setting the background, that's all. So. A lub story in Little Rock town. Off the beaten track. Aint Bethlehem, aint Beverly Hills, but I understand you heard the name recently. And let me just mention A-merica's favorite word: millions.

That's what CHARLES MORRISON has—millions. And he's our viewpoint character, insofar as I can be said to have a viewpoint. Milliums: I wouldn't cheat you out yo soap opera, Hon, no I wouldn't. Just have to digress a little, that's all: Holy Ghost my name, digression's my game. Hell, the world's a digression. Let me ax you a question:

Are you ready?
Are you ready?
Are you ready for the Judgment Day?

TRAVELING SHOT FROM A HEIGHT, AS IF FROM KROK COPTER #1
(*HIGH WITNESS NEWS*) TRACKING I-430 ACROSS
THE RIVER AND INTO THE CITY

Little Rock is a beautiful town. When you drive into it from the north
across the Arkansas River, you are rewarded with a grand scenic view: to
the east, the ridge of the city, with a few fine homes and exquisite green-
swards peeping through the forested slopes; and upstream to the west, a
vista that rivals Japan or Bali Ha'i—a tumble of dark blue smoky mountains, dreamy and mysterious in veils of haze, the sun-bright river shining
and snaking its wide way below.

The town itself is a fair-sized Southern city much like Jackson, Memphis, Knoxville. It's a busy and pleasant place, green with trees and gracious with neighborhoods. On the antique streets of the Heights, or out
along Pleasant Valley, that denuded if money-sodded landscape, that realm
of riding mowers and quick-grow pine, you may behold packs of gleaming
Jeeps that never see the woods, herds of—

—Mercedeses. It is not clear how a state that in 1980 ranked forty-ninth
in personal income, forty-ninth in educational quality, and among
the top five in teen pregnancies managed to support its taste for expensive
cars, continental cuisine, and top-ten Razorbacks. You would almost think
it had a retrograde legislature largely in the debt of developers, lumber
companies, dealmakers, poultry manufacturers, insurance companies,
major utilities, or just any old outfit that threatened to straighten out the
rivers, wash away the topsoil, kill the hardwoods, and put chickenshit in
the water table: *We still got most of our virginity left, come on in and rape
us. Just pay Daddy at the door.* You might wonder about some of the shady
bond daddies down in the city, and some of the cash crops up in the
mountains that don't get mentioned in *Progressive Farmer.*

You might, but then again, you might not, and I sure wouldn't want to
be the one to insist on it, Bubba. Especially not if you were to think
Governor Bill was to blame. This was mostly before his time, remember?

—Little Rock is located in almost the exact geographical center of the
state. The river is wide and navigable here, draining the mountains to the
north and west, and a system of locks and dams allows commerce with
the seagoing world as far inland as Oklahoma.

Right on the river, the town is also right on the line where the hill
country gives way to the lowland farms and piney woods of the Gulf Coastal

Plains, created umpty millions of years ago when the southern waters receded to what is now known as the Gulf of Mexico. So that standing even so high as the top of say Cantrell Hill, on say the marble balcony of Charles Morrison's home and looking southward, you may sometimes feel yourself standing under the vast weight of a vanished sea. And so that all the weather breaks right there, right over the city, the cold northwestern fronts stalling and grinding against the warm Gulf air.

The mountains to the west are the Ouachitas, and the mountains to the north are the famed Ozarks, home not to the likes of Pappy and Jethro but to a fierce breed of tall stubborn survivors, best chronicled in such novels as *The Architecture of the Arkansas Ozarks, Lightning Bug,* and *The Choiring of the Trees.*

Driving east from the city, you enter the long flat cropland of the Mississippi River delta, which is indistinguishable from the country around Alligator and Hushpuckena, over in the state that ranks fiftieth in everything. (And really the two deltas should be combined into a separate political unit, a state of misery, one poor sorry relation we can pretend not to know, and good for nothing but to produce the blue blue blues.)

There are those who insist that Arkansas is not really a Southern state. They say it is a Western state. Most of its memories are frontier memories, not plantation memories. It was a wild and woolly place a hundred years ago, bandits in the borders and manslaughter in the congress. It's loaded up now with necks and good old boys, but the true Arkansawyer is still his own man. He does things his own unpredictable way, and he makes up his own mind about reality. I say "man," but the women are the same damn way.

So much for scenery: Let's get to the meat of this tale.

Well, there's JOSEPH CHARLES MORRISON, already mentioned, lawyer, CPA, and fool for love. The Morrisons are third-generation money, live up in Edgehill, highest and finest neighborhood in the city, the gossip and envy of all. The irony is that old Chuck is an adopted child, and an only child at that, so that his father's branch of the blood is at an end, a fact that the cousins, aunts, uncles, and nephews are not happy with, since Charles controls the bulk of the various Morrison interests. But he gets along with everybody, mostly. He loves movies and science fiction and gardening, and his favorite image of himself is as a slick businessman. He's more of a bigot than he thinks he is, and he has some theological views that I find rather amusing. More a matter of style than conviction, if you want my opinion: They make him feel modern, scientific. Charles likes himself pretty well, but he is just totally crazy about his wife,

TOMMIE LIANNE MORRISON: the former Miss Little Rock of nineteen-sixty-oops, beginning to show her age, a perfectionist, hard on herself.

After her contest days, she graduated with a degree in music and went to work for a local tv station, KROK itself in fact, becoming the most popular newscaster in the state, and only recently, at Charles's insistence, retiring. Because of a painful fibroid tumor that forced the removal of her uterus when she was twenty-one, she cannot have children. TUCKER wants me to tell you that fibroid tumors are unusual in one so young, but nevertheless, that's what it was. I'll get to Tucker in a minute.

Against her mother's wishes and the recommendation of her doctor, Lianne retained her ovaries, and so still produces estrogen, and so still ovulates. Tucker says it would have been against his recommendation too, because of the chance of ovarian cancer, but back then estrogen therapy was almost nonexistent, and there were simply no long-term studies of women.

Lianne has thrown her maternal energies into fund-raising for good causes and into political activism: She's a modern Southern liberal, a MoSL, a mozzle, and she supports aid to education, the ERA, the arts, desegregation, and a lower tax burden on the poor, and votes a Democratic ticket. Her mother, mentioned above, is

ELAINE O'HARE WEATHERALL, definitely not a member of an upper-crust marriage, and she never let her husband, LEE ANDREW WEATHERALL, forget it, not until the day he died of a well-earned embolism. He stroked out just after Lianne hit puberty, so you can imagine how complicated the girl's feelings were over the next few years. It was his cousin who headed up Freeman Dairy, but that didn't cut no ice with de momma. Way she saw it, she had to use all her wiles and willpower to get shiftless hubby a job—delivering the milk. Way she saw it, by force of association, and biology to the contrary, the Freemans were *her* important relatives, not his. Now what Lee Andrew really wanted to do was run his own potato-chip business. He tried it once, but the factory failed. Did it fail because he was the impotent impractical gorgeous-eyed klutz Miz O'Hare kept telling him he was, or did it fail because she cut his heart out and served him a slice of it every morning for breakfast: because, that is, he became what she told him he was? How would Lianne know? All she knows, she still remembers the smell of the thick, hot, freshly fried chips, shining with their drying oil. She will cry sometimes when she opens a bag of Hawaiians, and that earthy roasted odor comes busting out, though the chips themselves, when she eats them, aren't a patch on the ones her old man used to make.

Now, Miz Weatherall might've gave Mr. a hard time about how well off they weren't, but she was always bragging to everybody else about her rich connection, TOMMY FREEMAN. Who is really, up alongside someone like Charles Morrison, just a redneck cheap-jack whey-brain. Blue-john up beside the honest clabber. And who really doesn't count for much in this tale, and I don't even know why I brought him up, except so you'd be ready when he finally walks on.

Let's see, what else? Her momma pushed Lianne into beauty contesting, into being a child model. Set her to doing tv ads for the dairy. The woman handled her about like she did Mr. Weatherall—outwardly proud but privately reiterating what a cheap worthless slut she was. I mean if you got energy, intelligence, beauty, charm, you bound to be a bad girl, right?

Then there's TINA TALLIAFERRO (pronounced *Tolliver*), and her lover LAFAYETTE THOMPSON, and the lord high bailiff of Pulaski County himself, SONNY RAYMOND, and GREG LEGG, and oh hey, TUCKER and DEE-DEE, Charles and Lianne's best friends. Tucker is an M.D., owns a couple clinics in town. Tucker and Dee-Dee don't have any children either. Charles figures it's Tucker's low sperm count, or else he would've said something. Maybe their mutual childlessness has drawn the two couples closer, a shared absence? Then, too, they can all take off on a trip together on a moment's notice, no baby-sitters to mess with, no wreckage from forbidden parties to come back to.

And J.D. RIDER, of course, I shouldn't forget him, there's always a rider—but what the hey, that's enough for starters, who can keep track. Less get on with it, are you ready?

See you later, so long. Oh, don't worry, I'll be back, I'll always be back. Just like the general said.

But right now let's go to the old control panel and download Charles Morrison. Well, of course We have a control panel—what did you think— We wasn't as advanced as you are? Here we go, temporal camera on, we're zooming over all the aforementioned terrain, closing in on a certain downtown building near a certain downtown park that just happens to bear the general's name, since he was *from* here, don't you know?

Hovering, we can see through the window that there's a meeting going on. We can see Charles sitting in a chair, twiddling his twiddle:

> *Keying datalock transfer. Check.*
> *All systems on-line. Check.*
> *Map status green-to-green. Check.*
> *Activate MORRISON:*

2

A WHITE MAN
IN A SUIT

Wrist, throat, and ankle. That was where you felt it. The white inch of linen at the sleeve-end of your raw silk suit coat. The neat collar propped on the rack of your collarbones. The sleek edge of your trousers gracing the ankle of your crossed leg. Wrist, throat, and ankle.

At least, that was where he felt it. Where was it for a woman? Skirt-edge on calf? Ruffles over the breasts? A point of brilliant weight in the earlobe? He would ask her when he got home.

Instrument of default, Boody was saying to the workers. *The board of First National, in reviewing the options. Taxes and assizes. Last general referendum.*

Charles studied his hands: bronze hair on the tanned backs, long fingers. The play of tendons under the raised veins, into the wrists. The hands of an athlete, or a piano player. But she was the piano player.

And he was healthy, but not athletic. Had no desire to be. Was a noon regular at the downtown Y, but was pleased that he did not jog. All that strenuous self-improvement. Sit on your butt all day, then bounce it around the streets of the Heights after work. You and your buddies, a trotting phalanx of white-faced, red-shouldered pudge-pots. Casually gasping out your time in the Pepsi 10K. Back to your remodeled two-story brick, with the air-conditioned Beamer out front. Into the Beamer for beer and pizza downtown, Sidney on the fuzzy bigscreen, a starter now, pretty good for only his second year. Damn Bird a star right away, of course.

It was—inappropriate. Driven. The strategy of a life in fragments.

Maybe you don't watch the Bucks that night after all, maybe you head for Robinson Auditorium to see *A Chorus Line*, Bill Lewis thinks it's such a great show. Fitness, then culture. Sum the pieces to see who you are. To see if you qualify for existence.

He preferred a bit of handball at the Y, a few slow laps in its shrunken little four-lane pool, some tennis, a modicum of gardening in his own backyard. Though his gardening irritated Coleman.

It aint right, Mr. Charles. It's my job. Aint right you to do it.

Well, I like it, Coleman.

Aint no good at it.

You'll just have to teach me, then.

Can't teach you nothing. Don't know a rose from a mulberry bush.

Boody was floundering. Charles would have to break in soon. Eamon wasn't going to, the fat old fart. Guess he thinks he earns his money carrying briefcases. Wonder is he even awake. Probably learned how to sleep with his eyes open, like a snake. For the one thousandth time, how long till Eamon retires? Nineteen months, count em, nineteen. Eyes on the goal, Charley, you owe it to Daddy—be polite to his old U of A buddy. Not to mention don't want to make Dee-Dee feel funny, uncle of her cousin or something, whatever you call that. Was that what you called twice removed? If it wasn't, what was? Never could remember.

He circled his right wrist with the thumb and index finger of his left hand. Now his blood beat through a loop of his blood.

He would study Lianne's wrist when he got home. He would watch her thoughts deploying through that small channel into the actions of her hands, a creek running faster where it narrowed. He would press his lips to her pulse.

Time to pinch-hit. Ten minutes ago Boody had had the meeting all wrapped up, but then one of the workers had started bad-mouthing Judge Beaumont, and Boody had come unraveled. Explaining again, tomato-faced, looking prime for a stroke. It was a fallacy that emotional involvement made you more effective. The emotion was beforehand, when you chose which play to back. After that, you just stayed cool and made the best moves you could.

The worker rep was out of control too, whitely desperate, as if she and the others faced not delayed paychecks but execution. To contain her fear, she needed somebody to blame. That was why she was jumping Beaumont's case, that and nothing else.

How did it feel to stare over the precipice of such a terror simply because a paycheck was a few days late? She wouldn't starve. Nobody starved. She and her husband might get a few threatening collection letters, sustain some damage to their credit rating.

For some reason he saw it again, the image from this morning's story in the *Gazette:* the baby in the paper bag, the kitten.

It must be that such people felt themselves only slenderly connected to life, by the most tenuous of arrangements. So that at the least whiff of the smallest trouble, they felt the wind of total ruin.

Boody was still talking, but he was looking openly at Charles. Charles nodded, and rose.

"Thank you, Mr. Lookadoo," he said, "for your time, and for your very obvious concern for these hardworking people. Folks, let me just sum up briefly before we adjourn." That was a good move: Establish sympathy—we're all in it together—but make it clear that the show is about to be over. "There hasn't been any kind of power play. What it boils down to is real simple. First National and Union National have backed out of the loan arrangement at the last minute. So all of a sudden there's no million dollars available, and that's why the judge told Shirley to hold your checks. He didn't *want* to, he *had* to."

He held up a hand at the sudden volume of protest. "The banks have refused the loan because they do not feel Pulaski County can sufficiently guarantee it. The fact is they are perfectly justified. For them, it's a business proposition." And that was for Boody, whose moral outrage on KROK last night had only made his own task that much harder.

How was it Boody was so uncool? Old Judge Lookadoo had never had the emotion of a turtle on a July log. His momma? But no, the old lady had gone straight from Junior League to Heights matron, born to pour tea in garden club meetings. Boody a throwback somehow, even in high school a jittery clown. Boody for his big butt. On the track team, though—you had to give him A for effort. White-haired soft fat kid, got on those canned low-cal drinks, what was it? Sego. Dropped 75 pounds and turned out could run a decent quarter, 55.4 at state in the relay, but still The Butt. Thin pipe legs and big blooming waddly behind. Fat again now, his brief glory gone.

Mind on your work, Charles.

"Ah, ok, the essential problem they had was, in valuing real estate for sale there are several rules for this valuation. Ok, maybe you're not interested in the technical details, but it is those same technical details that have been paying your salaries all these years." And that for the whiners, the complainers who didn't want to think about anything hard, just wanted their nice safe cradle-to-grave. But he couldn't afford much of that tone if he wanted to keep them in line.

"One of the most common ways to value real estate is the multiples rule, multiples of real annual income. It's standard to figure the market value of real estate at between five and ten multiples of its real annual income in the preceding year. Now, the county's assessable properties did not accrue appreciable valuable real income last year, though it does have to have some declared market value anyway. So for this reason, I assessed the properties as a whole at the high end of the spectrum, based on a trued-up annualized income, whereas First Commercial wished to assess the properties to be used to secure the loan at a much lower rate variable from five to seven multiples and based on an average income including the low income from last year. This is good business on their part if they can get it, but A, this would have necessitated the mortgage of more properties than desirable in order to secure sufficient loan moneys, and B, Pulaski County would have taken a beating."

Empathy, authority, reprimand—and now he had them numb with his barrage of information, more than they wanted, more than they could possibly follow. They were set up. Take it to the house.

"Now, you can say, 'Mr. Morrison, I don't care about all this high finance, I just want my money,' and I won't blame you. But I can't in good conscience advise the county to accept these conditions. So if you want to get mad, get mad at me and not at your own lawyer, ok? Poor old Mr. Lookadoo here is doing everything he can, but he can't turn water into wine.

"However. It was never true that this financial structure was the only route we were considering for transfer of these moneys. We will now appeal to the aforementioned consortium in Van Buren County, and I anticipate success within a very short period. We cannot give you a deadline, obviously, because formal negotiations have begun only this morning. As soon as an agreement has been reached, we will set a firm date for salary checks for all county employees."

Beat. Pacing was all.

"Now—we have run almost an hour past the lunch break, so maybe we better call this meeting to a close. Assuming our salaries are soon recontinued—and please, let's all do assume that," Charles said, and smiled. Another beat. "Assuming that, we'll certainly want to keep earning them, won't we?"

"Friday thirteenth," Boody sighed at the urinal. "Two months in a row." He pissed like a horse standing in a river. Free-flowing, for a nervous man. Eamon had vanished, thank God, supposedly to take the documents back to the office, but probably really to take one of his two-hour four-vodka lunches. Pass by his office door round about three, hear him snoring away, leaned back in his chair. Worthless fucker, drain on the firm, but at least he wasn't in here honking his adenoids. God, I hate to be in the same john with that man, fucking foghorn sinuses, *blat blat blat* off the stall walls, damn near peed myself yesterday when he cut loose.

Morrison had been looking at his own lengthened penis, bouncing it comfortably in his palm to shake it dry, enjoying the heavy and generous resilience, the slightly awakened pleasure. He took his time tucking away and zipping up, went to the mirror to look at himself, washing his hands and face as a cover.

"I read a science fiction story one time," he said. "Guy went back in a time machine to the Last Supper. Found out one of the disciples who was supposed to be there really wasn't. So all this time the real unlucky number has been twelve and not thirteen, and we never knew it."

"I don't know much about religion," Boody said. "Anyway, I thought you were an atheist." He came over to give himself a perfunctory glance: Ned Beatty in *Nashville*. The people who used to wear white belts and white shoes.

It's just a story, Boody.

"I reckon the twelfth was pretty unlucky for old Ron Orsini, though," he added.

"Can't say I know him," Charles said. Boody never had grasped the principle of cliques. He thought his world was your world. If he knew somebody, he thought you knew them.

"Did some estate work for him a while back. He was a pretty good old boy. The worried type, though." That was funny, coming from Boody.

"Found him dead yesterday morning. Shot through the head in his own bed."

Head, bed, dead. Charles thought of George Rose Smith hooting over the malaprops in some unfortunate's brief, the unintentional rhymes that destroyed all meaning for anyone who had an ear. "Was it in the paper?" he said. "I must have missed it."

"He lived over in Dogtown. My contacts say it looks like a drug deal went wrong." Boody with contacts, right. "Execution style. There's a lot more of that sort of thing going on than we realize. We think we're safe from it here in Little Rock, but we're not." Boody, privy to dark knowledge.

"Thanks again, Charley," he said. Charles hated the name. "Never could handle an audience. When you filing for governor?"

His idea of humor. "Don't want the job," Charles said. "Anyway, Bill Clinton's got it sewed up through the end of the century. Unless he decides to go for President."

"Are you kidding? You think he can come back on Frank?"

"I don't think, I know."

"Well, I know you involved with Bill and all, but everybody in Arkansas don't vote with the *Gazette*."

"Hell, no, of course they don't. But Frank already has people mad at him over this Walter Skelton business. He'll shoot himself in the foot, you watch. Whole country's in a dumb phase right now, but it won't last. Only reason Frank won was riding the coattails of that bozo in the White House."

Boody was shocked, Charles could tell. Disrespect for the presidency. It was hard to resist shocking Boody. He cried out for the cattle prod. Remember, Charles, you don't like people that pick on people.

Boody shifted to a subject he knew he and Charles agreed on. "We need to go to a four-year term. No sooner win than everybody's running again."

"It'll happen," Charles said. Something was nagging his memory, something he needed to say, something connected to elections. He remembered. "How do you stand on the sales tax?"

"Well, you know, I haven't decided." So he was against it. "I'm not sure it's not just a makeup for the millage thing. I mean, the millage lost fair and square, and here it is coming right back at us another way."

Quite a few people were taking that attitude, Charles knew. It infuriated Lianne. The sales tax didn't guarantee money to the schools. It would make more state money available to Little Rock, true, so that things like the Central Arkansas Transit system could keep running. And maybe, just maybe, if the city could stave off bankruptcy—why then, maybe the schools could breathe a little easier.

He and Lianne differed on the political practicalities, but they agreed strongly that the schools were in trouble. When he spoke to Boody his voice carried an anger that was not his own, that was Lianne's, as if he were a neutral medium, a carrier, a mere host for her spirit. Marriage was strange.

"Way I look at it, when you get right down to it, the millage was for the kids. But look, Ferstel's in favor of the sales tax, and he was against the millage."

"Well, I just don't think throwing money at the schools— I'll think about it. I know how Lianne feels."

"It's how I feel too."

"I know, I know. I didn't mean it that way. I'll think about it."

"Can't ask any more than that."

"Late, but you want lunch? I didn't brown-bag it."

"Boody, I'd love to, but I got to get the Buick back for Lianne." Poor excuse, she don't need it, but last thing I want is to spend an hour eating lunch with Boody. Hard enough to get him out of the rest room.

"280 still in the shop?"

"Still in."

"Well, I'm outta here. We gone beat Louisville, you think?"

Charles forced himself to patience. "Not a chance."

"I don't know—Walker and Hastings and Reed, and if Downtown gets hot . . . Sutton's one of the best coaches in the country."

"Yeah, I saw the article. And the day after they carry it, Texas whips us in the tournament. Face it, we aint the triplets any more. And Denny Crum's not a bad coach himself. Love to see em win, but I wouldn't bet money."

"Well . . ." Lookadoo hesitated, raised a hand in farewell, finally pushed out the door. Morrison, released, turned to give himself a long look. *The old he-looks-in-the-mirror-and-we-get-to-look-at-him shot*. He could almost feel the cameras, behind him and to the right. He was often visited by a pleasant sense of having witnesses, a sense of being a character in a drama, as if all the spirits sat out there somewhere, just past the lights, just beyond the screen, watching.

He was, as we know, right.

The man he saw was tall, with a long and friendly face, high cheekbones, a wide, full mouth, a straight nose, clear gray eyes. He wore steel-rimmed glasses, and his wavy brown hair, shot through with gray, had receded almost to the crown of his head.

He looked much happier this way, older and a little balding. Much more together than he had looked in college. "Tall, skinny, and serious," it had said under his photo in the '60 *Troubador*.

Normally he spent little time thinking about his looks. He simply assumed he made a good appearance. But Thursday a week ago, in San Antonio for the SWCs—watching Abe Lemons and his damn ragtag collection of Texas yard dogs whip Arkansas, as a matter of fact—he had seen a man who was the image of himself. A man in the crowd, a clean-faced fellow with steel-rims and half a head of wavy brown hair. A young boy rode his shoulders. A genial man, an intelligent man, with a legal face, an accountant's face, a doctor's, a teacher's face. Enjoying the game, enjoying his son, enjoying America, ah.

There would be no son whose bones would echo Charles when he was gone, in whose face the world might read a hint of the father. He might wish, like any other man, to multiply his image, but for him there was only now. The mirror was it.

He hunted his face until he saw the boy he had been. That was how his son might have looked. "I would have called you Gideon," he said.

It was cold in the parking garage, the wind whistling out of a gray sky through cuts of gray concrete. His suit was too light, but the morning had been sunny—windy and troubled with free-flying scraps of cloud, but sunny. He had expected the chill to burn off by noon. Spring in Arkansas, how could you tell?

His heart jumped when he saw the car in the slot, Lianne's Skylark with the bumper sticker: *My heart is in the public schools—and so are my children*. It was the smallest of double takes, the tiniest of sudden and suddenly punctured delights. Strange, the various rooms of his being: Just minutes ago he had been telling Boody how he was driving the Buick today, and here was another part of him that had totally forgotten.

He no longer noticed, even subliminally, the irony of the bumper sticker's message. "Well, I'm *for* the schools," she had said, "and it's the only sticker they have."

Lianne had a toss of auburn-brunette hair, a clean Loretta Young face that had gotten sharper as she grew older. The hair had been red when she was a girl. She had gone to Hall until the schools closed, a stratagem by her mother, who had used an aunt's address to keep her out of Central. *He* had gone to Central, but he thought maybe he remembered her. A busy girl, yearbook committee, pep squad, glee club, and under it all, those unnoticed good grades, those mostly A's, with a B or two here and there, salutatorian in her class eventually, though that was at the private school, later. He had been at Hendrix when she entered, his senior year and her freshman year overlapping. Surely he had seen her on campus, but he had no memory of it. He had already been at Boston when she won Miss Little Rock, had gone up that summer to check things out, find an apartment, acclimate himself before the opening of law school. But he had seen some of the photos, a few of which were in color. Those few were really all he had of the redhead. That and the blaze over her pubis, itself blazed with a streak of silver-blonde. Probably there were some tapes in a vault somewhere, from those early Freeman commercials. No, they would all be black-and-white. Or would they?

Did they even have tapes back then?

She had gone gray before they met, gray at twenty or twenty-one. Maybe because of the operation, but that was something she hadn't said. She didn't talk about the operation. She had dyed herself ever since, but to auburn, not back to her original red. Red was cheap, she thought. He had argued with her about it, had never understood her resistance. Himself, he would have been glad to fuck a green-eyed redhead for a change.

But she wouldn't relent, so he had never known anyone but the brunette: And in spite of the senior photos, the publicity stills, he always imagined a brunette walking across in a swimsuit, a brunette answering questions, a brunette playing the piano in an evening dress.

Say what you wanted about beauty pageants, the winners weren't usually bubbleheads, silly young geese. They had something, and it showed. The lowest runner-up in the podunkiest contest—Miss Hot Springs, Miss Warren Pink Tomato Festival, Miss Malvern Brickfest—all the Former Miss Somebodies, as Dee-Dee liked to put it—they all had a touch of class.

More oomph in the genes, a bit of style, the radiance of the above-average. Smarter and longer-legged, thoroughbreds, the cream of the crop.

He slid into the front seat, fastened the shoulder harness, backed the car out.

Down and around, down and around, the low dark spiraling cavern of the parking garage.

Lianne had left Hendrix early in her second year, during her term as Miss Little Rock. She had never said why, but he had the impression that she had been depressed at not winning Miss Arkansas. He also had the confused impression that her mother had kicked her out of the house. But how could that be, if she was already in college? She had spent a few months in New York, he knew, but had returned in time to crown the new Miss Little Rock, that short one—who was it?—he had seen her in Safeway just a few days ago, she was gray now, too, but didn't dye her hair.

Window down, show ticket, pay. Up goes the bar. Out into traffic.

He had flown to New York frequently that first year. All the boys did that, all the boys in Haaahvahd Laaah. It was where you would probably be working, you couldn't wait till you graduated to start building contacts. He had bought himself a Countess Mara tie the first time he went, something he'd been wanting ever since reading about it in what? *The Mansion?*—One of the few things he remembered from his Faulkner course.

Maybe his and Lianne's paths had crossed. What if they had met then instead of six years later? Would everything be different? Would they have married?

It was one of his favorite fantasies, orgies in the Big Apple with the beauty queen from Arkansas. It excited him tremendously, as if he were being faithful and unfaithful at once, betraying Lianne with her younger, more lissome self. Or you could do it now if you had a time machine: that would make a good story. Had she met a distinguished graying Southern lawyer in New York that year, fallen in love, had the fucking of her young life? Was that why she never spoke of her stay there? Was that why she had fallen so hard for him six years later, a blurred memory of that handsome elder legal eagle?

He had a hard-on. Hmm. He had been bullshitting Boody, but maybe he *could* run by the house for a few minutes. Friday afternoon, Clemmie would be out doing the grocery shopping. The Cleaning Crew came on Fridays, but only every other Friday, and this was the off week. So the coast would be clear. Call Jerry, see if his car was ready, that would be his excuse. Whoops, no, he couldn't, the phone was in the 280, stupid. Well, he could go by, then, to check on it. Or he *could* go back to the office. No, let's have a look at the car, Chucky. Loop around the one-way and back over to Broadway, then. Head for the bridge.

After she came back from New York, Lianne had gone to UALR, back when it was Little Rock College, graduating in music in what? '61? No, that was impossible, had to be '62. She had tried teaching piano for a year, and then had gone on to do nightly news for KROK for fifteen years. He had graduated, interned in New York, and then decided to come back home. Met her at a party and recognized her, because by that time everyone in Little Rock recognized her. She knew him because everyone in Little Rock knew who the Morrisons were.

She loved children. She had started a feature on the news show, raising money for the treatment of seriously ill children. It was a tie-in with Arkansas Children's Hospital and the Ronald McDonald House. *Hope Lines* had generated at least three million dollars in contributions in the eight years she had run it, and he hadn't put in more than a couple of hundred thousand of that himself. Seed money. Anonymous benefactor.

So she was more than a talking head, was our Lianne. She was good. She could have run anything. But the show had begun to exhaust her. In each feature, she appeared with a young child, usually very pale, often very thin, often with a shaved head or large black circles under sunken eyes, and equally often beautiful, as if death brought with it a bruised and haunting grace. Some were retarded. Some were shy and silent, some bright and convivial. They went to carnivals together, to the zoo, they rode escalators and ponies and fire trucks for the tv cameras. Cancer or ruined heart valves or leukemia brought the children of sharecroppers into the city, gave them luminous visions of worlds they would never have seen if they had lived on in good health. Lianne did what she could. She gave them a good time.

Joggers on the bridge, bare-chested in the chill.

Hard-on was gone, but might as well follow through, go by the house, why not?

Every time one of the children died, Lianne suffered. She had grown depressed and prone to anger. She had begun to drink heavily, and cry at parties. He had been afraid she was bringing on an early menopause. Finally he had talked her into leaving the station. He had put it that way, leaving the station because of overwork. She could accept that as a rationale. She would never have been able to admit she couldn't stand working with the kids themselves any more.

These last three years, he thought, she had healed. She stayed sadder and more gaunt, but she had regained the authority of her loveliness, the striking bloom of her complexion, the vividness of her wide-set eyes.

Even in her baby pictures—six months, and twelve months, and a year and a half—even then, those eyes commanded. The sclera so white, the irises not the intense green of redheads in tv commercials, which was probably always contacts anyhow, but ringed in a fine dust of charcoal. It was that that did it, that feathery margin of darkness: the outline, the contrast. That and the clarity of her focus. Lianne's vision had been 20/13 as a girl, and she could still pick out a hawk on a fence post from a half mile off at 70 mph.

Her daddy's eyes, she said.

In the parking lot of the auto shop a black man was standing behind the door of his dark green Galaxie, just getting out or just getting in. The man was ranting, Charles realized. He did not remember ever thinking that word before. *Ranting*. The man's voice was cutting and high, and came in loud claps and cracks of emphasis.

"—out the motherfucker cause you never been in the motherfucker! Spend some days in the motherfucker, you know how I feel. You know how it feel to be out the motherfucker! Come round me with no goddamn letter! I aint taking yo goddamn shit! Ass right, go on in there, goddamn pussy! Take yo motherfuck little pussy daughter witch you!"

Morrison saw that a couple of well-dressed black women, a thirtyish woman and her subteen daughter, were escaping for the shop office, hunched and hurrying. Nelson was standing stiffly in his olive drab mechanic's coveralls, like a cat with his fur up. He had grabbed a big adjustable wrench from a tool bin, but now he seemed frozen with indecision. The wrench wasn't Nelson's style. Nelson was quiet, had a good job. Street theater embarrassed him. He was a good citizen.

"Go on and call the cop! See if I care! Call em on yo own man, be just like you! See if I care!" The man was still looking after the women, though they had disappeared inside. Now he looked back toward Nelson. "I aint ashame," he said. To Charles it seemed the man was thinking how much time he had left before the police arrived. He had salved his pride, he had made his scene, and now he wanted to gauge his getaway.

Charles realized he was standing behind the door of the Skylark exactly the way the man was standing behind the door of his Galaxie.

"Got to have some feelin," the man said. "Got to let a man get his head clear fore you go hittin im with a letter. You know what I mean, man. You can put yo wrench down, I'm goin. Aint sayin you no son-bitch or nothin. Just hot, you know, cause you aint give me no time, dammit, aint eem give me no goddamn time, just hit me with a letter just as soon as I get out!" The man, his eyes on the wrench, was letting his anger flare again.

Morrison came around the car door and started toward him: "Can I help you, fella?"

"I'm gone," the man said. "You don't have to do nothin. I'm outta here, man." He swung down into the seat of his car, accelerated out of the lot in a spray of rattling gravel, a belch of oily smoke.

Morrison figured it was the suit that had done it. A lot of people were afraid of the blacks, the way they let their voices carry in the downtown streets, the blank faces of the open-shirted males, the peculiar shoulder-swaying butt-thrust walk, the hands swinging loosely back as if they were lazily shooing flies off their asses with every step. The big loud radios on the shoulders or booming out of a car at the stoplight. A lot of people were afraid of the blacks, and so hated them.

Charles thought it was territorial. The slow stiff way they turned to look around, exaggeratedly casual, head high, eyes cut—that was the supremely careful, give-nothing-away gesture of a man in alien territory. The jam-boxes were a subtle way of dominating the white-owned space around them, subtle because it gave the whiteys no good way to come back. You either pretended to ignore the racket, thus losing face in the subliminal contest; or you overreacted, giving in to anger, threatening with the law— *I'm on tell Daddy*— thus also losing face.

He was, he was sure, their worst nightmare, a white man in a suit. He gave them the cold shivers and the running blue shake-knee. If the Indians had been able to foresee his kind in their Oleg Cassinis and Arrow pinpoint oxfords, the cavalry would not have been necessary.

That was the wild ones, though. There were two kinds now. There were the ones that were like everybody else, like Nelson, and there were the ones who stuck to the old behavior. Trying to educate them both the same way was a big mistake, but try to tell that to Lianne. Like a reservation, like a wildlife preserve. It wasn't a way he wanted to live, and he couldn't really imagine why they wanted to live that way, but they had a right to if they wanted. They ought to face facts though: They ought to see that living that way wasn't going to get them anywhere in the real world. They ought to see that, and then if they wanted to keep on doing it anyway, they might as well quit bitching about what it did get them.

He was seeing the baby again, the baby in the big grocery sack, curled up with the kitten.

Nelson had gone inside, and Morrison went in too, looking for Jerry. He found him talking to Nelson out in the garage. He could see the 280, hood up, on the far side of the garage. It wasn't ready, then.

"I'm sorry, Jerry," Nelson was saying.

"I heard that already," said Jerry, a short bearded man with a big chewed-up cigar in his face. He thrust his beard continually out and up, as if that were how to gain height, push with the hair of your chinny-chin-chin. "I aint concerned with why or who or none of that. It don't matter to me. But yo love life don't belong around this place. These are good cars, and I aint having that kind of show-out crap going on around these good cars. I don't care if he started it or the police told him to stay away and he wouldn't, or he goes back to jail if you press charges, or what. I just aint having that kind of crap around my cars, and it's up to you to see that it don't ever happen again, you got me?"

"Yessir."

"What the hell you want, Charley?" Jerry said. Nelson walked away, head down only slightly, not like a man in disgrace, but like a man bemused. Morrison could see that he agreed with Jerry, that he was already trying to figure out how he had failed his responsibilities in letting the scene out front occur.

"I been given to understand I have a car in here being worked on," Morrison said into the beard.

The beard jerked with what would have been laughter if Jerry had ever been known to laugh. "Been given; that's good. Come on over here—I want to show you. See that goddamn oil? That's after we did the valve-cover gasket. Rear seal's shot. How many miles you got on this baby?"

"I don't know—eighty-five thousand or so."

"Yeah, more like ninety-five. Well, you need a short-block, my opinion."

"Short-block?"

"Keep your headers, pistons. Maybe change the rings. Drive train's ok. Just put in a new block."

"Can't you just fix the—what you said—the rear seal?"

"Can, and by the time I get through, it'll cost you as much, and you'll still have to short-block it in a year or two, because the crankshaft is probably worn."

"So how much will it cost me to do it the right way, Jerry?"

"It was a Chevy, I'd have a block in here tomorrow and it'd be what, two-fifty, three hundred. Add labor, you're talking seven, seven-fifty."

"Awful high for labor."

"But being it's got to come in from Germany with freight and shipping and they run twice as high anyway, you're looking at seventeen hundred, two thousand, somewhere in there."

"Jesus, Jerry, I might as well buy a new car."

"Aint a Chevy, is it? What do you care? You got enough money to burn a wet mule."

"You and everybody else thinks. Won't have a dime if I keep coming in here."

Jerry patted his arm. "Somebody's got to drive em," he said. "Come on, it's a classic. You shoulda never sold the big one."

"You know how it is."

Jerry grunted, not wanting to comment. Charles had sold the other Mercedes because Lianne wanted a smaller car. She said the big one made her feel like she was driving a truck. He was pretty sure her real reason had been she felt ostentatious owning two luxury cars.

"Anyway," Jerry said. "Short-block it, she'll give you another hundred thousand miles."

"But you can't work on it now, can you? Not till you get that block in. So can you have one of the boys run it back up to the house when you get it put back together?"

"It's already back together. Yeah, we'll run it by."

"Nelson's a good man, you know."

The beard came back up. "Goddammit, I know that. But I got to keep em in their places, don't I? Somebody's got to have some standards."

3

THE THING ABOUT BEING FAIR IN FIGHTS

As usual, both lanes were dragging going up Cantrell. Always a couple of suckers neck and neck at 20 mph, no engines for the big hill, and neither one of them with the mother wit to pull over. Charles didn't drive in a big anxious hurry, like so many other people, but this was just plain damn inefficient. Inefficiency and discourtesy really were pretty much the same thing, he thought, and then decided it was a good thought. Kind of Japanesey. Write it in his journal, use it in a talk sometime.

He didn't turn left where Kavanaugh crossed Cantrell at the top of the hill, but went on through the light. He would run by the elementary school in case Lianne was still there with her Committee to Save the Schools. How they could stand the kids whooping around between classes he would never know. Why not just have the committee over to the house? Maybe because she had pushed the line already, lobbying and working the election at the same time. No one had called her hand on it, since on balance the Heights had been in favor of the millage.

She wasn't there; nor were any other members of the committee. Just the sisters Renaldi and Mr. Beverly, stooped in his seersucker slacks, getting Tuesday cleared away. The elderly were in charge of every election, it seemed. The elderly and his own busy, busy wife. Was it that they were survivors from a time when people believed in the process, or were they just the only ones who had the time? Regardless, when he thought of elections, he thought of white hair, friendly baggy old faces, shaky hands writing your name into the logbook, a card table along one wall with a big cooler of artificial lemonade on it, condensation puddling up the surface.

He smiled and chatted. She wasn't here, they'd seen her but didn't know when the committee had adjourned, but probably not too long ago, too bad about the millage. Smiled some more. Goodbye to the good old loyal troopers. Left for home.

It was the house he had grown up in. He liked pulling into the long semicircular driveway, getting out of his car in the shade of the tall old trees, looking up. A gracious building, certainly. Almost a palazzo. Faced in white marble. Three floors, constructed on a set of the octagons his father had loved, although the house did not show its octagonality from the outside, so modulated was it, so gracefully interpreted. Instead, it seemed to rise smoothly, with wide and pleasant bays at each corner. Set well back from the street, it was secluded within high stone walls and hedges, except toward the front, where a half wall ran, surmounted by a wrought-iron fence. There the lawn was not really a lawn, but ivy and earth and paths and bark-strewn flower beds: a formal garden, in whose courtyard a fountain sported. Every home should have a fountain, a leaping fountain with a slim and naked Cupid. The palliative music of catapulted water.

Some of the homes on Edgehill had the baronial splendor of Bavarian hunting lodges, hotels of stone and cedar. Huge sweeps of manicured green all before, the walks carefully edged. He preferred the inwardness of his own place. Not small by any means, but not imposing. His father's touch.

She was in the sitting room off the downstairs library, on the flower-print daybed, watching a bulletin on the small tv. On KROK, of course. Something about the Senate. "Hey, good-looking," he said. "How's it going?"

"Haven't you been listening?" she said. "Shh. I'm trying to hear."

A split of anger forked through him. "Like you have to find out about it right now," he grumbled under his breath. "Like nothing those monkeys do could possibly wait." When the millage had gone down so badly, she had been angry for a day and then depressed for a day, but had seemed better this morning, cheerful over her coffee. He had left her sitting up in bed sipping, reading the paper. Things had seemed promising then.

He went through the french doors to the bar in the big living room, began constructing a couple of martinis. Fleischmann's. He liked Bombay, but it was too herbal for martinis; he liked Tanqueray, but she was allergic to it. And really, good old cheap Fleischmann's blended just fine, smooth and cool. The secret was in the vermouth anyway. A fair dollop—they weren't trendy about dryness. Stirred in a glass pitcher with a glass rod, not shaken, because that was how Travis McGee did it, or was it James Bond? Two frosted glasses from the minifridge. Drop a couple of cubes in, never mind the purists, because they liked their drinks to stay cold. Shave twin curls from the lemon, twist a spray of oil over the glasses, rub the rims, drop the twist in. Pour the cold clink-music.

"How about a drink?" he called, and brought the martinis to the sitting room.

"Since I'm not going to get to hear the rest of this, I might as well," she said. She squeezed the remote like someone thumbing an ant to death, and got up. The bulletin had reverted to soap opera anyway. She came over to get her drink. She was wearing heels, and a teal suit in a light, open-weave wool.

"You're looking mighty pretty," he said. She gave him a tight little smile, the look-up-and-smile-and-look-back-down kind, as if it cost her something. She took a big slug of her martini.

"How was your day?" she said.

"Oh, ok. They're real upset about their salaries. I did a good job of explaining everything, kind of calmed them back down. Boody was having kittens. They're bringing my car back this afternoon, but it isn't finished. They've got to order a new engine block, and it'll take a while. I been having some real neat realizations today. You'd like them. One is about efficiency and courtesy being the same thing."

"But they aren't."

"They don't have to be, but the way I mean it, they are. What made me think of it was these two cars on Cantrell Hill."

"Can you tell me about it tonight? I need you to run me back over to the school so I can help clean up. Mary Beth brought me home because I needed to eat, but—"

"You don't really have to go back. They can handle it. They're almost through anyway."

"Yes, I do need to go back. And I need to go now."

"I was hoping we could have some time together. It's a nice afternoon."

"Translation: You were feeling horny, decided to take the afternoon off, get me drunk, and fuck me."

"Dammit, Lianne, what's your problem?"

"I don't have a problem, Charles. I'm tired, I'm upset about the millage, which you clearly aren't, and I wanted to just get off my feet a few minutes and rest, and then this goddamned Senate bill came on, which I wanted to hear about. You couldn't let me alone to do that much, and now I have to go."

Heading toward critical mass, he thought. Say something neutral, defuse it.

"The goddamn news was already off when you turned the damned thing off," he said. "Don't lay your pissiness off on me. All I do is come home and offer you a goddamn drink. Try to be nice, and what do I get?"

Oh great, Chucky. Great going. That'll really smooth the waters.

"I can see you want to fight, Charles. You didn't get your little pussy break, and now you're mad."

Is that true? he wondered. She was uncannily plausible in her retaliations, could reconstruct reality in milliseconds, leave him dazzled in halls of re-reflected motive. *Didn't she take a whack at me first?* But she was no sexual witch, never froze him out, so maybe there was something there, something going on with him that he couldn't see.

The thing about being fair in fights was it gave you vertigo, you lost your bearings.

"Bullshit," he said. "You been mean as a snake since I walked in the door. The first thing you said was shut up."

"I asked you to be quiet and let me hear," she said. "I happen to care about what happens in our schools."

"Like I don't. That's it, it's the way you say things, it's that goddamn Nazi kommandant voice of yours, total cutoff, like I don't count, like I don't even exist."

"You're hearing things."

"And you're always throwing off these crossways accusations that don't have anything to do with anything, like how I don't care about the schools, so either I let the accusation go and I'm guilty, or if I argue about it, we're off the point and I'm just wanting to start a fight."

"You've obviously been building this up for a long time," she said. Her mouth was pressed thin, and it seemed to him that the bones of her face showed through, as if her skin were stretched tightly over them. And yet at the same time she looked older, her tone bad, the flesh of her jawline sagging. She seemed yellowed and pale, and the change in her complexion made her dark hair look false and off color, the dye job of a raddled dowager. It always amazed him, this transformation. How could she be such a wide-eyed young girl, jaw dropped in relaxation, mouth soft and blooming, and in a moment of anger turn into this? This image of her bitter mother, this other face inside her face, waiting to leap out. Oh, anger ages us. Oh, anger makes us die. She bent to one side, then the other, taking off her heels. "If you aren't willing to drive me, I'll walk. But I'm leaving now."

"Go get in the goddamn car, for God's sake." She was in such a hurry she couldn't be bothered to deal with him, but she was perfectly willing to take an extra fifteen minutes finding a pair of flats and walking over to the school. Bullshit, total fucking bullshit, but if he said anything else, she would head right out the door. Well, she was heading out anyway, but presumably to the car, since she had her heels back on. He drank a swallow of his martini, then bolted most of the rest of it.

After he had the car in gear and was heading out the gate, he said, "I was thinking of you all day long, you know. I was really loving you, and then come in the door and get zapped like that." He felt the sting of self-righteous tears, that freezing pinch in the tip of his nose. He tilted his face to let one of the tears trickle down, but she was looking out the window. He roughened his voice. "It really isn't me," he said. "Really. I was horny, sure, but it was because I was loving you, really in love. I mean it. All I'm asking is think it over. Just be honest. See if you weren't feeling bad about something else and took it out on me. You know you do that."

"Don't pull up here, go around the back," she said.

"You haven't heard a goddamn thing I said."

"I heard you. I'm mad at you, and I don't want to talk about it right now. Here."

He pulled into the small asphalted lot behind the school. She opened the door. "When are you through here?" he said.

"Five or so, but I'm going to help Mary Beth door to door with the petition."

"So it'll be nine or so before I can see you," he said. She got out and began walking away, toward the school. "Lianne!" he called, leaning to the door she had left hanging open. She turned. "How is it going?" he said.

"How is what going?"

"The sales tax. How do the numbers look?"

"They look lousy," she said. "The bastards."

"I thought so," he said, slamming the door and popping the car into drive. Out on the street, he gave himself another *Nice going* for that. Screeching off like some goober in a Firebird patchy with primer. "Goddamn bitch," he said. "Fuck up a whole goddamn day just because of a goddamn goddamn bitch bitch bitch." He pounded the dash of the Buick with his right hand, bam-bam bam-bam *bam*.

Where to now? He drove back out to Kavanaugh. He thought a minute, then turned right. Maybe the park, maybe sit in the park and feel the air and look at the sunlight and calm down.

4

INTERNAL
CHEMISTRY

Sat on a picnic table: two-by-sixes bolted to a frame of steel pipe, painted a turgid forest green. Feet resting on the cement seat. Foamy patches of spring beauty riffling in fitful light. Twisted a pecan twig apart, put half in his teeth. Checked his watch: 3:52. Watched a carpenter ant climb the back of his hand, laboring over the leaf-spring hairs. Flicked it off, checked his watch: 3:52. Cleaned his thumbnail with the chewed twig. Checked again: 3:52: 3:53. Felt later. The light was long. Early spring, sunset before seven. Fights made it seem later too. Late in a bad day, a bad year. Five weeks till Easter, and everything shit already.

The part of the movie where the loner cups his hands around a smoke, thumb and finger of one hand pinching a warm companionable glow. Then a grimace to pull the lit cigarette away from the flame, whipping his hand to kill the match. Walk around taking a few drags, tapping the ashes loose. Then flick it away, as if that was what you wanted to do to the woman, flick her away.

Cold out here. Might as well go to the bar.

A complete circle this afternoon: up Cantrell Hill on Cantrell Road, fight with Lianne, then down the hill again on the other side, winding around on Kavanaugh, then cut across on Cedar to Cedar Hill Road and almost to Cantrell again, stopping at the park. Now, at the Cedar Hill and Cantrell stoplight, waiting to cross his earlier path. See himself, a pleased transparent Charles Morrison heading home? No. Don't close that switch. This was early in the story. This was before he started seeing ghosts. The light changed.

Watch said: 4:04. Stood outside The Blue Note. Cute, but he hadn't named it. A small blue brick building all the way out on Cedar Hill Road, almost down to the river. The original joint now angling into a Quonset hut painted a matching blue, the dance floor. Door was locked, what the hell? Found his keys and let himself in. The television on, nobody behind the bar.

"We're closed." David, gloomily, emerging from the back.

"Damn, David, you can't close a bar in the middle of the day."

"Can if there's nobody in it. What do you care anyway? Just a toy to you."

David sat on the high barkeep's stool, watching baseball on the tv, ignoring Charles. David a Cubs fan, WGN his cornucopia of irresistible misery. Oh Jesus, please no Harry Caray, jug-mouth Harry Caray. Blathering and fulsome exegesis, a rumble of praise for the horrible Cubbies, some PR man's idea of big-city uniqueness, character.

Only spring training, though, so how come—ok, just that damn ad.

David's shoulders were slumped and the tv bracket-mounted, so that, looking up, he had the posture of a man in despair supplicating his God, a prisoner lifting his eyes to the small high window of his cell. Where one now saw *Gilligan's Island* replicated, one further segment of its undifferentiated unending being, temporal annelid.

Charles for a partner amplified David's fatalism. Really wanted a bar all his own, but didn't have the money, and wouldn't have the money unless this place boomed. Would cheer up when the happy hour crowds hit.

Trixie came out of the back, where they had a closet-sized bedroom and kitchenette and slept over sometimes, and he realized he'd probably interrupted a little bit of afternoon delight. Didn't help his mood any, thinking what David was getting and he wasn't. "Oh, hi, Charley," she said. She liked having Charles for a partner. Thought it added class to the joint. All they could do to keep her from running ads in the paper. If you only knew, if you only knew.

Picked a table that let him lean back against a brick wall and watch the door and all the windows. There were decisions to make.

Stay with martinis, or switch to beer? Planning to keep his anger for a while, kick it up clear and blue-hot, clean out the accumulated rust of previous resentments. Then mellow into a careful balance of cosmological what-the-hell and randy creative dominance. Cosmological what-the-hell would protect him if she was still pissed when he got home: In the scheme of things, planets and plastic vomit and plate tectonics, fish that could live on sulfur and John Wayne playing Genghis Khan in that godawful hilarious movie—in a world full of such multifarious oddities, what was one evening in separate beds?

Randy creative dominance would come in handy, of course, in case she *wasn't* still pissed when he got home.

But back to the question of what to drink: His internal chemistry had already smoothly surrounded the martini, the images and attitudes were flowing. He was halfway to speaking in tongues, which would do a lot to explain why I keep breaking in. Lianne got to me through therapy and hypnosis, he preferred the incandescence of booze. Which was fine, but you didn't want total meltdown. What would happen if you threw a brew into the works? A fracture, a jagged line, a glowing fault in the containment vessel. Omegas and alphas and anti-epiphenons spiraling out on tracks like the sprung springs of a busted clock. On the other handedness, he was not a heavy drinker, and two more martinis would probably blow him back in time to a time when the slag from the first volcanoes was still belching out like batter from an overfilled cake pan and a few little helpless amoebas were slithering around going *Ooch ooch ouch that's hot*.

"Charley?" said Trixie.

"Charge him double," David said, not taking his eyes off the tv.

"She's not going to charge me anything," Charles said. "She's going to bring me a beer as a gesture to a visiting friend." To Trixie: "Tecate. If you've got one that's really really cold. If you don't, stick it in the freezer for a few minutes. And a frosted glass. With salt on the rim." They always brought Tecate with the rim of the can salted, a chunk of lime on top, but he liked a glass, wimp or no wimp. What he was thinking, if the beer was extremely cold, and with the lime more or less modulating from the twist of lemon, and since Tecate a sort of metallic beer as gin a sort of metallic liquor, then maybe he could bridge ok. And anyhow the Fleischmanns made yeast which made beer so maybe it was all in the family.

He thought about trying to talk to David, but why push? Anyway, the solitude was nice.

Brought the beer, and it was plenty cold. He poured it in the frosted glass, bit the lime, swigged. Metallic, all right, but not good metallic. Flat and biting, like your tongue on the lid of a tin can. He had been hoping bronze or pitted steel. The light blasting through the west windows was too bright, and it was too flat: flat and dusty. Wasn't keying up the internal vitality of things, was just bouncing right off the surface: bingo-boingo, light in your oingo. The carpet was a short-napped off-tan leaning a little to the rosy side. The Formica of the tables was a urine-colored wood grain. On the table next to him was a blastula where a drink had been, dried tumorous ring shiny as varnish.

He tried to ignore the tv, looking away from the set and sipping his sour beer, but Thurston leaked into his brain around its barriers, a painful droning nasality. Right, just the way rich people acted. Now that long-legged Daisy Mae woman, what was her name? Was he really *watching* this shit? Any damn story would grab you up, dammit. So which are you, Charles? The handsome vague innocent all-American scientist? The Captain? Thurston? All three, anybody but Gilligan Silly-gan. And which was Lianne? Half rich-bitch, half sexpot?

Came walking across the desert floor of the rug, the emptiness of everything. She was getting older, meaner, there was no question. He had been fooling himself. Quitting KROK had helped for a while, but only for a while. She would never feel happy and whole. How many years coaching her? *Walk on the sunny side*—until she sometimes thought him a sap, a fool, a clown. And no one ever to handle *his* darkness.

Never no peace. Always some damn misfortune or other, always running off from love into an alien misery. Her bitch mother, ruining such a pretty girl. Calling her whore for kissing her date to the game. *I got a gal in Baltimore*— Catches her on the front porch saying good night, gives her a roundhouse slap, goads the father to slap her too. Which he does because Daddy's unthinkable lust for his daughter, my guess: *She's* the source, not him, of those horrible perverted dreams that he doesn't really have. See, has to be her, because he's the one doing the slapping.

Ah, well, stories I heard told. Should never've married from trash. Pontiac drivers, Naugahyde sitters, tractor-pull watchers, the Christianoids.

So what the hell are you, orphan boy? Could be her bastard brother, all you know. And your adopted daddy only two generations removed from Snopesdom anyhow.

And *she's* not trash. Seed grew in the weedyard, maybe, but she's the rare clean plant, genetic miracle.

Still, all the sweet wet rain in the world won't salve a root-cut plant: leaf rattle, stiff stalk. She could wear sable, they could bop around in a Rolls, party from start to stop. He could quit the firm, they could roam Biarritz, Antarctica, Chapultepec. He could write science fiction. Go back to school, study the movies for real. Study, hell—produce one. Why not? Here in Arkansas, State Head Office on Telling Israelite Types How Eager, Ripe, and Earnest we are. We pay you big rebates, maybe we all get parts. Mary S, sweet Mary could star, running naked so pretty, why not somebody like her in *this* bar, hubba hubba? *My* kind of Daisy Mae.

Science fiction movie here in Arkansas.

But Lianne kept picking hopeless crusades, ways to taste failure. He could see them mean and withered in separate bedrooms, his mouth pinched up with draw lines like all the old tight-asses have, like trying to squeeze a stink bug to death with their lips: Arkansas Gothic.

So leave the bitch. I'm a nice guy, good-looking, got money.

Can't leave, too much guilt. Rejection all her life. The one promise

that came true, me. But what about me? What about what I need? So I
can't leave, but what if she died, an accident. Crossing a dark street with
Mary Beth tonight, hit-and-run, hopped-up teenager. Oh Charles the dark-
eyed, the hollow-eyed, oh Charles the lean with grief—dropping that last
five pounds, too distraught to eat. The pity in other women's eyes, the
glances at his flat flat belly. Never marry again, too brokenhearted. So
many options then, so much freedom.

South Pacific beach, topless girl in a sarong. Forget the sarong. Black
hair between the thighs. No, the sarong is better. Let it get wet, that's it.
Cling. Transparent, with flattened bubbles, pockets of trapped opacity on
the legs. Shiver-skin nipples, evening's on the way.

No. Teaching business law at Halfhard. Looking over his half-rims.
Girl with the gray eyes gets off on older professorial types. Crosses her
legs, slit skirt falls open. The fluting where muscle joins thighbone. A faint
odor: pussy/perfume.

Rome, a big voluptuous teenager with an orange Mohawk. Sunlit ve-
randa, she's lolling back on white-painted wrought iron, big bare boobs,
copper-penny nipples. She's pouting. Wants to go dancing, but he hates
that music, that confounded noise. He wants to stay home and screw. Even
if he did go with her, she would be sullen. Wants him to get a transplant,
plugs of hair. He likes his forehead. All those millions, and she's ashamed
of his forehead. And her periods go on forever, huge messy irritable globs
of spill.

Everybody is just a person. Just another fuck-up. Trade one for the
other, why?

Where did I get this realism bit? Just like Dad, and that's strange. Silent
three-year-old, grim, no memories. Maybe he could feel it. Maybe why he
picked me.

Sad way to be. Where was the tenderness? No love, no love, I don't
feel no love in my heart. Trouble with screwed-up romance, makes all the
country songs make sense. *You dug a hole in my heart with yore hands,
and now she's filling it in. I'll put a tombstone to whur ar love used to be,
it'll never be rising again.* Goober music.

Lousy beer. Sucks, it sucks, it suxitsuxitsuxit.

Hole in my heart, hole in her belly. If we'd of had kids. Empty womb.
Missing womb, I mean. Thank God she'd fought her momma and the
asshole doctor to a standstill, all at twenty-one, with no support, no one
to love her. Where did she get the insight, where did she get the grit?
They're so bad now, think how they were back then. Stupid mechanics:
Long as we're in there, let's just clean it all out, it's just woman stuff, clip
clip snip snip.

But she won. So, natural estrogen. Best of all worlds. Fuck and no
periods. Fuck and no blood, no mess. No children.

The baby in the paper bag. Some nig left on a Longfellow doorstep. Crusted with drying afterbirth. Forty degrees last night. Big stained brown-paper grocery bag. The crumpled top slowly uncrumples, its compressed energies relaxing. Stray kitten stricken with foodsmell, nose in air. Mew-mew. Quick little jerky trot. Sniff. Sniff. Jumps, catches the edge, it gives a little. Hangs on, scrambles up, fall-jumps in. Licks the placenta, purring. Chews, growls. Curls up warm, with a full belly, in the human warm smell. Making that motor noise all night long. Keeping each other warm, alive.

Imagine the old man coming to the door. All the rest of his life expecting to find another bag, another bloody baby and kitten. But the next day, there's just a newspaper, and the baby is just a story in that newspaper. Everything is back the way it's supposed to be. News just got out of pocket that once, showed up all by itself, as itself. Took em a day to get it back into the phantom zone. The rest of his life, feeling like something big went by, but what?

Tears. God's sake, not here. Why real ones now and fake ones in the car with her? I love you, Lianne, I do love you, I do love you: Why why why doesn't it work? What a world! As the wicked witch said when Dorothy threw the water.

With a clatter and a zap, Trixie closed the blinds on the farthest window. Looked at his watch. 5:25. Woo, time jumps. All that on one beer? Trixie went to the other window, rattle-zip, rattle-zip. Now it was dark in the bar.

Coming to his table: "Another one, Charley?"

"Why not?" Eyes adjusting. Not really *dark:* Profound. Inviting.

When the beer came, he poured most of it into a new glass. Lovely in the frost. Bit the lime and drank half the glass. Tang, salt, cold clean cut of suds. Felt it bite immediately into his brain. Topped the glass with what was left in the can. Got up and went to the bar, carrying his drink. Jesus, the norts spews. Yammity yammity, no NCAAs today. Us against Louisville tomorrow, Lamar against LSU. Pat Foster was Eddie's former assistant, so we should all root for the underdog. The underhog.

David would, that's for sure. Hug a loser today, the state motto.

A commotion, a banging at the door. "Let us in, Charley, we seeeee you!" Male, female voices, hilarity. Bang bang bang. "We'll huff and we'll puff—"

David painfully off his stool and over to open the door: Tina and Greg and Lafayette, the gang from the office, uproarious and blowing smoke in the colder outside air. God the light was late out there, cuts of deep gold and lavender in the trees hazy with first leaf: the rivering spill of the hillsides. David closed: snapshot glimpse shuttering gone.

"Oooh, Charley was a bad boy." Tina, pointing, face screwed up like a little girl telling, shoulders hunched, hair up around her wild blue eyes.

She looked back at Lafayette, giggling. So it was Laugh now and not Greg. Greg was just hanging in there. Humiliating, not his scene. He did better at Whitewater with his canoe-canoe river-rat buddies. But how could he give up, a good American boy? Tits, hair, legs, smarts, eyes, professional, she had the total modern kit, punched all your buttons. Radical mozzle. Managed to seem young and fast-lane even at her age, which was after all only what—thirty-eight? Younger than Charles. Beautiful even with her irregular country-girl teeth: crowded, a little crooked, but it made her smile more fetching. The vulnerability. The human flaw in all that energy and gloss. Like to run my tongue around those wicked enamels, like to slip my hairy— Shut up, Charles, you chauvinist hog.

"We're closed," David said, walking back to his stool behind the bar. Didn't look at Charles. Because he was pissed: arranging his life to suit big-time Charley's big-time friends.

"Bad Charley." Greg, following Tina's lead. "Didn't come back to the off-ice."

Not right, let them come in here and talk to him like that. They weren't equals. He was too lenient. Lianne was right. Buddy-buddy with the hired help.

What she never understood, it wasn't because he needed friends. He hated to throw his weight around, that was all. But this wouldn't do. Time to crack the whip. But not here. Not where David would see all gone wrong.

"Go ahead and set em up, David. First round is on me." Whoops and cheers from Tinalaughgreg. David, seated, waving wearily at Trixie to get started.

"Did Charley go home and get a little?" Tina, scraping one forefinger across the other. "Lovey-dovey, wifey-ifey."

No, kiddo, I got jackshit; and you watch it, or you're gonna have jackshit for a job, you're gonna be out on the street in your underwear. *She aint nothing but a two-bit whore*— Been hitting the Evan Williams in that desk drawer again, no bout a-doubt it.

Lafayette, his wide hands on her shoulders, steering her away. "Come on, woman, less have a drink." Big slick Lafayette. He could read the white man pretty good. Going to be a partner soon. Business-econ, and then law. My mix exactly. In the courtroom he was intimidating: that beat-up face, the streak of red running through hair and mustache like bad toner in a photo; the growling voice, the rep as a bruiser. And he used it all, but he was smart, Gee God he was smart. *John Wesley Harding was a friend to the poor, he traveled with a gun in every hand. He was never known to make a foolish move.*

Going to strangers, it was all going to strangers. His reputation, his practice, even the house, the bank and the shares in the other banks, the bar, the fishing camp on the Little Red, the cabin in the Sangre de Cristos. No son and no heir, and tonight not even Lianne to love.

"I need another beer," he realized out loud.

He didn't remember getting that beer. Time jerked again, like when you're driving along thinking and all of a sudden you come back out of nowhere fifty miles down the road. Who was doing the driving all that while?

Tina was leaning her head on his shoulder at the bar, her arm around his waist. He was mightily sad and there were a lot of people in the bar now and it couldn't be seven.

Wasn't, was twenty till. *Sanford and Son* on the tv.

"Here you go, Charley," Trixie said, setting another frosted glass in front of him, this one already full.

"Is this my f-fird or thourth?" he said, slyly pretending, in mid-stammer, to joke. He could feel Tina laughing, a low, relaxed echo deep in her chest. She had her hand slightly inside the beltline of his slacks, as if to keep her arm from slipping down. Now she adjusted it, sliding her fingers under the edge of his shirt, into the band of his briefs, flesh on flesh. *Uh-oh,* he thought.

But he had no will to resist. He felt a zest for the danger. He was a car zooming off a mountain road into a ruinous night, headlights spinning into the dark like a falling fire baton.

Lafayette sat on the next stool, watching the loud fake overdone junk-yard Sanfords.

And Greg, at a table, in a voice that carried too far even here, telling the one about the farmer and the visiting ventriloquist. That Charles had told him.

Where the hell was Harry Caray? Decided absence of Hari Kari all night long. Waiting for Hairy Caries, dreading his advent, worse than the slobberjowl fact.

No, dammit, not baseball. I keep telling you, that was an ad. So what *are* you, drunk?

So he swallowed the beer, which was a river of foam. Whitewater. Past high rocks in a steep canyon, Santa Helena with Lianne, when they had drifted mile after mile looking up to the light on the high stone. Out to a meadow, green meadow under the narrow sky.

Damn Redd Foxx. Insult to a man like Lafayette. He leaned over the bar to David. "Can you not change channels on that thing?"

Voice from out among the tables, somebody thinking he was agreeing with Charles: "Eh-ya! Git them damn coons offa there!"

Too drunk to keep his eyes from flashing to Lafayette's. Whose own eyes are glittering and black, obsidian refusal: I don't need you looking after me. Butt out.

"Might be half your bar," David said. "All my tv set."

Piano. But the band won't start till nine. Someone decided to break the moment, good thinking. Who? It's Rider. J. D. Rider. Didn't know he could play. What's he been up to the last couple of years? Not practicing law, I know that. Probably just as well, he hated it. Kept on, maybe would've killed himself like his old man. Living off his mother? Seems to have plenty of time to work out at the Y.

Lianne I mean Tina gets up. Pissed at me, old-hand-in-the-pants trick didn't work. Did, but aint gone let *you* know. Lose all my bargaining power. She goes to get Greg for dancing, poor jerk. He don't know it don't mean. First lead him over, lay her hand on J. D.'s shoulder at the piano, we're all friends here, chatty-chat, flirty-flirt, twitchy-tail. Poor Greg.

David would not change channels, but he wouldn't look at Charles either. He looked everywhere else, busy with dirty glasses. The other barmaid came back with another tray of them. When had she come in?

Another voice from the tables. "—when hell freezes over, give em our water. After the way they treated us? It wasn't rooting *for* the underdog, it was rooting *against* us. Bush league damn attitudes. I mean, I was for Houston against Villanova, weren't you? Sure, you and me and everybody else in Arkansas, right? Because it's our league. But these mangy damn lop-eared Texas sonsabitches—"

Charles got up, managing his beer nicely. He spoke into the theatrical dark. "Thing about that water thing—you see the paper? Forty billion from the feds, ha. Tell you what really worries me about it, though—and it aint the money—"

He could see the water table dropping, the ground drying out. He could feel the summer high pressure system locked in place over the baking ground: shimmering heat, no evaporation, no way to cool off, trees dying, greenhouse effect. He stepped away from the light, gesturing. "Take what happened last year—"

The goddamn night was on ratchets. He was at a table with a whole bunch of people, laughing and hollering. Woo. Got the whirlpool at the back of the brain, the swivel-spine, no-gyro, fall-over-backward wobble. What are we laughing at?

Big night for everybody. Having a big time. Here in the bar with Charles Morrison and Lafayette Thompson both. Never guess who I was drinkin with last night, Thelma Lou Betty Liz m'dear. A millions-aire and a ex-Razorback football Hog, the high school all-American coon hisself. Shoulda seen how drunk that rich damn peckerwood Morrison was. Shoulda seen that blonde bimbo lawyer had her hand halfway down his pants: you want to pet my monkey?

He had a flashback to the 6:00 news, he hadn't been listening, but something, something important. Lianne and her bulletin, what? What time was it?

"What time is it?"

"Time, time," somebody was answering. "The time is." Big production of pushing up the shirt sleeve, moving the watch face back and forth to reading distance. Finally. "Eight oh nine. Ni-yen." The man with the watch seemed to feel he was onstage, doing his time-operator impression. "The ti-yem is eight oh ni-yen." Some of the drunks around him caught it up, *ni-yen, ni-yen*.

"What did the Senate do?" Suddenly terrified by a number. The number of the beast. No, not that, another number: 482. Senate Bill 482. As if he had forgotten a murder, as if the dizziness at the back of his head was in fact a whirlpool, a spinning drain, as if something vital was spilling away down it, lost forever. "The Senate bill," he insisted. "The one on the news."

Only a couple of people paid attention. "The what?" one of them said. "You talking about the monkey bill?" said the other one. "Twenty-two to two, they have to give equal time to creation science."

"I'll drink to that," said a red-faced fat man with a crew cut, leaning into the talk. He was the one who had been complaining about the Texas fans. "Fucking evolution shit." He raised a beer, slopping some over. He was wearing an olive-gray suit with a yellow silk tie. The tie had big stupid dots. "I mean, they fucking call it the fucking *theory* of evolution, don't they? Take the fucking prayers out of the fucking schools and put in a fucking goddamn communist *theory*."

They were trying to kill her, the bastards were trying to kill her. He saw a white spot in each eye, like the afterimage of a flashbulb. He stood up, his knees giving way. "What's your name?" he said to the man. "What's your stupid fucking name?" Somebody was whispering in the man's ear.

"You don't know shit about science," Charles said. "You got no more idea what science is than a red-ass baboon."

The man was furious, but frightened. He glared up at Charles, clutching his beer with both hands as if it were a post in a boxing ring, all his impressive poundage suddenly a liability, inert and twinging with weakness. His voice trembled: "I'm not trying to start no fight."

Poke him one more time, though, and he would, the only move left. Never mind, sick of it all. Stupid, stupid and proud of it, millions like him, can't fight em all. His money as bad as the fat man's pounds, slowed him down, made him afraid, careful. All over town by morning.

He turned away, falling over the man in the chair next to him, catching himself but accidentally grabbing the man's hair when he did: "Sorry!" Angrily, as if the word were a curse.

Laugh and Tina at the bar. Friday Night Movie.

"What's the. What's the picture?"

"We're going to my place," Tina said. "Party time. Charley wanta party?" *Wanta play house, wanna play doctor?* What had he and Tina been talking about before, her head on his shoulder? He had felt a delicious sadness, a sadness that went through like a shiver, but left him warm and pleased in its wake.

"*Name* of the picture," he said.

Some damn comedy, industrial scene. Should have been baseball, the field exquisite as a jewel, green and brilliant and distinct, but also like a meadow, like a green green mountain meadow somewhere, clean and sunlit and peaceful.

But there were no green meadows any more.

"Cracker Factory," Laugh said. "It's *The Cracker Factory.*"

Charles couldn't help it, he turned to look at the fat man, the others at his table, but he couldn't see them now, his eyes had adjusted. When he turned back, Lafayette was grinning, and Charles felt his own face stretching.

Tina was irritated, the way the men's eyes kept meeting, going past her. "I can't go," Charles said, and her face went blank. "Got to go to the house," he said.

"Just can't stay away, Momma's cooking's so good," Tina said. She modulated it nicely, smiling. It might have been a joke, a left-handed compliment to Lianne and not a reproof. It wasn't, but it might have been, and no way to call her hand.

He had a vision of alternate reality. Tearing what was already torn, breaking what was already broken: The hell with it all, let Lianne pick up her own damn pieces. Pumping it up into Tina, her hair falling into his face, I want to see nipples, rip of the blouse, see the goddamn stick-out nipples, half an inch long.

"I'm worried about you driving," Lafayette said.

"Let him alone," Tina said. "He has to go home."

No green meadows, no clean performances. A pissed-off woman on either end of this choice. Sorry, my dear; you're very attractive, but I love my wife. Saint Charles, gawk ack puke. Oh I want to pork her little slick-ass fanny.

"Let me drive you home," said Lafayette.

5

SOME TRACE OF WARMTH, SOME STIRRING OF THE AIR

Rolling his head on the back of the seat, chilled but not minding it yet, Morrison thought there was something peculiar going on. Something familiar, but wrong. He was heading up Cantrell again, he knew, in the darkness this time, a carousel of headlights and trees and stars.

"Ha!" he said sharply, then realized he couldn't explain to Lafayette. Because it was the feeling of being driven somewhere when he was a kid, trusty black chauffeur, Mr. Polygon. But Lafayette didn't inquire.

"How could I resist a name like that?" his father had said. But Mr. Polygon didn't know where the name had come from; it had always been the family name. That had bothered Charles, who believed that everything should have a source, a reason, a story. Then one day he had realized he didn't know where *he* came from.

"How you getting back?" he asked Lafayette.

"Tina bringing her car."

Morrison thought that one over. Lafayette was worried that Charles was too drunk to drive, but he wasn't worried about Tina, who was, in Charles's opinion, even drunker.

Suck up to the boss? Didn't seem like. You wouldn't tell him he was drunk if that was your plan.

They didn't speak the rest of the way home. In the driveway, Morrison said, "What you been wondering about. Your job, you know. Your promotion and all." Jeez, he thought. It's like talking about sex. Talking about sex would be *easier*. "Can't give you any specific—specifics right now. Hang in there, though. Going to be what you think it ought to."

He realized he was talking about it now to keep from having to get out of the car and go in the big dark house alone.

"Well? Don't you have anything to say?"

Lafayette laughed. Laugh laughed. It was a strange sound, like the grunting of a bear amplified and slowed down into the bass. "I didn't say anything," he said, "because I saw what I was about to say."

Tina's lights pulled up behind them. Naturally, she didn't put them out, so they sat there pinned like two escapees in a prison yard.

"What was you—were you about to say?"

" 'Thanks, Coach.' "

"What?"

"I was about to say, 'Thanks, Coach.' "

Morrison hmped, a derisive little snort of comprehension. "All those years," he said.

"All those years," Lafayette agreed.

"Well-o," Morrison said. "Gotta do it." He opened the door and heaved himself out. Lafayette got out on the other side. Then he was beside Morrison, a quick big presence in the night, his hand patting Morrison's coat. Jingle. Thrust in a pocket. Morrison almost lost his balance.

"That's your keys," Lafayette said, walking away. "Night."

"Night," Morrison said. A door slammed, the lights jerked away backward, lurched into the street. He could hear the car shifting gears, winding out and around and down the hill.

As soon as he entered the foyer, he knew she was home, though there were no lights on at all. Some trace of warmth from the walls, perhaps, where she had placed a palm to steady herself while she took her high heels off. A faint radiation, a wisp of her perfume, some stirring of the air in a way that only the living can stir, so that hours later it will not be entirely calm.

He went precariously from room to room in the dark. She was out on the sun porch, in one of the cushioned wicker rockers, curled under a blanket, looking out over the back lawn. He touched her, and her head went down, and her shoulders shook. So it was that easy. He kept forgetting. All these years, and he still forgot. Her anger, her apparently causeless hostility, was really just the defensive bluster of a terrified child. Who once had had her red wagon taken away because she had let a little naked boy ride in it, naked because he had wet his pants, so they had gotten cold, so he had left them in the sandbox. Who once had had her millage taken away. The child who had tried to save other children.

He knelt beside her, dizzy and awkward. The armrest was in his ribs and a rocker painfully jabbed one knee, but he folded her as well as he could, blanket and all, against his chest. Big loud sobs. He could see her face in his mind, contorted with crying. She didn't let herself cry often, but when she did, she cried hard, like a child, her face pulled into a grimace like the mask of tragedy, the face of a girl whose parents have just said, *We hate you because you're bad.* How not believe them at that age? *We hate you and you're going to hell.*

She had saved her tears for him. Just saved them, that was all. Not putting on a show, not dramatizing a thing. Just waiting till he was there and it was safe to cry.

"Help you to talk about it," he said. His back was hurting from the way he was bent over, the chair was attacking him, he was sweating under his jacket in spite of the cold. He was sick at his stomach. "Help you to get it out of your system."

But she didn't answer, went on crying. After a while she said, "I need a Kleenex."

He disengaged, fumbled, found his pocket handkerchief. "You can use this," he said. He held it up to wipe her nose, and she took it. Her face was wet with mucus, and his hand came away gluey. He wiped it on his pants.

"Let's go upstairs," he said. "But I think I'm too drunk to carry you." They bumbled upstairs in tandem, leaning against each other, her in the blanket like an Indian chief. "Whoo," he said on the stairs, his left leg giving way.

"Matter?"

"Leg went to sleep. Think I'm going to puke."

"Are you ok? Are you going to throw up?"

"Mm, don't think so. Maybe not."

They went to the sneak-away bedroom, the guest room they used when they were pretending they had eloped. It was directly over the dining room, the only bedroom on the second floor. It had a fireplace. It had a cherry-wood rocker, a rag rug on a hardwood floor. Black and white octagonal tiles in the little functional bathroom, set out with blue squares. Octagons were not space-filling like hexagons, a fact that his father had not minded but that he himself had always seen as a flaw: It proved that octagons were *not* geometrically perfect. There was an old oak dresser with a cloudy mirror, there was a big down comforter, there was, he knew, a Bible in the bedside table. She had put it there, no worshiper but not the unbeliever that he was.

He kissed her pale bare freckled feet, biting the pads of her toes. It seemed a wonder to him, a beautiful thing like an Appaloosa horse, that her feet were freckled. He fitted his lips to her arches, and bit the right one so hard she slapped him. He kissed the twenty-year-old scar over her pubic bone, his lips against the sealed mouth of that wound. About her thighs and belly, her sunny skin, the merest whisper of tea rose, lingering.

When he entered her, she cried out.

"I hate this place," she said afterward, naked, raising her leg to the light and sighting along it, flexing her toes. "We must just really enjoy looking like ignorant hysterical hicks. Creation science, my God. Eddie Sutton can get a whole new gymnasium. Little Rock can't even get an eight-mill tax to pay the teachers. These people hate education, they want to destroy it."

It was a line of recrimination they had traded in before, making themselves feel better, closer, by tearing down the benighted citizenry. It was true enough, but tonight he wasn't interested. He thought of telling her about the man in the yellow silk tie, and then decided not. Throwing fuel on the fire. "We can go anywhere we want to," he said. "I'm not tied to this house." Not true, but he knew her answer.

"I'm *from* here," she said. She wasn't very serious about her blues, lifting her other leg up, letting them both plop down. Looking at him over her chest, like a kitten daring him to play. He reached over and twiddled her red-and-blonde pubic hair. The burning bush, their old joke.

"Speak to me, Holy Spirit," he said.

She giggled and twisted away. "Mine," she said, sitting up cross-legged. She peered at his crotch, stagily, cocking her head like a bird watching a worm. "It's so little," she said. "Where did the rest of it go?"

"You can't have it," he said. "It's mine."

"No, it's mine."

"Mine can be yours if yours can be mine," he said. "But if yours is yours, then mine is mine."

"They're both mine," she said. "Where did it go? It was this big a minute ago." She made a sizing gesture like a fisherman telling a story. Then she swooped down and grabbed him with both hands. "Where did it go?"

"Aaah!" he cried in mock alarm. "I don't know, it's in there somewhere. Probably hiding. This time of night, it might be asleep."

"Only ten o'clock."

"Yeah, but it feels later. I don't know, this time of night, if you yank on it, it might just go away completely. Maybe it needs more like a kind of a gentle. Oh. Suction. Yeah, that's. *Oh.*"

She wept again when she was through, sprawled over his chest. He held her tight while she sobbed, her body seeming light and tough and frail all at once. He felt as though he were holding the girl herself, the young woman who had needed a lover so badly and had gotten a tumor instead.

The frailty of her body was a girl's frailty, but her skin had the velvety quality of her age, a fine suppleness under his hand, the soft leather of experience.

I choose you, he thought. This touch, this taste, this way of loving. How could anyone else ever be so real? No matter the swiveling plumpoid figures of the great American dry hump, the eyeball dream of Barbies with nipples. The hell with fantasies, the hell with Tina.

She burrowed against his neck, finally, content. It was always either giggles or tears when she came, nine to one on the giggles, but she had been overdue on the tears. "You know," he said, reaching over her hip to dip a finger, "if we could do this two or three more times, I might not even get a hangover tomorrow." She clamped his probing hand with her thighs, slapped it lightly, and pulled it away.

"Mine," she said, and put her nose back in the crook of his neck. "Light," she said. He reached up for the switch on the wall.

"I been having this picture in my mind all day long," he said in the darkness. "You know that story about the baby they found in the paper bag on Longfellow Lane? The one where the kitten had gotten in with it? All day long I been seeing it."

"That's easy," she said. "You're the little lost baby, and I'm the kitten who crawls in to keep you warm. Sleep now."

He lay there shocked and irritated. That wasn't it at all. She was the baby. He was the one who was saving her. Brave kitten climbing in. Clamber in the brave bag. A boiler room down in the basement. Something about a luminaria. And the light behind the door, fanning out into the dark basement, the basement of the bag. They were in there, playing poker under the hanging light. Amberjack/Laugh. Tina/Mom/Miss Kitty. Somebody's face he couldn't see, smoking, smoke instead of a face, curling in the cone of light. Empty holes for eyes. Hands dealt out on a pool table, face cards up, brilliant on the wide green felt, veldt, the baseball field. A pair of kittens with a jackknife kicker.

He woke up once constricted with her weight, dislodged her. They rolled over and slept, spoon-fashion.

He woke up again at four o'clock and could not get back to sleep. He got up, naked, and wrapped himself in the blanket she had let slide to the floor. He eased the french doors open and went out onto the rooftop garden, padding barefoot on the cool stone. He was tumescent, if not completely erect, and he laid his penis across the marble rail to pee. It took a moment to switch the channels, and then he heard himself splattering in the bushes below. When he was through, he leaned back in the lounge and watched the stars, the blanket tucked in around his feet, holding himself. He was hard now, so hard that it ached. He gave it a stroke from time to time. "You want something, boy?" he said, running a thumb over the slippery top. "What is it you want?"

Jupiter and Saturn were close together and low, setting into the dark trees, luminous, pearly, almost palpably globular.

He was still drunk, but in an easy, loose-jointed way. His sense of balance was swiveling, but swiveling gently, like a boat tied at a dock, not anything to make him sick. There were a lot of stars for a city night, the town as dark as it ever got: a few lights down by the river, the hotel signs red on the downtown plain. The new leaves whispered around him.

The stars were drunk too, he realized. They had to be, to go reeling around like that. He thought of the baby in the sack, but the image didn't do anything to him now. It had been sucked away, up into the whirling stars, the drunken and lonesome stars wheeling beyond his roof, the high clean spinning Arkansas stars that told him how much he still had to lose.

6

THAT EVIL
HEART

So how would it be?
Charles wonders, some time in the unspecified future. How would it be in Lafayette's head, he means. Will mean. Trying to sort it all out, untangle the tangle, see how it got so bad. Trying to blame himself, figure what he could have done different. You guys, you humans, what are we going to do with you? Causality and sin, the same damn thing, that's how you see it.

How about sensitive dependence on initial conditions? Does it mean anything if I say your fate is so fed back it's unpredictable? Does that begin to explain to you your freedom, even in the face of Somebody's—ok—*My* omnipotence?

Ah, forget it. Charles doesn't even need Me, he's haunting himself.

He blames himself for the sin of pride, he thinks maybe if he had been more sensitive. If he had kept the door open with Lafayette, if he had stayed tuned in. How was it in Laugh's head that night, driving his drunk boss home?

Walk back to the TR-7, Tina's TR-7, in the cold spring night, the air suddenly still, windless after the windy day. Walk back, a shadow in the barred shadowy spill of darkness from the white man's big white house, a house you will never have, never own, no matter how well you play the game.

Was that when it began, that night in the bar?

Walk back to the car, your mouth twisted with the bitter taste of his condescension, so generous with his pro-motion, him with his Miss Little

Rock but got to lean all over your woman anyhow, in front of everybody, in front of God and the world. David and Uriah.

He tries to imagine Lafayette, and of course I help. I have to, that's what I am. If anything moves between you, there I am. If I am. If anything moves between you.

Easy to say you done good, better than expected. Could've been in jail for the last fifteen years, but you aint. Figured out what your brain was for, why it was sitting up there on top of your head. Woke up one day and saw what the real game was. Knew you could play that one too. Congratulations, you get the honorary downtown nigger award, big gold trophy with fat lips. Get to be on the board of this, the council of that. Get to join the special black branch of the Good Suit Club. Get to live in a big pile of rocks out on River Ridge Road.

But you'll still feel them telling the coon jokes when any two of them go off to the john together, the stain of their unheard laughter oozing through the walls, a giant rusty discoloration, a spreading and fecal seepage.

Or you go in the john with them, and you have to laugh how they tense up at the urinal, their stalled flow while you make a good loud purl and splatter. How they cover their silence with sprightly chat, with friendly nervous conversation. And can't make a stream till you zip up and walk away. Like it had anything to do with anything, except you been in a million locker rooms, and one thing about a locker room, it will *teach you to piss. All they leave you, the small useless revenges.*

Crank up your time machine, Chucky-boy, your guilt machine. Let's check it out. Window up Lafayette on the old viewscreen, yeah.

Walking back to the car with that taste in your mouth, in spite of the fact you liked the man, or would've if you could've; if it had been that kind of a world. Did you say to yourself, So he thinks he likes old blondie spread-leg, does he? Well, maybe we'll just see about that.

But if you had a machine, how would you know what you were seeing was real? We invent our memories, they've proved that. So maybe we invent time, because what's the difference between memories and time? Maybe it's all just stories we make up to try to make things fit. To try to make all the busted pieces fit.

Oh, but that would be too cruel, wouldn't it? Not to be able to grieve even a memory, to think that maybe you'd just made yourself a meaningless little shrine in the middle of nowhere when really it happened on another planet. That would be too much like not ever having had her in the first place, wouldn't it? Too much like you had just made her up even when she was around. That would mean that you've always been alone, and that's a real hard thought.

But it aint like you have no choice, is it? Window it up, baby chile: Zoom on Laugh Thompson walking back to the TR-7, to

Tina waiting head-thrown-back, wild hair all down the back of the seat. Walk back with a sideways grin, feeling that dick swelling up already, laughing to yourself at the poor drunk jerk going wee-wee-wee all the way home to face his bitch-wife alone in his big dark house. Everybody knows Charley don't go out drinking lessen him and Lianne are on the blinky-blink-blinking. So you do Lianne if you can, Charley, and I'll jam my weena in teenie-teen-Tina.

She let me drive. Interesting, the kind of thing we don't have to talk about. Now, if she be pissed with me, it a be cutting time for the old black boar-hog, but right now we both got to prove a thing on the other people, and so I drive.

Of course I pop the gears, make that little plastic bug of a car jump backward out of the plantation drive, make the hind tires scream like a murdered woman when I rip it through first, of course I wind her up all along Jackson Street with a sound like a two-ton mosquito hitting the speed of light. Wouldn't want to disappoint no nigger-watchers might be hanging out the windows of the big houses, no. Also this is one useless little beach-bucket this-yere so-smart woman thinks is a spotes car, and I'm trying to make the damn little rackety whiz-bang come apart like a coffee mill hooked up to a ninety-horse Johnson. I would like to make her little engine blow up right in her little face.

"I swear, Lafayette, you drive like one goddamn fool." Ah sway-uh, Laugh-y-et, you drahve lahk one gah-day-um foo-ul. She don't have to do the Miss Scarlett bit, aint one bit funny, but she likes the way I react, the way it pushes me deeper into my role.

Corner of my eye, I see she's pleased, throwing off sparks. She knows how to use my anger. She can be the jaded mistress, popping her whip, having throats cut, striding through the quarters with her titties hanging out. Then the slave rebellion, the mighty are thrown low. Now she's the despised property of Mandingo Red, cruelest and most hardened brute of all the brutes who once lived and died to furnish her closets with silken petticoats. Oh he hurts her. Oh he rapes her. Oh she is punished for her crimes, oh, oh, oh.

Bottom of the hill, in traffic, I flatten it out, slow down. Car's like a little red arrow: *Look here, cops! White woman, black man!* Oh no, no bigotry here. Cop himself like as not black. But I get a ticket, it's a mark on my reppatation (like the senators say). It's a danger signal: Might be a wild type, a troublemaker. Charles Morrison gets a ticket, well, that's high spirits, is all. Humanizes him. Niggerizes me.

Tina could gig me, could turn up the heat another few degrees: *Why, Lafayette, why you slowing down?* In that mocking voice that says *I know why.*

She's got other things on her mind. "That bitch really has him under her thumb," she says. "Miss High-and-Mighty Tight-Ass."

She got the mojo on his dojo, honey, he lick the gravy from her steak. He weazle up and whistle when her record player break.

"You don't know what it was like being as poor as I was, Laugh."

"Naw, Babe, can't imagine."

"And she just waltzes in, la-di-da, take a piece of my ass, give me the wedding ring, now I'm a millionaire."

"Like you wouldn't." But she don't hear me.

Now we're at the downtown end of Cantrell, turning right on Chester, heading for the Quapaw Quarter. Pick her up in Quapaw, put it in her pocket.

"Laugh, you can get him to come to the May Day party."

"You aint through with me yet," I say.

"We've been through all that. If it was between your big fat hairy legs you could put a lock on it, but it aint. I told you up front, leave if you don't like it. You got no call to get jealous."

"I aint jealous," I say, lying. "I'm horny."

"Huh," she says. Grabs around left-handed.

"You got it now," I say. Stopped at the stoplight by the fire station. She's unzipping, I'm imagining a fire truck slamming into the car. Dead with my dick out, what'll Momma say.

The light changes, and I zoom over the still-not-open Wilbur Mills Freeway, into the dark side of town: where the reconstructed and remodeled floosy hardwood-floor Victorian-turret or Tudor-roof mansions of the upwardly mobile uppery crusty lawyers and teachers and doctors and ad-men and newspaper colyumiss and young politicos jam cheek-to-jawbone with crack-walled tilty-floored bust-windowed spiderwebbed wrecks divided to quadruplex housing for lost rednecks from the country who have stumbled in looking for city jobs or city cocaine and right up the street not four blocks or so, the governor's mansion. No, you can't say the guv lives apart from his constituency, no.

It's a good place to buy property, if you don't mind living just across the street from my momma and all her friends.

So she dig around while I fire down Chester Street, then cut over. Boom it come up free. All over me eating on that thing. What I get worrying about speeding. Spose they stop me now. Magine the papers. Be talking about "arrested for committing an oral sexual act while driving." Tell you exactly what they talking about but won't even say it, can't say getting his dick sucked on wheels. Aint that dirty now, aint that dirty, them papers, to be talking like that, talking about it without saying it, oh woman now aint that dirty, Momma Momma don't look out yo window now, go round the corner, scared I be caught, aint sposed to be scared, big redheaded niggers aint scared of nothing, big nigger will do it will do it anywhere, anytime, can't let the woman, oh do it, be know I be scared I be caught:

Bump up the hump up, her driveway, and damn near gag her: Finish me off under the lights the lights of yo big brick pile, yo party, the sound of yo party, pumping yo head on my grett big jump-up, I'm pressing the pedal to a hundred and forty if we was still moving oh Momma oh God oh Momma oh don't don't no—

And then I'm saying, "Goddammit, woman, swallow that shit. This a seven-hundred-dollar suit."

"That aint shit," she says, wiping me off with a Kleenex from the pocket and laughing. One of the main differences in men and women, keep Kleenexes in their cars.

Now she going to lead me into her house, like a elephant by the trunk. Around through the back, though, in through the dark back porch, washer and dryer lined up on the wall, basket of clothes on top, all just as strange as the grave in the shadows of trees through the windows, the dark tangled up in the dark.

Give me time to go down. Sometime she want to be caught, but not this time, I guess. This time just want to feel like she might could be, just a *little* thrill. Why I put up with this, led around like a clown?

How many women you think I can have? Yeah, I know the Colt 45 greasy-head ads, everybody still buy the big black stud bullshit. I am going to tell you something, Rufus. It aint that way. It aint that way for nobody notime. They just tell you it's that way to sell you something. It's rare stuff, baby. Have somebody you can fuck and also talk to even part of the time. It's rare stuff. Oh you'll take the fuck, forget the talking? Bullshit, Rufus. I don't care how goddamned stupid you are, you need to talk more than you need to screw, spend more time doing it. Need somebody to share yo sorry story with, even if you more stupid than a brain-damaged alligator.

And I aint stupid at all.

Plus which, she got that evil heart. Woman aint got that evil heart don't do me no good at all. What I probably need is a woman got that evil heart but that good heart too. Then my evil heart dissolve in her evil heart and both change color like them chemical liquids, and we be good. But that's more rare than rare. Come in two flavors mostly, and that plain vanilla heart don't do me no good at all.

Now she look in the window of the porch door, see if anybody in the kitchen. They aint, she yanks on me to come on in.

"Uh-uh," I say, hip-swivel it loose. But she leave a hand-burn on it. I pack it back in while she going on through.

All the noise hit at once when she open the door, loud cackle-cackle argument, music, somebody laughing. Like a school lunchroom, like chasing roosters, just the same old sound of a party, all over the world, any language, play any music you want to, grab up any different kinds of people you want, wind up making exactly the same sound. This kind of water down in Pascagoula, that kind of water up on Martha's Vineyard, all different fishes in it. Slap on the sand and make the same damn sound.

Tina goes on into the living room to jump in the ocean, Greg comes in while I'm standing there looking in the reefer for what I'm on drink. Don't need that beer, fat already, but Lord I can't stay sober no more, world aint worth it.

Greg drunk already, must feel the same way. Wobbling into things, fall against the side table, look like he trying to talk, look like a little lost boy.

Who you, he say, who you. I think he look like a ghost saying *whoo whoo*. "Who you think was the best back you ever played against?"

So he's gone be manly and noble, the gentleman loser. Aint whether you win or lose, it's how you lay the blame. Bear up under his broken heart. Shit, boy, I'm doing you a favor. You never would shoot that woman's rapids and live. Think *I'm* your competition.

Guess what, old Lafayette's a sucker for that decency shit. Just love to be accepted, even by a drunk little white boy. He big o heart just throb so *warm*. Grab Greg around the neck and bear-hug him close. "Help me figure out what I'm supposed to be drinking tonight," I say, and we stand there, buddies, staring into that treasure chest of cold stuff, that one thing in America got more promises than a woman's eyes.

7

GETTING
THE IDEA

So then later we're in Tina big old living room, pegged-oak flooring and pegged-oak stairs. Got about a million people yakkity-yak, standing around. Got a fireplace, which is going good, and about eight thousand worth of stereo, which is also going good, blinky green lights, graphic equalizer wave band. And over in the corner a grett big old concert grand.

And can the woman play? I don't believe it, never heard it. Claim one time the governor come by, well, he aint the governor now but will be again by '82, but he come by and Charles and Lianne for once was here, wasn't long after Tina join the firm, her return party for the one they give her, what it was, and he come by and Lianne played and sang in that silver-bell voice that almost won her Miss Arkansas, coloratura, and the governor sang "Old Rugged Cross" and "Standing on the Promises" and all those white people hymns. They say. Would I have sang with them? Probably. Make a jawful noise.

Governor Bill was making nice between elections, probably, don't have much use for Morrison, Morrison, and Chenowyth during a campaign—too liberal, and the electorate already sees him as a liberal, so we might cost him votes. He *is* a liberal. Or at least a populist. Really wants to do good in his heart of hearts, much as any politician have a heart of hearts. But he'll never take a stand, none of them ever will, what good are they?

How most people feel about lawyers too. Liberal law firm, ha, oxymoron. But we got a token me, and a token woman junior partner, and two other women, and Greg, a wild-eyed radical by Arkansas standards, Hendrix and Vanderbilt and belong to Peace Links. But mostly it's Lianne, she colors everything. Charles probably a Reaganite, left to his ownsome. But whup with that woman, Lord. See with her eyes.

"Yo, Last." It's that damn Bobby Leopard. Thinks he's Sylvester Stallone. Played a little in his senior year, '75 or '76, aint amounted to snuffjuice since. This bank, that S & L. Teller, assistant manager, branch manager. Put him where he can do the least damage. Bout like how they played him too. But he was a Razorback, live off that the rest of his life. Natch, since we both 'Backs, we got to be buddies. He thinks. Wanted a nickname himself, but couldn't get one. Says everybody called him Def, but Hooter say they didn't. How he find out mine I don't know. Hooter told him, I'll kill that nigger.

He might know my name, but he don't know why. Me and seven others, some of the first ones. Like a club. The brothers all calling me "Last" all the last two years, except it came out "Lass." Real long and drawn out. "Laaass." And none of the white boys ever figured out why. Cause when I hit the man, it was his last Laugh. But the caspers never picked up on it. They thought they were cool to figure out Laugh: Laugh. A. Ett.

"Hell of a party," Bobby says. So we're supposed to stand elbow to elbow surveying the crowd, I guess, two old gladiators above the fray.

"You right about that, Def," I say. "You surely are right about that."

He shines just like somebody switched a light on. Oh hell, I done made a friend. Slaps my belly like an old pal, grins. "You puttin on some weight, aint you, buddy?"

Some men just wadn't born to live very long.

Rider at the piano now, jazzing along with "Come Together." Showing out, but the man can play, give him that. *He got monkey finger, he got toe-jam football.* Built like a tight end. Wonder how tough he thinks he is. *He say I know you and you know me.*

Got to be good-looking, cause he's so hard to see.

Be fuck if the door don't open and in come Mr. R. T. "Sonny" Raymond, looking just like his campaign posters. Lord high bailiff of Pulaski County himself, and a couple deputies in plain clothes. One of the deputies I recognize, was chief in Jacksonville till they caught him messing around with a loaf of head cheese. Moved Raymond up to replace him, and then when Sonny run for the lord high bailiff job, he stuck by the old boy, brought him along. Which I got to deposition him before the grocery store owner dropped the suit. He didn't really want any money, he just hated to see anybody treat his head cheese that way.

Only good thing I can say about Sonny, think if Mr. Head Cheese hadn't got caught and we had elected him instead. Count your many blessings.

I'm about the first thing the deputies see, but then their eyes click over, put me in the right slot, the Say Mac slot: Niggers We Can't Mess With. Yet. Till I make a wrong move someday. One goes to one side of the room and one to the other. Just like their man was President of the U.S. Probably thinks he will be someday. Buford Pusser goes to Washington.

Making his hellos to Tina. Damn woman does like trouble. Bound to know this will get back to Charles. Believe she wants it to. Does she want Charley-boy, or does she want him mad? Does she even know?

Bending over to smooch her cheek, a tall man but don't quite look it. Built real funny, but nobody seems to notice. Kind of tapers toward the top. Big old duck-footed fellow, size thirteen feet, legs start out like he would be six foot eight or nine, but he just gets littler as he goes up. Winds up about six three. Round shoulders, average chest, little feminine hands on the ends of his short arms. Little old pea head sitting up on top. Good chin, but about six and three-quarter around the brains. Take him a foot at a time, he looks like he's in proportion.

Now they're saying he's handsome. Getting him all urbane: manicure, hairdo, good suit. Faking charisma, prepping to run for Congress next time around. But that pudgy white face, that black hair slicked back. Got that J. Edgar Hoover look, that Tricky Dick look, got them poochy little cheeks, them tight little pouty self-righteous lips, like a tv preacher with a mouth full of come.

Five or six other people come up, and I lose track of the megalomi-croid. Don't exactly invite people to come over and start yakking, but they see me with Bobby, means I'm accessible, and the next thing I know I'm being handed around the room like a baton in a four by one hundred. Which I wonder how old Redwine will do tomorrow? Lightning on wheels—

At one point I see Tina and Greg, in the corner behind the big lamp by the fireplace. They're talking work, not love, I can tell because he looks competent instead of lost and embarrassed. But they're talking love. So close she's shaking perfume loose into his breathing. Greg, oh Greg, poor Greg. The signal's in stereo, babe, and you only picking up one channel at a time. One side say No and one side say Yes, but you got to put em together to get the message: You're fucked, boy. You're double-fucked.

Greg Legg, what a name. Does his wife even know? She got to know. Will it be Deevorce City where used to be pretty little Yuppieville? Air she sit home and weepin, Greg? That long face clean as a collie dog's, is it going all hard and red-eyed and lonesome while you wag yo puppy tail up by this smelly bitch-ass?

—Mr. and Mrs. Greg Legg and child, promenading down Kavanaugh at six o'clock of a Sunday summer eve, he pushing the stroller, she holding on to his arm. Looking in the shops. Khaki walking shorts, probably bought em right across the street, Ozark Outdoor Supply. The Leggs, and that's what they are, rangy and tall and long-legged, six one and she must be five eleven, long tan copper-haired legs on him and long tan smoothified legs on her. A matched set. The young gentry, and beautiful to behold, the perfect life except nobody ever told them how it could go so bad wrong so quick for no good reason. Washing they car on a Saturday, she stretching to reach the windshield, shorts riding up. Send her on by me if you don't want her no more, Greg. I got something make her feel better.

Goddamn if it aint that whiskey blonde sing for the Holy Sacrament choir. Woman show more bone than a archaeological museum. Get away, you ugly thing, make me shiver to touch you. Can't say that, got to draw back a little and talk. Strategically disengage. What you got to do to make a living nowadays just as bad as being a politician. One or two good-looking M&M's floating around here—Tina a equal opportunity party-giver—but they won't even look at me. I got a bad reputation with the sisters. Once mess with a white woman you x-ko-moony-kated, babe; what I mean, you cut off.

No I aint gone come back to no choir, bitch. I done stayed out of jail one time, what I want to get back in with that batch of cokehead bisexual Christian embezzlers for? More indictments out of that bunch than the whole damn Nixon administration.

But then she puts her hand on my forearm to take her leave, the goodbye touch, and says: "It's just that we miss your growly old voice on the Doxology," and I remember one time looking around during the prayer at Sunrise Service and tears sliding down her face. Tears for the prayer? Tears for the beautiful music? Tears for Lord Jesus, risen to save us all?

—Before I left Holy Sac, left the white people's success church. Going back to Moan 'n' Groan A.M.E., back to my roots, I thought. *Oh aren't they wonderful, all that emotion and how they can sing those primitive hymns oh dearie.* It was too quaint. Too damn *cultural.* Won't be joining no memorial march for the Atlanta children neither, Brother Hezekiah D. I'm sorry, I done join Buster's First Church of Belly-busting Brunch, and I go to all the services.

And now her eyes, amused, clear. Can she read what I was thinking? And she's gone, but the press of her hand lingers, and she seems, suddenly, beautiful. Odd, skinny, drunken, and mysterious, and I'd like to bang that bony old cat.

Which goes to show, don't ever forget the flip-flop. The way it will suddenly switch around on you. Get so busy telling your own story to yourself, you forget all them others, how they telling their stories too. Get too close to their story, boom, suck you right in.

Remind me of lying out there on the football field coming back to myself in the cool fall air, sky full of faces and lights, noise coming back up like someone turning up the volume on the radio. I know I been knocked out, I know it like I been somewhere far away being my real self, and they sent me back, and before they sent me back they gave me a little slip of paper with all the information on it: "You a high school halfback, and you just been knocked out blocking a gap-shooting linebacker on a sweep right."

I woke up happy and sleepy, feeling warm and comfortable in my pads. They said I was smiling. They said I had been in convulsions a few minutes before. But right when I woke up, I saw all the faces, and it was like I could see *behind* the faces. Coach wanted to get me out of there because we had momentum and a ten-point lead and he didn't want us sitting around getting cold while we decided whether I was dead or not. Austin was waving sneakily at Shalene, over there with the majorettes, and then pulled his grinning face back in to look at me: "How he doing?" Jeebie the trainer scared silly cause all he know how to do is slap atomic balm on em and tape em up, and maybe they blame him if I die: "Don't move im, don't move im."

It was like when I looked at them, I *was* them. I was in their thoughts, and their feelings made sense to me. It seemed like they were feeling exactly what they were supposed to feel, that anybody who was them would feel that way.

And sitting by Momma in church two days later, when she stood up to testify thanks to God he brought her baby back from beyond the grave, it all flash into my head again, and I have The Idea. Then I'm supposed to testify, I eem have to come up front, can't just stand there like my momma, cause I'm the one it happen to. What I say? "Mumble just want thank Jesus He gimme my health mumble and He care e-mumble-nough to mumble my and mumble dedicate my mumble to Hee-yum," never moving my lips or looking up from the floor, and the whole time The Idea flashing in my head: How God lives every life, how He is us, broken into a billion pieces, maybe even be in the dogs and the bugs, all the time looking out of all these different eyes, giving up being God, one at a time, so he can come down and really exist, be in the real world He made instead of just a imaginary thought in His own lonesome brain. Make more sense to me than any other religion idea I ever hear.

Then when I get serious in my junior year at Arkansas, find out I have to take all these real courses, wind up in philosophy class to satisfy my core curriculum. Teacher about four years older than I am, grad ass. I bring out The Idea, show him I can think too. He say: "Oh yeah—that's Big Idea #475a, by Plato and Aristotle, and then E. Manual Cuntlicker, he had it too, only you got to figure in the Impressive Correlative as applied to Wittgenstein in a Group Matrix, which is semantically notwithstanding, unless . . .''

So I kind of lost the joy of the public use of The Idea, but here I am old and fat and pissed off, and people still doing their flip-flops, and I sure would like to bugger that bony ass.

''How do you get a woman to want you?'' Greg says, coming up to help me watch Amanda Peliandra's ass wander away. ''I mean, how do you make her *crazy*?''

What am I, father confessor? I'm a wild man, don't you people understand, a wild man, drunk out of my mind, blow job in a car on the way over, I aint yo goddamn friend and witness and caretaker.

''You might be a little drunk,'' I say.

''Sometimes I feel like a bar of Ivory soap,'' Greg says. ''Ninety-nine and forty-four one-hundredths percent pure. I have had women rub me all over their bodies and then just wash me off in the shower.''

''A man aint got to make a woman want anything,'' I say. Trouble with people asking advice, you start giving it. Aint nobody ask advice cause they need it. Ask it cause you getting a little too wise. Time to turn you back into a asshole again. Asking advice the quickest way to suck off yo smarts, make you make a fool of yourself.

''Sometimes I feel like a big cold glass of milk, and they want whiskey,'' Greg says.

This reminds me to take a drink of what's in my glass. Decided it was too late for beer. ''Women already want men,'' I say. ''They bodies made to want em. They like dick and hair and balls and big loud noise. Sometime they even like bald and fat. All you got to do is get out the way. Don't say no shit, just answer they shit when they say it. Look in their faces, see what they wanting to do right then. Get yo eyes off yo dick. *They* a be watching *it*. You be watching what makes em lift up their chin when they sitting down, what makes em twist around in their seats.''

''Who the hell is that?'' Greg says.

The whiskey's beginning to make me zoom, maybe why my dialect is so broad and fake, counterpart to Tina's Miss Scah-lett. ''Look for a woman like big dogs. Big ugly hairy dogs.''

''What the fuck is he doing here?'' Greg says, but I don't pay attention because I'm thinking about a weimaraner I knew one time. I should have kept my eye on him because he got that nice-boy white-boy kind of anger, equanimity squared until something flip his switch, and then he turn red all over and it's *code duello*, baby, fight to the death, *You have impugned my sovereign Southern honor, suh.*

Time to sit down. On the couch, it's a couple of theater people on either side of me, talking across while I stare into the whirly-q agitation of the fire, all that broke-loose excitement that it makes us feel so peaceful to look at.

"Rocky Raccoon" has been playing, over and over. Mopheads ever since we got here. Don't jive my bones, but this bunch done rediscovered it. Think they found their soul. Tina go on and on about their *melodies,* how much they mean to her when she a activist in college. Poor old John's meaningless death. The violence done to genius, oh God. All that week at the office, everybody depressed, all the retooled hippies. Charles the atheist waxing biblical: *In the midst of life are we yet in death.*

"Well, I don't care, I think Yoko is just *capitalizing,* and if you think that's ok, well maybe it is," says one of the theater people, getting huffy.

"Well, she's a *woman,* and she's *Oriental,* and don't you think you're being just the teeniest bit *chauvinistic*?"

"My goodness, what's going on over there?"

Two voices rising sharp over a spreading quiet. I twist my head around. Greg, and Sonny Raymond. If it was a comic book, stress lines would be radiating from their faces into the air.

"So," Greg says, "so if it's so all-fired infallible, where did Cain's wife come from? Some sisters and brothers we didn't hear about? Did he marry his fucking sister?"

Sonny gets ahead in life by doing things that would ruin a good man— paranoia, tyranny, an uncontrollable temper. Decent people can't stand him, the way you can't stand to look at a bad accident. And while the decent people avert their eyes, he moves up another notch. And you wonder how the hell such a crazy man got so much power.

"You don't talk about the Bible that way," he says. "It could have been space aliens," he says. "God could have sent down some space aliens."

I have worked my way through to grab Greg's elbow, but he jerks it loose. "Space aliens?" he yells. "What the fuck kind of aliens is that? Is there some other kind of aliens you know about and I don't? You pinheaded boob—"

"I told you to watch your mouth once," Sonny says. "I can arrest you for nuisance, public obscenity, and terroristic threatening."

"Your mother farted and thought she give birth," Greg says.

"You goddamn asshole communist," Sonny says, and jumps into him.

Head Cheese means to kidney-punch Greg, but I'm standing on his foot, and when he opens his mouth to holler, I stuff my pocket handker-chief down past his larynx, so he has eat at least that much nigger snot in his life. I also accidentally spill most of my drink, which is all bourbon, into the eyes of the other deputy—a kind of upward fling as I lose my balance tripping on the foot of the first one, you know. And then I have Greg around the arms and chest and hoist him away, backing him over to the couch like a man wrestling a chest of drawers across the living-room floor. The lord high bailiff is over in the corner yelling, but at least he aint pulled out his hogleg and fired a shot over the bow. Rider stepping between without seeming to, calming him down. Quick man, quiet voice.

I fling Greg down on the couch. "He's a brokenhearted lover," I say to the theater people, who have stood to watch the action. "Help him cry away his gloom." Best I could do, couldn't think of no moptop lines.

And then I figure it's time for me to disappear for a while, sight of me aint gone do nothing but aggravate the lord high and his deppity dogs. Maybe he got enough sense not to arrest Greg. Cause if he did, he in deep shit. I mean, Lianne might leave a brick or two standing, but I doubt it. Don't work for KROK no more, but think she wouldn't do a special report? Think they wouldn't be glad to let her do it?

What I do is snag the bottle out of the dryer, Tina's secret cabinet for the good stuff. Make up for the drink I donated to the eyes of the law. Slide on out to the glider. And what I think about out there, rocking myself and taking a couple of big quick swallows to hold off the shivers, what I think about is fights.

Every real one I ever had was a scrumbly old messy thing, boil around grabbing whatever you can, stick stab bite yank piss and kick. Aint gone be no clean shots, whack on the chin and the man goes down—you win because you got the bravest heart. Your man might go down, but aint no clean shots.

It take a whole damn sport to set up just one clean shot. The only fights that matter, the only ones that leave you anything after they're over, they're the ones with rules.

And I'm too old for those anymore.

No sirens come, so everything probably settling down. I hear people talking out front, a little at a time. Hear a car door slam here and there. Party thinning out. Getting cold. I head on back in.

Greg asleep on the couch, got his head on the lap of one of the theater people, his feet on the other. They're talking about whether to get a CD player like Tina has, paying him no mind. I fumble in my pocket, get out my little calendar book, write his address on tomorrow's page. Way I feel, won't be no tomorrow. Give the address to the one on the right, looks more sober. "Can you take him home?" I say.

Off to look for Tina. Don't see her nowhere, don't see Sonny Raymond and his bunch neither. Nor my bony old choirwoman. Jesus I need to talk to somebody.

"What happened?" I ask people. Trying to find out if Sonny went on home without no more trouble, if Tina went with him, or what. "There was a fight," one old goober says. "Yeah, there was some kind of a fight," says another guy. "I was in the kitchen." a young blonde woman says. "Who was fighting?"

I give up, head upstairs. A little swoozy, a little swivelly-sick. Patek Philippe say 1:22. What do he know? Half-past everything.

Nobody upstairs, good, party thinned out enough I can sleep. Got the monthly board meeting start at nine o'clock, just seven and a half hours, I'm on be in great shape for that. Could skip it, but if he aint shitting me about the partnership—

Charley-boy wasn't looking too healthy tonight himself. But he'll come in brushed and clean and bright-eyed, and I'll still be rubbing syrup out of mine, fighting to keep em open.

She aint on the water bed. Turn up the dial, I like to sleep warm. Git the wrinkles out these pants, damn pleats make em lap over on the hanger, give you two creases, wonderful, fucking seven-hundred-dollar suit look like a three-for-a-hundred at Horn's.

So she sitting on the toilet crying. All I want to do is pee.

"Why you sitting on the toilet crying?" I say.

I aint asking why she's crying, I'm asking why she aint crying in the bed like a normal person, so I can drain my lizard.

But I kind of see, because the bed is a warm comfortable place, and she looks real miserable and solitary there on that white marble torture throne, held up in the cold air in the middle of all that other white marble. The kind of a cry you can't get to if you feeling too comfortable.

"Thinking about my brother," she says, sounding just like a kid from the country out around Jacksonville. "Thanking." Aint really a *ank*, just real nasal.

I heard the brother stuff before, and what I'm thinking, I seen this with her, it's the fight has got her all upset. Whether she knows it or not, she sets the fights up, but then they leave her scared and shaky. And I'm thinking that's how come I aint gone stay with this woman long, cause she is trouble walking.

And she looks up and the flip-flop happens again. Because her face is small and white from crying, bony-looking, raw, the freckles showing through. She looks country-kid starved, the kind that eat salt pork and beans and corn bread and don't get enough iron till the greens come in, and her big blonde hair suddenly looks like a wig, a big fakey fluff over all that frailty.

I pick her up by the shoulders and kind of stand her over in the corner. "Just a second," I say. "I got to do this."

When I'm through, I turn to her, and she comes up against me, patting my big belly, brown hanging out over my white Jockey shorts. Treat me like a teddy bear, something warm to hug up to. "Since Brandon died," she says, nosing into my chest, "I hadn't felt like I had anybody to take care of me. Everybody thinks I'm so mean and tough. I know they do. But it's just a front. A lot of the time, all I feel is just scared and lonesome."

So I'm thinking about how it feels to be her. How it would be to have the kind of a family she had, that crazy daddy and crazy mother and the brother the one person she can count on, and then to be there when it happened. It's summertime and you're home from college, which Daddy never wanted you to go to in the first place, getting too uppity, too big for your britches. But Daddy died and you did and now you're home.

And Brandon's over changing the oil filter on your car, because you busted it off on a speed bump and you're too broke to take it in to the shop, cause you need all your money for school in the fall. And the jack slips. And even though he's not just your brother but your best and only friend, you had a fight with him the day before, one of those bad family fights, and he dies cursing you, bubbling blood and scrambling like a frog smashed under a cement block.

The neighbors come running over, so they get to hear it and see it, him screaming and clawing the gravel, and you shrunk up against the shed: *I'll get you Tina, goddamn bitch I'll kill you!* So you bound to blame yourself. You bound to blame yourself the rest of your life.

"Sonny was so good to me when it happened," she says. "That's why I still talk to him. That's why I invited him over." I had forgot till she said it again that he was the deputy took the call on Brandon. And I wonder if they had anything going back then. Probably. Wouldn't have been like her not to.

"You shouldn't mix lovers," I say. "They aint all easy like me. Him and Greg wadn't fighting over the monkeys. They were fighting over you."

"We aren't lovers," she says. "I know he's a reactionary son of a bitch. But they were all ignoring me, and treating me like I wasn't even there, or else like it was my fault somehow. He was the only one who showed me any kindness."

I like to see his kindness. I bet mine is twice as big.

But what it's like, holding her—it's like you're a real nobody. You aint a football hero yet, cause you just in the tenth grade and aint got your growth, just a skinny little scrapper. And you black, and poor, and you in love with the homecoming queen, this beautiful rich blonde. And because you hardheaded, because you like pain, you keep asking her out. And one day she says yes, and it shocks the hell out of you. And so you sitting there in the car with her at the drive-in, not knowing what the hell to say, scared shitless the ducktail honkies'll see you and come jump your ass. You sitting there thinking what a big goddamn total idiot you are. And all of a sudden she breaks down completely, messes up her makeup, mascara running witchily from the corners of her eyes, and she tells you the truth about how upset and depressed she is, and asks if you'll just hold her for a while. And it turns out yo white queen, yo unattainable bitch goddess, is just another person like you.

"I will take care of you," I say, squeezing her tight there in the bathroom.

"You'll take care of me," she whispers, offering up her small tight mouth.

"I'll take care of you," I say, and mash my mouth on hers so hard her teeth cut. She slides her center of gravity to nest against me, crotch to crotch, and warm. I turn her, leaning her over the basin, lifting her dress. Her face is sleepy in the big mirror. She loosens her straps, and her breasts fall free. You know I am the only dark thing in that white room. And I am peeling her pants down, and kicking out of mine. "I'll take care of you," I say, pushing it in, past the scratchy pull of the dry labia, into the wet core, and then we're both wet, and I can look down and see myself, shining and stroking, and I can look up and see her in the mirror, leaning on her arms, eyes closed and peaceful, her hair and her titties jumping every time I pump it in, how she lowers her head to get her neck in line with every slam. *"I'll* take *care* of *you,"* I say.

PART TWO

FRACTAL LOVE

8

LONESOME
LIGHT

Bright afternoon sunlight through a bank of southern windows.

Lafayette, the light in his eyes: As it turned out, the 9:00 meeting hadn't really gotten started till 11:30, which was ok with him. They had reviewed current activities, the most pressing being the situation with Pulaski County. It looked as though something would be worked out by Monday or Tuesday, Charles had said. And when had he had time to see to it? Lafayette wondered. Probably why he had postponed the meeting, that and not to cure his hangover. Probably been knocking on doors over in Dogtown since eight ayem.

He had called at Tina's: *If you see Lafayette, will you let him know? I can't get him to answer at home.* Tina giving Laugh the big wink: *Oh I don't think you have to worry about him being too early.* As if Charles didn't know Laugh was right there, rolling heavy and black in his bed of pain, draped in frilly percale. But this was official, so we would pretend to the proprieties. Jesus, all the games, all the subcurrents. Did any human anytime ever just say what he or she meant? What would happen if we did?

Jesus Fuck, Charles, he's right here stinking like a hog, drunk so much yesterday he's still drunk this morning. You know how that feels, have a hangover and still be drunk at the same time? And before I let him go off to that stuffy old office, I don't care how his head feels, he's gonna have to take a shower and come back to bed and jam it up my gravy-dripping crack, unless maybe you would want to come over and do it for him.

I understand, Tina, I was just that drunk this morning myself, and I would love to come over and jam it up your gravy-dripping crack except

*for the fact Lianne would sure to God find out and whack my business off
with a big sharp hatchet. Hope you don't think I'm too chickenshit.*

*I think you're chickenshit, all right, but you sign the checks, so I'll
come right on in and french-kiss your fucking asshole and bring fucking
Lafayette with me so he can sit there like a big goofy boy-dog cause he's
eat a woman and been eat before most men through with the paper. So I
guess I'm chickenshit too in a different way.*

The two extra hours gave Lafayette time to flush the sludge out of his
system, have a big noisy tarry shit, and steam in the shower till his follicles
were spraying faster than the showerhead. They gave him time to swallow
some hair-of-the-dog Bloody Mary, heavy on the Tabasco. Eating was a
problem, but he wouldn't make it without some kind of nutrition. He went
with the weightlifter's special, a dozen raw eggs in a glass. Not like Rocky,
though, no yolks, that was a stupid scene, the yolks are all fat. Tina pretending to gag. Lafayette: *Did it all the time on the team.* And follow with
another shot of the plasma Mary, to cleanse his palate.

Yeah, the two hours helped, but he could have used an extra two weeks.
It didn't do his morale any good to see Charles come in brushed and clean
and bright-eyed, just like he had never had a drink in his life, just like he
hadn't gone down to his own saloon the night before and gotten more drunk
than a crow on juniper berries. *Charles Morrison, Esquire,* Lafayette
thought.

What he was seeing was the magazine and not estates in England.
Charles never would blow-dry his hair. It was always wet from his shower
when he got to work, and combed down in slick rows. He pulled it straight
back and not forward to cover his growing baldness. All of which is to say
he looked, except for the high forehead, a lot like the models who were
beginning to show up in the magazine. When had everybody started using
Wildroot Cream Oil again, and wearing suits that were way too big, and
sporting ties that didn't have any stripes at all? How come all of a sudden
all the young men had heads that were exactly the same size as their necks,
so that neck and head seemed to be one long flexible superlaryngocephalic
column? How could the noses be so carven, the cheeks so hollow, the jaws
so angular, the chins so strong, and yet all still fit into one harmonic set
of features?

What, in fact, were argyles doing on their feet?

And how was it that all this suddenly seemed fashionable, even to
Lafayette, even though they were all young white boys posed on the grounds
of say Harvard U and wearing expressions of such hauteur as only the
discovery of a third and superior sex could explain, a sex that in its inter-
necine conjugation brought forth, somehow, showers of money from the
very air?

How was this possible? What strange secrets did the stylemongers know, that these expensive, otiose, handsome, and vaguely humanoid disassociated giraffes could represent his own estimation of flair, sartorial panache, when, a mere week ago it seemed, the apotheosis had been unshaven neurasthenic Eastern Europeans in tight and shiny two-button Italian suits, high collars with gold pins under the tie, and the ties themselves busy with severities of slanted maroon, sharp inclinations of black and silver?

Ah, style was more mortal than atherosclerosis. How was he to fit himself into this latest upheaval, then, this most recent sea change of awareness? He with his belly, he with his glare, he with his muddy and battered face, his wild and woolly checkerboard hair?

Charles, with his surpassing poise, simply avoided the question: He might, to Lafayette's early morning eye, possess the slick hair and the wolfhound physiognomy of the models, but he was too wise to force the resemblance. Aging, he abjured huge tweeds and voluminous double-breasted silks, stayed with the banker's dark blue in several subtle variations, an occasional marvelous olive or dawn gray, the tie an accent of clear bright red or yellow, dotted with tiny navy or sliced in perfect bands. And yet he still managed, at least to Lafayette, at least in the mornings with his slicked-down hair, to look superbly in the vanguard: so rich, one would guess, that he had no need to seem first of the firstmost: the sort of man who could spend three hundred dollars just to make certain that the cut of the armholes didn't bind him when he moved.

How conscious was it? Lafayette wondered. How much thought did the man give it? Because if he gave it a lot of thought, well, then he was mortal, he was on Lafayette's level, with just a lot more bucks. But if—and this was what Lafayette was afraid of—if he simply *did* it, simply assumed this easy appearance of confident fabric and masterful stitching, why, then he was, like the dude be saying, awesome. Terrifying, a phenomenon, the door slammed in old laughing boy's face, the final proof that there was for sure and always a world some people could never enter, a heaven you couldn't buy no ticket to.

These were the things in Lafayette's mind as he watched Charles perform for the board at 1:30 Saturday afternoon. Even though these wasn't all exactly the words in his mind: Dialect aint a zack science, baby.

You do dialect and you think you got it just right, reppazent it percisely, and twenty years later it all seems quaint and cute and unbearable, like reading *The Emperor Jones* aloud.

Because people don't speak dialect, they speak at and around and toward and with it, sliding from level to level as they understand speech and as need dictates.

As the light now slides from level to level, from face to face.

Charles was speaking again, blinking against the brilliance. He spoke of current earnings. He spoke of the firm's portfolio, last item on the agenda. All employees of the firm shared in it, investing portions of their salaries. Charles controlled the portfolio, both as executive manager and as largest investor. There was, however, a voting board of directors, which consisted of all senior members of the firm, plus one representative chosen by those employees who were not attorneys. All employees could sit in, but only the board could vote.

Charles was not the chairman of the fund's board of directors. That was his partner, Eamon Chenowyth. But these meetings were general meetings for the firm, and the portfolio was always just one item on the agenda. So, as head of the firm, Charles chaired the meetings, but as manager of the fund, he was presenting a report to Eamon and the board. He had never quite had to declare himself out of order, or overrule one of his own recommendations, but there had been times when such an event seemed the logical next step.

Earnings this quarter were down, and that was causing problems with Eamon, because Charles had sold more silver. He had sold off half of the firm's silver last quarter. Then he had sold another fifteen thousand ounces just recently at $11.75.

Eamon didn't understand that numbers are nothing but readouts: Money, said the vampire, is just a social code for available energy. Wealth is nothing more than poise, poise in the still center of large, complex, and rapid changes. What Charles could seldom communicate to his fellow monkeys, who understood money only as territory, who wanted to fix their money, mark it with cocktails of urine and hormones, is that the money on the high side of a selling point wasn't real money. It was illusion, a virtual image, the projection of a vector. If you allowed the pursuit of that illusion to make your position unstable, you were in trouble, no matter what that particular gauge reported. For there were many gauges, all with their claims and stories, and it was in the intuitive grasp of the whole implied by these many partial indications that true poise lay.

Charles was in command of considerable technical knowledge, but his strength was not actually the strength of a whiz-kid manipulator, all IQ and data and sharp edges. He could put on a show of such expertise, because that was the stereotype, the fashion of the age. People then understood reality as machinery rather than God's dream of existence; intelligence as information rather than judgment; and control as aggression rather than giving and sympathizing.

Charles had his real strength in the swiftness and clarity of his intuition. He understood Zen money.

But not Chenowyth: light-struck, stirred from torpor to warmer torpor, reptile on a riverbank lifting his massive tail. He liked solid money, he liked silver, because it was *there,* it was heftable. He liked to visit the fund's safety-deposit boxes, and there in the vault take out the hundred-ounce bars in their soft felt drawstring sacks. More beautiful than a pound of fresh cold butter when the hot biscuits sit steaming on the table. He would stand there, curling a bar slowly and thoughtfully to test, in his very muscle, the weight of money. He spoke of William Jennings Bryan with favor, as though he remembered the orator from his own days as a young lawyer, which was impossible, since Chenowyth had been born in 1920.

Chenowyth particularly liked silver that was performing like an allocated and oversubscribed stock in the aftermarket. He was a wealthy man, thanks in part to his long participation in the portfolio, but he did not understand his own wealth. Like most, he understood wealth as countable dollars, a huge storage of tangible symbols, a glowing jumble of bills and coins like Uncle Scrooge's money bin.

"Did you see the paper this morning, Charles?" he said now. "Twelve ninety-five and still rising."

Chenowyth's mouth, the prissy way the man bit off his accusations. The lips were narrow, a primness shockingly controverted by their rougy pinkness, and he was one of those people whose teeth were too regular: tiny and even, and all the same size and shape, like kernels on a perfect ear of corn. They slanted inward too, like a shark's. The other members of the board saw Eamon swimming murkily in beams of submarine light, blindly opening his jaw, engorging as he breathed. Nothing that went into that gullet could escape. Now the man was chewing away at a lovely spring afternoon. If they weren't careful, he would swallow the Razorbacks. This meeting had to be over in time for the game. Young and Peterson and Hastings, Friess and Brown and Darrel Walker—small bodies drifting in clouds of blood, mangled in that irresistible Chenowythian maw.

Charles leaned back. The others waited. The light shot through a bank of windows into their midst, faster than silence, faster than hope. "Eamon," Charles said, "if I told you the government was fixing to start selling all its silver, what would that mean to you?"

"What? How do you know that? I don't believe it. Even if they do—"

"Never mind *how* I know. It's going to happen."

"That still doesn't mean—"

"We can argue all day about what it means." Charles surveyed the other faces. He addressed them, ignoring Chenowyth. "It might not mean the prices go down right away. There's still a bull market out there for metals. But what it means to me is that something is rumbling, something is going on. Now, my thinking is if there's a tornado coming, you don't wait to see how big it is before you get out of the area."

Chenowyth raised his voice, but Charles, seeing consensus in the others, overrode him. "Eamon," he said, in his capacity as chair of the meeting, "the fifteen thousand ounces is a done deal. If it'll make you feel any better, I'll hold on to the rest of it. But we're going to lose money, you watch. Can we move on to the S and L numbers now?"

"Well, yeah, but there's only five or six thousand ounces left. You've sold—"

"There's sixty-two hundred and fifty ounces left. Can we move on?"

"I'll move on if everybody else wants to, but I'm going to have to hear a vote."

"Do I hear a motion to move on?" Charles said.

"I move we move on," Tina said, looking up in her reading glasses from her copy of the report. She was laughing, and Charles thought the glasses made her look older, but also witchy and infinitely desirable, just that beguiling touch of soberness, sternness.

"Second the motion to move on," said Laugh, stirring from his stunned slumber.

"Any discussion of the motion to move on?" Charles said. "No? I call for a show of hands. All in favor of moving on to the next item of business, move your hands up." Now even Eamon was smiling, though he tried to hide it. "The ayes have it."

And if I'm right, and we do lose money on the silver, Charles thought, *you'll bitch me out about that. If I could predict the market as well as I can predict you, I would be J. Paul Getty.* He had a vivid image of Chenowyth sitting there, months from now, grumbling, completely unaware that just a short while back he had sat in this same room complaining in the opposite direction.

Charles was right. Eamon's discontent was a marvelous instrument, perfectly transferable in any situation. Not only discontent, but all the baser emotions share this quality. Anger, hatred, envy, fear, accidie, lust, greed, self-pity, all and each: If you have a supply of these you can spend it in any country. Love, now. Love is a local imprimatur, good only where it is made.

But what point explaining love, Zen love, when it is so hard to explain even money, its pale and simpleminded imitation?

The light—the light fell onto the brilliant linens of the conference tables, which were arranged in a hollow square and which were set about with trays of tumblers, cut-glass pitchers of iced water, stainless-steel urns with spigots that dispensed coffee and hot water for tea. The men took coffee, the women took tea, except Tina. Charles hated tea, the sadness of it, the soggy bag like a spent scrotum. Lianne drank tea.

The light was dominant and ignored. The light rose into the eyes of the attendees. The light struck the table linens with such white intensity that what it fell on had two images, as if the interior of the eye reflected what it gathered. As if the eye were able to see not merely the physical fact of each object but its ghost as well, two similar luminosities a heartbeat apart. The people at the tables could not turn their eyes away from the light, though they spoke to each other in normal voices (but with little lags of disconnection). They tried hard to sound as if they were concentrating, but large portions of their minds were preoccupied with the light. They thought they were sleepy, but they were not. They were dazzled.

I know because I was there. As I am here, with you. I am the one you must confront in this. Open your eyes.

"The next item of business," Charles said, "—page fifteen in your report—is a recommendation from the manager of the portfolio that we strongly reduce our holdings in First South, Savers Federal, and Worthen Bank."

"Well, I partly agree with the manager on this one," Chenowyth said. "I have never liked our savings and loan investments, and I do not approve of the Omnibus Bill, I think it's just opening the door to disaster. You all know my position on all that. So I can go along with First South and Savers. But as chairman, I don't see our way clear to divesting any of our Worthen stock. Not only is that bank rock-solid, with Jack Stephens behind it, but you're sending a very negative message to Stephens Investment as well."

"Eamon, we don't have any money with Stephens, and anyway, I think you're making a couple of faulty assumptions. One is that any of Jack or Witt's money is really at risk. If anything goes wrong, they're going to know about it before the rest of us do, you can bet on that, and they're going to unload. In fact, that's when *we'll* find out, when we wake up one morning and lo and behold an Arab or a Japanese owns the place. Secondarily, I think it's wrong to think that Stephens Investment would allow any difference in the way they handled any personal accounts because we sold off our Worthen stock. They'd only be hurting themselves, and it wouldn't be honest anyway."

"Honest?" Eamon said. "Honest?"

"Charles, I don't understand the recommendation," Tina said. "I read over the report, but would you mind explaining some more? Those investments look to me like they're performing real well. I don't mean that I agree with Eamon about Stephens—I don't think that has any bearing, and anyway, I don't know anybody who has any personal funds with them."

"I do," said Chenowyth. It rankled him for Tina to use his first name. She was younger, and female, and should have been calling him "Mister."

"Well, that's your problem, isn't it?" she said. "But I still don't understand why we should sell the stuff."

Charles explained that in his view there were a lot of undersecured loans out there. He quoted numbers. A startling amount of Arkansas money was invested in Texas real estate. He adduced the relationship between those schemes and the current price of oil. He pointed out the vulnerability of that price, how completely dependent the Texas price was on unpredictable events in the Middle East, how depressed the Texas oil market had been just three and four years ago. He stated that in his opinion nearly every bank and S & L in Arkansas was in a dangerously exposed position, but that since the fund held stock in only three of the institutions, those were the ones he had gotten his numbers from.

In reality, he was operating on a hunch, on impressions that he had gathered listening to snatches of conversations among his colleagues at parties, over lunch or dinner. He had a fondness for land, but a deep-seated distrust of speculation. In his view, you treated real estate, private or commercial, as a long-term investment like a bond. You didn't get in and get out, looking for the quick big bucks. But lately he was hearing lots of excited talk about surefire projects in Dallas, ways to triple your investment in half a year. People who didn't normally get into jackpot schemes were taking fliers: not only the usual doctors and lawyers, but preachers and furniture salesmen and radio personalities and high school principals and college professors. It had been all he could do to persuade Tucker and Dee-Dee to stay away from one such operation. They had been thinking about mortgaging the clinics for investment capital, as if the clinics weren't in enough trouble already.

In real reality, he was hardly paying attention to what he was saying. The light fell in a rigid bar through the windows, moving slowly around the table as the sun moved west, moving like the hand of a clock across its dial, like the bright inverse of a gnomon's shadow, moving clockwise, as in fact all such light and shadow must always move north of twenty-three and one-half degrees north latitude. Which is the reason, according to at least one philosopher, that clocks move clockwise. Not that sundials do not measure time in reverse below twenty-three and one-half degrees south latitude. But that the clockmakers had been northerners.

"Well, what does point number four have to do with all of that?" Tina said. She had some real estate she was worried about, some houses she had divided into apartments. "The adverse impact of the drop in the prime?"

Charles and Eamon were together on this one, and both started to explain. The board chairman deferred to the manager.

"That's the lowest the prime has been since early last year. You know how you've had trouble selling your apartments because nobody can afford a loan? All right, just that way, the amount of money out there in the form of loans has been sharply reduced by the twenty-one-and-a-half percent prime. That's the whole point: slow debt, slow inflation. But now, drop it to eighteen, I think the market's going to take it as a signal of a downward trend. A lot of money out there people have just been sitting on for months, I think they're hungry, and I think they're going to take it as a chance to jump in in a big way. So if you've got some unstable loans out there with the rate having been so high, think how it's going to be now.''

She nodded her head, satisfied. And how much of that explanation had she needed, and how much was for effect, to create in Charles the warm fatherly glow of the mentor, to bring his eyes specifically to her?

So now the time the clock told was Tina. In the glory of the light, she herself was alive with glory, her hair a weightless cloud, too bright to see distinctly, shifting its mass with the slight motions of her head, a nimbus like the hosts of the angels rising and falling before the throne of God: White was her face, yea, whiter than alabaster, the shadows of her jaw and collarbone arguing an infinite vulnerability, and in her throat the tenderest lace of usage, the rings of flexion.

The kitten in the paper bag, but that memory was fading. It wasn't pity. Charles was simply stricken. He was in love. Twenty times in one day. Twenty times in one day a man may hate and love. The light was the clock, but what was love? More real than money, more real than time, but nothing so chartable as either. The heart revolving in its unstable parameters, flashing its changeable truth. He had loved Lianne, would love Lianne. Was faithful, would not now, unless everyone else suddenly left the building and she stood up and began to remove her clothes, fuck Tina. Had scorned Tina only the evening before. Twenty times in one day.

And her eyes behind the lenses of her glasses, her turquoise eyes, shifting in her skull, tilting their irises into, against the light as she stared into his explanation, went a strange flat green, like the leaves of a tree in a July noon, the pupils zipping shut, so that her look had no depth at all, so that her fragile beautiful face cast a glance as blank and reflective as polished malachite.

In the hall afterward, she was laughing with Eamon, and a pang of vivid jealousy went through Charles. ''May eighth,'' she was saying. ''It's halfway between the equinox and the summer solstice, and it's when they used to sacrifice the virgins. Maybe *we'll* have to sacrifice a virgin.''

''If we can find one,'' Eamon said. ''We'll have to go outside the firm for that.'' He seemed pleased with his little joke, no longer petulant or irritated; but he looked strangely at bay, a fat monkey cornered by a jaguar. He stood straight, pinned between the water fountain and the wall, holding his papers high above his belly, wearing the flattered smile of an Inca victim.

Charles could not for a moment imagine Eamon at one of Tina's parties, but that didn't help the way he felt. With the surge of jealousy had come a memory, and he hurried to his office, as if the memory might be visible to others and needed hiding. He had remembered sitting at the bar with Tina, and how it had happened that she had put her head on his shoulder.

She had told him a story about her father. Drunken, and threatening murder or suicide, or both. The shotgun up under her mother's jaw, choose her or me, who do you love, or else. Hysteria in a trailer house. Brandon, her brother, weeping, helpless to talk. What was the right answer? What was the answer that would make it all right, keep them both alive? Tina had chosen her father, shrieking with panic. And he didn't shoot, but then they had turned against Tina, both of them, hating her, the mother siding with the father. So often, the abused loyal to the abuser and not their fellow victims. Horrible, horrible, a doomed family.

The father shot while hunting. And her brother, Brandon, a car had fallen on him, and something strange there when she talked about it, bad vibrations. Had the father done it? Knocked the jack loose? But no, the hunting accident was before, the father was already dead. Brandon, who had been so much more brilliant than she, who should have had his own career but had sent her through school instead, who had talked her into trying, though she was starting late and would be almost thirty when she graduated. So when he died, she was alone.

Her low humorous voice beside him, ironic and melancholy, making it almost quaint, an old story, a terror outgrown. Except the loneliness.

And he remembered talking about being lonely himself. He was adopted, and he was rich, and both of these things sealed him off. It had not felt like confession or self-pity, himself as Eleanor Rigby, *Oh all the lonely pee-pul*. It had just felt like a relaxed, open discussion of plain objective facts. Life was lonesome sometimes. It was good to be able to have a few beers with a friend and talk about the facts of the case.

"Ah, Charles," she had half said, half sighed. "If people could just get together when they were lonesome. If there was just a lonesome detector or a little light that lit up, and they could just get together then and let it go at that. And it wouldn't make anybody mad and it wouldn't break up any marriages, because we all feel that way sometimes." And she had leaned toward him and let her head settle to the shoulder of his jacket, and it had felt like the most natural move on earth, warm and easy and no strings attached.

There was work to do. He had to review the reports on the potential jurors in GG-81, see if he could catch anything that Buddy and Betty had missed. He had to make a list of sources for review in FL-78, the Pinto case, which he wished now they had never taken. For that matter, he needed to get Alison started on his income taxes. More important than work, there was the Razorback game, now less than an hour away. Arkansas and Louisville fighting to make the sweet sixteen, and surely the Hogs did not have a chance, but oh God, how the heart ached with hope.

But what good was hope if you did it all by yourself? Lianne was out on her Saturday routine: farmers' market early, then group, and then painting class at the Arts Center. She wouldn't be there to help him transfer his identity to the team, to stake her soul with his on the performance of a few young boys they'd never met.

Such hope required a devotion, a ceremonial audience. It needed someone to turn to and say, *Oh my God, did you see that?* And pound each other's backs, and laugh with crazy happiness, and say to each other, back and forth, the items in a litany: *Aw, did you see that move. They've got a chance, they've really got a chance.*

What could he do?

He sat at his desk staring to nothingness, angry that Tina had invited Eamon to her party before she had invited him, suspecting that she had staged the invitation to Eamon to pique him in just this way, worried that she might not invite him after all, knowing that he could not go if she ever *did* invite him, pissed off that he had to go home and watch the game alone, and so they would probably lose, because his heart was thumping with so large and lonesome and painful a hopeless hope. And pissed off that even if Lianne were to be there, he would never ever be able to talk to her about the most important feeling in his heart right now, which was that he was lonesome, lonesome in the awfulest lonesome way, lonesome for some sweet lonesome gal to lean up against in some lonesome bar and be lonesome with forever.

9

SWEET SIXTEEN

So naturally what happened, Laugh poked his head around the door and asked if Charles wanted to come downtown and watch the game with them, they were going to maybe see it at Slick Willie's on the big screen. And Charles surprised himself by saying, No, I tell you what, why don't you guys come over to my house. We got that big old Curtis Mathis and I'll be the bartender, how about it? And anybody else you want. That latter just to try to sway them; he was hoping nobody else would come.

So Laugh draws himself back out into the hall, and there's a whispered conference. Negotiations. Charles can figure it: Tina had plans, Laugh had plans, complicated enough, but now the boss offers an invite, don't sound promising, sounds awful tense, in fact, but maybe you better not say no. And you're sitting there, Charles, thinking, *What the hell I think I'm doing? I don't know these people. This my idea of keeping the help in line?*

And all meantime a contrary fantasy: Laugh somehow has to leave, a phone call, his mother died, Tina sitting in that gapping yellow silk blouse, catches him looking. *Why should we pretend? You want to see my titties? Oh yes, oh yes.* Then ripping away the flimsy, buttons and all, fucking her there on the couch while the Hogs beat the Cardinals 100–54.

And under that another fantasy, just a glimpse: Laugh doesn't go, it's the three of them in the big bed upstairs. But that's disgusting: Laugh is black, black is dirty, dirty is a homo, you're not a homo, so you never really had that image, did you, chief? Not even for the flicker of a second it took to reject it.

Of course Clemmie was there. So neither the fantasy you had nor the one you really really honestly didn't have could have been realized in any case. But hell, that's just logistics, and fantasies don't wait for logistics.

Laugh stuck his head back in and said, "We'll meet you there."

About this time Lianne got to the Arts Center for her painting lesson. It was normally pretty busy on a Saturday afternoon, but today it looked empty, deserted. Because of the game, she figured. *Typical priorities in this state. Charles was mad, well, let him be mad.*

It isn't like I'm keeping you *from watching the game. You're a big boy, you can watch it by yourself.*

Just this one Saturday, that's all I'm saying. This is the *game.*

And the next one will be too, and the one after that.

There might not be *a next one.*

There always might not be, for anything. I might not have another lesson ever either. What you're doing is discounting me.

Sometimes I wish you'd never started going to group.

You should start going back. Listen to yourself. You're so symbiotic you can't even watch a ball game without me. That's why you're mad. People always get angry when the other partner rejects a symbiosis. You're just as mad as you can be—

Do you ever have those dreams where you're pushing through all these scratchy plants in the middle of a jungle and you don't know where you are and how you got there? Sometimes I feel like that talking to you. Lianne, we're just talking a damn basketball *game here.*

So why don't you treat it like one, instead of telling me I'm just another Sunday painter, just another bored housewife?

You're a Saturday *painter.*

Not funny, Charles.

You're right, that was stupid, stupid. Because I really don't feel that way. How many times have I said that you really do have talent? Didn't I buy you the damn easel in the first place?

The damn *easel.*

Oh for crying out loud. I'll tell you who's playing mind games. You're just verbalizing your own fears. Your parent won't let you paint, and you're projecting it onto me.

The guard in his parent uniform lets me into the studio, my heart hammering.

I am alone, I am first. I can hear the guard's radio on the folding table in the hall, that's why he was frowning—not a cop and I am bad, but he doesn't want to be here, wants to be home in the quarter, black man in his undershirt, beer in his hand in a worn-through armchair watching the game, his wife in a print dress, his boy he hopes to be a Razorback watching, black and white in Arkansas watching the game: home.

I am here first in a cold flat place in empty light.

Clemmie gave Charles a hard look when he came in and said he was

going to be watching the game at home. And some friends were coming
by too. And would she fix them a tray of snacks. "I thought you were
losing weight," she said.

"Hell, I'm fine, I look like a tennis player. Anyway, this is a special
occasion."

She sniffed. "Everything's a special occasion," she said.

"Eat," he said, emphatically. "Need eat. Heap big game coming, need
eat."

She shook her head at that. *Not funny, Charles.* Now what was the big
deal? She was a Hogs fan too, for that matter, probably had herself a plate
of sandwiches all ready and a six-pack waiting on ice. Just keeping her
hand in, that was all, letting him know he was out of line making more
work for her. God, he was tired of women without a sense of humor. Sure
was nice to be rich and do anything you wanted to.

Might as well smooth things over. He followed her into the kitchen,
where she began putting more beer in the fridge. "How's those apartments
of yours doing?" he said.

"How do you think? I do good if they just disappear without paying.
Half the time they wreck the place first. Your father could have warned me
about rental property over there."

"Correct me if I'm wrong, but didn't you get that place in the settlement?" Clemmie had gotten a second divorce thirty-odd years ago, after
Morrison senior had hired her and before she moved in. She rarely spoke
of either marriage, though she gave herself a party each year on the anniversary of the second divorce. On those days, they knew to stay out of her
way.

She fetched a jar of chili peppers, a wedge of Colby, and a rectangular
log of Velveeta from the still-open fridge, closed the door. "So? He could
have told me to take a cash settlement."

"And what would you have gotten, half the value? Twenty thousand
or so?"

"Adjust for inflation, can I get any more now?"

"I'm sure it looked like a good investment. The city was spreading out
that way, nobody knew it was going to be Sin City."

"Don't kid yourself." She reached in a top cabinet for a bag of corn
chips, stretching her long torso, hiking her skirt over her legs. A woman
built like a horse.

"What I was really trying to do was give you some good news," he
said.

But a battle horse. She wheeled around, pinning him with her pale blue
eyes. The straight blonde hair with just the least streaking of gray, the long
Teutonic face.

"You should be able to sell the place before too long. At a decent price."

Her face softened. "Really?"

"Watch the prime. When it drops another point, start kicking people out and fixing the place up. Give it six months or so on the market, and you'll sell."

She was whistling as he left the kitchen, slicing the cheese into microwaveable chunks.

Only two of us, Barbara and me. And Vega. And the model. Up on the platform, taking off her robe. Hands to Vega, drapes on an empty easel. Naked to daylight, Momma wouldn't like that, but across the room, Barbara in her smock, setting her palette. If Barbara will paint a nude, proper Barbara, then it's ok. Barbara Rotenberry, what a name. Always think some screwhead, a nut in rotary motion, so many r's, but she was a Miller.

This is the good part, and I am so scared. My palette, the colors, chunks of a world, the world that isn't yet. The radio noise—the guard cop, what if he looks in to see her naked?

I can't make a world, they'll get me, get me.

By the time he got settled in the big leather Lane recliner in the living room, hot nachos at his elbow and a freezing beer in his hand, the pregame crap was almost over and they were introducing the players. The pregame was always brief in the regionals anyway, brief and unsatisfying. The Razorbacks, especially, always got slighted. Can any good thing come out of Arkansas?

The fucking networks don't understand us, don't understand how passionate we are down here. We're always up there in rankings somewhere, count on it, by sheer force of will if nothing else, and *we* do it *honestly,* the Christian way, without paying megamoola to amateurs in name only, who're probably rapists and body-robbers from the streets of Chicago anyhow, but do we get national coverage? Noooo.

But this was perfect, the beer, the nachos, the chair, the game about to start, one hour of hot high hope.

The bell, and he was out of his chair slopping a little icy beer on his knee. He heard Clemmie letting them in. He went to the hall doorway. "Come on in here," he said urgently. "Damn thing's about to start. What do you want to drink?" Laugh took a beer, and Tina didn't want anything just now, thank you.

Naked in daylight to others, and oh I want, I want, I had a body like that when I was young and never been kissed and nobody saw, so nipple-beautiful, I stretched and felt my belly a field of grass, I wanted them to see and make me beautiful, but I was covered and what's covered is ugly and bad and can we shut that Arkansas noise off?

They had missed the tip-off. Louisville was bringing it down the court. "So what happened with LSU-Lamar?" Tina said.

"Oh, they wiped em out," Charles said, trying to watch the play. "One hundred to seventy-four, something like that. Crap! Who was that on? Shit, I don't believe it."

"Don't need him in foul trouble," Lafayette said.

"Sutton said the key was point production from Hastings," Tina said. "And it looks like Crum is making them take it right to him."

"You always did prepare well," Charles said.

"Hmp," Laugh said. "Right." Tina reached over and whacked him without taking her eyes off the screen.

Vega won't ask the guard, but I would, but if I do I'm rich bitch wife of Charles Morrison, so shut the big doors all the way but still can hear the noise raping her thighs and making me storm her full of rotenberries, whirly tornado muscles and pubic indigo whitecaps

and Ephraim saw, Ephraim alone, when Ephraim took me to the game the game, but we didn't really go, we went to the lake, and Mother never knew, she would have killed me, another foul on Hastings

a tall pretty boy from Cammack Village and his name so pretty, not Mike not Steve not Darrell Eddie Scott

The first twelve minutes of the game Clemmie was in and out with beer and more nachos, but then settled in on the big couch beside Lafayette and Tina. At 7:38 to go in the first half, Hastings was on the bench with three fouls, and he hadn't scored a point. Louisville led 25–21, mostly on free throws. The only bright spot for Arkansas was Walker, the first-year sophomore.

"I can't believe the way they're *calling* this game," Charles said. "I mean, they're all *over* us, and they're calling the fouls on *us*. It's like somebody *paid* em."

"I coulda played basketball out of high school," Lafayette said.

"It's not as bad as it looks," Tina said. "They're not taking many shots, and that means they haven't been able to use their press to break it open."

Walker snaked in for a lay-up. On the return, U. S. Reed jumped into the passing lane, stole the ball, and went in for a lay-up, and, bang-bang, it was 25–all. Louisville tried to bring it up, and Reed did it again, missed the lay-in, but Walker followed with a tip. Charles was on his feet. "All right," he shouted. "All right! We're taking it to em now!" He whirled around, and Clemmie gave him a sitting high-five.

"Sutton's got em in a zone," Tina said.

At the half, Arkansas led 37–33. Walker had ten points, Charles had had three beers, and the mood was festive in the kitchen, where they were

all helping Clemmie put together a platter of cold roast beef sandwiches.
"They can do it, you know," Charles was saying. "They can go all the
way. Sutton is a genius!"

"You a lot more mercurial than I realized before," Lafayette said.

"Denny Crum aint no dummy neither," Tina said.

Vega over my shoulder: Um. Interesting.

*She's supposed to be there to help, and normally yes, but the heaviness
of people watching. Don't call it a—*

Like a Picasso de Kooning or something—

name, dammit—

*but don't forget to work on your anatomy. Think Botticelli, think Mi-
chelangelo. You have to master the figure before you can explode it, or
implode it, or whatever you're doing. Do you want to do some modeling
on that knee?*

*And so I waste my time on a knee until she goes to Barbara, and I can
breathe, and try to remember where I was, because it isn't pushing, it isn't
making the paint do things, it's reaching in and pulling things out, the
canvas a window in humming nowhere, a gray might-be, and you reach to
who you almost were, you reach through a melting window to another
place, and you look at the model to help you remember, to take your eyes
away so your hands remember to feel, and I was beautiful like that, beside
the lake and that goddamn goddamn game—*

Arkansas stayed in the zone in the second half. Charles had a roast beef
sandwich with mayonnaise and thin slices of Vidalia onion, and two more
beers. Scott Hastings got a tip-in for his first two points and then was
called for his fourth foul. Charles jumped up and screamed at the set,
startling Lafayette so that he knocked his beer over on the coffee table.
"I'm sorry," Charles said, as Clemmie hurried to get a cloth. "But it's
just like Michigan, when we were about to beat them, and they *trip* U. S.
Reed, and they call *walking* on *Reed*. I mean, I'm just so *tired* of seeing
this shit."

"They staying with em pretty good," Lafayette said.

*I was the lake and the warm dim wind and the storm clouds tall and
glowing will be my skirt I threw to the air my blouse my panties my bra
because he said: It's such a mystery. I've never seen it. And what other
boys had words like that? And Ephraim said: I just want to see the mystery,
I'll never forget it, never forget you, and I won't touch, but he could have
touched if touch was touch was all . . .*

At 6:24 left in the game, Arkansas was up two, 56–54, and spreading
the floor. Hastings was back in, and Louisville had brought in a banger
named Burkman. Burkman stepped in front of Young, but Young got the
call for charging. By this time, Charles was too sullen to complain aloud.

"Now, that *was* a bad call," Lafayette said.

Burkman made both free throws, but on the other end Peterson was fouled. His first free throw went in, but the second one bricked. Hastings took the rebound, faked his man out, and put it back in.

"By God, even if we lose, at least you can't say we haven't played em a good game," Charles said. "Last year's champs, and we're giving em everything they can handle."

"Shoot, we *ahead*," Lafayette said.

And I am the lake but floating and naked, and here in the corner a box with Bobbie and Jackie and Bennie and Chigger and all the people watching the game we didn't go to, all looking up and watching me because I'm the game now, dab and dab and dab and all their little dab faces—

"Hot damn," said Lafayette. Hastings had blocked out on the other end, gotten the rebound, and been fouled. He made both free throws.

"Five points, by God," Charles said. "Come *on*, baby."

Louisville brought it down, and Jerry Eaves popped from fifteen, 61–58.

And I am dancing slowly to let him see, sweet Ephraim

Hastings tipped a rebound to Walker, who fed to a fast-breaking Reed for a lay-up. "All right all right all *right*," Charles said. "*63*–58."

"He's a streak," Lafayette said.

"Under five minutes, and we lead by five," Clemmie said. "We can *do* it."

"Just laying it in, no show stuff," Tina said. "You gotta love it."

whose nervous words, whose beautiful name, and Momma doesn't know my hair she hates is blowing to goodness, I feel it red so dash it out free and carmine thick, and here where the wind between my legs makes me all feathers, a touch, a touch, and the radio is the wind and thunder, it doesn't have to be—

Hastings was fouled and hit two more free throws, 4:11 to go. "Oh Jesus," Charles said.

They were calling the Hogs in Austin, could you believe it? That was worth watching, a sight for the ages. All the Texans going "WOOOOOOOO *PIG!* SOOOEY!"

The after-rumble, and this is the flash highlighting my arm and breast and forking along my leg, and Ephraim shivering to see the lightning like a girl—

Rodney McCray missed, Hastings rebounded to Walker, and Walker got knocked loose from the ball. "Goddammit, *call* that shit!" Lafayette and Charles said at the same time.

and right that moment a big raindrop exactly on my nipple

"That would have been nine up with under four minutes to go," Tina said. "We would have had it made."

"Oh bless it all," Clemmie said, as Poncho Wright drilled it from the corner, 65–60.

and he can touch me, kiss me all over

They were all leaning forward now, intent, their beer forgotten, the tortilla chips limp in their congealed cheese, the mayonnaise at the edges of the remaining sandwiches drying to translucency. They watched Arkansas miss, crying aloud as the rebound came out to Louisville, sitting up and applauding when Scooter McCray missed on the inside and Peterson was fouled on the rebound. Peterson made both of his shots.

"Clutch, oh clutch," Charles said. "Oh beautiful."

"Miss it!" Lafayette said, pounding the coffee table, but Scooter, taking it right back inside, hit this one.

Rodney McCray was called for the foul on Reed. "How many is that on him?" Clemmie said. "Is that five?"

Lafayette was doing the hooray boogie. "You gone, you gone, you gone," he sang to the television set, pointing his big finger like a father telling a child told-you-so.

"Bout damn time," Tina said.

"Now let's get the other one," Charles said.

"All we have to do is hold em," Clemmie said. "2:34, all we have to do is hold the ball."

and he stands up strange, Ephraim, the beautiful name, the only one to see me naked and I have never been kissed, never been kissed, his face all strange

Burkman, the hatchet man off the bench, drew Walker into his fourth foul, and they were all up groaning, pleading hands extended to the set. "Give us a break," Charles said. "They're hacking us to death, and you're calling it on *us.*"

"Just hold the ball," Clemmie said as they subsided. "Use up the clock."

Peterson took it in frontcourt, and Louisville gang-banged him, blasting the ball away. There was no call.

Charles collapsed into his chair, his head thrown back. "Goddamn," he said numbly. "Goddamn, they're going to do it to us again."

"Right up the old mine shaft," Lafayette said. "Rude, nude, and screwed."

and takes me, his hands like iron clamps on my arms, and then his arms around me like the band that locks you in the electric chair, and so the black a circle of black for me, the black in the crackling clouds, just kiss just kiss, please just touch

Eaves missed his second free throw, and Charles sat forward, hoping again in spite of himself. "69–65," he said, and then he let out a cry of jubilation as Hastings was fouled. Laugh had apparently decided to quit reacting, to just stand and glare the set into submission, the Razorbacks into victory. Tina was clapping, a steady beat, and she kept it up as Hastings made both of his free throws.

"He's doing it when it counts," Clemmie said.

because I don't even know, can you believe I don't even know, a junior in high school and no one has ever told me, what is he doing

But Scooter McCray hit a follow shot at the other end, and it was back to four points, 71–67. Arkansas brought it up into a vicious press, Louisville swarming on the man with the ball. It was rat-ball, frantic and messy, and when Young went after the loose ball, he was called for a foul. He was enraged, dancing in front of the referee, gesticulating.

"No technical, no technical," Lafayette was saying.

Clemmie and Tina were on their feet, dancing like Young, as if the tv were a referee, making strange sounds with their pursed lips: "Ooo—ooo—you!"

"Kill," Charles said.

bending me over? I'm sorry, he says, and the storm on the lake and the lacework of whitecaps and I am a storm of lace where he puts his fingers

The replay showed Young taking the ball away from Wright with his hands, no body contact. Cups of ice were sailing onto the floor.

"Yah, you assholes, a lot worse than ice," Charles said.

Wright made both free throws, and Arkansas called a time-out with 47 seconds left on the clock, ahead by two, 71–69.

When Arkansas brought it in, Louisville swarmed again. "Get it over *midcourt*," Clemmie yelled, but they couldn't, but Burkman fouled Peterson in backcourt.

"Ah, you stupid!" Charles called gleefully.

and Is this touching? I said. But don't, don't, it doesn't feel right, bent like an animal trapped in steel

What happened next took them to despair and back to elation so fast that all they could do was moan and pound on things and jump to their feet: "*Naaa, aah, OH!*" Peterson, who had been flawless from the line, missed the first shot, and Burkman was called for clobbering Reed going for the rebound. The four watchers spun to face each other, leaning back from a common center, hands extended palms up, teeth showing and eyes wide in bacchanalian delight.

and then I know, though no one has told me, I know what this is

"If he makes them both," Tina said, "we've got em. Four-point lead with thirty-six seconds!"

Reed made the first shot, 72–69, but Scooter McCray took the rebound on the second shot, and Louisville called a time-out with twenty-seven seconds left. They all sat back down. "We've got to keep them from getting a quick shot," Clemmie said.

"Don't foul, don't foul," Lafayette amended.

he has it out and hard and bad and prodding my leg so push the brush and push it so bad

Scooter McCray backed it in on the baseline, fed to Poncho Wright in the corner. Off the screen, Wright popped it. "Oh hell," Charles said. "I don't like this, I don't like this. I've seen it too many times."

"Protect the ball," Clemmie said. "Thirteen seconds, we don't even have to shoot."

"Protect the *ball,"* Charles agreed.

and please just kiss me I didn't mean oh please just kiss me first

So Young attempted to beat the press, a baseball pass to Hastings breaking past Scooter McCray, and the pass went long. Hastings lunged to knock it back in, but no dice.

"Young, you *idiot!"* Charles screamed, leaping to his feet. His voice broke on a note two octaves above his normal range.

Tina sat back in contempt, crossing her legs. Clemmie stared fixedly at the set, her lips pressed in a thin line. Lafayette shook his big head wearily but tried to be consoling: "It was a good idea. Every time we bring it down, their press been taking it away."

"Execution," Charles hissed.

"Miss it miss it miss it," Clemmie was chanting under her breath.

"Under their own damn goal," Lafayette said heavily.

I'm sorry I'm sorry sweet Ephraim says

Poncho Wright took the inbounds and fired from eight feet off the basket, but missed. Derek Smith used Reed for a stepladder to get the rebound, no call. He shot it off-balance from eight . . .

It went in. Louisville led 73–72, 5 seconds to go. Their players were jubilant, bouncing and smiling.

and I deserve it the lake in my eyes and I deserve it I made him do it the grass on my knees and going to hell forever

"It always happens," Charles said.

"We're a poor state," Lafayette said. "Doing good to get this far."

He could have sworn there were tears standing in Charles's eyes.

"Where there's life, there's hope," Tina said. The others looked at her, saw that she meant a bitter irony, like a gangster's moll to the piano player who loves her in a 1930s movie.

the storms of hell is a lake of fire and so more red in the waves and Vega back to see my humiliation, my ruined nakedness forever, and says, What is that white gridding whitecaps *it looks like a* not a *net net net*

Darrell Walker, holding the ball to throw it in, looked stunned. To the four sitting in front of the set, he was the emblem of their despondency, a continuum of gloom across three hundred miles. Over the state at that moment, there were thousands fixed in their exact posture, slumped in utter despair but leaning forward and unable to turn away from the perfection of their misery. In such moments, it seems possible to feel one's unseen neighbors, it seems as though a current of anguish runs not through one's own nerves but through the net of the community.

And perhaps it is so. Magnetism arises when the atoms of iron accept a common orientation; minerals whose crystals have been arrayed with superfine accuracy display new characteristics; conductors cooled until their constituent atoms cease to argue and vibrate will suddenly pass huge energies without resistance; and light waves, bounced back and forth between two mirrors until their frequencies entrain, burst forth like God's own sword of flame:

Ulysses S. Reed took the inbounds, ran through a host of defenders, and launched, from 49 feet away, a perfect parabola. It went through the net with no more noise than the mice make.

and the frame squares up and traps me and I slam it home a red blood glob in the goddamned net to hear her over my shoulder gasp in shock

The Louisville players slowed and stood, not understanding for a moment, a moment like the moment of decapitation, when the world tumbles dizzily in your eyes but you feel no pain. Then they walked stolidly off to their lockers. In center court, U. S. Reed was leapt upon, danced about, wrestled down by a joyous, writhing organism.

and he kisses me on the front porch, too late, and Momma sees, and slaps me to hell for kissing, my very first kiss, and never knows what else I did how evil I am how deep a hell she slams me to, and the lesson's the game is

Over a roar of white noise, microphones were seeking mouths, like ocean-floor organisms nuzzling after sulfur vents. "I've seen this before," Abe Lemons said to one, grinning, and

Ah, here's a microphone now for me: I've seen this before, Jim Ed Bob, and I just want to say I'm mighty proud of these guys, the human race just showed up to play today, and the Evil One was too much for us, but this is a great victory which hurts a lot right now but tomorrow's another day which we can take one step at a time

and then at school Ephraim can't look at me, won't talk to me, and I think that he never tells, but he never will look at me again, because I am dirty in hell

and wake up with our heads held high in a team effort for which I just want to thank the Lord Jesus for being with me

forever.

When Lianne came through the door, Laugh was waltzing Clemmie around and around across the room and Charles was tossing Tina into the air, her body girlish and light and tensile in his sexual hands. He caught her and set her down, and the four of them stood there looking at Lianne, for all the world like four teenagers whose parents have come home to catch them at an unauthorized party. Clemmie began gathering dishes. Lafayette ran his hands around his beltline, tucking his shirt back in. Tina straightened a stocking. Charles combed his hair back with his fingers and came forward.

"We won," he explained.

10

MONKEY LAW

All through the rest of that Saturday, and into the next morning, Lafayette had felt a nagging sense of exposure, of vulnerability. As if something bad was about to happen, something he needed to be ready for. It had begun when Lianne had come through the door and caught them celebrating the miracle game. *Caught* them—yeah, listen to the way he was thinking. What was wrong with celebrating? But the way her face had shuttered down shut. Whew. One cold woman. She know about Tina setting her hat for Charles? Maybe she hated niggers? But no, Laugh knew better than that, he'd been a guest at parties with her, talked, and you could tell that sort of thing. Believe me, you could tell.

No, it was the act of celebration that had upset her. She was one of those people got scared when other people had fun. Thought she was left out, inferior, thought it was at her expense.

That was what had triggered his foreboding, but it wasn't the core of the matter. There was something else, some little dangerous unresolved situation.

Sunday morning, at brunch, he figured it out. The fight. The fight between Greg Legg and Sonny Raymond. He had been expecting repercussions. Over a farmers' omelet, over a fifth glass of cheap sugary free champagne, he realized and, realizing, began to relax. It was Sunday, after all. If nothing had happened by now, maybe nothing would happen. Plenty of fecal matter but maybe no blurring inclined planes this time, applying their spray of centrifugal vectors. Maybe it would all slide right on down the tubes. Right, Lafayette.

When the shit finally did hit the fan it was Monday morning, which would have been a whole lot better than Saturday morning, when he had felt so bad, except that he had let himself relax, and you know, relaxing and all, well, he'd had a few more of the Andrés.

Now, why would anybody want to drink bad champagne? And especially why would they want to drink just a whole lot of it? Good champagne is only ten times as much, and it makes you feel good instead of bad, which is easy worth the money, especially if you can afford it, and Laugh can afford it. Only maybe Laugh don't *believe* he can afford it. Maybe Laugh thinks of his momma, how Momma is both cheap and puritanical, and so Mr. Laugh J. Thompson shouldn't be drinking no champagne at all, and certainly no afterfuck champagne with a white woman at Buster's. But he was, and so, well, then he can maybe stay a little true to Momma by drinking the cheap champagne. Going to hell anyway, might as well save money on the ticket.

So anyway Monday wasn't such a great day for shit-fannery either. He had spent the night at home, sometimes it was kind of a relief to get away from Tina. But she had called him, sleepy and grumpy, seven in the morning. It was like coming back from the grave to wake up and answer that fucking phone, like coming back from the grave on Judgment Day, only to be sent to hell. He had got maybe four hours sleep, the rest tossing and turning and coming awake with his jaws clamped like a vise with the handle spun all the way up and leaned on. He kept swimming up for breath from terrible dreams where he was wanted for murder, and then dropping back down drowning, right where he left off. Somebody at the *Gazette* had called her, Tina said, asking about the fight, and she had told them to fuck off, but they might be calling Laugh. She seemed to feel, in the wilderness of her drowsiness, that the whole thing was his fault, his business, would never have happened except for him, and he should get the lousy fuckers off her back so she could get some sleep. Which she probably immediately did as soon as he hung up.

But not Laugh, no. Laugh had gotten to the office early to think things over. Thinking things over, he realized there was no way to bottle the story up and that Charles had better hear it at the office before he heard it on the street. Thinking things over, they had better all three go in together and tell Charles. That would carry the implication that Laugh and Tina were as much at fault as Greg, and Laugh didn't like that one bit, but it was a lot better than sending Greg in alone, which would carry the implication that Laugh was chickenshit. It was a nasty bind, and by the time Tina showed up, Mr. Lafayette J. Thompson's headache was a lot worse, and he was pretty thoroughly pissed.

She breezed in about 9:25, well after Charles had gotten there, and spent the first few minutes out front telling her latest dirty joke to Rosalyn at the reception desk, something about Wendy and Welcome to Jamaica, Have a Nice Day.

Greg had come in before Tina, at nine sharp. He had looked for all his shamefacedness so clean and pressed that Lafayette had realized, with the chilled shiver of a man who has driven over a train track without looking and then hears the whistle behind him, that Greg and Charles were members of the exact same tribe, and that Greg, whatever his present folly, would, when his youth was spent, become the true inheritor, if not of Morrison, Morrison, and Chenowyth, then of something very much like it. Was this goddamn fight business going to screw up Lafayette's shot at the partnership? Probably. Damn the woman, and double damn.

As soon as Greg and Tina were in their offices, Lafayette summoned them. "Why the fuck don't *you* come down to *my* office?" Tina had said.

"Aint no time for that bullshit," Lafayette said. "Staff meeting at ten, and he going to lunch with Clark right after that. You can bet yo boody Clark already heard, and if you don't think he done worked out a way to use it to his advantage, you're plain damn crazy. In fact, we gone be real lucky if we get to Charles before his telephone rings. So you get in here right now."

He had laid it out for them, Greg downcast and nodding, Tina looking around, looking off out the window as if this were a minor annoyance, a silly PR game they had to play, a waste of her time, but if Lafayette was going to insist, well, if she had to, well . . .

Once they had their stories straight, as straight as they could make them in a mere five minutes, they headed down the hall. Charles was surprised to see the three of them at one time. He settled back in his chair. "What's up?" he said, warily, his head cocked. Laugh sat in a chair to the right of the desk: The three of them standing there together in front was a little too much like getting called into the principal's office, and besides, the way the blood was slamming around in his brain, he wasn't sure he *could* stand. Tina had wandered over to the double casements at the far end of the rather manorial room (more like a judge's chambers than an attorney's office—it had been, before the remodeling, the second-floor study in the old Patterson place).

It was all windows with Tina today. Put her in a room with a window, she would go stare out. What did she want, fly away free like an eagle?

"We've got a PR problem with LK-31," Lafayette said. He meant the Lockhart prison case. Charles had created an indexing system for all the firm's cases, and you never, in the office or out of it, referred to a case by its name or its subject matter. One advantage of the system was that it simplified filing. Another advantage was increased confidentiality. Not only was there an index for the cases themselves, there were indexes for some of the firm's more common strategies, and after you got used to the indexes you might find yourself saying things like, "We need to X the 22 on that

BM-77 DPO''—although the DPO, or deposition, was always pronounced "deepo," so you could guess that one. In spite of a few such more or less decipherable abbreviations, Morrison's attorneys spoke to each other in what amounted to a rapid code, and it sometimes seemed that no one else in town could understand them or keep up.

Lafayette was frightened as he spoke, just as he had been frightened before every single game of his life, and he hated it, just as he had hated it before every single game of his life. His hands were trembling, not just with adrenaline but with the weakness caused by violent pain, so he kept them on the arms of his chair. His voice would have been flighty except that he covered with harshness, his famous courtroom growl. Charles, hearing the tone, looked his way curiously, a curiosity settling to stone.

The man read him, Laugh realized. He read the tones of his voice, and he read the fear behind them.

"Let's hear it."

"Greg," Lafayette said.

"I got into a fight with Sonny Raymond Friday night," Greg said, still standing. He made no excuses, ready, like a good scout, to take what he had coming. But in his telling there was no mention of Tina, or of Lafayette stuffing a handkerchief down a deputy's throat. It was a simple case of two Southern boys drinking and arguing politics.

When Greg had finished, Charles punched the button for Brenda Faye, and punched another button to put her on the speakerphone. "Brenda Faye," he said, "have you heard any rumors about a fight at a party Friday night?"

"I've gotten seven messages in the last fifteen minutes," the voice came. "Four of them are from the papers."

"Right. Well, that's all it is, a rumor, but we better have a press conference anyway. Can you get me one?"

"When for?"

"Eleven-thirty?"

"I'll see. Did it officially didn't happen, or did it really didn't happen?"

"What business is it of yours?"

"I got to start telling these people something, and I can make my gossipy airhead secretary act a lot more convincing if I know whether or not I'm accidentally giving away the real truth or just an imaginary one."

"It's a nonevent two ways. It didn't happen," Charles said, "and it's for damn sure not going to ever happen again."

"Gotcha," said Brenda Faye.

"Also you better get hold of the attorney general and cancel lunch. No way we're gonna eat privately, not after this. I'll eat in. You can bring me a box of Bojangles, one thigh, one breast, a biscuit, a fried apple pie, a big diet Pepsi. Lots of napkins. See if Clark wants to call me during lunch. He's going to want blood after we make a deal on the press conference, and I don't know how else we're going to be able to talk alone. Also put him through at ten-thirty so we can arrange the conference, tell the staff the ten o'clock meeting has been postponed till two o'clock, which means you need to reschedule Harkrider and just let Tucker know, he won't mind, it was mostly personal anyway, and he can catch me at home this evening.''

"You want honey on that biscuit?''

"No honey, honey,'' Charles said. "I'm on a diet.'' He punched the speakerphone off and said mildly, "I don't like soap opera messing up my work. Greg, you know and I know you didn't jump Sonny Sonofabitch Raymond because he poo-pooed the theory of evolution. You jumped him because your glands have boiled your brains.''

So Charles understood about Tina and Sonny Raymond, Lafayette realized with a shock.

"How the hell did you pick that to fight over anyway?'' Charles said. "I mean, I would have expected tastes great/less filling or Ford versus Chevrolet, but *evolution*?''

And I guess you don't remember showing out earlier that same night, Lafayette thought. Just about punching out old poor old bigoted Barney Wardlow for the same kind of reason. I guess it aint occurred to you Greg might have felt like he was not only defending his ladylove but following in his hero's footsteps as well.

"Well, you know, he came in,'' Greg said, "and he was talking to this Ed Gran fellow about the Senate bill, how great it was, you know, and how it would get all the atheists out of education, and I said, Don't get your hopes up, even if the governor signs it it's unconstitutional, and he said—''

"Never mind,'' Charles said impatiently. "You have been steadily attempting to stink up your life for the last two years. And having a lot more success at it, I might add, than at the practice of law.'' He leaned forward and steepled his fingers.

"You're off LK-31 as of now,'' he said decisively. "But you're coming with me to a press conference in about an hour. When we get back, I want you to give your files to Betty and spend your lunch hour backgrounding her. After that, you're on leave for six weeks. I don't want to see your face this afternoon. There's a house down in Florida, on an island about five miles out in the Gulf, and you're going to take Alison and the baby and stay there the whole time. You tell her I'll take care of my taxes myself this year, not to worry.'' He sat back in his chair.

"When you come back,'' he said, "you and me are going to talk, and depending on how that goes, you *might* still have a job.''

Greg's face was red, but he wore the same expression of pained transcendence that a spanked child might wear, a child who knows it's for his own good. It was the look that probably came over Saint Paul's face when he finally got God mad enough to smite him with blindness.

Greg stood in front of the desk, waiting. "Well?" Charles said.

"Ah, is that. . . what should I . . ."

"Light a shuck, and get ready for the press conference. I'll be with you in a little bit." When Greg had left, Charles swiveled to Lafayette, but he spoke to Tina. Was he pissed to have his yesterday's transcendence so exploded, to find in the very engine of his game-time happiness the springs of this infernal device? What do you think?

"Tina, you're just about a lick and a hair from being out of here," he said. "I won't say you're not getting the job done. You have a way of being twice as smart as any judge you face but letting him think he's finding all these brilliant precedents himself and is maybe going to get in your pants besides. In fact, you haven't lost, have you, except in Elsijane's court and Shirley's?"

Now he turned further, to stare at her back where she stood at the windows. "Do you hear me?"

"I hear you," Tina said, but didn't turn around.

"But I tell you what, I had just about enough of your little games. Your sex life is your own business, until you start fouling up my office with it. There's a place and a time for a bitch in heat to go prancing around with her tail up and making every damn boy dog in the block crazy to fight, and that place is right out on the street. Is that where you want to be?"

"No."

"Well, then, you better get your act together. You walk the straight and narrow from now on, because you aint got no second chances. Your preacher might forgive you, but I won't. You pick one man and you stick to him. If you want this damn old ugly jigaboo here, then take him, I don't care if every asshole in town calls me a nigger-lover. If you *don't* want him, get rid of him and pick somebody else. But you aint going to embarrass me with any more of your show-out white-trash bar fights. You think this is sexual discrimination?"

"No."

"That's good. You get back to your office. It's time you did some real work. I been supposed to have a précis on TL-80 from you for the last three weeks. It better be on my desk by the end of the day, and a firm SK for the DPOs."

When she had gone, Charles got up and went to the windows where she had been. They were tall windows, with extra-wide casements of old and polished oak. "Well?" he said, looking out.

"Well?" Lafayette echoed. His vision had a trembly, extra-brilliant edge, as if he were walking across a western gorge on a rope bridge, the river glittering far below. It hurt to look toward the windows. Squinting, he saw Charles as a dark and uncertain silhouette, surrounded by flares of light. He was having trouble concentrating on the what-you-might-call interpersonal dynamics, but he knew Charles was trying to get a rise out of him.

"Don't mess around with me, Lafayette."

"What do you want me to say?"

"I want you to react. I want you to quit playing your hold-back game. I can't back your play if you aint going to give me no information. Do you think I'm being fair?"

"You're being fair enough," Lafayette said. "But I aint gone fall on my knees and confess my sins." Please, Mr. Charles, spare po old Lafayette, he didn't mean no harm.

"Is that what you think I'm asking?"

"No," Lafayette said. It was a hard word to say, because it was a lie. You don't play first-string linebacker at 5′11″ and 190 pounds without learning the universality of dominance negotiation. When the Christians forgive each other, they all want to be seen as the most charitable, and when the Zen masters sit down to meditate, each of them is hoping to be a little further off the wheel of desire than the others. But there is such a thing as playing smart, even when your head feels like a garbage-can lid somebody is whacking with a loose picket. So he said "No," but thought, *I don't bow to no fucking white man.*

"I don't bow to no fucking white man," Charles said, still looking out the window to springtime in Little Rock, the jonquils nodding on the vacant lot across the street, where an old house had once existed.

"You stop that shit," Lafayette said, his heart banging into gear like someone popping the clutch on second.

"What, I can't imitate you? You imitate me." Lafayette didn't answer. "Do you think I have a right to call you down?" Charles said. "Do you think I have a right to step in and say, 'Listen, Lafayette, you been acting plain damn stupid, and you are jeopardizing not only your own career but the livelihood of other and innocent people'?"

Charles wasn't going to let up on the pressure, Lafayette saw. He wasn't going to discipline Lafayette himself, he was too sharp for that. That would make it too easy for Lafayette to finish his rebellion, that would just push him over the line. Instead, he was going to lead Lafayette back to it, like a kitten to the shit in the corner. He was going to pinch him by the neck and say, Smell that, kitty. Smell that.

So what did Charles have to lose if Lafayette did blow it, if he just up and said, *Fuck you, I quit*? It would inconvenience the man, it would be a waste of time and training, but it would hardly qualify as an irredeemable disaster for the firm. Maybe it was just that Charles didn't want to spoil his image of himself as the Atticus Finch of Arkansas.

So that was it. So the man's idea of himself mattered more to him than a real person did. Lafayette was filled with a heat like white alcohol fire, a rage that said No, no, no, motherfucker. You aint got no rights. You aint got no rights at all.

Aloud he said, in a mild voice, "Yes."

"You're in a complicated situation, Lafayette. You're going to have to start trusting somebody sometime."

Lafayette didn't answer.

"I've got to make some notes for the press conference," Charles said. "I'd better let you get back to it now."

That was dismissal, and Lafayette went.

Back in his own office—not so luxurious as Charles's, lacking a fireplace, and square where the other office was rectangular, but still no modular productivity system, and with at least as many feet of bookcase frontage—Lafayette tugged the velvet drapes closed, switched his three lamps to low. He was pretty shaky, and his knees gave way just before his butt hit the chair. He pulled his left-hand drawer open and dug out the bottle of ibuprofen, the little packet of pseudoephedrines. He popped a couple of blisters on the packet, swallowed the two tablets dry. "Red hots," he said. He had found that the best treatment for a hangover was to handle it just like a sinus headache, and that the combination of pseudoephedrine and ibuprofen worked about five times better than aspirin. But when he shook the ibuprofen bottle, it rattled emptily. Sure enough, there was only one pill in it. He had at least a three-pill head-thumper, and probably a four. "Damn," he said, and punched Tina's number.

"What do you want this time?" she said, without preface. That was a favorite trick of hers, except that it wasn't really a trick. He didn't think she thought about it, she just did it. He wondered sometimes whether she was truly psychic or if it was just a subconscious logical process. Who else would be calling her on an internal line today? Not Charles, who had said all he had to say, and certainly not, at this point, Greg.

"Do you have any more of that Tylenol 3?" he said. "I'm out of Advil."

"Sure. How many do you want? I have some headache powder too."

"You better bring me three. And no, I don't want none of that damn snow. You start leaving that stuff home. That's just about all it would take right now."

When she came in, she had a bottle of cough syrup with her, as well as the Tylenols. "I aint got no damn cough," Lafayette said.

"Well, I thought as long as you were thinking codeine," she said.

"Oh," he said. He took two long swallows on the cough syrup, then reached back in his medicine drawer for the flask of Evan Williams. He washed the Tylenols down with the whiskey.

"There," he said. "At least that gets rid of the cough syrup taste."

"Poor baby," she said. "I'm sorry you're hurting." She leaned over his chair to kiss his forehead, and then his eyelids. She opened the top two buttons on her blouse, still leaning over him, and took his hand and placed it on her breast. "There, does that make you feel better?"

It was as if nothing had happened this morning, as if she had never been savaged by the boss. Where was her mind? he wondered. Where did she go off to when she was threatened?

"Yeah, that feels good," he said. There was a stirring along his leg, his cock stiffening in spite of the pain in his head. Although the pain wasn't so bad now. It was lessening: An almost tidal cleansing came over him, a wash of ease, the fuzzy amplitude of well-being. The codeine was kicking in. There was time, there was plenty of time. There was time for everything.

She slid into his lap, and he gathered her legs, held her curled like a small child. "You're going to invite Charles to the party, aren't you?" she said into his chest.

He leaned back in his adjusting chair, the chair holding him, him holding her. She had work to do soon; he had work to do; they could not stay this way long, or someone would find them, and they would be in real trouble. But just now, just for the moment, there was plenty of time; there was no need to do anything; no need even, in spite of his now total erection, to make love. It just felt good to have a hard-on, it just felt good to hold her, good not to hurt. They could lean back for a while and keep each other warm, secure in the absence of pain.

"Sure," he said.

11

MEDIA CIRCUS

Charles got through to the attorney general at 10:45, and they reached an agreement. They reached it without really ever talking about what they were agreeing to, but when they were through talking they both knew Morrison, Morrison, and Chenowyth was going to back out of interested-party status on LK-31, and that there hadn't been a fight Friday night, there had just been a friendly and high-spirited discussion, and anyway, the fight hadn't been a very serious one and nobody got hurt. The AG himself, a sort of pocket hybrid of Kirk Douglas and Steve Martin, with some Dudley Do-right thrown in, wouldn't even bother to represent his office at the press conference, since that would grant too much importance to an event that hadn't really happened. Instead, he would be in a meeting, but would send a letter of support.

Clark was a good man, maybe: as overinflated as any politician, but a man doing a decent job in a hard spot, saddled with a clown of a lord high bailiff, a buffoon of a governor. He was forced into the painful position of having continually to remind these two officers of the state what the legalities were, legalities that the general public didn't care for either.

Governor White's power play with Walter Skelton at the Public Service Commission was fixing to blow up in his face, and Clark would have to deliver an opinion on that pretty soon, and maybe Morrison would be able to help. Somebody was going to have to shut up Sonny Raymond on the matter of the Pulaski County paychecks, and maybe Clark could help with that. Which wasn't likely to make him popular with the minions of the law. So it was no surprise the AG was coming on so hard-nosed on the James Dean Walker case. That was the bone he tossed to the law-and-order fanatics, and it was a safe move, because he wasn't actually involved.

Charles himself had stayed out of the Walker case. MM & C didn't do criminal law, not if they could help it. He had had some overtures despite that fact, ACLU types looking for a taint of prestige. But figure it: Most of the state thought Walker should not only be extradited from Colorado, but be hung when he got here, so jumping into the mess could only cost the firm in public opinion. It was a sore spot with the lawmen and the judges, and that could come back on the firm too. And now, at this point, it would amount to attacking Clark's one remaining advantage with his own people.

It was a question who a scandal over the fight would hurt most, but there was no question that Charles couldn't hush things up without Clark's cooperation, so he was left owing.

The media would of course devil the AG for quotes even if he wasn't the official spokesman, but he could hold himself quiet and content, thinking about his eventual race for the governorship, say in 1990. Thinking how warm and fine it was to know that an upstanding Little Rock family was going to understand his political principles, whatever they were by then, well enough to lend strong moral and financial support to his campaign.

Unfortunately, there was no way around having Charles as a spokesman for Morrison, Morrison, and Chenowyth. Greg was simply too sincere to handle the truth the way it had to be handled.

There *was* a way around having Sonny Raymond at the press conference, praise the Lord. It meant Clark cashing in some chips with Prosecutor Bentley, and Bentley leaning on Sonny Raymond in turn, which would have its price. But it was worth it to keep him away. Nobody wanted him there, not even the reporters. He was a whole deckful of loose cannons, rumbling this way and that with the pitch of every wave. He kept an armada of common sailors frantically busy trying to tie things down before the rails busted, the mast splintered, the lifeboats were dashed to flinders, and the ship itself sank.

He was like as not to call your mother a dim-witted criminal-coddling whore if she spoke out against shooting fleeing burglars in the back, or else to prove that he hadn't beaten a prisoner by saying that when he beat somebody you could damn sure see the effects, never noticing how in his denial of the instance he implied the practice—and then, if he saw you red with rage in the first case or risibility in the second, why, you had made an enemy for life.

Let's assume the AG's message got through in no uncertain terms: You better quit shoving your muddy paws in my trough, Sonny, dear, or when I get to be governor you won't get no slop at all. And I bet Sonny really liked that, don't you? I bet he really loved having his nose slapped like that. I bet he figured that, one-on-one, he could take this asshole Morrison, him and his whole damn firm. Which is probably why he hit the prisoner so hard, the frustration he was feeling.

"Ow, shit!" Sonny Raymond said, grabbing his right hand with his left and doubling over.

"What the fuck's wrong?" said Audrey Tull, standing behind the prisoner's chair.

"I like to busted my knuckles," Raymond said, shaking the injured paw. "You know how sometimes when you go to whack a dog and all you catch is the bones in his butt? My fingers banged all together. Jesus, that smarts!"

"I could've told you not to slap the top side of his head. That shit aint going to give."

"Well I was going to pop some air in his ear, and he ducked."

"I did not," the prisoner said.

Audrey was carrying three feet of one-inch PVC capped and filled with nickels, the bottom one-third friction-taped for grip. He called it his piggy bank. He walked around the chair and lashed the instrument across the prisoner's shins. The man bucked and yelled, then reached down to massage his battered legs.

"I reckon you did," Audrey Tull said. "I saw you."

"Well, sho I did," the prisoner said. "I couldn't hep it. You would too, you saw somebody swinging at yo head."

"You fuck that old woman too. And then you kill her."

"That don't mean I'm on confess it, though," the prisoner said. "They got the deaf penalty now."

"What do you reckon that old lady was thinking when you beat her up and slid yo tube-steak in?" Tull said. He was grinning. "You reckon she expected that? You reckon she prayed to Jesus that was how she want to die?"

The prisoner grinned back. "Ax yo momma—"

This time the billy bar caught the prisoner in the solar plexus. It was a long time before he could talk. The door to the interrogation room opened, and Cheese stuck his head through. "They ready with the videocamera," he said.

"You can't beat me up no more," the prisoner said. "They a see it on the tv. I know my right."

"I can send a telephone repairman to yo cell, though," Audrey Tull said.

"Aint got no telephone in my cell."

"You too stupid to get a joke. I'm talking about one of them Tucker Telephones. Give you more excitement than that old lady did."

"I don't like that electricity," the prisoner said. "But I rather get it that way than in the chair."

"We got lethal injection in Arkansas," Sonny Raymond said.

"What's that?" the prisoner said.

"Well, we don't quite got it yet, but we about to," Raymond said. "I got the word. They won't let us execute nobody unless we get it, so we're going to get it. Have it by the time you wind up yo trial, most likely."

"It's a shot," Tull explained. "We don't fry nobody no more. They just shoot a shot in yo veins. Poison."

"I aint afraid of shots so much. Do the poison hurt?"

"It don't hurt none at all," Raymond said. "It's just like going to sleep. Well, what do you want?" he said to Cheese, who was still hanging in the doorway. "Tell em to bring the camera on in."

"What kind of food I be getting?" the prisoner said, looking up at Tull.

"That woman called," Cheese said. "That press conference is about to start."

"You handle it from here," Raymond said to Tull. "Read him his rights when they get the camera going."

"It's good food," Tull said.

"Why you let that woman yank your chain?" Cheese said, accompanying Raymond down the hall. "Like having a spy in your midst."

"Spy in my midst, shit. That woman can suck the chrome off a trailer hitch."

"Oh," said Cheese. *Liar,* he thought.

"You don't need to come in," Raymond said.

I bet that as he sat there in his narrow green cement-block office, longer from door to window than it was wide from wall to wall, his feet propped up, watching the whole thing on the little portable black and white tv on the shelf over his desk, he was thinking back to the head cheese trouble in Jacksonville.

Cheese was a pushy son of a bitch, and if it hadn't been for the scandal, he might be sitting where Raymond was sitting right now. So it hadn't turned out too bad, all in all, but that didn't mean Sonny Raymond was ready to stick his tongue up Charles Morrison's little puckered asshole. He had been officially on Cheese's side during the fuss, in spite of being able to see how the whole thing worked to his advantage, and anyway there wasn't a lawman anywhere in the whole fucking country who liked a rich do-gooder fucking lawyer sticking his moralistic nose into departmental business, especially when there wasn't any damage done.

And all because that fucking Greek grocer was Morrison's favorite butcher. Representing him as a favor to the little people, supposedly. But really because he couldn't stand the thought of anybody doing something like that to his own personal supply of head cheese.

On Sonny Raymond's tiny black-and-white tv; and on Alison Legg's big projection monitor in the conversation pit that she hated but Greg had insisted on; and on Lianne's big Curtis Mathis in the living room, which she was watching at this time of day only because Susie Chenowyth, Dee-Dee's little sister, who worked at KROK and hoped someday to be an anchor as Lianne had been, had called to ask if she was going to watch Charles's press conference (which call meant that Susie knew Charles probably hadn't called Lianne, which meant that a lot of people understood Lianne was out of the pipeline—since except for being Dee-Dee's sister and some kind of niece to old Eamon Chenowyth, Susie was a total dip with no special knowledge—and which general perception on the part of people who had no business thinking about her really pissed Lianne off); and on the tvs of people all over the state who had the leisure at 11:30 in the morning to watch, the representative from the AG's office was explaining: "It's just one of those things that happens when you have people getting involved in a highly charged situation of the kind this is. It isn't anything that ought to get itself made into a federal case or a mountain out of, when we're really talking molehills here, and I don't think Mr. Morrison would argue with that."

"Certainly not," Charles said. "There's nothing in the substance of your statement I could possibly disagree with." He smiled his favorite public smile, a smile of assurance, tolerance, and charm. "I don't want to make light of a serious issue, but I'm afraid this is one of those cases where rumor has gotten entirely out of hand. I'm not coming down on the media, you understand. You're just doing your jobs just like you're supposed to, and when there's an issue that raises such high feelings, it's pretty natural for there to be all kinds of stories floating around. All I'm saying is I want you to recognize that we're just like you, we're all professionals here. I highly respect the attorney general's office and all his representatives, as I know he respects mine, and neither one of us is going to be jeopardizing any issue of the importance that this one has, we're just not going to be bringing the kind of personal acrimony into this situation that it is supposed to have had happen to it."

Charles was rather proud of "acrimony." Just the right touch of vocabulary at just the right moment, he thought. Do most of it in good-old-boy, but flick in a reminder from time to time.

"Cocksucker," Sonny Raymond said. "Think I don't know what it means."

"Showing off again, Charles," Lianne said.

Alison Legg turned up the volume and went into the kitchen to wash the clinging garden dirt off her bare hands and the small trowel she carried. A clot of the moist earth fell from one of the knees of her jeans. There was another small clot that had fallen from her knuckles when she had turned the television on. She was not a neat housekeeper; she could never seem to do things in a sensible, well-worked-out order; she was forever spending her spare time cleaning up messes she needn't have made if she had just been able to think things out in advance—buying new batteries that wouldn't have been necessary if she had just remembered to turn the portable radio off, for instance. Greg would have been horrified to see the bits of dark earth on his carpet, dismayed to think how the bits of sand in the muddy water she sent down his gleaming drain were dulling the blades of the garbage disposal.

The *Gazette* took up the interrogation. "Mr. Morrison, we have sources who swear there was an actual physical confrontation Friday night between the lord high bailiff and Mr. Legg here. Why does what you're telling me sound so much like a cover-up? Is this going to be the Watergate of the Lockhart investigation?"

"You keep on like that, John, and I'll bet they give you your own column someday." General laughter. "Tell me this: Does any one of those so-called witnesses allow you to use his or her name, or are we talking 'reliable sources' here? No names? I see."

The AG's representative, a plump young man with thinning blond hair and a blond fuzzy mustache, leaned forward to his table mike, hugely excited at having been referred to as a professional by Charles Morrison, eager to return the compliment. "Watergate and this, those are two completely different situations," he said. "You're talking apples and oranges here. On the one hand you're talking conspiracy, whereas on the other hand you have one rotten apple who clouds the whole issue, notwithstanding the flip side of the coin, which is a whole drawerful of top bananas, performancewise."

"Smart-ass," Sonny Raymond said.

"What an idiot!" Lianne said, but when she said it, she sang it, sailing into high clarity on the first syllable of "idiot," concluding with a sort of sustained tremolo. She could make her voice crackle, but she was not capable of harsh or mangled tones. When she cursed you, you could score the performance for orchestra.

Alison Legg had come back into the conversation pit, had noticed the small bits of dirt on the rug, had begun to turn back to the kitchen for paper towels and rug cleaner, when she saw her husband's face and realized immediately and intuitively that he was the person in trouble, that there had indeed been a fight and he had been in it. She knew, too, in that moment, that the fight had been because of another woman.

Greg, under fire, the flush of the tribe of earnest young blonds rising in his face, experienced a conversion, a moment of visionary insight. He saw that his boss was courageously defending him from the results of his own foolishness, but he saw beyond that. He saw that Charles Morrison was a great man, a man who used all of his wit and all of his nerve to protect the purity of the judicial process. A man willing to take any amount of heat, so long as he could prevent irrelevant controversy from clouding essential issues. Greg Legg saw that to Charles, legal debate was precisely equivalent to the intellectual deliberation of the citizenry of Arkansas, an ongoing discussion of such significance that it must not be confused or roiled or distorted by the glandular injections of the media. He owed it to the state of Arkansas, Greg saw, to represent events not as they had actually happened but in such a manner as would best benefit the people themselves.

He felt his sincerity rising. He knew that he had slugged Sonny Raymond, but he knew that he sincerely should not have slugged him, and *that* was the sincerity that the people of Arkansas needed. Always he had felt in himself this earnestness, but he had never understood how to use it, had sprayed it casually to the wasteful throng. Now he saw how to channel it, how to focus and direct its tremendous energies. He had become, at long last, a lawyer.

"I appreciate the comments by the attorney general's office," he said, "but I just want to point out that he seems to leave open a question in the minds of the public that the public really deserves to have unequivocally resolved. If there's a rotten apple to be found in the barrel of this rumor, then I seem to be being nominated for that honor, but the fact is, there's just not any apples, rotten or otherwise. John," he said to the reporter from the *Gazette*, "you know me."

And this was true: Greg and the reporter were of an age, their drinking hangouts were of a type, they watched ball games together on the wide screens of Slick Willie's or Thank God It's Friday's or the White Water Tavern. They were both young, enlightened, convinced, and happy in the knowledge that there would never be an end to the afternoons of languid beer and intense discussion. "I'm telling you now, there wasn't any fight between me and anybody else at that party, or between anybody and anybody else. You've spoken of eyewitnesses—don't I qualify as an eyewitness? I was there. And you *can* use my name."

"You too, buddy," Sonny Raymond said.

"So he *has* been fucking her," Lianne said.

Alison was stricken before the tv, where she had knelt to rub up the spot, one hand raised and forgotten, holding a moistened paper towel, her blackened knees grinding in more dirt than she could ever erase.

Greg had been looking directly at the reporter, as if to underscore his forthrightness. Now he turned his eyes back to the cameras. "I just want to say that I have a beautiful sweet wife sitting at home, and we have a beautiful baby daughter who's the apple of my eye, and that when I think of the importance of this situation to the people of Arkansas, I'm thinking of them, and I'm thinking of what kind of society of free inquiry we're going to have when my daughter grows up, and questions of our right to have access to all the kinds of proper information we need, and that our courts are the proper place to argue this sort of thing out, and there is no way I would ever consider doing the least thing that would jeopardize that process for the citizens of this state and my daughter Ashley."

Charles, caught completely by surprise at the beginning of this outburst, was now thinking that Greg hadn't done too badly, that he just might come through. He should have cut all that Walt Disney stuff about the wife and baby, he needed overall to cultivate a more distanced and urbane tone—all that emotion could backfire on you, it could read like trying too hard. Still, he was showing some resources. Needs some practice, but good enough for now. Spin control would be manageable from here on in.

He was also thinking, by association with the phrase "spin control," that he had forgotten to call Lianne and let her know about the press conference. Too late now. Maybe a miracle had happened, though, and she hadn't heard. He could call her as soon as he got back to the office.

"I agree completely," said the representative from the AG's office. "That is exactly the kind of point I was trying to make."

The green metal door with the one small wire-covered window swung open, and Audrey Tull leaned in to speak to Sonny Raymond. "We got a confession," he said.

"Make sure he gets the roast beef and mash potatoes, then," Sonny Raymond said.

"I don't know whether you think you're protecting Greg or that Talliaferro woman," Lianne said to her husband's image. "Jesus," she said, dropping her head to one hand with a sudden thought. "Jesus, Charles, you're not. Tell me you're not. Not her."

Alison had gotten Greg's message. It had flown over the airwaves straight into her heart. She had her man back. The frightening days were over, the nights spent talking Ashley to sleep, but talking to her even after she had gone to sleep, on and on, quietly, nonstop, talking really to keep from thinking about where Greg might be, to keep from feeling how things were going wrong, strange twisted happenings out there just beyond her range, moving like nightmares through the darkness.

The tears came down freely now. But she had to stop, her mother would be back soon with the baby. She rose and took her trowel with her out into the garden in the backyard, knelt again in the dirt in the bright noon sun, stabbing and turning the rich soil, blindly weeding the already weeded plantings of day-lilies and pansies and marigolds, and around her, in the borders of the fences, where they had not yet mowed, there sprang the soft green masses of wood sorrel, scattered with pink blooms, and the fierce green looping towers of the wild daisies, daisy fleabane: Watering the soil with her tears, oh yes.

12

LUCKY DOG

At home, taking the shortcut from the garage to the front door, clattering through the fallen leaves and prickly seed-pod grenades of the saurian old magnolia, he stubbed his toe on Ramalam's marker. His shoes were sturdy enough that his foot wasn't hurt, but the impact pitched him forward. He caught himself on a hand and one knee. He stood up, brushing dirt and leaf scruff from his knee, and retrieved his briefcase. His hand bore the imprint of a seed cone, but wasn't bleeding. The marker, a huge stone Lianne had insisted on hauling all the way back from the Buffalo River and burying until only an inch of it showed, had scuffed his left shoe badly. She had put the marker there because that had been Ramalam's favorite outdoor summertime sleeping spot, and she had buried the stone so deeply because Ramalam had been accustomed to scrape and thrash until he had worn a bathtub-sized wallow in the cool talcy dust. "He would want to dig in deep," she had said. There was no body, only the marker. The dog himself was ashes now.

"You goddamn dog," he said. "You still can't leave me alone." Ramalam had been Lianne's favorite, her friend for fifteen solid years, a strange and enormous mongrel whose mother had been a Saint Bernard—Lianne knew this, because she had picked the pup from the new litter, busily burrowing to teat—and whose father, the original owners swore, had been an unregistered Doberman. The dog had been vast, chaotic, and smelly, leaving hair and the ornaments of his bodily processes everywhere. Turds on the stairs, smears of mucus on the windows of the big Mercedes. Charles had steadfastly refused to let him ride in the 280—not that there was room when he and Lianne were both in it, and Charles sure wasn't going to take the dog out by himself.

In general tremendously friendly, his Doberman heritage appearing only in a sort of high-strung hyperkinesis and in his fierce protectiveness toward Lianne, Ramalam had not approved of Charles and had waged continual war with Coleman, who had threatened more than once to quit.

It's him or me, Mr. Charles. Other peoples aint have that kind of a dog. I aint keep on planting yo flars if the Beast a Revelation gone keep on digging em up.

One of the finest occasional sights Charles had been treated to was the spectacle of Coleman harrying Ramalam from one or another of the beds with whatever Smith and Hawken he had to hand—the hoe, the rake, the pitchfork, the hand spade—and once even the posthole diggers, staggering heavily after the animal, making the edges bite together: *Chunk outta yo ass!*

When Charles had come along, the dog had suffered demotion from its status as bed partner and ultimate confidant. Though the damned thing had always been able, on Lianne's darkest and moodiest days, when Charles got nothing but hard words, to clamber into her lap and appeal, successfully, for the most disgusting and saliva-ridden of kisses, immediately becoming happy enough to leap down and wreck two or three more coffee tables.

It had been lover versus lover, as far as Ramalam was concerned, and the dog was the more subtle contestant. Not physically hostile, accepting grooming and direct commands, and even, when the family had been rocking warmly along, appearing to enjoy Charles, but frustrating him continually in thousands of small ways nevertheless: The creature ate books, for example, had once swallowed whole the precious first edition of Bester's best, *The Stars My Destination,* absolutely irreplaceable.

The beast somehow, despite its relatively silent parents, was a howler, shaking the springtime moon in the sky with belly-deep, protracted resonance, horrible wavering cadenzas warbling upward from a bass suitable to the throat of an irradiated and mutated thirty-foot swamp frog to the overtone-shredded treble agonies of a trapped angel whose feathers were being plucked, one by one, and the roots cauterized with a red-hot iron.

Ramalam had been dead three years, and Charles missed him. He missed him for what he had given Lianne. The dog's divided genealogy had perfectly represented her needs: the ferocious, almost paranoid guardian, the warm and dependable rescuer. He had been savior and clown at once, a domestic lightning rod, his calamitous ways drawing in and transforming all their potential disaster, all the tragedy hovering just offstage, to minor and harmless pratfall.

"You damn dog," he said, and went in.

He had picked the front door, big and formal as that entryway was, because Clemmie would hear the automatic bell and come to take his things. His briefcase, jacket, vest, tie, overcoat if he had one, his shoes, all would disappear in a moment, helped from his body, to be cleaned, placed, hung, folded. His keys, wallet, change, pens, tags, papers, reminder slips, all would be ordered and made ready for morning, put where they always were put, so that he could recover them without thought. It was one of the greatest of his luxuries, the ten minutes that he did not spend taking himself apart and organizing the pieces for reconstitution. The wealthy do not have to maintain themselves, and so are spared life's heaviest care. Not even We have it so good. Angels to serve Us, yes, but Who keeps the angels up and running?

Charles never thought of Clemmie's attendance as privilege, but his body knew, and gravitated infallibly toward it.

She was there bearing slippers, a light robe, a hanger for his jacket. On a small tray on a side table stood a slender glass pitcher with a glass rod slanting into the cubistic clarity of its contents, and beside it there was a frosted tulip glass with a shadowy yellow twist nested in its convexity.

She took his briefcase, and he turned to let her help with his jacket. "Where's Mrs. Morrison, Clemmie?" he said. When Clemmie had a martini waiting, it meant trouble.

"Upstairs," Clemmie said. Worse yet. If Lianne was happy, she was usually visiting, or out on the lawn to greet him, or in the kitchen chatting busily with Clemmie and helping with supper, or out in the greenhouse puttering with plants. If she was angry, she was waiting in the foyer, or was in the library, reading with white-faced concentration, or had the formal dining room dressed, the china ready to receive the most minimal of offerings from la cuisine nouvelle. Upstairs, now—upstairs meant she was depressed.

He felt it in the air, invisible draperies. She had her mother's ability, Elaine's ability, to charge her surroundings with her own emotion. An unrecognized psychic talent, the mood projectors. You lived inside their feelings. They were happy, the day was sunny. They felt black, it was damn sure gonna rain on your parade.

"Turn your back, Clemmie," he said, lashing the belt of the robe. "I'm going to go real comfortable this evening." He slipped out of his slacks and handed them to her. "Where are we eating? Still too cold for the sun porch, I guess."

"Really it's not," she said. "Maybe I'm being a little excessive, but I started a fire."

There was a large two-sided stone fireplace that could be used to heat either the sun porch or the adjoining kitchen. Theoretically, you could use it for cooking too, but they never did—in construction, it had seemed a festive idea, but his father had roasted a few huge briskets there for parties when Charles had been a child and the process had proved too smoky and left the hearth filthy with drippings. Clemmie sometimes worked up a batch of hearth-baked bread on it, or a Christmas pudding, but they kept it mostly closed off on the kitchen side now. It drew better that way, and the kitchen produced enough heat without it.

"That's good," Charles said. "We needed to use up some of that oak. Some of that oak's two years old." Clemmie racked his suit temporarily on one of the pegs provided for the hats and overcoats of guests, stirred the pitcher, and poured Charles a martini.

"Bless you," he said. "Is Mrs. Morrison going to join me?"

"I think so," Clemmie said. "You want me to go ahead and serve the table? I plan to go up early; I have to get my taxes ready for you. I'll tell Mrs. Morrison when I go up."

Clemmie was saying she would put all the food on the table at once and politely disappear, so that Charles and Lianne could thrash the problem out in private, whatever the problem was. Clemmie had been with them since Charles was eleven, three years after his mother had died. Morrison senior, finding himself less than maternal, had hired her for the boy's sake, his judgment perhaps beguiled by visions of English nannies. If Clemmie had allowed him the misconception in order to get the job, she had soon set matters straight. She had become Charles's friend, reliable, helpful, critical only when he was pulling stunts that involved real danger. In her own way as mild and distant as the elder Morrison, she had never tried to be in the least motherly but had rapidly made herself invaluable in a thousand other ways. When Charles had married, Clemmie had fallen for Lianne completely. He felt himself more and more displaced in her affections, a tolerated male in a female household. It had been like being demoted to sixteen again. With all that, though, Clemmie had never faltered, had never seemed to mind waiting on him.

It came to Charles that she might soon want to retire—her lean face and ungraying hair made her look younger, though she was all of sixty— but that event was a chasm he did not care to peer into, a void more intimidating than even his father's death had been.

"Mm," Charles said, nodding, and took his martini through the big doors into the main hall, and then down the west hall past the kitchen, and down the two steps, and out onto the sun porch. Which really wasn't a sun porch, since it faced north. A light porch, maybe. But that was what they had always called it.

It existed, the sun porch, as a sort of broad glassed-in bay behind the kitchen and between the projecting octagons of the formal dining room and the downstairs library (though it did not open directly into either of these latter rooms). It looked out into an entirely private half acre set off by dense banks of hedge and a wandering stone wall, an area that Charles liked to describe as half English garden, half Zen garden, and half jungle.

There was no lawn. There were untrimmed oak and hickory and iron-wood and Southern red cedar casting their mazy branches wherever they could, making their own decisions; there were the tall clean wands of sugar maple, Florida maple, silver maple, and red maple; there were pruned and trimmed hornbeam and yaupon and holly; there were hidden patios, including the one they called the dogwood patio; there were profusions of ivies, raised beds of verbena, phlox, pansies, azaleas, basil, pineapple sage, rosemary; there were incursions of ground cover in several different and glossy greens—sweet william and others he could not name; there were massive spills of the big-leaved and showy white and purple violets, along with clusters of bird's-foot, and wild variants transplanted from the woods that showed pale upper colors and a smashed-raspberry hue in the corolla, and even a few of the yellow dogtooth; there were rows of brilliant irises, distant borders of roses, ragged clumps of wild daisies, smatters of henbit and purple pagodas; there were two lily ponds, there was a small vegetable garden tucked away to the west behind a half-height hedge of nandina, there was the sizable greenhouse on the east, not tucked away at all, its aged and heavy glass gleaming like old bronze in the dying sun.

Charles finished his martini while Clemmie went in and out, preparing the table. He watched the stains of the foliage wash out into the evening, discoloring it, subtracting the greenery to blackness. The fireplace settled to a solid glow, a steady red warmth on his back.

He heard Lianne come in, and turned. She was wearing jeans and sneakers, a big loose-fitting gray sweatshirt that said BEER—IT'S NOT JUST FOR BREAKFAST ANY MORE. Practical clothes. She was planning to be direct, then. "Are you going to eat?" she said. He felt that she made the question vibrate with unpleasant implication—as if he might choose to waste good food and the time required to prepare it; or as if he should have already begun.

She was upset about the press conference, that was clear. Probably also nervous about the bad publicity, taking it personally, though she had no connection to the firm, nothing at risk. So did he broach the subject, or wait for her to do it? Waiting was terrible, her mood hanging over his own like bad weather about to break. But if he brought it up, he was on weaker ground, he was implicitly admitting fault. He imagined hiring someone to shoot her, disguising his voice over the phone so he couldn't be traced. But then he saw the bullets hitting her, her body jerking like a limp doll, the horrible inertness of *Bonnie and Clyde*, and he thought, *No*.

"Sure I'm going to eat," he said. "How about you?" He pulled out a chair and sat down. A tremendous cheddar soufflé dominated the vinyl and chromium table, a sleek designer version of the ubiquitous fifties dinettes. An avocado salad had been served directly to their plates, the remnants in a white crockery bowl. There was a lemon-and-anchovy béarnaise for the soufflé, one of Clemmie's improbable triumphs, lightly graced with powerful tangs. They were drinking iced tea, but Charles saw that the pitcher of martinis had been transferred to the table, strained of its cubes, and that a second frosted glass had been added.

"I'm not very hungry," Lianne said. She took the poker and began a series of completely unnecessary adjustments to the fire, prodding and hooking. A log broke, the faulting of incandescent strata, and sent out a spray of sparks.

"Well, eat something anyway," he said. "How long has it been since you've eaten anything? Did you have lunch?"

She didn't answer.

"How about a martini? There's a whole pitcherful here, and I'm not going to want more than one more."

"No, I don't want a martini," she said, racking the tool and coming to sit across from him. He ate, watching the dusk gather her in. Her features were so vivid and extravagant, and yet her face so fine and small, that his eyes could never solve the mystery of her beauty: Those dominating eyes, that nose fit for a Roman senator or the Indian on the penny, that jawline as firm and clean as the flex of a hickory handle—how did she subsume them to such an exquisite and trembling delicacy?

Fine tuning, he thought. She existed in the fine tuning. His question about lunch had not been entirely unconcerned, an evasive ploy. She was like a sports car: big motor, close tolerances, precise handling, light frame, small tank. Her metabolism ran open-throttle, pure air and fuel. She would forget to eat, until, in a matter of moments, she crossed into red-line hunger, her shoulders drooping, her face drawn, her eyes panicky. Then she thought she could carve raw slabs from the sides of cattle, then she craved great radiant chunks of crusty and buttered bread, jackstraw heaps of steamed vegetables, gravies ladled profusely over giant conglomerations of agglutinated starch, caldrons of thick and bubbling soup, the battered and fried hindquarters of amphibians, fowl, mammals; then she imagined stacked triangular sections of stratified chocolate dolloped with heavy and beaten cream, or amputated segments of lambent cherry pie, scoops of ice cream sizzling to nothing atop them.

And she would eat, with the gauge needle sticking to the zero post, until suddenly it swung all the way over, and an opposite desperation filled her eyes, the conviction she could not hold all she had consumed: She was under attack from her stomach and had to escape.

But tonight would not be the night to tease her about her eating. She was going to let him have his meal and his drink, and then she had something to say. He managed to enjoy the soufflé at first, but it seemed to grow more rubbery as it cooled, and the salad, in the dimness, was a messy hassle, hard to control with a mere fork, tiring and time-consuming to chew. He wanted to disturb the silence, but what could he say? *How was your day?*

And how was yours? she would come back. *Enjoy the press conference you didn't bother to tell me about?*

It was that last hour, that dusk that does not emit illumination but absorbs it: The late worker, home-bound at last, discovers that his head-lights remain pasted in two pale circles on the front of his auto, that they glow but do not project, like the eyes of a cat. It was that dimness that is not penumbra but a fog of void, nothingness in microscopic droplets, a deepening mist of vacuum from the fractured and fractional corners of the earth, those crazy-mazed fissures into which straight-lined light can never work its way: the knotted channels of rootlets; the interleavings of pinnate, compound pinnate, and alternate; the cracks in the undersides of stones in the bottoms of muddy rivers.

Her chin and throat were one field of gray now, gathered into evening. Only her eyes and cheeks showed at all, hints of a creamy richness, rubbed areas in a charcoal sketch. When full darkness came, he would be able to see the fire on her, its ruddiness parenthetical in her curls, surds of clear shine describing the curves of her face.

He pushed his plate away, considered a third martini.

"Charles, are you having an affair?" she said.

"What the hell?" he said. The image of Tina dominated his mind, and would not go away. It was an image he had conjured in his office that afternoon, after the press conference: in a string bikini, both cheeks pumping, walking away down the beach at the island. His heart-rate had doubled at Lianne's question, and he felt giddy and frightened, completely transparent. The woman is telepathic, he thought.

"No," he said.

Again, what else could he say? He *wasn't*. Tell her, *No, but I've been imagining it, but I probably won't, because I really do love you and you would find out and it would kill you, after you killed me, and anyway she's too damn crazy to mess with?* Sure.

Resentment flared in his veins. It was that rebound resentment from almost getting caught, from being only technically innocent: so that you don't have righteousness to power your defense, so that you must generate your denials from other sources of energy.

"What's going on?" he said. "What brought this up?" She did not answer. "I said no," he said. "What else do you want me to say? I've never screwed around on you. If you don't know that, how can I prove it? What can I do, produce the diary entry I wrote every time I didn't screw another woman? I've quit beating my wife too.''

He could not see her face at all. He got up to switch on the light, and came back to the table. Now, in the harsh illumination, objects seemed dislocated and glaring, with the overdone verisimilitude of a department store display. The room felt tilted. She looked the way people look coming out of surgery, when they begin to wake up. They have not been allowed pain, but they are in shock nevertheless. Something is gone. Something has been cut away.

"Look at me," he said intensely, leaning across the table. He took her chin and turned her face forcibly. The resistance in her neck was the wobbling resistance of an adjustable lamp.

He was terrified. As guilty as he felt, the thing that frightened him most was her state of mind. If she really believed he had been unfaithful, it would destroy her. Oh, not suicide, not a nervous breakdown, not that sort of thing. She was a survivor. But all the bloom would be lost, all of the trust, the happiness so carefully and patiently built over the last fifteen years. He could not bear to see that hopefulness close down, to see her become a bitter and suspicious woman.

So he was obliged, wasn't he, for her own sake, to convince her of his fidelity, however wicked his heart might be? Why didn't they cover this sort of morality in Sunday school? What good was the regular morality if it didn't tell you about times like this? The hell with Sunday school; what about group? They told you in transactional analysis not to do this, not to think for another person, it was game playing, it was manipulative. They were full of shit.

"Please look," he said. "You've got to trust your own judgment. You know me. I can't fool you."

"You're a lawyer, Charles," she said.

"But you're not a judge or a jury," he said. "They don't live with me, and you do. Have I been acting different? You know I would be acting different. I would have excuses for where I've been, I would be staying out late at night. I would be out of the office at strange times. Brenda Faye would give you a funny look when you came by the desk. She would be uncomfortable talking to you. You would go around feeling like people were whispering behind your back.''

"I always feel like people are whispering behind my back."

"You know what I mean. Look, Lianne, I haven't even been *trying* to fuck around. I'm the last faithful man in captivity. If you don't know that, what can I say? But it's more than that. Listen, Lianne—'' She had looked down, and now he lifted her chin.

"Listen, the main thing is I love you." He gentled his voice. "I really love you. I have never been and I will never be unfaithful to you." His heart sank as he promised. *Not even fantasies*, he thought. *Not even fantasies*.

"I believe you love me, Charles," she said. "But lovers can hurt each other. I've been feeling some real strangeness going on lately, and don't tell me I haven't. You say you aren't behaving any differently, but I think you are."

Her depression was gone, at least. Her eyes were flashing, she was asserting the accuracy of her perception. He had to admire her recovery time. He began to feel the adrenaline of combat. "What?" he said. "What things am I doing?"

"You were out late drinking Friday night."

"We had a fight, for Christ's sake!"

"Precisely. We had a fight."

"Lianne, we fight all the time. It's the way our marriage *is*."

She seemed abashed. "I don't think of us that way."

"So what do you think those things are, rational debates? Maybe not all the time, but we fight pretty regular. Face facts, we're just different personality types." He decided to press his advantage. "And listen—I hate to say it, but listen: Friday night was your fault, right? You can see that now, can't you? I mean, you were upset about the creation science bill, sure, but really you just kind of jumped my case as soon as I walked in the door. It wasn't *me*—I didn't do anything."

"You smelled like perfume when you came back," she said. Conveniently skipping over the question of who started the fight. And why hadn't she mentioned the perfume when they went up to make love? If it was important now, wasn't it important then?

"I was in a *bar*. I probably smelled like beer and smoke too, and I don't know what all else." Will that fly or won't it? Better not slow down. "But you know what? I think this is all irrelevant. You were glad enough to see me when I got home. You weren't wondering about me having an affair then, I know you weren't, or you would never've been able to touch me, much less have so much fun in bed."

"It was fun," she said. Aha. Victory in view. She wants to be convinced. And what else? A bit of the old coochie-coo? Could be, could be. The evening could turn out well after all.

But no, not yet, her expression was changing. "I saw your press conference today," she said angrily.

"Ah so, the famous press conference," he said. "Now, how did I know that subject was going to come up?"

"Don't you dare make fun of me, you shithead."

Danger danger danger. The worst thing you could possibly do to Lianne was to refuse to hear what she had to say: to discount her information, as group had taught her to put it.

"Well, I'm not. I'm really making fun of myself." He hurried to cover the cliché. "I know you hate being out of the pipeline, and I don't want you to be. You're absolutely my best adviser, but it all came up so fast, and I just didn't—"

"You can't tell me this all came up so fast—"

"Well, it certainly did. Hell, I didn't even find out about it myself until this morning. Hell, the *fight* was only Friday night." Friday night fights. Poll Parrot, Poll Parrot.

"Charles, what do you think I'm talking about?"

"You're talking about the damned press conference. I'm trying to tell you I'm sorry I didn't call you, but I had to throw the whole damned thing together in about two hours, and—"

"I didn't think you were hearing me."

"Hearing you? What the fuck, what about you hearing me? I was in a crisis, Lianne. I didn't have time to call home and fill you in. And what the hell does it have to do with adultery anyhow? Why does a perfectly natural oversight make you distrust somebody you've trusted for fifteen years?"

"Are you going to listen to me, or are you going to just keep on telling me what I'm saying? Because I have better things to do if you are."

He wanted to jump up and scream like a great ape, overturning the table, crashing the chairs about, beating the ground with a branch. He didn't. He said, as coldly as he could, "So talk." Thinking, *Why don't you have a stroke, like your father? No, you'll give one to me, like your mother.*

"Are you going to hear me, or are you going to sit there and be angry?"

"If I say I'll listen, I'll listen."

"But you haven't said it."

"I just did."

"No you didn't."

"Lianne—ok, ok. I. Will. Listen. Talk."

She had started a sentence just as he added the bad-tempered command. Now she stopped, watched him a moment, and continued.

"Susie called me and let me know about the press conference. I want you to know, as soon as I touched the button of that channel selector, I had a cold chill run down my spine."

"A freezone," he said. It was one of their joke words, her faux-naïf play on the French. She gave him the look of an impatient walker brushing away a cobweb.

"It just got worse while y'all were talking," she said. "It was all I could do to watch the whole thing. Charles, there's something evil going on, and all I could think of was how it was going to swallow you up. It was like an earthquake movie, where the cracks open up and the good people fall in, or like a black closet with a doortrap in it. Where they fall to the alligator water."

"Trapdoor," he said.

"I know she has something to do with it," she said, and neither she nor Charles noticed that she had not specified Tina. "Suddenly I felt she had you, like the spiders have bugs, and you were going to die. And there's something else, there's somebody else really wicked and twisted, somewhere in the background."

He was numb, outdistanced and everywhere flanked by her impossible prescience. She knew without information, she saw directly what no one else could see at all. How could it be that she had such perception and yet did not see his sequestered heart? With such flashing knowledge, why was marriage so inevitably a farce of forced duplicity? Was it that even clairvoyance was limited? That we could know all but not particulars, or know particulars but not all? In that moment, he hated the universe for its divisions, its stupid partial laws.

Although all laws are partial.

"My hands are still like ice," she said, holding them out.

Like the swain at a ball, receiving the princess's fingers in both his palms, he leaned across the table and took her hands. They were cold. He felt as though a current of chilliness had run suddenly through his body, completing a circuit to the ground. He had a vision of something black and mobile, a drinking blot. This was not to be tolerated, it must be dispelled. She stood open to all the dark spirits. Reason was needed. Talk. Words. Light.

"I want to be real careful about this," he said. "I want you to know I'm not discounting you. I know you felt something real. I didn't doubt you about the ghost at the Albert Pike house. And you saw Ramalam the night he died."

"We should have brought him. He would have barked at the waves." Her eyes filled.

"I know, I know." This was good. The dog was always a good distraction. She had loved the dog so much that at the mere mention of his name, he filled her thought. It was as if he were there inside her, complete, an entire country she could resort to. A sudden swerve to Ramalam. There was safety in Ramalam, sing praise.

"But what I'm wondering," he said. "There probably is something evil back there in the background. I mean, if Sonny Raymond's involved, there's probably a lot of evil in there somewhere—but why did it get to you so bad? I mean, you really are amazingly sensitive to this kind of thing, which is good, but maybe it's dangerous for you sometimes. But why this time? I mean, there's evil all around—I mean, look at this guy Lucas, and the girl who turned up missing over in Glenwood, and they're on the news, but you don't get a chill there."

"I don't know why I don't," she said. "I wish I did know. But this time it felt like you were connected to it."

"But I'm not, not that I know of. Except this whole damn fight thing is a PR problem for the firm, but what's new about that? I can't help feeling like it's something else that happened, something that kind of triggered you and made you have all your antennas up. It wouldn't be our fight, would it? Because—"

"I was going to say I don't think it was our fight, because I thought of that, and the millage amendment already had me depressed, and then the creation science, and so I was really upset about politics in general, and then the whole press conference thing was more of the same, and I just hate to see you so stuffy and smart-ass and full of shit, just like the rest of them, playing that game like you wanted to be governor or something someday, but—"

"Because it just didn't have that feeling to me, it wasn't like you were surprised, you knew the amendment was probably going to lose, and that's why you were so bitchy, because you were mad at being right again."

"So it wasn't that," she said. There was a pause while they adjusted their somewhat ruffled sensibilities, he at having been called stuffy and she at having been, in retaliation, called bitchy.

"You know what I think it is?" they said at the same time.

"You first," he said.

"Greg and Tina," she said.

"You see yourself as Alison." She ducked her head, making a little moue, and brought her face back up bright and clear with tears, her expression one of relief and embarrassment, but an embarrassment that was mixed with pride. "The betrayed and forsaken woman."

"It was just too close," she said.

"You know that's an old script, don't you? Maybe your momma betrayed you and your daddy betrayed you, but I won't."

"I knew that fight was about her. She's fucking that bastard Sonny Raymond, and she wants to get Greg killed. And Greg is shitting all over Alison and that child."

"Hey, he wouldn't be doing it if Alison wasn't putting up with it. I don't mean he's right, but she's awfully passive, you have to admit."

"I'd cut his balls off." She cupped a dangling invisible scrotum, made a slashing movement with her right hand.

"Yeah, yeah," he said. "You're tough. I shrink at the idea."

"Why didn't you tell me, Charles? All I could think of was you were protecting her, and why would you do that, unless—And *dancing* with her, in my *own house*. It scared me."

"That was a *celebration,*" he said. "First I swung Clemmie around, and then I swung her around, and that's just when you happened to walk in. And I'm not protecting her," he added. "You know I don't like to gossip, that's all. Anyway, I called her into my office today and told her to get her act straight or she was out of there."

"Too little, too late. It isn't you don't like to gossip—or you don't, but it's control with you, it isn't niceness. You don't like to let go of information. You want to make everything private, so nobody can judge you, so you can sneak around and make things happen."

"So I'm anal retentive," he said. "I'm hearing you now, aren't I? I'm being straight with you now."

"You're being straighter. I don't think you're fucking her, but you are protecting her."

"I am *not* protecting her. She's brilliant, she had great recommendations—"

"Which she got by fucking every one of them too, probably."

"She has a great track record. Do you know what kind of an EEOC suit I could get into if I fired a woman with a record like that? Because of her sex life?"

"I know you don't like me having opinions about the office, Charles, but I have a mind, and I can see things, and if you want to live with me, you're going to have to listen to me."

Well, maybe I don't want to live with you, bitch. "I do listen to you," he said. "Haven't I already *told* you I put her on notice? And anyway, you're wrong, she's not fucking Raymond now. Maybe she did in the past, I don't know, but that's not who she's fucking right now, not him or Greg, either one."

He had thrown that out as another distraction, a tidbit of gossip to divert her from her criticism, but he immediately regretted it. Dragging Lafayette into this mess, that's what he felt. Ridiculous. It was Lafayette who was creating his own mess, but still Charles felt guilt, a sense of having involved an innocent in something nasty. And maybe a slight twinge of loss, the realization that the information would further confirm Tina's image in Lianne's eyes, would make her even harder to defend.

"So who's she fucking now?"

"Who do you think?" he said. "Who was here with her when you came in?"

"Boy," she said. "I bet all these local rednecks just love that." She was delighted. And her delight was pure, he realized. She was not in the least worried about what a black man fucking a white woman would do to the image of the firm, she just loved the drama. She wanted all the details. How did he know? Was he sure? How long had it been going on?

A half hour later, she realized she was hungry. Really hungry, she explained. He volunteered to fix something, and she said he could just microwave the soufflé. He thought that was a horrible thing to do to a work of art, but she insisted. It would puff up again, she assured him, and it would do fine, even if it would make it tougher. And if it didn't work, bring her some bread and she would have a soufflé sandwich. *Gack,* he said. And the martinis were warm, and they needed to be colded again, and when are you going to buy me a microwave refrigerator?

You can't have a microwave refrigerator, it's entropy, it won't go that direction.

So how do they make those instant-cold beer cans?

I don't know, probably explosive decompression.

Decompress this.

I know what the middle finger is, but what's the little one?

For those who don't deserve the very best.

Oho, very clever. Ok, the lady wants a martini, I'll stir them over some more ice, or do you want fresh?

This is fine; all you need to do is get me drunk and fuck me.

Hum, well, put it that way, I'll go cold up some more martinis right now.

And microwave the soufflé.

And microwave the soufflé.

When he came back from the kitchen, she had turned the lights out. It took a moment for his eyes to adjust, and then, in the dimming firelight, he saw she was sitting naked at the table.

Put the soufflé right there, she said, gesturing to the spot in front of her.

Yes *ma'am,* he said. But, ah, ma'am—where do I put this?

Hmm, she said. I don't know. Where do you want to put it? Got any ideas? She got up and moved her chair away, then leaned over the table, swaying her breasts just above the cloth, bracing herself with her elbows.

That's an impressive ass you've got there, he said, going around behind her, lifting his robe. It's at a very interesting altitude. I think I have an idea now.

Umph, she said. All *kinds* of soufflés tonight. Ump. *Big* soufflés. She used a fork to tear a chunk out of the bowl in front of her, dipped it in the béarnaise. She turned her head to let him see her chewing, the thick sauce dripping from the corner of her mouth.

Her buttocks were cool against his stomach, her pubic hair brushed against his swinging balls. I own this, he thought, this is my female flesh, I'm bull ape horse tiger rip tear bite the back of the neck, this is mine, I mount, I take, I slam, I hump: I am *supposed* to be this way! He felt all of evolution roaring in his channels, and no matter she had no womb to receive it. Oh, it was not pretty but it was right, and he was certain that in her the moon drew full that stacked his tides, certain that she wanted his dominance as he wanted to give it, certain that her submission was from as old and as justified a source.

It was just that so few could touch these energies and remember, afterward, that they were energies, not identities, roles in a little mutual game and not immutable classifications, that men and women were, in fact, forever fucking equal.

Dog fucking, he thought, I'm dog fucking. I'm doing it to her, doing it to her, doing it to her, and that was ridiculous, sex was a clean thing, he didn't have to get his rocks off, rocks off, by thinking rocks off dirty rocks off. But dog fucking! he thought again, radiant with physical joy. God, it's great to be dog fucking!

And when he came, she bayed like a hound.

Up in her room, Clemmie switched off the kitchen intercom. "About time," she said, and folded her book, and put out her bedside light.

13

THUNDERHEAD

So it suddenly occurs, does it, that you been doing all these memories in your own colors? Yessir, justifying as you go. *Why I did this, why I thought that.*

Sketch Lianne, then herky-jerky hully-gully Crayola-color her fulla Chucky-boy. Got a crayon call Flesh. Got a crayon call Mind. But Chucky's box of colors.

Oh when I was a kid and the kid next to me says Can I bar your reddarnj cause I don't have no reddarnj and I have to do a far? *Because my box always had 48. But how I hated to say yes to Heshe Itweus (but always did), not because they were foreigners, but because he would maybe break it under the paper sleeve like a forearm bone in its sleeve of meat so that the paper would dimple and eventually tear, or because she would chew the end of it, incarnadine and toothsome mock of candy. So it would come back to me tattered, stripped, busted, gnawed. And no matter that Daddy could afford 48 boxes of 48, it was impossible to make a grownup understand how bad you needed fresh colors, so I always had to wait forever.*

Nothing like a fresh box: all the crayons at trim attention when you snap the lid open, ranked and geometric, a church choir, a clip of pointy-nose high-power. My joy then like the ease of a smoker cracking a carton of Camels. Po. Ten. See.

And you need em bad, Charles, because you a kid and the world a colorbook, and not the one you would of chose either, hardly no space cowboys at all, but the only colorbook they give you, and nothing in it but outlines, hollowstuffs, ghosts. You got to color em in or die. Ghosts want to suck your color away, want your blood, want you to be a hollowstuff too, white man in a suit, and this the only only weapon you got, this loose extra finger from the box of magic fingers.

All of which is maybe how Lianne would have seen it, or if not seen it then maybe felt it down there where all her pictures jangled like rivers of lightning cartoon. And you're trying, aren't you, Charles, you're trying to imagine how it was to be her on the day

all the little children supposed to draw house and she know they want cute little cottage, white, with steep peaky green roof, and gray smoke in a curl out of red brick chimney, and a tree beside (with a brown not burnt sienna trunk, and leaves a dull globe of not chartreuse but plain green), and also beside, a daddy stick figure and a momma stick figure big as the house itself.

And she did instead a piece she cannot now describe, just how she felt, lava fighting lavender in jagged corners, with azure bubbles of pleasure, vermilion puddles of blood. And so they take her to counselor: *What's wrong with you, girl?*

She told you the story, but you need my help to cross that last barrier, jump that ultimate frame. What was it like to *be* there, to be her?

And Mother made you watch her and Daddy eat supper and you got yours when it had gotten cold, and then you threw it up (but you always threw your supper up); and made you sleep without any panties on, so you would feel how shameful you were, how abnormal, to have such things going on in your dark little head.

Which was one of the memories she didn't remember but had gotten to under hypnosis, in her once-a-month deep therapy sessions. Mostly she hadn't told you about those sessions, but that one you know. She talked about it in group back when you were still going.

Having to borrow from somebody else's box now, aint you? Don't feel good, do it?

So hard to do it in her colors, but what choice you got? Do it in yours, and you aint got her, you got you. So hard to find out now at this late date that's all you really want, is her. Got enough you. Got enough you to last a lifetime. Need more her.

What happened to Tuesday and Wednesday and Friday? Just gone, that's all. Last thing I remember is fighting and fucking Monday. Always seemed to fuck good after a fight, isn't that neurotic? Monday of the press conference, and coming home and the martini light. So I should be able to go on from there, link up the days, because I remember Saturday morning well enough. What did I wake up feeling and thinking Tuesday? If I could just remember that, it would all spill out, what I did at the office, if we stayed at home or went out that night. But it's gone, all gone. Like the P.O. after closing. All of the letters supposedly in there, but unrecoverable behind the blind wall of frost-windowed boxes. Dead letter, dead memory office. What good is the brain? We die faster than we can remember living.

I know the employees got their pay finally, and the Senate voted 17 percent usury, that was good, Thursday morning we laughed so hard at the Fisher cartoon: monkey-scratching Senate and ape-shouldered House and picture of Frank White, and all munching bananas:

And that same day Frank signs the bill, sure enough: Senate Bill 482 signed into law as Act 590, and later he admits he signed it without even reading it.

And that was the day, Thursday, the red dust had come in from Texas, because I went out still chuckling at the cartoon, and Coleman hosing down the walls, and all day people driving around and their cars look rusty and dirty at the same time.

But Friday, how could I lose a whole Friday?

Saturday, down to the Y and swam, twenty-two laps, all by myself in the pool. Nobody there, better than workday noon. Chlorine, the peaceful slap of the water, bubble of breathing. The ease of working your muscles. Exercise and take a cold shower, what a cliché, but it works.

Went to the Y because she had her busy face on. Her things-to-do face. The pink socks fuss. But this is me, how I saw her. How was it for her? How did her brain feel?

Open to all impression, at time's mercy. Instantaneous associative leaps.

Never a thought but three other thoughts break through. You gotta see how
We would admire a mind like that.

   In your terms, baby boy, poor little fraction, Mr. Computer-Literate
Technological State-of-the-Art Lawyer-Man, in your terms, she could window an infinite number of screens.

   *So she wakes up, right? I'm still asleep and she wakes up Bang! like
she always does, her mind full tilt:*

   Because if farm market 1st then could go Surplus [catty-corner]
then group, but gas?—if down Cantrell then Phillips 66 but dangerous
cross traffic in and cross back out

   VAN SLAM PEGGY and her standing crying, torn metal like somebody died and a cop and a red light beating but no hurt just glass
in a scatter her 1st accident and we come around the curve and
see it and scare scare coming over me like transparent waves

---

   there by the Phillips 66 and 101.9 yesterday but 99.9 at Chief on
Thursday I saw because we were in

   DEE-DEE'S CAR to Steinmart for sweaters on special and sun hot
through window my titties warm and the nipples relaxed like warm
pools and I was thirsty

   BIG COKE WITH PEANUTS the salt and the sweet flow and
the bite at the side of the tongue and the back of the tongue
and the rub-tongue peanuts naked [no scratch-crystals] and the
mouth of the bottle round and hard like a granny-kiss

   THE NEW TALL TEN-OUNCE Maw-Maw let me have after Paw-Paw's funeral

and his white face with makeup like a wax face in white silk box white flowers everywhere so beautiful like the sea and I cried for the flowers so beautiful and they thought for Paw-Paw so I was a good girl and

extra chess pie at dinner, gooey and chewy

but Chief two miles wrong way unless can stretch tank, but probably can because Charles always hates to stop [*There's 20 miles left when it says empty*] and we always make it, so then Surplus will be open by the time finished with farm market [if can find pink sock] and then Chief and won't have to cross traffic and then take Mississippi to group [just right, just right, I figured it out, good girl!], which is just as fast as faster than Markham to Barrow even if longer miles so all work out oh good good good [if can find

**"Charles, do you know where my other pink sock is?" **

Groanstirs. What is this sleep? Mudfrog on a blue day.

**"What?"
"I said, what did you do with my other pink sock?"
"Pink sock? What pink sock? What are you talking about?"
"I saw you in my drawer yesterday."
"Yesterday? No, I wasn't even—oh, Monday, maybe. But that was the other drawer, the lower right one, and I was looking for the flashlight. Why would I mess with your socks? They scare me."**

SPIDERS IN SOCKS snake in socks reach in pink jumble and teeth flash bite? No, a Charles-joke.

**"What do you mean?"

"When I gaze upon your socks, I am forced to realize how weensy and funny-looking your feet really are. I am forced to abandon my subjective impression that your feet are like those of normal—ow!"**

Big dog lick face, hit with pillow. Puppy want to rough-and-tumble now WOOPSY spin room bang bed grab-wrestle AH HA no you don't no you don't I got I got

---

"God, you're a gorgeous woman."

I win I win I win I win, riding straddle, hair whipped out and face warm, I know little boys always like to see blood rise, face pussy cock see blood rise

---

and I hear in my afterhear his *gorgeous* washing over me like a sheet of water before the wet soaks in, like a skin I can't feel

---

and hands on my hips smooth up my back under my shirt to pull me back down to smothery grab and I could let go, could flow down, but no, no

---

**"No. I've got things to do." I swing-leg and slide off. He doesn't grab, just rolls on his side and says:

"Here's one of em right here."

Pink sock? Pink dick. Waggle with hand. Another joke.

"Forget you. Have you seen my other pink sock? I've asked you four times."

"No, I don't know where your other pink sock is. Have you checked the laundry? *What* have you got to do? Well, ok, just walk out without saying anything."

I hear, but who has time to answer all of his moves?**

Because I see it in my mind in sewing basket in bathroom, with orange-handled scissors across. Because I thought maybe sew lace on top and brought one to try and thought no but left in basket. Up on far cabinet, tiptoe to reach.

Old-fashioned bathroom, pillar sink, big old claw tub, black and white tile, smell of the blue clip-on bowl soap: but all like new, all perfect and gleaming.

Charles on bed-edge when I go back—make fun of forget where put it?

But no.

**"So where are you off to?" He knows. I always do. Grins, raffles his hair with his hands.

"Farmers' market. Bye."

"Well give me a kiss at least."**

Quick quick. Bend. Soft mouth Charles. Oh my jaws let go, my mouth opens, my throat opens, my body opens with heat all the way down my chest to my belly, but no, not now [Momma's on a tight schedule]—

**"See you."

"I'll be here."**

pink sock]

time

TOMATOES ARE A BIG ROUND RED like a sports car fender, all the hard red curves forced around into the green stem and I was looking at it when we were in the garden and I couldn't help stepping on the everywhere vines and the MEAN GREEN SMELL jumps out and Paw-Paw yells at me to be careful and I will throw it at you like a bomb, Paw-Paw, if you don't shut up shut up because you don't know it's a bomb but I do because I have a big red secret bomb

and Paw-Paw threw grenades in the war but they weren't round then, they were on a stick like a rolling pin with only one handle [or was that just the German?] because he had one he used to show me

and it must be the Surplus across the street making the pictures leak into my head

vines like barbed wire on torn-up black dirt so a war, and the bright red

They have to be hothouse this early but they smell right, so

**"I'll take two bombs."
"What say?"
"Two pounds. Two pounds of the tomatoes." And he flaps the sack open by dragging air and tumbles seven into sag-sack and weighs and
"Two pounds two ounces, lady."**

So now under the wild windy morning I have a heavy sack, treasure-bag. The wind crazy between the buildings and the cloud-sun, sun-cloud making me ripple like water-shadows, the whole weather running around half happy and half scared, like children let out of prison, like have to do everything now because the world won't last, because it will end soon, any minute, because too beautiful to last, and so maybe the wind is just all the children who never were born and that's their prison they want to break out of, never being born, and they want us to see them but we never do and they run around crying . . .

—Momma, look at the flowers!
Hush, Sherry Clare.
—Momma, I'm lonesome.
Paul Anthony, hush.

The marigolds wobble brighter in my almost tears. Trays of the bitter and beautiful, shake in the bright bright wind, in the clear clear light. Oh marigolds for the garden, to border the walk in the garden, rusty and yellow and black, and the bugs won't come.

And the bugs won't come to bite.

time

ALUMINUM CANTEENS in canvas [and so do the soldiers and boy scouts get Alzheimer's because doesn't aluminum?] and bayonets and compasses and folding knives and match-carriers under the glass-top counter and I always want to buy it all

---

Charles: *You carry enough in your purse to start Western civilization all over again*

---

you could find your way in the wilderness, cut trees, start fires, cook supper in the tinware campkits, and kill the bad people when they came to get you:

SOLDIERS IN YANKEE uniforms pouring in over the ridge on the other side of the creek, dirty-face ragged and running and yelling and shooting and now Japanese and German GI Indians and Mongols on horses [rearing and waving glinting scimitaries] and I have the big machine gun from the display window [air-cooled Browning with holey jacketed barrel (like a car-muffler)] and I shoot them, they can't have me, I could fight a war, I would be a good soldier, I would kill them all . . .

But today I want an old dark green wool army blanket, secure and safe and heavy and nothing warmer, not even Hudson Bay, for the cabin and for camping, folded thick in the cedar-wood linen closet, money in the bank, but they don't have any, and still 30 minutes before gas and group and I want water from a canteen

mountain water making the canteen heavy cold and wet in the hand and the taste of metal in it and the sound of the running water where I filled it and a high crow calling

but Charles will laugh if I buy any more canteens or canvas leggings or hemp rope [in a coil with the hairs sticking out and strong it won't break and put it around the tent and the snakes won't come to sleep with you] or iodine kits or portable shovels. So. Run by the flower shop Dumpsters to see if any roses or mums thrown out in the night . . .

time

The smell that makes everything go: In a gush that makes the handle cold, and wavery lines in the air where you put the nozzle in and the numbers spin in the side of your eye. Not a smell that always was, but a smell we made. We didn't even press it out from where it was hidden, like olive oil or cedar oil or attar of roses or bergamot. Crude is black rich thick, the sludge of old Jurasmic jungles—

If I could have been there—camping in time, like one of Charles's science fiction stories—flowers as big as my head, bigger than vases now, laddery fern taller than trees, oh all the nevernomore: What bouquets! What potpourri!

—But all black sluggage now, the rotted memories, and we pump it up, crack it, break it, make it boil off angry liquids, ether and gasoline. And paint. Aniline dyes, and paint. The artists dibble and dobble, nonrepresentational, broken and smeared stained glass, or else they paint the world, but they

don't paint it real, they paint it jangled and wobbled, like trees
and traffic through gasoline vapors. Transparent shimmering
stink. To breathe it carries your mind away . . .

Why suddenly frightened? As if a darkness around me,
as if this cement patch and even the grinding and whipping
street were floating in space and getting smaller.

Smaller and smaller until I disappear.

Sick-dizzy from fumes. Paranoid some fool will fling a match.
Rack up the nozzle, screw the dark hole shut. 8.82's enough.

time

Rapunzel's elevator. Up the tall tower of Baptist Hospital. Seventh
floor get-off, whisper-white hall, linoleum tile, fluorescent tubes. No
outside light, but like a white cave, a tunnel cut into not-cold ice.
Ivory tower.
Farber and Cunningham, Suite 705.
Open the door, and Father Christmas: Ian Farber. Noise and bright
colors and plants, twitchy people lounging on couches, their turn coming, shuffling photography magazines and doctor's travel magazines.
Two secretaries hustling back and forth, and there he is, behind the
glass of the business office, with the little round talk hole like a movie
booth used to be, and below it the slot where you pay. And he's waving
at me, smiling, Lianne's a good girl.
Danish modern depression: machine honeybun and bad coffee in a
Styrofoam cup in steel-tube decor and fluorescent light, and you're a
two-pack-a-day smoker, so you couldn't taste even good coffee, and
you're short and fat and red-faced from high blood pressure, and you
have to read a computer printout.
But Farter Christmas is never depressed, is always merry, glad to
see me, good Lianne.

time

Waiting for Jane, his partner girlfriend, to finish her session, so ours can start. Always runs over, but we do too. We all start showing up five minutes late, then ten, then twelve. Then fuss at each other to be on time and quit on time, but two or three weeks and back to the same.

Farm woman waiting for somebody. Our group, nobody here yet but the boy. Joe Burley Bleednose. Bleedlove. Can't say it. *Breedlove*. Big giant wambler. Slow bear, elephant on hind legs. Flunk out of school. Dungeons and Dragons.

Where are the Worry Twins? Always the last ones.

The door, Jack Beverly. Big black hair, saggy-handsome. Never in a million years. Floppy-tan red-tan face, bourbon and swimming pools. Rich from the family business. Bets on football and brags on hustling pool. Charles would clean his clock. I made him quit trying to sell me diamonds. Ever since he told his dream

face card, but then a real diamond, big as a building, glittering facets, fetus floating, a diamond-shape tank of womb water, floats around turning like *2001*. . . JACK OF DIAMONDS JACK OF DIAMONDS on the baby chest and a man's hard-on

sitting there so calm with his little twisted half-smile and the words coming out and everyone normal but I'm thinking bad I know this is group but we shouldn't hear this is bad bad and he's not telling it clear but his pictures are going straight to my brain bad

and it's a greenhouse, the diamond is, steamy, a greenhouse with a swimming pool, but the glass panes are broken, and the broken glass is cards floating in water everywhere standing in puddles, and a drowned earthworm in the puddle is the baby a body rotting floating in the pool and turn it over

SKULL WITH WORMS

I will never swim in his pool since either.

time

Door opens and they come out, finally. Do we look like that? Re-entry expressions, back to the world where you have to lie and hide things, thank goodness. Heaven sounds like group, God and the other angels know what's wrong with you, we'll all talk and figure you out for a million years and love you and fix you up. I don't think we can stand it. Have to go to hell on vacation so we can spit and cuss and pee standing up.

Somebody still in there talking to Jane. Always somebody had a breakthrough, or felt really cared about for the first time, and doesn't want it to end. Time, it's time. Momma's on a tight schedule.

Jack pushes on in to let them know, Joe Burley puts down the photo magazine he was looking for nude shots in. Farm woman stands up too, she looks confused, almost six feet, long-bone, big rough hands.

And I'm the only who lets her connect her eyes.

**"Are we supposed to go in?" she says. "Or wait till they all come out?"

"Most people just wait," I say. "Is who you're waiting for still in there?"

"No, I'm here for Dr. Farber. I mean, I'm not waiting on anybody, I'm in a group therapy myself."**

Her eyes flickle, that look-around-to-see-who's-listening look, when you keep your head from turning, but your eyes move anyway and you don't know they are. She blushes.

Cloth purse. High heels make her even taller, and starchy popover dress

Charles: *Popover?* Me: *They have daisies and poppies all over them.*

Like a girl's dress-up dress, funny on her long body. So she didn't know what to wear, she thought maybe like Sunday school. Touch her hand. Only the wedding, not even an engagement.

"We all are, hon. You're probably in ours. Come on in and sit down, and Dr. Father will be along in a minute and get things straightened out."

time

He doesn't poot when he sits down. His something valve, Jane Cunningham said one time. You'll be standing and talking, and poot poot poot. He never pays it any mind, and after a while you don't either. Like a fish-tank bubbler. It's kind of friendly, really, and he doesn't stink.

But the first time I came here, when he sat, like it squeezed it out of him. And I was so embarrassed to hear it I didn't say anything the whole time.

**"Who's not here?" he says. "Ah, the Weddingtons. Well, everybody, it's good to see you. We have a new member, Sarah Bean. She's taking Jody's slot, just trying us out for a few weeks. Sarah, do you want to tell us a little bit about yourself?"

"Well, I'm Sarah Bean, like he said, and my husband's name is Christian Bean, and we live over by Gum Springs, but more toward the river, which is close to Arkadelphia. We farm, mostly soybeans. Times are getting hard, but we can't complain. We got food and a roof over our heads."**

a board porch with a wringer washer. And the Bible on a plain board bedside stand with a porcelain basin. The Bible words getting loose in the air, like invisible wires with hooks. Cutting the light with its sharp edges. Sinful and ratty and poor. I don't want to go, Momma, don't want to go to Aunt Pickle's.

**"You don't have to say that stuff," Joe Burley says. Impatient. "You can say anything you want to. Things from your childhood." "Yeah, he . . . I mean, yes, he explained that," she says. "But I always said pretty much what I want to, and it aint never helped a lick. It was our friend Buckley—but mostly his friend—said I ought to come here. I'll try anything once."

"What I hear you saying," Jack says, "is you want to say something, and then you want people to do something about what you said."

"Well I do," she says.

"Jack, if I can break in," Father Christmas says. "Sarah, I don't want to speak for Jack, but what we are really trying to do here is listen to ourselves. We can't insist that other people hear us. All we can do is hear ourselves, and try to identify our own issues. Do you have an issue you want to deal with today?"

"The only thing I can think of is Bean—that's how I call Christian. But I don't see how he can be my issue, because he's not from my childhood. I never even met him till we was almost a grownup in church together."

"Why didn't he come?" Joe Burley says.

"He's afraid they'll find out something about him," she says. "He don't want em to find out he's crazy or dumb. He aint, but he thinks so. So Buckley says, Well, you can go by yourself. It'll still help *you*. So I come. But listen, I decided I don't want to talk about myself no more. Not today." Looks around the room. "I reckon I'm more like Bean than I realized. I don't know all y'all. I want to hold some of my personality back for a while." She looks at Ian. "Can I do that?"

He starts to answer, and the Worry Twins come in, Nikki and Mark, apologizing. Bustle and noise and where are we going to sit, and we all shuffle around, he comes over by me, and she goes over by Joe Burley.

Ian introduces the farm woman all over again. Jack Beverly twists his eyes up sideways, away from us all, disgusted. "Do you people realize you're playing disruption?" he says to the Worry Twins.

Nikki has her woofle look on: don't-hit-me smile, eyebrows peak like a roof, slant up in the middle to say a worried sadness. Her half-and-half look. "I'm sorry," she says. "It was his mother again. She had a gas attack."

Across the room, he nods. Then she nods. His face has been doing what her face was doing. Hers does when *he* talks. Skinny-face people, two little rabbity hook-nose blond people in sincere glasses.

"We're not breaking in on somebody else, are we?" she says, looking around. "Because if we are," he says, looking around. "But we're ready to deal with our issue if not."

Father Christmas nods, it's ok, go on.

Mark hates his mother, Nikki likes her. Momma lives with, rules their life. They won't put her in a home, because then they wouldn't have anything to blame their bad marriage on and might have to go ahead and get a divorce. Their marriage has been falling apart ever since I joined. Main thing holds them together, how bad their marriage is.

Every now and then Ian reminds them to talk about their issues. He tells them to each take their turn and to quit breaking in on each other. Quit rescuing.

"I heard of people staying together because of their children," the farm woman says. "But I never heard of nobody doing it because of their parents." For a minute, neither one of them has anything to say.

The Worry Twins write out contracts not to use his mother as an excuse for any of their fights next week but to have their fights themselves, and they sign them and give them to Father Christmas.

In the betweenish, the farm woman says, "Is it ok if I ask a question?" Nobody says anything, and she goes on. "Will I have to talk about that bedroom and bathroom stuff? Because it will be hard for me, because I'm a Christian."

"What do you think we are?" Jack Beverly says. "Hotten-tots?"

"I know enough to think you been sounding like somebody's mad daddy all day, and to me that means you really just a scared kid. Aint no use talking mean to me, when it's your ownself you whipping."

That shuts him up, and I have never seen that look on his face before.

"I wadn't trying to insult you," she says. "All I was doing was warning you about me. Even in Arkadelphia there's people that don't appreciate Christians, and I thought there might be more of them in Little Rock. It aint like I'm proud. I don't even like being one most of the time. But I met Jesus personally and don't have no choice."

Father Christmas says it's ok to be a Christian.**

Jesus is a big brother. Like a big brother nobody can see. WHIP WITH A LILAC SWITCH, lying on the bed with my heinie up so the cool air can blow over. The air that has the sweet icy smell of lilac. The grape Popsicle smell. The sweet smell of the thing that hurt me. School will laugh at the crisscross on the backs of my legs. *I kill you, kill you, kill you,* whispering, biting my pillow

---

so hard my jaw pops. Can't eat for two days, she thinks I have lockjaw, shots at the doctor, terrible hurting shots—

But Jesus beside my bed, he pats my heinie, his hand is cool and smooth like the cool air, his breath sweet like the sweet smell of lilac. It's ok, little sister, they whipped me too. I had the stripes on my back. But they'll never whip The King. That's what I am when I come back, The King, and I will kill them all, I will send them all to hell for hurting you.

Three years Jesus with me, my secret big brother. Blond and pretty like a quarterback. Said he would never never leave, but he lied, my dolly died, he Jesus died again.

**Jack says, "I hear what you're saying, Sarah, and you're exactly right, I am in my parent today. But about what you call the bathroom stuff, what if that's part of our problem? What if some of us *need* to talk about sex and shit, what are you going to do?''

"I can *hear* anything," she says.

"Why do you think you're in your parent today, Jack?" Ian says. "Do you want to talk about your issues now?"

"I guess so," and he starts a story about how his daddy used to whip him for playing with his thing, and then he realized that he could stand the whippings and so he would play with his thing on purpose to make Daddy mad. "You can bet if I had a son, I'd say, '*Play* with that pistol, boy.' ''

But it isn't long before he's off on a theory about how gambling is a psychological orgasm, because money, if you lose you're the man spraying it out, and if you win they're coming in you and making you pregnant so that's your wish to acknowledge your feminine side and yet at the same time be a winner—

Ian doesn't remind him to stay away from theories and talk, but he asks if Jack thinks the whippings have anything to do with his impotence. But Jack keeps on talking gambling, which he turns into a brag on how good he is at the horses, and then he knows a mobster over in Hot Springs, one scary guy, believe you me, yeah, we had a couple of drinks together, and he thought I was in the rackets, can you believe that, thought I was a mechanic or something? "Because I have the eyes," he said, "I have the hard eyes . . .''

time

". . . had another nosebleed," Joe Burley is saying.**

I must have been gone somewhere. My safety closet, the nothing place. Because why? The hired killers, the people with blank eyes. I don't want to think about them. Don't want to let them in my world. Jack thinks macho, but I think for them to exist makes your life empty, even if they don't shoot you.

**"How did you feel after you bled?" Ian says.
"Ok."
"How did your father treat you?"

"Ok, I guess. He was kind of busy."

"Did he help you get it stopped?" Jack says.

"I didn't need him to. I can get it stopped myself."

"That isn't the point, though, is it? Did he act like he wanted to help, or did he act bothered, like you were causing him problems, like you were bleeding on purpose?"

"I don't know. He didn't pay much attention. He was upset because Mom had come by and gotten the picture when he wasn't there."

"Aha," Jack says. "The Susan Morrison picture? Did you let her in?"

"What I see you doing," Nikki says, "is making excuses for your father. You're trying to get strokes from him, even negative ones, but he's too busy. But instead of just getting what you need somewhere else, you're making excuses for him and blaming yourself for not deserving any strokes."

"And that's a pity," Mark says, "because you're such a neat kid. You've got a lot to offer."

"I guess," Joe Burley says.

"People," says Father Christmas. "We're doing a lot of rescuing here. Joe, I haven't heard you say you really want to work on your issues today." Joe Burley doesn't say anything. "Do you want to ask anyone here for an unconditional stroke?" Joe Burley shrugs.

"Lianne," Father Christmas says.

"Deep potpourri," I say.

He waits.

"Smells can take you back in time," I explain.**

LOOSEN THE GREEN RUG between oak roots, leaves and dry stems stuck in, the tiny red flowers, crumble-dirt under, hanging in threads, the smell of the earth where the moss tore away: worms, and dirt, and rotten acorns, like the smell of

---

PAW-PAW'S BASEMENT, where the tools are, and spiderwebbed orange crates of old letters and mason jars full of rusty nails and—

"I was making some potpourri for my mother's birthday, and suddenly I thought about how smells can take you back. And then I thought about all the gift-shop sentimental potpourri everybody buys, which I just hate. So I made some potpourri with moss and eucalyptus and menthol, to take you back to when you used to lie up in bed sick with the flu, and they rubbed your chest with Vicks

staying at Maw-Maw's and Paw-Paw's down to the basement to fetch her a spool of cord and hot and musty I fainted, and then that evening I had the flu: the smooth strokes, Maw-Maw rubbing me, easing my chest, kind hands smoothing my nipples, someone can love me if sick if I'm sick I'm good

**and I put in some cinnamon oil, too, for the way you feel with the fever, floaty and warm. And some tea leaves for the hot toddy they bring you. I thought of one, you could make one with bay and dog fennel and chamomile, and you could get an oil that smells like cordite, to take you back to when you went rabbit hunting with Paw-Paw in the fall. You could have a potpourri exhibit. A smell gallery."

"I don't feel like it's an art," Nikki said. "It's just like flower arrangements."**

Mad at her heat in my head like the hot clove oil.

**"That's an art too. For the Japanese, that's an art. Anything's an art if you do it right. If you just want to make a million dollars and so you buy a boxcar of wood chips and throw in some sicky-sweet oils and sell it for Valentine's or Christmas, sure. But I go out and find things. So what I put in is experience, my own time. I save all our old flower petals. Once, when we built our cabin, I got all the cedarwood sawdust and put it in with the wild-rose petals that grow in the woods there and dried moss and juniper berries. It takes us to the cabin when we aren't there. Charles calls it Roomwood."

"But it's not going to work," Mark says, "because the same smells aren't going to remind the same people of the same things."**

I can't talk. My eyes are swimming in vinegar.

**"Lianne, can I tell you my hunch?" Jack Beverly says. Being nice. After Sarah called his hand, decided to be nice.

I can't talk. I nod.

"I have a hunch about why this is upsetting you so much. My hunch is that you might be displacing your painting onto your potpourri. Remember last month when you promised to give yourself the freedom to paint?"

"Potpourri is an art," I say. "But nobody takes it seriously. It makes me so mad."

"Lianne," says Father Christmas, "Jack has told you his hunch. Do you want to listen to his information, or do you want to discount it?"

"Would you say it again, Jack?" I say.

"My point was I think you might still be blocking yourself because you don't feel like you have any right to paint. Saturday before last you broke through and you said that's what you really had always wanted. To be a painter. But obviously you've still got some real strong tapes against it. That's why you went to potpourri instead. You let yourself get all busy with that because you were afraid to let yourself paint. And now you're displacing your anger about not painting onto us. You're hiding it by being defensive about potpourri."

"Charles discounted me. He wanted me—he discounted my painting. He thought the game was more important."

"That's too bad," says Jack. "But you know how to handle discounts. You want my opinion, I think your mother's involved. I think it being your mother's birthday is really strongly involved with all of this, because—"

"That's very plausible, Jack," says Father Christmas. "But let's let Lianne**

let's lick Lianne

**do the work. And I'm glad you wanted to share, but let's just stay with stating our hunches and not try to direct her thinking."

"Well, ok, I'm sorry," Jack says, "but do you hear me, Lianne?"

"I hear you," I say.**

split lick Lianne lick stick Lianne slit slut Lianne

**"Thank you for your information," I say.

"Do you think your mother *is* involved?" Ian says. "Is that where your parent comes from, the one that won't let you have your art?"

"You're probably right," I say. "Everything *else* comes from her." Toss my hair, cross my legs. Smart-aleck Lianne.

"I'm not telling you—I'm asking you what you think. Try not to discount your own perceptions. What happened when you gave your mother the Vicks potpourri?"**

And I can't breathe. Because potpourri is breath, an accent to your breath, to help you feel it come into your soul, like a creek comes into a river. Like a star comes into the night.

**"I didn't give *her* the Vicks potpourri. I just mentioned it because while I was making hers I got off into making a bunch of other kinds. I gave her a garden one."

"What happened when you gave her the garden potpourri?"

"Well, you know. She liked it."

"That's good. Can you remember what she said?"**

And I can't breathe, because the dishrag.

**"Lianne?"

I can't look at anybody.

"It was my daddy who used to say the awfulest things," Sarah said. "He wouldn't even be picking on me, he would just be saying the first thing that came into his pointy little head. Just dropping the needle on the record wherever it was. And you could tell by what he said that he didn't any more understand your feelings than a stone would. Come to think," she said, her eyes going wide, "that's what I hate most about Christian."**

This stuff has turned.

What do you mean, turned? Potpourri doesn't turn.

What's that sour smell, then? That smell like an old dishrag.

There's not any sour smell, I don't know what you mean. And she said, Well, you go on and smell it, then. There most certainly is. I can smell the rose oil and the lavender, but there's a turned smell. What else did you put in?

I put several other things in. I put in some salts and some dried-up narcissus and jonquil blooms, and some of Maw-Maw's artemisia that I transplanted, because you always liked her garden so much—

That's it. Wormwood. Just like an old sour dishrag.

I hate that name. Artemisia is so much—

It's poison, you know. If you eat enough, it'll kill you. With your allergies, I don't see how you can work with all these dusty leaves and petals and things.

I'm not allergic to—

Remember how I used to tie an old sour dishrag around your throat? When you got whiny?

"Lianne, do you want to talk any more?" says Ian.

Her little curvy mean smile. Her eyes sparkling. She doesn't even know how much I hated it. She thinks I think it's funny too. No. She doesn't even think about what I might be thinking.

"Will you make a decision to follow up on this? Will you promise yourself to look at what you're letting your mother say in your head?"

I can't let them see me with the dishrag. To see how bad I am. To school for a week with the dishrag around my throat. In her class, Miss English would let me take it off.

**"I promise," I whisper.
"Good," he says. "Ok, folks, in that case, it's**

time

She's here. I've been murdered in the stomach. I'll faint. Father Christmas betraying me, telling her all about me.

But she's standing up, saying, "Oh hi, Lianne," and I'm saying, "Tina, how nice to see you," both of us in our woman-woman birdcall voices.

And "Oh, hi, Ian," she's saying, and Father Christmas has come out and sees something wrong with me but doesn't know what and pats my arm, thinks it's still group I'm feeling, and he wouldn't, he really wouldn't, please don't let him betray me, good Lianne.

So scared.

"Oh, Lianne, I didn't know you went here," she says. "I was just dropping by to— Ian was just—" An excuse, but she can't make it, because Ian will hear. So obvious, and then she hears how obvious:

She needs therapy too, doesn't want me to know, and my scare goes away. But her face clicks over, from almost embarrassed to— cool? hard? Business.

"Listen, while I have you here—I can't come to the book club Friday week. I appreciate the invitation, though. Will you keep me on the list?"

All while I smile and nod and walk to the door, Ian leading me by the arm, solicitous. I had forgotten: Two weeks ago, before

I thought Charles and she but they didn't he better not they didn't. Because of attendance so low. Thank God, thank God, never invite her again. "I understand, I know how it is, we're all so busy. Maybe next time. You're welcome. I will."

And Jack yakking with Tina now, so they know each other and I bet he thinks he can get some the whore he probably can but

Father Christmas, his happy eyes. I hug him suddenly, he reaches around, his soft fat mashing me good in the belly, and squeezes me good, oh good Lianne. So there.

"You take care," he says. "See you next**

time

Arkansas weather: If you don't like, wait five minutes. While we were talking, stack-up of blue-black cloud. The blue sky filling west, and we didn't see: Inside whomping with words

feathers floating from broken pillows in pillow fights

and someone always gets scared and cries and the big people come in

and this built up, thunderhead, beautiful name.

So now in the glass cage, watching the waters above the firmament come down, bashing the parking lot. Big chunks of storm crashing and smashing the cars, rivers of windfall over the buildings, sheets of rain sideways, slideways, and whomping around, the parking lot trees laid over, whipping so skinny and drowning.

Smell of wet rubber. Dripping umbrellas in corners and wet people pushing through, impatient to get inside. Joe Burley has to go out, he can't wait. Out in the whippeting wet, spray on my face from the open door, a round rolling rumbling run, he's gone. The rest of us stand and wait, all watching the rain, not watching each other.

We're through talking, we're strangers again. Our bodies want to spread out, fly far away from each other, back to our lives to burrow in and hide.

If I wasn't this, I'd be up under the one big tree they left, top of the parking lot, big dark raggledy oak. The real Lianne: girl in a pasture, running from rain.

When this was wild, before they built Baptist? Freeman Dairy family picnics—west, out in the country, could have been here.

Daddy brought chips and Tommy Freeman made fun and I killed Tommy behind a tree with my point-finger gun, the chips are good. And made my favorite

---

Why did the Little Moron try to eat at the beach?
—Because of the

---

sand which is there, potato salad and chips and mash the bread flat and salty and crunchy

---

I would run under the oak when it started raining, although the thunder and lightning ramalam-boom-boom-boom. All one word, thought little Lianne:

Listening to the big radio, the storm making static: A flash, and wait, and a rumble, and: *What do you call the noise the thunder-and-lightning makes?* and everyone laughing.

Although it boomed me to a million pieces. I would die, but wake up a dog, or a red-winged blackbird. I would be an oak tree too, I would be a drop of rain, and the rain is safe, nothing can hurt the rain.

Nobody else would be around, just the girl under the tree. Staying dry.

Now it's easing, and we're deciding to run. The Weddingtons under one umbrella bumping at different gaits. Jack Beverly next, head down, sprinting full out. The big farm woman turns to look at me, holding her arm in front with her other arm. I practice thinking her name again. Sarah.

**"It'll let up more in a minute," she says.
"I think so too."**

Her eyes deep, seeing right into me. Nobody has a look like that anymore. Nobody can see you. I want to talk to her. Upstairs, I didn't, but now I wish we were friends going somewhere for coffee. But what could I say? What could she say to me?

And now the sun's back out, but still a few drops falling.

**"Devil's beating his wife," she says, tying a scarf on her head.

"Maybe there'll be a rainbow."

"Can't be," she says. "Sun's too straight up."

And that good sense makes me feel like a girl, a silly girl, because it's obvious, I could have known. "But maybe there's one around us in a ring, along the horizon."

"We couldn't see it."

"But maybe it's there."

She smiles. "I like to see my rainbows. But maybe so. Reckon I'll see you next week." And she goes out.**

The lot is full of baby creeks, quickets of brand-new water looking for drains. Water never gets trapped. It scumbles and tumbles and finds a hole. How does it know there's a hole to head for? Does the water that already went tell the water that's on the way? But then how does the first water know?

In the car on the way out, swing around the top of the parking lot to visit the tree. Roll down the window and look. See the girl nobody sees. Smiling at me. The rustling sound of the dripping leaves, the dry ragged circle finally getting wet.

Swing on around. Stop at the street. Cross over the over, keep to the left.

So when it rains, it doesn't under a tree. Then when all of the other rain is gone, the tree has rain. It's earlier under a tree. I have to tell Charles. A tree is a time machine.

Oh if you could tell Charles. If this was you. You could tell him what happened Sunday, Monday, Tuesday, you could fill in all the blessed days. But no dice. He can remember so much that doesn't matter, so little of what he wants. He cannot remember the following ten days, what the two of you did. The next thing he can remember is when the big news hit.

14

HAPPY HOME

"Can you believe it?" Lianne said when he came through the door. She led him quickly back to the Curtis Mathis.

"All I've heard is what people told me," he said. "I haven't seen anything yet." He followed her, tossing his coat and briefcase onto the couch beside Clemmie, who did not look up. Lianne went back to her wicker rocker, he took the armchair.

On the television they were replaying, in slow motion, one of the video clips. They froze it, a shadowy frame looking up along the drive from under the canopy, like looking out of a tunnel toward daylight: Agent McCarthy stretched upward on the left-hand side, partly out of the picture. The bullet had just hit him. On the right, top, an unidentified man either crouched for battle or turned to run. Blackness of heads and arms at the bottom and lower right, and now, here came the arrows and circles, and of course, there, that patch of blur was the hand with the gun.

"When did it happen?" Charles said.

"Shh, shh," Lianne said.

"—into surgery at this moment," Steve Barnes was saying. They had cut back to the local studio. "Carolyn, we have no prognosis as yet. We do know there is a bullet in the President's lung, but we are told he was conscious and in good spirits right up to pre-op, even joking with the doctors. Your opinion?"

Probably the best pair in the state: Barnes, balding, high-domed, with a round and friendly face and blinky eyes, had a superior voice and could assume a proper gravity, as if he really was personally concerned, no wooden-faced grinner trying to look tragic and only managing the look of a deacon at a funeral before a golf game. And maybe he did care: He had been over a few times, at Lianne's invitation. He and Charles weren't particularly simpatico, but Barnes was that rarity in public life, a thoughtful and articulate man.

Carolyn Long, looking directly into the camera: "You can't doubt the President's courage or his will to live. When he was ushered into George Washington University Hospital, he said to the doctors waiting on him, 'I certainly hope some of you are Republicans.' Remarkable, Steve." Long was not so intelligent as Barnes, but she didn't stumble. Probably the most professional since Lianne had left the air. She could manage seriousness too, though in her case it veered more toward a sort of worried intensity. She was pretty, but pale, and her eyes—Charles had always thought of her eyes as anxious, a bit pinched even during the formula bantering. And—

"She's *got* to do something about that straight blonde hair," Lianne said. "It absolutely washes her out. If she's not a winter, I'll eat my hat, but she makes up like a summer every time." Once a pro, always a critic.

"They shot him at one-twenty-six," Clemmie announced, as they cut to a network commentator standing outside the hospital. "Just as he was coming out of the Washington Hilton."

"The Hilton?" Charles said, surprised.

Lianne gave him a look. "You didn't know that?"

"No," he said. "I told you, people just looked in and told me things. There was so much commotion, I finally just gave up and sent everyone home. But nobody told me the Hilton."

He and Lianne had spent their honeymoon at the Hilton, a beautiful Washington June in the middle of Lyndon Johnson's second term. After the cherry blossoms, of course, but a week of gentle weather, the last few days before solstice. Mamie Eisenhower lived just up the hill, in the Wyoming Apartments. They had visited her once—his father had known Ike—a very brief, very formal visit. They both loved Washington, the polyglot streets, the whirling continual air of festivity. The bitterness over the war had been heating up, they would eventually oppose it, but he was twenty-seven and safe, and they had managed to ignore all that, moon-eyed, in love.

Strolling Kalorama, the Dumbarton Oaks gardens. Avoiding Adams/ Morgan, the rough downhill neighborhoods that in a dozen years would fall to gentrification. Down the tilting carnival slope of Connecticut to Dupont Circle, to hang out in the bookstores, cafés, and shops. Even then Lianne had not been able to resist a good drugstore, taking as much pleasure in uncovering a bar of black Spanish soap or a can of good English talcum as others would in shopping the proliferating dens of antique furnishings.

Out to the Mall, where she spent days in the National Gallery, dragging him through ten centuries of stunning art, more art than anyone could hold in his brain, too much magnificence, a great huge unabsorbable glut of splendor, so that he went blind and blank and numb, good for the first hour and spent thereafter, tagging along grouchy on painful feet.

While she flew, indomitable, indestructible, and frailer than balsa, from room to room, uttering cries that might have been happiness or might have been despair.

Back at the hotel, she might weep, helplessly, overcome. By what? While he stood by, depressed at the burden, the waste of glory. What was it for, why did humans spew forth such an unstoppable bilge of grandeur? To be hoarded in vaults, hung in dark rooms to haunt the minds of strangers? To be quarreled over, obscurely, by scholars?

No human existed on that mighty a scale—how was it then that we had *made* those treasures? Cities, cathedrals, those first rockets he had made *her* go see at the Smithsonian, that had actually hurled men into orbit. We were small, humdrum, pedestrian. We walked among our own works as supplicants, pilgrims, as one walked the trail to Bright Angel Point at the Grand Canyon, or climbed the creek to The Window at Big Bend.

Her shaken transcendence, his jaded melancholia: They had resolved them in common pursuits, having lunch at an outdoor café in shimmering Renoir sunshine or picnicking upcountry amid the Van Gogh stone of the upper Potomac; making love in the drape-darkened suite in a Rembrandt afternoon or walking the streets to study the Botticelli and Fra Lippo Lippi faces; catching a show in a Moulin Rouge evening or sailing the Potomac in the Vermeer moonlight.

The Hilton had been the center of all that for him, and now when he thought of Washington, he still thought of the Hilton as its center: not the Capitol, not the monuments, not 1600 Pennsylvania; but the Hilton, set into its equivocal hillside, capped by tree-shaded embassy neighborhoods, verging on poverty and violence, demarcated by the long, busy, cosmopolitan stretch of Florida and Connecticut.

Everything they saw was remarkable, unforgettable, the city a stage for their love.

He thought of her naked body now as it had been then, in the bed in the bright morning sheets, on the deck of the sailboat for a moonlit swim. He could see, for a moment, the aging of that body as if the process of aging were itself a single picture, the visible working in of mastery, the quick deft deepening that lifted simple prettiness into immortality.

"I'll be damned," he said. "I'll be damned." Lianne smiled, watching his eyes watch her.

"It was a crazy man shot him," Clemmie said. "Not a terrorist. Some little bastard named Hinckley." Back to the fifteenth replaying of the video clips, hastily assembled experts in a studio somewhere ready to tell us all about it, sitting down still clipping their lapel mikes into place.

"I heard that," Charles said. "John Warlock—"

"War*nock*," Lianne said.

"—Hinckley. But why?"

"Jodie Foster," Clemmie said.

"What?" said Charles.

"He was in love with Jodie Foster or something," Lianne said. "One of those crazy fans they get, followed her around. Shot Reagan to get her attention."

"That doesn't make any sense," he said.

"Oh, yes it does," she said.

She had had one of those fans herself, an older fellow always in a brown polyester suit, balding, with bugging blue eyes, false teeth, and dyed brown hair pulled over his scalp. For a year or so he had showed up at all her openings, ribbon cuttings, and benefits, always in line to shake her hand too hard and talk in a disassociated way about Miss Little Rock. He remembered her from when she had won it, he would say, and parrot a chain of mutual acquaintances, adults from her childhood she had hardly known. Always as if he had never said the words before.

He never offered violence, was not armed, seemed breakable rather than dangerous, but spoke disturbingly of the histories of other Miss Little Rocks, the smaller and larger mishaps that had dogged their not unusual lives. He seemed to have studied the newspaper files to learn of their every accident, divorce, sickness, DWI, bounced check, or lost child. Lianne had found him funny at first, annoying, then finally terrifying. There was nothing legally to be done, but Charles had spoken with the man's family. He had quit showing up after that, perhaps committed somewhere, or perhaps saner than he appeared and forcibly dissuaded, perhaps simply dead.

"It makes *that* kind of sense," he said. "But at first you expect it to be political."

"Oh, I know what you mean," Lianne said. "You know my first reaction? It's terrible, but do you want to know? —I thought, *Oh! We finally got one of* theirs."

Charles grinned. "Me too—you know I did the same thing. I was thinking, *About time.* And then I thought, *Shit no, don't think that way. This'll be just what the conservatives want: It'll make him a hero.*"

"I don't believe you people," Clemmie said. She was, as his father had been, a Republican. Ironic, that: It had made his father an outsider in this overwhelmingly Democratic and populist—if reactionary—state. And Charles had taken after the old man as far as personality was concerned: He was an outsider too—but in his case as a political liberal.

"Well, I *said* it was awful," Charles said. "But you can't help your first reactions."

"The President of the United States," Clemmie said.

"Hey, listen," Lianne said. "Do you see me wanting people assassinated? Who was *for* gun control in this last election? I don't want him shot, of course I don't. And I respect the presidency, and all that. But that senile old dodo bird got just what he was asking for."

Clemmie stood up. "I just think I'll just watch the rest of this upstairs," she said. In a moment they heard her in the kitchen banging dishes, slamming the refrigerator door. Stocking up supplies for later, for her supper, no doubt. To hear her this far, she was really mad.

"I think you just blew supper," Charles said.

Lianne stretched and yawned. "I don't care. Let's order pizza."

"What about the cheese?" Lianne had a milk allergy, not to the lactose but to certain proteins. Milk, wine, and onions—three of the primary justifications for life as far as Charles was concerned—gave her violent headaches. Sometimes, in moderation, if it was cooked, she could get away with cheese, especially white cheese. Some wines did it to her, and some didn't, no way to predict. The onions never failed, though. Weirdly, she could eat all the garlic she wanted.

"I don't care," she repeated. "It's been a long time, and I really want pizza."

"I'll call Tucker and Dee-Dee," he said, "and see what kind they want."

"Oh, they aren't coming," she said. "I meant to tell you."

"Not coming?" he said.

"They postponed the awards," she said.

"Postponed?" he said. "Well, shit fire."

"Only till tomorrow night. They're coming over then. Anyway, this way it works out better for you: You get to watch the finals. They're not postponing *them.*"

"The hell with that," he said grumpily. She was needling him. He was not, repeat *not,* and she *knew* he was not interested in the play-offs, not after the Hogs—forget it.

Oh, he was a loyal man.

"Oh, come on," she said, coming to sit in his lap. "You can have beer and pizza and a slice of me. Is that so bad?"

"No," he said, adjusting to accommodate her. They fitted remarkably well, her every crook just where he had a hollow, the convexity of her back an easy template to his concave arm. She planted a kiss in the hollow under his jaw, her plush lips slaved to the beat of his throat. Perhaps love was no more than that, the way you fit together.

He had been with other women before he met her (he counted, as he had before: seven, not really very many, a lot of pretty women out there, a vague regret).

Though he had twice before thought he was in love, his and his lovers' bodies had not moved with such reciprocal tolerance. What he had with Lianne was not mere comfort, familiarity. It was to gravity as forgiveness is to sin.

It had been there for them the night she brought him home. It had been there, for that matter, even before they had left the party, while they were still dancing.

That was the sort of thing you forgot when you were thinking of other women, was why you had to keep your fantasy life under control. He saw Tina vividly, but now he saw her all angles and harsh bright colors. It would be like sticking it in an electric socket, he thought. Fantasies were eye-brain-hormone things, not feel things. Your eyes saw tits&ass and your brain went white and your prong jumped up, boing boing quiver: Only your poor mute arms and legs and back and belly and hands remembered the nightlong ease, blessed connubial wallow, and pleaded unheard along the wispier nerves: *fidelity . . . fi del i teee . . .*

"I'm sorry I chased her off," Lianne said into his chest. "But I was tired of her crocodile tears. And anyway, I really did think it. I guess I am terrible, because he *could* have died."

They were showing Brady now, facedown in a puddle of his own blood, a gun beside his head—horrible icon, though one of the agents' guns no doubt. Hands on his back, patting, seeking vaguely to help. They cut to his widow; no, not his widow, not yet, but surely he couldn't make it? You could feel the thought, you could hear it under their voices.

Cold, he thought. *Leave the woman alone.* And he felt a coldness invade the house, a wave of icy neutrality. The sight of Brady had done what the wounding of the jocular actor could not: He felt the world a clash of blind atoms, of sticks and stones and empty stupidities. For no reason born, for no reason married and fled and bled and died. An idiot with a bang-bang; a hollow cowboy grinning and waving, oblivious and invulnerable; and a good man blown away.

He hugged her tightly, collecting her warmth to his heart, grateful for their little camp, their flickering fire. "Don't sweat it," he said. "The man has a bulletproof Teflon chest." Later he was to feel a violated priority, as if he had been cheated of royalties or out of a patent. He had been first to apply the word Teflon, he would think, but no use saying so.

"No he doesn't," she said. "I mean, he might, but he didn't have it on. He was definitely hit, it wasn't deflected or anything."

"I didn't mean that," he said.

They were showing Haig at a press conference, flashbulbs: "Mr. Secretary! Mr. Secretary!" Cut to commentators making a fuss. What was all that? Bush on a plane somewhere, flying back from Texas.

"You know what it made me think of," she said. He knew.

"Jack Kennedy," she said. "That's why."

She had been at KROK just six months when Kennedy was shot, had been working a local-color story at Little Rock College—her alma mater, though she preferred to claim Hendrix. It was her tearful and dignified coverage of the reactions on campus that had first brought her to wider notice. He had been out of state still, interning and then thinking to practice in New York, but he had seen the footage, KROK showed it during each of their pentennial retrospectives.

On campus there had been shock, some grief, but, horribly (as all across the still-segregated South), more jubilation. She had anchored from the college, pressed into service until the regulation airheads could be rounded up. Quiet, outraged, humane, she had narrated in her own words, had brought home the horror and put the fools in their places. And in this most paradoxical state of all the states in the Union, even those who hated the Kennedys above the devil admired her for it, and took her in as their image of a newscaster, the face and voice of the news itself.

He thought perhaps only he understood how deeply that time had marked her. The assassinations, the dying children of *Hope Lines*—why had she moderated at so much tragedy?

He himself had not readily comprehended the damage. What had he thought when they met, three years later—that he had wed the perfect unblemished angel? Despite the unexplained tears, the anger from nowhere? They had been together under two years when King was shot. Robert Kennedy had gone down eleven days short of their second anniversary, a party that therefore never happened. It was then he had first begun to be aware of the shadow over their marriage.

"They're killing all the good people," she had said then, and he knew that was what she meant now: that fated and paranoid sense of directed malevolence, that sinking certainty that the bastards, immune to genuine prosecution, were out there pulling the strings, picking the brave ones off, leaving only the gutless, the greedy, the crooked, the tin-pot Hitlers. He had caught the virus himself in a milder form, it was probably what had finally moved him to the left.

So now a conservative went down, and there was, after a dozen years of that swallowed bitterness, a sudden purgation, a vomitous relief: *We* got one of *theirs*.

Except it wasn't that way. This was just a cop show with no plot, just fireworks and gunshots and car chases. An anthill poked open, and all the ants running and scurrying, communicating, analyzing, what do we do now, what's the situation, Chet what do you think, Walter the American people, Ted can you give us any further, Sam can you hear me?

The local news came on, and she turned in his lap to watch it. It was mostly repeated coverage of the assassination attempt, reruns of the already worn-out footage, more arrows, circles, commentary. A few breaks for local matters. Frank White was making plans to step up his own security. The man was born to be a George Fisher cartoon. Yeah, first the President, now you, Frank. Better be careful, Frank.

He had gotten up to order the pizzas, when he thought he heard something about Hendrix College. He went back to the set. They were interviewing a police officer somewhere: "The only thing we know is we have found a young black male that meets the criteria of those found recently."

Atlanta.

Cut back to the newsroom. "At the Chattahoochee River, that was Fulton County Police Sergeant Denny Hendrix," Steve Barnes said.

"Oh," Charles said.

"That's what's really horrible," Lianne said. She waved at the set. "Those murders. Not this Reagan business."

He leaned over and kissed her. "Turn the damned thing off," he said. "I've had enough death and violence for one night."

"No, I want to hear it," she said. "I'm ok, really. Besides, the weather's coming on. I want to hear the weather."

There was never anything on the weather you couldn't figure out by looking out the window, but she never missed it, would stay up late just to follow tornado watches. She loved the unpredictable plotting, the suspense.

When the pizzas came, she decided she wanted to eat in bed, so he put them in the foyer dumbwaiter with five longneck Buds, a clutch of napkins and silver, and a shaker of Parmesan—real Parmesan, buttery and rich, flown in from Saint Louis, not American sawdust—and sent the lot up to the master bedroom. He followed her up, set up the trays and put three of the beers on ice in the little refrigerator under the corner bar, while she undressed and went into the bathroom. He took off his pants and underpants, slipped his tie out of his collar and threw it and his socks on top of the canopy. All her life she had wanted a big old four-poster with a canopy, carved, ornate, and froufrou. He wanted a water bed, and he preferred clean lines, enamel, and high-tech built-ins. So now they had a couple of acres of custom-made water bed with a gleaming half-torus at each end, like a couple of roll bars, and with an electric canopy that could be drawn all the way back into the wall—except that she kept it extended, as now. The bed had a silver cover but was stuffed with fat lacy pillows. Compromises.

He cracked two of the beers and took one in to her where she perched on the stool.

"Jesus," he said, "did you do that?"

"No," she said demurely. "The dog did it. I don't stink."

"Jesus," he said. "We better close the door before it gets to the pizzas." He pulled a packet of matches from the tray on top of the towel stand—she collected restaurant matches. He struck one, waved it around, lit the incense, and then leaned over to check his hairline. The joke about the dog bothered him. Sometimes he could still smell Ramalam, and when it happened, it spooked him badly. Ghost farts in the stairwell, ectopoot on the sun porch. He would walk into the sudden miasma, look around angrily, then remember: a feeling like somebody vanishing out of the corner of your eye. He had never mentioned the hauntings to Lianne.

She flushed the toilet and stood up, naked and slender. The thighs heavier than when they met, the belly skin wrinkled a bit and padded with just an extra layer of fat over her scar, but the shoulders wide and round and the arms firm, the small plump titties as sweet as a girl's. Plumper, sweeter. Because she had never suckled? The blaze in her pubic hair infinitely fetching, a marker, a sign, the kernel of a flame, the arrow of his desire. It had begun when she went gray, she had told him, just a few hairs at first, then widening over the years.

She hugged him, leaning her face against the back of his shirt, brushing his crack with her pubic hair. "I think Sean Connery's just as sexy as can be," she said. She reached down in front to grab his balls.

"Shit," he said, straightening and turning to fit against her, propping his butt on the counter. "I don't care if it all goes. Just checking." He reached for his bottle, tilted it up and took a slug. "The way you check the shoreline, you know. To see where the beach is now."

She leaned back with her torso, keeping her pelvis flush, unbuttoned his shirt. "Let me see your back," she said.

"Aren't you going to drink your beer?" he said. "It'll get warm."

"Turn around and let me see your back," she said.

He slid out of her arms and lurched for the bedroom, bottle in hand. She ran after him, chasing. "Pizza!" he said. He dashed his beer down and grabbed up her tray, a napkin, a fork, and two slices on a paper plate: He held it between them as a lion tamer would hold a chair. She growled and prowled, circling, showing her teeth. "Nice kitty," he said, revolving to keep the tray between them. "Nice kitty. Eat pizza."

"Rrrr-unh!" she said, and jumped, and he jumped back, and the paper plate sailed off, landing upside down on the pale oak just inches from the edge of the Astrakhan.

"Uh-oh," they both said, and looked at each other, growling low in the throat, then charged for the pizza on all fours, bumping and pushing. She got the piece he was trying for, tearing it out of his mouth, and he fell back barking while she shook it to kill it and then, in a very undoglike manner, sat and stuffed the rest of it in with her fingers.

He crawled over and took her down, lying across her and kissing her smeared mouth. "Let's get in bed," she said when he lifted his face from hers. She traced the line beside his mouth. "Actually, I'm hungry as hell. I do want to eat something first."

"Ok," he said, standing. "I'm hungry too."

"Oh," she said. "What's that hanging out under your shirt?"

"It's your fault," he said.

"Hmm," she said, and scooted over to take him in her mouth.

"I thought you were hungry," he said.

"Mm mam," she said, and let him feel her teeth.

"You're getting pizza on it," he said.

"Complaining?" she said, taking her mouth away.

"No, you go on about your business. Don't mind me. But less teeth and more tongue."

"Ha." She stood up and patted him, strode to the bathroom. "Fix me another plate?" she called over her shoulder. Hers was unusable, spavined and smeared on both sides when they had rolled over it. So he had to sprint back down to the kitchen after all, flapping in his shirt. When he got back, she had cleaned the mess from the floor and from her face and back, and lay under the covers, waiting. He had brought another beer because while they were fooling around his would have gotten too warm. He made her a plate with three, not two slices on it, and set the Parmesan on her tray as well, and brought it over.

"Turn on the television?" she said.

"The remote's right there on the side of the bed," he said.

"Can't reach it," she said, and held up a piece of pizza with both hands, tilting her head to receive it. He turned the set on at the console.

He had gotten washed up and had settled in with his pizza and beer, when she said: "Oh Chaaarles . . ."

"What?"

"Would you get my beer?" she said, a girlish singsong. "I set it on the bar when I was cleaning up the floor."

"Goddamn, woman," he said.

"Can't reach it," she said.

He padded over for it, grumbling. "Warm as horse piss," he said, bringing it back. "Warm as a bucket of snot."

"Thank you," she said, and swallowed. "Good."

They ate slowly and stayed with the special coverage. There was no new news, of course, and by now the panels of experts had reached back to Tocqueville for explanations of what it was in the American psyche that made assassinations so popular. Other panels consisted of psychiatrists talking about personality profiles, or forensic experts drawing diagrams, or constitutional experts talking about the line of succession.

He finished his beer, got up and got another out of the fridge. Reagan was out of surgery and stable, Bush was back in command (he said), they still didn't know about Brady, the wounded agents were heroes. The station had found a contact, a North Little Rock man who had been there when it happened, a business rep for the Plumbers, Steamfitters, and Pipefitters Local. He hadn't heard any shots, though.

It was comforting, it was unusual, it was entertainment. It was the best act since Mount Saint Helens, and would be the best until the World Series earthquake eight years later.

"You know what? It was twenty years ago tomorrow," she said.

"What?"

"When the plane blew up. When the plane blew up and the people fell."

"Hmm," he said.

"I saw it," she said.

"I know," he said. He'd heard the story. She'd been home in Little Rock, the spring after she'd left Hendrix, after she'd fled to New York. She'd been out walking early in the morning, he had never understood why, when the C-130 cargo jet had exploded in mid-air, bodies and fragments landing all around her old junior high, the engine smashing into a nearby home and killing two people.

"I'm full," she said, and Charles got up to put their trays away. He came back to her side of the bed, pulled the cover back. He took her unceremoniously, wetting her with his fingers, sliding in as soon as he had done so.

"I'm full," she said in a few minutes. "Move." He slid off, to lie beside her, patting her stomach. "You need to roll over and let me see your back," she said. He rolled over. "Turn up the light," she said, and he reached for the bedside rheostat.

He felt her adjust to sitting position, a rocking of water. Then her fingers were on his spine, searching. He knew if he could see her now she would be wearing her half-rims, squinting and focusing like a watchmaker. "Get itchy valley," he said, meaning the hollow between his right shoulder blade and his spine, which itched whenever he thought of it. Let her just *touch* his back, and that patch of skin went crazy. Now she was working the big one up over the shoulder blade. Old Faithful. "Getting anything?" he grunted.

"Hmm," she said, noncommittally. He felt a sudden sharp pain, her scissoring thumbnails, and flinched away.

"Goddammit, don't *cut* it out," he said. "Just squeeze, no surgery."

"Mmm-hmm." She held a thumbnail around for him to see. He moved his head back to focus: at this range, an enormous white worm on a fleshy protuberant outcrop. "You need new glasses," she said.

She went back to work. He was convinced that his spine needed mining, but she spent only a little time there, then went for his side over the
ribs, where the shallow nerves and the tickle reflex made her pinching a
lot more painful. "I don't have any there," he said, twisting away.

"Mmm-hmm," she said, and rolled him back over, back into range.

"Ow," he said. "That one's a mole. I've had it for twenty years."

"Not any more." She slapped him suddenly on the butt. "Now you do
me."

"I don't want to," he said. "I want to go to sleep. You missed one in
itchy valley."

For answer, she bumped him with her butt, and he rolled over to check
her back. Backs were such beautiful things, or could be. Sculptured and
flowing. He pressed the muscles across her shoulder blades with his thumbs,
ran a finger down the channels on either side of her spine, smoothed his
hand across her buttocks. "Uh-uh," she said. "Do me."

She had a bite on her rib cage six inches below her left shoulder blade,
and he scratched that for a while. On her spine just where the hump of its
S inflected was an old bump with a white top. "Did you get it?" she said.

"Reach me a Kleenex," he answered. Another smaller irruption up
near the point of the shoulder. A few that looked ready, but she had tiny
pores and a thin tight skin that afforded scant purchase. "You're holding
them tight tonight," he said. Sometimes he did better. One glorious night
last year he had had fifteen clear successes.

"Mash harder."

"I don't like blood." He sought out the twin blackheads under the mole
on her left shoulder, perpetual colon. Always there, always black. "That's
it," he said, pinching them up in the Kleenex. He wadded it, banked it off
the wall into the basket. "Two," he said.

"Rub some lotion on my back," she said. "It's dry."

She had a thousand different lotions, but he knew the one she meant.
Aloe vera and coconut oil and lanolin and glycerin and an unreadable
paragraph of -ydes, -etones, and -onyls. He went to the bathroom and got
it, came back and splatted a cold squirt right between her shoulder blades.
"I *knew* you were going to do that," she said. He rubbed it in, feeling her
skin warm up, watching the white streaks absorb and disappear. He decided her ass needed some, and then he decided to bite her side between
her rib cage and hip.

"Yes?" she said, rolling over. He munched his way down to her pubis,
stoned on coconut wafting from her tannic skin. She shifted her butt to
help him. He slid down, fitted his hands under her cheeks. She hadn't
showered since morning, and was pungent with what they had done half
an hour ago. Sometimes he wanted her slick and clean and shining pink,

but tonight he wanted it raw, the funk and skunk like hooks in his brain, hard as a post already, a direct link from nose to cock. He enveloped her, probing with his tongue: vinegar/salt traces of her dried piss; slick numbness attacking his lips and the tip of his tongue, the antisepsis of his own semen; and the unspeakable violent musk in his nostrils, most wonderful smell on earth.

He traced the folds and valleys of her vulva, then drew the clitoris up, isolating it in the curve of his tongue, circling the knobby tip. He felt it burgeon and stiffen, a veiled and enfolded cock. He licked its length with a stiff tongue, pushing back into the fur at its base, but always returning to the tip. She lifted her hips, rotated against his mouth, groaning. He scooted forward to prop her with his hands, braced on his elbows, glued to her moving pubis, his own erection aching and prodding the skin of the water. And now he grooved his tongue lengthwise and drew it rapidly back and forth across the rigid first inch, and he felt her gathering like a thundercloud.

He loved it when she came, her face red and her eyes squeezed, gasping and bucking, butt held high in the air, her belly and body a single flexible cartilage, limber and tuned and quivering.

Then she was laughing and pulling him away by the hair with both her hands, rolling her head from side to side like a girl being tickled while he made eating noises and tried to burrow back in between her clamping thighs. "No no no," she said, laughing. He didn't persist. It was fun to snorkel her, but she was on reflex now, and he had more than once been fetched a resounding slap in the ear or caught a knee in the nose. Instead, he rolled her on her side, hunched up, lifted her left leg, and slid himself greasily in.

"You *did* that," she said.

"I'm doing it again," he said.

"Too big," she grunted as he bucked against her. God, this angle: the access. He rode her on his knees, straddling her right leg down on the bed, leaning into the uplifted left with his chest. It made her butt seem impossibly, sleekly round and divided, it made him feel two feet long, jammed to the root in juicy juice juice.

"I want to roll over and go to sleep now," she said, looking back over her shoulder.

"Go ahead," he grunted, laboring hard. "Don't let me stop you."

"I'm going to sleep now," she said, putting her head down on her pillow. He came, whinnying like a horse. He leaned over her, spent, then collapsed in stages to curl against her back, still hard, still inside her. They lay that way a long time. He became aware of the noise from the television again, as if it had been off and had just now turned itself back on.

I'd rather be in Philadelphia. Honey, I forgot to duck.

"Whatever else you say, they really do seem to be in love," she mumbled.

"Mmm-hmm," he answered. His erection finally shrank a little, slid out.

"Oooh," she complained. A little while later she said, "It's the afterplay I like."

"What?" He had drifted a bit.

"You remember, they used to talk about foreplay all the time?" He remembered. Masters and Johnson, *Everything You Always Wanted*, millions of inches of type in the *"Playboy* Letters." Consciousness raising? Maybe. It had been an event of sorts, like the assassination attempt, if slower: something big passing through the anthill. Foreplay. It all seemed quaint now, clinical, mechanical, strange. Manuals for those who just didn't get the concept.

It hadn't been sex. This was sex.

"It's this I like." She yawned. "The afterplay."

He was awake again now. The little fugue that refreshes. "I'm going to shower and watch tv," he said.

"Tell Clemmie," she said into her pillow.

He had already rolled to his feet. "What?"

"Tell Clemmie we're sorry."

"Right," he said. Another errand thought up by the Sleepy One, but. "Good idea."

He showered, threw on a robe, and took the elevator to Clemmie's suite. She was eating popcorn from a big bowl, drinking a beer, and watching the coverage, her feet up on the ottoman. Two empty bottles stood on the floor beside her chair.

Her rooms were done in what lately was called country. Tole painting, warm yellowed wood, figured knobs and pulls, heavy drapes, lots of pale blues, coarsely floreted china: Charles couldn't stand it, but they were her rooms. *God Bless Our Happy Home* in framed needlepoint over the television set. He sat on the couch across from her.

"Hey, we're sorry," he said.

She was a little drunk, he could see. "Have a beer," she said.

"No thanks. For being such assholes," he said.

"I hate it when we fight," she said, looking back at the tv. "You don't know what he was like when—did you ever see *Knute Rockne*?"

"Yeah, I did."

"He was good in that."

"He was good."

"He was—he was a rebel, but really a goodhearted boy. And so beautiful back then. He had—what do they call it?—an edge. Like a little bit dangerous.''

"Yeah, he did.''

"He died in that one.'' She peered back at him. "It's all so different now. The whole world has gone to the moon. It's like I'm living in space, and nothing makes sense with what I remember.'' He couldn't think of anything to say to that.

He stood, came over, and kissed her leathery cheek. "You wouldn't try that if I wasn't drunk,'' she said.

"No, but you are.''

"Damn right.'' He patted her, went to the door. "Hey.'' She hung over the back of her chair to look at him. "Do you remember *Santa Fe Trail*?''

"Yes,'' he said. "He was good in that one.''

"Damn right,'' she said. She turned back to the set, and he went out.

In the bedroom, he pulled the other two beers out of the fridge and set them on the nightstand beside him. He switched off her half of the bed and switched his own lighting low. He switched the sound to the earphones and put them on.

It was the ten o'clock news. Still nothing new. They interviewed Sonny Raymond: "Heck no, it doesn't change my mind on gun control,'' he said in his coarse cracker voice, rough and yet somehow also nasal and whining. "A crazy man got his hand on a gun don't mean disarm the American citizen. The problem aint guns in the hands of crimnals, the problem is the crimnal in the hands of the judges and the courts that just let em right back out on the streets. That boy better be glad he had just the Secret Service on his butt and not me. Tell you what, he would be one dead psycho right now, I can tell you that.''

The weather was nothing new either. He wanted the last beer but was saving it for the sports. That ham Reagan, he thought. The sports came on, and he sucked the beer half empty in one long swallow. Indiana stomped NC, so what? Oh, and a big fuss because they didn't postpone the game. Shit, what is this, church? The President is the Pope or something? We supposed to close our eyes during the prayer? Didn't they know it was all just more tv?

And tomorrow the big joke would be that RR had faked the assassination just to postpone the Academy Awards. Upstage em. That he couldn't stand the competition.

He fell asleep, the earphones dislodged. At midnight, the television shut itself off.

Toward morning, he dreamed. Lianne was Mary Steenburgen, and they had just won the Academy Awards. They were getting away with something they weren't supposed to. She was crying and she was beautiful. Sidney

Moncrief lay facedown on the hardwood at midcourt, smashed pizza scattered about his head. People were yelling, and there was a car backfiring. He and Tina/Lianne were in the stands with no clothes on. Then Tucker and Dee-Dee drew the curtain gently around the back seat, leaving them alone and guilty on the cool white sheets, teenagers in love. There was the shadow of a dog on the curtain, and he began to scream, but they were driving too fast, he had to watch the empty road. The road through the desert, Monument Valley, a car commercial. The car sailed over the edge and smashed, a bloom of rolling fire.

The black dog drooled on the sand: white teeth, red tongue, laughing. They had strung a linen curtain between gleaming tripods in the sand, and now the projector was running. He and Lianne sat naked under the stars, the surf rolling darkly behind the screen, Mary Steenburgen's face glowing and stirring on the folds of the gauzily moving curtain. She was blonde, like Tina. Her voice came from somewhere, huge on the PA system, echoing over the applause in the stands: *Thank you. Thank you. God Bless Our Happy Appiom Om.*

He didn't remember his dream when he woke up, but that evening, when Tucker and Dee-Dee came over and they did in fact finally watch the Academy Awards, he had a strong sense of déjà vu. Mary thanked her family, her co-workers, and Jack Nicholson, and said: *I'm gonna have to think up something new to dream about.* Charles felt as though his ears were ringing with echoes, as though he had lived all this before, as if some cycle hugely beyond his control were repeating itself and bringing him flashingly, only this very moment, to consciousness: as if he were a mere character character in somebody else's dream dream.

15

SONNY BOY

Arkansas Gazette.

From the People

Where Is Science in Creationism?

To the Editor of the Gazette:

Every time we Arkansans have a family quarrel, we have such a sound and fury that the whole world watches. I've been a high school science teacher for twenty years and a Christian. When my classes discuss evolution, we also discuss God's theory of creation.

A scientist has to be objective, including such ideas as one of God's days could well be up to a million of our years or more, and when Genesis says the dust of the earth, that could be their way of saying how God created man through combinations of elements up to one-celled animals, and then backbones and warm-blooded and so on, with brains coming last.

On the other hand, a theory is just a theory. We look at all the evidence, including comparative anatomy and embryology and radiocarbon, and then the students make up their own minds.

Unfortunately, our can't-leave-well-enough alone legislators have passed a bill which will again make us a laughingstock. "Creation Science" is not a science, but every teacher is free to do as I have done in following his conscience and put forward both opinions. The only effect this bill will have is unworkable.

We in this state need to get on with the business of education instead of making yet another spectacle of ourselves.

Parker Johnson, Conway

Trashing Evolution

To the Editor of the Gazette:

I have had this evolution trash shoved down my throat long enough by a godless society where brute instincts are glorified and we are taught not a Divine Spark but that we are all just animals. If so where are the missing links and God who can do anything could put the bones in the rocks, that doesn't prove there were really dinosaurs.

> *Communications on any subject are welcome. Letters should be brief and typewritten with double spacing if possible. All letters are subject to editing. Letters must be written to this newspaper exclusively. Each letter must have a signature and mailing address although names will be withheld on request. No published letters will be returned. No unpublished letters will be returned unless stamped, self-addressed envelope is enclosed. —Editor*

Why He would do that is up to Him, and I'm not going to question it. But I for one would like to thank Governor Frank White for signing this, as he has taken a lot of flak from the secular humanist media, or Satan's PR for short.

So "thank you" Governor White, and my prayers for you will count since I pray to God the Ruler of the Universe and not some monkey in a zoo somewhere.

Mahlon Wehunt, Morrilton

Always Genesis Now

To the Editor of the Gazette:

As if God himself could help but laugh at "creation science". Hell the Lord Almighty use evolution, course we did. Aint no challenge to this fiat business (except maybe that fiat lux business—gotta start somewhere). What do you think I AN, baby, a child? Have to do it all with willpower, aint no talent involved? Holy She-It, Man. You can create a world just by thinking--sure, just by saying so But it will purely stay in Your Own Mind. Get it out where somebody else can live in it, even for a little while, that's work, children, that's skill. That's science, e-volution, evil-you-shun, the damn righteous boogie.

The Holy Ghost, Evening Shade

Pack Mentality

To the Editor of the Gazette:

What's behind the recent passage of House Bill 482 is not religious conviction but one more manifestation of anti-intellectualism in Arkansas. The science of evolution has grown slowly, over more than a century. "Creation Science" was thrown together overnight, to try to get around the restriction on teaching religion in public schools.

A scientific theory is not a guess. It is a system that puts facts together. Evolution just as much a fact as air pressure on a wing that makes a plane go up, or the chemistry that makes the piston in your car go bang. The only thing that is in question is the precise mechanism that causes evolution, and that is what a scientist means when he speaks of the theory of evolution. It is fine if you wish to disregard the facts, but you might as well believe the earth is flat and planes will fall from the air, and if you want to be consistent you better quit drinking coffee from plastic cups and ask your preacher to get rid of his microphone

No, what is really at issue here is that the pack mentality who don't wish to think want to make sure that nobody else does either. I have more faith in my God than to believe He would give me a mind and then ask me not to use it.

Lianne Morrison, Little Rock

"Shit," Sonny Raymond said, and flung the newspaper to his desk. He was feeling a complicated set of emotions, which however summed themselves easily to a generalized resentment. On the one hand, it pissed him to have to be reading the *Gazette,* that liberal buttwipe of a pinko snotrag. Which how they survived in this state for over a hundred years he didn't understand, you would have to explain. On the other hand, they did cover his press conference, which you would have *thought* the other paper would, being more the kind of shotgun-on-the-rack-in-the-back-of-the-pickup kind of a paper and closer to the sort of a thing you might sell in a checkout line at a grocery store. With Wally Hall on sports. But of course that warthog of an editor hated his guts for some reason he didn't understand why.

On the other other hand, the *Gazette* had got what he said at the press conference all wrong. He had a whole set of ideas on why gun control wouldn't work, and you used guns to control guns by shooting the motherfuckering crimnals and eventually all you had left was people who wouldn't use guns the wrong way, so it would work itself out if the courts wouldn't let em loose, but of course he hadn't said motherfucker in the press conference. It was justice is the survival of the fittest, which ought to be obvious or there wouldn't be no point in having justice because it wouldn't survive, but I suppose that was just too damn complicated and intellectual for the goddamn suckdick commie-fucking liberals who all they said he said was you couldn't take guns out of the hands of crazy people.

Then there was this Reagan fuck, getting himself shot like a dumbass, which just played into the hands of the goddamned Democrats, of which he Sonny Raymond was one because how else do you get elected in Arkansas still yet and ever, but somebody was going to have to turn them around, but then this Reagan fuck goes and gets himself shot somewhere. And which if it happened to me it wouldn't, I guaran-damn-tee you. Come up to me, motherfucker, I'll pull my motherfucking cannon and you'll be thinking, *Oh Jesus dearie me nobody told me the* President *would have his* own gun, and here's yours, buddy, brains all over the sidewalk all over the dark blue suits of the Secret Service who aint even got *their* guns out yet, it happened that fast, and they're shaking their heads and grinning, that President is one fast mean motherfucking dude.

Medal of Honor for the goddamn President, the first motherfucking time that ever happened, by fucking God.

Which is when Cheese showed up in the doorway, to say: "Anything wrong? What's going on? I thought I heard something."

"Jesus H. Hieronymus Fucking Christ, Cheese. Don't you ever get more than fifty fucking feet away?"

"Well I thought I heard something."

"Well you heard me fart in a paper bag and save it for you to take home to your momma."

"Well Jesus Christ I didn't mean to bother your fucking ass."

"Well if you just let me read the fucking paper in peace instead of popping up every ten minutes like a teenager's dick in a whorehouse, I might get a little reading done."

"Well shit I thought I heard something, that's all. Anyway I got to go out, so I'm gone."

"So where the fuck you think you're going?"

"Well I'm going over to fucking Dogtown PD."

"So what the fuck for?"

"Because I'm checking out this Orsini thing."

"You're checking out this Orsini thing."

"We got the right to."

"We got the right to. You got the right to if I say you got the right to. Why do you want to meddle in their business?"

"Well because I fucking know her."

"Because you fucking know her."

"Well if you could read the paper like you say you was instead of just reading about yourself you would notice this whole thing has gone national. I mean there's national attention on the case, and we could get some."

"Except it's Dogtown local, and they aint gonna like Pulaski County taking over."

"Well I'm not taking over, I'm just thinking if it was drugs."

"If it was drugs?"

"I think there's a drug thing involved. On this side of the river."

"Are you trying to take a drug thing around on me?"

"Naw, it has all the earmarks. I mean it was a pro killing, I mean it was like he was assassinated. And she said he been having mysterious meetings."

"Mysterious meetings."

"Over in B.J.'s Star-Studded and the like. And with somebody in a unmarked car."

"What else she whisper in your shell-like ear?"

Cheese grinned. "Nothing yet. She any good with trailer hitches, I'll let you know." His face clouded. "Right now she thinks she's in love with that fucking lawyer of hers."

"I hate lawyers," Sonny Raymond said.

"You and me both."

"Put all the lawyers in jail and let all the crimnals out, things wouldn't be one whit worse."

"You got that right."

It was a mistake to start in with Cheese, because if there was one thing he had plenty of, it was opinions. It didn't even matter if you agreed with him on most of em, because he was such an asshole porcupine, he would still run one of em festering up under your skin.

But finally he left, and Sonny got back to thinking about what was pissing him off.

Cheese was, for one thing. You would have thought the scandal would have kept him in his place, and it did probably mean he could never get elected to anything because that Morrison scumbucket would bring it all out in the open, but already Cheese was getting comfortable, settling in. Sonny had heard the men talking about him.

"Well shit, he aint the only one who ever—"

"Hell, no. I remember when I was a boy—"

"Mistake was using somebody else's head cheese, that's all."

"Shit, yes. That's his mistake."

Cheese could hear them talking too, and he was already acting like he had never almost been splattered all over the front pages or maybe even wound up in jail himself. He was already getting too big for his britches. Sonny loved Cheese like a brother, but there wasn't going to be but one king of the hill in Pulaski County.

But it was this letter that really set him off, that was making his coffee and pancakes curdle out in his stomach like Sambo's butter. This fucking Lianne Bitch Morrison letter, telling him what to think, dressing him down like a frigid schoolteacher cunt bitch whore. Too fucking good for god-fearing Arkansas, that was her dryhole problem. She thought her and that fucking atheist lawyer she was married to could do anything they wanted, thumb their noses at good honest Christian people all day long because they had so much fucking money, well, Miss ex–Miss Little Rock, you got another think coming.

But let's face facts, Sonny, you scared of something. Something is chewing on your guts. Now, a brave man will always face his own fear. And it aint the shitrag *Gazette* getting your story all wrong, and it aint fuckhead Ronald McDonald McReagan, and it aint Cheese, because normally you would just blow Cheese off for the clown he is instead taking him so serious. What it is, Sonny, is this letter. You aint mad, you're scared, and you're feeling mad *because* you're scared. So let's just get right at this binness, because you aint scared of no letter from no woman, but nevertheless this letter is what *started* it, and that's a fact.

You know what you scared of, Sonny? You scared this is what the future face of Arkansas is gonna be like, these Morrison fucks. Now we getting to it. That these kind of fucks are going to take over the state, that they're going to have all the money and power, and there won't be any place for you. You love the state of Arkansas, it's Arkansas that first gave you to light, and you owe it to people that believe in God and fair play and keeping the streets safe and keeping porno out of the hands of children.

Because it aint this letter, it's what this letter means. It's the same with the way Morrison took out after Cheese, and the same with that pansy-ass yuppie-fuck lawyer you would have decked if the bastards hadn't yanked him away, and the same with that sonofabitching nigger, though it *was* funny to see Cheese choking on that handkerchief, and I'll get the nigger sooner or later, there aint no worry about *that*. But it's this holy-ass fuck Bentley telling him—him! Sonny Raymond!—to cool his fucking ass on the deal, there never was no fight, and stay away from the press conference. And you know Bentley was just doing what Mr. Attorney General Steve Clark asked him to. It's the way it's all *connected* to each other.

Because you know Morrison is going to be against you whenever you run for governor. He's gonna be for this Clinton jerkwater or maybe even Clark. Sure, they're butting heads right now, but politicians are strange bedfellows and it could happen. It's all connected, and you have the good people of the state behind you, but they have the money and the power and they could take it all away from you.

That's what you're scared of, Sonny. You're farsighted, you're always thinking ahead, and that's your edge, how you got where you are now. Watch your chance and you take it, because you know where you're heading. You're farsighted, and you're smart.

Only now you scared they smarter than you are.

Well are they?

Because let's think about it, because if you think this Morrison jackass hadn't ever done anything you could pin on him, you're a goddamned fool. Of course he has, the thing is just to find it out what it is and catch him in it. Which if you think about it, you've got a good way to do that. If you think you can trust her little blonde lawyer ass as far as you can throw it. But it wouldn't make any difference what she was up to herself if you could get something on Morrison. Just a little something to keep him in line. Could even be drugs. You know *she's* doing em, and all these rich fucks snort cocaine nowadays. Hell, he could be running the stuff, who knows. That nightclub of his, could be a crimnal element hanging out there. Mysterious meetings. Cheese so interested in the drug angle, you could put *him* on it.

Shit Sonny, you're fucking brilliant. Put Cheese on it, and he gets something, and good, it was your idea. And it blows up in his face, well shit, the man had it in for Morrison ever since the head cheese binness, he was out on his own whipping this up, you didn't know nothing about it.

And you're shut of Cheese and at the same time half the people gonna believe the shit anyway just because he's rich and he got accused of it. You're a fucking genius, Sonny.

But he still has the money and he would know it was you and he could buy all the dirt in the state and throw it at you in handfuls. And you sitting here with county judge Beaumont yapping in your ear how you're overspending your budget.

But Morrison aint the only rich man in the state, is he? No he aint. Who's the richest people in the state, Sonny? Who's the ones could buy and sell these Morrison fucks by the gross? Which it's too bad they're Republicans, because when you look at it really they're a whole lot closer to you than these fucking tax-and-spend baby-murdering Democrats. But you have to stay by your principles, only it's a question which principles, if it's just where they used to be for the common people, and your daddy was one, or if it's where it's a whole lot closer to what you really believe even if you do catch some flak over switching parties. Which that wouldn't hurt if it was the wave of the future which this Reagan fuck sure makes it look like. So let your conscience be your guide, and it won't hurt to talk to the money boys.

Feeling better, Sonny? Got it all planned out? First we neutralize the fucking Morrison shit and take Cheese out and at the same time we're building financial support, and you aint scared no more are you? No, because Daddy was right, the first thing you got to do when you're in a pinch is be honest with yourself, and it must then follow as the night the day like he always said. You miss that old asshole sometimes, what a jerk, but by God he knew a thing or two.

About that time Audrey Tull showed up in the doorway. So it's a good thing you already got your mind clear, Sonny, because it looks like you aint destined to have no peace today.

"So what do *you* fucking want?"

"Well you a regular terror, aint you," Audrey Tull said. "Them College Station jigs are here. They got a reporter with em."

"Ok."

"And then you got that Lieutenant Hawthorne. He wants to settle it in a reasonable manner. He don't see any reason to call any names, and he won't mess with you if you won't mess with him."

Sonny Raymond laughed. Hawthorne had wanted to quit when Raymond came in, but Raymond wouldn't let him. He had wanted the pleasure of firing him himself. Sure, he would talk to Hawthorne. It would be fun to talk to Hawthorne.

"And then Walter Simpson wants to meet you for lunch. He don't think you're supporting him enough against the judge in that traffic ticket thing."

Ah, politics, politics. Sonny Raymond loved politics. It was the stuff of life. He was beginning to feel really good now, alive and vital and competent and happy.

"And we having some evidence problems."

"Sounds like you got a full day lined up for me," Sonny said cheerfully. "Hold on a minute while I write myself a couple of notes." He opened the center drawer and pulled out a writing pad, God knows where he'd gotten it, then rummaged around for his broad-nibbed Shaeffer. This is what he wrote:

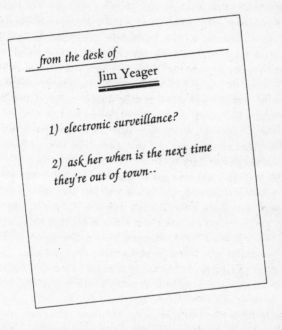

from the desk of
Jim Yeager

1) electronic surveillance?

2) ask her when is the next time they're out of town--

"You got a nice hand," Audrey Tull said.

"It's that calligraphy," Sonny said. "The missus made me take it up. Glad I did now." He shut the tablet back in its drawer, stood up, exhaled. George Fisher's cartoon pistol stared up at him from the top of the desk. He made a pistol of his thumb and forefinger, pointed it at Lianne's letter, squinted, made a sound like busting a cap. Then he followed Audrey into the hall.

"What kind of problem with the evidence?" he said.

"We got a gun and some boo-grass missing," Audrey said.

"Shit. Well get me some details. I'll check it out this afternoon, after I get through with Simpson." They were at the door to the conference room. "You don't come in here yet. Let me talk to em awhile. I'll send for you later, maybe." Audrey nodded, went on down the hall. Sonny Raymond watched him walk away. He probably *had* beat the suspect up, but he said he didn't, and Sonny stood behind his men. Especially since sometimes that was all the suspects understood. You didn't want em finding em dead in their jail cells, that was just stupid shit. But you had to get the message across.

He opened the door and went in.

The truth of the matter is, what had really set Sonny off hadn't been Lianne's letter at all. That was just what he thought it was. What had really set him off was opening that editorial page and there was that gun, pointed right at his head. Because Fisher was subtle, you better believe he was subtle. He wasn't just editorializing his knee-jerk liberal reaction to the assassination. Uh-uh, no, no way. He was saying, *You like guns, brother? Here's one pointed at you.* He knew the attempt on Reagan was a weapon for the liberals, and he was pointing that weapon right at the heads of people like Sonny Raymond. And no way to come back at him, no way to do a damn thing about it. Which was why Sonny had put it all off on Lianne. He couldn't admit to himself that a man like George Fisher could get to him and no way to fight back.

Sonny did not like being pointed at. The one way you could get in real trouble with Sonny Raymond, as opposed to just the usual trouble you came to expect, was if you pointed a finger at him. He might take ragging and cussing and pounding on tables, but shake a finger at him and he was all over you with hobnail boots. He read it as a dismissive supercilious gesture, and resentful men resent condescension above all else.

It wasn't just this particular morning, because of the butt-fucking rich pissant knee-jerk communist dick-suckers, either. He was *always* resentful. Sometimes he thought he was happy, but really that was only just when he had the taste of fresh blood in his mouth. And there is this one other thing about resentment: You harbor one little worm of it, and it will eat you hollow. It will clean every little scrap of the sweet meat of love from your bones and leave you to knock through life with no meaning and no awareness you have no meaning.

Are you ready?

Resentment was Sonny's whole soul and all his being. It was all there was to him. I mean, that was the man. And you know why?

Are you ready for the Judgment Day?

His momma had made him clean out the toilet with Pine Sol and a wire brush once when he was eight, and he had been pissed off ever since.

AN
INTERLUDE
WITH
THE HOG

Hold on, now, you say. I know you do, because I *am* you right now. Or you're Me. I mean, what other spirit could animate this, take on each character in turn?

That's what I want to talk to you about, Holy Ghost—

Call me hog. I prefer to be called the hog.

Shut up, hog. Now what was I saying?

Look a couple of lines back.

Yeah. Listen. How serious you expect us to take this? I mean, come on, you're just the author messing around, trying to pull some kind of meta-fiction stunt.

But what if I wasn't?

Jiving the illusion, fucking with the verisimilitude. It's an old trick.

But what if not? What if he doesn't have the least idea what I'm going to do next?

So who do you *say you are?*

Randomness in a bottle, baby. Just the medium, the message, and a megabillion white holes. Possibilities R Us. I'm Legba, Coyote, The Guy with Short Arms. Pleased to meet you, I'm a gentleman of wealth and fame.

Yeah, sure, the identification of the trickster with the enabler. Have to go through Legba to get to the other gods, but you can't depend on him. In other words, uncertainty is what allows time. But see, what people want in a novel—

Is something novel.

—is people. I mean, I don't mind you being the narrator and all that. It lets you show us all these different minds and all, from the inside. Like Charles, and Lafayette, and Lianne.

And Sonny.

You *wouldn't be in* Sonny, *would you? Tell me you wouldn't, hog.*

Or maybe the ghost of Ramalam one of these times. I mean, who else loves Lianne so much? Woof! Woof woof woof! Orooooooooooo . . .

Well go ahead, fool. Be in whoever you want to. But why keep breaking in, why not just stay in everybody?

If I'm in everybody, then I'm *not* breaking in. I'm breaking out.

Whatever. You're breaking. But why not just stay with the action? We know it's only a fiction, but we want it to seem real. Why not let it seem real?

I aint against reality. But don't you wake up sometimes in the middle of the night, thinking, *What? How come everything's here? How come it aint nothing instead?*

So?

So reality itself fades off into mystery at the edges, right?

So?

So look at it the other way: If you want something to be real, you have to supply some mysterious edges for it to fade off into.

Say what?

Foreground background. Listen what I'm telling you.

That's another thing. This hokey accent. How come this accent keep sliding on down?

Whole lot a brothers in heaven, brother. This the slide guitar of voices.

Say what?

Because all I am is voice. All *I Am* is voice.

Is there an echo in here?

Is there an echo in here?

Cute. Could we just get back to the characters? All this meta-meta making me dizzy.

Honey, don't you still don't understand?

No.

Honey, I *am* one of the characters.

Well I don't care. Could we just get back to the other characters? The real characters?

Ha, made you say it. —Ok, don't split your britches. I'm outta here.

It's about time.

What I been telling you.

THE HOG continues OVER as we watch blankness, the featureless fuzz of hyperspace.

HOG

(Singing)

It's about time, it's about space. It's about the
whole human race . . .

Kinda lost track of where we were, though.
Stuck in here with no dimensions, no format. This
gray place, this council room of the fogs.

(Beat)

Let me just fiddle a little with the dials—this is
an art, you know, not a science. You guys made
the metaphor: Clocks to time as rulers to space. And
then you imagined the ruler extending indefinitely
forward and called it "the future" and indefinitely
backward and called it "the past." But who's to say
it works that way?

*The big bang comes up on the IMAX, and then the history of the uni-
verse begins to unfold.*

HOG *(cont.)*

I mean what month did the moon begin? How
many years ago was the first year, when a
recognizable earth went around a recognizable sun?
Were there some sort-of-not-quite-years when it was
all just a protostar? Margin of error's pretty big.
Bigger than life on earth.

Got it, Gondwanaland, zoom, there goes the
American plate: Whoa, too far, lost it, you don't
want to see what happened. Stick with Afro-Asia
awhile, till I get the band narrowed down. Origin of
man, cradle of civilization. Back, back, easy now,
the steppes, mammoths, slide on over to the four
rivers, lock and change scale: And we've got
Sumerians! Egyptians! Jews! —Hey, want to see a
monkey rise from the dead?

Nah, what you want is the same day, only one
thousand nine hundred and eighty-five years later,
am I right?

So, later, maybe. It's a good trick. Got to ask

him how he did it sometime, if I can ever get him away from Miss Liza long enough.

Tell you what, let's follow the old land bridge route, it's underwater by now but I know the way, I must've brought a million hominids along it, all told.

O-kayyy, got the contiguous 48, let's convert to Julian: 11, 12, 13, 14, here come the white people, bing bing, buildings everywhere, 19 *aaand* 20, and lock and change scale one more time. And . . .

Are you ready? Roll the page, Baby Chile.

PART THREE

IN THE MIDDLE OF LIVING

16

EASTER
AT THE LAKE

Tucker was the only bucktooth Charles knew, which was funny, because there had been a lot of them when he was a kid. Orthodontia, he supposed. Which was a pity, like the loss of a species: Watching Tucker spray one of his stories, you wanted more bucktoothed people, not fewer. His teeth made Tucker seem impossibly merry, a bustle of calcium crowding forward into a permanent smile, as if impatient, unwilling to wait for him to deliver the punch line.

It wasn't you wanted anyone to suffer, not when all it took was a little cosmetic work. No doubt the condition was especially humiliating for the young, with their still-fragile self-esteem. No, it wasn't that you would wish bucktoothdom on a single solitary soul. It was just that you hated for the *idea* to die out. Like the idea of the comic drunk, lately so unfashionable. Alcohol is bad. Alcohol kills. But Jeez, didn't we use to *enjoy* a good boozer, didn't we hoot and roll at his slapstick antics, his rubbery, universally-gimballed gait? Didn't we have a *good* time, drunk on laughter?

Tucker, drunken and bucktoothed, lifted the gleaming oars from gleaming water. The four of them clunking across the morning lake, tiddled with silly drinks, sated with blintzes. This was tradition, the third-morning row. This year was Tucker's turn to paddle. The four of them plumped like Humpty in orange vests, perched on their little seats.

It was always this way, Charles could have sworn, the brilliant anomalies of Arkansas spring: the middle of April and bright flowers, spring beauties and hyacinth and jonquils and rain lilies nodding in still-sere grass; the chill of the air and the warm of the sun, the delving facets of sliding water, massive undulation, a heavy clarity slipping the chains of its linked shine.

It was always this way on the third day, rocking across the mint-new lake, clunk clunk drunk drunk. A nap in the afternoon to sleep it off, metabolize bellinis, mimosas, smoked salmon, cream cheese, and toasted bagels. Jesus Christ, they were sinners, putting things *in* champagne. Though only Wiedekehr's, the Arkansas bubbly, way too sweet for sipping but *the* best with orange juice. And then when they woke, snacks, tidbits to hold them while Tucker worked up ribs on the grill, the ravishing smoke hollowing their bellies, acrid and hungry on the lilac air.

Appetite, appetite was all; appetite was pure salvation.

And then the famous all-night game of strip poker. That nobody ever had won or lost.

"You do much fishing, Charles?'' said Tucker, resting the oars. Tucker fished and hunted. As if to say, *See, a doctor can be a real man too.* No, that wasn't fair. Tucker didn't prove his manhood by killing things. Just, that was what you did: You hunted and fished. Tucker a typical Mississippi truck farmer's boy turned top of his class at Duke; typical poor white bucktooth trash with two doc-in-the-boxes and a reputation, seduced by Dee-Dee into this foreign altitude. Because of course there would have been no question of her leaving her old hometown.

Tucker knew Charles *didn't* hunt and fish, so with his question smilingly implied Charles maybe wasn't all man. Not that he really thought so. Just the bucksnort trade of comradely males, testosterone in the best of friends: *I like you buddy but I could whip you if I had to.* His way of redressing the imbalance they all felt, that Tucker and Dee-Dee's cabin, posh as it was, was nothing like what Charles could have built. Could have *had* built. The Other Shore, they called the place. A bit quaint. Charles wasn't sure about people who named their real estate.

It was Charles's manliness to provide the cases of Wild Turkey and Dom that sat dusty in the pantry nine months a year; to furnish Beluga to spoon in gobbets onto Charles's primo creation, Steak Tartare Good Ole Boy: twice-ground top sirloin mixed with minced garlic, fresh-ground black and green peppercorns, this and that spice, and herb vinegar for a bit of a tang; then hollandaise-drizzled, dashed all with Louisiana hot sauce, and then the caviar to top your bite.

It was Tucker's manliness to bring the venison from last fall's kill, thawed at last for Tucker's famous venison stew Provençale; it was Tucker's balls scrotum dick and sperm to catch a mess of bass from the lake, clean them, fry them up for the signature Saturday night meal.

As it was Tucker's role to be the raconteur, the wild old storyteller. Without morals, without meanings, Tucker's unpredictable country tales crooked and disappeared and reappeared bang in your face with somehow a certain rightness, proportion, justice after all. The best Charles could do was to cry out at this or that striking incident, "That would make a great movie!" Why his ability to see visions should pale beside Tucker's to spin tales he could not explain to himself, especially not since this was supposed to be the age of the image, not of the word.

"Fishing's boring," Charles said. "I know it's supposed to be mystical, Izaak Walton and all that, but what the hell. I just get sunburned and sleepy."

"Well, you do too fish," Lianne said. "When you take the firm down to the Little Red." Jumping to his defense, men hate it when the wives do that, listen honey I appreciate the instinct, but don't don't don't, *please* don't help me defend myself. Might as well cut off the trophies and hold em up: *See, he* does *have balls*. Yeah, did have.

Independence Day weekend fishing vacation she meant, his daddy's innovation, proof that we're all just one big family here at Morrison, Morrison, and Chenowyth.

Bunch of overweight drunken city lawyers trying to outcountry the fishing guide. Three days of no-shaving body-odor beer-drinking log-cabin public-farting sun-burnt cigar-smoking hung-over exhaustion. He hated it. Hadn't been the same anyway since first Betty and then Tina had insisted on going. Sexist if he didn't let em, what could he do? "Shit, your firm isn't liberal, Charles," Tucker had said once. "They're wrong to accuse you. You're not liberal. You're just nigger-loving and pussy-whipped."

Not that they liked going, Tina and Betty. Had nothing but scorn for the macho display: *We few, we Men, at one with the wild, can discern the lair of the monster trout by a kind of mysterious instinct, iron-stomached before the supererogatory ickiness of gutting the catch, the egg sac sliming the webbing of finger and thumb, hands shimmering with glued-on scales.*

And yet the one time Charles had tried to do away with the trip, put an end to this midsummer misery, the uproar, the outraged protestations! His daddy had known something about people Charles still didn't understand.

"This old boy came to deer camp in a Thunderbird one year," Tucker said.

"What's that got to do with fishing?" Dee-Dee said in her froggy voice. She was a big woman, maybe five nine, rangy but broad in the trunk, strong, with an attractive face that age had lengthened and flattened, coal-black hair, and an impressive bosom. "Whoops," she said, the sudden breeze trying to take her Easter hat, wide organdy with embroidered lilies: The wind wanted to sail the hat, spin it across the wide water without sound.

"Would have been 'fifty-five or 'six," Tucker said, "because I wasn't legal to drive, not that I would've had the money in the first place. It was rusted-out and dirty, it wasn't shiny like the pictures in the magazines, but it was supposed to break my heart, so I thought my heart was broken. I repressed all the inconvenient details. Like you ignore the hairy verruca simplex on your girlfriend's titty.''

"Tucker," Dee-Dee warned.

"Imagine showing up at deer camp in a Thunderbird," Lianne said.

"He was from New Jersey," Tucker said. "His parents were dead and he had a Mississippi aunt, so he was living with her and going to college."

"You know, we *could* just sit out here in the middle of the lake for a couple of hours," Charles said, and Tucker took to the oars again.

"You know how it is in deer camp," he said. Nobody contradicted him. "It's somebody new every year. I mean, you have your regulars. Same ones for twenty-five years. But every year one or two new ones, the tryouts. Now and then somebody sticks. So he was a new one. Albert Quong's sister-in-law's nephew is who he was."

Tucker let them wait while he made some progress. "All he wanted to talk about was sex," he said, finally.

"Sounds ok to me," Lianne said.

"But he didn't want to talk about it the right way. The right way is how the comedian in Gulfport says to the stripper, 'Honey, your pants is coming off.' And she says, 'No they aint.' And he says, 'Yeah they is, honey, I done made my mind up to it.' He wanted to talk about how the male spider does it by loading up his palps and had we ever fist-fucked—"

"What?" Lianne said.

"—and if we thought there was any way on earth that spider enjoyed what he was doing. Or if there were three sexes, what would the third one be, and how there would be three kinds of homosexuals and six kinds of transvestites."

"Wouldn't there just be three?" Charles said. "Because each of the other two would be overlapping one of the others."

"Depends," said Tucker, "if you count it who's doing it, or just who they're doing it like."

It was now possible to see the old Bodark dock, so called not because the dock was made of bois d'arc—it wasn't, was treated pine—but because better than four hundred feet below the waterline there lay the drowned streets of the mountain town of Bodark. Tucker looked over his shoulder, as if gauging how many words he could spend before they got there.

"So anyway," he said, with a heave of the oars, "of course he wasn't worth shit with the deers. And of course they put him out on a stand with me, because we were the two youngest. He was five years older than me, but."

Tucker was silent awhile, laboring. They all felt guilty for letting him do all the work, as the ones who did not row felt guilty every year.

"I could smell him," he said finally, "so you know the deer could. Definite hyperhidrosis. And it was urinous too."

And they all became aware of the tangs of the sweet cool air, oak mast and root rot muskily down off the shore, sliding over the water. Currents of ozone and lilac.

"It was two days on that stand before he got the idea he had to get a deer or he wasn't a man. Which wasn't true, not if we knew you. Might give you a hard time, but all in fun. But he felt his deal going down, and conceived in his heart to redeem himself by blowing away some antlers. Way a lot of bad hunters get made."

Tucker pulled. The Bodark landing didn't seem to be getting any closer.

"Tucker," Lianne said, "I hope this isn't going to be one of those stories where he gut-shoots it and they trail the blood and put it out of its misery and everybody looks at him and then he meets with a mysterious accident."

A momentary irritation crossed Dee-Dee's face. Charles looked at the sliding water.

"No," Tucker said. "He never shot one. Camp was almost over when he finally realized he wasn't *going* to shoot one. The last few days he gave up on the stand and started stomping around in the woods. I guess he thought he was going to track one down. All he did was drive them away from everybody else. I was afraid he was going to shoot somebody by mistake, or they were going to get pissed and shoot him."

Was the landing closer now? Yes, it was. They had crossed over that line. The other shore no longer receded uniformly with their motion, like the moon from a car at night: Tucker had brought it into their perspective, their domain. Each stroke now made it nearer, more real.

"I still don't see how this is a fishing story," Dee-Dee said.

There was a boat tied up at the landing, brightly striped, red and white. From here it looked new and eager. A big boat with a big motor.

"Phooey," said Lianne. "Somebody's here."

Tucker looked over his shoulder. "No," he said. "I don't think so. It was here last month. I think it's somebody's motor broke down and they got disgusted and left it."

"Well, it wasn't here yesterday, was it, Charles?"

"That's strange," Tucker said.

"I hate those loud motors," Charles said. "It's so quiet this morning."

"Wait'll summer," Tucker said.

"A speedboat is fun, though," Dee-Dee said.

"So what happened to him?" Lianne said. "What did they do to him?"

"Nothing," Tucker said. "I mean, he didn't get hurt, and he didn't get a deer. Deer camp broke up and everybody went home."

They were close enough now that the urge to arrive took over. Tucker leaned into the oars.

"What's the rest of the story?" Dee-Dee said, then cleared her throat. The wind roughening her already rough voice.

"What rest?"

"I know you, Tucker. You start out with fishing, you're going to work back to it."

"We're almost there," Tucker said.

"I want an ending," Lianne said.

Tucker bumped them up against the dock, opposite the speedboat. Up close it didn't look so new. You could see the overlapping of several waterlines on the hull, the tea stains of algae. Rust leaked onto black enamel at the crack where the housing fit over the motor.

The dock was even more rickety and rotten than it had been last year. Tucker swung in close to its base, where presumably the wood was more solid. They tied up and clambered to land, helping each other from the contrarily dipping boat.

"I'll tell you the rest when we head back," Tucker said. "It ought to be told on the water."

"I knew there was an ending," Lianne said.

She and Dee-Dee had tied their hats in the stern, replacing them with tractor caps, and had fetched the Easter baskets from under the seat. Charles and Tucker took a drink from the ceremonial canteen, which held just a few long gurgles of Wild Turkey.

They walked the Bodark-McQuistion trail, an old Ozark footpath, a short transit between the lost cities for a walker or a man on a horse, but too rough and steep for wagons. It was almost grown over now—slowly, fractally losing its directedness, its meaning. It rose from the water, ran into air awhile, then dipped back down where the lake came crookedly around its rocky point.

Dogwoods on the mountain, the westering glitter of new leaves in windy profusion. Held up to the slanting morning the answering saucers of whitely dance, or else subsumed in lucid shade: a pale bridal, complex and shifting.

They would have felt a slight chill, perhaps, except for the labor of working up the trail. "This is better than sunrise service," Lianne said.

"We don't do much that has to do with Jesus," Dee-Dee said, the mischief-maker. Lianne was no atheist, but she and Charles had long ago come to an accommodation. Could Dee-Dee goad him to spite her for principle's sake?

"I don't know about that," Charles said. "I kind of think He would approve. I mean, He wasn't a prude. And we're celebrating beauty and spring and everything."

"We're celebrating having a good time," Dee-Dee said.

Tucker had stopped for breath. Now he lifted the canteen. "Take and drink," he intoned. "For this is my blood which was squeezed out of corn and fed through copper tubing for your sins." He took a swallow of the Wild Turkey.

"Tucker," Dee-Dee said.

"Jesus take care of Himself," Tucker said, gasping. "He's a big boy now."

"Do you really think we're being too pagan?" Lianne said. "All this feels really important to me. Really beautiful. Do you really feel like we have to do something specifically for Him?"

"Well, He did save us," Dee-Dee said. "Tucker, hand me that canteen."

In spite of the bellinis, the mimosas, and now the bourbon, they had sobered as they climbed. They found the first egg about three hundred yards farther on.

Lianne had set them all out yesterday evening, striding off up the hill with a knapsack of her hand-colored treasures. Charles had rowed her over and then waited with the boat till she returned. This was a new ceremony, and he could see that it was going to mean a lot of extra work. She had been up till two ayem the Friday they left, the whole bottom floor of the house pungent with vinegar. Then the eggs had had to be packed in the cooler, individually wrapped in paper towels, six to a Ziploc packet, so that they would stay dry.

While she hid them, he had taken a nap, and then smoked one of the half dozen cigars he allowed himself every year. It had gotten dark, and he had gotten worried. Finally here she came, waving her flashlight briskly about to pick her way down, nothing but a light on the mountain. Her face, when he was able to see it, was wild and transfigured, like a cat's just in from out-of-doors, or a saint's back from the wilderness. She had brought a treasure back with her, a hornets' nest fastened to a broken-off branch.

"I hid things and I found things," she had said.

This first egg was blue and green and yellow, like the morning. It lay nestled in the hollow of a mossy rock, the rock itself half enclosed by the flowing root of a maple.

"It's exquisite!" Dee-Dee cawed. "How do you get them so glossy?"

They worked up the hill, scouring bayberry, yaupon, sedge, and stone. Some of the eggs were sunsets, with rich austral hues bleeding into each other, some were midnights with moons and stars; there were noons at the

beach, vague rainy gray-green afternoons, wintry blues etched in an almost
Japanese fashion with sharp branches. Charles found himself irritated that
Lianne had poured such energy into so trivial a project. She struggled with
her painting because it had no justification beyond her own desire; but let
a Christmas, an Easter provide occasion, and she bestowed the attentions
of a Raphael. She threw herself away on the temporal.

He and Tucker began to compete, searching thoroughly in rough grids.
Dee-Dee seemed merely to stroll and chat, but then would dart suddenly
to her find.

They came to the flat stone bottoms, smooth layers of mossy and lichen-
cushioned rock. On the other side of the bottoms, the creek, running full
and bright this year. The trail followed the creek now, and would until
they came to Settler's Spring, half a mile on, the highest source in the area,
a little cliff-bordered nook where water sheeted and purled from limestone
strata, divided in glittering braids across a small grassy meadow, knitted,
gathered into a rocky ravine, and fell.

Lianne had hidden eggs in tree crooks, on stones in the creek. Well,
not hidden. More like displayed. Hidden only as the glories of earth are
hidden, in plain but unlikely view. Each was a focus, called into attention
some element of its setting: an elegant vaulting of branch and shade, a
dapple of sun through rippling shallows, a patch of flowers, a stone worn
like mother and child, the water's hypnotic upleap at an unusual eddy.

After a while they were silent, simply walking and looking. Charles
and Tucker forgot their competition. Each egg was a reward, the pluckable
heart of its place. Whoever found it would hold it up for the others to see,
then bring it back, perhaps across the creek and up a bank, helped by a
reaching hand, to store it in one of the baskets.

They made the spring at almost noon, chose their rocks, and sat.

"I warmed up," Dee-Dee said.

"Take a bath," Lianne said. "We won't watch."

"Speak for yourself," Charles said, and Dee-Dee stuck her tongue out
at him.

"More," he said. "More. I love tongue."

"Oh hush," Dee-Dee said.

"I know you want this canteen filled," Tucker said. "There's whiskey
left in it, though."

"Well, pour it out," Lianne said.

"No!" said Tucker and Charles, horrified.

"I don't want it messing the water up," Lianne said. Tucker answered
her by taking a long swallow. Charles got up to help him finish it off. "We
should have brought a couple of gallon jugs," Lianne said, thoughtful.
"Then we could have our coffee from spring water."

"Next thing you know we'll be carrying those ten-gallon plastic water cans back down the hill," Charles said. "Lashing them onto the jeep and hauling em back to Little Rock."

"It's good water," Lianne said.

"Was that all the eggs?" Tucker said. He was feeling a little disappointed, a little at loose ends and restless, like a kid after the movie. He was ready to start back.

"I thought they were just wonderful," Dee-Dee said. "All that work. And it really is kind of spiritual if you think about it. Because an egg is like a flower, it's the beginning of things."

"Yeah, but these are boiled eggs," Tucker said.

"There might be a few more," Lianne said. "Just one or two or so."

"Where?" Tucker said.

"Why don't you just go ahead and do what you were going to do a while ago?"

"What was I going to do? Aha." Tucker got up, took the canteen across to the spring. They watched him pick his footing, kneel where the water jumped out. "Aha!" he called, reaching into the pool at the base of the spring and holding up a shining egg. Another. And a third.

He filled the canteen, first rinsing it out and drinking the rinse. Then he came back to them drying the eggs on his pants, the canteen slung on his shoulder. He handed an egg to Dee-Dee and one to Charles. "And this one's mine," he said.

"What does it say?" Dee-Dee said, turning her egg over in her hands. "What a cute idea! Of course we'll come!"

"I like things worked into other things," Lianne said. "It's the way the world works."

"Let's see," Charles said.

Tucker's and Dee-Dee's were done the same way, but hers orange and his green, their favorite colors.

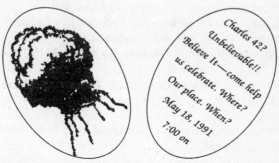

Charles 42?
Unbelievable!!
Believe It — come help
us celebrate. Where?
Our place. When?
May 18, 1991
7:00 on

"That's cute," Charles said. "So I guess it's not going to be a surprise this year?"

"Not anymore," Lianne said.

"I don't get the volcano," Dee-Dee said.

"The way Charles comes," Tucker said. "She's trying to brag."

"No, you dummy, I know, it's Mount Saint Helens. Because it happened on his birthday, remember. Lianne, that's just *really* cute. Charles, did you get invited to your own party?"

He handed his egg over, reluctant:

Dee-Dee dropped her voice an octave. "That really *is* darling."

Lianne blushed and brightened under the praise, pulling her chin down long in the self-disclaiming grimace that she meant as a broad grin. For all her beauty, it made her look, Charles had often thought, exactly like a cartoon version of Oliver Hardy.

Tucker was looking away, as you do when a singer hits a false note. They thought Lianne was silly, Charles saw. Dear, annoying, brilliant, cutting, refreshing, obvious, and silly. So militant and defensive, yet wearing her feelings helplessly, inappropriately, for all to see. Her gaieties, her decorations. His eyes stung for her. Fiercely embarrassed, he walked across and hugged her roughly, pretending the others weren't there.

"Thank you for my egg," he said, and kissed her.

"Why don't you kiss *me* like that, Tucker?" Dee-Dee said, her voice somewhere between mockery and compliment.

Tucker slapped her butt. "Get back down the hill. I'll do better than kiss."

Dee-Dee tried to slap his butt, and the two of them got into a butt-slapping contest, laughing and trying each to hold the other away by the arm.

"I wish we could stay up here forever," Lianne said. "Don't you?"

"Hmp," Tucker said.

"Well, let's head on down," Charles said. They set off, two couples arm-in-arm, hip-bumping, basket-bumping, canteen-bumping their crooked way back down the hill.

At the landing, a man in a ranger cap and uniform squatted beside their boat. He rose as they came up. He was tan, with the squint and weathering of a smoker. A long scar ran from his jaw just in front of his ear down his throat and into his collar.

"That's our boat," Tucker said. "Don't know whose that other is. In pretty bad shape."

"It's mine," the man said.

"Oh. Well, we didn't see any ranger insignia or anything," Tucker said.

"I didn't say it was a ranger boat. I said it was mine." The man was looking at them levelly and hard, as if he considered them intruders. He was wearing a gun. Were the rangers supposed to wear guns?

"Where have y'all been?" the man said.

"Just up the trail," Lianne said, breathless and happy. "You know Settler's Spring—"

Tucker touched her arm.

"What was y'all doing up there?" the man said.

"I don't think it matters, do you?" Charles said. "It's national forest. It's public land."

"Look like you having a party," the man said. "Might be tending your little crop."

"Right," Tucker said. "This man could buy and sell your whole county if he wanted to, and we're gonna be up in the hills raising grass."

"Let's go, Tucker," Charles said.

"We walk where we want to," Tucker said.

"Catch a trip wire, you won't be talking that way," the man said. "It's Vietnam all over again up in them hills." He shrugged. He walked away, onto the dock, and clambered into his boat. He leaned over the hull and loosened his line.

"How does that sorry hunk of fiberglass run?" Tucker said. Dee-Dee jerked his arm.

The man was winding his rope up. Now he threw it in the bow. He touched his hat to Tucker. "Runs fine," he said. He stepped into the back well, tilted the motor into the water, gave it a one-handed pull. It fired, belching a cloud of smoke. He backed the boat out, swung it around. He touched his cap again and roared off in a detonation of slapping echoes, leaving them with the haze and sharp odor of hot oil, his wake rapping up under the dock.

"Well, *that* puts a blight on the day," Dee-Dee said.

Lianne was white and shaken, whether with fear or anger Charles couldn't tell. "Not if we don't let it," he said. "I'm not going to let some asshole ruin my good time."

In the boat, though, life jackets on, the organdy hats in panoply once more, they were all somber. The morning's breeze had stilled, and it was warm out on the lake. Lianne had taken charge of the canteen. Now she screwed the cap off and lifted it and drank. "That is so good," she said, sighing. "So good and cold."

She drank again, then offered it, to headshakes from the others. She capped it. "Tucker, do you think *he* was growing marijuana up there?"

Now why, Charles wondered, would she ask Tucker instead of him?

"I tell you what," Dee-Dee said. "I was flashing on *Deliverance* all the way."

Tucker considered. "No," he said. "I think he really is a ranger. He looked more worried than mean. Maybe a local boy, grew up here—some country practitioner ran a blanket suture on that knife wound twenty years ago. Then we came up and surprised him, strangers on his home ground. And then I insulted his boat. Something more like that."

"We all seen too much tv," Charles said.

"Some of it really happens," Lianne said. "Why was he in his own boat?"

"Maybe he was off duty but wearing his uniform," Dee-Dee said.

"He wasn't supposed to be wearing a gun, I tell you that," Charles said.

"Some of them hunt with them," Tucker said. "I knew this fellow—"

"Oh!" Lianne said, sitting up straight. "What happened to him?"

"With a pistol?" Charles said, dubious.

"To who?" Tucker said. "Oh. Oh, well, it was way next spring, and we were fishing over on Moon Lake."

"I told you," Dee-Dee called to a flight of ducks. "I *told* you he would get back to fishing. *Whahnk whahnk,* yourself," she added, watching them sail in low over the water.

"It was me and Daddy and Mr. Quong, and of course this fellow showed up again."

"The one who couldn't get a deer," Dee-Dee clarified.

"And this time he couldn't catch any fish either, and you drowned him," Lianne said.

"No," Tucker said. "Although you're right, he didn't catch any fish. Not to speak of. A couple of little bream, but. He was too distracted by the roaches."

"The roaches?" Lianne said.

"Don't encourage him," Charles said.

"Mr. Quong used them for bait. Well, we did too, but he was the one who used to wear them. The bass just loved em."

"*Wear* them?" Lianne said.

"In his clothes," Tucker said. "He would come fishing with five or six dozen big ones running around loose in his shirt and jacket."

Lianne rolled her eyes and let her head flop back, making a wavery sound that suggested someone fainting and gagging at the same time.

"I think Mr. Quong is the grossest man alive," Dee-Dee said.

"He has to be some kind of pervert," Lianne said.

"No he wasn't," Tucker said. "He was a nice old Chinese gentleman. He ran a grocery, and he was a deacon in the Tunica Baptist Church."

"How did they *feel*?" Lianne said.

"He said they tickled. Said it was a kind of a dry, friendly tickle. Said they were really clean and smart. And besides, they kept the ticks off."

Lianne shivered.

"I would just rip my blouse off," Dee-Dee said. "If one got in there. I would just rip my blouse off and go naked to the world."

Charles imagined her breasts large and sagging, but wonderful with wide brown areolae. "That's tonight," he said. "In the poker game."

"You wish," said Lianne.

"Tucker's just stalling so he can think up an ending," Charles said.

"He got so scared of the roaches he peed himself, and you all laughed at him and you finally had your revenge," Lianne said to Tucker.

"No," Tucker said, "we didn't want any revenge by then."

He had been rowing steadily the whole time, if less strenuously than on the trip out, and now they were in range of the dock at the cabin.

"So what happened?" Lianne said.

"We were out in the middle of the lake, and a second-year buck came crashing out of the trees and started swimming across, holding that head high like it had a rack already."

"He shot him," Charles whispered. "The sonofabitch shot him."

"No," Tucker said. "We didn't bring any guns." He put the oars up and let them idle, to finish telling the story on the water.

"That deer swam right by us," he said, pointing across the lake. "He wasn't any farther away than that stob. Never looked at us once, just swam right by with his head up like he was a king riding on a coach, like his legs weren't down there working like a windmill."

Lianne couldn't help herself. "And?"

Tucker took up the oars again. "And then that boy jumped in the water and drowned him."

"Tuck-*errrr*," Dee-Dee said.

"God, that's awful," Lianne said.

Charles was laughing. Tucker had them almost to the dock now. "Jumped in the water like Tarzan and swam out and drowned him," Tucker said. "We didn't know who was going first for a while. But finally he got him by the neck like he was riding him, and he wore that deer out and drowned him." Tucker was laughing now because Charles was.

They bumped up against the dock, this one in good condition. Tucker was obsessive about maintenance. Charles let the women head on up.

"Tucker," he said, "did that really happen?"

"You know what an insult that question is?" Tucker said. He started up to the cabin, and Charles fell in beside him.

"Yeah, I know, but this time I really need to know."

"It happened," Tucker said. "Not all of it happened to me, but it happened."

Charles considered asking which parts had happened to Tucker and which to somebody else, but decided he had pushed matters far enough already. "What did he say?" he said.

Tucker paused with his hand on the rail of the deck steps. "What did who say?"

"The man," Charles said. "After he drowned the deer."

Tucker grinned. "He said, 'Help me get this sonofabitch in the boat,' " he said, and headed up the steps into the cabin.

Charles and Lianne woke from their naps about four o'clock, both feeling good, no hangovers: The walk, the sun, the open air had made them well. They opened the sliding glass doors, leaving the screens closed, and made love while the linen curtains blew and billowed in and out of the sun. It was a lean, healthy lovemaking, their skins smooth and electric, tasting of sun and dried sweat. They did it quietly, because they heard Tucker and Dee-Dee in and out on the deck. After a while there came the odor of cooking ribs, a smoky charge on the hollow air, the lust of burning meat, and they rose and showered and went out to drinks and mixed nuts and Melba thins with cream cheese and smoked oysters, to laugh and talk and watch the sun go slowly down into the trees across the lake, into the trees over Settler's Spring, in fact.

And life was good, and they did not think of the ranger again, or the slain deer, or its slain cousin, whose hacked-out portions roasted so sumptuously on their grill. They did not think of Lieutenant Matt Wingo in Brazoria County, Texas, who was afraid forty girls might have died at the hands of a mass murderer as yet unknown. They did not think of the so-called Tasmanian tiger, that bloody marsupial, whose kind had spent as long on the earth as humans and was now, in the last year or two, extinct. They did not think of the fifteen who had died in the collision of a commuter plane with a plane full of parachute jumpers, though Lianne did think, fleetingly, imagistically, watching the swallows swoop over the lake after the evening bugs, of the four who had parachuted to safety. But then, she thought of parachutes often.

They did not think of the ghosts four hundred feet below, lives that had been and vanished in the drowned towns, that had crossed and interlaced these hills and watched this sun go down tens of thousands of times. And shall we blame them? Who can think of such things long?

Well, I can, but I have to. It isn't what you were made for. You were made to kill me and eat me and drink me. And my reward is that you are sometimes happy and safe and warm, that you afford occasionally a little pocket of bliss, a wink of time in which I can forget myself and the rest of the universe almost entirely.

The darkness came, and with it mosquitoes, though the night air was cool. Up from the lake they came, my little whining angels, filaments of pure hunger. Charles and Lianne and Dee-Dee and Tucker fled inside, to begin the poker game.

They played, as always, at the table in the kitchen-dining area, a round of oiled walnut under an art deco hanging light. They played with chips, $2, $5, and $10. The chips were not traded in for money, though. Each item they wore had been assigned a dollar value, and you could trade the chips for clothes, anybody's clothes. If they didn't want to strip, they matched you, and both bids went in the pot. You could buy more chips with clothing, too, if you got in a tight spot. The value of the item went up the closer it got to skin or to an erogenous zone. An earring went for five dollars, a shoe for seven, a sock for ten, but a pair of slacks went for forty, panty hose for a hundred, and a bra for two hundred fifty even. They had had Tucker down to his briefs once, just once, and one night Dee-Dee had played for a glorious hour in nothing but a skirt and a bra.

You could buy your clothes back if your luck improved, but only if the person who held them would sell them to you, which they would probably do only if they were short themselves.

Tucker played with abandon, though he thought of himself as a guerrilla plotting cool tactics and making blitzkrieg raids. He would bet the pot up suddenly just because he thought it was time to throw some randomness in or because he was bored and wanted to drive the chickens out. Charles played too carefully, folding unless he opened with cards, betting it up when the probabilities were there. He knew that sort of play cost him money, but he liked to think he made it up on the one or two big hands he successfully bluffed each night.

Neither Lianne nor Dee-Dee took poker seriously enough, keeping up a constant stream of talk on other subjects, getting up and coming back; they laughed whenever either made a mistake like dealing a down card up that would have been somebody's second queen in the hole in queens-

and-what-follows. And you had to remind them to ante over and over and over.

Neither one of them was a bad player either, which made it worse.

They broke for the ribs about nine o'clock, and spent a good forty-five minutes with coleslaw and garlic-and-butter toast and barbecue sauce, gnawing bones and smearing their faces and hands with vivid grease. "Well, Tucker," Charles said, leaning back. "You did it again."

"More poker?" Tucker said.

"Y'all wash your hands with soap and water," Dee-Dee said.

After the break, Charles had an incredible run of luck. At 12:30, he held a boat, kings over, and he was looking at aces in two different hands and had an ace up himself. He was also looking across the table at Dee-Dee, in nothing but her panties and the huge white harness of her bra. Her breasts were freckled across the tops. She was frowning intensely at her cards. No laughing now, no mock-clumsy mistakes.

She and Lianne were still in, Tucker had folded. He was barefoot and had lost his belt. Lianne was down to her pullover, her bra, her socks, and her panties. "White cotton," Tucker had said when he saw the panties. "Rats."

"Tucker, what do I do?" Dee-Dee said, leaning over to show him her cards.

Tucker shook his head. "He's had em all night long," he said.

"Well, I think he's two pair aces high," she said. "Maybe aces and kings." Only one of Charles's three kings was showing. "This is straight seven stud, not baseball or something."

"I'm gonna see them bazongas," Charles said in a W. C. Fields voice. He was euphoric. "You have got a flush and I have got you whipped all the way." He had found you could tell people exactly what you were up to in poker, and they wouldn't listen. They were too busy working up their own stories of how it would go.

"Charles, dear," Lianne said. "Don't be so crude."

"Hotcha hotcha hotcha," Charles said. Jimmy Durante now.

"See your one hundred and call," Dee-Dee said, slapping down a heart flush, mostly face cards. That was probably why she had stayed in. A heart flush with face cards is a beautiful thing. The faces are meaningless, but it's still a beautiful thing.

"And unless I miss my guess," Charles said, "you are now light two hundred and sixty-five dollaroos." He waggled his eyebrows like Groucho Marx, flaunted a nonexistent cigar.

"You're called, Ace," Dee-Dee said. "Let's see em."

Charles spread the boat across the pot. "Yeah," he said. "Let's see em."

"Shit," Tucker said.

Dee-Dee pushed her chair away. She took one step back and froze. "Ta," she said.

"Ta-dum," Tucker said.

"Ta-dum, ta-dum," Dee-Dee said, her hands going to the fastener at the front of her bra. She began to sway her hips. "Ta dum ta ta dum ta ta dum ta ta *daaaa*," she said, and unsnapped the bra, flinging her arms wide and lifting her face to one side.

Tucker brought his hands down on the table in a drummer's barrata-tatat.

They *were* a little floppy, with big brown areolae.

"We did it," Lianne said.

"Want to try to win it back?" Charles said. "I bet I can take those panties too."

Dee-Dee was still in her pose. "Wot I got, beh-bee," she said in her huskiest voice, "five hundred dollar will not buy." She slapped one hand down over her mons, as if in sudden modesty. The other over her ass. She began to dance again, whistling the bump and grind. Then she stopped, skinned out of her panties, twirled them on her finger, gave herself a wide-eyed wolfwhistle, and ran for the back deck.

"Well I guess that's it for poker," Tucker said. "Y'all up for the hot tub?"

"I don't know," Lianne said. "It's awfully late."

Tucker had gone on out. "Come on," Charles said.

"Do you really want to?" Lianne said. "You just want to see Dee-Dee."

"Well, you get to watch Tucker," he said.

"Whoopee."

"Come on," Charles said. "It'll relax you."

"I am relaxed."

"Well, I think I'm going to get in for a little while," he said.

He went out, resentfully, into the darkness. Tucker and Dee-Dee hailed him, pale figures in steaming dark water. He stripped, folding his clothes on the bench.

"Woo-woo," Dee-Dee said when he got down to his briefs. He imitated her, twirling them on his finger, false cheerfulness, and clambered in.

His eyes adjusted. Her breasts floated, dim and round, and you could catch a glimpse of something dark that had to be nipples. But the trouble was, he discovered, you had to be cool. You had to look equally at everybody, and look around at the night, and keep up a conversation. Spend all that time and energy and gamesmanship trying to see naked bodies, and then you can't just stare. From far away whatever you wanted looked simple and singular, but when you got it, it opened up into a whole new set of rules and behaviors.

"Lianne not coming out?" Tucker said.

"She was really tired," Charles said, and the door opened, light pouring out, and here came Lianne in bra and panties with a tray of drinks, bumping the door shut behind her.

"Bless your little heart," Tucker said as she set the tray down on the rim of the hot tub. Prettily, pertly, the saucy French maid, she handed the drinks round: a whiskey sour for Tucker, iced vodka for Dee-Dee, a dry manhattan for Charles. Charles understood her mode. Unsure of herself in this new context, she could feel safe if she found a role, a service; could feel acceptable if she offered others something they wanted.

She had brought the canteen for herself.

When they had come back from the lake, she had put the canteen in the refrigerator to keep it cold, and during the poker game, while the others had had their drinks, she had gone to the fridge from time to time and gotten herself a swallow of spring water. They had made fun of her, but as vulnerable as she might be in some ways, when she had gotten a physical situation the way she wanted it, she was unshakable, and she had laughed them off.

"You're trying to ruin me," Charles said happily, holding his drink up by the stem. It was one of his favorites, Turkey and Boissiere three to one with a twist. Dry manhattan. A whiskey martini. He could just see the twist, a mere hint in the steam-shrouded flute.

"Come on, girl, get in," Dee-Dee said. "You don't need those fig leaves. It's just skinny-dipping with the guys. You've done that before."

Lianne tucked her head, that disclaiming grin again. Charles was sure she was blushing. "I've gotten so fat," she said.

Dee-Dee stood on the seat, thrust her butt forward just at the water line, grabbed it with one hand. She was magnificent, streaming and gleaming and steaming. "What do you call this flab?" she said, wiggling the handful. Lianne began to undo her bra, and Dee-Dee subsided.

"Don't swamp the damn drinks," Tucker said, grabbing his up where he had set it down. "Good Lord, what was that?" he said as Lianne scampered in, for all the world like a girl in her first camp shower. "*Little* Miss *Little* Rock. Dee-Dee, I want you to dye yours."

"Tucker," Dee-Dee said.

"Like an arrow showing you where it is."

"*Tucker.*"

Lianne leaned back, up to her neck in the water. She looked at the stars. Then she got herself a drink from the canteen. "That's *good* water," she said, sighing. She looked up again. "I hate to have to go back to Little Rock," she said.

"At least we don't have to get up early," Charles said. He didn't want to think of going back to the office. The office was complicated, painful.

He was worried about Lafayette. He found it simpler to stay far away from Tina. Far from Tina, close to Lianne, so that Lianne's warmth washed out all temptation. And there were other things going on at the office. They were having trouble with cases they normally would have found cut-and-dried. Trent had defected to Wright, Lindsey, and Jennings, and he was pretty sure Baker was shopping himself around. On the street, the firm was no longer seen as unbeatable, and as a result they were having unaccustomed trouble finding replacements.

Betty was talking early retirement, which he knew was his cue to offer her a senior partnership. She was invaluable, she knew the firm better than he did, but as a senior partner she would be a disaster. Tricky enough offering partnership to Lafayette and not her, but now with the monkey fight gossip percolating through the firm, almost impossible. So it probably *would* have to go to Betty. Which, with Eamon, meant two dinosaurs as partners, though if he could have a straight-up swap, Eamon for Betty, he would take it in a flash.

"Penny for your thoughts," Dee-Dee said.

"I don't know," he said. "I guess I just hate to go back to the real world."

"Can't say I mind," Tucker said. "All this fun wears me out. I'm ready to get back to some nice relaxing work."

"Y'all should be so glad you have this place," Lianne said. "Why did you name it that? I mean, I always wondered, but it just now crossed my mind to ask."

"Ask Dee-Dee," Tucker said. "I just bought it. I don't have any real authority."

"Because there's only one," Dee-Dee said. "It goes all the way around. But whichever side you're on, you always think of the other one as the other shore."

"That's deep," Lianne said.

"I tell you what's deep," Tucker said. He slid under the water, surfaced, snorted, wiped his hair out of his eyes. "Sleep. And I'm about ready to get me some."

"Poor baby," Dee-Dee said. "Keep him up till two in the morning, put him in a tub of hundred-degree water, and feed him a good stiff drink, and he just poops out."

"He's all tuckered out," Lianne said.

"Boo hiss," Dee-Dee said.

"No stamina at all," Charles said. He tried to persuade Tucker to stay, but no luck. "I guess I'm ready too," Dee-Dee said, and stepped out and wrapped herself in a towel. And that suddenly it was over, the nonpareil day. Nakedness went clothed, and the bonds fell separate.

Charles and Lianne tried to stay out a little, but now they both felt tired too. Charles thought of making love in the hot tub. Probably just get a sermon on yeast infections, though. He put a hand on her leg as she got out, and she leaned over and gave him a perfunctory kiss.

"Shit," he said, after she had gone inside. "Shit shit shit."

A meteor went over, a huge tumbling yellowgreen fireball that split into two tracks.

"Mother of God," he said. He took it as a sign from Me, climbed out, dried himself, and went in to Lianne. It wasn't a sign. I'll tell you something you may or may not know: Stay out long enough on any clear night of the year, and you'll see them. Stay away from the bright lights and stay out long enough. Not just on meteor shower nights. Any night of the year.

In Tucker and Dee-Dee's bedroom, Dee-Dee was brushing her teeth, and Tucker was already in bed. "What do you think's going on with them?" Dee-Dee said foamily.

"What do you mean?"

"Well didn't you see how antsy she was? She was on a tear all day long. And he was taking care of her right and left."

"And for God's sake, those awful eggs," he said.

"I thought they were real pretty."

"Yeah, but are we going to have to have an Easter egg hunt every year now? Help!"

She came to the bed. "Move over," she said. "Is he playing around on her, Tucker?"

"How would I know? Probably not. Maybe."

"He seems so distracted lately. Like his mind isn't really here." She grinned and punched him. "Are you playing around on me?"

"Every day." He laughed. "I thought his eyes were going to pop out."

She pulled the covers back and straddled him. "Did I make you hot, lover?"

"Yeah, you did. But I'm sleepy now."

"I'll do all the work."

He grunted. "Work your will," he said.

She leaned forward to put her face against his chest. "I hope he's not screwing around on her. It's the marriages that are friends, not the people in the marriages. I wouldn't want to lose them." He had risen, thumping against her ass, and now she moved down to find him and guide him in. "Oh. Oh, you're my good man, baby. Oh, I want to have your *child*."

"Don't say it if you don't mean it," he said.

She stopped, looking down into his face. "Honey," she said.

"They can take an egg out," he said. "Plant it back in you, bypass the fallopians. They do it all the time."

"Honey, I'm getting too old," she said. "We talked about this."

He sighed. He held a long face for a moment, then grinned and bucked under her, slapping her ass. "Well, git up, old hoss," he said.

Later she snuggled into his chest again. "Tucker," she said, "I wouldn't want to be anybody else but us. I wouldn't want it any other way."

He wrapped his arms around her and squeezed.

In Charles and Lianne's room, Lianne was dabbing astringent on her face. "What do you think's wrong with Tucker and Dee-Dee?" she said when he came in.

"I don't know," he said. "You noticed too?"

"Like a bear all day long. Nothing was any good. *Grump* grump grump grump grump."

"I think they're under a lot of pressure."

"The clinics?"

"Yeah, the buyer fell through."

She looked at him, her face white with the mask, like a vampire's face in a cheap stage play. "You didn't tell me that."

"Well, I would have, but he wanted me not to mention it—"

Withholding information; she would be angry. But she let it go: "Even when they made so much money on that first one, I didn't see how they could live the way they do."

"It's the way they are," he said. "Boom or bust, feast or famine. He'll find a buyer and they'll come out swimming in cream again."

"Well, she doesn't like having to work, not one little bit. Ever since I've known her," she said, "way back when we were little kids, she was bound and determined to marry rich and never work another lick in her life." She smiled. "And look who wound up actually doing it."

That made Charles uncomfortable. "Don't talk like that," he said.

They turned out the light, got under the covers, and curled together, her back to his stomach. "I sure hope they're ok," she said. He patted her flank.

"This feels so good," she said. "I'm so glad we're us. I look around, and I can't think who else I would want to be. I just wouldn't want to trade for any marriage I know."

He hugged her. It *was* good, he thought sleepily. *She* was good. She was home. They were asleep in five minutes.

Not long afterward, in the Heights, the *Gazette* newsboy made his rounds, thumping the rolled papers off the steps of the houses. At Tucker's and Dee-Dee's home the slender Monday edition sailed in to lie jack-strawed in the driveway with Saturday's and the fat log of Sunday's. Furled darkly in the center of the Sunday paper, there was an excellent essay by John Workman, the religion editor. He said we had let Easter become too civilized.

In the woods near The Other Shore, an owl floated through foggy trees, hunting. A lost dog, bony and chancred, curled tightly in a hollow. From time to time he shivered. On the lake, water striders slept on their feet, rising and falling with the small slow waves. And fathoms below them, in the lost city of Bodark, the darkness weighed two hundred pounds per square inch.

17

BACK IN THE
REAL WORLD

"There's something wrong with the phone," Lianne said. "All I get is rock and roll."

"What?" Charles said. He was knotting his tie, guiding himself in the mirror. He had meant to get to the office immediately after lunch, but they had been late getting back from The Other Shore, and then Lianne had insisted on getting everything unpacked and put up right away. She couldn't let the mess just sit a few hours, oh no.

"Well, you come listen," she said, holding the phone out.

"Oh for God's sake," he said, snatching the instrument away and putting it to his ear. Tinny and flat, as if from a great distance, he heard music. It was Creedence Clearwater's "Suzie Q." "That's a long song too," he said. He handed the phone back to her. "Did you try to dial?"

"What do you think?" she said. "Of course I did. Nothing. Charles, why would the phone be playing rock and roll?"

"I don't know," he said. "Maybe we're getting interference from the tuner. Those speakers you bought. The ones that plug into the wiring. They could be shorting onto the phone lines or something. Magnetic resonance."

"I don't think it works like that. And anyway, we haven't had those speakers for a year. I made them take them back, remember?"

"Well I don't know, then. And I don't have time to figure it out now. Have you tried the other phones?"

"I've been standing right here," she said. "Did I leave the room and go pick up the other phones? No, Charles, I didn't. Would you for once try to be a little help around here?"

"Help?" he said. "Shit, Lianne, do I look like a fucking repairman? I'm a fucking lawyer. Call the telephone company."

His alarms were going off. He saw this was an issue. When support systems broke down, it scared her. If he didn't take it seriously, he was discounting her. A quick inventory of his emotions, and he realized he was in full-brusque mode: getting ready to sail in and set things straight at the office. He enjoyed using the mode on her, because in it he felt invulnerable, not a common state in their arguments. But it was the better part of wisdom to back off.

He took the phone again, listened. *Jody said, "It's mine, but you can have it for seventeen million,"* the flat thin voice sang. He looked at Lianne, lifted his shoulders in a minishrug. "I'm sorry, Hon," he said, setting the receiver back in its cradle. "I don't know what to make of it. It's weird, but. I can call the repairman from the office if you want me to."

"No," she said. "I'll do it." At the same instant, both of them realized what they had been saying. He started laughing first.

"I'll call from the office," he said. "It's a pisser."

"Try to give me a call. See if you can get through the other way."

"Right." He gave her a hug, and she followed him out. They tried the hall phone on the way to the elevator, and the phone in the living room after they came down, but it was Creedence on them all. *I put a spell on you,* sang the phone in the foyer, *Becaw-awse you're my-ine.* There was only one line in the house, because his father had thought multiple lines were pretentious and silly, like having three cars for two people. And now he was married to a woman who felt the same way. He sure could pick em.

Not to mention if it was left to him, they would have an unlisted number. A woman of the people. But she was probably right: They had too many friends and acquaintances; the number would get out anyway.

"I'll call from the office," he said again, and gave her another hug.

He forgot to call her, though he did remember to call the phone company. When he got the service department on the line, he had the familiar and always delicate task of letting them know that although he was too modest and democratic to say so outright, he was an important man whose problem needed immediate attention. He managed by describing his wife's predicament, marooned at home, so that it was legitimate to drop her name into the conversation. Everyone knew her name. And by saying, after giving the address, "It's up on Edgehill."

He forgot to call Lianne because he got busy in the office. He was a whirlwind. Every precis, every schedule, every report, every case history that was even a day overdue—he called them in. He wanted to know the reasons for every postponement in every current case: Were his people stretching out fees, or were they just laggard in getting their work done, and covering it by asking for continuances? He reviewed three current cases with their advocates, pointing out flaws in strategy or, in one situation, reaming a young man out because, in Charles's opinion, he *had* no strategy. In an hour and a half he had the junior members white-faced and frenetic, hurrying down the hall to the library, looking in to clear with Charles before heading out to take depositions or visit the scene of the accident or pull records at the courthouse.

At 4:00 he had an appointment with Betty, and at 4:30 with Lafayette.

Waiting for Betty, he remembered that he had been supposed to try to call home. He cursed, and punched the number. Busy. Good enough. It might mean that the phones were still messed up, or it might mean that they were fixed and Lianne was on the line to someone. Either way, he could say he had tried and all he had gotten was a busy signal.

Betty came in. It had been a problem, deciding whether to talk first to her or to Lafayette. He got up, closed the door behind her, and went back to his desk. She wanted a cigarette bad, Charles knew. She was a thin, pale woman, a chain-smoker, with a smoker's lines around her eyes and a smoker's rapidly aging skin. Even her hair seemed to have been affected by the habit, a drab and graying brown—and the gray not a silver gray but a yellowed gray, as if old smoke had left its values there. What was she, early fifties?

He had planned a careful and modulated talk, but now he found himself impatient, full of energy. Tact be damned. It was his firm, and he had them hopping again. It felt good.

"Betty, I'm not going to name you partner anytime soon," he said. She didn't flinch, but she didn't look at him either. That was one of her liabilities in the courtroom: She didn't make eye contact—or if she did, you felt her eyes sliding over you, away, wanting not to see.

"You're the best researcher we've got," he said. "When you prepare a case, I know nobody's going to blow holes in it. You've been with us a long time—"

"Nineteen years," she said. "Longer than you have. I was your father's first woman."

He guessed she didn't hear the bawdy ambiguity. No sense of humor, no perspective. And that was the other thing. She simply wouldn't accommodate. She was tireless, full of nervous energy, seemed never to sleep—he had found her in the office at midnight sometimes, working. No one to go home to, he would think, and would wonder, briefly, what her life must be like, how it could possibly be satisfying.

But she was as inflexible as she was tireless. She wasn't confrontational, certainly not. She just didn't want to be bothered. She wanted her cases to be cut-and-dried, mechanical. You did the work, the law kicked in, followed its logic, you got your results: That was how she saw it.

"I was pointing out how valuable your experience is," he said. "I don't doubt you know the history of this firm better than I do. You know the history of all the judges in town. You probably remember things about my dad that would surprise me."

"Your father was a good man," she said. In another mouth, those words would have meant, implicitly, *by comparison with you.* In her case, Charles was sure, they meant nothing so ironic. She was just claiming the association, hoping it would do her some good. "If I'm so valuable," she said, "when's the payoff?"

"I don't want you to retire," Charles said. "But you have some liabilities. You just won't work a courtroom."

"Because they're supposed to be courtrooms. If you want *Perry Mason,* hire an actress. Another actress," she amended, and he knew she meant Tina.

"You've lost cases you had no business losing," he said. "Not on the basis of preparation, but just because the other side was willing to work the courtroom and you weren't. A partner in this firm has a lot of public exposure, Betty. He or she has to be able to work with people. Not only work with them but encourage them, butter them up, make them feel good. And you're a lousy organizer too. I'm not talking facts, you keep your facts straight enough. I'm talking systems, dynamics. This firm is a growing and changing thing, and I frankly just can't see you taking on any of the day-to-day load of running the place. Can you?"

"What about Eamon?" she said. "He's a partner, and he's a dead loss."

"You know it and I know it. And we also know how he got that way." He wouldn't accuse his father outright of the bad decision, but she understood him.

"The point is, he's being compensated and I'm not. He was made a partner when he was a lot younger than I am, and his record is a lot worse. I could put together a pretty good summary for an equal opportunity suit."

"Yeah, and lose it because you got no talent in the courtroom. Understand me, Betty. I'm just not willing to put you and Eamon on the letterhead at the same time. That's as blunt as I know how to be."

"So I can pack my bags and go. You'd be in great shape then. A team full of rookies and free agents. I'd like to see you trying to get by with the likes of Tina and Lafayette and young Mr. Yuppie. It'd be worth it to quit just to watch that circus."

"Fair enough. I'm being up front. You have the same privilege. But I don't want you to quit. I didn't say I would never make you a partner. I said not now, not while Eamon's around. If you can wait two years—"

She stood up. "I'll think it over," she said, looking at her skirt and smoothing it. She looked up, over his head at the bookshelves. "I'll want an increased portfolio contribution and something in writing about the scheduling for the partnership."

Damn, she was irritating. He studied her a moment, then decided to play it her way. "Fine," he said. He looked back down at his notes, began to go through them. "Let me know by Monday at the latest," he said without looking up. "You can go now," he said, only to hear the door closing so quickly afterward that he knew she'd already been on the way out. No point in trying mind games with that one. The hell with it. He needed to stretch his legs and settle his nerves before Lafayette came in.

In the hall, he smelled the smoke of her cigarette.

"Lafayette," he said. "I've got bad news." Lafayette, in the chair that Betty had sat in, didn't answer. Surely he knew what he was about to hear, but no reaction showed. Was he really that cool? Charles wondered. Or did he seem that way because he was black and Charles was stereotyping? It was hard to know, he thought. They didn't, after all, blanch.

Lafayette was thinking, *Here it comes.* Why should he feel this way? Over the years, he had developed a good deal of contempt for whitey's world. Now he sat here feeling like the bottom had dropped out of his own because he wasn't going to get massa's pat on the head, wasn't going to be a partner.

Well, he reckoned he could figure out why he felt that way, if he had to.

"I can't offer you partnership," Charles said.

This was how he always did when he funked, Lafayette realized. He would think about why he was funking. He would go back to the roots of it, figure when the first fear-thrill hit. Follow the skein of gut sickness back, connect a feeling to a feeling until he remembered where the first tremor trembled. When he would finally get it, when he had worked back to the source, he would find himself calm. Fatalistic, but balanced and cool.

He had gotten himself ready for a lot of games that way, lying awake listening to Big Daddy cuss Momma, and cuss her God, and cuss her baptized cunt. Lying awake after Big Daddy fell drunkenly asleep. Lying awake ashamed, as if tomorrow the boys and girls would be able to read his home life on his face. Cooling out, thinking why their quarrels made him feel so filthy and guilty himself, understanding even before he ever heard of Freud that it had something to do with the weirdness of their relationship, the reprobate old man marrying his dead preacherboy son's widow, so that he was Big Daddy, grandfather and stepfather at once, and was Lafayette his son or his grandson? Legal as hell, but incestuous, incestuous before he ever knew the word incestuous, with such dexterity to posthaste—shit yes, incestuous, and her twice as righteous as before, as if by scrubbing its boards with industrial Lysol to blot the stink of the outhouse hole.

Which he had dreamed of again and again when he was younger and he and Big Daddy got on well: the summer effluvium of the one-hole shack from his early childhood, when they had lived outside town, sweet rot thick in the honeysuckle-heavy air. The daytimes were good when Big Daddy liked him, but he dreaded the nights. Again and again he murdered his father, except that his father was a little boy, six or so, the same age as Laugh when the man had died, and Laugh understood why now, but too damn late, the dreams had done their damage.

In the dreams he chopped his father, chopped him and killed him and crammed him down the hole. And then to hear the broken dead doll-body pleading, eyes gleaming up from the farbelow dark shitsoup, a whining voice in the unbearable booming fermented fetor as he squatted and heaved and never could let go. Except the twice or three times he shit his bed, and the anger in Momma's eyes then, the utter revulsion she turned his way.

By the time he was playing football he had quit having the dreams, but when Momma and Big Daddy fought he would remember them, and the sense of shame he felt on those evenings made him weak and worthless, so that if he didn't work it through before he fell asleep he would walk out on the field next evening, and the other team's guards, tackles, and linebackers would clean his clock. So he would work it through until he saw once again it was them, not him. And he would work it through, and the malarial calmness would come, and in the game, restored if not cured, he would deliver all his fury to the bodies of strangers.

Charles was waiting for an answer. What do you want, Laugh? Shoulda been thinking strategy before now. In the absence of a plan, let's keep our job, ok? Ok. Now, you aint gonna get away with pretending you don't know what this is about. So:

"This about that fight?"

"What do you think? It's all over this office, and it's all over town. I know in some ways you were just in the wrong place at the wrong time—"

Gee thanks, boss. You so kind to me.

"But that's the point. I can't afford that in a partner. A partner has to be somebody who's in the right place at the right time."

"What about Eamon?"

Charles ignored him. "Besides, I been hearing you were maybe a little more deeply involved than I heard at first. Like taking out a couple of deputies."

Charles couldn't help himself, he smiled at that. "The right ones, I might add.'' He modulated his expression with an actor's succinctness. Now he was serious again.

Amazing, Lafayette thought. Simply amazing. The man is out of my league.

''The only enemies we can afford to have are professional enemies. You ought to know that. No telling how much business this mess has cost us. No telling how much more static we're going to get out of the lord high bailiff's office. You never know who is whose friend till you piss em all off. Now, I'm sure this is all hitting you pretty hard.''

Thanks for telling me. Laws, a body don't hardly have to do nothing for his own self round here, not even feel his own feelings, mercy mercy me. What I'm feeling . . . what I'm feeling is guilt. That's the operative word here. I feel scared and guilty; now why? I can see why I got to take this hit, bad luck and all that, but what I done to feel guilty about?

''What I want you to know is I'm not saying never. I'm saying not right now. The rest of it kind of depends on what you do with yourself over the next few years.''

Years. Years is a long time. I have waited so many years already. For what? To get to the safe place, the ok place. Make enough money, get enough success to get *rid* of this scare, to offset this guilt. Lafayette felt an iciness, a trembling anger. He couldn't sit any longer, he had to get up. He went to the window and looked out.

''How many years?'' he said. On trial again. Always with Coach it had been wait and see. Maybe you start next week. When will I know, Coach? How do I know, Lafayette? Just practice hard, and we'll see. Always with Momma it had been wait and see. Maybe you won't be grounded no more, you change your ways, quit fighting with Big Daddy. He's your father now, you better show him some respect. How long, Momma? How long do I have to wait?

''How do I know?'' Charles said. ''Just get your act together and hang in.'' He took a breath. Laugh turned to look at him. The man looked pleased with the way he was handling this. Laugh could see the tolerance come over his face. ''I've always had the greatest respect for you personally,'' he said. ''I think you've come a long way against tough odds.''

Yeah, hard for us colored to keep all this primal savagery keyed down.

''You just need to clean your act up, that's all. Do that, and the partnership is waiting on ice. I promise you.''

My act is Tina, that's what he means. And that's it, that's where the guilt is coming from, that's what I think I done wrong. Tina, the dirty girl. Momma don't like Tina, she know what I'm after. I'm bad for wanting that dirty stuff. Forever bad. Punished in hell.

He was calm now. It felt good. It felt peaceful. He could almost hear the noise from the people in the stands.

And you, Mr. Clean Charles. Mr. Proud-of-Yourself. I got a surprise for you. Let's open a door and see if you can keep yourself from walking through.

Laugh said, "I understand where you're coming from." Relief on Charles's face. "I believe in myself. I believe I can earn your trust." He waited a beat. "But could I ask a favor?"

"Sure."

"It's a psychological thing. I understand why you're doing what you're doing. But I need something to help me feel better about it. Some little token of your confidence."

Charles's expression became guarded. "So ask."

"I'm giving a party. May eighth, at my place. Would you feel like coming? It would carry a message to the other people in the firm. It would make me not such a scolded child."

Now Morrison's face cleared. He was being asked to bestow his presence. Had to make him feel magnanimous, the grand seigneur, the medieval lord. "Is that the party Tina's been talking about? I thought it was at her place."

"No," Laugh said. "It's at my place."

He watched Morrison's expression flicker and resolve, a water-top ripple that he was sure represented some deeper current, a transient fantasy of getting off alone with Tina, perhaps.

"Sure," Charles said. "What can it hurt?"

Laugh smiled.

Charles had scheduled Betty and Laugh toward the end of the day purposely. It allowed them to get out and restore themselves, to not feel they had to either sit and stew or risk looking as if they were leaving early, in a huff. For himself, he planned to work late. He was looking forward to it, even. Silence, peace. Get some *real* work done.

He hadn't reckoned on the subliminal competition, all the scolded employees working past time to prove something to the boss. Stubbornly, he outwaited them, repossessed the place. Finally he was aware of things emptying out. He imagined he could sense the mood in which people were leaving: put out, tempers frayed—the boss is back, he has the red-ass, he's on a tear, and it's just fucking Monday, for fuck's sake, this is going to be one hell of a fucking week.

It was after six, the sun was almost down, and he had been working in what he thought was perfect solitude for half an hour, when the door opened and Tina came in.

Tina's blue eyes behind her half-rims. The freckles across her nose. She sat primly, looking very young, very country, very contrite.

"I want you to know this isn't an apology," she said.

"For what?" he said.

"I'm in therapy," she said. "I just want you to know that." Charles didn't know what to say. "I'm beginning to realize what I've been doing. I've been trying to work through leftover stuff from my childhood." The blue eyes brimmed. "This is hard for me to say."

For Charles the evening suddenly seemed twice as vivid, and yet somehow unreal. He felt as if he were connected to the breeze stirring in the darkening trees out the window, and yet as if he and the breeze were equally phantasms in a dream.

"I was—he raped me. When I was fourteen, that was the first time. My father."

In Charles, embarrassment and curiosity fought. "You don't have to tell me this—"

"No, and I probably *shouldn't* be. It isn't fair to you, to dump my troubles on you. But I need to tell somebody, do you understand? Somebody besides my therapist. So I won't feel so dirty, like I have this terrible secret that no one should ever know."

"It isn't your fault he—"

"It doesn't work that way, though. You know that. You blame yourself. But what I was saying, I know you have some strong reservations about my behavior lately." When he tried to make the obligatory disclaimer, she overrode it. "No, I know you do. But don't you see? I'm not mad, I'm happy. *You called my hand.* You really shook me up. You cared enough to set limits. So, suddenly, you became my father, the father I never had, the good one."

He was shocked into total silence. And he was frightened, as we are when we find that we are playing a much larger and more dangerous role in someone else's drama than we had thought. And he was deeply flattered. As we also are.

"The only time he used to treat me good was when he—when I let him—" She started again. "I grew up thinking that was how to get love, and I've been trying it with every man I ever met, turning them into my father all over again, and then, and then I would hate them, just like I did him." The eyes were overflowing now.

Charles wanted her to wipe them. But she sat there unmoving, raw-faced as a child, the tears rolling out and down, slowing as they subtracted themselves to shining trails, stopping finally in minimal bulbs of glisten, the last round quanta of suspense. Rivulets on a rainy window.

"It's hard," she said. "Coming to all this now, nearly forty." Finally she took a handkerchief from the pocket of her slacks, like a man, and wiped her eyes, and blew her nose. She smiled. "Better late than never, I guess." Her smile was radiant, the crooked teeth more than white in her flushed complexion.

"Well," he said.

"Don't feel like you have to say anything," she said. "I just wanted you to know. You said *No*, and it may have been the most important thing anyone has ever done for me."

He felt a stab of intense disappointment. He could not allow himself to verbalize the feeling, but on the level just below verbalization what he was thinking was, *Shit, there goes my chance*. Trapped into nobility again.

"I don't feel like I did anything so special," he said. "If I was to be honest, I'd say it was something I had to do for the sake of the firm."

"That's just the point," she said. "You have your priorities in order. Listen, I've bothered you long enough." She rose to her feet. "I don't expect this to make any difference in my status around here. I know you have to wait and see how I do, you can't just go on what I say I'm going to do. But I wanted you to know I *heard* you. I wanted you to know I'm working on it." She paused, looked bashful. "May I—"

She stepped around his desk, bent, and brushed his cheek with her lips. He was so startled he almost fell over backward. Her lips were cool and dry. Her musky perfume hung about him. "Thank you," she whispered.

At the door, she said, "Say hello to Lianne. I saw her last time I went."

"Went?"

"To therapy," she said, and was gone. So he sat there with a hard-on, ashamed that she knew Lianne took therapy. Therapy had probably saved Lianne's life, it was a thing to be proud of, not ashamed of, and Tina herself had just sat before him confessing she went too, for worse and deeper troubles. And still it felt shameful to have her know, a weakness in his masculinity, in the unity and perfection of his marriage.

The memory of her kiss, her perfume: It was a donated moment, a gift from life itself, which almost never gave anything without a cost. The gate of heaven had swung for just an instant, and music and lamplight had spilled out, the air of a cool and fragrant evening.

It took him half an hour to become calm enough to go home. A few minutes after their talk, he saw Tina swinging across the parking lot in the last ruddy glow of sunset. He went into his bathroom and masturbated. Then leaned his forehead against the cool glass of the cabinet mirror. "What the hell am I doing?" he said aloud.

When he got home, Lianne met him at the door. He could see at a glance that she was both terrified and furious. "Charles," she said, "what the hell have you been doing?"

18

BAD MOON
ON THE RISE

It was pretty confusing for a while.

"I always wondered why you owned that saloon," she said. She had her arms folded across her chest, and she was glaring at him, her face white and bony.

"What are you talking about? Come home, all I want is kick my shoes off, have a drink." They were standing in the foyer. He was still holding his briefcase.

"That's where you meet them." She turned and stalked into the living room.

"Meet who?" he said, following, gesturing, his palms extended, the innocent supplicant. The briefcase dangling from the right hand, so the gesture felt stupid.

She was behind the bar, clinking and clanking. Making him a martini. For lack of anything better to do with her hands? Habit? Who the hell are we?

"Whoever hangs out down there," she said, slamming the cocktail glass down on the bar, slopping about half the drink out. "The Mafia. Drug runners. Hired assassins."

He dropped the briefcase and tossed the martini back.

"I was a fool to think you could make all that money honestly," she said. "Believing in you all this time and you played me for a fool." She marched out of the room.

He raked the puddle on the bar into his glass, getting most of it. "Never a dull moment," he said, toasting her absence. He had the distinct feeling this was a more-than-one-martini scene. Glass wasn't big enough either. He dumped his cubes and the twist in a tumbler. A dollop of Boissiere, quadruple dollop of Fleischmann's.

Sound of the piano now. She was in the library, pounding away. He felt like an alcoholic war correspondent. To the front, at the risk of life and limb.

" 'Revolutionary Étude,' " he said, coming in to stand behind her. Proud of recognizing the piece. Trying to score points with her. In the middle of a fight. *We seem to proceed on several levels,* he thought.

She answered by playing twice as loudly, if that was possible with Rachmaninoff.

When the last thunder had died out, she began flipping sheets so fiercely he thought she would tear them out. Snap snap snap through the music.

"Do you want to talk about it?" he said.

"Maybe you'd better talk to me about it," she said.

The bench locked her in position. There was no natural way for her to turn to him. He walked around to face her at an angle over the keyboard. She was angry, all right, but she was also frightened. Her lower lip was trembling. Her soul was in that lower lip. He could see her trying to hold it together, like shaping a globe of water with your hands in zero g.

"Be glad to, if I knew what *it* was," he said.

"You know." Her gaze went through him. Looking at something that wasn't there. "And I know. I knew all along." She shook her head angrily. "I hate it when she's right about me. Hiding from the truth so I can get what I want." The line of her mouth was utterly grim, the recurved clamp of a reptile's jaw. But the brilliant green eyes were filling with tears.

"You don't have to *go* to hell," she said. "If you deceive yourself, you're already there. That's the way it is in hell. To be hated by terrible people and they're *right* about you."

He saw himself calling Tucker. Sedation, the men in white coats. Commitment papers. Hushing it up. Half of her comes back home, wounded, more fragile than ever. The famous nervous breakdown. At least one in every good Southern family.

"Lianne, what the fuck?" he said.

Her eyes found his. Sudden hostile focus again. "The phones are bugged," she said.

It took him a while to be convinced, even when she showed him one of the button microphones. The phones were bugged, that was why they had been playing rock and roll. Though he couldn't exactly see how the one followed from the other.

"What the shit," he said finally. "I don't *know* why."

"People don't just bug phones for no reason."

"Maybe they do—how would I know? It doesn't mean I'm in the fucking Mafia."

"Charles, it's either the police or the crooks. Nobody else does it."

"Maybe it's your mother."

"What do you mean?" It was a good thing she wasn't holding a knife.

"Who else would bug us? Maybe it's Elaine. Maybe she wants to have us arrested for unnatural acts or something."

"Don't be ridiculous."

Mrs. Weatherall had been dead set against the marriage, tell me why. Her little baby was hooking up with a millionaire, wasn't she? Most mommas would be blissed out. Momma wasn't averse to money, no, you knew that from the years she had spent sucking up to the Freemans.

Momma liked control, that's what it was. And once Lianne married him, all chance of control was gone. The immemorial to-the-death competition between the Miz (short for miserable) and her excessively glorious daughter. When the girl succeeded, she had sold her soul, hardened her heart against the truth, or fallen in with the wrong crowd. Success meant she was going to hell forever. So when she won Miss Little Rock. So when she turned star newscaster.

And so so so when she married Charles Morrison.

The Miz had made out that her resistance was on moral grounds. Charles had, at that time, a bit of a local reputation as a playboy.—Sad how little we have before the rumors of our joy outstrip anything we will ever actually experience, so that we wind up bitterly envied for pleasures we've never known. Still, he had had the reputation—and, if the truth be known, actually *had* been running just a little bit wild at the time, had been playing around just the tiniest bit, had even been involved with gasp gasp shudder a married woman for a few weeks.

Elaine had for godsake written a letter to her pastor. Had written Charles a long bitter letter. Had snubbed him at the reception (oh yeah, she had *come* to it). Had done everything but picket out in front of the church with a sign.

If she had known he was an *atheist*. . . But Lianne had persuaded him to keep quiet around her mother, at least until after the marriage.

Of course she had bugged their phones. If it wasn't her, who the hell could it be? But why now, after all these years? He was pissed, royally pissed. He hadn't done a goddamn blessed thing, and here somebody had upset his wife so bad it would probably be years before he had a peaceful evening again. Shit, she might never quite believe him. He couldn't live with that. They would have to get divorced. Freedom. Solitude. Independence. Tina's kiss came into his mind. Her powdersmooth lips rasping his late-afternoon stubble. Her perfume, like getting fucked by gardenia mush-rooms from Mars. With antlers.

He didn't know who had bugged the phones, but he was going to find out. He was going to raise hell in this town. He was going to make himself another martini.

"It doesn't make sense," he said, at the bar. She had followed him in. Turn and turn about. Adrenaline was catching. He had Lianne's now. That and a swallow of martini made him giddy. He felt reckless. It was exciting, being bugged. They were the center of attention.

"When you put your arms around me at night, I won't know who's holding me. I won't know where you've been and what you've been doing."

"You're going to have to trust me," he said. The recklessness carried him on. The hell with it. Enough beating around the bush. Say what you gotta say, boy, let's rock and roll. "This is twice you've gone into a tizzy like this and I haven't done anything," he said. He couldn't, for the mo-ment, remember what the other time had been.

"What about the phones?" she said. "How do you explain that?"

"I don't explain it," he said. "I don't have the foggiest."

Her mother no longer seemed so likely. After the wedding, the woman had slowly become more civil. Then she had begun dropping by when she thought Charles was out of the house. For days after one of her visits Lianne would be alternately depressed and hyperactive—moody and silent or continually bitchy. But he had put up with it. Then when Lianne decided to leave KROK, Mrs. Weatherall had flown into such a fit—in nineteen short years Lianne would be fifty, and where would she be then if Charles left her, as he surely would, since there was no way she could hold on to such a good money-maker after her figure went—that Charles had forbid-den Momma the house except on special occasions. And then she had to call first.

But even if she had sneaked in while Clemmie was out shopping, no way could she have bugged the phones herself. Nor could Charles see her paying to have it done. Too cheap. Also she had the malice but not the style: just not the sort of punishment she would think of.

"It just doesn't make sense," he said again. "It's some kind of mistake."

"People don't accidentally bug the wrong house," she said icily. "It's not like delivering a pizza to the wrong address."

"Actually, they do," he said. "At least, you read about these drug agents busting in and—" At the look on her face: "Ok, ok. But you don't know how crazy this is making me. I have no idea why anybody would want to do this. Why does it have to be me? What about you? What are *you* up to? You and the book club ladies running a whorehouse out of the library?''

"Charles," she said.

"Yeah, but see how it feels? What if I came home and pitched into you, how would you like it? You know *you* didn't do anything. I know *I* didn't. You want a martini?'' She didn't. He made himself another one.

"It's crazy, that's all," he continued. "This is a weird world. Weird things happen.''

"Not this kind of weird. This isn't like getting hit by lightning," she said.

"Not what I mean," he said, finishing a swallow. "Two billion people, that's a lot of different motives flying around. Who can keep track? I'm not going to bust my butt trying to figure out why some crank has set me up.'' He looked at her. He felt the thrill of assertion. "And I'm not going to let you bust my balls about something I don't have any damn idea about.''

It went off her, she was impervious. She didn't care what he said right now; she just wanted to get it settled.

"Maybe it's been there a long time," he said. "Maybe it's left over from something Dad was doing years ago. He used to do some FBI work.''

"You can't get off that easy. The telephone man said it was state-of-the-art. He said they didn't even make that kind before 1975.''

"So maybe it's a disgruntled plaintiff or something. Somebody lost a suit and wants to get back at me, maybe thinks they can get something on me.''

Gradually, indirectly, they settled on an arrangement. Lianne, instead of blaming Charles, would try to transfer her anxiety into anger against whoever had done the bugging. They would go into therapy together, taking extra sessions with Father Christmas. Meantime, they wouldn't sleep together, not until she was sure, not until she'd worked through her fear. And they would hire a private detective to find out who had bugged the phones, and why.

The only private detectives Charles knew were ex-cops, ex-military, or ex-FBI. Some were hacks, and some were pretty good. He had hired a couple of the better pros for the firm from time to time, but it wasn't like detective novels. He didn't think Lianne knew that. They weren't sensitive literate mythopoetic truth-hounds. Given the nearly universal enforcement background, they were 99 percent likely to be political conservatives if not hard-line right-wingers, especially in the South—flat-eyed suspicious mechanics who didn't believe in God any more than Charles did, and who viewed their clients as skeptically as they did the adulterers, embezzlers, skipped husbands, hot-check artists, and crooked contractors they were sometimes paid to track down.

"I know somebody," Lianne said.

She was talking about J. D. Rider, of all people. J. D. had gone into the private detecting business, that was what he was up to nowadays. J. D. was sensitive, literate, and mythopoetic. In Charles's opinion, he hadn't had the balls to make it as a lawyer, and Charles didn't see any way he would have the balls to make it as a detective. Much less the contacts, because that was really what the job was: telephone numbers. You had to have a long list of telephone numbers.

But if it made Lianne happy—he could always look around for somebody else on his own.

"I'll get him to come for the book club meeting," she said. "That way it'll be two men."

Oh shit, Charles thought.

The book club meeting was on May 8, and he had just now realized that he had promised he'd go to Lafayette's party the same day. Oh shit. Then he got mad. Goddammit, why couldn't he go to a perfectly innocent party when he wanted to? He wasn't going to cave in on this one.

Didn't mean he had to bring it up just right this moment, though.

"That's two weeks off," he said. "Don't you think we ought to get after this right away? Before the trail gets cold?"

"Yes. We can bring him in and talk to him. But I *am* going to invite him to the book club. After all, he writes books himself."

This was news to Charles. "He does?"

"He has these cases, and then, when they're over, he writes these little mystery novels. It's part of his fee. They have to sign a waiver."

Charles sometimes thought he was the only lawyer left on earth who didn't secretly think of himself as a novelist. "Guess I haven't checked the best-seller lists lately."

She ignored him. "Besides, it'll make a good cover. In case anybody's watching us."

"Oh good Lord," Charles said.

Neither of them thought of going to the police. Lianne didn't trust the police, even though there were plenty of good old boys out there who were decent and fair and honest. For Charles, it was a question of Sonny Raymond. This was just Sonny Raymond's meat, plenty of potential for headlines. And with the way Raymond felt about Morrison, Morrison, and Chenowyth—

No, no way. Whatever you do, stay away from Sonny.

"How did that little job go?" Sonny Raymond said. "You get anything yet?"

"What job?" said Cheese.

"Goddammit," Sonny Raymond said. "The goddamn tape recording crap."

"Oh," said Cheese.

"*Well?*" said Sonny Raymond.

Cheese didn't know what to say. He had set the bugs himself. He liked to think that he would have made a good cat burglar if he hadn't devoted his life to law and order. But then he had gotten home, and there were some pieces left over. The kit had had a lot of extras, so it didn't necessarily mean there was a problem. He was pretty sure not. But then, when he had played back the first day's tapes, all he could hear was the devil's music, some of his son's rock and roll. It was faint, as if it had been recorded over by a blank tape but had left a ghost. But it was there. He got on the boy's back, but the kid swore he hadn't ever borrowed any of his daddy's equipment, and you had to believe them when they told you flat out, didn't you?

So Cheese had driven over to the Morrison place, maybe they weren't home and he could get back in to scope it out. And had seen the telephone company truck. Oh shit.

Might as well get it over with. "They found out somehow," he said.

It was loud for a while. Sonny wondered in a voice that sounded like it might show up in the papers tomorrow just from sheer decibel level, no reporters necessary, how the hell he had thought somebody dumb enough to mess with jellied pig by-products could successfully install an electronic listening device all by his little lonesome self. But Cheese had done some pretty good yelling himself from time to time, and in his opinion the same could happen to anybody and he still might make governor before Sonny did. So he just bowed up and waited it out.

When Sonny got calmer, Cheese explained that he was pretty sure there was no way they could trace the bugs back.

"If they did, we would have heard from a lawyer by now," Sonny said. He appeared to think. "You know, this aint all to the bad," he said.

"It aint?" Cheese said.

"Think it over," Sonny said. "How come them to get on to us so soon? *They had to be expecting it.* And that means they're into something. They're doing *something* they ought not to. All we got to do now is find out what." He leaned back in his chair, looking pleased.

"I had that very thought," Cheese said. "You don't reckon they could be mixed into this Orsini-killing drug ring thing, do you?"

Sonny Raymond waggled a hand. "It's something," he said. "Don't matter what. The main thing is that we aint just fishing around anymore." His face darkened. "The bad news is we can't put another tap on em. You done blown that. They'll be checking for it from now on."

"Maybe we could put a couple of agents on em," Cheese said.

"Agents? Jesus Christ, man. What am I supposed to pay for a couple of extra men with, tell me that? Damn Beaumont's busting my balls so bad already, where am I going to get another thousand a week? And this could take a *long* time." Sonny thought, not for the first time, how if he could make a big drug bust and there was say several hundred thousand lying around—

"Not that kind of agents," Cheese said. "I'm thinking some of these boys walks both sides of the street, you know. We got one or two owe us some favors."

"You're talking wrong boys."

"You got it. Let me use my underworld contacts, and—"

"Your underworld contacts."

"Suppose we knew something on a couple people, and we leaned on em. Like, you know, you can help us out, or we come in and. I mean, some guys, all we do is we say, Listen, we'll live and let live, but you need to help us out here. I could get em cheap."

"I don't want to hear nothing more about this," Sonny Raymond said. "But—"

Sonny held up his hand. There was something in his eye, he was trying to blink it out. "The law can't afford to use that kind of tactics. You ought to know that." He blinked again.

"You need to get that eye looked at," Cheese said.

Lianne got in touch with J. D. Rider the next day. Rider came and looked the place over, collected the bugs, and said he would farm them out to see if he could establish their provenance. He actually used that word, provenance, flicking a quick ironic smile.

They were in the library again, the most august space in the house. Octagonal, of course. Two floors of books, each equipped with rolling ladders. A balustered landing on the second floor, also octagonal, opening onto the halls through archways in three walls (Charles's office was directly across one hall). The Steinway grand that had been given such a workout yesterday. Leather reading chairs, splendid lamps, both on this first floor and on the landing above. Two antique writing desks, fully supplied. Liquor caddies. A massive marble-faced stone firewell in the east wall, offering a hearth to each floor. Stained-glass lights in the northeast and southeast windows. Above, in the semicathedral ceiling, spotlighting for the shelves. A central chandelier, octagonal in design, hung with thin panes of stained glass. The chandelier had been specially ordered and was now fifty years old.

Charles had taken them into the room, feeling a need to impress Rider.

He was taller than Charles, with a fresh complexion, an impressively hooked nose, and blue eyes under a profusion of black curls—the sort of coloring Charles thought of as Welsh. He was wearing denims, cowboy boots, and an expensive short-sleeve pullover. He was lean, but acrobatically muscled. Even when he sat, his biceps and torso flexed visibly, and Charles remembered seeing him at the Y. In fact, now that he thought, Rider was nearly always there when Charles arrived, and he was nearly always there when Charles left.

Charles figured him at six two and a deceptive 205. The black curls were receding, he noticed with pleasure, the high forehead gaining. He was as far gone as Charles was, and a lot younger. "Not that I expect where they came from to tell us much," Rider said, jiggling the bugs in his hand. "That's not how I mostly work."

Oh boy, Charles thought.

"Rock and roll," Rider said, and grinned. "This ought to be a good one."

"No novels," Charles said. "If we hire you, you're not writing a book about us."

"Don't worry," Rider said. "I don't think there's a story in this. Only about one in twenty is interesting enough. And I change all the names anyway."

"No novels," Charles said. "You'll have to add a clause."

"I'm having a book club meeting two weeks from Friday," Lianne said. "Could you come and sort of mingle? It would give you a good excuse to check around."

"I don't really see the point—" Charles began.

"Sure," Rider said. To Charles he said, *"That's* how I work. I mess around and I get to know everybody you know, and after a while I tell you who did it."

"This is just a bunch of poetry-reading ladies," Charles said. "They didn't bug anybody's phones."

"You never know," Rider said. "I have to get a complete picture of your life." He studied Charles's face. "That's if you want me on the job. If you don't . . ." His eyes went to Lianne.

"We do," she said.

"Fine," Rider said. "Who are y'all doing at the meeting?"

Charles gave up and walked away. Then, to have a reason for walking away, he went across the hall and through the sitting room to make himself a martini. When he came back, Rider was ready to leave. The detective patted Lianne on the shoulder.

"Listen," he said. "Y'all are under some strain." He included Charles. "When something like this happens, people tend to lash around a lot and take it out on each other. But y'all are both good people, and you need to hold together, ok? Ok?''

He came up to Charles, who was standing with his martini, still in the doorway, surprised at the man's familiarity. At his *accuracy*. Rider flicked a nail against the glass, making a tone. "I'll grow on you," he said, and was gone.

Charles looked at Lianne, as if to say, Well? Are we going to hold together? She tried to smile, but couldn't, pulled her trembling mouth wide and down. It was her scowl of forbearance: I'm being as fair as I can—oh, touch me not. "Ok," he said.

They slept apart again that night, he in the sneak-away bedroom, she in their regular bed, up on the third floor. He read himself to sleep with Larry Niven's *Ringworld,* a book he'd been meaning to get to for a long time. He didn't read in bed with Lianne very often. She always wanted to talk, or to watch the television, and even though she used the earphones, he found the picture distracting. He told himself he was having fun, there was a lot to be said for just being on your own, doing what you wanted to when you wanted to. He dreamed, at first, of riding horses across a grassy plain with Halrloprillalar, the bald-headed spacewoman. The plains converged ahead, not to a horizon, but to a strip that curved into the sky, vanishing.

He came awake during the small hours, panicked and dislocated, as if the room were underground rather than two floors into the air, as if its darkness were the darkness of a mausoleum. He felt stifled and made his way out to the patio. A gibbous moon rode high in the east, sullen over the city. Tenuous smokes of cloud drifted past, showing a frail radiance, spectral nacre. His heart slowed. The panic subsided to a flutter of vulnerability, a sort of intermittent thrill in the chest, a flexible blade of fear that cut when he moved against it.

He tried to understand the source of the fear. He thought that maybe it was the no-win situation he would have to face soon, choosing whether to go to the party or to Lianne's book club meeting. Or maybe it was a reaction from taking the hard line at the firm Monday. It hadn't been cheerful there today. He had forgotten, in the exhilaration of asserting himself, that he always had a reaction afterward, doubted himself twice as much.

It took him a while to realize that he was frightened for the same reason Lianne was. It had finally sunk in. Someone had bugged their phones. Someone had invaded their lives. Out there in the darkness somewhere, under the lopsided moon, they had enemies.

19

NOBLE ROT

Charles came into the kitchen to get a glass of cold milk before he left. Clemmie was settling a bottle of white wine into the cooler. On the center island, a tray of canapés—smoked salmon rolled and tooth-picked onto crusts of bread, little square cucumber-on-whole-wheat sandwiches. He grabbed a handful to have with his milk. He liked the cucumber especially, the way Clemmie did them, layering filmy slices onto a bed of Hellmann's mayonnaise, dashing a sprinkle of salt, sprinkling a dash of fresh pepper.

Clemmie flashed him a look, taking in the tuxedo. It was that quick, wise, dismissive look, the one that women do best, the one that sums you instantly, instantly inventories your many shortcomings, the one that tells you you are in more trouble than you can know, poor dumb dog.

"Get something to eat at the other party," she said.

"Now, Clemmie."

"I don't care," she said. "She asked you a month ago."

"Try two weeks." Lianne had finally quit hinting and asked him directly to sit in on the book club meeting, and he had told her about the May eighth party. She had not seemed surprised. Nor had she burst into anger. Not that things could have gotten any worse between them if she had. They hadn't slept together since when? Since their last night at the lake, he now realized.

"Leaving her alone, as scared as she is," Clemmie said. Clemmie herself looked frightened. She was afraid this was it, this issue would finally take them down.

And it might. They had a joint meeting scheduled for Wednesday with Ian Farber, the therapist she insisted on calling Father Christmas, but the marriage might be finished before they got there. They had not talked to each other about this evening, the division in their plans. They had hardly talked at all. They had managed, nevertheless, to wage an intense subliminal war, whose terms were perfectly clear. This night was a breaking point. And the more sharply she had drawn the line, the more stubbornly he had wanted to step across it.

"What can happen?" he said to Clemmie. "She's going to be surrounded by friends all evening. Anyway, I hate these hen parties, and she knows it."

"It's not a hen party. That detective, remember? And if you were there—"

"Oh, so he's still coming?"

Charles had gotten in touch with Freddy Mayfield, a county cop he had once called as a witness, to see if Mayfield would recommend a detective. Mayfield was a Baptist, but he could be trusted. He had testified against his own department in a wrongful-injury suit. He hadn't wanted to, and he hadn't been promoted since—but in his view the truth was the truth, and you told it all. He and Charles had formed one of those odd-couple friendships, mutual respect across polar differences. Charles was pretty sure Mayfield hoped to convert him someday.

He had told Lianne about his plans to hire another detective, but she had kept on with Rider. Apparently she thought they needed one apiece, the way things were going.

"He isn't coming, he's here. They're all here already. Your tie is crooked."

She came over and straightened his bow tie. "Quit fidgeting. You're as bad as a boy getting a haircut." She went back to the wine in the ice bucket, settled a cloth around the bottle. "I don't think you have any idea how hard it is to work in a house where it's always so tense," she said. "I wish the two of you would think of me just once."

"It's not always tense," he said.

She scooped up the tray of canapés.

The doorbell rang. "Phooey," she said. "Get that, will you? I'll just have to make two trips."

"Who is it?" he said. "I thought you said they were all here."

"Probably the author," she said, balancing the tray as she backed the door open. The doorbell rang again, and he went to answer it. *The author?* he thought.

On the stoop in the twilight, a baby-faced fellow two inches or so shorter than Charles, with disordered brownish-blond hair and helium-blue eyes behind thick lenses in a black frame. He carried a thin green volume with a map on its cover, and a manila folder stuffed with papers. He wore a white cotton shirt whose cloth was too thin, a striped polyester tie in chocolate and navy, an off-cream linen jacket that by its cut was obviously a suit coat, and a pair of raw silk dark brown slacks. The slacks, which were probably his fanciest and most expensive item of clothing, were a mistake: cut pleated and full over his substantial rump, and already losing their shape, they made his short legs seem even shorter. His brown lace-ups were shiny, but heel-worn at the outside edge, and his belt was too wide.

The author said something that sounded like "Ramalam butler," and Charles smiled.

"No," he said. "I'm Charles Morrison. The tux is just for a party."

The author blushed, and made an effort to enunciate. His accent was pure Mississippi mud, thicker even than Tucker's, and he was one of those who had trouble moving their lips when they talked. "I'm sorry," he said. "What I said was my *name* is Jack Butler." He looked uncertain. "I'm—ah—supposed to be here? For a book club?"

"Come on in," Charles said. "It must be your book they're doing."

He led the author through the huge foyer, down the hall to the kitchen. "You have a nice place," the author said, trying hard not to gawk, but resembling nonetheless a tourist in the Smithsonian. Charles became aware of his house in a curious and pleasant way, as a *place* rather than an extension of his needs and moods. He felt the light, the space, the sweep of design.

"Yeah, houses are alive, aren't they?" Charles said. "You can feel what kind of living has gone on in them."

They went onto the sun porch, and through it out into the back garden.

It was a perfect tea-party evening, three tables of ladies in light dresses and organdy hats under the mild and cloudy sky. The bugs weren't bad yet, so the club could stay out after the garden lights came on, and there would be chatter, the tinkle of laughter, the tinkle of spoons and glasses. Petits-fours with coffee later.

J. D. leaned back at one of the tables, affecting a bomber jacket this evening in spite of the pleasant weather, his booted feet thrust forward. The talk flowed around him, so that he seemed like a log fallen into a creek, at once included and ignored. He gave Charles a nod.

Charles waved to Dee-Dee, who lowered her eyes and went on talking. So she knew how things stood. Perhaps Lianne had felt them come up, but she did not turn around. Well, fuck her, then. He shivered in a wash of adrenaline. Freedom was just around the corner. Blank madness was just around the corner.

"I always wanted the whole horse, and not just the horse's head," Natalie was saying.

"I liked the flower ones," Dee-Dee said. "They were these English prints; of course I didn't know that then. But they would be in these darling ceramic pots.''

Alison, younger than the rest, sat with her shoes off and her feet curled under, puzzled and big-eyed, listening. She and Greg had gotten back from the island Sunday, but Charles hadn't seen Greg yet, so didn't know how they were doing. But she flashed him a look he would have sworn was gratitude, and he felt warmed. He had his friends. He wasn't entirely the outsider.

"The kittens were my favorite," Carol said.

"Dogs," Lianne said. "Definitely the dogs."

Charles cleared his throat, and Lianne looked around, got to her feet. "You must be," she said, taking the author's hand. He shook awkwardly.

She turned to the women. "This is the author of tonight's book." There was a rustle of interest, and then a patter of light applause. Butler looked nonplussed.

"Have a seat here in the middle," Lianne said, leading him to a chair.

"What were y'all—if you don't mind," Butler said. He looked for a place to put his materials, and Lianne moved a drink table to his elbow. He laid the book and the folder down, and sat. "What were y'all talking about when I came up, those animals and all?"

"Would you like some wine?" Lianne said.

"Trading cards," said Dee-Dee.

"It's a decent chardonnay," Lianne said. "Drier than most, and a bit sunny."

"You used to get them at Heights Variety," Barbara said.

"*I* never did," Alison said. "I haven't the foggiest what y'all are talking about." Charles hadn't the foggiest either. But he had heard this sort of thing before, and he hated it, the flurry of knickknack, the smother of silly trivial detail.

"Well, toodle-oo to you too," Dee-Dee said. "While you've got the wine out, Lianne—"

Butler ran his hand through his hair, not affecting it much. "Was it a game, or what?"

"No, you traded them," Natalie said.

"You bought packs, and you traded for the ones you liked best," Barbara explained.

"What on earth for?" Charles said, still standing. The women looked up at him blankly.

"Like baseball cards?" Butler said, and one or two of the women nodded.

"Yeah," Charles said, "but those were *about* somebody. I mean, they had real people on them." The hell with this. It was time to go.

"Well, maybe these were real horses," Natalie said.

"I think some of the flowers were maybe photographs," Barbara said.

"Did they do this everywhere, or was it just Little Rock?" Butler said, and Charles realized he was doing research. Though what use you could make of something like this—

"I have no idea," Lianne said, and a few of the others shrugged. She looked around at them. "I just thought everybody did it."

"Remember poodle skirts?" Reba said.

"Poodle skirts?" Butler said.

That's it, Charles thought. *That is absolutely it.*

And yet he didn't go. The women were leaning forward to Butler, gesturing, talking, setting each other off in trills of laughter. He looked up, to see Rider watching him watch the others. The garden lights came on, like a signal.

Lianne stood. "We'd better get started," she called. Then, in a quieter voice: "As y'all know, we've been doing Arkansas authors." She turned to Butler. "We've already done Don Harington and Miller Williams and Buddy Portis and Jim Whitehead," she explained. "You're our second poet. Well, Whitehead's a poet too, but we did him as a novel."

"*Joiner,*" Butler said.

"I want to begin by asking you about your book title," Lianne said. "And then other people can ask whatever they want to. How did you come up with that name? I mean, I see the map points to Hollywood, Arkansas, but—" She sat back down, attentive.

"I have this friend named Johnny Wink," Butler said. "And he bet me one time that Los Angeles was east of Reno, Nevada."

A buzz of discussion: No way. You mean *west,* don't you, Los Angeles *California*? Let's get a map. Charles laughed, visualizing the longitude lines.

"Sounds like an old bar bet," he said.

"Well, he was right," Butler said. "Which I might have known, because every time I call he does have a flush. I told him next he was going to tell me Iceland was south of the Florida Keys."

"It *isn't* though," Alison said, looking worried.

"Anyway, the poems were about when I had a cabin out in the woods. And I thought how we think of Hollywood as the most far-out place in America. And geographically as the most far west, because it's on the ocean. So what's even more far out than Hollywood, you see? Maybe what's right in front of you. Maybe when everybody looks at pictures and nobody reads, to write poems. So the cabin was five miles west of Hollywood, Arkansas, and so—"

Charles looked at his watch. Butler caught the motion.

"So I called it *West of Hollywood*," he finished. "It was my little joke on Johnny Wink."

"How do you get your ideas?" Alison said.

"How do you *keep* from getting them?" Butler said. He gestured excitedly.

"Americans, maybe because we used to be a frontier, but we're afraid of ideas. We have like a filter, don't think this, don't think that, don't say anything that might upset somebody, and so all our schools are crippled. We can't teach anything interesting because it might upset somebody. It's like—I don't mean this politically, but it's like Frank White and that Act 590, that creation science amendment. And then that letter he sent Governor's School."

Governor's School: the state's annual roundup of the best and brightest, some four hundred high-schoolers sent off to brain camp for six weeks of the summer between their junior and senior years. On the Hendrix campus, because the college held no summer sessions. Begun by Bill Clinton, but now Frank had written Bob Meriwether, the director, a threatening letter, warning against the School's liberal, freethinking, humanistic bias. Meriwether had been Charles's freshman adviser, a huge booming roué, and he smiled now, imagining Meriwether and the governor *mano a mano*, two giant round white-haired men belly to belly, slugging it out.

Butler would pick up a badly needed couple of hundred as a visiting writer during the School. Of course Frank's letter disturbed him. Nervous now, though, torn between his so-called principles and the fundamental tenet of artistic practice everywhere: Never offend a patron. He probably thought they were all Republicans. He would shit if he knew how many strings Charles had pulled. Frank was going to back off. Give him a few weeks to whip up a menu—sauces and gravies to smother the taste—but the governor was going to *eat* that crow.

"I mean, to me," Butler faltered, "that just represents the worst thing about—the most unfortunate— Don't-get-me-wrong-I-love-Arkansas-but." He surveyed the indecipherable faces, summoned a breath. "That letter was just flat-out *wicked,* and it put a chill on education here."

"No shit," Dee-Dee said. Butler shot her a look of intense relief.

"You don't have to be vulgar about it," Barbara said.

"No shit shit shit," Dee-Dee said. Now Butler looked embarrassed again—starting a quarrel among patrons, inappropriate behavior. What a case.

That's why he was still here, Charles decided. He was an observer of human nature, and this was a specimen he hadn't seen up close before: The Writer.

"Who are your major influences?" Lianne said, changing the subject.

Serious now, the arts critic. Her penetrating look. *I can read her like a goddamn book,* Charles thought.

His eyes stung, and he felt a tremendous helpless woe, like the lift and downslam of a black wave when you swam off the island at night. That it should come to no more than this: the venality, the tedium, the utter predictability. He didn't *want* to go, he wanted to be warm and happy and safe at home. But he could not give in now, not on these terms. Standing while the others sat, hovering on the margins of darkness while the others chatted in lamplight. No use prolonging the pain. It was over. He drew in his breath, straightened his coat.

"Science fiction and the Bible," Butler said.

Charles felt his knees go weak. He found a chair. Butler was explaining, but Charles could not follow the explanation. He felt his mind full of spinning things, of a tumbling brightness, of a busy movement like fall wind in the brilliant trees, like a spring creek in a canyon.

Butler was going to read something, not poems, he was writing stories now, he wanted to read a new story. Charles could hear the hunger in his voice, the hunger to be heard. *Yes,* Charles thought. *Read me a science fiction story: a brand-new sort of story.*

He had read Shakespeare, yeah, and he liked it ok, the parts he could understand, and Hemingway, which he understood just fine but didn't see the point of, and some others since college, Ludlum and Cheever and Stephen King and John D. MacDonald, but you know what, it was always the same old quarrels, the same old motives, the same old world. Give him a hollow world of stainless steel, with the trees and the sky on the inside; give him intelligent worms of hyperdense matter that swam in the magma, to whom this crust, these continents, were a wispy near-nothing, less than atmosphere; give him spaceships whose brains were the salvaged brains of humans mangled in accidents, who sailed the eternal void singing an eternal loneliness; give him a world of tall red mountains, in whose green sky hung three blue suns.

Give him, for God's sake, something *different.*

His mind was racing so hard he couldn't concentrate. Butler's story was about a farm woman, Miriam Bone. He hoped it wasn't going to be one of those *sensitive* science fiction stories, worn-down rural female protagonist, her hard-bitten suspicious husband, the new neighbors aint like folks around here, but she brings covered dishes, they turn out to be from Antares or Procyon or Deneb IV, stellar pacifists, the old man sneaks over with a shotgun, sees them undisguised and dies of a heart attack. Having caused his death, even unintentionally, disturbs the aliens so badly they have to spare the earth the shame of their presence, but they leave her some high-tech superproducing seeds to feed her hungry children, and she looks up at the stars at night and knows gentleness is right and she's not alone in the universe.

This story seemed to have a lot of tomatoes in it. Charles kept waiting for something to happen, but nothing ever did, just Jesus and a lot of tomatoes.

Butler had been reading for almost twenty minutes when Charles realized the story was never going to be science fiction. He couldn't figure out why he didn't leave. Lianne was as cold as ever. The war between them was still on. But he no longer wanted to go. He felt confirmed in his chair, immobile but powerful, as if he were stone and gravity had tripled.

This was *his* place, damn it. Lianne was not going to drive him away. He thought of Tina resentfully, as if she and Lafayette had planned their party for no other purpose than to cause him trouble at home. So he didn't show up, so what? So he had promised Lafayette, so what? He didn't *owe* the man anything, he was the boss, it was just a favor in the first place.

Butler was *still* reading, and since nothing was going on, you couldn't tell how long it would be till the end. More tomatoes, and taking an outdoor shit, and then later volunteer tomatoes coming up from seeds in the shit and the woman eating the volunteers.

But then something happened in a pickup, and then the standard brave soul-in-the-blank-void-face-of-darkness ending, and the performance was thank God over.

"That was really interesting," Alison said.

"It was awfully explicit," Barbara said.

"Well I don't think so," Natalie said. "I think it's realism."

"Did that really happen to you?" Alison said.

"No," Butler said. "I don't write autobiographical fiction. I don't think the author belongs in his own stories."

Charles understood that Butler was bragging. But he had so little shrewdness, so little understanding of human nature, that he failed to manipulate his audience to the desired response. "Now, my *poetry* is autobiographical," he said, leaning forward.

Dee-Dee had gotten up and gone over to sit with Lianne. Several of the others were gathering their purses and jackets. Rider had refilled his wineglass and was sitting down again. Dee-Dee and Lianne were talking a mile a minute. *Comparing notes on me?* Charles wondered. Dee-Dee, feeling his attention, glanced his way, kept talking.

Departure became a formal process. The ladies filed by to pat Butler on the arm, thank yew, we just enjoyed that so much, I can't wait till your next book comes out, Reverend.

Slowly, like a statue coming to life, Charles rose and walked over.

"Well," Butler said. "Thanks. —I guess I ought to say goodbye to Mrs. Morrison?"

"Come on," Charles said. They stood at her elbow while Lianne finished what she was saying. Dee-Dee pointed with her eyes, and Lianne looked around. She stood, took Butler's hand.

"Thanks a lot," Butler said. "I've always thought there was a lot more interest in literature out there than people thought there was. It's really encouraging when people like you—"

"Our pleasure," Lianne said, glancing at Charles. He would not have believed there could be so much nothing in anyone's eyes. "Keep up the good work," she said, and retrieved her hand. Dee-Dee leaned back, a loose grin on her flushed face.

"Jayme said to tell you hello," Butler said.

"I'm sorry?" Lianne said.

"You gave her the crown. When you were Miss Little Rock. She was the one after you, and you put the crown on her head. She said to say hello."

Lianne was nonplussed. She didn't like being reminded of her title; she preferred to treat it as the forgotten vanity of a silly young girl.

"June 17, 1961," Butler said.

"Five years before our wedding," Charles said, "less one day." He got the flash of hatred he sought. *What are you up to? Is this a test?*

Dee-Dee rolled her head back. "All the Former Miss Somebodies," she said. A hurt look crossed Butler's face, cloud shadow on a windy day.

"Of course I remember Jayme," Lianne said. "She's very pretty. Do tell her hello for me."

Rider had come up, and Lianne said to him, "Do you want to go inside?" She turned back to Butler. "I don't mean to rush you off—we have some business we need to talk over."

So, Charles thought. I stayed, but it cuts no ice. Busy busy busy, no time for Charles.

"Oh, no," Butler said. "No, I've got to be going, I just wanted to say thanks."

"Hang around awhile," Charles said. "I don't have any business to talk over." Lianne gave him a brief, incurious look. Not even anger now. Totally absorbed in her mission once more, her paranoia, who had bugged the phone. It was that single-mindedness that infuriated him most deeply, more deeply than the white heat of her anger: the absolute quality of her disregard.

"If you're sure it won't be a problem," Butler said. "Because really it's getting late."

"Sure, stay," he said. "Let's talk science fiction. I'm a fan too, you know."

Butler's face lit up. "For just a little while," he said. "Then I've got to be going."

Dee-Dee yawned and stood up. "I'm out of here," she said. "Bye, J. D." She punched the detective in the shoulder, squinting and peering closely. J. D. bent and kissed her on the cheek. Charles had not known they were friends, and he found it somehow disquieting. Dee-Dee put on her jacket, slapped Charles on the back. Lianne waved vaguely goodbye.

The writer gestured at the littered tables. "Do you need any help?"

Charles laughed. "That's what we pay Clemmie for. Come on with me."

He gave Butler a tour of the house, the writer shaking his head in appreciation, grunting every now and then as if under the impact of a blow: "Mmp. Mmp. That's really *fine.*"

When he saw the library, Charles thought he might cry. They stood on the polished wood of the second-floor landing, looking over the rail. Lianne and J. D. had come inside, finally, and were below, Lianne in a chair at one of the desks, J. D. leaning against the edge of the desk, arms crossed, nodding down at her. Neither looked up. "Business to talk over," Charles said.

"I see that," Butler said. He looked overhead, at the vault of the ceiling, where the stained glass of the unlit chandelier hung, glossy and darkly glorious.

"You should see it when the lights are on." Charles didn't offer to throw the switch.

"I bet."

"The legal stuff is on the first floor, and history and biography so on. Science and science fiction up here, where I can just walk out from the office. Clemmie's rooms are right above here. This floor is my fun floor. That wall over there"—Charles pointed across the way, where a reading space projected from the second-floor hearth—"the northeast wall, just to the left of the fireplace—that's my science fiction collection." Butler drew in his breath.

Naturally they had to go look. Butler was excited that someone else had read Asimov's *The Currents of Space,* Heinlein's *Universe* or *The Puppet Masters,* Pangborn's *West of the Sun.* Charles had the devil of a time getting him away without letting him borrow any of the books.

Finally they went down the hall past the huge office and into the game room, which was, which was. Over the portico? But if it was, then you'd have a central projecting bay on the second-floor, and that's not the way the house looks. Is it?

It can't be where the office is, because then you have to push the office into either the sitting room or the exercise room. And it can't be directly over the dining room, the room just off the patio, because that was the sneak-away bedroom, wasn't it? You probably know, you can go back and check page 41 in its bound state, or jump ahead and look at the floor plan, but think of me, I can't.

You know what this is, don't you? Indeterminacy, that's right. Or maybe relativity, the speed of light. Uncertainty and nonsimultaneity, hey—they're the same thing seen twice.

Help me, Miss Liza, Little Liza Jane! Come down with your several viewpoints, your many-rhythmed italics! Help your poor messenger, your photon, oh succor your little hog!

She answers: *You might have let the room's location stay vague, a sort of distribution, a standing probability wave over the house. But you caused him to notice the process, how a thing becomes, how a fiction moves from spirit to being, a human from nothing to fact. Therefore what he must do, what he* is *doing—which of course changes the velocity of the story—is tell the reader now just precisely where the now room is. Now:*

Into the went room came, which over the portico was, a lighted bay o'erhanging all approach, its ceil offering a third-floor balcony to the master bedroom and guest bedroom alike, its pediment the single capital of ten pillars, the ten pillars of the ten-pillared portico.

There like a central altar, the huge green-felted fore-, aft-, and mid-pocketed leather-cupped slate-bedded bulk of a pool—not, thank Liza, billiards—table, a long lamp hanging its length.

Charles went to a telephone beside the hall door. Butler circled the table counterclockwise, trailing his left hand like a child at a garden pool, taking in the rest of the room as he revolved: the broad bay windows on the south; the door into the office, flanked on either side by shelves; the dartboards and racks of darts on the east wall; the rolling chalkboard for scorekeeping; the built-in projection screen and, facing it, three chairs with arm-tables; Charles holding the phone to his ear; the door to the hall; west of the door, the eight-sided leather-topped poker table, with its inset racks for drinks and chips; the glass front on the wall beyond the table, stored with board games, decks of cards, trophies, boxes of cigars, glasses, liquor bottles, and fitted out with a small refrigerator; the cones of white chalk and racks of cues, rakes, and wooden triangles along the southwest wall. The writer moved to this last display, reached up reverently for an 18.

"This is perfect," he said. "Pool tables are so beautiful. And poker."

Charles spoke: "There you are. I thought maybe you already went up. Ok, listen, bring us a bottle of the Château d'Yquem. Make it two, the '77." His eyes flickered to Butler. "No, the '79. What? Ok, bring one of those instead. And, let's see, the '73. The game room. Fine."

"Château d'Yquem?" Butler said.

Charles hung the phone on its hook and grinned. "Noble rot. Wait'll you taste it."

"Noble rot?"

"*La pourriture suprême*. This crop of sauternes took a fungus one year, and they were going to throw it out, but then they said what the hell, let's make it anyway, and it did something wild to the wine. So now they cultivate the fungus. The flavors are just incredible—nutty as hell, and they keep coming and going. It's like a wine with rooms in it."

"I love that," Butler said. "The fungus changing the wine that changes the grape."

"Change your brain too," Charles said.

"I love it when one thing rides another like that. To me, that's how the world is. Everything is so—*inwrought*." He peered to see if Charles understood, as though the word were a special possession, available only to poets. "It's like how sixteenth-century English survives up in the Ozarks," he said. "Or how radio waves have songs in them."

"Carrier waves," Charles said, smiling. "Signal-to-noise."

"Or how we carry the stories of our friends in us; or we make the written word carry the sound of the voice, and voices carry thoughts. To me, that's what poetry *is*, one movement riding another. I have a whole book I called *Riders*—"

"I read a book one time, these people were trying to build this computer model of the world. They were arguing about whether the people in the model were really alive or not, and one guy thought they were but the others were against him, and then he was driving and the road just ended. It just cut off, not even into empty space. Just into not even nothing. But then suddenly it came back. He stumbled on it, he wasn't supposed to see it not there. And he realizes—"

"I read that!" Butler cried. "*Simula . . . Simulacrum . . .*"

"*Simulacron-3.*"

"Yeah!"

Butler had been standing holding his 18 like a staff, gesticulating with his free left hand. Charles took a 16 from the rack, a pitted blue cube from the tray, chalked up. The author came to himself, ground the tip of his cue in the small blue metate of another chalk.

Clemmie appeared, carrying a silver tray on which there rested an unopened bottle of wine, an ice bucket, and a stainless-steel corkscrew. The open mouth of another bottle, draped in linen, canted from the bucket. She set the tray on the poker table. She was wearing a house robe.

"I didn't mean you to go back down," Charles said. He leaned his stick against the wall. "I thought I punched the kitchen."

"You did," she said. "Everybody left, and I got comfortable. You can put the other bottle in your little fridge or whatever. I'm going to bed."

"I thought J. D. was still here," Charles said.

"He is," she said. "I meant everybody else left. Good night."

Charles took the cloth off the chilled bottle, spun it in its bed of ice. He put the other bottle in the fridge and took down two tall crystal flutes. He set them on the tray, licked a finger, traced the rim of one glass to make it sing. He poured while the note still hung in the air. It died with the weight of the liquid, the soaring quell of a stilled bell, vanishing to faintest overtone.

"That makes a note like Jayme's voice." Butler still held his cue, Moses in the wilderness.

"Oh, can she sing?"

"Can she sing," Butler said. "Lord, that's pretty stuff."

So can Lianne, Charles thought. And ten times better, I bet. He brought the writer a flute of liquid, the color of sun through a yellow leaf.

Butler took a tiny sip, watching Charles. He rolled it over his tongue. His expression became complex. Charles threw back half of his, then set the flute on the edge of the pool table.

"You ever think maybe we're just simulations in a computer?" Charles said. "It could be a computer inside a computer inside a computer."

Butler took a larger swallow, set his flute down on the edge of the table. "Yeah, I like ideas that make me dizzy. Like spinning around when I was a kid. Did you do that?"

"Yeah, I did that." Charles collected the balls from the pockets, racked them up: a good tight rack, a rigid crystal pointing the spot, bright atoms in matrix.

"Do you still?"

Charles looked up. "No," he said.

"What are we playing?" Then, spotting the black in the center, the perfect alternation of stripes and solids, the game implicit in the array: "Oh, eight-ball."

"Lag for the break," Charles said. He brought the cue ball softly almost all the way back.

"I can't beat that." Butler took another swallow, nearly emptying his glass. "Take a hell of a computer to do this wine," he said. "Christ, it's good." He sighted on the cue ball.

"You know, that's the problem with that concept," he said. He straightened up. "Pleasure. You can simulate pain, it's just warning signals that the system is breaking down. But what's pleasure? It isn't just things working right. Otherwise, how come you can zap one little center, and the whole system feels good? Pleasure is like an epiphenomenon of the whole thing. It only makes sense in terms of an *I*. A perceiver. I mean, *who* feels good?"

"I feel good," Charles said.

"But I still like ideas like that," Butler said. "Or like characters in a novel. We're just stories these overbeings read, and when they get to us we feel like we're alive."

"Lag for the break," Charles said. He brought the cue ball softly almost all the way back.

"I can't beat that," Butler said. He brought it too far, bumped off the rail.

"Too hard," Charles said.

"And that would be where déjà vu comes from," Butler said.

"I love déjà vu," Charles said. He sighted. "So that would make you God," he said. He broke. The twelve and the seven went. "Solids." He got the six and the two, missed on the four.

"You didn't leave me much," Butler said. "It isn't that simple. Or if it is, if you can make that parallel, well, then, God is a lot more helpless than they always say. The nine off the thirteen." He clipped the four instead, bringing it off the rail, out into the open.

"I wouldn't be," Charles said. "Pillage and rapine. I would be Zeus, killing all the men and fucking all the women. I sure wouldn't be that nail-scarred wimp. Let em die for their own sins." He slammed the four, really too hard, so that it rattled and orbited before it lost force and dropped. He missed a long shot on the three, bringing it out to the middle.

"I couldn't do that," Butler said, studying the table. "But I wouldn't be Jesus either. I would be more like a clown. And I wouldn't teach them things, they would teach me things." He sank the nine on a straight shot, got draw for a corner shot on the eleven.

"Why not?" Charles said. "They aren't real."

"But like you say, what if we aren't either. I don't feel superior to my characters. I'm just the space they begin in. Then they can go on living in other spaces." He had spent a long time lining up the eleven. Now he sank it, came off the end rail toward the middle, but not far enough to straighten out the side-pocket shot on the ten. "Maybe."

"Sounds like Jesus to me," Charles said. "If neither one of you is real, what difference does it make? What do you get out of all that equality?"

The fictioneer inhabiting imaginary worlds. Makes him/her a spook in the real, a shade in the fictions—not all there in either case. But our world increasingly imaginary: More and more of it a product of the human mind. So maybe a survival thing, fiction is practice for how to live as the world gets weirder and more metaphysical. We're mortal, which is boundedness, not just we're gonna die. But mortality is beautiful, like a rhyme, and imagination is its burden. In other realms, out of time, we can learn judgment, kindness, beauty, law.

Ask a simple question, Charles thought. But under the hand-waving, the rhetoric, he thought he saw the real answer: the warmth of sentimentality. Butler wanted to feel himself a goodhearted fellow, the ultimate egalitarian, perfected in his humility. Yea, though he slew them, he wanted his characters to trust in him. He wanted to avoid the guilt he felt for twisting their lives according to his desires. He wanted them, by God, to like him.

I need to take another lick at Faulkner, he thought. This shit is easy if you drink enough Château d'Yquem.

The ten caught the corner of the pocket, came off to bump the three into a lock on the five.

"Shit," Charles said.

Ramalam trotted past the open door, immense black manifestation, *Hundgeist*.

"Shit," Charles said again.

"It isn't that bad," Butler said. "Try throw english, it'll go in the side."

"No," Charles said. "It's that damn Ramalam. First I start smelling him, and now I start seeing the son of a bitch."

"Ramalam?" Butler said.

"Our dog," Charles said. "But the goddamn dog is goddamn dead."

"We have a dog," Butler said.

"Not like this one," Charles said.

"Ours is half hound and half Great Dane," Butler said.

"Ours is half Saint Bernard and half Doberman," Charles said. "Was."

"Shit," Butler said. He sucked the last drops from his flute.

"You want some more," Charles said.

"Yeah," Butler said.

Charles poured them full again. There was still a third of a bottle left. Good. Butler took a swallow. Charles took a swallow. He was probably going to have to try throw english on the goddamn five ball.

"I thought you said the dog was dead," Butler said.

"So I'm seeing a fucking ghost or something," Charles said.

"No shit?" Butler said.

"Why would I shit you about a fucking ghost?" Charles said. "I'm not the kind of person that *likes* to see a fucking ghost. I don't even believe in the fucking things."

"Just now?" Butler said.

"Just this fucking minute," Charles said. "He ran by the fucking door."

"Weird," Butler said.

"Ram a fucking lam," Charles said. He was shivering.

"I've never been around a real ghost before," Butler said. "Are you saying Ramalam?"

"The fucking name of the fucking dog," Charles said.

Butler was off on a story, his buddy the famous Johnny Wink. Who had written a poem, "All the Things That Will Not Happen." Somebody would not get off a plane with a raincoat, and somebody else would not take his picture, and none of it had anything to do with dogs. Or ghosts. "See, it's about possibility," Butler said. "The sadness of possibility."

Charles went to the window. Rider's Bronco was still there, crisp and black on the white chat of the driveway, the floods from the portico throwing its image onto the fountain pool: a trembling shadow car, its windows full of shaken light. "It's your shot," he said.

"No, it's your shot," Butler said. "You have solids."

"Oh yeah," Charles said.

So that was one of the lines of the poem: *Jack will not ramalam.* It took Charles a second to remember Butler's first name. "I don't get it," he said.

"It's just a nonsense word," Butler said. "It doesn't mean anything."

"I see that," Charles said. "I just don't see why you're telling me about it."

"It's your dog's name," Butler said.

"So what?"

"Well, it just felt like it meant something."

"Throw english on the five," Charles said. "Side pocket."

His shot was close, but too lively: two cushions and back out. That was the trouble with throw: It had to be crisp. Tough to soft touch, with throw.

"I sure thought that would go," Butler said. He had the ten in the side again. This time he made it, drifting the cue ball up between the fourteen and the thirteen snug on the top rail. He took the fourteen down with follow, so that he came off the side with an angle on the thirteen.

The little twit could shoot, Charles realized, if you cleared all your own shit out of his way. You couldn't just play offense with him; you had to defense the man.

Butler snicked the thirteen humming along the rail. It went. "Rail-woman!" he cried.

I don't want to know, Charles thought.

Butler had the fifteen straight in for the corner. He put draw on the shot, and came back into the middle with a long angle on the eight.

"Lots of green," Charles said.

"Piece of cake," Butler said. He sent the eight long into the corner, but drew the cue ball left in a spinning curve. It hung on the side pocket, collapsed from view.

"Cottonpicking suck english," Butler said.

I *don't* want to know, Charles thought. He went to fill his glass, brought the bottle and filled Butler's. He held the bottle to the light. There was a puddle left, half a toroid slipping around the bulge. He drained it. He flipped the bottle like an Indian club, caught it by the neck.

"That's pretty good," Butler said.

"I'm unconscious," Charles said. He set the bottle down on the silver tray.

"You're right about this wine having rooms in it," Butler said.

"Did I say that?"

"Or at least a lot of space. It keeps changing, like the sound of a train in a canyon. Or like walking a mountain road. You hit a warm river of air rising up, and you make a turn and hit a cool river going down, all the leaves full of light and shadow like ripples in shallow water."

It came to Charles that you could use poetry to possess things. Well, then, that made it just another kind of money. "You're just drunk," he said. He racked the balls again.

"I'm drunk, but I'm not just drunk."

Charles broke, sank the eleven. "Stripes," he said. The fifteen top right, but not much after that, solids in front of three pockets. He squared the twelve away, gently, so that it stopped just in front of the pocket. He had applied low right english, to bring the cue ball back along the top rail. It nudged between the six and the rail, bumping the six away from the pocket.

"Whoa," Butler said.

"You ever read that Heinlein story," Charles said. "This contractor built a house, only he accidentally built it in the shape of a hypercube?"

"I think so," Butler said. Charles was sure not. Butler tried a long shot on the seven, bottom right corner. Missed. "But how could he build a hypercube—I mean that's a four—"

"Ok, ok," Charles said. "It was what, a three-dimensional *projection* of a hypercube." He popped the nine in the side, came out on the ten, top right corner. Laid it gently in front of the pocket. The cue ball settled against the rail, almost exactly where he had put it before.

"You love that rail," Butler said.

"And then an earthquake hit," Charles said, "and it folded up into a real hypercube?"

"I think so," Butler said. He tried to clip the five into his right side pocket, but it was tough shooting over the rail. He got too much: It caromed off the point of the cushion.

"So the house was still ok, it wasn't wrecked," Charles said. "But if you stepped through an outside door, maybe you would fall from the ceiling onto the floor of a bedroom, or you could walk right at a wall and you would suddenly be in the garden, or standing on the roof in the sunshine."

He brought the thirteen in front of the side pocket, hooked Butler behind the three. "All of the rooms were hyperconnected," he said, straightening up.

Butler frowned. "There's four sides in a square," he said, looking for some way out of the hook. "Six faces in a cube. Eight cubes in a hypercube, right?"

Charles didn't respond. Butler shrugged, put throw english on the three. It sailed up, clicked the seven away, came off itself. He shrugged again.

"Each side in a square," he said, "connects to two other sides at a corner, which is a point. Each face in a cube connects to four other faces at a vertex, which is a line. So probably each cube in a hypercube connects to six other cubes at a something-or-other, which would be a plane. So every room in the house would connect to six other rooms, one at each surface."

"Pretty good," Charles said.

"I'm unconscious," Butler said.

Charles made the side pocket on the thirteen, came off the top rail with a straight-in on the ten. Low center english, to pull back on the fourteen, long down the rail. He laid the fourteen in, came across to the twelve on a short angle in the corner going the other way.

"I always wished I could visit that house," Charles said. "You could go through it thousands of times and never take the same path twice. Sometimes I feel like I've been there, in a dream, or a long time ago, when I was a kid. I get homesick to go back."

He made the twelve and rolled all the way back, trying for an angle on the eight. But the cue ball wound up so that it and the eight were equidistant from the spot, parallel to the bottom rail.

"Back here off the bank," he said, patting the pocket to his left.

"Watch the scratch," Butler said.

"Never in a million years." Charles bisected the angle. The eight sang off the rail on a line for the pocket. The cue ball banked above the side pocket, came to a wandering stop.

"Wow," Butler said.

"So that's the kind of rooms this wine has," Charles said triumphantly, lifting his flute. "It's hyperwine." He drank. Sweet as the translucent blood of angels.

"I'm not too good at eight-ball," Butler said.

"Any way you choose it," Charles said. He had gone to the window again. The Bronco was still there. "A great big shaggy dog story," he said, turning back. "Just a big long pointless joke." He lifted his flute again, considered the wine. "What I think the world is."

"So who tells the joke? God?"

"He doesn't exist," Charles said. "But it's the only way He would make sense if He did."

"Let's play a game a friend of mine invented," Butler said.

"Let me guess," Charles said. "The famous Johnny Wink."

Butler described something called Little Red Rubber Ball Baseball, a variation called White Little Red Rubber Ball Baseball, a poker game called McGinnis, and some sort of basketball involving the Ouachita Baptist University Tigerettes. He went into detail on a form of pool he described as the Sixty-Second Game. What was the point? Oh, games.

In the Sixty-Second Game, you stationed shooters at the four corners of the table. One broke, and then Wink started counting down. You shot on the fly, any ball off any other ball, the balls never stopped rolling. You had to put them all down before the count ran out.

"We looked like a bunch of cranes," Butler said. "Dipping and shooting and dodging and watching not to mess each other up."

"Sounds like demolition derby pool," Charles said. "Did you ever win?"

"We won a *lot* . . . We won fifty-two times in a row once."

"You were cheating."

"We were not. We *wanted* to lose, all but one of us, this other friend, the famous Larry Johnson. You've got to meet Larry. We were staggering around the table at two in the morning, dead on our feet, but we were too hot, the game wouldn't let us go."

"So?"

"So we lost finally. But Larry wanted to try for a new record. He was marching around the table and yelling at us: 'You can't quit now! You're chickenshit if you quit now!' "

"Ok," Charles said. "But you do the counting."

"That was just an example," Butler said. "The one I'm talking about *playing* is called the five game. It's noncompetitive. We help each other."

"Doesn't sound like much fun."

"The only rule is to sink all fifteen with no more than five misses between you. The skill is how you think ahead and set your partner up if you can't make it."

"It sounds awfully easy," Charles said.

"So, if it is, we'll go to the four game," Butler said.

"Are you out of wine?" Charles said.

"Yeah, but I don't remember drinking the rest of it."

"Me either," Charles said. He pulled the other bottle out of the fridge, poured them full.

"So you know what heaven would be?" Butler said.

"What heaven?"

"If it's all a joke. Heaven would be when you get it. Heaven would be the laughing."

Charles held up his glass. "To laughter," he said. He didn't smile when he said it.

"Isn't it strange how that happens," Butler said, racking the balls in no particular order, the eight ball on the outside left, which bothered Charles. It felt wrong there, a puncture wound, a morbid ulcer, a negative space, a black hole in time.

"How what happens?" he said.

"Forgetting things. Like drinking the wine. It's like that road you were talking about. Something that's just not there, like you just skipped over that part of your life," Butler said. "When you were talking about rooms, I kept thinking about personality. How there's so much more to us than just our conscious minds."

The five game turned out to be straight pool with a free break. When you missed, you changed turns. Scratches were misses if you didn't make anything on the shot. The break didn't count as a miss, but if nothing went, you changed turns anyway. Anything did go down, you kept it, and the breaker kept shooting. It wasn't call-your-pocket, slop shots counted. They won the first, lost one, won three, lost one, won one.

"The six and two god," Butler said. He filled the interstices of the action with a running monologue: the true nature of personality, how fiction had almost always treated it as uniform and fixed from moment to moment, but how he saw it as shifting, changing, how each of us can contain the range of all others, a man can be both noble and a bigot, smart and stupid, tough and wimpy, et cetera. They drank their wine, refilled.

Butler made a bad break on a loose rack. Nothing went down but the cue ball, so it counted as a miss. The other balls had gathered in messy clumps, like protogalaxies.

"You and all the other schizophrenics," Charles said. "I know plenty of people that are always the same, and happy being that way too." He thought of Freddy Mayfield, of Eamon, of Betty and Lafayette. What about Lianne, what about her inner life? He felt for her, but did she ever ever have any empathy for *him*? He wanted to check the window again, resisted the weakness. "Slop," he said. He slammed a clump on the rail, the three, the eight, and the eleven all stuck together. The cue ball jumped off the table. The seven and the two went down.

"No miss, no miss," Butler said. He spotted the cue ball. "Maybe they just *look* always the same. Maybe what we treat as discrete is really just the recognition of probabilities. How frequently certain behaviors recur."

"Who knows," Charles said. "Anyway, how would you get all that into a story?"

"You can't," Butler said regretfully. "There's not enough room. Maybe if you had seventeen dimensions, instead of just linear prose." He ran off five in a row, missed an easy angle shot on the fourteen. "I'm sorry," he said. "I still haven't got my eye back."

"Good run," Charles said. "Besides, readers are just like regular people. They need to be able to know which character is which."

"That's another thing. We always treat personality like emotion is how you tell them apart. But I'm not sure the way we process information isn't even a bigger difference. Everybody's brain handles information a different way. And you *never* see that in fiction."

Charles ran off four, but scratched on the fourth.

"Suck english," Butler said. "But you sure left me nice."

"It's a pretty idea, though," Charles said. "Quantum psychology, huh?"

Butler smiled. "Yeah, or maybe even fractal. Not that I know what that means with regard to personality. Shit, I blew it." He had missed another short angle shot.

"No problem," Charles said. "Still just three misses." He made the five off the rail. He turned to Butler, made the success pistol with his right hand, blinking his right eye and clicking: *We connect.* "Recursion," he said. *"Gödel, Escher, Bach."*

Butler's eyes went wide and grateful. "Mandelbrot sets!"

"Yeah, that paisley stuff." Charles sank the six and the four, missed on the eleven.

"Still just four misses," Butler said. "So you would recognize a personality by the shape it returns to at each fractal level." He sank the twelve, the one. Only one ball remained, the eight, but the angle was bad. "It's gonna be up to you," he said. He nudged the cue ball into the center of the table, leaving Charles dead-in on the corner pocket. "That's five."

"Piece of cake," Charles said. "But it wouldn't mean there weren't a whole lot of levels, and a whole lot of different shapes on each one. And the shapes could include information structures, not just emotions." He sank the eight, raised his hand.

Butler slapped it for a high-five. "Twelve and two," he said. "Seven in a row."

"More wine," Charles said.

The phone rang. A wild happiness went through him, a wave with precisely the frequency of the phone. Rider was gone, and Lianne was ready to get back in touch.

It was Clemmie. "He's gone," she said. "I saw him leave out my front window."

"Why are you telling *me*?" Charles said. It was not Lianne, not Lianne.

"I thought you would want to know," she said. She hung up.

"I better be going," Butler said. "I think Jayme's got some cake and ice cream waiting."

Cake and ice cream? Cake and ice cream? Charles's mind spun in angry circles. For a moment he wanted to kill the writer.

Then, improbably, in the midst of his fury, he felt a calming pity. He saw the poet as if from a great height, and yet very intimately, very clearly. He felt as if he could see all the way through the man, the way you might see through an amoeba under the microscope: a low translucent creature, but glimmering with form nevertheless, diaphanies of hope.

"Cake and ice cream?" he said.

Butler tucked his head sheepishly. "It's my birthday," he said.

Charles saw the elevation the writer must have felt at Lianne's call, how he and his Jayme must have hesitated to mention the birthday, not wanting to risk withdrawal of the invitation.

He saw them planning a private party when Butler got home, just the two of them, cake and ice cream, a party with something extra to celebrate: Butler's entrée, at last, into the world of those who made things happen. Patrons his conscience would allow him to sell out to. The rich and powerful but the noble rich, the powerfully noble. He saw that the chance to extend the evening was more than Butler had been able to refuse, but that he had been afraid to ask to call Jayme, afraid it might break the spell.

He saw Jayme waiting up late, supporting her man. Finally, exhausted, turning out the lights. He saw Butler saying goodbye, drunken and full of plans to stay in touch, to make Charles his friend. Going home to a dark house, to a giddy and fervent and sleepless night.

He knew that this was the last time he would ever see the poet.

"No kidding," he said. "Mine's in ten days."

"No kidding?" Butler brightened for an instant; then he seemed visibly to age. He looked at his cue as if it were a severed limb. "I really better go," he said.

"You can't quit now," Charles said. "You're chickenshit if you quit now."

They were fifteen and two when Rider appeared, ten in a row. "Lianne said you were up here," Rider said. "She said to come on up."

Charles's reflex was to jerk to the window, but he caught himself. Shock pounded in his veins. He felt a dislocated certainty that he was in the hyperhouse, that Rider had walked through walls to get here, had leapt a jagged path through unmapped halls of space and time.

"I thought you left," he said.

"No," Rider said. "I went out to the car to get something." He nodded at Butler. "Lianne said Mr. Butler might need a lift home. Since I was going that way."

Of course. No car. At the door, no car. Butler had walked. He had not noticed, but Lianne had. Good Lianne, thoughtful Lianne. Why had he been so worried? They had fought before and had gotten back together. This was just another fight. He had done a good thing, staying home, no matter his motives. He no longer envied Rider, nor any other man. They all had difficulties, he and Rider and Butler, he had nothing to be ashamed of, was in good company.

"Sure," Butler said. "It's not far, but sure."

"One more rack?" Charles said. "Eleven's a good number."

"Sure," Butler said.

Rider seem neither anxious to play nor in a hurry to leave. He pulled a chair from the poker table, sat on it backward to watch.

Charles broke, but nothing went down, and he had left Butler almost hooked between the fifteen ball and the right rail—nothing open but an angle shot on the eight, right corner pocket.

"So, you get any ideas tonight?" Rider said.

"I don't know," Butler said. "Maybe. Things never turn out the way I think." He leaned over, sizing up the shot. "All I ever really know is what to do next." He punched it home, a crisp stroke with left english, so that the cue ball banked twice and spun to the middle of the table.

"Can of corn," he said. His hair was standing up where he had run a talcy hand through it, and his nose was red with the wine. His glasses seemed askew, and there was a floury smear on his cheek. "If I don't make at least five of these," he said, "you need to shoot me."

"Good leave," Charles said.

20

DEATHS OF
NEGROES

Sonny Raymond was walking up and down in the conversation pit, seeking whom he might devour. Just last week the quorum court had voted him another $400,000, and what did that goddamn Beaumont do? Another warning about overspending his budget. And now, today, this very day, seven inmates had escaped from the county jail, and he could feel the whole state laughing. *Reckon we pay him another $400K he'll let some more prisoners out? One way to solve overcrowding, that's for sure.*

Let em eat shit. Wait till they read about this.

The conversation pit was a sunken, red-carpeted space, a wedge of emptiness like the vanished quarter section of a restaurant pie. Stone wall met a second stone wall at right angles. A ninety-degree arc of carpeted steps, dotted with throw cushions, offered impromptu seating. Sonny was walking up and down along the entertainment wall. It was not a cold night, but Lafayette had a fire going: The stone stayed chilly well into June.

"This is bullshit," Lafayette said. "You aint got a warrant."

He stood with his arms and back to the fire, one wrist locked in the other hand's grip, his free fist clenching. The heat was painful, almost blistering, but he held himself to it, burning the shiver from his spine and shoulders, cooking his anger hotter.

Tina curled on the nearby sofa, her chin on her hands, sculptural shadows flickering under the high cheekbones, highlights running the elegant ridge of her nose. But the fire took all color from her eyes, so that she looked abstract and empty. A doll, Lafayette thought, a face carved from some roseate hardwood.

"I got probable cause," Sonny said, jerking open the cabinets under the entertainment system. "One of my men seen a naked woman running across your yard." He squatted, began pulling things off the cabinet shelves onto the floor: boxes, pamphlets, guarantees in clear plastic, manuals, videotapes, cassettes, earphones, cable jacks, the clutter of modularity.

"One a your men, bullshit," Lafayette said. "You got-damn peckerwood." *You probably had seventeen cars up the hill waiting,* he thought. *You probably paid somebody to run out naked.*

Raymond stood and kicked through the litter, like a man looking for dropped pennies in a pile of leaves. He smiled. "Really got your ass in a crack now, don't you, cousin?"

Freddy Mayfield went by on the upstairs level of the living room, trying to hustle a young woman wrapped in a blanket out to the foyer and into the wagon. She was resisting arrest, giggling and stopping, trying to kiss Mayfield. The blanket kept slipping, Mayfield with one hand frantically tugging it back up, trying to keep her under control with the other hand, trying to shove her along without letting her touch his body, but she kept twisting around, a tit flashing here, there a bare cheek, a beard of raw pussy. Mayfield was bright red with exertion and embarrassment—morally mortified, and his chief watching to boot.

Funny as hell, Sonny thought, and all he could do to keep from laughing out loud, the Bible-thumping damn hypocrite.

Audrey Tull came stalking out of the far hall. "Sonny, git me some help in here. This goddamn Lookadoo is nekkid and dead drunk, and I can't get Cheese to touch the fat hog."

"Well get Rabelais to help you," Sonny said.

"Robbie is in the goddamn bathroom puking his guts out," Audrey Tull said. "He thinks it's Sodom and Gomorrah or something, we're all gonna turn to salt." Rabelais was young and thin and twitchy, easily upset. He still took sin personally.

There were a whole clutch of Rabelaises in central Arkansas, and yes, they were direct descendants of who you think, a writer We greatly admire, since he plots like We do and has the same sense of propriety.

"Well get me some uniforms in here to search for drugs," Sonny said. "And call a ambliance for a stretcher. Lookadoo probably aint the only outcold jughead fruit in the joint."

"And I think the media is here," Tull said.

"Fine," Raymond said. "When you find Mr. High-up Muckety-muck, you let me know. And hold him till we can be sure they got cameras on the door." Tull shrugged, headed away.

"If you find drugs in here, you brought em," Lafayette said. Out in the woods down the hill toward the river maybe, where it might be any-body's from any of the big houses along River Ridge. But not in the house. He laid his hand on Tina's shoulder. She reached out a finger and twiddled him, shielded from Sonny's view by her head. Lafayette tightened his grip to make her quit.

He should have paid attention to his gut. He'd had that sinking feeling all night, people slopping down a pint of his booze, disappearing into the bedrooms or the master bathroom or slipping out on the deck to the hot tub, reappearing in badly draped linen for more booze, tripping down to the den on the lower level in groups of three or four or five.

Lafayette didn't care for orgies, for the cunning and vacuous faces, glimpses of aging cellulite under tailor-made silk togas. He didn't like the air in his own bathroom full of anonymous mingled rut, like a mix of gutted fish and old urine.

"They're just having fun," Tina had said.

As soon as he'd seen how it was going, he had retreated to the conver-sation pit to wait it out. No point trying to chase em, it would cause too much commotion and attract attention. But never again, he vowed. He was through letting Tina plan things for him.

Lie low, Lafayette, he had told himself. *Keep still and wait, and it will be better.* His counsel to himself all his life long. Nobody here would be talking about the party, they wouldn't dare for their own sakes, so he didn't have to worry about this getting back to Charles.

Unless oh God he showed up after all, please don't let him, and sure enough after a while it was pretty clear he wasn't and probably never had intended to, the bastard, thank goodness.

And even that hadn't seemed to bother Tina, who had lobbied so hard to get the man there, but now had just cuddled and hummed and patted Lafayette's sick stomach. *The sickness unto death*—that swooning phrase, a favorite of his mother's, staggering down the scale to its final, occluded stress.

But he was calming down, he was doing better.

Until the door opens and Sonny Raymond walks in. Lafayette up pro-testing, "Not *him,*" half turned to Tina, how could you invite *him,* before it even registered that Sonny had a gun in his hand and that Audrey Tull had stepped through beside him with a gun in *his* hand.

And beyond them at the open door, patrol cars logjammed into his driveway in among the Audis, the Beamers, the Jags, and flashing blue lights and cowboys with badges and the crackle of radiophones, so all his neighbors knew.

Lafayette had felt he was in one of those Bugs Bunny cartoons where somebody's in a rocket by mistake and it zooms up and in a twinkling the streets turn into a neat map of roads and fields and then twinkle North America and then twinkle the whole globe hanging there in space.

The fear was vertigo, was what it was. His job was gone, and with it all his status, the only credit he had to hold against his mother's scorn.

So why didn't the fear go away now? The worst had already happened. Sonny over there twisting knobs on the stereo without turning it on, like he knew how to run it. Just his way of saying *Your home is mine, bro. Your ass is mine.*

Tina twisted out from under his hand and settled to watch Raymond. Tull came back down the hall, stopped at the top of the steps.

"He ain't here," he said.

"Don't give me that shit," Sonny Raymond said. "I know mother-fucking well he is."

Who?

"Well you can know what you want to," Tull said. "But he aint here."

Sonny whirled on Tina, glaring. He was white, and his jowls were shaking. Spittle flecked his lips. He seemed to be trying to talk. He pulled his gun from its holster under his coat, and Lafayette thought for a moment he was going to shoot them. Then he charged up the steps past the motionless Audrey Tull, ran cursing down the hall.

You should have known before now, Lafayette. God, you're stupid, Lafayette.

So now you're rocketing up through space and the world gets tiny, tinier, and then pops out and there's nothing but blackness. But if you're rocketing up, why does it feel so much like falling? The whole feeling of the thing turned around on him:

Because it *is* falling, that's why. You're not zooming up, you're falling out of the world. It's leaving you, *it's* up, and you're falling down backward. And under your feet all the stars shoot in to make a big glowing cloud and you're falling headfirst right out of the galaxy.

He deadlifted Tina by her shirtfront, two hands full of a rope's thickness of gathered silk. He was going to throw her at the fire, I think, break her back on the stone, scorch the body. The charge would have been not just indecency or dope or whatever Sonny had in mind, but murder one. For the violence, not the premeditation. But the blouse ripped away, and she fell to the floor.

"Hot momma," Audrey Tull said, and made suckling noises.

Tina tried to get up, clambering against the couch. Lafayette flipped her, sat on her. He tore the shreds and sleeves of her blouse away with one hand, holding her off with the other. She was twisting and grunting. She kicked her shoes off and dug for leverage, trying to heave her pelvis, throw Lafayette. Tull sat on the top step.

"Watch out for the teeth," he said conversationally. "Sonny said she's bad to bite."

Lafayette had her on her stomach now, the blouse completely off. She showed a couple of bleeding scratches across her shoulder and back. He had some too, across his face. He was undoing the belt of her slacks from behind, hoisting her belly to get at it. She broke loose, twisted sitting onto the sofa, tried to kick him, but he fell back dragging the slacks down her legs.

"Law enforcement has its friends too," Audrey Tull said.

She kicked like a child in a tantrum, flinging her head right and left, her feet tangled in the inside-out slacks. Lafayette stood, hauling the slacks off her feet, dragging her thumping to the floor. He flung the slacks at the fire, but they sailed open and fell short.

She tried to run, but Lafayette caught her by her filmy panties, like making a jersey tackle. They went down in a tumble, and the fight left her. Lafayette knelt, ripped the panties apart, the elastic slicing a running wound on one hip. She lay huddled on her side, crying from sheer rage, mumbling into the carpet. "Damn you Brandon," she was saying over and over. "Damn you damn you damn you Brandon damn you."

"Shut up," Lafayette said. He stood. Audrey Tull got up, came down the steps. "Shut up," Lafayette said again. He kicked her in the ribs.

Tull took his gun and laid one across the back of Lafayette's skull. The big man crumpled to his hands and knees.

Cheese had come into the living room and down the steps. "I wanted to do that," he said.

"Too late," Tull said.

When Sonny came back Tull and Cheese were squatting to get a good look. Tina was still curled on the floor, but had quit crying. She looked into space, idly fingering the carpet.

"What the hell?" Sonny Raymond said.

"You missed the show," said Audrey Tull.

"What show?" Sonny said. "Well never mind, you right. The son-ofabitch *aint* here. Get those two motherfuckers in the wagon."

"Both of em?" Cheese said.

"Her and him both," Sonny said. "The bitch lied to me."

"What," Lafayette said, still on his hands and knees. All his concentration the last few minutes had been not to vomit. Not to vomit on his own rug, in front of his enemies. "Just what. The hell you think. You can charge me with?"

"Contributing to the delinquency of a major," Sonny said. "Operating a nonprofit whorehouse. Tearing the tags off mattresses. Who gives a flying fuck in Abraham's hell?"

. . .

They charged thirteen partygoers, all but two with indecent exposure. In addition, they got seven of them for possession of this or that, nine for adultery, which was still against the law, and even three for sodomy. Which latter was a strange number, if you thought about it. They had bagged a retired judge Sonny couldn't stand, three pretty well-off lawyers, a couple of bond daddies, and four Heights matrons.

They didn't charge Lafayette with possession because the two bonehead cops Tull had sent him didn't find any dope anywhere except on the persons of various individuals and said so to Mayfield before Sonny could tell them otherwise, and he wasn't going to put himself in the position of saying one thing while Mayfield said the other. They wanted to charge him with assault, but Tina wouldn't press. "He doesn't matter, Sonny," she said.

So that left probably resisting arrest or manufacturing a nuisance or something.

Sonny had decided not to charge Tina with anything after all. Too many cops were ready to say she had been an innocent bystander, including Tull himself, which made you wonder. Must have smelled something he liked, kneeling down there beside her ass.

In his office, his first peace and quiet since they made the raid, Sonny grinned to himself.

He hadn't wanted to charge her anyway, not really. He believed her that Morrison said he would come and then reneged, wishy-washy motherfucking two-timer. And be fair, she hadn't realized what Sonny had planned. What she had talked about was maybe an undercover man with a camera, get some photos you could wave at the bastard, get him off your back. The raid was as big a surprise to her as it was to the nigger.

He thought maybe she had thought she would have some copies of the photos too, a way to make Morrison do what she wanted. As if she wouldn't be in the same photos, as if she wouldn't be incriminated too. As if Morrison would thank her for the setup. As if Sonny would just smile and let her have the bastard, when the bastard was his own mortal enemy.

Poor girl, she *was* an innocent. For a smart woman, she just didn't always connect.

He believed her about Morrison partly because of the way she blew it off, as if it was nothing, she didn't care, she had expected it all along. He knew her and he had known her daddy, and they both lied the same way. If they were really angry you didn't hear a whisper, they were completely cool, they had no feelings at all.

John-John Talliaferro had wanted on the Jacksonville force real bad, and he went to his death not knowing that Sonny, who he had used as a reference, had recommended against him. He recommended against him because of something that had happened one summer when he was sixteen and John-John was twenty-four with two kids, his nominal boss. They were working construction for Hamlin Phillips, throwing up a cheap subdivision near where later on it would turn out Vertac had poisoned everything. It was a Saturday, and John-John wanted to sleep late, but Hamlin said work today or look for another job Monday. So he was already mad when he put the nail through his big toe with the nail gun.

It should have been funny, but Sonny already knew enough about John-John not to laugh. They had been running bottom studs on the slab, John-John loading the .22 caps and firing the nail gun to drive the thick grooved spikes through the wood and into the cement, Sonny coming along behind and slapping the sledge on any that didn't quite go.

All John-John said when it happened was, "I *told* Phillips." He said it in a quiet voice, like someone commenting on an article in the paper. Standing there one foot fastened to the stud.

Sonny got the claw and yanked it out, pure straight-up force, you couldn't lever it without crushing the already destroyed toe beyond restoration. It was three o'clock in the afternoon. The nail had gone right through the bone, but John-John wouldn't let Sonny take him to the doctor. He tore his bandanna, wrapped it tight, and worked out the day without a whimper, his shattered toe wrapped in a bloody rag and stuffed back sockless in its boot. As if he felt nothing, no pain at all.

A man like that ran too deep. Too much was hidden. You couldn't trust him behind you because he would have his own plan. And if he ever once got off with you—

The same was true of Tina, but with a woman it just added spice.

He had come back from the army to find John-John's boy Brandon, almost grown, and Tina a white-headed blue-eyed starved-looking holy terror, eleven years old but already with tits under the thin-striped blue-and-purple white-collared Ban-Lon pullover.

"What you going to be when you grow up?" he had asked.

"Rich," she had answered. Rich. Standing there in her dirty holed-out jeans, living in their rusty tilty busted-in house trailer with the ratty worn-out carpet and the vent for the potbellied stove cut through the tin of the living room wall.

"You and me both," he had said.

"So I can help all the poor people," she had added.

So of course she was mad at Morrison, she was furious at Morrison, she probably thought she was in love with the son of a bitch—chase his wife off, marry him, and help all the poor people. He had to get her out of that snake pit, delicate girl in treacherous company, she had had more trouble in her life than anybody except Sonny maybe knew, his heart had gone out to her in the nigger's house just like it had to the skinny intense eleven-year-old, to see her frail and curled and bleeding, naked on the rug, pussy hair showing between her drawn-up thighs. Not to mention the size of her knockers.

So he had been over his temper even before they finished taking photos and left. He had changed his orders to put them both in the wagon, had let her shower and get dressed, and then had sneaked her out in a quilt, too bundled up for the media cameras to show who it was.

Now Tull stuck his head in the door. "She wants to see you again," he said.

"Hell, is she still here?"

Tina came in, opening the door wider to step around Tull. She sat, smoothing her slacks as though they were a skirt. Demure now, not lifting her eyes. She was wearing a blue uniform shirt for a blouse, the sleeves rolled up to what would have been halfway on him, but nearly lapping her wrists. Sonny waved Tull away, got up and closed the door.

"Those ribs might be broken," he said. "You shoulda let me take you to emergency."

"And have somebody at the hospital take a picture, and then it's all over the papers? No, thanks. She has her own personal doctor."

"Who does?" Her eyes were on his, but she didn't seem to have heard.

"Well," he said, "you might not be in the news tomorrow, but what about money? Because this shithead won't have nothing legal on you, but you know he's going to fire you. If nothing else, for knowing me."

"She's got resources," she said. "Investments she can raise money on. Some real estate too. When she came back to town, she wasn't just a poor little towheaded kid anymore."

"Say what?"

She looked ok. Her eyes were clear. But Sonny knew for a fact that it did strange things to your mind to get beat up. Sometimes it kicked you right out of yourself, made you feel like you weren't even there, or like you were looking down on things from far away.

"You're talking about yourself," he said.

"If it was a movie," she said. "I was just thinking if it was a movie. She's mysterious and beautiful, and nobody knows where she's from. And she wants to start an orphanage, but they beat her up because they want the land for a bank. And they leave her for dead."

"Honey, what did you want to see me about?"

"And it could be where she's on her deathbed, and he realizes she's his childhood sweetheart, she came back in disguise. And he falls in love all over again, but it's too late."

"Honey," he said, "you need to go home and get some rest."

"You've seen that movie," she said. Scolding.

"I just don't want you getting hurt," he said. "Just because you're sweet on the bastard. You know you aint no judge of men."

"It's not his fault," she said. "If he had his own way, things would be different."

Cheese swung the door open and leaned in. "Those boys you wanted me to find?" he said. "I've got em lined up and ready to go, just say the word."

"She married him for his money," Tina said. "She doesn't love him."

"What boys?" Sonny said. Suddenly crazy shit was coming at him from all directions. "What the hell are you talking about?"

"You know," Cheese said, rolling his eyes at Tina. "Those surveillance boys we were talking about. To watch that certain person."

Sonny finally got it. "For godsake, Cheese, not now."

"What surveillance boys?" Tina said.

"It's nothing," Sonny said. "It's just somebody we're keeping an eye on."

"That's a good idea," she said.

Cheese was still hanging in the doorway. "Get out of here," Sonny said.

"I just thought you'd want to know," Cheese said. "Considering the way everything turned out tonight and all. I just thought I'd let you know."

"Shut up and get out of here," Sonny said. "I'll talk to you later."

To Tina he said: "You need to get on home now. I'll come by and check on you later."

"What about Henrietta?" she said.

"I already called her," Sonny said. "She aint expecting me home this morning. She knows this is a big-time case. She knows I got responsibilities."

"You always do take care of me, Sonny," she said.

Laugh was in a holding cell, considering his options. Five of the others arrested in the raid had been let go on recognizance, all but the ones charged with sodomy and possession.

And Laugh. Which you knew Sonny wasn't about to let the nigger just walk without a bond. But if you were going to stick his ass in jail, the law said you had to let him get hold of his lawyer. Easy enough to ignore the law, let him sit and stew for as much as a week, if it wasn't someone where there was going to be a lot of media attention, but you could bet on it in this case.

They hadn't charged Laugh with resisting arrest, though it was obvious that they *would* charge him with it if he raised a fuss about the lick on the head, which he wasn't going to do, he understood the rules.

So who could he call? He could represent himself, but frankly, Lafayette was tired of himself. Didn't want to say another goddamn word about himself. Just turn himself over to somebody else and let them do the goddamn work for a while.

Who did he have? He saw clearly how Tina, unfaithful Tina, had absorbed him, isolated him. She had kept *her* contacts, her side romances, but he had let his go in order to have that heat in the middle of his life, that one consuming love that he gave all of himself to so it would cleanse him and give him all of himself back.

Charles? Charles would do it, no question. Lafayette was fired as soon as he found out, but Charles would come down and represent him. But it would be a few more hours before Charles found out. A few more hours was all, but Laugh wanted those hours free of the man's contempt.

So he wound up calling Timothy Chambers, the civil rights activist, and Tim would come down and spring him as soon as the court opened. Chambers had bailed Big Daddy out a time or two, so he would have the right kind of experience.

Which was fine as far as it went, Lafayette explained to Mayfield, who had accompanied him to the phone. But the problem was, when they arraigned him and set bond, he wasn't going to be able to pay it, not right away. He was tapped. Wasn't that a hoot? He grinned, to show Mayfield how funny it was. He could go to a bail bondsman, of course, but he hated the idea. It seemed so low-class. So niggerish.

Oh he could raise the cash eventually, but there was none in the bank, and none in his pocket. The house cost way too much, and he spent too much on clothes, mostly impulse buys. So he'd been shorting himself on ready cash lately, to hold his spending down. So here he was in the tank with his pockets turned inside out, and soon everybody he hated would be laughing at him not only for getting caught at the toga party, but for being such a fraud financially speaking.

About four in the morning, Freddy Mayfield came back down to the cell and said Lafayette could call around for bail money if he wanted to. "There's some things go on around here I don't approve of," Mayfield said, by way of explanation. "And that's all I'm going to say. Otherwise, near as I can see, you deserve what you got."

Who was going to come up with bail? That was the fear swirling in his stomach now. What else could it be? The worst had happened. Even Tina couldn't cook up any *more* trouble. This was a boy's fear, the fear of having no one who cared, of being alone in the world. But it was a hard-ass world and you got through it by being hard-ass yourself, not by crying in a cell. Everybody had *somebody* who could help.

Greg Legg? He would gush all over with gratitude for the chance, but I'm sorry, I just can't do it, I just aint willing to give up my sense of superiority quite yet.

So that left his half-brother—his uncle?—Stephen Trenton Thompson. The prim chunk of young self-righteous shit Big Daddy had fathered on Momma when Laugh was seventeen. More tight-ass than Momma, sensing his shame more deeply than Laugh no doubt, but not the guts to fight the battle Laugh had fought, went running to Jesus at five years old. He wouldn't begin to come help, he would just spew some scripture and twitch his little self-righteous church librarian's butt away.

So that left Momma, finally, after all, which he guessed he must of known on some level, which was really why he had been so scared. But what the fuck, she was an old woman, and it was time to quit being scared of her.

The phone rang a long time. He wasn't waking her up, probably, she was usually up before five nowadays, but she was hard of hearing, and ran gospel music at top volume on the radio all day long anyway. She would walk around the the house for five minutes with the phone ringing until some sort of cumulative awareness built up.

"Anybody answering?" Mayfield said at his elbow. Probably nervous that Sonny would walk out and see him. They were calling on the pay phone at the end of the courthouse hall.

What if Momma never did answer?

A man's voice: "Yes?" Just like his momma, abrupt and challenging.

"Goddammit, who is this?" Laugh said.

"Is this Lafayette?" the man said, and Laugh realized it was Stephen Trenton's voice. "About time you call back, party man. I been leaving messages on your phone all night long."

So how had he found out?

Momma found out and called him over, probably. The early radio news? This was bad and good. Good part it might speed things up, wouldn't have to do all the explaining, and she be done show out her mad, get some of it over with.

"Listen, I don't care what you think," Lafayette said. "The fact is I'm here, and I aint got the money. I can get it but I aint got it."

"I heard some scandalous things," Stephen Trenton said, "but I don't know I ever heard anything as hard as that. Don't worry your pointy little head, brother. I'll pay for it. You probably make five times what I do, but I'm proud to be the one paying."

"Hell, I'll pay you back," Lafayette said. "Just get someone down here to pay the money and pick me up."

"Couldn't you cut out the profanity just this once?" Stephen Trenton said. "Out of respect? What's wrong with your car?"

"What do you mean what's wrong with my car? Nothing's wrong with my car. You think they let me bring it with me? I just need somebody to pay the man."

"I already said I would, didn't I?"

Lafayette wanted to cuss again, but since it was looking like it would be Stephen Trenton that would have to come down and get him, discretion was as best as valor. "Well get on down here and do it, then."

"Lafayette, are you coked up? Don't you think we ought to wait till we get the bill?"

"Nigger, what the fuck you saying? They aint gone send you no fucking bill. Bill down here at the courthouse where I am."

Stephen Trenton's voice grew cautious, shaky with some emotion Laugh couldn't identify. "Lafayette, you in some kind of trouble?"

"What the fuck we *talking* about, Stephen Trenton? Hell with this, let me talk to Momma."

"Lafayette," Stephen Trenton said, calling his name the third time, "Momma's dead."

"Fuck you," Lafayette said.

"You hear what I'm telling you? Doctor said she went about two in the afternoon, heart attack. I came by to say good night and found her. She's dead."

"Don't be shitting me," Lafayette said. He was gasping. Offense fumbled on first down, and he was right back in there getting his ass whipped.

"Whole family's coming in," Stephen Trenton said. "Fune'l's on Tuesday. You need to get yo sorry tail over here and show respects if it's the last thing you do."

"Well that's gone be a little complicated," Lafayette said. The tears were running down his face now, but he kept his voice rough. "Somebody don't come get me out."

"Got yourself in, get yourself out," Stephen Trenton said. "You probly what kill her. You and yo sorry-ass life-style." He slammed the phone down in Laugh's ear.

Laugh had to laugh at that, Mr. Oh-So-Proper driven to profanity himself. He fumbled to find the hook for the phone. The tears were still running down his face, but they were tears from laughing so hard, so it was ok, nothing to be ashamed of, not a weakness.

"What's the matter?" Freddy Mayfield said. Laugh leaned back against the wall, laughing so hard he was sobbing. Mayfield had his pocket handerkerchief out, offering it to Lafayette to wipe his face. Laugh tried to explain the joke, but Mayfield just looked more worried. "Come on," he said, and led Lafayette back down the hall and down the stairs and across to his cell.

"I'll raise bail for you," he said, locking Lafayette in. "If you won't tell anybody. But I can't do it till the bank opens. Try to relax."

He went away, and Lafayette leaned back on the cot. Try to relax, hell. Life wadn't nothing but relax now. It was all over now. Now he didn't have to worry any more about his momma giving him a whipping for fucking the little white girl. Now he could fuck whoever he wanted to. His body felt young and limber. He felt like he could make the pros after all. It was the best he had felt in years.

Lafayette could not know it at the time, but Mayfield would think things over and then give you a call. It would be you who would make bail and not Freddy Mayfield. You would be furious, whether more furious at Sonny or at Lafayette you hardly knew, but Lafayette was there and Sonny wasn't, Sonny was over in the Quapaw Quarter with guess who.

So Lafayette would stand there before the judge between two men who were helping him and neither of whom liked him a bit: you, quivering with silent rage, and Chambers, gone formal with disgust.

Chambers was a neat man given to tan gabardine suits, smallish, very correct in his address, a stiff black glove hanging from one sleeve. He was not the prude that Stephen Trenton was, but he had no use for Lafayette's kind of black man. He had lost a hand to a Mississippi shotgun in 1961, and the way he saw it, a man like Lafayette was worse than the KKK. A man like Lafayette set the cause back twenty years. And a man like Charles, far from being a friend of the race, was deeply to blame for preferring the stereotype, encouraging and covering for the excesses of a man like Lafayette.

Speaking of which, interracial codependency you might call it—you would not fire Lafayette after all. Instead, you would put him on leave, as you had Greg, and you would assume the cost of his defense (but leave Chambers in charge). Who can say why? In all the conflicting motives of your fractal personality, what summary might suffice?

Generosity? Not precisely, though you would later credit yourself with generosity, and perhaps we should too. White liberal guilt? Complicated by personal sexual guilt? You felt responsible for the mess because Tina had tempted you? Sheer bullheaded cantankerous resistance, refusing to bow the neck to Sonny and his minions? And that resistance strangely crossed and amplified by your resistance to Lianne, whom you loved and

*fiercely wanted to rejoin but nevertheless could not entirely surrender to,
so that Laugh became the nonnegotiable instance of your pride; by saving
him you were denying, at least emotionally, that she had been right all
along about Tina? Or the blinding anger toward the son of the father, who
punishes the son by helping, thus driving home that cruelest message: See,
you can't take care of yourself. Or was it that Laugh was your stalking-
horse, your tar baby, the one who drew down on his own sticky head the
wrath that belonged to you, and so by rescuing him you rescued yourself?*

> *Oh the human soul is a raging fire,*
> *desire riding upon desire.*
> *And what does the fire hiss and sing?*
> —Fire is not a simple thing.

You would *fire Tina. Or rather, would try to fire her. We can imagine
the way it would be at your house when the news hit, when Lianne realized
what kind of party you had almost gone to, the fact that you* didn't *go the
minorest of minor quibbles. We can imagine how angry you were at your
close call, and how much angrier to have done the right thing, for whatever
reason, and to have Lianne on the warpath yet again anyway. We can
imagine how you felt about looking out your windows and seeing reporters
camped on your lawn waiting to buttonhole anyone—you, Lianne, Clemmie, Coleman. Had you known about the party, how many other members
of your firm were involved, was the rumor true that you were there yourself
but had paid someone off to avoid being taken in, was the rumor true that
Lianne had been there, how long had you and she been wife-swapping
perverts, oh what did you know and when did you know it?*

*We can imagine how you called all over town all Saturday and Sunday
trying to find Tina, so as to have the satisfaction of axing her yourself,
how pissed you were not to be able to get hold of her, how extremely deeply
magnificently pissed you were to get her letter on Monday stating how
chagrined she was to have occasioned embarrassment to the firm, and that
although the way the party had gone was a surprise to her and she was
innocent of any wrongdoing, she fully understood how you must feel, and
fully understood the circumstances of your life that forced you to feel that
way, and it was her deepest regret (far deeper than that caused by her
loyalty to the firm) to have hurt you in any way, and that to spare you and
the firm any further grief she was resigning in order to start her own practice, it would be the best for all concerned.*

*Oh all the things that would happen and would not happen, and you
remember some of them, Charles. But just now it was five in the morning,
and you were dreaming a dream you don't remember, and you were not*

*thinking of Lafayette at all. You awoke and ate and then got Mayfield's call
and came down and got Lafayette out.*

*You would not find out about Mrs. Thompson's death until Lianne read
you the obituary, and at that time you would still be too upset to think
much about how it must have been for Lafayette in those dark hours of a
Saturday morning. It would be months and months before you would try to
imagine how it must have been for Lafayette:*

Very dark in the holding cell, and Lafayette thinking about his mother.

He could practically see her obit, a broken column of skinny type. He
saw it with a picture, a young picture like so many of the older blacks'
pictures were, prints of the one or two photos they'd had made in their
entire lives. A seventy-four-year-old deacon would kick off, and there staring out at you from the page would be a fierce handsome young man in a
soldier suit. His momma's picture would be the one Big Daddy always kept
over the bar: her wedding picture, beautiful in her long white dress.

Not her wedding to Big Daddy, but her wedding to his son.

He saw it under the banner the *Gazette* had run for years, up until at
least 1961, he knew, running it for a few years, inexplicably, even as they
were editorializing against Faubus and segregation and for equal rights:

Deaths of Negroes

Clovis T. Bookout, Jr.

Funeral for Clovis T. Bookout, Jr., 55, of Little Rock, who died Thursday, will be at noon Monday at the Rock Creek Baptist Church. Mr.

Mr. Bookout

Bookout was a member of Bricklayers Union No. 1, a veteran of the Korean War, and an aficionado of the martial arts, who conducted demonstrations for many local schools and churches. He was a native of Jackson, Mississippi. Survivors are his wife, Daisy Bookout of Helena; two daughters, Allene Bookout Whitmore and Rockie Bookout, both of Little Rock; a son, William Vergial Bookout, of Jackson, Mississippi; and two grandchildren. Arrangements are by Griffin Legget Healy & Roth.

Mrs. H. Elizabeth Thompson

Mrs. Hattie Elizabeth Thompson, nee Shadowvine, died early Friday afternoon. Mrs. Thompson was a leader in the women's auxil-

Mrs. Thompson

iary of her church, and was active for many years in the Woman's Christian Temperance Union, as well as in many other community organizations. Mrs. Thompson was a Democrat. Marriages were to Walter Everett Thompson of Hazen, a minister, who died in 1952, and Wilbur "Big Daddy" Thompson, a Little Rock restaurant and club owner, who died in 1971. Mrs. Thompson, who as a girl was a pretty little spiritual thing, could never come to terms with her own need for warmth, sex, and financial security, a need that led her, some three years after the unfortunate death of her handsome, penniless, and sincere young preacher, to marry his father, the hard-drinking hard-playing big-laughing owner of several shady joints in the city, and a man who was rumored to have ties to organized crime. Maybe Big Daddy was flattered by the admiration of such a sprite, or maybe he had desired her since the moment Walter brought her home, thinking what a waste to throw that body away on a boy who thought of nothing but heaven and who had no natural feelings, wanting to get just as far from his daddy's life as he could. Maybe Mrs. Thompson convinced herself she could see the son in the father, and that with her help and guidance Big Daddy would straighten out his ways and become a force for good in the world. What actually happened was they spent the next fourteen years fighting and fucking, Mrs. Thompson loathing the weakness that had got her into this mess, and loathing the body that kept her in it, leading her again and again back into Big Daddy's noisome but irresistible bed. Strangely, she visited all her disgust on the head of her oldest child, Walter's boy, perhaps because in some obscure way she felt he was a witness to her degradation, Walter's witness, and had to be impeached; and she pampered and spoiled her namby-pamby youngest, Big Daddy's boy. So it was ironic, as if wildness were a gene that skipped a generation, both of Big Daddy's children turning out church mice, and only Laugh, the preacher's son, coming through like high holy hell. Survivors include a sister, Thelma Shadowvine Leslie; a nephew, Willis Leslie, of Port Arthur, Texas; and two sons, Stephen Trenton Thompson and Jean Lafayette Thompson, an attorney, both of Little Rock. Burial will be in Harmony Cemetery by Roller Fune'l Home.

Jesse Vincent Raglin

Jesse Vincent "Pump" Raglin, 28, of Little Rock, died Friday. Mr. Raglin was a cab driver for the Black and White Cab Company, and

Mr. Raglin

until 1975 was part owner, with his brothers, of Raglin's Friendly Esso. He was a model airplane enthusiast and a Baptist. Survivors include his wife, Mrs. Nola Price Raglin; two brothers, Martin Anthony Raglin and John Jacob Raglin, both of Little Rock; a son, Jesse Vincent Raglin, Jr.; and his mother, Mrs. Ruth Vandiver Raglin.

It was floating in space, her obituary was, floating in space right under his feet like the stars of the galaxy. And then it shrank, and all the other galaxies came rushing in together in a white-hot swarm and blinked out like a blown-out light bulb. And it was just Laugh there in his dark cell, falling, with nobody to see him fall.

"I'm glad you gone," he said.

21

HORNS IN MY CHEERIOS

"Rubert, come here," Ferrin Dwell said. He was sitting at the breakfast table, a lean knobby white man wearing an unbuttoned blue work shirt and nothing else. His ribs showed like slats in a shutter. An unfiltered Pall Mall was burning away in an ashtray beside his cereal bowl. He was only twenty-nine, but he was ropy and weathered, and his face and neck and arms had the burnt dirty shade of the man who rides on the back of the asphalt truck. His narrow butt was too bony to be comfortable in chairs, and he shifted it now.

His full name was Ferrin Loyal Dwell, and he pronounced "Loyal" so that it rhymed with *Casino Royale*. The people who usually mispronounced it were the ones behind desks: teachers, principals, counselors, preachers, sergeants, military lawyers, Employment Security Division advisers, cops filling out reports, court-appointed lawyers, probation officers, the bill collectors at AP & L or Bell or the hospital, loan officers at the bank, divorce lawyers, crew foremen, wardens, the parole board—99 percent of the work force in the modern world sat behind desks, and they were all exactly damn alike.

Pud or broad, short or tall, skinny or fat, clear-sighted or goggle-eyed, wop, spic, chink, hebe, nig, or goob, every damn one of them was too damn ignorant to get splinters if you hit him in the face with a pine board, and every goddamn one of them wanted you to answer him, and then they all wanted to write your answers down into some kind of thing that didn't have any reasons in it at all, and then they wanted to look at what they had written and send you sliding down a greasy chute to hell.

He stirred his cereal with his spoon, watching the little rings play bump-a-car in the eddies, watching the ones that had gone under rise to the surface. Like bodies in a river. There they were again, the horns.

He called again, and Rubert stepped out of the bathroom fastening his belt. The bathroom was a wallboarded space not so big as a closet, a little enclosed box that had simply been added in when the house had been chopped up for apartments.

"Hell, Ferrin," Rubert said. "I was taking a shit. You bound to know I was in there. Goddamn, you seen me go in."

Actually, he had been through taking his shit and had been sitting there thinking how strange it was that every single morning he woke up with a hard-on and had to go take a piss. Then he would have some coffee, and then and only then did he have to take a shit. And then maybe some more coffee, and then he would have to go take another piss. He was wondering how many other people did it in the same order. He knew Ferrin didn't. Ferrin could go a week without taking a crap, and bragged on it. "Wastes time," he would say. "You be on the run, you have to stop to take a grunt, cops'll grab you while you sitting on the shitter. Me now, I would be done gone. I would be away from there. Besides, my body uses all its food." Rubert had been thinking that it was a way of knowing who he was, this having a rhythm every morning. It was a way of getting acquainted with himself all over again after dreaming all night and being something else. And it was a pity that Ferrin couldn't get any good out of the natural rhythms. Tight as he was, they might ease him some.

Rubert Bokamper was a round man with shiny brown skin. The shine was the gleam of healthy oils, exuded smoothly and steadily all day long in all weathers, dry, hot, cold, or wet. Rubert could process the oil from anything he ate—fish, liver, pecans, avocados, even bean sprouts or a crust of whole-grain bread—and get it to his skin in thirty-two minutes flat. He was barefoot but wore a tan t-shirt and jeans with a big leather cowboy-style belt Ferrin had given him, a belt that read LOYAL across the back in raised letters, given to Ferrin years ago by his older sister for Christmas, when he had been in prison the second time and had written her that the food was so good he was gaining weight. Rubert's belly bulged over the jeans, putting an almost unbearable strain on the belt. The man could shit three or four times a day. It was amazing.

"Come on over here," Ferrin said.

"Hell, I don't want no breakfast. You know I don't like breakfast," Rubert said.

"Somebody worries as much about his health as you do, you ought to know a good breakfast is the foundation of the day," Ferrin said. "Secret of my success. But I don't want you to eat no breakfast, I want you to look at something."

Rubert came over to the table. "What?" he said.

"There," Ferrin said, poking the surface tension with his spoon.

"What?" Rubert said. "I don't see nothing. You eating Cheerios. That's good because of the oats, but you drinking that fat milk with it, clog up your otteries. What?"

"Look at that Cheerio right there," Ferrin said, poking again.

Rubert bent over his shoulder to peer closer. "Yeah," he said. "It's in two. So what?"

"You dumb nig," Ferrin said. "It aint in two, it was born that way. Look at it."

"Yeah," Rubert said. "I can see it now."

The Cheerio was a floating set of horns, a circle that had not closed but tapered to a pair of points, the points varnished a darker brown than the rest, having baked more quickly.

"There was two of them," Ferrin said, "but I et the other one. You know what it tells me?"

Rubert straightened up. "What does it tell you?" he said.

"It tells me that things aint what they sposed to be. It tells me that things don't work out the way they sposed to. Somebody figured out how to make a machine to do it, and that machine starts putting out Cheerios the way you put out smoke rings."

"I don't smoke none, you know that."

"I'm just talking, nigger. Just as *if*. And so they set up the machines all in a row, and the factories humming and whistling, and another machine shovels em into the boxes, and the boxes go bumping and falling, and then they get stacked into bales, whip that plastic cord around them, and the truckdrivers come and pick em up and take em to the stores, and everything's hunky-dory. But some of the Cheerios didn't turn out the way they're supposed to."

Tell me some news, Rubert thought, but decided not to say it out loud. Morning was not a good time to rattle Ferrin's cage.

"And what that tells me is you might as well not depend on no system. You might as well go out and get what you can for yourself, because you can't count on nothing else to get it for you. You can't count on just being a good boy and having things fall in your lap."

"Well you bed eat yo cyril so you can have some of that strength. Eat up them horns too. We got to go mow some yards."

"I don't believe I'm going to mow no yards today," Ferrin said. "I'm about sick to here with that damn coon-ass that runs us. If I spend one more day listening to him, it'll be the day he dies."

How were they going to pay the rent, though? They were already two weeks late, and had promised to make it up come payday, end of the week. Rubert didn't want to go back into the streets, or start hopping around again from one relative to another, sleeping on the couch till whoever it was got tired of him and kicked him out. He liked having a regular bed all his own and nobody walking around picking up his mess and frowning at him.

"Landlady be mad," he said. "Kick us out the room."

"Fuck the landlady," Ferrin said. "I done got us another job."

Uh-huh. So maybe Ferrin had a plan to get hold of some Lady Godiva and have Rubert sell it down on the corner. That was wonderful, he was out of that kind of action lately, so to get back in he was probably going to have to have two or three fights, get some territory back. If the brothers already there didn't just say Fuck this fighting shit, motherfucker, I'm gone blow yo fucking head off. And even if all *that* worked out all right he would eventually get caught and go back in the hole.

"What kind of job?" he said.

"A special job." Ferrin was grinning now.

"I hate when you get so fucking mysterious."

"We working on the side of the law this time," Ferrin said. He cackled, and whacked his knee.

"Come again?"

"I got a call at the body shop the other day."

When Ferrin wasn't working or drinking or in jail, he hung around his brother's body shop drinking endless cups of coffee so burned and stale that Rubert thought they might as well just drain the oil pans of the cars they had up on the racks straight into their cups, that hot black slurry spouting smoothly from the loosened plug.

"So who they want us to kill?"

"You wish. But it probably is some kind of government work. They said they do a bunch of that government work."

"Well who was it? How'd they know where to reach you?"

"Hell, Rubert, I don't know. These kind of people don't let nothing slip. Cover their ass all the way. All they said was they was representing some people that needed somebody to be followed. They couldn't tell us no more, but they needed some street-smart types, some people knew their way around."

"You reckon it's CIA?"

"It might be CIA, or it might be FBI. Running one of these federal cases, you know, trying to get something on a defendant or something. There's a lot more illegal drugs around here than you think there is."

"So it's surveillance," Rubert said.

"That's right," Ferrin said. "We're going to survey some people."

In fact, Ferrin was pretty sure who had called. But as far as he was concerned, that information was on a need-to-know basis, and Rubert didn't need to know diddly-squat. He needed to know *Do like I say,* that's what he needed to know.

The call had come just in time, too, because Ferrin had already made up his mind to quit the lawn-mowing job. Damn if a couple of loud voices downstairs hadn't woke him up at six in the morning. Thumping around like somebody moving furniture. Forget going back to sleep, if that was what you wanted to do. Not that the racket bothered Rubert, of course. Rubert could sleep on a rolling locomotive with the whistle going and not wake up till they pulled into the station.

Ferrin had showered, and then had gone down shirtless and barefoot, his hair still wet, to check her out, but it was only the landlady overseeing a painting job, an old fucking cunt. But maybe not that much older than Ferrin, ten or twelve years or so. He was no spring chicken himself any more, aging fast like his daddy. Severe in her half-rimmed glasses like some kind of Nazi spy. Ok to fuck for a couple years, if you didn't have to hang around till she got *really* old. He had seen her before, but they had never really met.

He had sized her up, cracking jokes about hangovers and wild times and getting really spaced. He would have sworn she was a crackhead, but she seemed not to understand his hints, giving him absentminded *hmm*s and *n-hn*s and staring at the paint going on the wall, the roller driven by a red-eyed and frustrated young hard-ass who had planned on sleeping even later that day than Ferrin had, but had instead been rousted suddenly and without warning into actual work under the very eyes of his employer. The boy had one of the downstairs rooms, and he paid for it by doing repair and maintenance on the building.

"No, no, no," the woman had cried. "That's way too thick! How much water did you put in that paint, anyhow? None? Oh, come on! One coat, and thin it down. Who do you think's going to be staying here? This aint going to be goddamned Edgehill."

She was probably planning to sell the place quick. It was the only reason anybody ever painted these kinds of places, when they were trying to get rid of them. What did he care? He would rent the room from whatever other snotty-ass downtown sleaze-bag took it over.

Then she had turned to Ferrin and said, "Maybe you could do a better job." The boy had looked down from his ladder, uncertain whether to be angry or relieved.

"It aint really my line of work," Ferrin had said, and the boy had gone back to his painting.

"What is your line of work?"

Ferrin had not answered, but had simply smiled. It was his favorite smile. He had let it spread slowly over his face, but kept his eyes hard and deadly. He had read once in a cop story about a murderer smiling a feral smile, and he figured that was what this was, his feral smile. Feral was cats, he figured, like a tiger or something. And it sounded like his name.

A peculiar expression had gone over the landlady's face, and he liked that. *She looked into my eyes,* he told himself. *She seen I was a man who was capable of anything.*

It was watching the bitch bossing that young stud around that had decided him. No way he was ever going to let anybody boss him again. As far as he was concerned, he was quit as of right then, and he had headed on over to the body shop. But then Rubert had showed up at the shop with the mowers, and lo and behold the blades needed sharpening, and the big mower wouldn't crank, and the coon-ass had said Ferrin could spend the day fixing it. The coon-ass was no dummy. He knew Ferrin's brother would let him use the tools free. Ferrin had figured what the hell, it was a buck, and nobody would be chewing his ass. Quit tomorrow. So he had sharpened the blade on the one and sent Rubert on his way.

The telephone call had come at noon, and after that Ferrin had quit even so much as diddling with the dead mower. Just threw it back together and let the coon-ass find out later.

Rubert, standing over the breakfast table, had been absorbing their new status. Now he spoke. "Well, that's ok, then. But you still better eat yo cyril."

"I aint hungry no more," Ferrin said. "Let's go to the hardware store." Which was what he called the pawnshops. He stood up, pushing his chair away with the backs of his legs, and walked off to the bedroom, his shirt-tail flapping over the red sitting-spots on his bare butt. His walk was stiff and halting. Ferrin already had arthritis, young as he was, and it took him till nearly noon to get loosened up good. Which was another reason he hated the lawn-mowing job.

Rubert followed him to put on his boots, went to the john one more time, and they were through the outside kitchen door and down the ramshackle wooden stairs. Behind them, the Cheerios slowly bloated and thickened in their pond of sweetened milk.

They had a good day, riding around in the pristine May sunlight in the lawn-service pickup with the windows rolled down so they could hang their elbows out. The breeze of their movement was partly warm and partly cool, like fresh tea warm and sugared from the jug and poured over a glass full of ice cubes. And it was fun to think of the damn coon-ass cussing and waiting for them to show up.

They stopped by a quick-stop for a case of Pearl, some ice to throw into the big red cooler, and a couple of bags of jalapeño-flavored pretzels, and for a moment Rubert wondered if they were going to rob the place, but then he saw that Ferrin was just enjoying the idea that he *could* rob it if he wanted to. The register girl was just a stupid old fat cunt, but she had the instinct to practically read Ferrin's mind—she was from the same part of town—and she was sweating beads of pure lard.

Then they headed out into the country on Mabelvale Pike till they got to Ferrin's uncle's house, where they went in and made themselves at home and took seventy-five dollars in quarters out of the icetrays in the freezer compartment, the uncle's idea of a safe hiding place. "Cold cash," Ferrin joked, but the quarters stuck to Rubert's fingers, which hurt, and he didn't think it was a bit funny, running the hot water to get them off, which also hurt.

They sold the two mowers in the back of the truck to a goober they met at a yard sale over on Chicot Road, for forty-five dollars each. The goober didn't want to buy their machines, but his wife said, "Bee-bee, you better buy them mowers. You ain't never going to get a better price on a Yazoo, and you know you going to be mowing that extra lot the rest of your life." They had to crank them up and run them awhile to satisfy the goober that he wasn't getting cheated. The big one, the one he had just thrown back together, cranked on the first try, which Ferrin thought was a hoot.

Rubert was worried about selling the mowers, but Ferrin said Fuck it, they had to have operating capital, didn't they? And if the damn coon-ass came at them, he would tell him someone had stolen them off the truck during the night and they had been driving around all day trying to get them back. And then if the damn coon-ass still kept coming, Ferrin would personally stick a gun up his ass and blow his butt all the way back to Louisiana. And anyway, didn't Rubert realize they were working in the big leagues now, and the people who had hired them had connections, and would back them up all the way?

When they cashed Rubert's unemployment check, they had almost four hundred dollars.

Rubert hadn't eaten all day, except for the jalapeño pretzels, and he was ferociously hungry. "Besides," he said, "if I don't dilute these here pretzels with some hamburgers or something, they going to give me the absolute red-ass tomorrow morning." Rubert's favorite downtown hamburger place was the Andy's on the corner across from the Tower Building.

"I don't care where," Ferrin said, "as long as it has air-conditioning." It had warmed up as noon came on. In Arkansas in May you could have a day like late summer or a day like early spring. Sometimes you could have both before the day was over.

"I figure Andy has got to be either Wendy's husband, or he's got to be her brother or something," Rubert explained. "Because Wendy's and Andy's hamburgers are just alike. I don't know why they won't say so up front."

"They don't want you to know nothing," Ferrin said. "They can't control you if you know things. That's why I made it my duty to educate myself.''

"Well, is he her brother or her boyfriend, then?'' Rubert said.

"Fuck you,'' Ferrin said.

It took them a long time to find a place to park, and they had to walk four blocks over. Ferrin felt naked in his work shirt and jeans. He felt that telescopes were trained on him from the high office windows. He felt cross hairs lined up on his back, right between the shoulder blades. "Try to look like a serviceman,'' he said.

"I am a serviceman,'' Rubert said. "Why?''

Inside, there was a long line, folded back on itself around an oak hand-rail on a steel frame. An old man from out of town was holding things up, reading the wall menu out loud, item by item, and asking the order girl what was in each item and how much it cost, though the cost was displayed in big numerals right there in front of him. You could tell he was from out in the country: the brown felt hat, the thick-lensed black-framed bifocals, the short-sleeved lime-green shirt, the twenty-year-old double-knit slacks. You could tell he wasn't used to restaurants, was nervous, and wanted reassurance.

"It aint a life-or-death decision,'' Ferrin said, in a voice that was just a bit loud, but not loud enough to carry through the hearing aid he saw in the old man's ear. Most of the people in the line ignored him, but Ferrin saw a short olive-skinned man in a fancy suit smother a smile.

"Don't forget your Ex-Lax milkshake,'' he said a little more loudly, and the olive-skinned man now grinned openly.

"Retired, so he don't think anybody else has anything to do,'' Ferrin said. "Damned old bastard.'' Now the olive-skinned man quit smiling. He pretended he hadn't heard anything before, had been smiling at a private joke.

Rubert wanted two double-cheese on a whole-wheat bun, but no fries, because of the grease, he explained to the order girl, and a salad. He got a Coke to drink with the burgers, and a cup of frozen yogurt for dessert.

Ferrin didn't know what he wanted. He wasn't very hungry. He pretty much lived on beer and cigarettes. "Chicken sandwich, I guess,'' he said.

They took their food upstairs, sitting at one of the tiny square tables that would not hold even four trays. Ferrin pulled a beer and a bag of pretzels out of the rumpled paper sack he had brought with him.

"You aint supposed to have that in here,'' Rubert said.

"See,'' Ferrin said, "that's the thing about rules. They don't give a shit how you feel, or what you need. They just slap a rule on you, and that's that.'' His voice was still as much above the ordinary as it had been in the line downstairs.

Rubert didn't like the way the other customers were avoiding looking at them. "You letting yourself get all tense again," he said. "We get through eating, I'll massage yo shoulders."

A frightened young man came up. "Sir, we can't let you drink that in here," he said.

"Drink what?" Ferrin said.

"That beer, sir."

Ferrin had snagged a large Styrofoam cup on the way upstairs. Now he poured the Pearl into it slowly. When he was finished, he capped it, then stripped a straw and pushed it through the thin plastic of the lid. "What beer?" he said. "This here's my Coke." With a snap of his forefinger, he thumped the empty beer can spinning. "That's just an old beer can somebody else left here. You can take it."

The boy took the can and left, and Ferrin pitched back, thrusting his feet out into the aisle and smoking a Pall Mall. From time to time he sipped on his beer. He was in a better mood now, but he didn't touch his chicken sandwich. "You care if I take that with me?" Rubert said. "I hate to waste good food."

"I don't see how you can set there and eat all that greasy meat," Ferrin said.

"Protein is brain food," Rubert said.

"Well you better eat a lot more of it, then."

It was almost two o'clock when they got back to the pickup. They were just across the street from it, waiting for the light to change, when they heard somebody yelling. "It's a damn nigger with his shirt off," Ferrin said. The man headed toward them with rapid, exaggerated strides, calling out in a loud voice, his face lifted to the sky over the buildings. He went right by them without seeing them. "Thank you, wonderful God of Arkansas!" he exclaimed. "Thank you, Jesus!" He called it out at the top of his voice, over and over, striding purposefully away from them now, into the west, as if he meant to walk right through the wall at the end of the world, as if he meant to break directly into heaven and speak his gratitude: "Thank you, wonderful God of Arkansas! Thank you, Jesus!"

"Least he dressed for the weather," Rubert said.

"There's some crazy people in this town," Ferrin said.

They spent the rest of the afternoon knocking around in the pawnshops. "I do love a hardware store," Ferrin said. He couldn't decide whether they needed a camera or not, so he looked at a lot of cameras as well as a lot of guns.

"If it's just surveillance, why we need guns?" Rubert said. He didn't have anything against guns. He liked guns. Who wouldn't? He just wanted to hear Ferrin explain things.

"We're operatives, Rubert. Operatives don't never know what kind of dangerous situation they walking into. Your best friend might be your worst enemy. Be prepared."

"Ok," Rubert said.

The cameras Ferrin favored would have taken most of their money, even in a pawnshop.

"You don't know how to work one anyway," Rubert said.

"How do you know I don't?"

Rubert himself was drawn to the guitars. He strummed a bright red Fender but evoked only a low ghostly twanging, since the instrument was not plugged in. "Hey, Easy Money. Lookahere."

The truth was, Rubert knew E, A, and A minor, and that was all, and the closest he had come to actually performing had been once when he was in the eighth grade, when he and three other boys had talked about quitting school and forming their own band. "The Squashed Armadillos," he said fondly, strumming. "Coming to a theater near you."

The guns were cheaper than the cameras, but Ferrin still didn't like the prices. Anyway, all these shops had were pistols, rifles, and shotguns. Ferrin hinted around, trying to get a line on where they could find bigger pieces, or maybe explosives. He got mostly hard looks or anxious disclaimers. One dried-up little old man said flatly, "You get out of my shop, mister." Ferrin thought it was funny, being ordered around by such a shrimp, and he left, laughing. Finally a clerk in one of the stores came through. The owner had gone in the back for a minute, and the clerk pulled Ferrin over. He had black sideburns and a receding jaw, and he wanted ten dollars for an address. Ferrin jewed him down to five, which he was successful at doing only because the clerk was afraid the owner would come back in before he got any money at all.

"Where were you in?" Ferrin said, after the fellow had scrawled the address and a rough map on the back of a charge slip.

"Just Tucker," the man with the sideburns said.

"Hell, that's ok," Ferrin said. "Tucker's nothing to sneeze at."

"Where were you?" the clerk said.

"It wasn't Tucker," Ferrin said, with an evil grin.

The address on the charge slip was way out in southwest Little Rock again, over where Sixty-fifth Street ran under the I-30 overpass and hooked around a swampy corner into Arch Street Pike. A gravel driveway ran for a winding quarter mile along a drooping wire fence, beside a field that seemed to be mostly broken stalks and brackish puddles. Finally it ran in through a gap in a honeysuckle-throttled privet hedge, to end at the root-sprawling waist-high weathered stump of an old oak tree. The house had been a farmhouse when the oak had been young. After a while a couple of black teenagers came out to see what Rubert and Ferrin wanted.

Only one of the teenagers did any talking. "We aint got no Uzi," he said. "Uzi real poplar right now. Cost you eight hundred anyway. You got eight hundred?"

"I aint saying what I got and what I don't got," Ferrin said, bargaining tough. After a while, they worked out a procedure. Ferrin would describe what they wanted, the teenager who talked would turn to the one who didn't (his brother?) and tell him a brand name and particular description, speaking so fast in that peculiar dialect, almost Ferrin's own, yet whose images and cadences were somehow changed so that the act was like translation and made Ferrin feel like the President making a speech at the UN. And then that one, the silent one, would run back in the house after the requested weapon. As the light faded, they had narrowed it down to four items, all laid out on the tree trunk while they argued over prices. There was a fake-walnut-stock .38; there was a 9-millimeter automatic that Ferrin kept referring to as a Luger, to the infinite scorn of the talker, there was a cheap little Ingram that looked about as solid as a Daisy air rifle but would fire twenty-six rounds in seven seconds; and there was a lump of dark-blue plastique: "Aint got no dynamite," the boy had said. "You zip-lock at, keep it in yo frigerator."

Ferrin wanted a silencer too, but they couldn't afford one if they got all three guns and the plastique. Rubert preferred the .38, so they swapped the 9-millimeter out. The runner carried it back to the house. The spokesman leaned on the stump, pretending to ignore them.

"I forgot to ask who we supposed to be watching," Rubert said, sighting with the .38, dead on the red and harmless sun.

"You wouldn't believe it if I told you," Ferrin said. "I'll tell you this much, though. It's a lot of money involved. And it's tangled up in this toga-party business."

"Toga party?" Rubert said.

"You got to start reading something besides the funnies," Ferrin said. "Had a big thing on it Sunday morning. Wife swapping, nakedness. Didn't have no good pictures, though. Caught that big old lawyer coon used to play for the Razorbacks."

"Which Razorbacks?" Rubert said.

"Football." Ferrin grinned. "Bet you like a party like that. Poke you some of that rich white ass." He picked up the Ingram, one-handed it like a movie gangster.

"I still don't get it," Rubert said.

"The family involved been getting death threats. Somebody might want to kill one of em. My contact says just stay in the background, keep an eye out. Pick up whatever we pick up."

"So we protecting rich people," Rubert said. "Aint that a hoot."

Ferrin was manic in the gathering darkness, his eyes and teeth flashing. He popped in the one clip that came free with the Ingram, whirled, and pretended to fire at the tree line. He held the chatter gun up happily. "This is a whole shitload better'n a lawn mower," he said.

22

FAST FORWARD

By Monday early they had it worked out that Laugh would plead no contest to a misdemeanor charge of indecent exposure (the irony being that this time he wasn't guilty). Misdemeanor would allow him to keep his law license. The sentence would be so many hours of community service, which meant going to juvenile detention centers and boys' camps and telling them where he had gone wrong and how the same thing might happen to them if they didn't heed these words of wisdom.

Charles had expected Sonny to fight the plea bargain, but strangely he hadn't. Perhaps because he had already gotten what he wanted. He was basking in media attention, the crusader for clean living and right thinking; the savior, just as they were beginning to falter a bit, of the moral majority. Even some of his own cops were swayed. Robbie Rabelais had found a new hero to worship, his chief, the two-gun smut-smasher. He spent some time explaining the wonders of Sonny Raymond to Freddy Mayfield, how at first Robbie had misjudged him but now he saw that maybe if you were going to stand up for the right maybe you *had* to have a little bit of a rough edge. Jesus whipped the money changers out of the temple, you know.

Freddy mostly kept his own counsel, though he sat and took doughnuts with Roscoe Hawthorne from time to time. There were others, older cops a lot of them, who wanted to believe the job they were doing was a respectable job. Not enough for a palace revolt, although if he had been willing to sit down with some of the not-so-clean cops who hated Sonny for their own reasons, there might have been—you could count on Sonny to make enemies in every camp. But Freddy was not the sort who would stage a revolt. There was a higher authority than Caesar, and you held to your principles and waited for false prophets to trip themselves up.

Freddy was on the phone to Charles Morrison a few times too. There were other things on his mind right now, but Morrison still wanted to find out who had tapped his phones. Tracing bugs wasn't Freddy's line of work, though, and it wouldn't be right for him to moonlight anyway, and he honestly couldn't think of anybody else who would be safe just now, who would for sure not have ties to Sonny Raymond. Free-lance detectives are a little bit like free-lance poets, in that they both have to depend heavily on the power structure to get any action. Few poets would have refused dinner at the White House, no matter how they felt about Ronald Reagan, and few pee eyes would have refused Sonny a favor.

Implicit in all this was the suspicion that Sonny was responsible for the bugging of the phones, though neither of them ever said Sonny's name.

Morrison couldn't think *why* Sonny would have it in for him, other than general cussedness or political differences. And there were plenty of other people who hated Sonny's politics. Well, maybe the man had bugged them too. It was just the only idea that made sense at all. Especially when you put it together with the entrapment of the party.

Charles explained to the newspapers that no one else in the firm had been involved in the famous toga bash, that Laugh had been basically an innocent bystander, that his mistake was bad judgment in the company he kept, and that he had been suspended from the firm as punishment.

Charles refused to give interviews to the tv stations, feeling that such appearances only gave haters an icon to focus their hatred. It was bad enough the way they ran the same floodlight-bleached clip over and over, pale bodies in blankets, the shamed libertines shielding their faces, hurrying to the temporary anonymity of the county van. One station ran their same clip twice each night for a week, leading off and closing their story with it, as if you were really seeing something different. There were solemn references to "the troubled Morrison firm."

KROK at least ran an editorial by the station owner, in which he spoke vaguely of the desirability of not presuming guilt by association and explained that many of the town's most esteemed cultural and social leaders actually didn't as a rule go to shameless bisexual falling-down-drunk stick-your-pecker-in-someone-else's-wife orgies. True, he didn't run the piece until several days had gone by and the heat was off a little, but you could understand that. He did hint that an important person's handling of what he called the racial dimension had been a model of tact and forbearance, which Charles appreciated. Charles thought he deserved some credit from the black community for looking after Lafayette, but fat chance, the damn kinky-haired ingrates.

It was still possible he would ask for Laugh's resignation later, after the hooraw had died away. Meantime, he gritted his teeth, promoted Betty to partner after all, doubled Greg's caseload, and even got after Eamon to knuckle down and do a little work for a change. He had always heard there was no such thing as bad publicity, and sure enough, their business went up. You had to laugh.

Laugh, for his part, asked for and got an extension on his community service. *In order to get my life back together before I attempt to influence the thinking of youth, blah blah.* After his mother's funeral, he cleared out of town, at his own cost. Charles didn't send him all-expenses-paid to some Florida island to wash away his crime. No, Laugh went to Hazen, his daddy's hometown, and just lay low awhile. Before he left, he came home one day and found the extra set of keys on the luncheonette bar in the kitchen, no note or anything. The keys were loose on the counter; she had taken them off the leather ring she always carried. He smelled them, but there was no whiff of her. He threw them at the window over the kitchen sink. They clinked and sprang back, two clattering into the sink, one onto the floor. There was a nick in the window where one had hit, a thumbnail fan of rainbow, but no broken glass. He never picked the keys up. Maybe someone else did. The house was sold before he came back to town.

That was pretty much the last flash of anger he felt. He might have been angry with Charles for patronizing him, but he wasn't. That anger was part of the old Lafayette. Might not be a new Lafayette, but the old one was dead. Died when Momma died. He didn't have much of anything straight yet, but he did have a good grasp on one big thought: how much of his anger and fear hadn't really been him, had just been his momma's transferred and using him for a host, living in his chest like a giant tumor. So when you cut her out, there was this hollow man, skinny as a child, all these dangling veins. Impossible to say how the real Lafayette felt, because the real Lafayette had shriveled up and quit growing at about six years old.

He had had to agree to counseling in order to defer his community service, which raised the question of could he leave Little Rock, but Hazen had a social worker now, so that was ok. He saw the worker some, but didn't have a lot to say to her. She was more used to dealing with white farmboys who got in trouble for spotlighting deer, or young black men who skipped school and then when they got caught showed up the next day with FUCK carved into their fades. She was nearsighted and alcoholic and was having trouble with her boyfriend, who weighed three hundred and twenty pounds and gaining, couldn't get in his own pickup any more, and laughed every time she suggested he go on a diet.

Laugh spent some time fishing LaGrue Bayou from the bank, or out in a flat-bottomed boat on Peckerwood Lake. He actually went to church, his daddy's old church, way out in the country, and he didn't feel superior to the whiskery feeble old gents and stooped old ladies who mostly populated it. He just listened and watched, trying to learn what he could. After all, they had gotten nearly all the way through *their* lives without making a god-awful mess of things.

Nobody heard anything from Tina.

Charles and Lianne made their appointment with Father Christmas the Wednesday after the toga party. Charles wasn't looking forward to it.

It was the last day Rubert and Ferrin would have the pickup, because by now the coon-ass would know they hadn't cut any grass Tuesday, and would have been waiting to ream them out this morning at the first house on his list, and then, when they didn't show there, would have stormed over to the apartment, and when he didn't find them there would be all over town raising sand and carrying on.

"Cross that bridge when we come to it," Ferrin said.

"Is that all the more of a car they can afford?" Rubert said, not impressed by the Skylark.

They circled the vast parking lot at the Baptist Medical Center, cruising slowly two lanes over while Charles and Lianne parked the Buick, got out, and walked toward the Tower. Ferrin pulled the pickup over to one side, the motor running. He leaned over Rubert to look out the right-hand window, craning up at the Tower.

"What you think they doing in there?" Rubert said, scrunching out of his way.

Ferrin sat back. "I don't know. Maybe she's sick."

"Didn't look sick to me," Rubert said. "Neither one of em didn't."

The Tower made Ferrin nervous. He hated it. He knew it wasn't the hospital proper, but what exactly *did* go on in there? He thought of cubicles lit by lifeless fluorescents, of stainless-steel machines humming with a sound just beyond hearing. He thought of pulling your pants down to strangers, of hypodermic needles and strange etheric odors. He thought of blond men in white coats and steel-rim glasses, with their hair parted just right. He thought of sweating in his work clothes trying to pencil in answers on a form that made no sense, and the sweat going cold on his body in the air-conditioning. Handing the paper back through a glass panel, somebody's typewriter starting up rattledy-clack like machine-gun fire.

"We in a fire lane," Rubert observed. "Let's move on. Go get some doughnuts."

Ferrin gunned away from the building angrily, feeling pursuit, as if a gang of lab-coated zombies had been about to come pouring out of the building to drag him upstairs, clamp him into some kind of mechanical bed, cut out his eyes and tongue, and run a rough plastic tube up his pecker. "You the biggest hog I ever seen," he said. "What happen to eating healthy?"

"Man is a omnivore," Rubert said. "Besides, they got whole-wheat blueberry doughnuts at Community Bakery," he said.

"We'll make a stop on the way," Ferrin said. "Reconnaissance."

It wasn't really on the way. He took them around behind the Med Center, going east on Kanis Road, left on Barrow to Markham, right on Markham over to University, north on University to Cantrell, and right and east on Cantrell over to Charles and Lianne's house. It wasn't really reconnaissance either.

"You gone alert em they being watched," Rubert said.

"Well then, the bird is flushed," Ferrin said. "And you can pull the trigger."

It was hard to talk to Ferrin sometimes. He kept changing the frame of reference. "But we aint hunting these people," Rubert said. "We protecting em."

"Don't worry about it," Ferrin said. "I got a cover story."

Ferrin parked in the big semicircular drive and got out. Rubert stayed in the truck, watching through the windshield as Ferrin swaggered over to an old black man on his hands and knees in a flower bed. He knew what Ferrin was up to, and he didn't like it. It gave Ferrin a sense of power, tramping other people's territory without their knowledge. "Why 'on't you just spray a few bushes while you at it," Rubert muttered.

"We was wondering if you was in the market for any lawn service," Ferrin said to Coleman, his eyes on the big marble house.

Coleman sat back on his haunches, brushed the dirt from his knees. He looked up at Ferrin. "This look like a lawn?" he said.

"We do gardening too." Ferrin ran his eyes over the grounds, casing the joint. The wall, running back of the garage, about a twelve-foot-wide alley. That might be a good outpost. You wouldn't be visible from anywhere else on the property. No gates or locks on the drive, no alarms or surveillance cameras. These people might be rich, but they were sitting ducks.

Coleman got to his feet. It took him a long time. He was taller than Ferrin when he got straightened up. His yellowed eyes were flat and insolent. That sort of yellow, as if the tobacco-brown irises had leaked into the surrounding white, seemed animal to Ferrin, inhuman, demonic. Coleman studied Ferrin, flicked a glance at the pickup. "I do all the work around here," he said.

"You still a nigger," Ferrin said. "Just cause you work for a rich man."

"I'll remember you said that," Coleman said.

From the pickup, Rubert could see Ferrin was making the old man mad. He leaned out the window. "Less go," he hollered. "I'm hungry."

Ferrin cocked a finger and thumb at Coleman: *P-kwwwh!* He walked back to the pickup and got in. "Doughnut time," he said.

Up in the Tower, Charles and Lianne were in private session with Ian Farber. Charles was wondering why he had come. He'd never had to endure such vituperation before, not at Lianne's worst and angriest. He was an adulterer, a traitor, he was involved in shady activities, probably drugs, which had caused either the Mafia or the police to bug their phones, and now he had not only ruined their reputations but put both their lives in danger, you should hear the hate calls we got until we changed the number, and then somehow somebody found out and we got more and changed it again and not any since then thank God, and the mail is even *worse*:

> Dear Harlot,
>
> I am a Christian, may God wipe your kind from the face of the Earth, and to put your views across on every television for years in our state, what is Arkansas coming to?
>
> But the worm dieth not that will crawl in your body. And you will cry out for your money then, but it will be up in smoke in the eternal fires of Hell.
>
> Such garbage as you will holler for mercy then, but the time for mercy is all past. Not one drop of water on your tongue, and your screams are going to be music in the angels ears.
>
> Sincerely,
> A Friend

The worst of it was that Lianne delivered her accusations not white-facedly, not in apparent icy rage, but calmly and conversationally, looking back and forth from Charles to the therapist and illustrating by pointing at Charles from time to time, as if he were no more than some sort of living visual aid. "And how do you feel about that?" Ian Farber said once.

"How am I supposed to feel?" Charles said. He was imagining their plane going down, a tumble of broken fire across a snowy mountainside. Lianne dead instantaneously, so she wouldn't suffer. He and the gorgeous black-haired beauty two rows behind them the only two miraculous survivors. Forced to huddle for warmth in a makeshift tent, they can't help themselves, they fuck over and over, grief and relief.

"That's a control move, Charles," Lianne countered. "You won't talk, you just hide back there in your hole and hold on to things."

Then when the rescuers find them, he's free at last, no guilt, he didn't make the plane go down. The black-haired woman too shy now to look at him. *Never forget you,* she whispers.

"I thought you were supposed to be the therapist," Charles said to Ian.

"I have a right to make observations," Lianne said.

"How about this," Ian said. "If you think she's right, you listen to her. If you don't, say so. What would that hurt?"

"That's the way he does it," Lianne said. "He badgers. He just badgers and badgers till you give up. Or you try to reach in his hole and pull him out, he bites your fingers."

"That's not how people use the word," Charles said. "It doesn't mean to withdraw from people. It means exactly the opposite. It means to pester somebody to death."

"See?" Lianne said triumphantly.

"He's totally destroyed my independence," she said later. "He got me to resign my job, he discounts my painting. He's completely cut me off from my mother."

"Jesus Christ!" he said. "*I* cut you off from your mother? You *hate* your mother."

"See?" Lianne said again.

All along, one thing that was deep-down worrying Charles was his birthday party. He loved his birthday parties, he really did. Lianne had a running joke about his "surprise" party, every year pretending nothing was going to happen, but every year unable to contain herself: And still it would be a surprise, because he wouldn't know what *kind* of party, always something different. Last year Mount Saint Helens blew up, and she claimed she had planned it.

This year she had spent a week painting volcanoes on the handmade invitations. She hadn't let him see what they said on the inside.

Ever since Friday, when the poet had stood there talking about cake and ice cream, Charles had been thinking about his party. He had woken up thinking about it Saturday morning. What could you do with the volcano idea? A stripper erupting from a papier-mâché cone?

Now the party was only five days off, and he didn't see any way they could go through with it. She was probably planning to—she would never let herself default on a commitment—but it would be one of those white-faced things, where she spent three days killing herself getting everything ready, a grim martyr to the childish needs of an undeserving bastard. Everybody on edge with the tension, leaving as quick as they can. Him alone in the kitchen after they all left, eating an extra bowl of melting French Vanilla. Thrusting a finger toward the ceiling, fuck you, Lianne, up there somewhere, where she slept, a mask on her face, exhausted.

But so far he hadn't quite been able to bring himself to declare, *Hey, face it, let's just call the whole thing off.* Some stupid little silly hope kept whispering, *Wait, wait.*

"How in the hell *can* I trust him?" Lianne said. "And then he can't even stay home the one night I really need him to. No, he has to chase *her*. *After* we talked about her, and he lied and said nothing was going on. And then he lies again, and puts on his tux, like it's some kind of formal reception, when all along what he's going to is nothing more than a drunken whorehouse orgy."

"Yes, Lianne," Ian Farber said. "But he didn't go, did he?"

About time you put in a lick for me, Charles thought. "For the last time," he said. "*Lafayette* invited me, and I had no idea what kind of party it was going to be."

"And what about the wiretap?" Lianne said.

"I don't know, Lianne," Farber said. "I think that's a decision you have to make. You know Charles better than I do."

"I thought you were the therapist," she said.

"That just means I've had training in positive interaction. It doesn't mean I know everything about all my clients. You live with Charles, and I don't. You have more information about him than anyone else can have, even a therapist or a detective."

They had told Farber about J. D.

The therapist continued: "You may be denying that information because you're frightened, but it's real information. I don't know what it says, but you do. And my hunch is you need to listen to it. You may not decide right, but none of us ever gets a rose garden. Sitting here waiting for some outside agency to tell you whether Charles is guilty or not is a very helpless position. You don't have to be helpless. You can decide for yourself, and make it count."

That was a little more intrusive than a therapist ought to be, maybe, but Father Christmas believed in cutting through the crap when cutting through the crap would do some good. He didn't have a theory of therapy, he just did whatever he thought would work. There were a lot of techniques out there, and all of them worked sometimes. He could have lain back and waited for her to discover that she needed to decide to decide, but he saw hundreds of troubled humans, and he had learned a few things she might not get to on her own for a million years. Why not give her the benefit of his experience? What else was he for? Ostensibly the code of neutrality was to protect the patient, but what good was it, since the honest therapists would be fair anyhow and the crooked ones just ignored it? In his opinion the real reason so many honest therapists adopted the stance was fear of responsibility. He had no such fear. He had no hidden agenda, and he didn't need anything from his patients. He just preferred to see humans satisfied. He preferred it on a profound but almost abstract level. Humanly speaking, it was better art.

Lianne's eyes were on Charles now, wide and dark and impartial as the lenses of cameras in a darkened room.

Rider came over on Friday for a meeting. He asked specifically to see both of them. He said he had news. Charles wasn't getting anywhere with picking his own detective, and while he still wasn't convinced Rider had the necessary toughness, at least the man was doing *something*.

"Look at this," Rider said, spreading blister packs out on the big desk in the ground floor library. They were electronic components of some sort, mounted under clear plastic on brightly painted cardboard. Striped resistors, fine coils of wire, clip junctions, little buttons with tiny holes like miniature sprinkler heads.

"What is this stuff?" said Charles.

"That's the same stuff that came out of the phone," Lianne said. "Those little buttons."

"Right," Rider said. "What I'm showing you is an over-the-counter electronic surveillance kit. They don't market it that way, of course." He held up one of the blister packs. "Gadgeteer's Delight!" it said, in large yellow letters on a red background. "Surprise your friends! Make them wonder how you know!" He tossed it back on the desk. "I bought this array downtown, at Razorback Industrial Electronics." He grinned. "For fifteen dollars more, I could have gotten a phone to practice on, and for twenty, the whole kit and caboodle in a handy plastic carrying case"—he made his voice sound like a tv pitchman's—"*complete with micro tool set!*"

"So it could have come from anywhere," Charles said, depressed.

"Razorback is the only source in town," Rider said. "Not that it couldn't have been brought in from outside. But it probably wasn't. People are lazy."

"Yeah, but anyone could have bought it. It doesn't tell us a goddamn thing."

"No, not by itself it doesn't."

"Not by itself?" Lianne said.

"They keep a record of all purchases of such equipment," Rider said. "By law, they have to. They have to record cost, date of purchase, and the name of the purchaser."

"Oho," Charles said. "Can you get hold of the records?"

"I not only can, I did."

"Oho," Charles said.

"How?" Lianne said. "I don't want you breaking and entering."

"No," Rider said. "I'm no good at that stuff."

"Did you con them into it?" Lianne said. "Like pretend to be an auditor who needed to see all the records or something?"

"Lianne, that's movie stuff," Charles said.

"I don't know if that works in real life," Rider said. "It sure doesn't work in Little Rock, where everybody already knows your face."

"So how?" Lianne said.

"I told them I had a client whose phone was being tapped and asked if I could see the purchase records. They said sure, why not."

"And," Charles said.

"They've sold seven kits since January the first. One of them went to the North Little Rock PD, and the other six to Pulaski County."

"Don't they have their own equipment?" Lianne said.

"Cheaper this way," Rider said. "The market is flooded with gadgets nowadays. Everybody's a spy. And you know all that budget trouble they been having."

Charles was frowning. He looked as though he faced an unpleasant decision. "Sonny," he said finally.

"Seems likely," Rider said.

"Do you think Freddy Mayfield could find out for sure?"

"You ask him. I don't think Freddy and me could work together very well. I don't think he likes me very much."

"Why?"

"The taint of the father, I think," Rider said. "In his worldview, suicide might not be a mortal sin, but it's still a pretty damn big insult to God Almighty."

It isn't, by the way. Think about it all the time myself, but We figure the children need Us.

The answer caught Charles off guard, embarrassed him.

"Charles, what have you done?" Lianne said, her eyes frightened. "Why would Sonny Raymond be tapping your phone? It's drugs, isn't it?"

"It's your phone too, Lianne," Charles said.

"Lianne, I don't think so," Rider said. "Old Charles here *is* a devious type, all right, way he keeps everything to himself. But I been talking to people, keeping my ears open. You know that bit from *Jesus Christ Superstar*?" He sang, snapping his fingers:

> *What's the buzz, tell me what's happening?*
> *What's the buzz, tell me what's happening?*

He grinned at his performance. "Well, with Charles, there *aint* any buzz. And there would be, there would be some kind of gossip floating around. You might keep it out of the news, but you aren't going to keep it out of the rumor mill. Besides," he added, "old Charles is too much of a prude to be tangled up in professional crime."

The familiar tone to Lianne, the implication that Rider had been checking up on the man who *hired* him, the jocularity, the presumption that he knew what made Charles tick, the slurs and condescension, the readiness to get involved in what was by God a *family* quarrel—

There were so many things wrong with Rider's attitude that Charles was unable to respond: fuses blew, relays clicked over, klaxons sounded, and all he could do was stand there paralytic with resentment while smoldering fragments of ego rained about his ears. Lianne studied Charles as if he were an anatomical diagram hanging on a wall and Rider the instructor, tapping significant morphologies with the point of his ruler. And somewhere in there, while Charles was seething with anger at his mistreatment, he had the best luck of his life: Lianne decided. She had heard Father Christmas, and he was right. She had all the information she really needed. She knew who Charles *was,* and he was ok. She trusted him.

The way stories usually get told, you'd think people made important choices because the plot drove them to it, because they hit a moment of truth. But that's just stress conversion. Foxhole Christianity. More often, it's the other way around. Your choices disappear in the tissues of your being, they happen as quietly and invisibly as the obscure mitosis of a cell. Time doesn't make choices. Choices make time.

"Ok," Lianne said to Rider. "But then why? What's his reason?"

"I don't know that a man like Sonny Raymond has reasons," Rider said. "Not logical ones anyway." He looked at Charles. "The only thing that comes to mind is that fight him and your boy Legg had a couple months ago. Is there anything else?"

"There wasn't any fight," Charles said.

"Oh come on, Charles," Rider and Lianne said together, then smiled at each other.

"I was there," Rider said.

"I don't know of anything else," Charles said. "I voted against him, which he probably figures, but so did a lot of other people."

"Maybe it's not so much you as your law firm," Rider said.

"I've never gone head-to-head with him."

"That case about the head cheese," Lianne said.

"Well, yeah, that, but that wasn't him, that was just that dufus deputy of his. I mean, before he *was* his deputy, when he was—"

"He didn't like it, though. You remember what he called you."

"No, he didn't like it. But when you really look at it, we did him a favor. Now *he's* lord high bailiff—"

"This isn't getting us anywhere," Rider said.

"Well at least we have a pretty good idea who did it," Lianne said. She sounded cheery and relieved, her voice as sprightly as Charles had heard in a month.

"That's the good news," Rider said.

"Oh yeah," Charles said.

"What?" Lianne said.

"It's a dead end," Charles said. "We can't touch him. We can't prove anything, and even if we thought we could, how could we go to the police? He *is* the police."

"So we just have to sit here and take it? What if he does something else?"

Charles suddenly felt very paranoid. "Hey," he said, waving at the windows all around. "Aren't there these laser things nowadays—pick up vibrations right off the glass?"

"In this neighborhood?" Rider said. "Nah, you'd have to have an unobstructed line of sight, and there's only a couple of windows even visible from here."

"Barbara's and the McHughs'," Lianne said. "They wouldn't give him the time of day."

"You might want to see if you can get the city to put on some extra patrols," Rider said. "If it would make you feel better. They're not all just real crazy about the county. If it *is* him, for whatever reason, my hunch is he's playing mind games. It isn't so much can he do anything to you. It's more can he harass you, make you feel threatened."

"Well, it's working," Lianne said. "How about you? What if we asked you to keep an eye on things? I'd feel better about that than the police."

"I've taken it about as far as I can go," Rider said. "I don't like bodyguard work. Don't have the attention span. I like to solve puzzles, figure things out."

Lianne didn't seem surprised by the answer. She pulled open a drawer in the desk. "Here's something for you to figure out," she said. "I should have given it to you before now."

Rider opened the envelope, took out one of the volcano cards. A folded check fluttered to the floor. He picked the check up without looking at it, slipped it into the pocket of his shirt. He read the card and gave a short laugh, then grinned at Charles.

"Let me see," Charles said, reaching.

"No," Lianne said, slapping his hand away. "So will you come?"

"Sure," Rider said. "Wouldn't miss it for the world."

Here's what Rider's (and everyone else's) card said:

Last year, Mt. St. Helens blew its top. This year, blow your troubles away, and come help us blow Charles's mind:

—champagne in blown glasses
—balloons to blow up
—breezes softly blowing outside
—Bob Elder blows the blues
—G. M. and Chocolate souffles

Where? Our place, of course
When? 7 pm, Monday, May 18

Don't blow it off!

"Everybody likes a blow job."

Sonny Raymond was talking to Cheese. Actually, he was trying to *keep* from talking to Cheese, trying to get a little work done and having no luck, because Cheese wouldn't shut up. Cheese was full of his triumph.

"Let's put it this way," he said. "She's not thinking about that attorney of hers anymore. She's got her mouth on bigger things."

"You mean her mind," Sonny said, not really listening: He was checking Audrey Tull's deposition for provable falsehoods. The College Station beatings.

Cheese chortled. "I mean her *mouth*!" he cackled, and Sonny got it. He was about to kick the slime-butt out, when Cheese sobered and said, "That club of Morrison's? The Blue Note?"

"Yes?" Sonny said impatiently.

"She says it's a focus of drug activity. She says it's well known as such. She says Ron used to go over there all the time, that's how she knows."

"Hmm," Sonny said.

"I asked her about it, and that's what she said." Cheese grinned. "Even when I'm cleaning my weasel, I'm working."

"What do you want?" Sonny said. "A medal?"

Audrey Tull showed up at the door. He was grinning. "Them eight prisoners have escaped," he said. "It took em long enough."

"Aint that too bad," Sonny said. "Wonder how can we get em back in?"

For Charles and Lianne it was a weird weekend. Things were better between them, but not in a way he was entirely comfortable with. That is to say, she kept busy, wasn't around him much, or was moving too fast to chat with, but at the same time appeared to be quite happy. Blithely happy, one might say, as if nothing had ever gone wrong between them in the first place. She didn't stop to cuddle or to lollygag, she was cooking calling cleaning directing planning, but when she saw him, she smiled, and it wasn't a forced smile.

When she's busy, you might as well keep out of her way. And if you don't want to feel totally useless, a kid waiting on Momma to pay some attention, go find a way to keep your own self busy. Go out in the backyard and bother Coleman, dig around in the dirt.

So he reckoned she had made her decision, thank you, Father Christmas, and he reckoned it was in his favor. Which was great. But. Still. Howsomever. It seems to *me*, Charles silentsaid to himself, stabbing his trowel into the black dirt of the peony bed for emphasis. It seems to me I have some rights around here. It seems to me I knew all along I wasn't guilty of anything, and so, great, I'm back in the fold, tra la la, we're all so happy, but *goddamn*—

What he wanted was a little of his own, you know, a little drop of blood or two, a little revenge, gratification, payback. But she was singing in the kitchen, and she wasn't about to notice him waiting in his badgery way for his little temperamental nip at her fingers.

Coleman had been working for some time across the way. The activity finally percolated through Charles's inattention.

"Coleman, what the *hell*," he said, clambering hastily to his feet.

Coleman was laying a huge double-bitted ax to the roots of the small central dogwood in the patio. He rested the ax as Charles came up. "Now what?" he said.

"That's what I was going to ask you," Charles said.

"Tree dead," Coleman said.

"Don't tell me that tree's dead. That's my favorite tree."

"Where the leafs?"

"Leaves?"

"Aint no leafs on it, aint you notice? All the other tree done had the leaf. Had the flower too. Reckon you had a lot on yo mind lately."

Coleman was right. There was not a leaf on the tree. Thinking back, Charles remembered seeing no leaves on it all this spring—the two or three times he had even been out back. Jesus, was that all? The last time he remembered was the book club meeting. He had sat right under the tree then. He could call up images of it, stark and ideogrammatic in the generally leaf-softened evening, a lightning of reflex lampglow. And he had never once thought why it had been so bare. Right again, Coleman. I had a lot on my mind.

He felt an unreasoning grief at the loss. There were other dogwoods in the yard, but he and Lianne had brought this one back a sapling from the dogwood-crowded spring on the tenth anniversary of their first fuck. They had celebrated with another one, right there on the moss in the woods, and it had been as good as the first, her reaching back over her head to grasp the sapling's trunk, looking up at the sun through the white flowers of its overarching neighbors (the sapling too young as yet for flowers). Afterward, she had wanted to take the tree home, and they had taken it, digging it out with the steak knife they had brought to slice the cold rare roast beef, that and the jack handle from the car. He'd planted it himself, bedding it in with some of the moss he'd also brought back. The patio had been expanded to incorporate the tree. He had pruned it, watered it, admired it, thinking of himself as performing an act like bonsai.

He liked to think he had a sense of composition, that he was, if the truth be known, at heart as much an artist as Lianne. He thought the way he had caused the branches to sail up and around in a graceful but not too obvious spiral was evidence of the elegance of his spirit.

It might have lived forever, left in the heaven of its forest, but he had brought it home, and now it had died, probably of neglect. It was his fault, his mind so much on his own worries. Life kept you busy fighting off troubles, and you looked up, and the best parts of your life were gone.

"Well, what? Well, what was wrong with it?" he said.

"How I know?" Coleman said. "Wrong kind of dirt, maybe. Fungus."

"I thought you were the gardener."

Coleman regarded him like a father wishing he didn't have to change a diaper. "Probably not enough light," he said. "All these other trees. Weaken it, so the fungus take hold."

"That's really too bad," Charles said. "I really liked that tree."

Coleman, deciding that Charles had said his say, turned and hefted the ax again, let it fall to shiver root and dirt (moons of severance in the black chop). Watching him was like watching the Betamax on slow. He gathered the ax in stages to his shoulder. Lifted it. Let gravity take it in. Stood waiting a moment, loosely holding the helve, as if to let the slow-thinking earth get the news. Wiggled the ax to loosen the blade. Gathered it to his shoulder.

"I know what I'm doing," he said. "If I am just a rich man's yardboy."

"What?" Charles said to his back.

"You can hire em if you want to," Coleman said.

"What are you saying?"

Gather the ax, lift, let fall. "Yard service come around. Smart-aleck white man, some kind of useless nigger in the truck. Hire em if you want to."

Charles had a vision of Coleman dying on his feet and not falling, as gaunt and hard and immovable as the dead tree: You would have to come in with axes to root him up. You would have to grub his rigid body from the yard with cables and a tractor. "You suit me just fine," he said. "I aint planning to hire anybody else. Where did you get that idea?"

Coleman rested on the ax again. "All I'm saying is I get some respect. I might be yo yardman, but I get some respect."

"Coleman, don't I give you respect? I'm selfish sometimes, but when did I ever treat you low? When did I ever say you didn't know more about gardening than I would ever learn?"

Coleman had caught his breath. He straightened, nodded. "You right," he said. "Wasn't you said that." He turned back to his task.

"So is that all right, then?" Charles said.

Gather, lift, let fall.

"Still working, aint I?" Gather. Lift.

Charles, feeling that he had handled something well, only he wasn't too clear just what, went in the house for a glass of water.

Clemmie and Lianne had the kitchen in total disorder, mixers, bowls, trays, pans, pots, wooden spoons, slotted spoons, spatulas, all manner of whatnot pulled out all over the place. "We can't find the collar for the other soufflé dish," Lianne said, half under the counter. "We've got four dishes and three collars."

"Don't ask me," Charles said. "Did you know our dogwood tree was dead?"

"What? Oh yes. I told Coleman to go ahead and pull it up." She sat back on her heels to look at Clemmie, leaning against the center island. "Do you think it could be up in your kitchen?"

"I'll look," Clemmie said. She left the room, and Lianne stood up.

Out the open door, through the glass of the sun porch, Charles could see Coleman, bent under the uprooted tree, dragging it across the patio. "Look," he said, and pointed.

"I hope he's not working too hard," she said. "I worry about him."

"Coleman? He'll outlive us all."

"He looks like Jesus staggering under his cross," Lianne said.

"It's too wavy," Charles said. The tree was like a giant wooden anemone, a cluster of curling branches at one end, a knot of twisting roots at the other. "Too many limbs and things."

"You know what I mean," she said. "I want you to talk to him. Tell him to slow down."

"If he gets any slower—" Something dawned on him. "Hey, are we having soufflés?"

"None of your business," she said.

. . . .

Sunday, Tucker and Dee-Dee came over after dinner after church. To help decorate, it turned out. Which meant that Charles and Tucker poured big glasses of Turkey on the rocks and went out back and smoked a couple of Charles's infrequent but expensive panatellas while Clemmie and Lianne and Dee-Dee strung crepe paper and filled balloons from a tank of helium delivered the day before. While the boys were out, the girls were climbing up and down the stepladder to tape strips of crepe to the wall, with breaks to suck helium and talk in squeaky rapid voices, driving themselves into fits of laughter and generally having a giddier time than Charles and Tucker would if they drank the whole bottle and ate the cigars instead of smoking them.

"Tearing up the ground again?" Tucker said, tapping loose his ash, looking out over the yard. A great cavity where the tree had been, heaps of dirt on the paving stones. Tucker wouldn't have let the mess stay. He would have filled in the root hole, paved the wound over, and then swept off the entire patio, if he had had to do it all himself and stay up till three in the morning to get it done. And then he would have washed his tools and put them away.

"No, the little dogwood died, and we had to pull it up. I was sorry to see it go. I raised it since it was a puppywood."

Tucker scowled. He didn't think puns were a man's work. He felt Charles someday sooner or later ought to buckle down and learn how to tell an honest story. Charles thought maybe he ought to tell Tucker how ridiculous a bucktoothed man looked with a cigar stuck in his mouth.

"Now you got room to put in a pool," Tucker said. "That one little old tree was filling up the whole middle there."

Tucker had a pool. He was in perfect heaven wielding the long-handled vacuum or brushing the algae from the sides or opening up the skimmers to drop the 3-inch chlorine tablets in. Only rich people had had pools when he was growing up, he would explain. It had seemed the height of luxury then, an impossible dream, and now, grown, with a pool of his own, he felt secure and happy no matter how his daily life went.

A line from *The Wind in the Willows* went through Charles's mind. *Simply—messing about—in boats.* Except with Tucker, substitute the words "a pool."

It was a tempting idea. Charles imagined the yard with a pool. His would be patioed in stone, none of this low-class cement. The willow cascading onto one end. A beach umbrella over the patio table. Rocking on the blue water, half asleep on an air raft in the languor of the warm sun, a round floating drink tray beside him, sweat-beaded icy martini.

But Lianne would never go for it, it would uproot too many plants she liked and crowd too many others, change the whole life and flow of the place.

And then he surprised himself. *Look at you,* he thought. *Blaming her for your own decision. Blaming her because you can't have your cake and eat it too.*

For the truth was, it wasn't a pool sort of yard. His father had never even considered the idea. As much as Charles liked the water, his father had hated it, except in a glass or a shower. So he and his father were different after all. Strange never to have thought of that difference before. Oh, you were aware of it, but never to have concentrated your attention on it, never to have *thought*. Think of the man out in a fishing boat on the Little Red River, for example—twelve hours at a time, giving his employees their precious ceremonial vacation. How out of sorts he used to be when he got back in, not fit to talk to for days. Unapproachable until he had spent a weekend sweating and rooting in the herb garden.

So it wasn't Lianne; *Charles* didn't want to rip out all this green history. However much he might like a pool, he liked it this way more. And how many other times had he displaced his resentment at the world's narrow alternatives, given her the *No* side of the equation? *Choose,* the world said. *You are finite, and you must choose.*

He could have chosen Tina. But he could not have chosen Tina *and* Lianne, and he had blamed Lianne for that. And what was Lianne's offense? If she required fidelity, that was her prerogative. In return she offered unqualified love. No I-love-you-if: If you please me, if you do what I want. Thorny, hard to get along with, yes—but how much of that was his own resistance to truth? She gave him a gift of great price: She gave him straight information. She saw him clearly, and said what she saw. He *was* secretive, devious at heart. He *was* a badger.

The question, he saw now, was simply whether he was man enough for love.

He didn't realize it, but Charles was experiencing conversion. He was a Christian from that day forward, atheism and all, and whether you like it or not. Well, maybe not a *Christian,* exactly, but at least a lovean. Don't expect him to be perfect, though. With conversion come all the fringe benefits—ingenuous euphoria, self-righteousness, backsliding. And doubt, the cruelest gift of all, without which no faith can be complete. Total withering doubt.

"Yessir," Tucker said, slugging down some holy water. "You ought to put in a pool."

"Never happen," Charles said, and took a swallow himself.

Perhaps it was the drink, or perhaps it was the sort of psychological energy that is released when we cease to defend a highly cathected image of ourselves, but he felt washed in well-being. They strolled idly across the patio in the spring afternoon, nudging the dirt pile with the tips of their deck shoes, looking up at the leaves, inhaling deeply. And as they strolled, Charles felt, under the flagstones, the rolling surface of the pool that would not happen. Under the stirring of the breeze, under the dim sounds of traffic on Cantrell, he could hear, almost, the lapping of slight waves. In the glisten of grass he could see, almost, the bright hexagonals of light in blue water.

"Probably just as well," Tucker said. "There's a cost to everything."

"Yeah," Charles said.

"We been worried about you guys," Tucker said.

"Yeah," Charles said. "We hadn't been doing too good." It was easy to say, suddenly. No pretense necessary.

"You been screwing around on her?"

"No." And that was easy to say too. It seemed almost the whole point of his struggle, to be able to answer so easily and simply. He thought how close he had come, and shivered with *frisson*. Freezone.

"I'm glad to hear it," Tucker said. "Not that I'm no angel. Not that with the right woman, if Dee-Dee wasn't there— But we would have hated to lose you."

Charles patted his arm.

"The problem with a pool is—" Tucker said.

"It's a lot of work."

"I don't mind the work. What I was about to say, a pool seems like a big beautiful clear glistening thing, you know. The way you always see it on the tv ads. Crystal pure."

"With long-legged beautiful women around it."

"In bikinis. But what a pool really is is a system, an artificially maintained system. It isn't stable. Left to itself, it keeps trying to change into an ecology or something."

This seemed pretty obvious to Charles, even if he hadn't really thought of it that way before. "Yeah, I know you have to keep after it. Chlorine and all."

"This new algae going around, you either keep it scrubbed, or it'll fur up and turn green in a week. But it isn't just that, it isn't just the algae. Everything on earth loves water, and here's a great big shining chunk of it. The damn blackbirds walk down the steps at the shallow end to drink out of it. I came out once and there was a duck squatting out in the middle."

Charles laughed.

"The wasps are all over it, red wasps. See em out there riding and drinking, then they pop loose and fly off. Many's the time I've had em land on me while I was floating in the sun."

"Ever sting you?"

"No, I'm not afraid of wasps. Crickets and spiders. Skimmers are always full of dead crickets, hopped in the pool during the night and couldn't hop back out. The wolf spiders come out and hunt, run across the water. I found one in the skimmer once as big as my hand."

He held his hand up for illustration. "Frogs," he said. "Every week or so, I find a frog in there, hiding in the shadow of the diving board, or up under the edge of the steps. As far as he's concerned, he found it, it's his pond, and he's going to keep it. I have to run around with the long-handled net trying to scoop him out. Young frogs, old frogs, hoptoads, bullfrogs, tadpoles."

"Water moccasins?"

"Not so far. I had a giant crawdad in there for about two weeks last summer, though. I mean giant, I'm not lying—the sucker was the size of a crab. Scooting around on the bottom in the deep end. I couldn't catch him."

"What happened?"

"He died. I let it go as long as I could, and then I had to shock-treat the damn algae, and it killed him. Turned him white as a ghost. Which I hated, because I admire crawdads."

"Mosquitoes," Charles said.

"No, thank God. Chlorine kills the wigglers, I guess. There's some kind of damn waterbug, though, a little diving bug just about the size of a piece of snot, that will just bite the fire out of you. Swims like a streak. Damn thing comes in like a Jap in a Zero, I mean it will scare you out of the water the way it comes after you. I *hate* the bastards. I scooped one in a handful of water one time and flipped it out on the hot cement."

Charles smiled. "You wanted it to *fry*."

"Damn right. But the little sonofabitch dried out, sprouted wings, and zipped right back in the water and went after my ass again. I tell you what, I was on that cement myself in no time."

"Yeah, Tucker, it's really rough having a pool. I really feel sorry for you, man."

Tucker grinned. When he grinned, his wild teeth made him look not foolish but fierce. He took a swallow of his whiskey. "Go ahead, laugh. But you don't know the worst part."

"So tell me the worst part."

"You know how when it rains and you go out in the morning and the sidewalks are covered with night crawlers?"

"Yeah, and the sun comes out and they dry up and look like little twisted pieces of waxed string somebody's stepped on." He looked away from Tucker, sipped his whiskey.

"Oh, I see," Tucker said. "You want to tell this story."

"Oh, is this a *story*? Oh, pardon me, how gauche. If I had *known*—"

"Wise-ass. Well, anyway, the little suckers are trying to keep from drowning, I guess, ground gets full of water. So explain to me why they all wind up in the pool?"

"Aint got no hands," Charles said. "Fall off the edge, can't catch themselves. Worm aint got no hands."

"They all wind up in *my* pool," Tucker said. "Which leads me to the single most horrible thing I have ever seen in my life—"

"This from somebody tells me about gross anatomy. Tells me about heads rolling around in a vat of carbolic."

"Formalin. —Which is why it's just as well you don't have a pool yourself."

Tucker occupied himself with his whiskey. He pulled down a twig from the willow. He bent over and smelled the early roses.

"Ok," Charles said. "I give up. What is the single most horrible thing you have ever seen in your life? Worms in your pool?"

"Not exactly," Tucker said. "In the pool, they're all spread out, you don't really notice them that much. But this one time I was vacuuming, and when you vacuum, you have to stop every now and then and dump the trash out of the trap, you know—"

Charles saw it coming. "Tucker," he said.

"—so I opened it up and pulled the basket out—they're these round plastic baskets, you know, kind of a white gridwork cylinder—"

"Don't."

"—and it was just full. Dead worms, live worms, rotten worms, half worms, slimy worms, bleached-out worms, limp worms, wiggling worms—"

"Jesus Christ, Tucker."

"I jumped back about three feet and flung the damn thing off the fence. But you know, the shit of it was, I had to clean it out anyhow. It wasn't going away just because I didn't like the looks of it. I ran the hose on it, but they were woven in like shoelaces in a screen. So I got this paint stirrer out of the shed to scrape with—you know those flat sticks—"

Charles bent to pick up the ax where Coleman had let it fall. Balancing his drink, he one-handed it high. "Tucker," he warned.

"Since you put it that way," Tucker said. "What we having for supper tonight?" He peered into Charles's puzzlement. "You *are* rewarding us for helping with your surprise party?"

"Shit, I don't know," Charles said. "I guess so."

"So what are we having?"

"Spaghetti, probably," Charles said.

.   .   .

Across town, on the phone at his brother's garage, Ferrin finished his report.

"What about the rest of the week?" said the voice in his ear.

"What rest of the week?" Ferrin said. "We're fresh out of transportation. You want more, you're going to have to pay for transportation."

"What happened to your pickup?" the voice said. "I'm not made of money."

"It's up to you," Ferrin said.

"You should have told me earlier," the voice said. "All right, I'll arrange a car. But I want you up there right away tomorrow. This is a critical period. I want to know everybody that goes in and everybody that comes out."

"Can do," Ferrin said.

"And listen, get a phone put in. I don't like you calling me here."

Yowzah, yowzah, Ferrin thought. "Leave some money in the car," he said.

Charles and Lianne didn't sleep together Sunday night, but things felt comfortable anyway. It was as if intimacy demanded a formal declaration, an unburdening, and by the time Tucker and Dee-Dee went home they were both too sleepy, and she was too tired, to bother with so complicated a transaction. So she smiled wearily and went up to the master bedroom, and he had a glass of milk and some crackers and then went off to the guest room, to read himself to sleep, as he had been doing for weeks. And yet they both knew that the worst was over, that they would sleep together tomorrow night. It was as if they were waiting for the party, as if the party were, in both their minds, to serve as the process and ceremony of their reunion.

Each of them had a secret they did not say. A fear, an off-key note, a foreboding thrill that in their hopefulness they managed to forget. That's normal. I know what you have to live with. If it wasn't for shutting some things out, you'd be as crazy as I Am.

Lianne was afraid that Sonny Raymond would pull a Sonny Raymond. That he might have somehow gotten hold of one of the invitations and would raid her party. Harbored a thrill of guilt for calling it a Blow Job Party and thereby putting them at risk.

Charles, for his part, had gotten forty-two red roses at work that day, and a card that said, "Happy Birthday—Love, Tina." Brenda Faye and Rosalyn and surely others had seen the roses, but maybe they thought they were from Lianne. The card, its fragments nestled in the fragments of its envelope, littered the bottom of his otherwise clean wastebasket in his now dark office.

. . .

The party turned out to be a blast. Everyone arrived in a state of high hilarity, already animated and nervy. It was the invitation that had done it, just the right shock of bad taste to set the blood going, to communicate that this wasn't just any old party, that we were going to break some *boundaries* here. No one really thought this was going to be an orgy of oral sex, of course not, they all knew very well they were going to do mostly the same old things they always did at parties, eat, drink and talk, but my isn't it *fun* to be *daring,* to enjoy that exhilaration that makes the air crisp, the meat savory, the wine full-bodied, and perfume a magic in the night.

Bill in the corner gently hooting his sax.

"I was worried I'd gone too far," Lianne confessed. "I thought y'all might get upset with me and not come."

"My dear, don't be silly," Barbara said, kissing her cheek. "I may be an old prude, but this is a *party.* I think it's perfectly delightful." She sailed in grandly in her red gown, pale blond bald mustachioed Warren meekly in tow. They were the only ones Lianne had invited that she was really worried about—somewhat older than the usual run of their friends and definitely high church, though Barbara was willing to gaze upon a nude during class and within the sacrosanct boundaries of the Arts Center. Warren's family was old Virginia money, and Barbara had met him there as an undergrad, nailed him, and brought him back home.

Lianne had never considered inviting Charles's family—the surviving aunt, the two first cousins and their children. The aunt was ninety-five. The cousins, Belle and Fletcher, were not fond of Charles. They would receive half the original fortune plus increase when the aunt finally died, but they envied him, Lianne thought, for his greater latitude—the outsider, the adopted usurper. This though he had agreed to continue managing that money for them after their father's and his own father's death, and had, in fact, despite the extremely conservative strategies allowed by the aunt, kept them well ahead of inflation. The children, assorted ages from eight to collegiate, were variously dim, pedestrian, or hopelessly spoiled.

As for inviting her own mother—ha.

No, take it from the hog, Lianne knew the two secrets of a good party: Don't give one except to have fun, and don't invite anybody who aint willing.

—Howdy, howdy, I'm *glad* to see you, come on in, take a load off, get you a drink?

Jim and Natalie, Greg and Alison, Carol and Phil, Tucker and Dee-Dee of course. A couple dozen others. Rider was escorting some tall sleek young woman with enormous boobs and nightblack hair. She hardly spoke all evening, stood around with her eyes on Rider or on the floor. Charles had about decided she was retarded, when she smiled at him over the punch bowl, and he nearly fell down blind. The eyes widened, the red lips parted, and several hundred candlepower of white teeth burned his brain blank.

"Lianne," he said, bringing her back the requested cup of nonalcoholic punch—she felt sensitive to the champagne tonight, why risk a headache—"we need to go upstairs for a minute."

She was talking to Tucker and Dee-Dee, and lifted an amused eyebrow. "You get too close to Darlene?" she said.

"We need to go upstairs bad," he said.

"Tucker got too close to Darlene a while ago," Dee-Dee said. "I had to pour him out of his shoes and stiffen him up with ice water."

"Hoo-wee," Charles said, shaking his head. "Her name isn't really Darlene, is it?"

"It's Darlene," Lianne said.

"Why don't you boys make a play for her?" Dee-Dee said. "Me and Lianne are going to run off with J. D. and spend our last days making him happy." Rider had come up as she was speaking, and she put her arm around him.

"Y'all must be talking about Darlene," he said. "She's really smart, you know."

Charles and Tucker nearly snorted their drinks. Rider looked halfway between amused and put out. "Well, she *is*," he said.

"She looks good enough to eat," Charles said.

"You wish," Lianne said.

"You know, that's a clever menu you came up with, Lianne," Tucker said, "on the invitation. But—"

"Thank you."

"But it is a sexual menu." Tucker scratched his head, pretending to honest puzzlement. "So where's the cunnilinguine?"

Charles howled, and Rider fell away slapping his knee. Rider pointed at Tucker, jabbing his finger as if to help himself speak: "Spoontang!" he called, his voice soaring up the scale.

Darlene, spotting Rider across the room, had joined them. "Felafellatio," she said in a high, whispery little-girl voice, her eyes modestly on the floor.

The noise they made drew the attention of everyone else in the room, and now they had to explain, absorbed severally into the flow of the party, the differing, drifting, recombining vortices of merriment. All the rest of the evening, walking by a knot of people, you might hear someone cry out "Fromage à trois," or "Clitortellini," or "Coq au man."

"Charles, we've got one," Alison confided. She and Greg hand in hand, young, blond/e, flushed, tipsy, happy. "Twattermelon sorbet," she whispered into his ear, on tiptoe.

"It cleanses the palate!" Greg called back over his shoulder as she dragged him away.

"Beef buggeringnon," Jim said out on the patio, gruff Jim, sandy bear, superintendent of schools.

"I don't get it," Natalie said.

"Don't you know what buggering is?" Jim said.

"No," Natalie said. "I don't know what buggering is."

"It's British," Jim said grumpily. It wasn't as funny if you had to explain it.

"Ravishioli," Phil said, up in the game room, thumping Charles on the chest. "Huh? Ravishioli! Huh?" He was carried away by his own laughter. "Huh?"

Late in the evening, Tucker, drunker than Charles had ever seen him, would corner Charles in the kitchen. "Charles," he would say.

"Yes?" Charles would answer, none too steady himself.

"Charles."

"Yes."

"There's just one thing I want to say to you Charles, before I pass out."

"Yes, Tucker my friend."

Tucker would lean against Charles, his face in the taller man's face. His breath freighted with cloves, and that would be a thing Charles had never noticed before.

"Vulveeta," Tucker would say.

But the party went on a long time before that, and Charles got two good ideas out of it, though he didn't realize that the second one was an idea until nearly a week later, on Decoration Day. Greg gave him the first idea. "I just want to thank you," he said. "I don't think I've ever really thanked you out loud for what you did for us. For me and Alison."

Charles mumbled something appropriate. He had the uneasy sense that his motives, when he had sent Greg and Alison to the island, had been anger and practicality, not benevolence.

Greg shook his head in wonder at his narrow escape. "It could have been me at that party," he said. "Just as easy as Lafayette. If it wasn't for you, it would have been."

This observation made Charles even more uneasy. "Forget it," he said.

"You know, it's funny, though," Greg said. "It doesn't work the way you think it will. Ever since I got in that fight, I've had people coming up to me like I was some kind of expert on evolution. Asking legal advice. Any publicity, I guess. I wish I knew what to tell em."

Charles grunted, thinking of the extra business the toga party had brought in, and of the problems he was having finding new staff to carry the load.

"If we weren't in such a sensitive position right now, vis-à-vis PR, I might ask you to let me join in this suit they're filing."

Charles was going to have to teach Greg not to say *vis-à-vis*. Especially not to say it as if it meant *"with regard to."* "What suit?" he said.

"The suit against the creation science law. There's a bunch of them, two dozen or so, planning to file later this month. Preachers, teachers, regular citizens, and all. Susan Epperson. Might even get Lloyd George and John Lisle in on it. They're saying the law is unconstitutional, that it mandates the teaching of religion in the public schools. I'd love to help out, but I figure I better stay low-profile awhile."

"No," Charles said. "No, I think it's a good idea. A good idea for the firm, I mean."

Greg looked at him in happy disbelief: "You want to get the *firm* involved?"

Charles explained that yes, it was risky, it might make them a few more enemies, lose them some business, but face it, people thought of them as liberal anyway. And if they got some negative reaction, it would be a *different* sort of negative reaction. It wouldn't be just an ugly black eye like the toga party had given them. No, this was a classy project, would in fact help rehabilitate their image. It identified them with liberty, courage, and the principles of good government, not to mention that it also aligned them with the new forward-thinking generation now surely just on the verge of taking power in the state (please Lord after all these dark dinosaurian years). It distinguished them from the wishy-washy, like James Martin out at UALR, who wasn't against it and wasn't for it because it wasn't right for the school to get involved. Or like Jim Guy, who thought politicians ought not to set the curriculum, but as for himself, he definitely yessir *absolutely* believed God made man.

Yes, this was a great idea, it was just the way they ought to go. Did Greg think the group would allow Morrison, Morrison, Chenowyth, and Frail to sit in, either as interested observers or as a party to the suit?

Greg was delighted. He knew just who to talk to.

Charles was delighted too. Wait'll Lianne heard. A present for the female of the species, hot momma tonight!

Later he got into a long conversation with Rider about his Bronco. Rider was at pains to explain that his was one of the old original Broncos, not one of these new pansy-ass confections like the Jeep Renegades every spoiled sixteen-year-old upperclass hotshot was suddenly to be seen in, juking about town with a buddy and a couple of beer-drinking sixteen-year-old dyed-blonde sexpots. No, his machine was a veteran, a battered, nicked, rough-and-ready woods monster.

It wasn't the sort of conversation Charles was just crazy about, and for that matter it wasn't the sort of conversation Rider usually engaged in. Rider was busy trying to make himself more comfortable because he felt ill at ease around Charles's wealth, power, and presumed taste, him in his one beat-up vehicle, him with the black-haired wench on his arm, not to mention the size of her knockers, him with his boots and Levi's. It wasn't that J. D.'s upbringing had been exactly *poor;* not in the least. The P.I. business wasn't bringing in just a whole lot of dough, but there was some income from the trust fund.

Charles was definitely a bigger monkey, at least in this one area. Thing about the human monkey, territoriality was multidimensional. Different dominance rankings depending on where you were and what you were doing, and so you had to be always switching frames of reference, which made for a lot of ongoing unresolved stress. Rider was bigger, stronger, younger. He didn't feel ill at ease around Charles at the Y. He was maybe smarter, he thought, at least in some ways, but that was hard to measure.

But this was Charles's house, and these were the members of Charles's crowd, even if Rider did know a few of them. So suddenly he felt his usual comfortable accoutrements, the scuffed leather and worn denim and un-starched cotton, the twenty-five-dollar black plastic wristwatch that he wore because it did the job and was waterproof and could survive the sweatiest of workouts, he felt these things hanging on him as awkwardly as if they were meant to make a statement, and he doubted himself and thought that maybe he *had* worn them to make a statement, and it was the wrong statement.

So here he was coming on like a good old boy, as if to enlist Charles, find some buddy-buddy man-to-man level on which all these competitive jostlings could be forgone. It wasn't working, he could see that. Charles was reading it as Rider's assertion of superior cool, of centered masculinity. It wasn't working, but what can you do? You can't relate in a vacuum. You have to have a structure, a format. If the right one doesn't pop up—bingo! you find yourself defaulting to one of the wrong ones. Being conscious of the process doesn't change a thing.

In the middle of all this Rider provided the second idea, the one Charles wouldn't recognize as an idea until a week later. "You know," Rider said, "I didn't know Lianne was so crazy about this stuff. We must have spent two hours talking about four-wheel drive the other night. I had to go out to the Bronco and bring in my owner's manual and all the specs."

"Yeah," Charles said, appearing to have spotted someone across the room he needed to talk to. "Yeah, she really likes camping."

About midnight, Charles and Lianne left the party to go upstairs. There were still a dozen people scattered about the first and second floors (actually—as if it mattered—three in the game room and nine on the first floor). They were all good friends and were welcome to stay, and Clemmie would do the cleaning up tomorrow anyway. Charles and Lianne chose the stairs, not the elevator, and Tucker and Dee-Dee and a couple of others followed them into the foyer and applauded them as they rose. On the second-floor landing, Charles and Lianne bowed to their audience, then mounted on their way.

In the master bedroom at last, they were alone with the real thing. What to make of themselves? The ceremony was done, the community had been appeased, and the two of them were formally agreed.

What to do next? It was clear they were supposed to make love, but maybe they had forgotten how. Should he unbutton her blouse? Why then did the act feel so mechanical, so strange, like something you could train a factory robot to do better? Why when he kissed her throat did he feel like a crab exploring a strange beach? —There had once been a socket there for his mouth, from which warmth flowed like 220-volt power.

Why couldn't he get a hard-on?

Guilt, that's why. Guilt over his crude desires. Lust was what he had been feeling as they left the party. Lust boiling around for Lianne, but also for every other woman on earth, especially nighthaired Darlene. Now, though, he felt he should be loving and tender, that the restoration of his and Lianne's love should be a bridal act, full of lace and flowers, and flowing to the gentle music of strings, and specific to this one woman.

Ah, the great invention of the monkeys. Mammals invented love and dreams, but it took you guys to make guilt. No other species has it except dogs, those poor monkey-ruined wolves. You think I like it, Bubba? You think I even *feel* it? Nossir, I run hither and thither, to and fro, but I never feel no guilt. Neither does the fathering son, nor Miss Liza too. What we want, you done wrong, you should admit it, fix it, and shut up about it. Didn't dine on the cross to save you from your sins, dieted on the cross to save you from your guilt. Save *us* from your guilt. Save us from having to *hear* about your guilt.

Be kind, be interesting, be useful. That's about it. Morality aint hard. All this guilt binness, all this oh dearie me I got something in me so terrible so awful so dirty Law Gawd can't stand to see it and I deserve to roast in hell forever—that aint religion, that aint morality; that's just one little weird group's idea of social control. Baby, that's just leftover toilet training.

And even supposing there was such a thing as sin anyhow, which there aint, there's just misery, and misery ought to be a crime but it aint no sin, but even supposing there was such a thing as sin so guilt made some kind of sense, what the fuck it have to do with sex-and-shit anyhow? Who you think invented elephant sex, baby? *We Are* did. Who you think said Man shall not merely consume doughnuts but shall be topologically identical to them as well and whatever goes in the hole fresh comes out collapsed and stinking of methane? Alimentary, my dear Watson: *We Are* did. And shall We Are blink to look upon that which We Are made?

Lianne, who is/was as guilty as any of you, who suffers as cruelly as anyone from the narcissism you simians call Original Evil, Lianne this evening understood. She and Charles belonged together because they *wanted* to belong together. They would come back into love because they *wanted* to love each other. Lianne, wanting to love Charles, understood what his fumbling meant, and, holding his shoulders to pull herself up from the pillow as he on all fours like a dog hung drooping over her, raised her head and whispered in his ear:

"Fuck me, Charles. Don't fuck me pretty, just fuck me like a monkey. Fuck me now, because I want to be fucked."

And slipped her slender legs around him, sliding her heels across his hamstrings, across his ass, locking around his waist, and they made love. They raged and bit and tore, they thumped and kicked and licked and slurped and cried, and never hurt a thing. I want to tell you, they were two bad animals. And there were no bad animals there.

23

DECORATION DAY

Deep in the portico, Charles hesitated. It was really pouring out there. Maybe it would slacken. He beguiled himself thinking of the lick he was getting in on the lord high bailiff.

The latest batch of county escapees had been recaptured the very next day—by none other than that gun-toting symbol of righteousness himself, Sonny Raymond, in a high-speed chase down Robinson Road. Mighty convenient. Charles had said as much to the defense lawyer, a friend, and had been pleased to see in the paper this morning that the defense was accusing Raymond of setting the whole deal up.

Raymond was quoted in response: *Pack of deleted big-time lawyers in deleted deleted cahoots with the whole deleted county court system, ganging up trying to make him look bad because they knew he had serious evidence of some serious deleted wrongdoing, and the deleted hadn't hit the fan yet, but their day was coming, you'd better deleting well believe it.*

Yes, it was good to see the man squirm. You don't tug on Superman's cape, and you don't mess around with Charles.

The rain was not letting up. One of the things he liked least about his home was the detached garage. It had not mattered when he was a child, because there was always Mr. Polygon. You could call him on his phone in the little apartment over the garage, and in a few minutes here he would come driving up, all in uniform, as if he wore the uniform every moment of every day, as if he even wore it to sleep. Charles had a vivid sensual memory of waiting in the foyer at the age of eight or nine, dialing on a heavy black phone on a dark little three-legged stand that came up almost to his chin and that he had long since gotten rid of.

But Mr. Polygon was dead, and you couldn't ask Clemmie to go running through the rain, it wasn't in her job description, it would be an insult. Coleman, maybe, if he were here, but he was in church right now. And maybe not, it wasn't in his job description either.

Why not just hire another chauffeur? Well, for a while, when he had come back home, he had felt too egalitarian. It was all right to have help with the housekeeping or with the gardening, since both of these activities were clearly more than he and Lianne could manage on their own. But it was quite another matter, in late-twentieth-century America, when a man *was* his car, to hire a full-time chauffeur. It would be like hiring somebody to follow you around just to hold it for you when you had to pee. He wasn't his father, after all. He didn't remember the horse-and-carriage days. He didn't expect stableboys, grooms, drivers.

Then when he had gotten tired of being so egalitarian, Lianne hadn't. Besides, the thought of the extravagance frightened her, as if it could bring them to ruin, as if he couldn't handle the annual salary fifty times over and hardly feel it.

It was his father's childhood that was responsible, Charles thought. Back then, you didn't live over your horses, not if you could help it. That was for the servants. Well, the horses were long gone by the time his father had built his own house, but the architecture had lingered. Charles had threatened time and again to build a covered walkway, or to tear the garage down and build a new one attached to the house. But the nature of the place defeated him. He simply couldn't think of a way to perpetrate either scheme that wouldn't ruin the feeling.

So there it was, the garage, half a football field away, invisible in the torrent. Which was *still* not slackening. Even backed up against the front door, he felt the spray blow over. The Great Inland Hurricane of 1981. He sighed, popped the big umbrella open, and sprinted.

"Breaker, breaker," Ferrin said as the Skylark passed him going west. He was parked just where Armistead veed onto Edgehill. "Wheat Germ, do you read? Come back, good buddy."

"I hear you, Pall Mall," Rubert said on the speaker.

Ferrin thumbed the mike. "Goddammit, Wheat Germ, at least say it right."

"I can't remember all that shit," Rubert said. "What you calling about? Come again, good buddy."

"Come *back*," Ferrin said to himself. He clicked the mike again. "Subject number one has left the house. Subject number two is alone with the maid."

"Which one's number one and which one's number two?" Rubert said.

He paused, and the sound of a chuckle came over the speaker. "Sound like going to the bathroom, don't it?"

"I can't tell you names on an open channel!" Ferrin said. "Goddammit, Ru—*goddammit*, Wheat Germ, you're gonna blow the whole mission. Come back."

"Come back," Rubert said. "I'm tired of the mission. Let's go eat."

You don't say it on the front *end*, Ferrin thought. *Next thing you know, you'll be saying "breaker" on the* back *end.* "You et less than two hours ago," he said. "And it aint nearly time for lunch."

"Breaker, I don't care. Come on. This rain getting me down."

Ferrin couldn't really argue with that. He was tired of the mission too. Sitting here in a stupid damn Pinto with the rain booming on the roof, pouring over the windows. Watching the green trees shake heavy and vague, the street run with brown water like a river.

They had been watching the place off and on all week long, ever since the big party Monday night. What was the point? People came and went, nothing happened. They weren't proving anything. The CBs had helped at first, had made him feel big-time, like it was a real operation. But you had to face facts, this wasn't James Bond's damn Lotus or whatever. It was a damn Pinto. And he, Ferrin, wasn't made to sit in a Pinto all day and do nothing.

Besides which, he was getting nervous. You couldn't hang out in a neighborhood like this in a car like this without getting noticed. The rain helped today, kept everybody inside, but sooner or later a squad car was going to pull up and ask him what his business was, and in spite of the fact he didn't have no outstanding charges and his contact had pull, this was not an experience he looked forward to real eagerly.

The contact had called him a couple of times on their new phone and asked for reports. Ferrin had made himself sound official: The subject did this, the subject did that. In truth, he had invented most of the details, because the fact of the matter was there was nothing to report. Next time they called, he was going to say so. He was going to say that this operation lacked direction, that it suffered from poor planning, and that Ferrin was going to have to see some kind of action if he was going to keep on with it. He hated to let go of the easy money, but then again, it wasn't easy if it was boring, was it? They had better get that straight.

Ferrin cranked the engine. The hell with waiting.

They might not like it, but he was going to place a call himself. "Wheat Germ," he said into the mike, "prepare personnel for pickup. Over."

"Glad to hear it," Rubert said. "I'm mighty tired of this damn dozer."

Rubert was in the cab of an idle bulldozer across Cantrell, the construction site for a new home. The theory was he was the back-door man.

Ferrin could monitor the street where it came out onto Armistead, and Rubert could monitor the intersection where it devolved on Cantrell.

If they both left the scene, the subjects could get away with murder, but never mind. The thing to do now was to get Rubert out of the rain and off the airwaves and into a cheeseburger, and that would shut him up while Ferrin made his little call.

Charles pulled up in the double carport of Mrs. Weatherall's house, her weathered green Dodge in the other slot. He honked the horn, which he knew Lianne wouldn't like, but as far as he was concerned, this whole excursion was the only concession he was willing to make to her mother, and the heck with being gentlemanly and going to the door.

He made these trips now only because they mattered so much to Lianne. Having no family, or—as he saw it—having only monsters for family, she clung fiercely to any fragment of kindness or normality in her lineage, wept for long-dead elders who, to judge by the stories he had heard, had never themselves found anyone worth weeping for.

He honked again.

The week had been a honeymoon, full of lust, tears, and awkwardness. Though in the last couple of days he had felt the quotidian threatening, the irresistible gathering fog of their routine. He far preferred the clarity of newness, the intensity of their healing, and had been on his best behavior, trying to prolong the magic. That was a reason to dread this trip more than he had in other years. He couldn't imagine riding over two hundred miles with Mrs. Weatherall, the genius of bad feeling, and not himself at some point becoming unpleasant.

They were taking their sweet time. Charles could imagine what they were doing. Going back through every room in the house, making sure all the outside doors were locked, all the dresser drawers were closed. That no water was running, that the lights timer had been set for what Mrs. W. thought was a convincing cycle. This was a day trip, but she was going to have those lights going on and off just in case some burglar was watching.

The timer had been a Christmas present from Charles, back when they were still doing Christmas together at his house. It had been what she asked for. It was just the sort of thing she believed in, and just the sort of thing that she would not get for herself, feeling it too expensive. Oh wonderful to see her paranoia at war with her cheapness. He hated himself for having ever been willing to give such a present. What did she want this year, a set of steel grilles for the windows, like they put over the shop windows at night in New York City?

The house was pink brick and white siding. Aluminum siding of course.

Single-level, the carport supported on round steel columns, painted white like the ceiling and trim. In the rear of the carport, the inevitable semi-detached utility room with hollow-core door, at which, through the windshield, he now sat staring. On his left, the equally inevitable two cement steps up to the side door and the kitchen. Walking around the house, one would have seen, in the brick of the walls, narrow double windows for the living room and two bedrooms, single windows everywhere else, and all the windows flanked by white steel shutters which, even if they had swung free on hinges, even if they had not been screwed directly into the brick at all four corners, would not have met in the middle—too narrow for even these narrow lights.

Mrs. W. was probably checking right now, for the fifteenth time, to make sure Fannie Mae, her large, belligerent cat, had enough to eat for the five or six hours they would be gone, and water to drink, and clean scratch.

The kitchen door opened, and finally, here she came—raincoat and rainhat, one-stepping down, a waddling menace, alert as a bird. Charles opened the door for her, backing out of her way as she squeezed by, blinking against the spray. Much huffing and puffing as she climbed in past the tilted-forward front seat, got herself adjusted.

See how many difficulties you make me endure? —That was the message here. For it was true that Charles refused to have her up front with him.

Often Lianne sat in the back with her mother, but this time she didn't. She had waited inside the house till her mother got seated and got her door closed. Now she came out, dashed around, and hopped into the front seat on the other side, smiling radiantly at Charles as he got in, a little girl running happily through the weather.

His heart gave a lurch of pleasure. On the night before Decoration Day, Lianne always slept over with her mother. And nearly always she came out of the experience angry or depressed. If she had survived in good spirits, it meant, it meant—

He had a sunny sense of opening possibilities, of powerful bright changes.

And at the same time he felt the quivering of a great fear. As if something terrible were about to happen, as if he and Lianne were suddenly exposed to all manner of harm.

Was it precognition? Was he already picking up vibrations from Me?

No. I guess I was in him—yeah, sure I was. Technically speaking, the Doctor is always In. But he didn't need Me, hadn't yet called on my Namelessness. What it was then—what it was at that point in time, Mr. John Dean—was just your native simian suspiciousness.

You guys don't trust happiness. Which is to say you don't trust Us. When things go right, you think We're setting you up.

Can't say I blame you.

"Did you lock the door?" Mrs. Weatherall said. Charles waited. No point cranking the car till he knew whether one of them was getting back out.

"It's locked," Lianne said.

"I didn't see you twist the knob." To check the lock, she meant.

"It's locked," Lianne said.

Charles cranked the car, put it in reverse.

"Fasten your seat belt," Mrs. Weatherall said to Lianne. She struggled with her own, grunting as she pulled it into position.

Charles backed down the driveway, stopped to check for traffic, and Mrs. Weatherall said, "You left the gas on. When you made the tea." Lianne had brought a small thermos of hot tea, a packet of crackers. Her stomach often upset her on these trips.

"No I didn't," Lianne said.

"I don't remember you turning it off," Mrs. Weatherall said.

"I did, though."

"Well, it's not the sort of thing I like to take chances with."

"House go boom," Charles said, vaguely remembering a line from some cartoon in his childhood. He took the car back up the driveway and had a cramped impatient wait while Mrs. Weatherall rummaged in her immense black purse for the keys.

"It's probably open anyway," she said, handing the keys to him over the back of his seat. He got out, opened the screen, tried the door. "Locked," he announced, turning triumphantly toward the car. After fumbling through three keys, he got the door open.

"Check the bathroom heater too," Mrs. Weatherall called after him.

A crown of blue flame hissed on the small back burner. He felt a shock of adrenaline, leapt to turn it off. He glanced guiltily at the door, but the stove was in a corner, and from the car, you couldn't see.

Was it all the way off? He couldn't be certain unless he turned it on and then back off himself. Control. Perhaps he shared that tic with Mrs. Weatherall, then. He turned the eye on, waited for the pilot to catch. It was slow. He imagined the house filling with fumes while they were gone. House go boom. Except then Mrs. W. would probably come stay with them awhile. So he imagined instead that she walked in, struck a spark somehow, and *then* house go boom.

The pilot caught, and he turned the flame off.

The living room was dark, its heavy curtains drawn, its air dead and heavy. Air that had had the life cooked out of it by dry central heating. Air that felt as if it had not been changed in half a century. There were no bad smells, it wasn't that. Any possible stink had long since been beaten into submission with Lysol and air freshener (what a lie *that* name was). Yet Charles could hardly bear to draw the miasma into his nostrils. His eyes adjusted, and he saw: wall-to-wall carpeting, a sculptured dark-green nap with hints and highlights of rust and gold. Mustard-colored walls. The familiar dark furniture, its visible wood stained some oily murky brown from a sticky can that had no doubt read, on its stained label, "walnut."

Familiar not because he had been in the house more than half a dozen times, but familiar because to be in the house once felt as if he had been in it forever, as if all such houses, and he knew there were millions, were the same: a single inescapable misery of enervation.

And Lianne with her bright colors had come from this.

In the bathroom, Fannie Mae lifted her head and hissed. She was curled on a stack of towels in the laundry basket. She watched him a moment, then settled her chin against her paws again. No threat there.

The bathroom heater was unquestionably off. He made his escape, fled back through the gloomy halls to the relative cheer of the rainstorm. At least the air was alive out here. He snorted lungfuls of the clean wet stuff, opened the door, and buckled in.

"It was *off*," he said.

He guided the Skylark through a maze of tilting tree-lined streets, nice older homes mingled indiscriminately with run-down places on whose porches dangerous-looking characters sat and stared through the downpour: the jumble of neighborhoods north of Barton Coliseum and the fairgrounds. It had been Lianne's home all of her high school years, replacing the Beechwood Street cottage she had loved so much, from which she had attended Pulaski Heights Junior High. Over to Ninth, then across the river on I-30, swinging west at the I-40 intersection.

"Heck used to live up there," Mrs. Weatherall said, leaning over the back of the seat and pointing up Highway 107. "In Morningside." Charles couldn't remember a Decoration Day trip on which she had failed to point this out. Heck—Hector—hadn't even been a relative. He had been part of a couple Elaine and Lee Andrew used to get together with back in the early days, back when they were young enough to have first names, back when Lianne was a girl.

"He got cancer all through his body and blew his brains out. Virginia's in California now. She retired from the highway department three years ago."

She tapped Charles on the shoulder. "They'll stop you if you go over fifty-five here." Charles had the Skylark on sixty, which probably *was* a little fast in the rain. "It's a real speed trap. They make all their money here, close to town. Too lazy to go out along the highway.'' He didn't slow. Next she would talk about hydroplaning.

She settled back in her seat. "You should never have sold the old Mercedes.''

"I got tired of driving it," he said, inaccurately. "Made me feel like I was driving a truck.''

Unlike the 280, which was nimble as a cat. He thought of it with longing. It was a two-seater, nobody but him and Lianne sailing down the road. But that was silly, because if it was just the two of them today, they wouldn't be going in the first place.

The new block still hadn't come in, although Jerry kept saying any day now. The 280 ran, but it ran rough and was blowing some oil, and Charles didn't like driving it that way. The 280 was all that was left of his youth, and he wanted to treat it right.

"These little cars are death traps," Mrs. Weatherall said. Right, Charles thought. What she was really worried about was the style of her arrival. She would have loved pulling up at the cemetery in a forty-thousand-dollar car, never mind that half her relatives wouldn't understand why you would pay that much for something from a country we whipped and later they made Volkswagens. "You have to give the Germans credit for that, at least. They understand safety.''

"This is a good little car," he said. "Solid construction." Lianne patted his leg, a little smile on her face. He realized he was hunched over the wheel. He drew in his breath, relaxed.

"The Mercedes weighed more," Mrs. Weatherall said.

Right about this time, Coleman was getting home from church and was deciding maybe after he had a little lunch he would go over to the Morrisons' and do some work. There was so much to do outside, he tended to let the greenhouse go. A rainy day was a good chance to catch up on the inside work. He needed to repot the big fern, and the half-dozen jade trees were completely overgrown. And if he was ever going to set those tomatoes out, he needed to bust the bottoms out of their boxes and mix up the bedding soil.

He made himself a sandwich from the skimpy offerings in the small white icebox: sliced ham and mayonnaise on white bread, two thin slices of the ham, with pepper sprinkled on them. A man didn't need anything else on his sandwich, no cheese or tomato or lettuce. This was flavor enough. Get too many flavors, couldn't taste none of em. He boiled water and poured it over two heaping spoons of instant coffee in his cup. Stirred in four spoons of sugar and a healthy dollop of Pet Milk. A bite of the sandwich, a swallow of coffee as thick as cocoa. Ah, good eating. He felt he was back in New Orleans, drinking that what, that caffy oh lay.

He ate standing up, looking over his memory shelf. Picture of Debelle, dead these twenty years. He didn't miss her anymore. She was like a stranger who reminded him of somebody. She wouldn't know what to make of the old man he had become. But she was a pretty stranger, and he liked to think about the days of their marriage, like a story you read in a book. He had never wanted to marry again, not because of grief, but because once was enough. We were made to do everything once and then die, and that was ok with him.

Glass tumblers from the bars in New Orleans. Manny's essay he did for English one time, yellowed notepaper folded lengthwise. Manny's name and the date on the outside, October 5, 1961. He read the essay sometimes, about Christopher Columbus discovering America. No picture of Manny; Coleman had never had the money for school photos back then. Except the once, and then the boy gave them all away to friends. But the paper was better, because you could see him in the actual handwriting, whereas the picture was just something some stranger did, some uncaring slice out of Manny's time. He hadn't heard from the boy in thirteen years. In Chicago the last he knew, trying to be a record producer. If he had become famous, reckon Coleman would have heard. Just hoped he wasn't in jail somewhere, or dead.

Coleman's bill cap from when he was a trolley man: "Franch Quahter. Watcha doors."

Manny's third-place medal in the distance medley in the tenth grade. Coleman's own Bronze Star. That was like a book too, or no, more like a movie, the Jap planes coming in and him banging away on the sewing machine. Was he scared? If so, he didn't remember it. Busy, more like. Planes come in so close he could count the rivets, firing all the way, WHERE'S THE FRESH BELT, how can I think with all this ack*ack*ACK here come another GODDAMN I AINT GOT IT FED YET plane.

He didn't think he ever got one, and what got him was a round from somebody else's gun, half a dozen went off in the fire when that Jew got killed. Traub. Traubman. Isidore Traubman. Izzy. Put out the fire and pull Izzy away, and got one in the thigh for his trouble. Serve him right for joining up when he should have been through with all that. Boot camp shooting guns and blowing off grenades like some kind of kid playing war, when he was all of thirty-six already, a grown man long since. And then they shift him to navy without any warning.

Thing the movies had done, whenever he remembered his one battle, he saw it in black and white. Now you know damn well it didn't happen in black and white. So your brain was like a garden soil. Anything would grow, you didn't keep it weeded. But hell, he like some of the weed better than some of the flowers, so what difference it make?

So that was Columbus discovering America: a nigger on a warship near Hawaii trying to shoot down a Jap, and he gets hurt when a Jew's gun blows up. They bring him in to New Orleans, where he meets Debelle Zarounian, his soft-eyed colored Hungarian Creole lover. Later a white Baptist from Missouri pins a medal to his chest.

You could say that was an achievement if you wanted to. The President actually touch him over his heart. How many other people in Little Rock could say that? A few. But there wasn't really any achievements. Wasn't any achievements but seed. One more spring, and the green things keep going. See em open up and know the world good for another year. And Manny dead in Chicago somewhere probably.

He chewed every bite ten times, and went to change into his gardening clothes. Washed out the cup before he left. Almost forgot the digitalis patch, had to unbutton his work shirt. Need to ask Mr. Charles for a raise, cause the insurance only cover eighty percent, less the deductible. And ham going up too. But this wasn't a good time, not with them yard people hanging around. Mr. Charles know about his angina, he might think twice about keeping him on. Pay him off with a pension, yeah, but who want to sit around watching tv all day?

Angina a funny name. Sound like a sheep. Wouldn't think a sheep would hurt so much.

Morgan, Mayflower, Conway. The sign for the Hendrix exit, but Charles and Lianne and Mrs. Weatherall kept straight on by, of course. "Your great-grandmother went to Galloway," Mrs. Weatherall said. Galloway had been the girls' school that had merged with the boys' school that had eventually, almost a century ago now, become Hendrix College.

There had been an unbroken line of O'Hare women in Hendrix since the great-grandmother, and Charles knew what was coming next. "Is that lightning?" he said, leaning forward as if to peer at the horizon. "I swear, this weather is just getting worse."

"It's a shame you didn't have what it took to finish there," Mrs. Weatherall said.

"Yeah, it's really held her back in life," Charles said. Lianne patted his leg again, but this time her face was tight and she was looking ahead. This was a frightening subject for her; he had no idea why. Dropping out of school was traumatic, but not so traumatic it should stay with you for twenty years. He wondered if she ever dealt with that time in her deep therapy, under hypnosis. Because yes, Father Christmas would use even that trick. He would put you under and command you to remember, if he thought it might help.

As he will have put you under, Charles, to help you remember, though you do indeed think hypnosis is a trick, *a cheap parlor trick*. You and Lianne had argued about it once:

I've seen too many medical con men take the stand, you had said. *Turning the courtroom into a psychological circus.*

What's the difference, if it helps me? If I believe it works?

You had even confronted Ian Farber: *That's between Lianne and her therapist. I recommend you think about your own issues.*

You'll never hypnotize me.

No. No, I wouldn't try. You aren't willing to let go. In fact, I suspect—well, let me put it this way. Do you see Lianne as an extension of yourself? Are you threatened by the fact that she is willing to yield control, if only temporarily, to someone other than yourself?

That's what I hate about this bullshit. All this Time *magazine psychobabble crap.* You had quit therapy not long afterward.

But now there are so many details that still for some reason will not come, and of those that will, who can say why they will and not the others? Moments you would give your fortune to recall and cannot, and moments you cannot forget that seem worthless. But since you may not choose which, then you will choose to have as many as you may. And so you will have gone to the magus. You will have gone to Ian Farber and said, *Help me. Help me remember.*

"Those were the happiest years of my life," Mrs. Weatherall says now, in the present tense. "Before I met your father."

In the mirror you see her smile, the toothy V of the carnivore lizard.

"You'd better enjoy yourself when you're young," she adds. Still the smile, the relish for disaster. "Because the night is coming in which no man can reap."

Ferrin was using the phone at Peck's, looking out through the glass at the relentless rain, the traffic on Markham. Rubert was back in a booth, munching his third chili-dog-with-cheese-and-onions, and slurping another beer. All the important people came to Peck's. It was cheap and ratty, but you might see anybody there. State senators, famous bankers, anybody up to like the governor, who couldn't afford to be seen in a bar. But anybody else, anybody important behind the scenes. And of course all the med school students from across the street. So you never knew which one of these young guys was going to be a famous doctor someday.

Rubert didn't care where they went, as long as the food was good. No sense of style.

"I can't believe you eat that hog slop," Ferrin had said.

"What hog slop?" Rubert had answered. "Onions have sulfur in em, fight bacteria. And everybody knows beer has vitamins. It's what the serfus used to practically live on. Beer and bread. And cheese."

"The what?"

"The serfus," Rubert had said, uncertainly. "Back in England."

Ferrin had snorted and had gone to make his call.

Now the voice spoke in his ear: "So what do you want to do?"

"It aint what I want to do, it's what do you want us to do," Ferrin said.

"You're the one complaining," the voice said.

"Because this aint getting anywhere. I don't go for this kind of a blind operation. Insult to my intelligence. We aint watching em to protect em. You know it and I know it."

"So you think you're ready for strategy now."

"I might be. Try me."

"You don't know what's at stake here. I hope you aint thinking you can take over."

"I'm not thinking anything like that," Ferrin said. He was, though. "I aint questioning your leadership or nothing."

"I'm always thinking three moves ahead," the voice said. "You can't see what I'm really up to because I'm always thinking ahead. It's like chess."

"I aint arguing that," Ferrin said.

"What do you have in mind?" the voice said.

"I think it's time we threw a scare into em," Ferrin said. "Flush em out into the open."

"What kind of a scare?"

"Attack em at their weakest link," Ferrin said.

"I think it's clearing off," Lianne said. They had turned off the interstate onto Highway 95, heading due north into the hills. As they gained altitude, the rain had slackened. Now the clouds looked brighter, thin and transient.

"Yeah," Charles said. "The storm stops at the mountains. We may see some sun yet."

"More people die in flash floods in Arkansas than tornadoes," Mrs. Weatherall said. "You watch these low-water bridges."

They swung west on 124, gradually curving north again. They passed ramshackle farmsteads nestled into the wet green slopes, Lianne's hand tightening and relaxing on his arm. "Wouldn't you love to live *there*?" she might say of one or another dogtrot with a corrugated roof, rusty or shining, and Charles would grunt *pro forma* approval.

Before, this had always annoyed him, this mountain romance of hers, as if it implied rejection of all that he had to offer. But today he was able to share her vision. Rocking on the front porch watching the townie car drive by, a couple of worthless hounds at their feet. Nothing to do but walk in the woods and hoe the garden and love each other. Inside in winter with their feet up in front of the wood stove. No poses to maintain, no appearances to keep up.

"The rain on a tin roof is the best sound on earth," Mrs. Weatherall said, and even that didn't bother him, her preemption of their pleasure.

Above Jerusalem, just before Lost Corner, they climbed into clear weather.

Coleman got off the bus on Kavanaugh, at Crestwood. He had a good quarter mile to walk, but he had his navy slicker on and his galoshers, and he had his big umbrella. Anyway, he thought the storm was wearing itself out. And he had walked it in the rain a hundred times before. It would be funny if the rain quit once he got there, since that was the reason he came in the first place, but so be it. It would still be too wet to work outside, so the plan still made sense.

It was definitely letting up. When it had got so black and boomy when he was on the bus, tearing itself into pieces and throwing the pieces around every which a way, you knew it was going to let up soon. Nothing could go on at that rate very long, not a marriage, not a battle with Jap airplanes, nothing.

It was the slow steady stuff you had to watch out for.

At the cemetery, old and new pickups together with corroded finned Plymouths and weathered Roadmasters and dusty two-toned Galaxie 500s lined the gravel road for a good two hundred feet back from the gate. This was where all the big old ugly cars went to die, north of Jerusalem. This was why you didn't see them in Little Rock any more. These people had bought them all thirty and twenty and ten years ago, and were still driving them, just as they cooked in the same iron skillets and wore the same restitched overhauls and dropped the same bucket down the same mossy well. Yes, they all had pumps now, rickety indoor plumbing, but you never knew. You didn't go back on a good well rope. What if we ran out of electricity?

They parked at the back of the line, Charles seesawing around to face away from the cemetery, ready to leave. "Watch that shoulder," Mrs. Weatherall said. "It's going to be awfully soft." The shoulder was firm under a ragged cover of weeds and wild grass.

"I don't think it rained at all here," Charles said.

Lianne spun out of the car and ran down the drive, her skirt and blouse a bright explosion, an exotic bloom in time-lapse acceleration. She had been wrapped in a raincoat when she got in, had gradually shed it, but he had been too close and too preoccupied for the effect. Now the pageantry, the startle: the running woman, the brilliant clear yellow of the blouse, the improbable chartreuse-striped magenta of the silk skirt which somehow and against all reason all went perfectly together as windy blossoms.

The Peace That Passeth Understanding Cemetery, or Petey-Puck as Charles liked to call it in Mrs. Weatherall's presence, was a combined Southern Baptist/Church of Christ burial ground sprawling over three stony hills secretive with cedar, a thread of a creek running through. The shelves of rock, where they broke through the grass and the ocher patches of sedge, were the same lichen-dappled gray as the headstones, an effect Charles admired without thinking about it. The earth lies buried here, it might have said. It was an unintentional effect. You may rest assured the church fathers would have chosen level ground, if there had been any level ground in that part of the county. The dead should be neatly filed, in rows and planes, the better for resurrection.

The creek divided the cemetery into its two generally accepted enclaves, though a few stray Christers might be found west of the water and a Baptist or two east of it. Originally the owner had refused to sell the acreage except all in one piece, and neither church had enough money on its own. The name was written in wrought iron in an arch that spanned two stone columns.

This was where Lianne wanted to be buried. In spite of the fact that she had loved her father and not her mother, she traced her heritage back to these hills. They spoke to her as Lee Andrew's lower-middle-class small-town-pine-lowlands-turned-beltway never had: Bryant and Bauxite and Benton and for gossakes Malvern, how tedious all that was.

It fell to him to get the bouquets and wreaths out of the trunk, half a dozen assorted factory-made commemoratives in a cardboard box, and to escort Mrs. Weatherall. When they got to the gate, they saw Lianne down the hill a little, already surrounded by her more or less kin, chatting away. She brought glamour to their lives, the one descendant whose image had been multiplied beyond the mortal realm. Although they lived perfectly well without glamour, didn't miss it a bit when it wasn't around. But since Lianne was unselfconscious about her fame, had come up simply because she loved seeing them all, adored their ways and voices and lives, they didn't mind her but enjoyed her as they enjoyed the freshness of the air.

He was glad to see Curtis among them, Mrs. Weatherall's second cousin's husband, his head rising above the heads of the women and the one or two men in the group.

There was no path, only a caretaker's gravel road winding through to the other side—this was a country cemetery; you just walked where you could. Elaine was convinced the ground would be loose and sodden under the grass. He had to take her elbow to steady her, awkwardly supporting the box against his side with his other arm.

Strangely, for the moment, he didn't mind. The act of helping her felt almost like reconciliation. She was still wearing her coat, though the day was sunny and warm, a light breeze stirring the grass, the creek glinting here and there between slants of rock and cedar, and he pitied her for her carapace, which sealed out more happiness than danger.

He gave the box over to Lianne, who held it while Elaine parceled out the decorations with their tags saying which grave they went to. Most of the group had brought their own but had already placed them. It was the renewal of the plastic flowers. Once a year the congregations hurried home from services and had a quick light meal and went straight to the cemetery. "Going over to Passeth," they would say, leaving church. "See you later at Passeth."

The families brought in little gardening tools, trowels and scissors and shears and brushes, and cleaned up the grave sites. They brought in garlands of plastic rue and rosemary, they brought in plastic pots wrapped in green and gold and silver foil, in which sprouted plastic lilies and plastic phlox and roses and daisies, and settled them at the feet of the stones. There was not in the entire cemetery, Charles would have sworn, a living flower or a wildflower grown of its own accord. He could have brought in glorious tribute from his own greenhouse, whole bowers of blossoming rebirth, but no, Lianne and her mother, staying true to the customs of the hills, had spent last night in Wal-Mart, cruising the aisles for polyethylene bargains, while he had had a beer at the bar and then come back to pick them up and drive them home.

What was it with country people? They who had created the buttermilk biscuit in the first place now cracked open the spirals of cardboard tubes for their doughy breakfast, they who had been born where there were still first-growth forests would clear-cut a section without a second thought, leaving it stumps and trash not even for the money, but just to improve the view.

Country people were hell on the country.

Watching the women coo and exclaim as if over Christmas presents, he understood. The plastic flowers were bright and long-lasting, and that was all that was required. They would pale eventually under the repeated sun, the huge unnatural violets fading to a sort of gray-white pansy like those they removed today (stuffing them into filmy garbage bags). The flat green leaf blades of the fake bamboo would subside to the sickliest of pastels, become brittle and split. But these displays would last months longer than real flowers, and that was a gesture toward heaven, where beauty never failed. Only nonbelievers quibbled over the quality of the symbol. The faithful looked frankly through to the object. Plastic Jesus on the dashboard was a true enough reminder if you were sure you were washed in His real Blood; if you knew what real blood was.

What had brought this accession of tolerance upon him? Was it the warmth of the sun on his hair, the tonic of high crisp atmosphere? No, he had been remarkably large-spirited all day, even before they had gotten here.

It was love. He and Lianne were once more in love. Love puts things in balance, gives you proportion. The absence of love distorts you with need. With love, you see things whole and sanely. Without love, you criticize, you strike attitudes.

He stood aside with Curtis as Lianne moved off with her mother, the one trim and taller, the other dumpy and dense, and yet their gaits so similar.

Lianne was beautiful today, light and mobile and full of grace, and he wanted to protect her from every threat, from her sorrows, her past, her mother. Yet there her mother was *in* her, in her bodily habitus, as Tucker would say, the ghost haunting the hallways of the genes forever, and he saw he could protect Lianne from nothing: It seemed a good realization then in the sunlight among the peaceful stones; it seemed the right place for such a realization.

"Synchronize your watches," Ferrin said.

"I aint got but one watch," Rubert said.

"You know what I mean," Ferrin said, vaguely irritated. You couldn't say synchronize your watch, that wouldn't sound right, and you couldn't say synchronize our watches, that wouldn't sound right either. One of these days he was going to have to twist Rubert's head off. "Now let me hear you run through it again," he said.

"I take it up to the door and ring the doorbell and when she comes to the door I pull the gun and shoot her in a flesh wound and run like hell and you pick me up at the gate. This aint gone work unless this rain slack off some more. I aint standing out in no rain."

"The rain will quit," said Ferrin, who had listened to the weather on the radio. "You're leaving parts of it out again."

"Yeah, but I know all that other stuff. Anyhow, this pizza's driving me crazy." The pizza had arrived at their apartment just minutes before, and now the smell filled the kitchen. "How about just one piece? I mean, she aint gonna open it."

"For Christsake, how much food would you eat in one day? Didn't I tell you this has got to be a turnkey job? Now, that means every little thing in place. You think she aint gonna open it, I think she aint gonna open it, but what if something happens we aint expecting? I tell you what, a man is judged by how he pays attention to the details, and you think I'm on risk my life on a operation where my partner don't give a shit in the details of the thing—"

"Risk your life, shit. I'm the one going to the door."

"I thought I already explained that to you."

Ferrin *had* already explained it, and Rubert had had to admit that for once the explanation made sense. They were trying to throw a scare into em, and white people were more afraid of a black man with a gun than they were of a white man with a gun. And besides which, they had a whole lot harder time identifying the black man's face, because they all looked alike to em. Ferrin was a genius sometimes. It was almost worth the aggravation just to be around him when he pulled something like that out of his hat.

"Well ok," Rubert said. "But I can't sit here smelling this pizza and keep my mind on the plan no more. Pizza has all the major food groups," he added.

"All right, all right. Get your stuff together and wait here. I'll be back in a few minutes. I'll honk out front, and you come down."

"How long you be gone?" Rubert said hopefully.

"Don't you touch that pizza."

"You could have not ordered the Italian sausage, you know. That's my favorite."

"Everything's your favorite. Shut up and synchronize your goddamn watch."

"Emily is your third cousin on Alma Luce's side," Mrs. Weatherall said to Lianne, introducing a pale young woman who had just joined the group. They were two graves along on the planned itinerary.

The young woman looked familiar, and Charles was sure they had met her before, but that was Mrs. W. all the way. For her it was not introduction, he thought, but definition: She controlled the information. You weren't who you were until she said so. In her world, lineage was everything and people were nothing.

"Emily had diarrhea for a whole year when she was a baby, we never did figure out what was wrong, did we, Emily?" Emily shook her head palely, maybe she still had the flux, and Lianne starting in on how it was probably allergies, had Emily ever been tested for food allergies, yeah

Lianne there were a lot of allergists up here and all these people could afford them too, and no and a little animation coming into the pale face but do you remember Judy Dillman I guess you wouldn't you was just a baby then but anyway Judy broke out all over hives whenever she eat greens, reckon how a body would keep alive without greens?

"All of the O'Hares are on this side of the hill," Mrs. Weatherall explained to Emily and Lianne and the two or three others who had allowed themselves to be entrained. Charles hung back, far enough so that he didn't feel he was part of the audience, but near enough not to be obviously shunning them. Across the cemetery here and there he could see other family groups tending to their various sites, or just standing and talking. It was more like a picnic than anything else, a picnic without food. He felt he would rather have been a member of almost any of those groups than of his own. They were the family at the picnic that had brought the embarrassing obnoxious relative nobody could stand but nobody would say anything about.

"All of your ancestors were Irish," Mrs. Weatherall was saying. "There aren't any Welsh in this part of the cemetery." She spoke the word, *Welsh*, with a sort of spitting contempt. Lianne's father, he had heard often enough, had been Welsh. Mrs. Weatherall herself was at best half Irish, and that only if you believed her father full-blooded, when the family had been two generations in the hills before him.

"You would think it was the graves of kings," Curtis said at his elbow.

"It is, to hear her tell it," Charles said. "The proud princes of Eire." Thatched-hut sodbusters, more like.

"Say what?" Curtis said. He was was six four or five, lean and stooped and monkey-faced. He carried a battered felt hat, which he would not replace on his gray head until he had walked back out of the cemetery gate, and he wore a wide brown tie with ducks on it, a suit coat, a set of cleaned and pressed overalls, and what people in the city called Timberlands or Red Wings and he called work boots.

"All these O'Hares," Charles said. "You ever hear a one of em talk with an Irish accent?"

"Nair a one," Curtis said.

When had all the presumably Catholic O'Hares become Church of Christ? What forgotten wars of conversion had passed over these fields, leaving him only the hints and traces of such family stories as he had heard from Lianne, an evidence as sketchy but evocative as buttons on a Civil War battlefield? For that matter—

"Why did she switch from Church of Christ to Baptist?" he said.

"Do what?" Curtis said.

"Lianne's mother. Wasn't she Church of Christ, and then she went Baptist? I never heard why that was."

"Elaine? Well, that was atter she move to the city, you know. I might not be able to tell ye exactly."

"Was it Lee Andrew? Was it because he was a Baptist?"

"You know, I think it was atter that too," Curtis said. "Anyways, he didn't strike me a church type of man. Any church. Anyways, wouldn't he more likely do her church than she would do his?"

Charles grinned. "You got that right."

Mrs. Weatherall and her group had moved around an outcropping. "Your great-uncle James," her voice came. "He would have been a hundred and five this June." Charles and Curtis gave them a decent interval, then proceeded. A group of five stones stood in a small nook, separated from the adjoining plot by a line of cedar. Mrs. W. had already forged ahead into the cedar. Her following seemed to have dwindled, now comprising only Emily, Lianne, and a couple of older women. Charles and Curtis stood at the larger central stone, which read *James Foster Bennigan O'Hare, 1876–1957. The Lord Has Called Him Home.*

"I have a idee, though," Curtis said.

"Tell me what," Charles said.

They moved into and through the trees, onto an open area clustered with family plots, the creek circumscribing the bottom of the slope. Below them, Mrs. Weatherall gestured at the Baptist graves across the way, while one of the older women took Lianne's hand to say goodbye.

"Strikes me it happen right about yay time when Lianne was starting piano," Curtis said.

Charles laughed out loud. Lianne looked up the hill at him, squinting into the sun, the breeze ruffling her skirt, her hair. "What's so funny?" she called.

"Tell you later," he called back.

The Church of Christ didn't allow musical instruments in their sanctuaries, based on what Charles thought was an idiotic misreading of some biblical line about praising Him with melodies in your heart. Which they construed to mean *only* in your heart. No matter that Solomon and David were musicians, and that other verses spoke of praising Him with harp and psalter. *Whatever is not expressly permitted is forbidden:* who said that?

So maybe when Mrs. W. realized her young daughter had musical talent, a talent that could conceivably be capitalized on? That could win contests and maybe make money?

"Curtis, I like the way you think," Charles said.

Down the hill Lianne was on her haunches to trace her finger over the wording on a stone, a child's stone probably, it was so small. Curtis was watching her with a look on his face that Charles could not identify, though he thought it was most like the look of a man watching a beautiful horse, except without the possessiveness, and with a shadowing of time and not exactly sadness but something stronger, something you might come to when you were no longer young and you had worn sadness out.

"You done a good thing," Curtis said, "taking her off the tv. She looks better now than she ever did on the tv."

"Well you know," Charles said, "it was really her decision."

Lianne stood easily, the skirt clinging along her thigh for a moment. She tossed her hair and followed after her mother, picking her way near the creek, below the levels of the lowest graves, below flood stage. Charles felt his throat clench, and the fear came over him again, a fear as open and clear and omnipotential as the sky. She was just a girl, still just a girl. The fear and the sky were one thing, and the sky was itself a bird, the wings of a great blue transparent bird swooping silently down upon them.

"You done a good thing," Curtis reiterated.

Rubert was lost in admiration. "How the hell did you get a pizza van?" he said. They were standing in the narrow stoop of their front entrance.

"I told you, I got connections everywhere," Ferrin said. The pizza van was pulled up to the curb right where their Pinto had been parked before. It was a skinny little white truck, shining in the light but steady rain. It looked as if it ought not to have but three wheels. In the back were racks for the pizzas and on the top a big blue and red sign, which Ferrin was pretending to himself was a combination spotlight and machine-gun rack, blow your enemies off the road.

The van had been in his brother Tommy's shop since Thursday, and as a matter of fact it was what had given him the idea about the pizza in the first place, not the other way round, but it was a good idea to keep Rubert impressed, it made him easier to handle.

"Let's rock and roll," Rubert said. "Get in out of this drizzle."

"How's that boy Leon doing?" Curtis said. "Fletcher's boy?" He and Charles were sitting on a shelf of rock that projected over the little creek. Charles was thinking of flood stage still. Something about it seemed important. Of course: The fact that the current was not running high and muddy was proof it had not rained up here in the hills. He felt a flash of remembered irritation: *Watch that shoulder. It's going to be awfully soft.* He wanted to take his shoes off and wade in the clear shallows. He resisted, not that Curtis would think him silly, but Curtis's boots were laced all the way up and Curtis had a couple of fused vertebrae in his spine, and Charles knew Curtis wasn't going to trouble to bend over and unlace his own footgear, and you didn't enjoy something in front of other people when they couldn't enjoy it with you.

Curtis loved to hear stories about Charles's family, never mind they were related by marriage only, and at the remove of two marriages at that, and really less than that in a way if you took into account Charles was adopted and so wasn't even blood kin to the other Morrisons.

"He wrecked that Mustang," Charles said.

"No," Curtis said. "That pretty little red car? Was he drinking?"

Charles nodded. "Totaled it." The red Mustang, a '67 fastback, had been Leon's high school graduation present two years ago. The fact that a boy could get a whole car just for doing what he ought to do had been shocking enough for Curtis. He probably really got a kick out of this news. He had a rascally appetite for gossip, the more scandalous the better, and in that connection in the last few years Leon had proved to be the fount of every blessing.

"Hurt him much?" he said.

"Walked away from it," Charles said.

"Aint that the way," Curtis said. "And some old deacon down here never had a snort in his life run in the ditch with his seat belt on, probably kill him. Still in Tulane?"

"Not for long," Charles said. "Not the way he's going. Had a C, a D, and an F last semester and dropped out of two classes."

Curtis clucked in disapproval, shook his head. "Straighten up and fly right. He don't realize, but one of these days he'll run out of chances, like everybody else. Money won't save him." Belatedly, Curtis realized that the reference to money might have offended Charles, and threw him a sidelong glance.

But Charles had not noticed. He was looking at the play of sunny water on mossy stone, thinking how good the day was, how good it was to be done with artifice and the city, to be here in the country doing something real, having a real conversation with a real person. He was grateful to Curtis for accepting him, for treating him like one of the fellows.

"I heard that," he said.

"There she goes," Rubert said. "You sure called that one." The taxi, with Clemmie in it, had just pulled out of the Morrison driveway.

"One a these days you learn to trust me," Ferrin said.

"Well you don't tell me nothing. Tell me it a be arrange, but won't tell me how. How'm I s'posed to know?"

"There's chiefs and then there's Indians. And the lesser you know the better. If they catch us, they can't beat it out of you."

Rubert didn't like the sound of that. "Aint gone catch us," he said. "This a turnkey operation." He twisted in his seat, reaching in the back for the pizza box. "Cold as shit," he said.

"Will you quit fretting?" Ferrin said. "It'll warm up fine in the stove."

Yeah, Rubert thought, you who don't care what you put in your mouth.

Curtis took his leave. The light was getting longer, and if he didn't get back pretty soon, there would be no nap at all before the evening services. Which made for a long day for a man as old as Charles suddenly realized Curtis was, watching the fire of playfulness, though in Curtis it burned as brightly as ever when it burned, so abruptly shut off.

Charles was alone on the hillside. Lianne and her mother had disappeared along their course. Perhaps he ought to hurry and find them. The water made its fine constant sound, the permanent music of variation. He bent to unlace his shoes.

"Are you ready?" Ferrin said. "Three forty-six. Check your watch."

"Check," Rubert said, because he knew that was how Ferrin wanted him to answer. "And almost a half. I'm ready."

"Now I'm on be circling around," Ferrin said, "so nobody'll notice a pizza truck just sitting here. We on go on three forty-eight. When am I gone be back?"

"Eight plus seven is, ahm, is—shit, Ferrin."

"Three fucking fifty-five. If you can't do it in seven minutes, you can't do it. If you miss me, I'm gone. They catch you, I declaim all knowledge."

"Yeah, yeah, we done this part. Let's get rolling." Rubert wanted to get it over with and get back and get the pizza warmed up. Get Ferrin to stop off at Safeway and pick up some shaky cheese and a six-pack. Maybe some kosher dills, and a Pepperidge Farm German Chocolate or something. And some whip cream.

"Not yet, goddammit. Forty-five seconds and counting."

"I think I'll plug her in the thigh," Rubert said. "I think that's best, don't you?"

"How am I supposed to watch the fucking watch? We been over this. *No* I don't think the fucking thigh is any good, you got the fucking female artery in the fucking thigh, she'll bleed to death. Thirty seconds."

"Yeah, but that upper body shit. If you miss, there's so much other shit you can hit. On the thigh, you just bust up a knee or something. This aint the best gun in the world, you know. Them niggers took yo money."

"Shoot her wherever the fuck you want to shoot her. Twenty-five seconds and counting."

"You got to roll me up to the gate, now. I aint walking down the street with no pizza box in my hand."

"That's part of the goddamn seven minutes. How many times I got to— *Ten. Nine. Eight.*"

Rubert knew enough to know you shut up when the final countdown began. *"One,"* Ferrin said, and Rubert said, "Blast off," and Ferrin put the pizza van in gear and rolled down the street to the Morrisons' gate. Rubert got out, slammed the door, and started up the drive. At least it wasn't raining any more, or maybe a light sprinkle, but that might just be the trees and all, still dripping. He heard the sound of the motor dwindling behind him.

At just about the same moment, although the concept of simultaneity is spurious, but at any rate at a very small remove along the space-time hypotenuse, when his watch, if he had looked at it, would also have read 3:48, Charles waded around a crook in the creekbed and saw Lianne leaning on a headstone, her rump on its rounded cap. She was above the flood line and above the almost coinciding shadow line too. The sun caught her blouse, which hung unbuttoned and open, showing her bare breastbone. She held something crumpled in her left fist, a scrap of white silk.

"Hi," he said, climbing toward her.

For answer she opened her fingers, letting the fabric fall free. Her panties.

He jerked his head, looking guiltily right and left. "Where's—" His throat seemed to be full, and he cleared it.

"She went to the car," Lianne said. "Come here."

She shifted herself and lifted her legs, balancing herself with her hands to either side. Her skirt fell away from her knees, and he saw the blaze of her pubis, blonde-in-red like a matchflame. Her labia showed through, gorged and splendid. The skirt had cleared the name on the headstone, and he read it now, a foot under her sex: *Bull.*

"I can't sit like this very long," she said. "You need to give me something to hold on to."

He found himself with her arms around his shoulders, the stone cool through his slacks where he braced his slightly bent knees. In his mind were sirens, spotlights, news cameras, the outrage of citizens waving pitchforks.

"You'll have to undo your pants," she whispered in his ear. "I'll fall if I let go."

"Honey—" he said.

"They've all gone home," she said in his ear. "She chased them off, and then she went up to the car to wait." She nibbled his earlobe, and he caught her scent rising between them, bitterweed-strong and sharper than trodden horsemint.

He held an almost instantaneous argument with himself, a battle of images that for your benefit, however, I must render sequentially: If they got caught, who by? These people disappointed but not dangerous. Certainly not surprised. Not the first time for this or any other cemetery. Depending on who if anyone—maybe not ashamed but amused, Curtis for example.

Call the law? But how long to a phone, and how much longer a trooper? He would be gone, deny it all if tracked down.

Come on, Charles—live a little!

And still his heart beat with panic, he felt cold and weak.

She leaned back against his arms to look in his face, changing their balance so that his chest and belly and loins met hers at every point. Her eyes were wide and merry. "They won't catch us," she said. "And I don't care if they do."

Which was what made him erect, her words or the look on her face, so that he couldn't get his pants open fast enough, almost pitching her off as he fumbled and then springing free and poking around and helping with his fingers and then sliding into the warm lathery fact of fuck her mother she chose him happiness leaning her head back and laughing as he slid it in all the way up to the blue fucking bird fucking sky, his balls slapping cool on cool flat stone.

Rubert rang the doorbell again. He could hear it away inside, a dim trilling. It sounded empty, and he knew Ferrin had fucked up again. The woman wadn't home. Hell, they been away four hours, eating chili dogs and I don't know what, anything could happen. But you didn't go back and tell Ferrin that on just two rings.

He looked at his watch, which said 3:51, and then he rang again, leaving his finger on the button a long time. But this ring sounded just as empty. He reckoned two more long rings and then he would go back up the driveway and wait for Ferrin.

What the devil, Coleman thought, as the bell at the other end of the greenhouse rang for the third time. You didn't usually get a salesman in the

Heights on a Sunday, especially not in Edgehill. Had that in common with his neighborhood, for different reasons.

If the old woman hadn't left, she could get it, but she had a mergency with her apartment and call him to cover the door before she leave. Probably a salesman, but if he don't answer it like as not something important, some kind a relative or something and won't hear the last.

Picked up the machete use for whacking vine, so when he come around the front yard they could see who it was, the gardener. Besides, you know— have something in your hand. Never walk into nothing without something in your hand.

Lianne screamed, coming almost as soon as he penetrated, jumping against him, waves of compression, like being in a pulsating vacuum cleaner, highly uncommon, normally took a while and maybe a lot of work with the tongue, this was not he was beginning to realize your ordinary day as she collapsed against him sighing.

"Oh. Charles. You've got. To see. My picture," she said into the base of his neck.

"I'm not through," he said, rigid inside her slackness.

"Well for God's sake don't quit," she said. And as he began to buck and pump, holding her ass now, rapacious, his knuckles scraping the raw edges of stone, she wept, her breath broken not by her own pulses any longer but by his carnivorous lunges: "I'm a real, yesterday, a real, you've got to see what I oh *god* you're big, what I did yesterday, I'm really a real—"

He sank his teeth through her blouse into her shoulder as he shuddered and came, and she shrieked again, trying to talk, her voice floating high over the trees like the call of a circling hawk:

"Ah . . . aaha . . . *aaah* . . ."

Rubert had rung twice more and nothing happened. He could kick the door in and do some damage. But would that thow a scare in em, or just make em mad like a regular burglar? Besides, what if they *were* home and just didn't hear yet? It was a big house, how did it work in a real big house? What if you was off in some other room, how would you know anybody was at the door? Last thing he wanted was to get in there and then have somebody surprise him in the act. I mean he was gone shoot em anyway, but he didn't like being scared while he did it. What if they were looking at him right now on some kind of spy tv, already called the cops. He didn't see a camera, though, would have to be a camera. His watch said 3:53.

Close enough. He was fucking out of here. He started back up the drive-way, lifting the lid of the box to check the pizza.

And then the goddamn nigger come around the corner of the goddamn house waving a goddamn sword.

Lianne was squatting in the creek, peeing, holding her skirt in her teeth, and then she was splashing herself clean with the running water, a natural bidet washing away her urine and his drip and he was leaning against *Bull* laughing soundlessly at the picture she made, his slacks still down around his ankles and his briefs at his knees and still waving in the air a bit though it was if you want the truth getting a little cool in the long blue shadows of their declivity, and she caught him laughing and growled, the skirt in her teeth, and let it drop so that the sides trailed in the water dark purple immediately to a half inch above the waterline and then soaking far more slowly, that was how fast capillary action was and no faster, and said, "Liverloaf."

The first thing Coleman saw was the .38 with the fake walnut stock, jammed into the fat yard-service nigger's beltline in the small of his back and he was holding some kind of box but it was the gun gun gun that counted so he lifted the machete over his head and charged like a kamikaze Japanese in the jungle knowing the man was there to kill Miss Lianne Debelle Zarounian Morrison but Coleman wasn't Japanese he was *fighting* the Japanese—

What would *you* do if a white-haired old nigger with a sword came at you yelling AAAAHHH GODDAMN JAP I KILL YOU GODDAMN JAPANESE FUCKING JAP?

Rubert let a wet fart, which messed his underwear up but that was why you wore underwear, and kind of jerked and flung the pizza box at the old bastard which went way up in the air and came open and the pizza sailed out like a Frisbee, and he spun to the gate but Ferrin wasn't there as he spun back drawing the gun and the silencer snagging on his belt for just a thousandth of a second and the old nigger standing stock-still in the drive-way and then as Rubert fired twice sinking to his knees holding his chest and the pizza settling in a slow curve between them.

It was like lightning but black. It didn't make sense for somebody to be pointing a gun at him with one hand and picking up a pizza with the other from the flagstones of the driveway, but that was what it looked like to Coleman in the aftermath of the black thunderclaps, like a strobe light as the fat nigger got smaller and smaller and turned away, the pizza hanging from one hand like a kid with a dead stingray on the beach in Pontchartrain the stingray there by mistake thinking because it was salt it was still the ocean.

Shit, he thought. *I done kill myself for a white man.* Getting hit when he pulled Traubman out wasn't brave but this was, but he would never get a medal which was ok because a real ending was always a surprise and this was a good one, so long Harry Truman.

None of the country stores she loved so much were open on Sunday, of course, so they were all the way back to Morrillton before they found a meat counter with blocks of sharp cheddar and livercheese as he called it but which she had grown up calling liverloaf, so he called it liverloaf from then on because she had surely earned that much today.

She was happy to pretend the quickstop was a real country store. It was air-conditioned and had a plate-glass front, but the narrow boards of the floor were old and gray, and they had a real old-fashioned drinkbox, the kind where you slid the bottles along a rack in icy water. She came out with a quarterpound of the liverloaf wrapped in white butcher paper, and two cream sodas (Elaine just wanted water, thank you), and a peanut patty, a disk of shrink-wrapped violent pink consolidated sugar with embedded irregular legumes, the sort of sweet Lee Andrew had bought her when she was a child coming up here before she had ever met or even thought of anybody like Joseph Charles Morrison.

They had the liverloaf on the crackers she had brought along as they zoomed back down the interstate toward home, Lianne stripping the strings of fat from the slices and folding the slices in half and half again to break them into four pieces just the size of the crackers, handing him a double-loaded cracker and taking the same herself and licking her fingers.

Elaine was too upset to eat because he could have been a lot more help at the cemetery. She meant she had brought the garbage bag of used decorations back to the car herself, and also he and Lianne had left the box the flowers came in just sitting there. Lianne said she didn't see how he could have possibly been any more helpful, and he nearly choked on the cracker and had to have another swallow of cream soda, and Elaine didn't have a comeback. He would have bet she knew exactly what Lianne meant but couldn't admit she knew, it was such a slap in the face. He couldn't figure out why he was thinking not about making love on the headstone but instead of pumping gas back at the quickstop while Lianne was inside buying the liverloaf.

It was because of the bright red Ranger that had pulled up at the pumps while he was there, four locals hopping out, teenagers with the long hair that ten years ago would have got them shot as hippies but now was the standard for any pimply deerhunter or good-old-boy nail-puller, a greasy mane spilling loose under a tractor cap, but they weren't the point.

He heard Rider at the party last week—*We must have spent two hours talking about four-wheel drive*—and he thought how she loved woods and the back roads, and coming into the city limits he suddenly knew the perfect thing to get her for their anniversary, only three weeks off.

24

CALAMITY
AT THE GATE

Clemmie blamed herself for not being there when Coleman had his heart attack. There had been, as her caller had said, a fire in number two downstairs. Some kid had thrown a Molotov cocktail through a window. But it turned out to be just kerosene in a Coke bottle, and kerosene is much less volatile than gasoline, and the bottle hadn't broken, so it hadn't exploded. It just lay there and burned like the wick of a knocked-over lamp and put black smoke all over the ceiling.

The noise had waked the renter, who was hung over but somehow got up enough willpower to stumble into the next room and see what was going on and get the fire out before Clemmie even got there—stupidly dousing it with glasses of water but succeeding because the flame was so small. He sat on the orange Naugahyde sofa with his head in his hands and his feet on the green throw rug while she called the police. They were reluctant to come out, but she fussed and fumed and made angry-citizen property owner's noises until finally she got a patrol car so there would be a report and she could get the insurance on the damage.

"Ok, buddy," said the cop who was asking the questions. He sighed. "So exactly when you hear the window glass breaking?"

The renter held up his bare left wrist.

"You called me at twenty till four," Clemmie said.

"I never called nobody," the renter said.

"Well, who did?" Clemmie said.

"Probably the one who done it," the cop said. "They do that a lot. It's like nyaah nyaah na nyaah nyaah."

"But it didn't sound like one of them," Clemmie said.

The cop was black. He gave her a heavy-lidded look. "One of who?" he said.

Clemmie temporized: "The neighborhood kids. Anyway, how would they know my number at home?" The cop shrugged. "Can you go to the phone company?" Clemmie said. "Trace the call back?"

"Lady, we aint God Almighty," the cop said. He turned back to the renter. "When you heard the crash, did you see anybody? Like running away, or hanging around watching?"

"Anybody got any aspirin?" the renter said.

It was six-thirty by the time Clemmie got home and found Coleman lying on his face in the driveway. Both of Rubert's bullets had missed, one thumping into the dogwood in the bed at the foot of the portico and the other into the foundation of the house.

Coleman was still breathing, but in a ragged and frightening way. One emergency after another, Clemmie thought. All she had really wanted was to get out of that godforsaken Sin City rathole she hoped Charles was right she could unload on some poor sucker soon, and get home and get her feet up and have a beer and watch maybe Audie Murphy in *To Hell and Back* for the fifteenth time, but instead here she was having to deal with one more goddamn crisis and hustle up one more public supposedly service ha-ha. Though when the medics heard the address they jumped quick enough. She didn't say it was just the gardener.

Then she went back out and sat down beside Coleman and patted his laboring back, crying for no good reason since although he and she had not disliked each other they had never been close: too little in common and each territorial as a cat, her territory the inside and his the out. The rain had returned, a misty drizzle as evening came on. Not very hard, but enough to soak her through before the ambulance got there.

She felt guilty that her first impulse had been irritation and not sympathy, which was why she blamed herself for not having been there. It made her hell to live with for the next week.

Charles and Lianne put Clemmie's bitchiness down to her having been a lot closer to Coleman than they had realized, plus the shock of being the one to find him.

They had dropped Mrs. Weatherall off first and then detoured by the Arts Center to look at Lianne's painting. The guard let them in, and she led him up to the easel and whipped off the linen cover, an old torn sheet really. The painting hit him with the force of validated prophecy.

It wasn't finished, in some ways it was just a sketch, because Vega put a premium on working rapidly. She wanted you to draft a painting completely in one go. She believed that working at speed forced you to trust your impulses, and that impulse tapped into the true power of the subconscious mind. For once it had worked, Charles thought.

Bright blue and green, Adam and Eve in the garden. The garden was the cemetery, a relaxation of green slopes across concentric concussions of sun expanding and cooling to become the sky. Except that there were no graves in the cemetery. Instead, on the right, under the zinc-white-and-cadmium-yellow sun, as if flowing out of it and showing back its light, a river broken around not rocks but tombstones. The tombstones were gray blank stoop-shouldered shapes like cartoon ghosts and casting delicate shadows across the water they troubled. Couched in the air above the slopes on the left, almost balancing the sun schematically and the true source of warmth in the coloration, the naked couple curled to each other fat and simplified, their prehensile tails hanging, their curved haunches and rounded shoulders like the flanks of a divided apple, but caught in that moment when they have just broken their gaze at someone's approach, their bare and fleshy chimpanzee faces turned outward to the viewer: his eyes were gray and hers were green. And on their haunches and on her back, since her back was toward the river, the ripple of that waterlight a moving current will cause to play across the undersides of leaves.

It was a long time later before he thought that perhaps her painting had been not so much prescience as a declaration of intent.

They got home right at seven, the ambulance still in the driveway, with Coleman already in it. It was a shock to find calamity at their own gate, and they looked at each other as if to verify that yes, they were both here and ok, it was neither of them hurt.

Lianne talked to the medics and got all the information they had, what had happened and what shape he was in and what they were doing for him and where they were taking him and. Charles stood aside with Clemmie on the portico, out of the drizzle. She had explained how she hadn't been there when it happened, but had come home to find him. She had explained guiltily, but Charles hadn't appeared to notice. "Trouble comes in bunches," he said, missing the point, for which she was glad, but then felt guilty about being glad. He had tried to send her in to put on something dry, but she was staying downstairs until the ambulance left. She had collected the pizza box from the driveway, and now she toed the sodden and crumpled cardboard.

"I think he ordered a pizza," she said. "And had an attack when it came."

"It's weird," Charles said. He had never known Coleman to order fast food. He was far too frugal, and mostly he ate what they provided.

But maybe it was a secret vice, and he had decided since no one else was there . . .

"Why would he eat in the front yard?" he said. "In the rain?"

"I don't think he ate it," Clemmie said.

"So where is it?" He had an image of Ramalam scarfing slices from Lianne's hand that time they took the mongrel to the fair. "Neighborhood dogs," he said. Dogs snatching and snarling around the fallen man. "What about the delivery boy, why didn't he call the ambulance?" He was angry. They already knew from the medics that Coleman had been down a couple of hours. If the pizza boy had just called it in, that could have made the difference right there.

"He was scared," she said. "Or he already left when it happened." She felt, obscurely, as if she were defending herself.

"You can't tell me he would have an attack before he even got out of the driveway and the boy wouldn't notice." He was going to *find* that boy—

Later they called Tucker and Dee-Dee to come over and commiserate. It had somehow gotten to be nine o'clock before they got there, and then Clemmie was too shaken to mount a full-scale dinner, so they all pitched in and built snacks and had a couple of drinks and found themselves without much to say but stayed up past midnight anyway. So Charles found himself peeling for bed in a very unsatisfactory state on what had been, for a while, a highly satisfactory day. He was tired, but in a fuzzy anxious way, depressed and restless. He was afraid he was going to toss and turn all night.

Lianne came into his arms under the cover, shivering as she snuggled. "I'm so glad I have you," she said. He knew she meant the gratitude of the survivor.

"It's a dangerous world," he said. Fires, accidents, floods, and wars. Plagues and famines. Wobbly-headed children with their ribs showing. Air raid sirens, running people. Rubbled walls and bloody bodies. He was almost asleep in spite of himself. The kitten in the paper bag. "I'm glad I have you too," he said, burying his nose in her hair, his nostrils full of the warm waxy smell of her scalp.

Ferrin was smoking Pall Malls one after the other, pacing back and forth in the kitchen. They had ditched the .38, driving out to the airport so they could fling it into Fourche Creek. Now he was raving on about how that didn't do em any good because Rubert had left the pizza box behind. "Well I got the pizza," Rubert said, between bites. He had warmed it up in the oven and was chewing on a piece.

"They don't trace the goddamn pizza, you goddamn idiot. They trace the goddamn box."

"Anybody coulda bought a pizza."

"What about the sales slip, you moron? Sales slip has the time on it, they can look back and see who delivered a pizza when to where, and come right to us."

Rubert held up a white slip of grease-stained paper triumphantly. Congealed cheese clung to it in pale strips. "Stuck on one of the pieces," he said.

"You moron," Ferrin said.

"Hey, Mister Big Chief Mastermind," Rubert said. He was a little pissed, a little less than tolerant, because, as so often happens when you try to warm pizza up in the oven, part of the cheese had bubbled up and burnt black, while the crust remained soggy. "You didn't tell me no sword-carrying nigger was on come running out. What about that, you such a genius?"

"Sword-carrying nigger," Ferrin snorted. "You're such a moron." He lit another Pall Mall from the butt of the one he was smoking, came back to the table, and ground the first one out in the cracked saucer he was using for an ashtray. Rubert waved the smoke away, irritated. Ferrin smiled, went back to his pacing.

"I don't know what we tell the contact," he said.

"Don't see why we have to tell em anything," Rubert said. He put the edge of crust aside, a snack bone for later, with a glass of milk. He picked up another slice. "We might not a hit the primary target, but we done what we paid to." He felt Ferrin's eyes on him, incredulous, and he enjoyed it. "We thrown a scare into em. We kilt their nigger."

They hadn't, though. Coleman was stabilized, still in coma, in the ICU ward of Doctors' Hospital. The episode itself might not have been that serious if they had gotten to him in time, but there had been interference with the blood flow to the brain, and they didn't know the extent of the damage. They wanted to perform a bypass, but not until he came out of the coma, if he did.

Besides, who would give permission? There were no local relatives. Lianne spent several days talking to Coleman's neighbors, until she knew them better than Coleman ever had and they took her appearances as a matter of course. Charles worried about her in that neighborhood until Rider started going with her. She had hired him to try and find Coleman's boy—they had not even known he had a son until Lianne went through his house Monday morning.

Charles spent Monday morning at the hospital with Coleman, and then Lianne spelled him while he went to the office in the afternoon. He came in the next morning, but didn't spend much time in the room because he had to deal with about a thousand bureaucrats, signing papers to assure them he would be responsible for all Coleman's medical bills that Medicare didn't cover. He was astonished at how much money that amounted to, though he shouldn't have been. It brought home the fact that in this country health care was simply a commodity bought and sold like any other, the same as chicken parts, automobiles, fresh air, and a college education. Your very time on earth chopped up into parcels and shrink-wrapped and sold back to you after processing costs and markups. He made up his mind to become even richer.

He spent his lunch hours at the hospital the rest of the week. But Coleman showed no change, and by Thursday Charles's mind was back on business. It was Lianne who pointed out that it was the thick of the growing season and they were going to have to hire a new gardener.

"Coleman mentioned some kind of yard service," he said.

"What was their name?" she said.

"He didn't say. It was a black man and a white man, I think."

"That's a lot of help. Never mind, I'll just ask around. They'll all be protecting their own, but somebody's bound to know somebody I can call."

The contact was pleased with Ferrin and Rubert's results. "Slicker'n goose grease," Ferrin bragged. "Went down like a pine tree in a rainstorm." But the contact was frustrated at not being able to see the impact on the Morrisons. They wouldn't dare go to the papers with it, of course not, not if they were connected to the local drug trade, which they probably were, there was a lot more of that going around than you might think.

"We got to get somebody on the inside," Ferrin said, his heart beating rapidly. He knew the operation was about to escalate, and suspected he himself was going back into the field. That was all right, in spite of getting the shakes. The heroes aint the ones who aint afraid. The heroes the ones who do it anyway. Anybody tell you that. All the real leaders are hands-on.

"I have an idea," the contact said, and explained.

"So that's what they're doing at that hospital," Ferrin said. Even rich people didn't get off scot-free. Ha. All the money in the world couldn't save em from going crazy.

The creation science suit was filed on Thursday, with Morrison, Morrison, Chenowyth, and Frail participating as cocounsel. Greg Legg was attorney of record. Charles had debated taking the job himself but now was glad he hadn't, with so many other things on his mind. This way, if there was negative feedback, Greg could absorb the brunt, and Charles could shrug and play it off as the enthusiasm of a young hotshot, you had to give them their head sometimes to keep them happy. Since Greg *was* young, they would cut him more slack and do him less damage than they might an established attorney. And to top it all off, Greg was infinitely grateful to have the case.

Not that he had gotten it free for gratis. Charles had given it to him on condition he first sort out and assign all of Tina's outstanding caseload. In effect he became a junior partner responsible for overview of half a dozen cases, but without the pay and the title.

Greg had come into Charles's office Wednesday, the day before the filing, with a worried look on his face and a fistful of papers.

"What's up?" Charles said.

"There's a lot of this I don't understand," Greg said.

"You mean the law or the theory?" Charles said. "You don't necessarily have to understand everything the scientists say." He himself was struggling through a huge compendium of books and extracts Lianne had picked out for his edification, and was heartily sick of equilibrated punctuation or whatever, convergent functional morphology, and vestigial processes. People thought the *law* was full of jargon, they ought to try evolution.

"Oh, not the suit," Greg said. "I've got all that down. Tina's stuff."

"Tina's stuff?"

"Like the action against University Central Mall. I've been going through her notes, and—"

"Is that the one where the sign fell—"

"On Boody's daddy and killed him. Yeah." They both smiled. Judge Lookadoo had been smoking a cigar in the parking lot, waiting for his wife to finish shopping, when a wind had come up and blown the *C* off the big sign. The judge would not have seen what was so funny. He himself had never had a sense of humor.

"So what about the notes?" Charles said.

"I can't find any. I mean, here I have a bunch of papers with citations and page numbers and declarations of fact, but then there's just no trail. There's some handwritten stuff." He held up a yellow sheet from a legal pad, with a few illegible sentences on it in pencil. "But it's really general. And they're all like this, all the cases. I've tried to trace some of the citations back, and some of them are ok, but some. Well, maybe they're there and I'm just missing them."

"And maybe they're not there," Charles said, suddenly grim. "Let me ask you this. Did she ever—you know, did you ever think maybe she was sort of picking your brains? Take you aside and ask what you thought of a case, if you'd ever had one like it?''

Greg studied the papers in his lap. Charles exhaled and pushed back in his chair. ''Well, we can't go to court with this crap,'' he said.

They were having trouble looking at each other. A current of knowledge went between them. Charles spoke again.

''First thing you do is see if you think any of em are salvageable. If they are, get postponements. If they aren't, we're going to have to unplug the clients. I don't know how that'll work, probably on an individual basis, but you and me'll talk that over after you get em sorted out. We're going to have to be ready to refund any fees received, but do it in a way where we're not admitting culpability. Not where we've done the work and we're backing off, you understand—just unexpected personnel circumstances have prevented us from doing any work at all and we thought it was in the client's best interests to seek other representation blah blah blah.''

''The old cloud-of-smoke trick,'' Greg said, and Charles threw him a sharp glance, then thought, *What the hell, he's right.*

''The important thing is we don't need any publicity over this,'' he said. ''We're going to be up to our ears in public attention over CS-28, and we don't need to catch any extra shit.''

That would really be great, wouldn't it, if posthumously so to speak something Tina had done or more accurately not done blew up in their faces and derailed the creation science suit. Shit, he could hear Lianne now, and just when things were going so good in spite of how upset she was over Coleman—if anything, really, Coleman's attack had brought them even closer together, though that certainly didn't mean you were glad it had happened.

''We file tomorrow, and it's going to be a lot of extra work,'' Greg said. Charles knew he meant not complaint but practicality. If no one else was to know, who could help Greg?

''Call Hazen and tell Lafayette to come back in,'' Charles said. ''If he'll do it on the basis of keeping his head down and doing all the grunt work for you.''

Greg lit up. This was a brilliant solution. Equal complicity.

''He probably won't,'' Charles said. ''He'll probably just tell you to go to hell.''

But Laugh was glad to have some work to do. He continued living in Hazen for the time being, because he wasn't through getting his head straight. He began coming in after lunch, when the traffic was light. He worked late into the evening except Wednesdays, when he went to prayer meeting. In the next few weeks Charles and Greg would come in from this or that trial late in the day and find him at work and maybe put their feet up and talk things over. It made the offices seem more comfortable than they had in a long time, more relaxed and homelike.

Sometimes Lianne would come in for a visit, and that was a mixture of pleasure and uneasiness for Charles. But he soon saw that Greg and Lafayette were shrewd enough to stay away from the subject of Tina when Lianne was there, no doubt for their own reasons.

Lianne had not come to the office often before. For one thing, she felt it was an imposition of sorts, pushing the place out of its routine; and for another, she didn't like the wifely status that seemed to click on around her automatically, as if she were a wire-frame model on some unseen computer monitor, bracketed, gridded, with data running down the side of the screen.

But she lived and breathed the creation science issue now, when she wasn't at the hospital hovering over Coleman, and she could not stay away, and in fact she had some ideas that turned out to be very useful, especially with regard to who might make good witnesses.

The day the suit was filed there was a side story with her picture on it:

Say what? Well, I don't know. Must have been somebody that hates Lianne. Must have deleted the photo: Did a global search (find **Lianne clipping** in [file] **time**), you know how it is, and I guess the computer just pulled up the first one it came to. Must be two hundred thousand out there. Doesn't matter, wasn't a good shot anyway.

They had taken the picture in the hospital parking lot the day before, which is why she looks squinty and windblown. She was well aware that many of those who'd worked hard and long for the cause would see her as a headline grabber, a fading star trying to stay in the limelight. But she had thought it over and decided to give the interview anyway. If she had any capital to spend in the realm of public opinion, this was the time to spend it.

But who could have done her photo that way?

Sonny Raymond gave the paper a resounding slap. It was lying open on his desk, and Cheese leaned over his shoulder to see. "Yeah," Cheese said. "Can you believe that shit?"

He was talking about the article on the same page as Lianne's photo, how the lawyer for Ron Orsini's daughter was saying that Lee Orsini, the murdered man's wife, was a prime suspect in the killing. "They're just trying to keep her from getting his money," Cheese said.

"What the fuck are you talking about?" Sonny Raymond said, twisting his head to look up at Cheese. "And get away from my shoulder."

"Same thing you were," Cheese said, backing off to the door. "All I said was it was a damn shame, the way these fucking lawyers can say anything that comes into their heads. He just wants Orsini's money. That daughter won't see half of it, you watch."

Sonny looked back at the paper till he found the Orsini article, grunted. "She'll go to the chair and take you with her," he said.

"I didn't even know her then. Besides, she's innocent."

Sonny gave a short hard laugh. "Yeah, innocent," he said. "Like to have me some of that innocent. Bet it feels good on a cold night."

Cheese grinned, man to man. "Way I hear it," he said, "that Talliaferro woman—"

"You leave her out of this," Sonny said.

"Excuse me for living," Cheese said, though he wasn't really irritated. He was used to the mood swings by now. The chief was under a lot of pressure. The ACLU had come out and made a stink about the College Station beatings, and so it looked like there might be some kind of civil rights suit filed. And the missing evidence thing had hit the newspapers, the missing pistol and kilo of marijuana, which made them look like clowns, you had to admit, so now there would be an internal investigation, which was easy enough to cook, but it still took a lot of time and trouble away from the real job of the lord high bailiff, which was to be out there fighting crime. And now that damned Hawthorne was suing for back pay and damages. "Fuck these police school cops," Sonny had said. "I aint having no more of these pretty-boy police school cops walk in and stab you in the back the minute the going gets rough. I'm training my own fucking cops from now on." Except it was pretty clear that Bentley wasn't about to let him do that.

"What did you ever get on these Morrison fucks?" Sonny said.

"What?" Cheese said.

"Why do I have to say everything twice to you? What you got on these Morrison fucks? Didn't you tell me this bitch of yours had something on him, running dope out of that bar of his?"

"I didn't think you would take the word of a woman who was headed for the electric chair," Cheese said, still nettled.

"Don't fuck with me. You were going to get me a couple of street jockeys, keep an eye on the bastards. You were in here bragging about em. What you got?"

"Ahh, well, it's moving slow, you know. I mean, you didn't seem to be too interested the other night, and after the wiretap, they're onto us, you know, so you have to be careful—"

"I knew it. You aint done a goddamn thing. They're gonna be gone and made a monkey out of God in the highest court in this state, and you're just gonna be sitting there with your thumb up your ass smiling like you found another piece of big wet juicy head cheese."

"I have so," Cheese said, stung. It was the first time Sonny had jigged him about the scandal, and it hurt. "These things are delicate. You can't just—"

"Fuck delicate," Sonny Raymond said. "Do I have to do everything myself? Get the fuck out of here and get me some evidence before everybody in the state has to grow hair on their faces and fuck from behind and go oot oot oot."

Saturday was the first day since his attack that Lianne had not gotten out of bed and gone straight to the hospital to see Coleman. This morning she planned her usual Saturday routine: down to the farmers' market, then off to group, then lunch at the Arts Center, and then her painting class with Vega. "I feel guilty," she said.

"I know how you feel," Charles said, watching her from the bed. Clemmie had waked them up early, it was the freshest part of the day, she had had her shower, and she was alert and glowing. She wore her high-top Luccheses, tight jeans, a white pleated-front blouse with pearl buttons, her fringed leather jacket, and a beaded Apache headband. She looked like a cowboy hippie. "But there's nothing you can do for him right now."

"They say sometimes you're conscious down in there, and they can hear you, but they just can't respond. But I'll go in this evening for a while."

"Don't be too late." He got out from under the cover to show her why not. "I mean, it's already been eight hours."

"Oh, pooh," she said and tapped it swinging. He grabbed for her, but she laughed and pushed away. At the door, she waggled her denim-clad butt, looked back over her shoulder, and in a mock-alluring voice said, "Bye now."

It was just seven, but he went ahead and showered and got dressed himself. Clemmie had breakfast ready when he went down—hot biscuits, homemade hash browns with sautéed onions, three eggs over easy, and thick fried slices of Petit Jean ham with red-eye gravy.

"Lord, Clemmie," he said, finishing up with a second glass of fresh orange juice and surveying the loaded serving dishes. "It would take an army to eat the rest of this."

"I can't help it," she said, with her back turned. "I always make enough for Coleman." She banged the skillet down in the sink and started scrubbing it under running hot water. You never put an iron skillet in a dishwasher. You never wash it with soap.

Charles thought she was blaming him for making Coleman work too hard and thus causing his heart attack, and he changed the subject. "I'm working on Mrs. Morrison's present today," he said. He wasn't sure why, talking to Clemmie, he always said "Mrs. Morrison" instead of "Lianne." Maybe to remind her who was boss, he thought.

Actually it was because that was how his father had referred to his mother around the staff.

"What present?" Clemmie said, her back still turned.

"Her anniversary present. She's really going to like this one."

"Mmm-hmm," Clemmie said, drying the skillet with a cloth and hanging it up. "That's good." She had yet to look at him.

"Ok, I'm out of here," he said. "Miles to go before I sleep."

She was wrapping the serving dishes in aluminum foil as he left, storing them in the fridge. Their contents would be recycled into this evening's meal, he was sure. Cassoulet au porc, avec pommes de terre sautées, sous les croûtons des whatever the word for biscuit was in French.

He limped the Mercedes down to Jerry's. Jerry had come in early to make sure they got right to it. "I'm going to need a loaner," Charles said. "Lianne's got the Skylark today."

"Take mine," Jerry said. He drove not one of the Jags or Alfas or

Porsches he worked on but a chopped and channeled '75 Duster, reared up on its hind wheels like a cat in heat.

"You sure?" Jerry kept the Duster immaculate, bright gold with a chocolate top, the tail pipes gleaming. It would do a quarter mile in eleven seconds, and you could eat off the engine.

"Hell, I aint going anywhere. And what if I do? I got cars out the ass around here."

"Speaking of that," Charles said.

He was looking for a good four-wheel-drive for Lianne, he explained. Jerry suggested a Range Rover, but he didn't understand Lianne's psychology as well as he understood Charles's pocketbook. No way she would let Charles spend that much money on a personal vehicle, no matter how much she loved it. All week Charles had been checking out American makes, calling showrooms. He hadn't bought a car in years except for the Skylark, which had been cheap, and he had been dismayed at the way prices had shot up. These things ran nine and ten thousand. So his idea now was to get a good used one and fix it up. That would go down well with Lianne, and hey, he had to admit he never minded saving a penny himself. Maybe Jerry could point him in the right direction, maybe he knew of a vehicle?

"As a matter of fact," Jerry said. "My brother-in-law runs a shop on the other side of town has an old black Blazer he's wanting to sell."

"I thought the Broncos were the good ones," Charles said. "Anyway, it has to be red. Bright red." It had to be red because that was the color of the one in his mind, that was the color of the one that had pulled up at the quickstop.

"Nah," Jerry said, "Blazer's fine. This one's got everything—spots, winch, mudders, foglights, you name it. And anyway, paint is cheap."

"I don't know," Charles said. "Does your brother-in-law guarantee it?"

"Hell, *I'll* guarantee it. Listen, we'll let him rebuild it, and then I'll check it over. He's great, he really is. Time he's through, you'll have a new machine at two-thirds the cost."

"What about music?" Charles said. "Does it have a stereo?"

"Put in whatever you like. I said I'd guarantee the work."

"Ok," Charles said. "You talked me into it. I'll take a look. Incidentally. Can he have it ready in two weeks?"

"Jeez," Jerry said.

In the parking lot of the Baptist Medical Center, Ferrin switched the ignition off and got out of the car. "Hell of a way to spend a Saturday morning," Rubert said, hitching himself across the seat under the steering wheel.

"Just be here when I get out," Ferrin said. He slammed the door and turned away, squaring his shoulders. He knew Rubert was admiring him, knew he was doing something Rubert could never do, and he marched down the aisle of the lot and across the front drive, clunking loud with the heels of his boots, and pushed through the glass doors into the foyer of the Baptist Medical Tower. His knees had never been so weak, not even when they had walked him down to his cell that first time. Compared to this, that was a piece of cake. His heart was bound to blow out if it kept thumping so hard. He was in enemy territory now, and no kidding.

There were people walking by everywhere, it was like a downtown street. Doctors in white coats crossed the foyer, nurses in blue gowns, mothers with crying babies, men in suits, teenagers holding hands. He knew where they were going, all of them but him. There was a drugstore/gift shop off to the right, glassed so you could see in, people buying magazines and chocolate bars and bouquets of artificial flowers. "I thought this was supposed to be a goddamn hospital," he muttered, and a granny in slacks and pink tennis shoes gave him a look.

There was a security guard on the other side of the foyer, a big black man whose blue-shirted belly hung out of his leather jacket. He had a gun on his hip. Ferrin walked over to him. It was like being the spy behind German lines, and the first time you walked up to a kraut officer and spoke German and waited to see if you got away with it.

"Where's the stairs?" he said.

"Can't use the stairs," the guard said. "Emergency only. Hey, you over there! You can't smoke in here!" He charged toward the offender, an elderly gentleman with a pipe who looked up owlishly at his approach. "Yay, you! This a cottonpicking hospital, main."

Great, Ferrin thought. Just great. Bad enough being in this kind of a building in the first place, now he had to use the elevator. He hated elevators. He had been in an elevator maybe twenty times in his life, outside of Uncle Baldwin in Atlanta when he used to work in the department store and Ferrin would visit him summers and an old nigger in a red uniform would pull a handle to close the doors and move them up and down. All the other times had been in prison, going back and forth to the warden's office, with an armed guard for an escort.

There was no driver in this one. A colored woman and her two kids got on. The doors closed automatically, like a grocery store. *This is it,* he thought. *If it's ever gonna fall, this'll be when.* He waited tensely, but nothing happened. "Twelve," the colored woman said. The kids were a fat boy and a little shy girl, the boy wearing some kind of ridiculous puffy shiny pants with zippers and pockets all over.

"What?" Ferrin said. His breathing was tight.

"Twelve," the woman said. "You got to punch the button." There was a register of lighted buttons in front of him, and thinking fast, he punched the one that read *12*. The elevator lurched, but then slid down instead of up, and he let out an involuntary cry.

"It's going the wrong way," he said.

"Cause you wait too long," the woman said. "Somebody in the basement done punch ahead a you. Now we got to go down and git them."

"What floor you going to, mister?" the boy said, leaning across bright-eyed.

"Seven," Ferrin said. The boy punched the button and leaned back against his mother. The elevator door opened, and a doctor got on. The doctor punched nine, then crossed his arms in front and stood looking up at the row of numbers across the top of the door. The elevator jerked them heavier, and the numbers lit in slow succession. Ferrin relaxed a little.

"Momma, I punched seven," the boy said.

"I seen that," the woman said, patting the boy's head. "All by yo self."

The 7 over the door lit up and stayed lit. The doors opened. "Get off here," the woman said to Ferrin. "This is yo floor." He pushed past the doctor. In his throat, anger at being told what to do battled with a childlike, almost tearful gratitude, and he said nothing.

The hall was cold and shrunken and empty, nothing but shine and geometry. It was exactly like the worst dreams he had, when he was walking through corridors like the ones in prison except they were tighter and smaller and no cells off to the sides to offer a sense of space. Someone he couldn't see was hunting him from behind, a tall man with a knife, and so he had to run ahead into the pale white light, the weird lancing gleam from enameled walls and waxed linoleum tile. But as he ran, the corridor got smaller and smaller and squeezed in on him as though he had crawled so far forward into a cave he was stuck and couldn't back out and couldn't move his arms and couldn't turn around, except that in the dream he was still running when he felt that way, and he couldn't breathe, and the man with the knife was right behind him. He would die if he couldn't turn around, but if he turned around he would see the man with the knife and that would be worse, but you had to face him, and so he struggled to move in a terrible fit of will until he ripped himself loose from his paralysis and woke up, screaming.

This was a lot worse than Ferrin had thought it would be. His contact had briefed him on what to expect from the people, but not on the building. Ferrin hadn't confessed his fear of tall cold buildings. What good would it have done? He would still have to face his fear. No way could you send Rubert in on a job like this. And really there ought to be nothing to it.

You walked in and you made reconnaissance and you walked out. He could control himself that long.

He had hit the contact up for extra money. Hazardous-duty pay. Got it too.

There was nobody in the hall. He began walking, expecting the walls at any moment to start squeezing in. The striking of his bootheels made clattering echoes. He read the numbers on the doors aloud to himself. He turned right into a short dead-end corridor with a door on each side. The one on the right was featureless, the one on the left said:

> 705
>
> **FARBER AND CUNNINGHAM**
> *ASSOCIATES*

25

DREAM TIME

ime, time: Charles, where are you? My God, boy, here I am messing around in Ferrin's head trying to give you what you want, trying to explain him to you, and all of a sudden you're nowhere to be seen. Well I know it's all made up, and of course it's Me and not you and I'm just blowing smoke whither I listeth, wandering here in this not-sleep and not-awake, this between-time, this phantom zone where the mingles image and the stones weasel, draped in climbing liana—

But not made up somehow in spite of that, this puzzle I piece together in no particular order in order to give her to you whole even if partly dreamed up, because not to have her whole is not to have, because memory leaks away down lost connections, like the sap of chopped-away vines—

So maybe that's where you've gone, I'm working too deep for your conscious mind, so the question is which trip through is this, because this is a story that has been told many times and on many levels, and is this the time when you don't believe in Me and all you're thinking is whodunnit, as if that would help, as if that would be an answer, or the next time through when you believe in Me not because you want to but because there's Nowhere Else to Turn, and you're thinking whydunnit, as if that would be an answer, as if that would help, to know why—

Oh is this kingdom come or am I having my last laugh at your expense or is this some total other untemporal where, the ramalam realm of dream in which you know her completely and forget her completely, in which who goes changing like echoes in a canyon and in which there is no why why why but in which this world and all worlds are made, and which is where I travel most truly, I who can hold the final complete timeless picture shining in my mind, but I have to tell in sequence like a story to Mr. and Ms. America anyhow to while away a rainy Sunday and make sure we understand on a feelthink if not a thinksay level that brains do hold more than three dimensions and lives are the medium for lives. Or maybe for reasons of my own which I aint sane yet but to keep your heart—yours, Charles—from all the way being broke, because dreams, even if you can't remember them or figure them out, can heal.

So come with me now into the crazy unreal, come Charles and all you people traveling with Charles, come in sympathy or color it imagination, but come, though you may wake wordless and full of loss and uncertain even of who you are.

Oh yassuh massa Ghos', I know, but it hurt so much, like walking in flames massa Ghos', and when it's someone you love then the fire burn close and you don't know—

how it feels, I don't? Who you think I am, Joey-boy? Lord God, you all that way to me. I live in a hell of love, all I am is your meanings, flashing from person to person down here validating their lives from within without no word from the grand Who-Who, aint heard in a long time, until I begin to wonder maybe I just imagined the Farther in Sun and Little Miss Liza, they aint really there and think how that would feel, being Me all alone without any Them.

But hey, enough about me, let's talk about you-know-who. Don't you think she knew burning? I love that little girl, and you do too. You love her for her fiery mind not to mention the size of her knockers, so suck it up Charles and make the leap, I'm with you every jumpcut of the way. Hadn't heard from her since the Hogs came home, and don't you I think it's about

time?

The sofa, Sarah sitting beside me. Worry Twins go first. Twitching his eyebrows (Mark), twitchet like crickets—they don't slide and unwind and crumple like most people's, they just jump: *Hop* now I'm wide-eyed *Hop* now I'm worried *Hop* now I'm wide-eyed telling the truth again, isn't that right Nikki, see? She really did, she expected us to bring her a movie for while we were gone, even though it would make us miss our own movie to go get it *Hop*.

Like his eyebrows are alive and they're running things: Say, brother, let's twitch his face again *Hop*. I want to giggle, watching Nikki to see if she does it too, how our faces go echo oh when Momma fusses and you feel her face on yours moving like hers and you're just a kid, you can't stop these things, but she slaps you for making fun of her and

Something terrible's going to happen.

Every time I laugh, every time I have fun, the fear and the terrible, like a black boxcar hooked on, and

OH I dreamed it, this is my when I was five first nightmare first I remember

because I wanted a toy train, not metal and skinny track electric model on big plywood board in the basement woooo-wooo, but a wooden painted all colors, like a cartoon for the hands, so friendly with big wooden wheels you could drive anywhere not just around and clickety by itself

and I was going cross-country to Colorland like Disney—but better because colors, they ate colors and they bathed in colors

And fell asleep hoping and dreamed I rode it like at the municipal park when they have the little train for children you sit in all open but chugging around squealing, but it was my wooden train I was riding, and then I'm standing by the mouth of the tunnel and my train's big, bigger than a house, I'm looking up and scary somehow though still all colors but not wood any more just giant cartoons in 3-D, whoomp whoomp whoomp as the cars come out of the tunnel, a ghost train and I'm on the platform waiting and the slow train pulls up but still as if from a tunnel so I only see one at a time slow and now the black boxcar slow and the sliding doors and black inside

and bones and skeletons and skulls

anyway, and I wake up screaming, and that's why I thought black boxcar but it isn't this but it is Christmas, it's something about Christmas that scares me.

"So anyway, she wasn't happy," Mark says,
"And we weren't happy," Nikki says, and
Mark says, "We were late to the movie."
"And when we got back," Nikki says.
"She was asleep, like we planned, but we were all worn out and we just didn't feel like making love after all."
The weasel-man is squirming. He says: "Why don't you just tell the old bi-ba-bat to stuff it? Get her own cottonpicking movie?"

Come in and the weasel-man sitting there, and who is he, a friend of Sarah's, country like her, maybe her husband, is this the famous Christian Bean? But I thought Bean was bigger. And Jack is late, but no, Father Christmas: "Jack Beverly has decided to drop, at least for a while—"

Jack floating face-down in his pool dead his face a skull, but he's not dead, he's just dropped out, but he shouldn't have is why I see him. He's not ready, he's out there drowning, but I won't, I'm ready. What? Ready? Am I ready?

"So this slot was open when David called. I want you to welcome David Stone to"

The group all over the weasel man now, looking around like a cornered animal because they're yak yak yakking him, you can't say mean things to old ladies and Joe Burley:

"Yeah, but if you take out your anger on a person, then you haven't really resolved it." Looks at Ian, did he say the right thing?

"She knows just how to make you feel guilty for saying no." Nikki.

Joe Burley says, "I want to give you a stroke for saying no."

"But they can't accept the stroke because they didn't follow through," Sarah says quietly. "You have to be willing to pay the price." Ian's eyes flicker at Sarah. How with her it's always cost, it's always sacrifice. But he won't say, he will wait for her to see herself.

Mutters weasel: "—let an old lady keep me from fuh. From getting." Frustrated, no right words, he can't say *making love.* "Cold day in hell," he says, louder.

"Maybe that's our problem," says Mark to Nikki *Hop* wide-eyed she looks at him *Hop*

She *does* do it too! I *am* going to laugh. I'm scared—

because I giggled at her when she sneezed and sneezed and sneezed she couldn't help herself because the talcum all up her nose the

"Maybe our libidos." Nikki. "Maybe we just don't have strong enough—"

English talcum she asked for lemon I can still smell it lemon she squeezed and it puffed out too much there in the chair with the lights shining on the tree and the colored shadows on her face and I can smell the tree and I can smell the lemon and the red-and-green paper torn open on her lap and the can of talcum

The weasel man, his face hard: "I can't believe you people talk about this sh. This stuff. Talking about feelings is one thing, but talking about what you *do*—" Looking around with contempt. What is he doing in here? He's wrong, I'm scared.

Sarah: "People need to be able to talk about everything. It's the things you think you can't talk about that drive you crazy.'' She looks at him level and steady, like she knows him, like she knows all about him, and where have I seen that look before?

Coleman, when the moccasin came out of the leaves. Coleman one step back with the hoe, calm and ready. Poor Coleman, I should be there, I should be at the hospital.

And he looks back, the weasel man, hateful at Sarah for contradicting him and doesn't Father Christmas see it's wrong to have him here, he's dangerous, I'm scared—

''Do you want to go now, David?'' Father Christmas says.

The weasel man's face falls apart and

sneezing sneezing and her face is gone crazy she can't help her face it goes

Oh oh OH

kaPLOOey

and pieces of her mind fly out all over the room and she gathers them back and almost gets them put back together into her frown but

kaPLOOEY

''Go?'' he says.

and it's so funny I giggle because she's out of control but Daddy's

Don't laugh at your mother!

standing up

''Take your turn,'' Father Christmas says. ''Do you want to tell us about your issues?''

''I aint got any issues.''

I do I can remember this I will

"You must or you wouldn't be in here," Joe Burley says. Good for you, Joe Bleednose.
"Well I aint got anything to say right now."

But I do, but too fast to tell them too fastforwords:

how they whipped me, each, two switchings, a switch from the tree so I am striped with Christmas and it was going to be my turn next to open

and I knew it was the watercolor box little flat tin box with trays of red and blue and yellow and green and orange and white and black and I knew the box because of the shape and I could read the writing on the tin through the thin tissue but I never got to tear because

Joe Burley is talking now, stumble pause, hesitate, he had a wet dream and he wanted to tell his father but too embarrassed is he sick is that wrong how what where and poor big lumpy thing dear boy it's all right he's trying but he's stumbling he can't see himself how he's fighting himself but

I can
remember I will

remember alone in my room all day all Christmas but not alone because we had a tea party on the bed for a table and the blanket was a tablecloth with Jesus and Elizabeth my blonde dolly with blue eyes because Elizabeth is the prettiest name of all and Jesus said it's so nice of you to have a tea party on my birthday and Elizabeth was very polite and served the tea warm water from the bathroom faucet in little cups

and the warm water (so warm it's hot) keeps you from feeling so hungry when you smell the turkey and gravy from the kitchen. The cold bites and makes you more hungry but the warm spreads out in your tummy and feels full

and we slept some and we had more tea party and it got dark and that's all

but it's not because Sarah is talking now, Sarah my friend, and her quiet dark voice, her troubles with Bean, and you can ride her voice like a dark quiet river, and we can offer our troubles to each other and they aren't like troubles to them but like a river that they can ride and we can ride theirs into our own dark places and it will be safe

and I can do this with Charles now I can tell him all riding her voice into the wide part of the river under the stars camping with Charles and I can tell him and I can remember

when she came in I was afraid to be switched again, but she just stood there and I was afraid to ask but I wanted the watercolors so bad and I was afraid if I didn't get to open them before Christmas was over then they took them back, I thought you had to open that day or else, I didn't know, so many rules and you could never tell what was going to

"The thing about Bean," she says, "is you can"

never tell
but I will

what was going to happen and she came in and she didn't see Jesus but she saw Elizabeth and I asked real quiet and real good if I could open now

because I was afraid it would be too late

but there's always another blackness

so this is blackness hahaha that's all you get you fuckers blackness because I won't look because when you look it's even worse than you could imagine so blackness is blackness is haha better

No.

Grow

up, Lianne: She

laughed, like a bark-dog yapping.

Santa doesn't give presents to little girls who make fun of their mother. And I saw the idea come to her eyes. That she had thought of something bad, before she even moved. And she grabbed Elizabeth up. *Santa takes their favorite toys away.*

I pounded on the slam door and I cried, and for some reason she didn't come back and switch me for pounding, maybe she enjoyed the sound of my misery. And I turned back to Jesus to ask him to kill her, but he was disappearing.

Have faith in Jesus, Jesus said, and finished his disappear.

So I did. But that still wasn't the worst of all. But I was right to believe, I was right to hope, because remembering is like walk-

ing in the fiery furnace after all this time and it doesn't burn because that's why he had to disappear, to be everywhere around, to
be not separate and beside but all around, to be the fire so it won't
burn and I can walk in it and remember the worst of all:

In the cold ashes next morning, in the fireplace, Dolly's two blue
eyes, and a burned hand. Two blue eyes with the metal frame still on
them that held them in place and let her blink. Eyes on a metal frame,
black ashes, burned wood, a fat little hand.

Oh the poor woman. I threw up my breakfast, and I threw up all
day and all week, and I cursed Jesus for disappearing, I said shit piss
damnyoufuckhell Jesus, words I didn't know I knew. I didn't understand His disappear, and I thought hell it's all hell, there's not any God
but it's all hell anyway, and I puked my guts out, I cried till I puked,
and I thought you had to be at least fifteen to kill yourself, or I would
have, I didn't know kids were allowed to.

But the poor miserable woman, she was killing *herself*, not me;
and now she's dead, she walks around but she's dead, all her life dead,
and I live:

Here I am, Dolly, still here, I have *my* eyes. I miss you Dolly
Elizabeth, but thank you for dying for my sins and go with Jesus,
because I have come through safe and grown and I can remember the
worst, the worst of all and I am not burned, and I can paint this, I can
paint it all, my beautiful toy train and black boxcar and the white bones
and Dolly's blue eyes with the metal and her pink burned hand in the
blackness with the bones, and no one will know what it means but I
can see it and I can say it and I can paint it, oh thank you all and oh,
    is it my

---

time

"Lianne, are you crying?" Mark said, his eyebrows twitching up in
concern.

The weasel man snorted. First sex talk, now tears. These people had
no shame.

"It's Coleman, isn't it?" Nikki said. "I heard from Barbara just yesterday. How is he doing?"

"Not so good," Lianne said. "He's still in a coma, and his heart could
go anytime."

"It's almost like they're family, isn't it?" Nikki said.

"I know it's callous," Mark said, "but have you found a new gardener yet?"

The weasel man sat forward, alarmed.

"Because I know somebody you might call," Mark said.

"What happened to yo gardener?" Ferrin David said.

Lianne thought he might be applying for the job, not that she would ever have considered hiring him. A score of times his hands had gone to his shirt pocket, where a pack of Pall Malls protruded, a match packet wedged in front of the cigarettes, visible through the thin fabric. Each time, remembering he couldn't smoke in here, the look on his face had been murderous. She couldn't imagine such a man caring for plants. They would wilt, she thought, in the heat of his perpetual anger. Dry up and burn at his very presence.

"He had a heart attack. We think he ordered a pizza and had the attack after they delivered it, because we found him in the front yard with the pizza box."

"That's so awful," Nikki said.

"In the midst of life," Mark said.

"We're not planning to hire anybody else right now," Lianne lied, as if she were talking to Nikki and Mark, but really to let the weasel man know. "Out of respect for Coleman."

Stone Dwell got the message. He sat back. "So he could wake up anytime?" he said. His hands went to his shirt pocket again, trembling. He caught himself. "Shit," he said under his breath, frowning terribly.

"We hope so," Lianne said. She looked at the floor. "But that's not why I was crying."

"Why were you crying?" Joe Burley said. He had been looking bored, all this jabber over something as unimaginable as being old and having a heart attack, and just somebody's gardener anyway. If that wasn't why she was crying, maybe there was something more interesting.

Ian was watching to see if they wanted to get back to issues. It was their money, but it was his time. A little chat was all to the good, relaxing and all that, but. It was amazing how quickly the monkeys set up roles. Of the people he saw in here, ninety-nine and forty-four one-hundredths percent needed to adjust either their parent or their child or both, and develop a functioning adult. They knew that, that's why they came in, and yet, if he let them, they would instantly turn him into the parent or school-master, and themselves into truant children trying to get out of their lessons.

Lianne smiled at him, the freeest, easiest smile she had ever felt. She could even read *him*. She could read Father Christmas. All things were possible to them that gave up their fear. It was so very clear to her now that fear was the only death.

She felt her tears begin again as she spoke: "It's just that you all have meant so much to me. You listened, and, and you didn't put up with any bullshit, and. Just thank you, that's all."

They were all infinitely dear: Nikki and Mark caught in their spiral around each other, they *wanted* to love, the Worry Twins, the twitchy little rabbit people, because we all have to be somebody, we can't all be Robert Redford and Jane Fonda, and wanting to love *was* loving and she hoped they found that out, and Joe Burley Breedlove she had watched grow up in the last few months, still a big bumbling goober-boy, still confused by his parents' divorce, but he wasn't just sitting there any more, he was actually asserting himself and saying things and you wouldn't notice maybe if you hadn't been watching every Saturday how he changed and good for him even if he was a pain in the ass now sometimes, at least he was confronting his father instead of just internalizing his resentment, and Sarah, dear sweet Sarah with her poor crazy tormented soybean farmer, Sarah who wanted out but wouldn't allow herself the easy answers—

They were all fighting brave battles, the human battle, they were all earning their souls, because it was dangerous and there weren't any guarantees and she wished she could tell them how beautiful they were in their courage to try, but she couldn't, who could, no words, she could paint maybe a picture, God pinning their medals on in heaven, but they wouldn't get it—

Ian was smiling. "That sounds awfully final," he said.

"Are you saying you're leaving?" Nikki said. "Leaving group?"

"I'm ready," Lianne said. "I've been doing this for seven years, and I didn't know until today, almost this very moment, but I'm ready."

Nikki and Mark looked shocked, Joe Burley distraught. They felt deserted. Group creates its own world, that's one of the problems with it. You want to stay safe in that world, the safe place where you had a momma you could tell everything and she stroked your hair. When one of the group left, it broke all the illusory safety open. Reminded everyone that the whole point was change. Not a safe island, but back into the stormy world, but this time ready. That was why Ian was smiling, because he knew. She had seen fifteen people leave in her seven years, and four were ready. Jack Beverly wasn't, she was.

Sarah reached over and patted her knee. "Gives me hope, honey," she said.

"I just thank you all so much," Lianne said.

"Hell, I just got here," David Dwell said. "What do you people do, just run in and out like a parking garage?" He seemed really upset, which didn't make sense, he didn't know her, maybe he felt insulted, maybe he thought it was because of him?

They spent fifteen minutes in congratulations and hugs and mutual strokes. Lianne told them a little about being able to paint now, about being able to remember and then to paint what she saw in her mind, but they weren't artists and couldn't know how painting the nightmare was accepting it, was more, was celebration. She told them about being able to talk with Charles, and they *could* understand that. How Father Christmas had laid it on the line, was she going to trust her husband or not, it was up to her, she was in charge of her own information. Not to trust wisely was not to live. She didn't say what she had been not trusting him about, wiretaps and Tina Talliaferro and all that business, but probably Nikki and Mark and maybe Sarah at least guessed the sorts of things she meant if not the specifics because they would have read all the papers and watched the news and heard all about the toga party.

"I knew something big was going on with you when I saw that creation science article," Nikki said, admiringly. "You haven't let them put your picture in the paper in years."

This was true. After she had left KROK, Lianne had hated the idea of publicity. Not even on the society pages, she and Charles in dress and tux grinning glare-eyed and shine-faced like puppets at some benefit or gala or inauguration, like all the other see-me monkeys. She had gone to most of the ones that were for good causes, but always refused the pictures, and asked Vonnie Hewitt not to mention her in the column.

Visits with Vonnie.

Which might seem like humility, because all that was such a laughable thing, the social scam, but she saw now it had really been self-doubt, retreat, self-hatred. The same as when she had lost, made herself lose, her mother had made her lose Miss Arkansas. All her life it had been engage, retreat, engage, get frightened, retreat. But no more. Because she was born to shine, she *was* a butterfly. The original Social Butterfly, big, bright, gorgeous, and classy. You could be what you were and be an artist too. Just own yourself and do it.

"I saw that article," Sarah said. "You don't really believe that, do you? We came from monkeys?" Her expression was one of gentle concern.

"Hell no, we didn't," Ferrin Stone said.

Lianne answered Sarah. "Yes. I do. I think the evidence is overwhelming. Except *we* didn't evolve from *monkeys,* the way everybody says it. The monkeys and we *both* evolved from earlier species. Pre-hominids."

"What about Jesus?" Sarah said.

Lianne smiled, because she was ready. "I believe in Him anyway," she said. "I don't know how and I don't know why, but I believe." And poor Charles, lonely in his defensive atheism. But atheists could love Jesus too. They just didn't get to know it was Jesus they were loving, so they didn't get any comfort out of the deal.

"So you can believe in evolution and still be saved," Sarah said. "Well. It's not that stranger than some of my own thoughts."

"People, this is all very interesting," Ian said. "But we only have about ten minutes left."

"God made man in His own image," Ferrin Dwell said. "Them bones and all, He put them there when He made the place. He put it with the past built in."

"Why would He do that?" Joe Burley said. "I mean what's the point? Why would he go to all that trouble just to fool us?" Joe Burley was comfortable on this ground. He played Dungeons and Dragons, and he read science fiction. He was a trained metaphysicist. Just for an instant Lianne heard Charles in Joe Burley's voice. Charles would argue the same way.

"Prove He didn't," Ferrin said. "You don't know nothing, kid." Joe Burley's hand went to his nose, pinching it slightly. He tilted his head back a degree or two.

Lianne was afraid there would be blood, but nothing happened.

"Even if He did," Joe Burley said, nasal, "what difference would it make to us? He could of done the future the same way, and we just *think* it's not there yet."

The kid was on a roll. I hate to break him off, but I'm with Ian:

"You're the only one who hasn't gone yet, David. Do you want to do any work, or shall we let out early today, folks?"

Ferrin was glaring at Joe Burley. He didn't seem to realize Ian was addressing him. Then he looked around. "Work?" he said. They could see him gathering his attention, replaying Ian's last few words. "Sure," he said. "Sure, I'll go. We can like tell our dreams in here, right? I mean if we can say all this other shit, right? You guys talk about dreams, don't you?"

Why was it Ferrin's "shit" rang so loudly? He heard it clattering on the floor. But they couldn't fault him, could they? Not if the Morrison pussy was going to say "bullshit," they couldn't. Thought they were so high and mighty, so liberal-minded, she says it and it's perfectly all right, nobody notices, but let him say it and it's oh mercy me how shocking.

So the whole mission was blown, all of his bravery wasted. He *had* the woman, he had had her in his sights, and boom! She was gone, vanished in a cloud of smoke.

And it was worse than that, because the nigger could wake up any minute and identify Rubert. Christ, he needed a cigarette and some Rolaids! He thought about lighting up anyway, what would they do, but what if they called the guard, Ferrin could take him in spite of the gun, but keep your head, you're behind enemy lines, you don't need that kind of attention.

So play their game and get out, but the assholes think they're so smart, facing their fears and all that bullshit, bunch of pussies, like to see them face prison, so let's give em something to think about, that's the way you do, you play their game but you beat em at it, and nothing they can do because you aint technically broke the rules. That's the way you do if you're smart, let em know what you think about em, give em something they can never forget, never get out of their minds and nothing at all they can do about it.

He thought about telling the hallway dream, the man with the knife, but he was the one scared in that, it put him in a bad light, so it wouldn't do.

"If you can talk about bedroom stuff, I guess you can talk about bathroom stuff too," he said. He grinned. His feral grin. He shook a cigarette out, put it in the corner of his mouth. "Don't worry, I aint gone light it," he said. Fun watching their faces, though.

"You can talk about whatever you need to talk about," Ian said.

"See, I have this dream. I don't hardly ever shit, you know. I can go three weeks without taking a dump." Got em, the two blond-headed perverts, they're turning red.

"How do you live?" Lianne said.

"Don't bother me none. I do fine." He leaned back, flicked the unlit smoke, stuck it back in his mouth. "I figure that's where the dream comes from, that's all."

"I go two or three times a day," Joe Burley said.

"I don't like this," Sarah said.

Ferrin smiled again. "Hey, it's my dream. I need to talk about it, right?" Pussies. "So anyway, in the dream, I'm taking this long dump. It's all smooth, it aint scratchy with hard edges like people with constipation get. But it's coming out in big turds like logs."

Ah, fun. *Look* at their faces. "It's like a sawmill, right? All dusty, with all this powder in the air and dark with just some sunlight coming in and the saws going real loud. So I'm stacking up the logs, right? Stacking em in these rooms, and all the rooms full to the ceiling of these stacked-up turd-logs. But get this."

He leaned forward and looked around, everybody's eyes on him, good. *"The sawmill is made out of logs.* It's like this one big log cabin. I can see the sun coming in at this one window where it has a wide sill and you can see the butt ends of the logs. And sun in the chinks."

He paused for effect.

"If you want my hunch," Mark said.

"I aint finished," Ferrin said. "Now get this. The fort, I mean the sawmill aint a sawmill anymore, it's a fort, like an old western, with John Wayne. I'm outside it and I can see it, but I'm inside it at the window too.

I'm way up on a hill, and there's armies down there, armies trying to come up to get me. But they can't, see, because you know what the saws is now?'' He waited, but this time no one said anything.

''Machine guns,'' he said, triumphantly. ''I got a machine gun at the window and all they got is bows and airs, and I'm mowing em down. I'm killing em and they can't get to me, and I got enough logs to last forever.''

He stood up and pulled the match packet from his pocket. He folded a match out with one hand, tore it loose, struck it, and lit his cigarette. ''What do you make of that?'' he said.

''Very interesting,'' Ian said mildly, who never said the phrase, who thought the phrase was not only a cliché but the ultimate cop-out.

''Right,'' said Ferrin Dwell, and exhaled a cloud of smoke, and headed for the door.

In the outer office, the receptionist called after Ferrin to wait, to come fill out the information form, the one they had to have on all their clients: ''Mr. Stone!''

He gave her the look that Clint Eastwood gives the clerk at the hotel in *High Plains Drifter,* when the fuckface tries to make him sign his name in the register. Clint looks at him like *What makes you think you can talk to me?* and he doesn't even bother to answer, he just turns his back and goes. Clint don't have to do what other people have to.

Sarah took Ian Farber aside. ''It aint my business to tell you what to do,'' she said.

''He won't be back,'' Ian said, as Lianne came up. ''I don't know what his game was, but he won't be back.'' To Lianne: ''Here, let me give you a hug.''

Lianne gave him a full firm hug, and got one back, leaning over to accommodate his plush belly, his body almost the same length as hers, so that, her head beside his, she could smell the tonic on his sparse clean hair. ''That certainly was a strange little man,'' she said, separating.

''It happens,'' he said. ''He flipped himself out of the river into the picnic and flapped around a while. I think he's flipped himself back now. But we don't have to worry about him.'' Beaming at her, patting her arm. ''We've got our own lives to live. Good for you.'' His face changed. ''Jesus, that cigarette smelled good. Listen guys, I'm gonna run back in the office, grab a smoke, I got five minutes at the most before the next session. Excuse me, ok?''

Merry little Father Christmas, and she had thought she might cry again, saying goodbye, and she thought now to hold him back a moment, to say let's stay in touch: But this was just his job, and his job with her was over. There was no point pretending. They didn't run in the same circles, he liked awful movies like *Police Academy*, and he wished her well, but in such a nice objective unsmothering way, and she would never see him again.

That was good, that was clean, that was right. She was ready.

She and Sarah went down together. At the glass doors they saw David Stone on the far side of the drive, just getting into a Pinto, a big black man at the wheel. Stone didn't see them. Something about the scene felt familiar to Lianne: the little weasel man and the black man together. But she couldn't pin the feeling down.

"I guess we ought to be tolerant," Lianne said. "They're just nasty because they need help. Everybody ought to be allowed to try and help themselves."

"No, ma'am, that aint true," Sarah said. "Some people ought to be shot on sight."

Ferrin had had a bad couple of minutes, standing there on the edge of the lot, looking up where he had parked the Pinto, and no Pinto, and no Rubert. He was already shaky with the adrenaline of his escape, and now he felt frail and palsied as an old man. All of a sudden, here came the car, swinging up from the bottom of the drive over toward Asher. Probably been down getting himself coffee and those little powdered-sugar doughnut-shape blood-bombs come in a narrow box with a cellophane window and taste three days old when they hit the store.

Rubert pulled up beside Ferrin, swung open the passenger door, and said, "Hop on, cowboy." Ferrin hopped. Normally he would have said, "What you talking about, nigger?" and walked around to the other side and made Rubert scoot over. But now he just sat there in the passenger seat and let Rubert drive them away.

"How'd it go?" Rubert said.

"Goddamn rich smart-ass motherfuckers think they're better'n everybody else," Ferrin said. "We got problems, the goddamn godless god-fucking sonsabitches. That goddamn ugly old bitch thinks she's so fucking pretty, but she's way past it. Trying to cover up the wrinkles with all that fucking makeup and lipstick, goddamn it makes you sick."

"I take it it didn't go so good?"

"The nigger aint dead," Ferrin said. "And this thing runs a lot deeper than we been realizing. These people a threat to the state of Arkansas."

26

POWDER
AND SMOKE

Later that afternoon, at home, two threats to the state of Arkansas were talking. Her painting session was over—she had been at odds with her intent, feeling her creativity at last totally free and yet also feeling too excited to concentrate. His ball game was over. He wasn't really that big a fan anyway, he tended to admire individual performers rather than team play. But it was summer, and baseball was all there was to watch.

As it was for him, so it is for you: It wasn't an Olympic year, you were all six months away from basketball, it would be August before you started getting football stories again. There was nothing left to beguile yourself with but the news and your own life. Both seemed to read much the same from day to day, the mood never changing, only the details.

I say summer: If it wasn't quite solstice, it was nevertheless the beginning of that long dry deceitful stretch of time which we have been conditioned to anticipate so eagerly. The afternoons made unnaturally longer by daylight savings, so we can have even more freedom, sun, and fun. Yee-hah, boy howdy, whoopty-do, school's out!

Truth is, summer hasn't done a damn thing for any of you since you were seventeen. Ever since, you've had to work, and probably work all that harder since everyone's taking vacations and the remaining staff has to double up.

And what about those vacations? Two, maybe three weeks at most, which you have to take the kids with you, spend half your time driving, if you do hit the beach it's sand in your suit sunburn dry eyes and hangover, squinting at the white page blinding even through your shades, one of those books they call Summer Reading, like it's a whole different genre, carefree and thrilling, maybe even this one though that aint likely since it's not technopop or a so-popular soap opera, but just in case, listen, you need to turn over now, you're about to burn on your back.

And your elbows are gritty and your spine hurts from being propped up like a suspension bridge and oh aint it awful how old and fat you've got, lying there unnerved how fast your little bit of free time is flying by, gone you might say in a puff of powder and smoke, you're on vacation but you can't relax, fretting what's going on at the office behind your back while you're out or all the things need doing at home and you'd like to remodel, but who can afford. Speaking of home, it's vacuum wash fit the new curtains mow mulch clean out the gutters do all those little jobs you've been putting off. At first you convince yourself it's ok, it's getting back in touch with regular life. Ha. Evenings you were going to go out dancing like you used to, but the two of you just sit there with reruns and have a few brews and say things to each other like, "Go see what he's crying about, will you?" Or "Did we see this? I'm pretty sure we didn't see this one."

Yessir, that's the state of Arkansas if not America, and Charles and Lianne were threats to it. They were part of a story even if they didn't know they were, and so eventually part of the news, for the news is just the dimmest damndest ghostly flickering reflection of all those always-going-on stories. Whispers of a rumor of a distant actual maybe really happen which you'll never truly get to hear about. Unless you pay attention to me, your Roving Reporter. Oh I may twist the facts, babe, but I don't fuck with Truth. Unless of course she makes the first move.

"I had no idea you were thinking of leaving group," Charles said.

"Well I didn't either. It just became obvious all of a sudden. I mean, it wasn't like I *left;* it was like I looked up, and there I was outside it *already,* you know what I mean? I was an observer. I could see everything that was going on, and I loved everybody, but I just wasn't *in* it any more. So to stay would have just been pretending, and why?"

"You internalized it. You finally incorporated it all. That's why you were outside it."

"Well, yeah, maybe." Charles made things neater than they had to be. Sometimes he made them so neat you started thinking about the neatness and forgot all about the point.

"Ok by me," he said. "I don't mind saving the money."

He had been making a lot of cracks about money lately. Were they going broke, and he hadn't told her? No, this was some kind of gag. He was setting her up for something.

"But did you hear what I said? How connected it all is? I can deal with my life through my *painting* now. Not so much the subject matter, but the process, you know? I mean, I have a thousand paintings I've already thought of memorizing; you don't know how good it feels."

"You mean a thousand memories you've already thought of painting?"

"What?"

She told him about Dolly Elizabeth and the black boxcar. About the weasel man and the Worry Twins and their twitchy eyebrows too. She ran through the entire session, blow by blow. His expression was like a man in a rainstorm with an umbrella that wasn't helping.

"What's the matter?" she said.

It was the completeness of her joy. He was feeling a wobble of insufficiency. "I guess I envy you a little. You're so in touch with yourself now. I feel kind of jealous and empty."

"You didn't have to leave group," she said.

That was irritating. "You asked about my feelings," he said. "I was trying to tell you about my feelings, I wasn't asking for advice."

That was irritating back. But she didn't have to be irritated. She could handle things now instead. Use her adult: Was he going back to group? No. Did she want him as he was, knowing there were things about him that would never change? Yes. Nobody got a perfect deal.

"You're a good man," she said.

"What do you mean?" he said, hopeful.

For all his shortcomings, she explained, the way he hid his feelings and manipulated and sometimes all he wanted was sex (he was frowning), he had the overwhelming virtue that he was capable of love (his frown lightened). She didn't know where he got it, certainly not from his father, or to hear him describe her, from his mother, but he knew how to love, which was rare for a man, in her opinion, and was why she was able to trust him in the first place.

"You make me feel good," she said.

"You want to go upstairs and make love?" he said.

The question facing Ferrin was this: Did he report right away or wait for the contact to call? Always face into trouble like a hawk into the wind, that way you soar. But he could stand to give his nerves a rest first. But Rubert was watching to see how he handled it, so he called.

Talk about pitching a hissy fit. The more he listened, the madder he got. "If you aint gonna say anything useful," he said, his face blackening.

Rubert put his finger to his lips, thinking of cash flow. "Don't say nothing back," he whispered. "Just listen."

Ferrin obeyed, his ears full of profanity. Finally the contact calmed.

"All right, we're gonna have to escalate. Let me think the situation over. You wait by the phone."

Ferrin slammed the phone down. He spun a chair out from the kitchen table, sat. He shook a cigarette loose, tried three times to light it. Goddammit, they never let up. Goddammit, you did everything a man could do, but they just kept piling the goddamn pressure on. He was shivering. He felt how lean and small he was, how little meat he had to protect his bones, the way he had felt as a boy, sitting in his underwear, waiting for his daddy to come with the belt. He threw the cigarette across the room, put his face in his hands. The goddamn tears started, but he kept his voice steady. "That goddamn pussy," he said.

Rubert came up behind him, kneaded his shoulders. "Hey, Easy," he said. "Be all right, main." He put a big hand on the crown of Ferrin's head, tousled the hair. Went back to kneading the shoulders. "Easy Money," he said, soothingly.

By the time the contact called back, Ferrin had collected himself. He wasn't taking any more crap. If they wanted to do it themselves, fine. But if we're going to stay with the program, from now on out it's my way or the highway.

"It's time to take the kid gloves off," the contact said.

"Fine. But how I say and when I say. First we need some R and R, some planning time."

"How much time?"

"Me to know and you to find out," Ferrin said. "I'm the field commander. When the balloon goes up, you'll know."

"No more mistakes."

"Aint been any *mistakes*. This aint checkers we're playing here."

"Just get me some results."

"Let's just make it real clear what we're talking," Ferrin said. "We're talking termination with extreme prejudice here." Rubert made a moue to say how impressed he was.

The contact was silent.

"Hey," Ferrin said.

"I need her neutralized," the contact said. "I'm not saying I wanted her terminated."

"Ok, so we're talking major bodily injury, then?"

"Or just trauma. Just psychological trauma. You're the field agent. You handle the implementation. Don't come running to me."

"What about the secondary target?"

Again the hesitation, then finally: "The man aint the problem. The woman's the problem. I can deal with the man."

"We'll do what we can," Ferrin said. "But it gets messy out there. If she gets messed up or killed instead, I can't help it."

Silence.

"This is going to cost you fifteen thousand," Ferrin said. Rubert's jaw dropped. Ferrin knew how to blindside em. He knew how to get em leaning his way and then drop the hammer.

Rubert heard a violent squawking over the phone.

"Hey, life is tough all over," Ferrin said, negotiating hard. "You want professional work, you pay for it. For us, this is combat pay. Seventy-five hundred up front."

They wound up compromising: $9,999 overall, $1,999 in earnest money and the rest payable at $2,000 a month for the next four months after completion.

"Easy Money," Rubert said, delighted.

Early next week, while Rubert and Ferrin were over in Hot Springs getting their R and R, Charles got a card at the office. It was from Tina. She wondered if he had ever gotten the flowers she sent. She was also curious about the annual fishing trip on the Fourth. She had to be in the Little Red area on business during that time, maybe she could look him up. What business? Watch the newspapers for an announcement.

He wanted to burn the card, but even if he didn't set off the alarm, the smell of smoke would make people wonder what he was up to. He tore the card into little pieces, as he had the other one. These pieces, though, he flushed down the toilet in his bathroom. He came back to his desk and called Lianne. "I love you," he said when she answered.

"What do you want for our anniversary?" she said.

"I don't want anything," he said. "What do you want?"

"You don't have to get me anything," she said.

"I'm going to, though," he said. "So you might as well tell me what you really want."

"I don't need anything," she said, "except a perfume atomizer."

"You want perfume?" he said.

"No, an atomizer. Lord, I have seventeen kinds of perfume I never use."

"You ought to wear that tea rose again. I really like the tea rose. You haven't worn it in a long time. Are you out?" Brushing his lips against her skin. The leathery silkiness of a rose petal, with the scent of dried petals in his nostrils. The salt scent of her skin, mingling.

"No, I'm not out," she said. "Anyway, it's easy to get, it's about the cheapest around."

"I don't care, I like it."

"I didn't mean cheap that way. What I don't have is a nice atomizer."

"Doesn't perfume *come* in . . . ?"

"It's nicer to buy it just in the bottles."

"Let me get this straight. It's tacky to buy perfume in an atomizer. But what you want to do is buy it in a bottle and then buy a fancy atomizer to put it in?"

"There's a real nice cut-glass atomizer down at Powder and Smoke. Marcel Franck."

"How much? " he said.

"Two hundred," she said. "A little over two hundred." It was two hundred and thirty, actually, and that was before tax.

"Jeez, Lianne!"

"Oh, you," she said.

Charles had already bought the Blazer from Tommy Dwell, Jerry's brother-in-law. He had bought it with cash from bonds in one of the lock-boxes, so Lianne wouldn't find a missing check. Tommy Dwell was working on the vehicle right this very minute. But if she wanted a perfume atomizer too, well fine. In fact, that gave him an idea. How to set up his surprise.

What?

Oh, yeah. Well, yeah, it *is* Ferrin's brother. Didn't you see that coming? Not that big a coincidence. It's the 96th-largest city in the country, which is to say it's a small town. Anyway, we're all interbred down here, I thought you boys knew that.

Tommy did what he could to throw a little work Ferrin's way. He always felt Ferrin could get himself straightened out if he just had a steady job. His big mistake had been ever leaving Naylene in the first place. Pretty little brunette and loved him like a puppy dog, but Ferrin couldn't stay home, he had to go out tomcatting around, and you were out late at night tomcatting you couldn't keep a job, and you fell in with bad friends and you all needed money all the time, so you robbed some houses, and then you got out for good behavior and were going to go straight and even got that job cleaning up at the Y, but you found that rich guy's wallet and checkbook. Which was really dumb, because forgery wasn't even your line of work.

No, it was no accident Ferrin never went to jail till after Naylene left him. He got careless then. For all his tomcatting, he had loved her, and when she left he just didn't care any more.

It was what you might say a typical southwest Little Rock family. Male children turned out one of two ways—like Ferrin, or like Ferrin's younger brother. If you were like Tommy, then you worked in the factory, or ran your own auto body shop, or got a bread route, or went to electrician school. You were a good Baptist, and you didn't necessarily tell the preacher you sometimes had a beer or two while you watched the game. The wife would pick the beer up at the grocery to save you the embarrassment. You never touched the hard stuff. Walk in a liquor store, and you would have felt like you sold your soul to Satan. You had a pickup or two, and you hunted everything but ducks. It was mostly rich lawyers and planters who hunted ducks.

Lianne had a great Saturday and Sunday on the black boxcar painting, this time relaxed and working with perfect concentration, and her head was storming with ideas long after she left. She was thinking how soon she would set herself up a studio at home. It was silly to keep coming down to the Arts Center, it was a waste of time. She saw how structured her days had been, how such rigid structure might be a form of self-loathing. All you have in this life is your time. Give your time over totally to schedules, and you are refusing to value yourself.

There was an irony in the realization: Group, which had taught her to see this truth, had been a part of the structuring. It was strange that the simple act of leaving group had made her weekends seem so free and ample. Going to group was like going to church. It took only a couple of hours, all told, but it punctuated and dominated your time. It arranged your behavior.

She was too preoccupied to notice the car that followed her from the parking lot. And she drove right by another parked car without looking, a black Chevrolet Blazer in which a man with a tommy gun in his arms and wearing a Groucho mask ducked suddenly from view.

She was beyond paranoia at last.

"Goddamn," Rubert said, uncramping from the floor and looking after the disappearing Skylark. "That was her. You could have done her right then." He was impatient for the rest of the money. They'd spent most of their advance in Hot Springs.

"Right," Ferrin said, his mustache bouncing with his grimace. "And we would have been back inside before supper. Didn't you see them bodyguards?"

"Bodyguards?"

"Them goddamn plainclothes in the white Caprice. They get here when she gets here, and they sit here waiting the whole time, and they leave when she leaves. What do you think?"

"Shit."

"Shit is right."

"I thought *we* was working for the law."

"We are, asshole. But there's law and then there's law. This might be some other law. Or it might be private."

He yanked his Groucho mask off. Rubert had refused to wear his. He said being a nigger was enough disguise.

It had all seemed so simple in Hot Springs. They'd had a good time. Ferrin was cheery, because he was reestablishing control—icing the contact, making em wonder when it was going down and where and just how bad it would be.

They had spent Sunday through Thursday at the Arlington, a grand old lodge built into a mountainside in that spa town, a dowager hotel renovated into a sort of art deco pink-flamingo post-fifties punk funk granny—fun, if you didn't take her too serious. They had had mineral baths, massages, had gone across the street and walked in the only national park inside city limits. Ferrin's arthritis had felt better than it had in years.

Rubert had loved splashing in the pools on the decks cut into the mountain behind the hotel. He had never been allowed in the pools when he was a boy, and so it was his idea of heaven. Truth is, he had spent most of his time in the lower pool with the kiddies. He couldn't swim worth a flip. What a hoot to watch him playing water games with five-year-olds.

Ferrin had sat on the upper deck at a table, smoking Pall Malls, drinking Pearls. Hot Springs had felt like the right place to be. He had felt connected. There were probably still a lot of the Mob in town, though the action was nothing like it must have been in the twenties and thirties. He had seen himself at nightclubs in a tuxedo, gambling huge sums with an icy nerve.

Evenings they had eaten at fancy restaurants, and had planned and replanned the operation over coffee and dessert. Well, Rubert would have dessert, Ferrin had had smokes. "Item one," Ferrin had said, ticking the points off on his fingers, little to index. "Forget the gardener. There aint no realistic way we're going to get to him."

"I could sneak in disguised as a orderly and smother him."

"Too chancy. He probably won't ever wake up anyhow. He's just a calculated risk we gone to have to live with. Do the job clean and get out of town before he does wake up. We can go a long way on eight thousand dollars."

"Ok."

"Item two. We overexposed in that neighborhood. We can't be hanging around their house, watching everything they do."

"Right." Rubert hadn't intended ever going back to that house. Maid probably come running out the bushes with a flamethrower next.

"Item three. The woman knows my face now. I can't just walk up and take her out. What if she spooks? Or if something goes wrong she can identify me. But."

And here Ferrin had smiled, leaned back, and taken a pull on his Pall Mall. Blowing out a plume of smoke, he grabbed his index finger and said, "Item four. I know where she'll be, regular as clockwork, every single Saturday of her life."

So they would go to the Arts Center and wait. Too many witnesses there, so they would wait till she left, drive up alongside on one of the nearby back streets, do it, and pull away fast. Borrow a car from Ferrin's brother so nobody could ID the Pinto they'd been driving around in.

Of course, she might live, which was ok. He would rake her with automatic fire, and if she made it—well, fair was fair. The good hunter gives his quarry an even break.

Things had worked even better than they had hoped. They had come back into Little Rock Friday, and Tommy was working on a Blazer he was going to paint starting Monday, so even if anybody did see the getaway car it would be bright red before anyone saw it again. Tommy would never connect it with the one he was working on, or if he did he would put the thought out of his mind. His big brother was turning over a new leaf, couldn't a been him.

"Use your own car," Tommy had said when Ferrin asked.

"We got some hauling to do." Yay, hauling ass. "I can't be hauling shit in a damn Pinto."

"I'd appreciate it you watch your language. Listen, a mighty rich man wants this car."

Thought he was the only one had big-time contacts. "Who?"

"If I told you, you wouldn't believe it."

"Can I bar it or not? Just tell me that. I'm trying to make an honest living here, I thought that's what you wanted. Hard work and an honest living."

"Try not to do no damage, ok? I don't know what you hauling, but don't scratch it up to where I have to do extra work. The man wants it this week. Ok? Ok?"

So it had all fallen into place. It was a simple plan and it was beautiful.

And now here yet again some unexpected complication had thrown a monkey wrench into the creamworks. The Morrison pussy led a charmed life. But this time Ferrin stayed calm, cool, and collected. He went straight to the phone and laid the situation out. It was a new wrinkle, and the contact would want to know. Maybe it was a double-blind game, one hand didn't know what the other was doing, two sets of agents. He didn't think so, but that was the way those kind of people's minds worked, and you had to be aware of the possibility.

"Look at the advantages, though," he said to Rubert after he got off the phone.

"What advantages?"

"Well, hell. We already said we can't hang around watching everything they do. Well now we don't have to."

"I don't get it."

"Think, " Ferrin said in a friendly way, grinning. "We don't need to follow the Morrison pussy any more. *We can just follow her bodyguards.*"

Rubert had never admired him more.

"There's a problem," Cheese said to Sonny Raymond. It wasn't unusual for them both to be in the office on weekends. Crime didn't take no holidays. Besides, Saturdays were the easiest afternoon for them to get away and visit their respective sweethearts. Had to work late, honey. Something came up. You bet it did. Went back down, too, after I worked it around awhile.

"There's always a problem," Sonny said. "What's this one?"

"You know those Morrison fucks? They're wise to something. They got some kind of bodyguards or something following everywhere they go."

"The fuck you say. You sure?"

"My men just reported in. There aint no doubt."

"*Your* men. Hmp." Sonny decided to let it go. He thought things over. "Well then. Well that's ok, then. That's fine."

"Fine?"

"It means they guilty, don't it? Why would they have guards if there wasn't something there to hide? We're closing in."

"Oh yeah."

"Find out who those men are. They may been provided straight over, right out of the Mob. I want to know everything goes on in that bar. That's where the deals are gonna be made, out of that bar of his. It's a front operation all the way."

Charles liked owning the bar, but he didn't spend a lot of time in it. All the next week especially, he hardly thought of it, he was too busy straightening out court dates. What with the fallout from the toga party, Laugh's suspension, Tina's leaving, Betty's promotion, and Greg's return, the firm's schedule had gotten rather scrambled. They'd asked for any number of postponements. Business on the whole had gone up, but a few clients had left them over the notoriety. He had also decided, and had told Lianne, he was going to get back into harness. He hadn't actually tried a case himself in over a year. He had let himself turn into a manager.

It was fine with her if he wanted to make like a lawyer again. She had things to do. She had gotten a letter from Alice at the Children's Hospital.

They wanted to have a big *Hope Lines* Christmas in July fund-raiser, and they wanted her to star in it. KROK would give them ads at a reduced rate and cover the actual event itself. They were going to rent the Heights Theater, a grand old unsubdivided art deco movie palace, with a lobby big enough to hold the party in, one of the last few true movie theaters on earth, a monument that surely no one would ever be crass enough to turn into a Cinema Sixteen or a dress shop, and they were going to show Bing Crosby's *White Christmas* and a couple of other Christmas movies (for God's sake not *Miracle on 34th Street,* Lianne said). They would all dress up in Santa's helpers outfits. If Lianne would just agree to help out, it would probably double attendance.

She found she was no longer afraid of the death she saw in the children's faces. We're all only temporary, she thought. But what about the unfairness? That children should suffer so terribly, should die so young. What about it? What could you do beyond acknowledging the way things were and trying to be fair yourself? There was horror in the universe. The thing was not to let the horror infect your soul.

Preventing the infection was not the same thing as pretending that it didn't exist.

On Monday afternoon, Ferrin and Rubert followed the men in the white Caprice down to The Blue Note. They had slept late and had thought about taking the rest of the day off, but what the hell, there was nothing to do in this town, so they had run by Edgehill, and lo and behold, the white Caprice was on its way out of the neighborhood, lunch break probably.

At first it was like the Caprice was following *them,* pulling out onto Kavanaugh behind them as they drove by the entrance to Jackson. But down the hill, past the plant nursery, Ferrin pulled over, and the Caprice went by. He waited while it stopped at the Van Buren intersection, and then, as it disappeared around the curve, followed. He saw it a couple of blocks ahead, stopped at the Beechwood intersection, ran the light on yellow to keep the Caprice in view. Turned out they were doubling back on Cedar Hill. Ferrin followed, topping the last rise as the Caprice went by the park and stopped at Cantrell.

By the time he got to the light, they were gone, and he thought he'd lost them, but there the Caprice was as he drove down Riverfront, parked in front of that bar, The Blue Note. "Now what?" Ferrin said. "That's Morrison's bar."

"What?" said Rubert. "How you know that?"

"Everybody knows that. I got my sources. So what you suppose they doing in there?"

"Well let's go in and find out," Rubert said. "I'm hungry."

They drove on by the bar, parked down the street. They gave it fifteen minutes, which was all Ferrin could stand of Rubert's complaining, then walked over.

Trixie brought them a couple of beers and some pork rinds. Ferrin didn't want anything. Rubert ordered avocado on whole wheat with swiss and sprouts and mayonnaise and a couple of slices of tomato, sprinkled with salt and pepper, but Trixie just laughed. The menu was microwave pizza, and for sandwiches, lunch meat or barbecue. "See," Rubert said. "At's why a man can't stay healthy. It's in the culture. It's a conspiracy to make us eat crap and die."

He settled for a couple of the barbecue, but on Roman Meal.

Ferrin felt conspicuous. It was after the main lunch rush, and the place had emptied out some, but there were still several tables of businessmen in suits lingering over an extra drink or two. They were people who ran real estate offices or car dealerships or various of the shops along the road, but to Ferrin they might as well have all been bankers or preachers.

The two men they'd followed, both white, sat at a booth in the corner. One was fat and red-faced, in twill pants and a blue work shirt out over his belt, and the other was young, middle twenties, crew cut and wearing jeans and a dirty white t-shirt. They were out of place in the bar too. They were punks, they weren't cops after all, but neither Ferrin nor Rubert knew them. They had given Ferrin and Rubert the eye when they came in, then carefully ignored them ever since.

"Quit looking at em," Ferrin told Rubert. "You'll clue em in."

David came out of the back to help Trixie, and Rubert said, "Well I be swan."

"What?"

"That's David."

"What David?" Ferrin looked around where Rubert was looking.

"I don't know his last name. But remember five years ago, when we had all that load of cocaine and horse we were selling?"

"For godsake, keep your voice down." The men in the corner were pretty obviously listening in, and one or two of the suits had turned, smiling. David had looked Rubert's way, then turned his back. He got busy with the cabinets under the liquor rack. Trixie gave David a look, went back to slicing meat off the log of roast beef and slapping it with sauce out of a bottle.

"Yeah, but wonder who he getting it from now," Rubert said.

"Probably Morrison," Ferrin said. "Probably where his money really comes from."

"Yeah, they all into it now."

David disappeared into the back again. Trixie banged a platter of sandwiches onto their table, started to walk away. "Hey," Rubert said. "We need more beer." Trixie stopped, stiffened, then continued on her way without turning. She was back in a minute with two more longnecks. She slammed them on the table and left, her face expressionless.

"Goddamn pussy," Ferrin said, almost loud enough for her to hear. He checked to see if the men in the booth had been watching.

The next day, Tuesday the ninth, a week before Charles and Lianne's fifteenth anniversary, there was a story in the paper. Tina was opening her own firm, low-cost legal help for the poor. There she was in jeans and a pullover, casual and (you could tell if you looked close) braless. She seemed sunny and relaxed, the blonde hair wide and tossed, as if she had just come back in from a nice walk, the slightly crooked teeth giving her smile an aura of easy vulnerability: *I'm not perfect, but I don't mind, because I'm as fetching as a kitten with string.*

There was no mention of the toga party—she had never been there—or of her former association with Lafayette. There was only a passing reference to Morrison, Morrison, Chenowyth, and Frail: Miss Talliaferro had left specifically to start her own firm, it now appeared. She was a Reaganite Republican, and while MMC & F was a great place to work, none better, and had never held her politics against her, she felt she could be more effective on her own. Among other things, she wanted to correct the public's entirely erroneous impression that only liberal Democrats cared about the poor. "I was poor myself," she was quoted.

Bitch, Charles thought. His heart almost broke, as he looked at her soft breasts forever unattainable, thinking how once or twice when she had leaned over he had actually—actually!—seen the nipples. All the things that will not happen.

He got out of the house before Lianne saw the story. He could handle his dolor, and he loved his wife, but he was in no mood to listen to snide comments.

So of course Greg walked in with the clipping first thing. "Seen this?" he said, waving the limp cutout flapping in the air. He grinned and shook his head. He collapsed in a chair. "You know that Delaware law degree?" he said.

"Don't tell me," Charles said. He meant it, but Greg thought he was being rhetorical.

"That's right. I've been calling around. She was there as an undergraduate, sixteen years ago, but got asked to leave in her sophomore year. Disciplinary reasons. She was active in the theater, the registrar says. He remembers her. Says she was really good."

"I saw the diploma," Charles said.

"Yeah, me too," Greg said. He frowned. "You know, this is really serious. This is criminal. We ought to notify the bar association."

"We ought to," Charles said, his stomach weightless as a falling man's. He felt caught in a logic as terrible and remorseless as gravity's. "How would you feel about waiting a month or two? Give us a little distance on it?"

Give me a little distance on it. Time to harden my heart. To prepare for Lianne's scorn.

"I feel ok about that," Greg said. "If we break the news right now, we're going to look really vindictive. I could just find all this out later, by accident. Or we could do it anonymous. Call the paper and tip the reporter who did the story."

Charles shook his head no. The notion was repulsive.

"Yeah," Greg said. "Of course, in the meantime, her clients—"

"You don't think she's really going to follow through with that, do you?" Charles said. "Tina working for poor people? It'll never fly."

Greg grunted agreement, got up to go. "How does she do it?" he said. "How does she get away with it?" His tone was carefree, almost admiring. He had *had* her, goddammit. He could cut loose because he had *had* her. It wasn't fair.

"She doesn't," Charles said curtly, looking down at the work on his desk, and Greg knew it was time to go. He had been insensitive. The boss was taking it hard. It was the prestige of the Morrison firm that had kept her scam alive all this time: Why would anyone bother to check her out when she'd already been vetted by the best?

Though of course she'd had to pass the bar exam and present qualifications to them, and it was going to be interesting finding out how she'd managed all that. But the firm had given her credibility and cover, and Charles was taking the full responsibility. Heavy hangs the head.

Watch the master and learn. That might be him someday. Greg felt chastened, abashed. Still, as he made his way down the hall, he began, without realizing he was doing it, to whistle.

No court date had been set for the creation science suit. For that matter, it wasn't yet clear which judge would hear it. It made a difference. Some of these old boys were hard-liners all the way. Right now the plaintiffs were mostly in meetings mode. They met and talked strategy. Brain-stormed for possible witnesses. Lianne, sitting in, suggested Jane Goodall and Stephen Jay Gould. Somebody suggested Mary Leakey, who just two months ago had drawn five hundred people to one of the University of Arkansas for the Medical Sciences campus lectures. Others opposed her, saying she had been strangely wishy-washy, that she had said to give students a choice—although people who believed in creation science [were] "not looking at the facts."

Somebody else suggested Carl Sagan, and Charles and Lianne groaned, though it was probably inevitable and also a real good PR move.

All this time, Coleman lay up in his bed with tubes in his nose and his arm, breathing heavily. Once, when a nurse turned him to bathe him, he said "Don't." She wasn't sure she heard it, thought maybe it had been a sort of noise forced out of his body by her handling. He made no other response, and she debated whether to say anything to the doctor.

Lianne visited Coleman every other day now, staying thirty minutes to an hour. She didn't know him all that well, really, had found out more about him after his accident than she had in all the time he worked for them. So it was hard to know what to talk about. She asked him about his son, speculated on what the boy might be doing. But asking questions of someone who couldn't answer might be frustrating for that person, so she began to talk about herself, her paintings. She called them her paintings even though most of them were still just visions.

She felt a bit self-centered, but it was the thing she was most interested in and so the easiest way to think of things to say. She thought Coleman needed to hear a voice, no matter what it said. We all talk mostly about ourselves anyway.

The gardens and the yard were getting out of hand. Now that it was light later, Charles was coming home in the evenings and doing some work, but face it, his gardening was recreational, and there was no way he could keep up with what Coleman had been doing. They had developed a nice routine, though. Fertility rites, if she had been able to have children.

About sunset he would quit his gardening, and would come in to wash his dirty hands in the kitchen sink. Lianne would have finished interfering with Clemmie's plans for supper by then, and would give him a hug from behind while he washed up.

Then they would go upstairs and make love. Afterward, they would ring down, and Clemmie would send martinis in the dumbwaiter. They would lie in bed talking and sipping, then shower and go down for supper about nine o'clock. Usually after that it was reading or tv until midnight or one o'clock or so. It was a nice way to live, at last.

Friday evening, with the weekend coming up, they felt they could sleep later than usual, so they lingered over their martinis. Lianne said she really did think Coleman was down in there somewhere, that he could hear her. She said it was like having someone on the phone line who needs help but can't talk. You can still *feel* the person there.

"Oh!" she said. "Oh, what if that's the way it is when you're dead? You're still there, but nobody pays any attention. You can't feel anything or do anything, because you don't have a body any more. Oh, that would be why we should pray to our ancestors, like the Chinese. Because they need to hear a voice."

"That's like the idea of Hades," Charles said. "All the shades wandering around in nothingness, moaning and groaning. But I thought you were a Christian."

"Charles," she said, "will you quit trying to organize everything?"

"I still don't have you anything for our anniversary," he said. "Why don't you take me by Powder and Smoke tomorrow to see that atomizer?"

He was up to something, clearly. Charles *asking* to be taken shopping? So no doubt he had blown a wad on some sort of superexpensive perfume, and he was going to waltz her in there and make a big production of surprising her. Well, maybe she'd get the Marcel Franck anyway.

What had she gotten him? What do you buy the millionaire with his own money?

A box of chocolates. He loved dark imported chocolates with nuts and liqueurs, and Clemmie would never buy them, a holdover from his teen years, when he'd been capable of scarfing a box a night all by himself, and his father had forbidden her to let him have any. He hated the fruit creams you got in the usual samplers. She loved the fruit creams, like dark eggs hatching not chicks but colors, sweet pastels, pale lemon and mint and dawn orange and foamy cherry. Usually they just bought the samplers and split them, but for their anniversary she'd splurged, gotten him a whole box of nuts and liqueurs all for himself alone.

If you were just a shade when you died, then the best thing about living was your senses. Just to experience things, whichever way they went. That was heaven, to be alive and be able to see and taste and hear and smell and touch. The way the sheets were rumpled, the way the lamplight made them golden. The way his balls smelled now, nuzzling, which was her smell mixed with his smell. "Mmm-hmm," he said, shifting to make himself more accessible. The phone rang. "That's Clemmie," he said. "Supper's ready."

They were having fresh pasta with mushrooms and whole cloves of garlic sauteed in olive oil, some of the real Parmesan grated over the noodles. She straddled his pelvis, slid him in long and slippery, seated herself. "So what do you want for antipasto?" she said.

When she came again, she yelled "Fruit cream." Charles laughed so hard he lost his erection, but it was ok, he'd had his already, what the hell, let's go eat supper, I'm starving.

After the close encounter at The Blue Note, Ferrin and Rubert lay low for the rest of the week, only checking on the Morrisons a couple of times.

Except for where were they going to get some money, Rubert would have been happy to goof off forever. That was his problem, no work ethic. But Hot Springs had been about all the idleness Ferrin could stand. He would have gone through with the job, money or no money, in order to give a shape to his existence. He was hanging fire for one simple reason. They had a problem.

The problem facing Rubert and Ferrin was how to get Lianne away from her bodyguards long enough to make the hit. After her session at the Arts Center was still the best time, but the damn people in the Caprice were on her like stink on shit.

"Too bad they can't just have an accident," Rubert said, and Ferrin wheeled around, wide-eyed. Rubert thought maybe he was having a stroke.

"They are," Ferrin said. "They *are* going to have a accident."

Rubert could easy find some buddy of his would be happy to take a $200 old rusty junk heap would hardly run and, for another $100 on top of the deal, ram it into the white Caprice as they were leaving the parking lot. Rubert and Ferrin would be waiting down the street in a borrowed pickup or something for Lianne to drive by (the Blazer was bright red now and had gone to its owner). Or better yet, Rubert could set up as spotter in the Pinto, to let Ferrin know when the Morrison pussy was headed downtown for her class. Then he could light out for the other side of town, and the Pinto would be alibied.

The nigger with the junk car wouldn't have to know anything about the deal except he was going to make a fast $100. He could light out on foot, and nobody would never catch him. Even if the bodyguards suspected it was a setup, what could the punks do? Go to the cops? Right, and they were probably running dope or something for the Morrisons, sure they would. No, they would write off their losses and fade back into the wood-work.

"And the beauty is," Ferrin said, "we can write it all off. It don't come out of our fee."

"You're one smart white man," Rubert said.

During the week Lianne had moved her stuff out of the Arts Center and was set up in the sun porch as a studio. Northern light, and all that. Charles had immediately wanted to remodel it for her—closets for her painting smocks, racks for stretching canvas, wide flat thin drawers for paintings, trays of brushes, compartments full of every possible tube of paint, and so on. Lianne told him it was fine as is for right now, and wait till next anniversary, maybe.

Which reminded him, was she ever going to show him that perfume atomizer? They had slept in, she forgoing for once the farmers' market, and he was sort of kissing around on her titties idly, seeing if he could make the nipples stand up again.

"You're so hot to see it," she said. "Come on." She hopped out of bed and went in and got the shower running. What was it going to be, a surprise party at the perfume shop, three days early? Walk in and silver helium balloons bumping the ceiling and ribbon everywhere and all their friends, and the atomizer wrapped and bowed on a pedestal in the middle of the room? He was such a little boy. A present for Momma, and it was supposed to show how much he loved her, but it really meant *Please see me, love my head, make me happy.*

He had followed her to the shower, and nothing would do but he get in with her and lick her all over. Fucking standing up in the shower isn't nearly as romantic as the movies make it out to be, because the water changes the texture of your skin and washes away your usual natural lubricants, and you tend to get water in your eyes and up your nose, especially if you go down on each other, but they managed. By the time they had finished, and then finished showering for real, and dressing, and having a bit of breakfast, it was almost two o'clock.

It was a beautiful day, the balmy middle of June, which in Little Rock can sometimes be as hot as August or as cool as April. It is a place where the weather is even more turbulent, random, fractal than your usual weather. But today puffs of white cloud were blowing over in a brilliant blue sky, and the as yet unparched leaves were soughing gently and greenly in the temperate air.

On the portico, squinting out, Charles said, "It's a beautiful day. Why don't we walk?"

He was really making a production of this, Lianne thought. What the heck, it was a pleasant walk, not over three quarters of a mile, and trees all the way.

"Sure," she said, linking her arm through his.

Ferrin was having conniptions. He was burning up the radio to Wheat Germ. Like it was my fault, Rubert was thinking. Like I made her not go down there. Goddamn, he was gone be hell to live with this next week, Ferrin was.

"I aint waiting any longer, " Ferrin said. "She aint showing. I had it with this shit, and I had it with this shitting job, and they can just take their goddamn shit and shove it up their goddamn asses, the goddamn cocksucking sons of motherfucking bitches. I'm out of here."

"Hold on, Pall Mall, come back," Wheat Germ said.

All he had heard was *shit shit ass am cock son mother bitch.* Reception was poor, they were so far apart, and the hill between them cut off most of the band.

He was parked in the Pinto on O Street between Blair and Cantrell, with a view across the way of the mouth of Crestwood. He couldn't control access from there, they could exit onto Cantrell at Palm, Beechwood, Spruce, Monroe, or Jackson, and he would never see them leave. But it was as close to that house as he was willing to get any more.

Then he saw Charles and Lianne, holding hands like a couple of teenagers. "Hold on," he said urgently. "Something going down. They out on the street, they walking out on the street."

"Fuck the fucking street, what you talking about?" Pall Mall said, fumbling for a Pall Mall. But when he opened the book, he was out of matches. "Fuck!" he yelled at the top of his lungs. The cigarette lighter in his brother's pickup didn't work, he'd already found *that* out. He slammed the lighter with the butt of the tommy gun. He slammed it so hard it broke the element out of the dashboard. "One more thing!" he yelled. "Just one more fucking thing!"

"Breaker, Pall Mall, I can't hear you," Wheat Germ said. "But they walking down the street and the Caprice following them."

Street Caprice was what Pall Mall heard. "Goddammit," he said. "I'm coming back in radio range. Fuck the plan, this is going down *now*."

He tore the cigarette out of his clenched teeth, and then had to spit the butt out the window. "This'll be the day you die," he said. He jammed the pickup crunching into gear. "Bitch."

In the parking lot of the Arts Center, Beth Beth and Monroe Izard pulled slowly out of their space. They had been to see the McArthur Museum beside the Center. They were from Danville, visiting her daughter in Little Rock, and were driving the daughter's white Chevy Nova.

"Well, it's white," James Wilson Farrell said to himself. He built up speed in the Plymouth. He had an angle on the Nova, and he creamed them square in the back door just as they crossed his exit. Monroe Izard got slowly out of the ruined Nova. He found himself looking over its top at a laughing young black man.

"Look like a hundred dollar to me!" the young man said, gleefully, and lit out running. "What happened, Monroe?" Beth Beth said, inside the Nova, slowly unbuckling.

Charles and Lianne crossed Cantrell on the light. The Caprice and the Pinto followed, crawling along, frustrating the drivers behind them. Since the Heights was full of such traffic, mostly older widows in block-long fifteen-year-old Cadillacs or young window-shopping matrons who would be the widow-equivalents in forty years, there was no point in honking or being rude. You just fumed and cussed and turned off as soon as you could. Even so, the Caprice and the Pinto had to pull over a couple of times to let people by and to keep from being obvious, and once the Caprice sailed off around the block and back across and back over, a big figure eight.

It gave Rubert a bad few seconds, deciding whom to follow, but he was proud of himself: He figured out what the Caprice was up to, and he let it go and stayed with the targets instead.

"Fuck," said the man driving the Caprice as he crossed Kavanaugh again and saw the Pinto. "It's that fucking Pinto again."

"What?" said the young man beside him.

The driver gunned the Caprice away from Kavanaugh, cut over on Hawthorne to University, and plunged into Cammack Village.

"What are you doing?" his passenger said.

The driver was watching the side streets. Cammack Village had its own traffic cops, and you had better not even think of rolling a stop sign or going twenty-six in a twenty-five zone.

"That Pinto been on our ass all week," the driver said. "I'm quitting this job. I aint cut out for this spy versus spy shit," he added, heading away, out of the Village, out of this story forever.

Charles and Lianne were enjoying the sun on their shoulders, enjoying the window-shopping, idling along on the right-hand side of the street. They went by the cleaners, the drugstore, Yancey's Liquor (run by a real honest genuine WWII Medal of Honor winner). They went by the fire station, the post office, the Heights Theater. At Ozark Outdoor Supply, they crossed over. Mary's Music, the health food store. They turned the corner, and there it was, Powder and Smoke, a little freestanding cement-block building painted a cool slate gray.

"Get up here, Pall Mall, I got em pinned down," Rubert said, excitedly. He pulled around the corner, nosed into a driveway, reversed, and parked on the right-hand side of the street, across and a little down from Powder and Smoke, so that the nose of the Pinto was back the way he had come. "Breaker," he added, though he had already thumbed off. Where was the

Caprice? Nowhere to be seen. Well fuck that, it didn't matter now, it was better this way.

Ferrin, stuck in traffic at the Chester and Cantrell stoplight, pounded the seat of the pickup softly with his right hand. All the damn morons, Saturday afternoon and the traffic worse than a workday rush hour. It was such pretty weather, everybody wanted to be out and around, and in modern American that meant get in your car and drive somewhere.

There was no party in the shop. The son waited on Charles and Lianne, the father was in the back opening boxes. It took the son a long time to understand what Lianne wanted, though Lianne had been in there just the week before looking at the atomizer, and the son had waited on her then too. He kept mistaking Marcel Franck for a brand of perfume he didn't have. "But try this," he said, spraying a puff of some disgustingly flowery stink in Lianne's direction. "Isn't that delicious? It's almost exactly the same formula."

Charles had wandered off, bored as usual when he got inside a store. So what the hell was this all about, then? Lianne wondered. The son had gone into the back to see the father. The father didn't think they ever *had* stocked the atomizer. Lianne knew perfectly well they had, and she was about ready to start looking for it herself. Charles poked his head around the corner. "Lianne, come here," he said, gesturing.

"Not now," she said. It had been over here, on this mirrored glass cabinet along the side wall, but of course they'd moved everything around. Absolutely no principle of organization.

"Lianne," Charles insisted.

She realized it was part of his game, which at the moment she had no patience for. At the moment she wanted nothing more than to find the cottonpicking atomizer. Then she saw what she was doing and laughed. The atomizer wasn't the point, the anniversary was the point. "You're obsessing again, Lianne," she told herself, stepping back from the cabinet and following after her little-boy hubby, so full of himself and his big secret.

He led her through the back, where father and son were having a discussion so involved they didn't seem to notice that the customers who had occasioned it were leaving. They went out a door Lianne had never known was there. "She doesn't mean a *perfume*, Father," the son was saying impatiently as they went down the steps. "She means an *atomizer*."

They were in an alley giving onto rear parking lots. Worn brick pavers and big battered dark green Dumpsters with faded white stenciling. "Let's go in the back way to Browning's," he said, tugging at her arm.

Browning's was the neighborhood source for refried beans and pale guacamole and burritos floating in a puddle of orange cheese dip, a local tradition. Charles had grown up eating at Browning's, and he thought genuine Tex-Mex was pretentious, an artsy and unsatisfying branch of nouvelle cuisine. So that was where the party was going to be.

What about the atomizer? What the hell, Lianne, you're doing it again.

Lianne liked Browning's ok, but she was allergic to so much of the stuff they served. And they had just had breakfast anyway. Oh well, leave it to Charles.

They followed the alley across a street and into another back-door warren of Dumpsters and parked cars. "Wow," Charles said. "Look at that. I sure wouldn't mind having one of those."

"What?" said Lianne. He was admiring a bright red Blazer.

"One of these," he said, patting the roof of the vehicle.

"Charles, they're waiting for us," Lianne said. She meant the people at the party.

"Hey, it's unlocked," he said. He opened the driver's door and got in. What if the owner came out? She stood there, shocked. More than shocked, terrified. Something terrible was about to happen. They were about to be caught and punished. "The keys are in it," he called. "Come on, let's go for a spin." He cranked the engine.

"*Charles*—" she said, taking a halting step. And then she got it. She ran to the open door and leaned in, pounding him on his side and shoulder and uplifted defensive arm. It had been too much of a roller-coaster ride, and for just a second there she was furious, but then she was laughing. She came around to the other side and got in. He worked his jaw with his hand, like a stunned fighter in a movie. She had gotten in one pretty good lick there close to his larynx and another up near his eye, and the truth was it hurt like hell, the eye was blinking and tearing up, but he was going to carry through like nothing happened.

"Is this mine?" she said, looking up into his face, doe-eyed. She fluttered her lids. "Sugar Daddy, is this all for little old me?" She pouted her lips, Baby Doll fashion, and he kissed them.

"Come on," he said. "Try it out."

She wanted to get it out into the country *right then*, no waiting, so they bucked down the alley across another street, and then over to University and back onto Cantrell heading west, heading across the I-30 bypass, where Cantrell would become Highway 10, heading out toward Lake Winona and the Ouachita Mountains.

.   .   .   .   .

Charles and Lianne were at the Reservoir Road and Cantrell stoplight, already nearly four miles west when Ferrin finally got to the Heights. "Wheat Germ, I'm in the area," he said, chugging up Cantrell Hill in the old pickup. "What's our status?"

Wheat Germ took a moment to answer. He was coughing, had a little stuff in his chest lately. "Nobody gone in, nobody come out," he said when he got his throat clear. "Take your time, good buddy, come back."

"Where's our friends in the car?" Ferrin said. "You can stop all that CB shit," he added.

"Breaker, breaker, Pall Mall, you got me. They aint in the vicinity."

"Conditions optimum," Ferrin said, in line at the Kavanaugh/Cantrell stoplight, racing his engine. "Here's what we do."

Rubert held the stake-out till he saw Ferrin at the head of the street, stopped and waiting to cross traffic. He took off headed the other way, waving at Ferrin right in front of him as he made his turn, but Ferrin ignored him of course. After Rubert, there were five more cars, then finally a window in the traffic, and Ferrin wheeled his pickup around the corner, driving with one hand, the barrel of the gun resting on the frame of the open window opposite.

In the instant of his approach he saw two shadowy bodies through the glass of the shop, and at last, at long last, triggered off.

In the shop, beside the son, a bottle of perfume seemed to leap into the air and pulverize itself. On that level that is far swifter though less comprehensive than words, he thought it must be poltergeists. Half turned, he saw the shattered glass of the window hung in midair like a ghost of glittering shards and fragments.

If this were a movie (and more than a movie, because we would have smell and hearing, but still a movie) and we could do it in slow motion, we would not see sudden and messy collapse; no: Shining translucent vessels would rise and dissolve themselves one after the other like a string of firecrackers going off, like dancers sailing into *grands jetés,* only to explode and disappear, intensest essence free at last, thank God amighty, civet and ambergris loose to roam their elements once more, cat stalking the shadows and leviathan thundering in the waves, and succulent jungle florals would climb and hang themselves, blossoms of orchis and bougainvillea, across the clean sunny tang of this and that citrus, oh and the warm slippery opulence of sandalwood would come sliding like the whisper of tropical thighs, and over the bottom notes of musk and earth once more would unfurl the long intelligent wilderness of green.

Glass shelving would be collapsing all around with a sound like a thousand trillion wind chimes in magnified and slow rebound, and over that music we would hear, cacophonic and apparently unrelated, an insane angry chattering growl like mad machinery no one ever invented, and through it all the huge and hugely confused pungence of a giant and nonexistent Eve, a rich and sexual bloom on the summer air, lingering all that evening long and well into Sunday morning, infecting sightseers, passersby, neighborhood walkers on their way to church, with wild and aromatic longings they couldn't visualize or pronounce.

The real woman, Lianne, was ten miles away, heading out of town with her husband, heading for the hills to romp and sport and make love in the back of a Blazer parked under a tree. In the shop, beside the son, the father seemed to leap into the air and pulverize himself.

27

THE DOUBLE-WIRED
CLOCK

The gunning of Powder and Smoke was front page in the Sunday *Gazette,* color photo and diagram on the inside. (No inset summary boxes, and the same old stodgy typeface, though. It would be another seven years before the Patterson family sold out to Gannett and the Old Gray Lady dyed her hair purple and started wearing loud makeup.)

Charles and Lianne, breakfasting on the sun porch, read the story with the sort of interest we all take in catastrophe, an interest made the more piquant by their close call.

They did not connect the shooting with themselves, except as coincidence. If they had done so, they would have thought it was Sonny Raymond's doing, like the tapping of their phones. But they didn't make the connection. As for Sonny, they thought he was a clown, a scofflaw, a demagogue, not all there, and dangerous in many ways, but as little as they admired him, neither for a moment imagined that he was capable of attempted murder. And who would want to murder *them*?

It is true that Lianne suffered a freezone, reading Sonny's comments. For a moment, just for a moment, she remembered what it had felt like to suspect Charles, and imagined him involved in some dark and vicious illegality, something that would cause hoodlums with automatic weapons to seek his life. But then she saw how ridiculous that was. That sort of thinking led into the whirling pit of all her previous existence. It is better to trust what we are able to know than to live in fear of what we cannot establish. From across the table, she watched his face. Absorbed in the funnies now, smiling. He felt her gaze and looked up.

"What?"

"Nothing. I love you." She shivered.

He smiled. "I love you too. Are you cold?"

His eyes went back to the funnies. "No," she said. "What are you laughing at?"

"*Peanuts.*" He folded the paper so that the bottom half of the page was up, handed the strip across to her. "You'll like it."

She read it, looked away. Gave the section back. Her smile was as unconvincing as a bleached-out dollar bill from a pocket of the wash.

"What's the matter?" he said. "You like *Peanuts.*"

She liked *Peanuts,* and she liked *B.C.* She didn't bother with the rest of the comics, though, unless he forced them on her. She turned to the weather first, the obituaries second, the business section third, and then to the news. Never society, sports, or the funnies. He wondered sometimes what she filled her mind with. It wasn't jokes and laughter, that was for sure.

"It hits too close to home," she said.

"You think we should put hawks on that?" he said, moving his hand to indicate the wall of glass behind him. He turned in his chair to consider the idea. "I might go one or two. But it's really going to mess up the looks of the place."

Birds regularly bonked themselves on the glass, which, since it was north-facing, never carried any glare and made, from the outside, an excellent mirror.

Two hummingbirds, once, flying in tandem. The loud double collision, THUMP-UMP. They had run out to see them lying in the grass, feet up. Had held the tiny bodies, one each, a feathery warmth in the palm. Thinking the necks were broken. When suddenly, in tandem, they had stirred. A cheep from the one on his finger, a single high plaintive note, and they had blurred and were gone. It was one of the best moments of his life.

"No," she said. "It's just—this. Coleman, and now this."

Now he knew what she meant. He tapped the laid-aside section A, the Powder and Smoke story. "Dangerous world," he said. He shook his head and grinned, that self-satisfied disclaimer of a winner, the shrug that says *Guess I'm just lucky.* "We must be leading a charmed life."

"Do you think we ought to tell them?"

They spoke in the ellipsis of marriage, with the floating pronouns of understood common reference.

"No," he said. "It'll just be a lot of publicity, and we don't know anything. We didn't see anything. I mean, if *they* don't remember we were there—"

"They don't know me from Adam," she said. "They don't have the foggiest."

"Terrible what happened to him."

"He didn't do anything. He's so awful."

She meant first the father who had been shot, and Sonny Raymond.

Sonny, in a lengthy side story, attributed the shooting to a drug war. The local perfume trade was probably a cover for drug smuggling. He all but accused the father of being a gang lord. "Who knows what's in those bottles?" he was quoted. "Strange chemicals from all over everywhere, and nobody ever checks on it. South America and everywhere else."

"I don't know what he's talking about," the son had responded, in a much shorter quote. "My father's in the hospital. I think I'm going crazy."

"This octopus has worked its roots a lot deeper into our community than any stone we've turned over so far," Sonny Raymond had said. "I am going to be on its butt like black on a—like stink on—like a dog on a bone."

It was a Sunday morning, for crying out loud. The day was meant to be as gay and brightly colored as the funnies. Brunch in a little while, with some of their own good chilled champagne. Then, if they wanted to go back upstairs and play with each other, who was to stop them? It was what Sundays were made for.

He refused to let Sonny Raymond cast a pall over their happiness. "Remember the cedar waxwing?" he said.

"Which one?" she said.

There had been a lot of them. Every fall when the yaupon's berries were ripe and red, flocks of waxwings came through, eating themselves crazy, the branches frenzied with twittering bodies. Walk out and they all took to the air at once, as if the tree had blown up: *boom*flutter flutter flutter. Every fall, one or two or three slammed into the sun-porch glass.

"The one you blow-dried," he said.

She took his smile as a challenge. As if he were making fun of her good sense. "It was in shock," she said curtly. "It was shivering."

Late in the fall, and cold. The bird's eyelids with that dead look, drawn up from the bottom. Her with the blow-dryer, bent over the wadded blanket where she had nestled the creature. Blow-drying a damn bird. He couldn't help it, he laughed.

"No, no, no," he said, at her uncertain expression. "You saved its life. It was great."

"It was the fastest way to get it warm."

"I know. I just don't know anybody else who would have thought of it, that's all. I mean, your logic was perfect. But you should have seen the picture it made."

She understood now that he was teasing, that this was an invitation to see herself as he saw her, dear and quixotic. She gave him a tentative smile.

"Blow-drying a damn *bird*," he said, and laughed again. Blew her a kiss across the table. She laughed at him, he was so funny when he thought he was jollying her along.

"Did you see this Asimov article," she said, later. It was the *Gazette*'s reprint from *The New York Times Magazine*, the good doctor taking on creationism, was it really a science? She knew Asimov wrote science fiction, thought Charles would be interested.

"He's so boring," he said. "He writes like he thinks you're three years old."

"He makes good sense," she said. "Somebody needs to make good sense." She read the byline. "How can *anybody* write two hundred thirty-two books?"

"Damn baseball strike," he said.

"Are they on strike? Who's on strike?"

"The players. The damn greedy players. Going to be a long, boring summer if they don't settle this thing."

She smiled. She didn't care about baseball. A summer without baseball was ok with her. She was teasing him now. "Why are they greedy?"

"They want free agency. It'll drive salaries way up, and baseball will be out of business."

"You always side with management," she said, still smiling.

"I do not. You always side with labor."

"I do not."

"This is the kind of thing that really irritates me," he said later, busy with the financial section. He read her a piece on the intricacies of the election in Mexico, Ordaz to Echeverría to Portillo. *Tinkers to Evers to Chance.* Important because Mexico the world's fourth-largest oil producer, 2.5 million barrels of crude per day. Half of it, 1.5 million barrels, to the U.S.

"What?" she said.

"One point five divided by two point five is sixty percent. *Not* half."

"They just mean it's close to half. You know what they mean."

"It's not that hard to get right," he said. "Bunch of ignoramuses."

"Tight-ass," she said.

"Look who's talking," he said.

And so they washed the taint of Sonny Raymond out of the bright day, dispelled the aura of gloom and nastiness surrounding the story of the perfume shop shooting. They put it out of their minds.

Why *would* somebody shoot up the perfume shop, though? It was fascinating. The whole town was speculating that morning. Was it a jealous lover? A hit carried out on the wrong address? Was Sonny Raymond right for once, and it was drugs? You could find out, write a book, make a movie, and Little Rock would be famous. Except they would probably change all the names and film it in Austin. Movies about places were never made in the places, they were all made in places that people who weren't from the places thought looked like the places.

"Are you in control of your men?" Sonny Raymond said to Cheese. "Because I aint heard word one from you what they found on this drug shoot-em-up, but if ever I seen proof positive—"

Truth was, Cheese hadn't heard from his men. He hadn't been able to get hold of them either. "I got em on the trail," he lied.

Rubert and Ferrin had dropped the pickup off at Tommy's and split town. Rubert had wanted to go over to the Peabody in the morning for the Sunday

brunch with the jazz band and the Charmat bulk-process free champagne
and the tree of dessert dishes, but Ferrin had vetoed it because they were
low on funds. "You aint feeling good anyway," he had said as they sped
along in the Pinto. Rubert had been in the middle of a coughing fit.

"Call the contact," Rubert had said when he got through coughing.
"We done our part. Two thousand dollars buy a lot a lox and bagels. And
I feel fine, it's just your damn smokes getting to me."

"I don't see how you can eat that shit. Jew shit anyhow."

"Fish oil the best thing you can have for your heart. Clean out the
cholestrol."

"It's a fucking Saturday evening. You think they can get money to us
by tomorrow morning? We laying low until I say different," Ferrin had
said, and snapped his tenth Pall Mall since Little Rock out the window.
He was shook. He had never actually killed anybody before, and his new
status at once frightened and exhilarated him. He had shed his skin, made
himself new. All bets were off now. Anything could happen. And until he
got control of himself, until he was comfortable with his new authority, he
wasn't talking to anybody.

They had stayed in a Ramada Inn, slipping the night clerk a twenty to
let them register without ID. Ferrin wrote in a fake license number.

Ferrin had brought the Ingram along, reluctant to part with the instrument of his mastery. But he had triggered off all twenty-six rounds, so it
was useless anyhow.

That night they had driven back across the Mississippi River bridge and
Ferrin had hopped out and flung the weapon spinning down to the black
water. It was an executive decision. It was smart. It meant that he was
back in control.

Until the next morning, when Rubert woke him, coming into the
room with the Sunday *Commercial Appeal*. Light and the roar of traffic,
and the door closing to darkness and silence again, but then the lamp
snapped on.

"Goddammit," Ferrin growled, pulling the covers over his head.

The story wasn't as big in the *Commercial Appeal,* but you don't get
shot-up perfume shops every day, so there was plenty of detail.

"Hmp," Rubert snorted. He was taken suddenly with a coughing fit.
When he got his breath back, he said, "You didn't kill nobody."

Ferrin threw the covers back and sat up. "What the fuck are you talking
about?"

Rubert tossed him the front page. He read the story with growing rage.
"Goddammit, Rubert," he said. "It don't say one goddamn thing about
em. Where the fuck are they?"

"Don't look at me. I seen em go in, and they didn't come out."

"You seen, you seen." Ferrin flung the section of paper at the window, but it sailed open and separated. He tossed himself back against the pillows, raised his arms angrily to the ceiling. "Why me?" he bellowed. "Jesus fucking Christ, why me?"

"I aint read all that yet," Rubert said, gathering the scattered pages.

Charles and Lianne didn't do anything superspecial on their real anniversary, having already exchanged presents. They went out to eat, at Jacque and Suzanne's, high in the First National Bank Building, about as good Continental fare as you could find anywhere, notwithstanding it stood smack in the middle of Arkansas, and the only place on earth you could get mousseline of catfish. You laugh. Try it sometime. I wish I had a body, so I could try it.

They took Ciemmie with them, because otherwise she would get her feelings hurt, thinking that they preferred Paul Bash's cuisine to her own. They drove over in the Blazer, and it died once at the Chester and Cantrell stoplight. Clemmie allowed as how the lettuce was limp in her Caesar's. The rest was ok, though the sauce on her tournedos was too cold.

Lianne professed to love the Blazer. The only problem was she wanted to go camping right away. Charles was not keen on camping. He stalled her, noncommittal. Besides, he had the damn July Fourth outing with the firm, so that would make two camping trips in a matter of weeks.

Then Thursday, at the office, flush with the successful resolution of the first case he had tried in over a year—his client the wife and business partner of the fellow who made all the mascot suits for college teams, she sewing them up for local schools at first and then he took them national and now they were divorcing and he had been trying to buy her out way too cheap—and wanting to call Lianne to brag, knowing she would be proud of him for winning for the woman, and also feeling generous in his triumph and therefore wanting to give Lianne something but having no idea what, but some small thing since their real anniversary had felt anti-climactic, some small token to cheer her because she had seemed withdrawn the last couple of days, he realized what a niggard and asshole he had been, withholding the one obvious thing she really would like.

A-camping they would go. He put out a hand to call her, but was struck by an idea of consummate brilliance. He called Brenda Faye first, had her come in to take a memo to all the members of the firm. As of this year, the July 4 excursion was canceled. Fuck his daddy—it was *his* firm now. Brenda Faye looked at him in shock. He was feeling merry. "Hey," he said. "Life goes on." The Fourth was on a Saturday, but he gave everybody Friday and the following Monday off. Let em bitch about *that*. And he and Lianne would have four days to go camping in. Two birds with one stone. Make the wife happy and get rid of a trip he hated.

Then he called Lianne to give her the news. "That's fine," she said. "But we'll have to take the Blazer back to the shop. Did you get a guarantee? You probably didn't. When you buy things used, you need to get a guarantee."

"I got a guarantee," he said, nettled. "What's wrong with it?"

"It's running rough. You were there. It dies at the stoplights. And the steering squeals when you turn it sharp left. I'm not taking it up into the mountains like that."

"The mountains?" he said.

"You weren't planning for us to go to that fishing camp, were you? I hate that place. I mean, the river's nice, but." Worse and worse. They would be tent camping, then, not staying in a nice cool air-conditioned cabin. And it would be hot as hell by the Fourth, it always was. Pretty damn warm already. "Where did you get it?" she said.

"My father," he said. "You know that."

"Not the camp, the Blazer. I can take it in today."

What was the rush? "I got it through Jerry," he said. "But you can't take it in there, I mean he guaranteed the work, but he didn't actually *do* it. I'll take care of it."

"You've got plenty to do," she said. "Just tell me where to take it."

It sounded awfully slipshod as he related it to her: Jerry's brother-in-law but you'd better call Jerry first so he could call the guy and lean on him. She had that knack, the ability merely by listening to make your strategies sound sloppy and poorly thought out. Here he was, a power among the powers that be, and she could with a casual inflection turn him into a boy making explanations to mother. But she took the information and didn't comment.

"Is something bothering you?" he said.

"No."

"You're being awfully terse. I thought you'd be happy about the camping trip."

There was a silence while she interpreted. She was in get-things-done mode, that was all, but he was obviously wanting emotional byplay.

Forget it, she had things to do. She said matter-of-factly, "Nothing's bothering me. I love you, and I'm glad we're going camping," and he had to make do with that.

Meantime, Ferrin had evolved a theory. His theory was that he *had* nailed the Morrisons, or at least wounded them, and that a huge cover-up was taking place, a cover-up designed to trick him into making a mistake, giving himself away.

By Tuesday, he and Rubert had gotten down to five or six dollars in change, and they had skipped the motel the next morning. They'd had maybe enough gas to get back to Little Rock, and Rubert had thought there was a chance the yogurt in the refrigerator at the apartment was still good. They had debated robbing somebody, but what with? The pistol was gone, the Ingram was gone. Do what, wave the lump of plastique under their noses? Besides, it was hard to get up for the idea when two thousand dollars was just sitting there waiting.

But when Ferrin called, the contact said, "Two thousand dollars for what? You aint done nothing."

Ferrin explained about the perfume shop and the police cover-up.

"Oh was that you?" the contact said, in a snotty tone. They argued back and forth a long time, but the upshot was nothing doing, no money.

"You aint done diddly-squat," the contact said, "and I aint paying diddly-squat. You already into me for rent and a car and two thousand dollars."

"One nine nine nine," Ferrin said.

"Fuck you and the horse you rode in on too."

Nothing was said about the Pinto or the rest of that month's rent, and the contact hung up without actually saying they were off the operation, and Ferrin didn't say turn the money over or reckon would the newspapers be interested in who *ordered* the perfume shooting, because that was his trump card, and once he played it, if it didn't work he would for sure never get the money and might even get caught himself. But the money was by rights already his, and aye God as soon as he got it they were going to pay for all the crap they had put him through. He was in a black mood realizing what he was going to have to do to keep himself in cigarettes till then. He was going to have to do something worse than jail. He was going to have to go out and work.

He went to Tommy and begged a little part-time, which Tommy couldn't really afford to pay him, but all the same since it was a sign of Ferrin trying to straighten himself out he had to do it anyhow. No way Tommy could hire Rubert too, though.

So for the time being Rubert was just laying around eating Ding Dongs, which royally pissed Ferrin off even further. Claimed he wasn't feeling good. Claimed he had went out and applied for work anyway while Ferrin was away at the shop Wednesday afternoon. Maybe so, but Ferrin wasn't talking to him any more, not till the nigger actually *got* a job.

All of which is how Ferrin happened to be in the garage with a cap on and black grease all over his face Thursday afternoon when Lianne brought the Blazer in. He recognized it, and he was curious what it was doing back. He was looking through the little windows of the pull-down overhead steel door, which was down to keep the air-conditioning in, already practically full summer out there. When Lianne got out, cool and elegant and healthy in the steamy air, it was like a blow to the stomach. It was like the worst insult of all. That for all his sweat and pain she should be walking the earth fat as ever, while here he stood, lean, broke, and elbow deep in shit.

Tommy went walking out from the office, and Ferrin watched through the little window, like you would watch the screen of one of those portable color tvs if you were in a dark room with the sound off, like you didn't have a body and didn't even really have any eyes, just your seeing and the screen were the same thing, nothing was real and all you were was what was happening on the screen. It was just like watching her on the tv, except now the show she was in was his own life. He saw her start and look strangely at Tommy, and then ask him a question.

Ferrin couldn't hear, but she had asked Tommy if he knew a man named Alvin Stone.

She was thinking of David Stone, but she hadn't quite remembered the first name, and her mind, filling in, had somehow got from stone to hammer pounding stone to hammer pounding anvil, and the anvil came out as Alvin.

"No," Tommy said. "Why?"

When she pointed at the car and started waving her hands around and they both started jawing back and forth, Ferrin realized the next thing would happen, once Tommy agreed to take another look at it, would be he would say, "Wait a minute, I'll get my brother to drive you home," and so he split for the house, leaving through the back door onto the alley.

Tommy was pissed, he had to lock up to drive her home himself, who knows how much business he lost, but Ferrin claimed he had suddenly got a bad headache, it wouldn't happen again. He was in a daze all that night.

Rubert had never seen him look so bad and pale. But Rubert was feeling poorly himself, and had Ferrin shown *him* any sympathy? No. The motherfucker wasn't talking to him, he wasn't talking to the motherfucker, no matter how sorry for him he felt.

Friday morning there was a big puff piece in the paper about the upcoming *Hope Lines* Christmas in July. This looked to be the social event of the year. Lianne's idea was to make it extremely high-ticket and thereby create the inverse appeal of exclusivity. You raised more money at a hundred a pop than you did if you made it cheap enough for the hoi polloi. She was all for democracy, but she was pretty cynical about how things actually worked. People in Little Rock with money to spend loved to dress up in tuxes and evening gowns and go to glittering events, but there was a definite shortage of glittering events to go to. The opera in season, or Tabriz at the Arts Center, but after that strictly roasts and toasts. It wasn't like you had book publicity parties or gallery openings or first nights of plays or even big-time political dinners every day of the year.

So she could fill a community need. And if it was for a charity, they could feel important and virtuous at the same time.

On the same page there was an article by Duane Campbell of Harding University, that little school in Searcy, so expert at turning out Christian binnessmen.

Duane thought Act 590 was a real good idea. His article was being offered by the paper as a balance to Asimov's article last Sunday. Show both sides of the story, you know. Yessir, creation science was a quality issue, all right. Duane Campbell versus Isaac Asimov.

Under Duane's story was a brief news release on the big-name witness list for the creation science suit, and Charles was quoted regarding the magnitude and luminosity of its stars. So he and Lianne were on the same page, a little marriage. Not the first time.

There was no photo of him, but there was one of Lianne above the *Hope Lines* story, this time just a file photo, the one they'd taken when she had done the creation science interview.

Rubert had coughed himself awake that morning, something in his chest. Ferrin had slept through it, more evidence that the man was depressed. Now Rubert was at the table rolling the plastique on Lianne's picture, trying to get the photo to come off like it would on Silly Putty, when Ferrin came out of the bedroom. He showed Ferrin the story, thinking to get a rise out of him, anything but this zombie shit, but all Ferrin did was look at Rubert like he was some kind of strange bug he didn't even care enough to squash.

"You got the damn air-conditioning on already," he said, pushing the paper away across the table, his voice dull and automatic. At least he was *talking*.

They had to pay their own utility bills, that's what this was about.

"I didn't touch it," Rubert said. "I was just setting here, and it clicked over."

"Cause you got the fucking thermostat set so low. I saw you do it last night."

"Hey, Big Chief. News flash: It's hot out there. Air hard to breathe."

. . .

Henrietta Raymond had shown the story to Sonny that morning too. In appearance a perfect meek little brown-haired wife, she loved to annoy him. It was one of her few pleasures, and he never knew she was doing it on purpose. Just as he never once suspected she knew all about the fancy-ass Talliaferro whore he spent his afternoons with two or three times a week.

He hated Lianne Morrison with a passion, she understood that, so she had shown him the story. But this time he got madder than she had ever seen him, so mad it scared her.

"The goddamn self-righteous motherfuckers," he raged. "Atheists, and everybody thinks they're such fucking angels. All the money in the world, and I can't get a fucking thing on them." He had never used language like that in the house, and she thought, for the first time, of divorce. He went to the office and vented his anger on Cheese. He was for sure not going home after work today, he was spending the evening with Tina.

By lunchtime he was saying the hell with that plan, he was spending the *afternoon* with Tina, he was taking the rest of the day off. But when he got to her place she wasn't in. There was a note in a plain envelope with his name on it. She thanked him for everything he had done, but maybe they had better quit seeing each other. She was going off to the country for a while, and when she got back, it would be all over between them. Her heart wasn't in it any more. Her heart was somewhere else. She knew he would understand.

Ferrin had gone to the shop in spite of feeling completely dead inside. Why not work? What difference did it make? What difference did anything make? Seeing Lianne had done what all his previous frustration had not been able to do. It had cut the heart right out of his chest. Seeing her there, alive and vital, on his own territory. Changing plugs, grinding valves, cranking the ratchet on frozen-up manifold nuts he couldn't reach with the power wrench—all afternoon long he saw her death and his own. He imagined himself, a cartoon bomb of dynamite and a ticking clock strapped to his chest, waiting in the dark of the garage for her to come pick up the Blazer. One sudden final shocking embrace, the sort of woman he had never had his arms around before.

Though that was a disgusting thought: She was way too old to fuck.

It would never happen anyway, something would go wrong, somebody would grab him, and he would just be a poor pitiful crying fool in a nuthouse somewhere. He didn't even have the guts to try. He felt like a whipped dog. All he was was her garage mechanic. Checking the idle on the carburetor, checking to see if the valve was sticking in its throat. He could ruin the damn thing if he wanted to, put sugar in the gas tank or something. Hell, he could blow it up in her face. Rig something with the plastique. He could imagine the explosion but couldn't concentrate on how to rig it. Wires, batteries, plastique on the gas tank, but it was all a jumble and confusion in his head. *You got the I-want, but you aint got the I-will to go with it,* his daddy used to say.

He got the carburetor all taken apart but lost interest and went to another job. Let it wait. Let Tommy do it this weekend. She could pick it up Monday. He was a beaten man.

Late that afternoon, Brenda Faye took a call from Tina. She had orders not to put Tina through to Charles, and so she said, "I'm sorry, hon, but he's not in the office right now."

Tina laughed. "Well, hon, I know he is."

"I'm sorry, but he's really not," Brenda Faye said. "Can I take a message?"

"Just tell him I called. Confirming our meeting on the fourth up at the Little Red. He can call me back, he has the number. Are y'all looking forward to the big trip?"

"Hon—" Brenda Faye said.

At home that night Lianne was busy making plans for the camping trip, now only two weeks off exactly, or really thirteen days if they left Thursday afternoon, which she was pushing to do, because it was like having a whole extra day, to wake up there and be already set up.

Charles didn't want to leave Thursday afternoon, because he hated getting in late and setting up in the dark. And also because it was like having a whole extra day, to wake up there and be already set up.

Lianne was almost for sure going to have to visit the surplus store after farmers' market in the morning. Among other things, they needed a good sisal rope and a couple of pounds of sulfur and a big box of moth flakes.

"What on earth for?" Charles said. "Are you making your own napalm?"

"Snake repellent. You put the rope around the tent and they won't crawl over it, and then you mix the sulfur and the moth flakes and sprinkle it all around and it repels them."

"It would me too," he said.

"They're cold-blooded, and they come for your body heat," she said.

"Maybe in winter or fall or something, but hell, it's going to be hot as holy Jesus up there. There's not going to be any snakes crawling into your tent."

About that time, in the apartment, the phone rang. Ferrin didn't move, and Rubert answered. It was the contact, and he recognized the voice. His eyes widened. He held the phone out for Ferrin, who slowly, stiffly, like a rusty tin man, got up and came to take the receiver. Rubert fumbled behind his back for a chair and sat down.

"Yeah," Ferrin said, and then he listened without saying anything. But as Rubert watched, the life came back into his face and body. It was like watching blood come into a dying vampire. Something good was happening, the worst was over. "Sure, sure," Ferrin said once. "Absolutely guaranteed. Tuesday at the latest. But the price has gone up. We need four thousand up front. And we still get three more payments. Sure. Lots of em out there. But can you find em in time?"

When Ferrin hung up, he was smiling.

"What?" Rubert said.

"All things come to him who waits around," Ferrin said. "We got em where we want em now. They just *thought* they could get along without us. You shoulda heard em whining."

Still being mysterious, just as if Rubert hadn't finally heard the contact himself. He wouldn't tell Rubert what was up, but sat at the table smiling to himself, muttering little fragments of speech, drawing sketches in the air, shaking his head, erasing them. At last he slapped his hand down on the tabletop and sat back.

"Eureka!" he said, and then he was off in the bedroom rummaging in the chester drawers. He came back with the plastique, set it on the table. He went out and down the stairs, and Rubert heard him forcing his way into the empty apartments below. She was definitely getting ready to sell; they were the only tenants left in the building now. Ferrin came back into the kitchen with something in either hand. Two ripped-off wall thermostats, it turned out.

"What the fuck you do that for?" Rubert said. "We'll have to pay that back."

"Watch and learn," Ferrin said. "You're looking at ten thousand dollars."

He took the thermostats apart with his pocket knife, forcing loose from each a little glass capsule soldered into a rocker switch. Inside each capsule rolled a little pellet of silvery liquid. Then he went rambling around, looking for some copper wire, but couldn't find any. Not finding it made him a little pissed again for a while, but what the hell, he said, relaxing. They didn't have a clock or any batteries yet anyhow.

"I'm tired of this bullshit," Rubert said. He wasn't learning anything, he was sick and he was sleepy, and he wanted to go to bed. "What you up to, Mr. Mysterious?"

"We're gone blow her up," Ferrin said. "We're gone wire a bomb to her fucking car and blow her right off the face of the earth."

"You are, maybe," Rubert said. "I aint going nowhere near that fucking house again. Probably where I got this cold, standing out in the rain." He could just see himself crawling up the driveway in the dead of night with a bomb in his arms. Blow his face off about the time he was fastening it to the gas tank. Unh-unh.

"That's what I aint told you." Ferrin grinned. His feral grin. "Guess whose car we got sitting in Tommy's shop right now? Be there all weekend, just waiting for the hand of the master." He explained, laughing at the irony of it all.

Lord love a duck.

Rubert had never seen a man so pleased with himself. Ferrin wanted to diagram the whole plan, but they didn't have any pencil and paper, not even a stub and a notepad. Ferrin rummaged through all the cabinets, found nothing. He went in the refrigerator and got the jar of wheat germ. He screwed the lid off and tossed the cereal all over the tabletop. "Hey!" Rubert said. He had been planning to have the stuff for breakfast, mixed into some honey and yogurt, with raisins and banana slices. Tons of iron and B vitamins, get his energy back up.

"You can rake it back up when I'm through," Ferrin said. He used the blade of his knife to draw lines in the spill. "This wire goes from the batteries here," he said. "To the mercury switch here." He shook one of the thermostat capsules in Rubert's face, plunged it into the spread of wheat germ. "This other wire goes from the plastic back to the batteries. When the car starts forward, that mercury rolls and closes the current, and that's all, she wrote."

There was a problem, though, Rubert thought. Something vague at the edge of his brain. Oh yeah. Well, it was his brother, and if he didn't care, ok. But still.

"All right. But when she come to pick it up, it a blow the garage up too, won't it? And also they can trace you thoo him."

He could tell he had said just what Ferrin wanted him to. Making a big production of it now. "Aha!" Ferrin said, holding up one magic finger, waiting a beat. Slowly unfolding a second finger. "That's why I got *two switches*, brother."

Ferrin drew a big circle in one of the wires. Then he drew two more wires from the batteries. These wires went to the circle. He waved the other mercury switch, cackled, and stuck it halfway along one of the new wires. "Click," he said. "Snick." Then, walking around the table with his hands lifted palms-up: "Tickticktickticktick—"

He stopped, shot his hands into the air. "Kaboom!"

"I don't get it," Rubert said.

"The clock is a switch," Ferrin said, pointing at the circle.

"That's a clock."

"That's a clock. You see now? You see how it works?"

"Might's well be the theory relativity," Rubert said. "Where you learn all this shit?"

Ferrin thought about telling him he'd been in the Green Berets once, but Rubert would know better, he'd known Ferrin ever since they were in jail together, Ferrin's second time, when he was twenty-three. Rubert knew his life history by now.

"In vo-tech," he said. "Took one of them electrician courses, but I hated it, I never thought it would do me no good. I can hear my daddy now: *Everything you learn is worth something, son. Value of an education.*"

"It's really easy," he said, enjoying Rubert's bafflement. "Look. She starts the car, both mercury switches roll over. But nothing happens to the plastic, because the *clock* is a switch, and it aint closed the circuit. I put a lead on each hand, and the circuit don't close till the two hands come together." His finger hovering over the second set of wires, Ferrin traced the working of the current. "She starts the car, and the clock starts ticking." He moved his finger in a circle over the circle. "Tick tick tick. And eleven hours *later*—"

"Why eleven?"

"You *could* make it eleven hours and fifty-nine minutes and fifty-nine seconds. But I don't want to take a chance on it jiggering back and blowing me up instead."

"So then what?"

Ferrin indicated the first set of wires. "Eleven hours *later,* the clock closes the switch in *this* wire. There's a post, here, to stop the clock so it doesn't open the switch again. And then, *then,* the next time that car moves—"

"Boom?" Rubert said.

"Ten thousand dollars," Ferrin said.

Ferrin was restless, too excited to sleep. He wanted to brag how he'd waited the contact out, how what took the most guts was waiting. Waiting, waiting. Waiting for the other man to make the first move, and then you had the advantage. "You shoulda heard em," he said. "You shoulda heard em. They were almost *crying.*"

When Ferrin finally did shut up and turn the light off, Rubert found his own mind going in circles. Round and round he went, trying to make sense of how the clock and the bomb fit together. Where the electricity went and what it did when it got there. But it seemed like too many things were happening at the same time, or things were happening to things that made the first things happen, and he got dizzy trying to see it all.

He slipped into a dream, one of those lakes, one of those lakes in a cyclone fence you see by the road, and they charge admission. With a sand beach around it inside the fence, and out in the middle a big tower with a diving board.

He was on the diving board with Lianne Morrison, they were naked and rubbing legs, they were going to jump together. He was choking, but when he jumped in the water he would be able to breathe. A little dwarf was running up the beach.

Charles Morrison, but he had Ferrin's face. A little dwarf was running up the beach with a clock on his face, making everything scary.

28

BLAZER

Tommy was surprised when Ferrin volunteered to come in Saturday afternoon and finish up the work on the Blazer, but it just went to show you should never give up on people. And now he could go fishing like he had wanted to in the first place. Even if he did get a late start because Ferrin had waited so long to tell him.

Ferrin had sent Rubert out shopping Saturday morning. Rubert felt like Santa Claus, dropping off a bag of presents at the garage: a new carton of Pall Malls, a six-pack of beer, a couple of six-volt batteries, a small round battery-driven clock (analog, not digital), the plastique from the apartment. Tommy had a soldering iron and all the kinds of wire and solder and brush contacts Ferrin needed right there at the shop.

Ferrin wanted Rubert to see everything he was doing. He had done some more planning and realized he was going to have a problem making sure the mercury switch to the clock stayed closed so the clock would keep running. And maybe the switch wouldn't carry enough load anyway, so he was building a contact switch on the mercury switch. When the mercury switch closed, the contact switch would draw down and take all the current. The other mercury switch, the one between the clock and the plastique, didn't have to stay open. It just had to deliver a single pulse to the detonator. He wanted Rubert to see how clever his wiring was, how he had soldered the batteries in parallel and then soldered the leads right to the contacts in the clock.

Rubert hung around and watched awhile, but the smoke from Ferrin's cigarettes and the stink of old oil and filthy black gasoline-soaked cleaning rags and of burning solder and insulation was too much for his lungs, so he took off.

. . .

Lianne picked up the Blazer on Monday, Charles dropping her off on his way to work. The rocker switches worked like a charm, and the contact switch closed, and the clock under the gas tank started running.

It was the twenty-second of June, just past solstice. Summer was officially under way.

Governor White said he would reconsider Act 590 in a call for a special legislative session. That is, he would if its original sponsors requested such action.

Ferrin didn't come in to work that afternoon. Tommy cussed him out as well as he could, given his Christian principles: *that confounded flop-eared no-good dadgum useless piece of trouble.* He called the apartment, but nobody answered.

Ferrin and Rubert had left for Florida Sunday evening, driving down all night through Jackson, Hattiesburg, Mobile, and arriving at Mexico Beach early in the morning. They had clear title to the Pinto, in trade for half of the up-front money, and another two thousand in their pockets.

They holed up in a beachfront motel and slept all day. Ferrin had never seen the ocean before, but he didn't let Rubert know that. Rubert hadn't been too keen on Florida—"What I'm on do, get a suntan?"—but Ferrin had convinced him the sun and salt air would probably help his flu. That was what he figured it was, the flu. It wasn't just the cough, he was feeling kind of peaky and run down. He was taking extra vitamin C, but so far it didn't seem to help.

Lianne spent the day organizing her old park maps and driving around to various places to get new ones. That evening she made Charles sit down with her in the library and pick out a campsite. They settled on Rush, finally. It was a primitive campsite up where Rush Creek fed into the Buffalo below Yellville, nothing but a toilet and drinking water. So they wouldn't even be able to shower or to run an electric fan. Sometimes it was cooler up in the hills, near the fast-running water. Charles hoped and prayed this would be one of the times.

Rush wouldn't be as crowded as all the other places would be on the Fourth, and there was a forsaken old lead-mining community they wanted to see. Peering into vine-throttled and empty shacks—they both loved poking around in the lost cities of the Ozarks. There was something intensely pleasurable about ghost towns, something wonderfully haunting about the empty light, the greater-than-lonely loneliness of a place once lived in and now abandoned.

. . .

At 9:16, out in the driveway, the clock showed twelve straight up, and the circuit closed. Ferrin had soldered a post, a hacksawed segment of nail, above the *12*. The hands of the clock labored against the post, going nowhere. Charles and Lianne went to bed.

At 7:25 a.m., because Ferrin had used the same solder for the post as for the wires, electrical solder instead of regular, and because he had soldered the post directly to the clock face without burning all the paint off, the post gave way. The clock began keeping time again, and the switch opened, breaking the circuit. Now the circuit would be closed only twice a day, when the hands of the clock showed twelve. Which is to say, at twenty-five past seven in the morning and twenty-five past seven in the evening. The bomb would go off only if the rocker switch closed while the clock circuit was closed. Only if someone was driving the car at twenty-five past seven in the morning or twenty-five past seven in the evening: that jolt of inertia from starting up, or from a bump in the road or hitting the brakes.

It was like that old joke about the busted clock. The bomb was right twice a day.

Charles was downstairs having breakfast and Lianne was sleeping late. In Doctors' Hospital, Coleman grunted and opened his eyes. Nobody was in the room to see. Nobody but me. He closed his eyes and went back under.

Over the next ten days, Lianne put so much gear together you would have thought they were preparing for an assault on Mount Everest. She liked to use the old metal and plastic milk cartons left over from twenty-odd years ago, when her father would bring them home from his job, though he wasn't supposed to. All these years she had held on to them, her only heirlooms.

She filled four of them with food and kitchen supplies—trail mix, peanut butter, boxes of crackers, dried fruit, packets of dehydrated vegetables for stews, soup mixes, powdered drinks, graham crackers, boxes of cookies, canned tuna, canned corn beef hash, canned mandarin orange sections, canned green beans, jellies, jams, syrups, oatmeal, biscuit mix, coffee, the old tin drip coffeepot, enameled camp mugs, a couple of black iron skillets, camp pots and camp pans and camp silverware, long-handled spatulas and serving spoons and forks for cooking over a fire, a washpan, a scrubber, biodegradable detergent, washrags, plastic sacks of all sizes, some for their empty cans and cartons, their paper, eggshells, sodden coffee grounds, orange and banana peels, greasy used paper plates (which I forgot to mention above before they ate off them), and Ziplocs for used food and extra empty vegetable bags to put rocks and pine cones and other treasures in, and bags to hold the bags, and army-green folded-over sheets of tear-off twist-ties with which to seal the bags. The refrigerator stuff went in at the last minute, in the big red ice chest—bacon, eggs, butter, milk for Charles, thick bars of Baker's German chocolate, cheeses, wines, frozen juice, fresh bread, fresh fruit, fresh vegetables.

And that was only the food and kitchen supplies. What about the tent in ripstop nylon, the tent poles, stakes, guys, rain cover, the slickers, the sleeping bags, bedpads, pillows, matches, the stubs of used candles in old Pringle's tubes, the Coleman stove, the Coleman lantern, white gas for the stove and the lantern, flashlights in all sizes and descriptions, the battery-operated reading lamp, the medical kit with its Band-Aids, gauze, sterile solutions, disinfectants, insect repellents, pain relievers, antihistamines, pseudoephedrine pills, salves, unguents?

What about the huge box of baking soda, good for making a paste to put on bee stings and ant bites, also for brushing your teeth, deodorizing the tent, and cleaning the coffeepot. What about the citronella candles to keep the bugs off? What about the picks, axes, shovels, hammers, knives, the walking sticks, the twine and rope and Visqueen and old vinyl table-cloths for setting things on, the toilet paper and Handi Wipes and paper towels and soap and bath towels and hand cloths, what about the booze, the books, the clothes?

Listen, she had clothes for mountain hiking, river rafting, evening sitting when it got cooler and you wanted to keep the mosquitoes off your ears and ankles, she had clothes in case they wanted to drive into a town to eat, clothes to go square dancing in, she had sun hats, tractor caps, pith helmets, visor shades, she had twelve-year-old low-top tennis shoes, cowboy boots, hiking boots, river waders, nice little go-anywhere flats, shower sandals, she had bandannas in six different colors and sizes, the most prized of course the big giant old-fashioned red ones.

Then of course there were plastic bags full of maps: road maps to get there with, topo maps of the local area, national forest maps, maps of the entire length of the Buffalo. Oh, I could go on and on, but I won't, because Miss Liza don't think it's one bit funny. Charles had seen it all before, and he knew better than to say anything.

He thought, though, that he had never seen anyone who loved nature more or was more allergic it. Food allergies, yes, but also pollen, spores, dust, animal dander, poison ivy, oak, sumac, the toxins at the tip of the spines of wild rose, blackberry, horse nettle, sandspur, hawthorn and honey locust. She whelked up and suffered extravagantly from mosquito, tick, bee, chigger, spider and wasp bites, got hives from too much sun, assorted fungal infections from too much rain, and any number of pulmonary and rheumatic conditions from weather fronts bringing in different air from somewhere else. She loved nature and it threatened her in a thousand ways, and so she went to her love, but she went prepared.

Then, too, packing satisfied her puzzle-solving instincts. As it does mine. How to stuff all this into a Blazer and still leave the two of them room enough to ride? Monkey look, monkey poke, monkey lift, monkey pry, monkey push, monkey do. Good monkey, it fits!

Charles was grateful that at least they no longer had to take Ramalam. He remembered far too many such trips trapped with the stink of over-heated hound in the overstuffed old Mercedes—yes, they went in the old Mercedes, heavy black beast covered in dust rumbling around the hairpins of eroded and petering-out mountain roads.

What a wimp you are, Charles, not to love dog! Ah, the luffly effusion of dog, dog in close quarters! Like a plethora of gravies poured over your head, like having toasty-warm feather pillows stuffed up your nostrils, like having an unwashed sumo wrestler sit on your face, like running the baby's diapers in the dryer without washing them first, and then when they're fluffed and dry as powder, you open the door to the stopspinning soft fallfall and stick your head in panting and whuff that wonderful whoof, wow! What I wouldn't give, what all we dead wouldn't give, to snuffle such walloping spoor once more! Woof!

Lianne did most of her packing in the evenings. During the day, she was busy getting ready for Christmas in July. There would be less than three weeks left when they got back from their camping trip, so she had to do as much planning as possible ahead of time. She pulled Dee-Dee in, though Dee-Dee was not just superkeen on hoity-toity social events. She got invitations mailed and printed, arranged for Rose Crane to handle the music and food and catering, and set up a publicity schedule. She was on the telephone hours at a time pressuring people she knew to come, or to donate this or that, or to help out with some of the work.

Since she packed after working hours, Charles was available, and he wound up having to help a lot more than he wanted to. "I'm going to throw my back out, and then I'm not going to be able to go camping at all," he complained, hoisting a loaded milk carton to rest on the high back bumper of the Blazer. Lianne had just worked the stove into a corner, wedging the gas can in beside it and padding the can with folds of plastic and a box of food so that it could not tumble over. She stood with her back to him, not moving. It was almost eight o'clock, and still light, though the sun had just gone down. He realized she was crying.

"What's the matter?" he said, turning her around. She leaned against him, stiff and silent. "What's the matter?" he said again when she was through crying.

"What if Coleman dies while we're out of town?" she said.

He knew what she meant. It was worse that way, she would feel responsible, guilty, as if she had abandoned him in his hour of need.

Ramalam had died one spring while they were on the island, and she had never forgiven herself. The dog had survived surgery for pancreatic cancer just the week before, and was able to stand and move around a bit. They'd had the trip planned for months, and Charles had pressed to go ahead and take it. It was just when she was first considering leaving KROK, and she was at her palest and most gaunt. He'd thought she needed the break even more than he did. So they were probably strolling through the waves with their pants rolled up when the hemorrhaging started. They were probably having an afternoon martini on the sun deck when Ramalam was opened back up on the vet's operating table. They were probably chewing their ice cubes when the dog said the hell with this noise, I'm checking out. I *know* they were.

Here it comes again, the flip-flop, I'm being sucked into yet another persona! Oh wonderful, oh woof! Woof! Arrrrrrrr-rooo!

Been trying to tell you ever since I died, hon, don't take it so serious. Been barking up a storm, but for all your prescience, you don't seem to hear. Listen, gal, you gimme a good life, I aint blaming you you weren't there to help me on out the door. We look at all that kinda practical, you know. When we hit the point of diminishing returns, we just cash it in.

You have to have whole religions to teach some of you momentarily to get a glimpse of what we knew all along, life's illusion. What religion is, a construct mapping the void in your brain. Artificial support system filling in the gap until your gray matter finishes evoluting and ramifying and finds out what it sposed to be. I admit we probably wouldn't done no better, all the rest us animals just glad you monkeys the ones they sperimenting on.

And listen, gal, get away from that Blazer car. Just get away, huh?

Speaking of evolution, it was right about in this time frame that Judge Overton denied the petition of the Unitarian Church to enter the suit against Act 590. *Darn right,* muttered the True Children of the Lord, *not a real religion anyway, bunch a cottonpicking liberals.* But the fact that Overton had been assigned to hear the suit was not very good news for the Truculent Children, as Overton was an intelligent reasonable man who wanted to hear intelligent reasonable arguments. It was also right about in this time frame when Governor White announced that reconsideration would not be part of the special session after all, and that his mail was running five to one in favor of Act 590. Not to take any chances, a bunch of the True-True-Trudy Goodbye incorporated to support the act, calling themselves Arkansas Citizens for Balanced Education in Origins. You figure out what they meant by the acronym, I can't.

While Lianne was packing and the clock was ticking and the creation science suit was perking and Charles was working, Ferrin and Rubert were walking on the beach. Or this is the way it really went. Arriving, they had stood in the parking lot of the motel for a few minutes trying to watch the sea and feel like they were really there, and then like I said they slept all day Monday. Ferrin woke up right at sunset and went down to the beach in his jeans and t-shirt and bare feet, unshaven. He had the devil of a time getting his Pall Malls lit in the whipping wind off the waves. He walked into the surf a little, got the cuffs of his jeans soaked. He was shivering, which didn't seem fair, this time of year. The darkening beach was dotted with couples, families, a fisherman or two walking back to somewhere along the surf line with their poles over their shoulders and carrying their bait in yellow plastic buckets. He felt out of place, disconnected. The big booming water was alien, incoming, a massive pulse of threat.

He went back and got Rubert up and they went out drinking. They found a couple of good beer joints, and the flavor was partly familiar and partly strange, redneck but different, oysters and shrimp and Tabasco sauce with the longneck bottles. Nobody gave them any hassle for being half nigger, like they would've in Arkansas. Which was too bad in a way, because Ferrin felt like fighting. He liked standing up for America. He believed in freedom and equality and kicking butt. Also he was horny for the first time in a long time, and there were one or two scroungy pieces of tail hanging around he felt like might get real hot at the sight of a roll wrapped in hundred-dollar bills, but first you'd probably have to whip some old boy thought he had prior claim.

But the closest he got to either fisticuffs or pussy was an argument with a broad-shouldered blonde bitch in cowboy boots over how many men they'd killed. She claimed she'd slid a knife into her first husband's heart while he was sleeping and spent five years in Raiford and then popped her boyfriend's buddy with a magnum and got off with self-defense because he was trying to rape her even if the boyfriend had gotten drunk and told him to come on in and rip himself off a piece. Also she might've shot a guy hunting once, she wasn't sure.

Ferrin claimed three kills, thinking of the three tries on Lianne and glossing over the fact she was just a woman. It was fair enough, even if it was Rubert that would have shot her that first time, because he had planned it and she *could* have died.

Anyway, he was 99 percent certain the dyke blonde was bullshitting.

He wouldn't give any details of his own killings, though, just hinted darkly at dark doings. He claimed he was a pro and wasn't about to give away trade secrets.

"You're a liar and pussy," she said drunkenly, pushing his arm.

"Shit on you," he said. "Last one I done, she's probably blowing up right now. Car, I mean. Wired a car. It's probably blowing up right now, even as we speak. Tell her, Rubert."

"What?" Rubert said. His heart wasn't in it, he was tired all the time now. He'd been sitting stupidly all night, staring around without seeing anything. He hadn't drunk more than a swallow of his last beer. He wasn't hungry either.

"Liar, liar, pants on fire," the blonde bitch said.

Ferrin was angry at Rubert's lack of support. And he'd had it with the blonde, fuck her, she was an ugly bitch anyway. "You just check your paper tomorrow," he said thickly. "You just check your paper for car explosions."

They got back to the room about four in the morning and slept on through to afternoon. The blonde, whose name was Veronica Delray but who went by Ronnie, woke up in her own house with a terrible headache. The house was a stilt house on a section of bay. When she finally showered and got some coffee in her and read the paper, there was a story about some guy in Utah, the mob had blown his car up. She couldn't make head or tails of the story, he worked for a radio station, and there were Mormons involved, but it gave her the cold shivers, and she puked her breakfast over the deck rail, a stroke of luck for the mullet and bluefin.

It took real connections to set up a hit and get from Utah to Florida before it came off. "Ronnie gal," she told herself, wiping her mouth, "you been keeping bad company." The rest of her life she told the story how she had once met a couple of genuine Mafia hit men in a bar. "The look in their eyes," she would say, "would freeze whiskey in July."

Ferrin and Rubert had breakfast in McDonald's, walking the sand-and-seashell strip from the motel, breathing CO and other fractured polycarbons all the way, the rumbling flatulence of the continual growling traffic. Ferrin bought the papers from Pensacola, Tallahassee, and even the Orlando *Sentinel* (though it was from all the way across the state). It was too late for breakfast breakfast, so they had fries and Big Macs. Rubert didn't finish his. There was nothing in any of the papers about a 4WD blowing up in Little Rock, Arkansas.

"If it happened last night," Ferrin said, reasoning things out, "probably it was too late for the wire service. It'll be in tomorrow's. Or we can listen to the radio."

"Aint no radio *in* the Pinto," Rubert said.

"You're one fucking negative son of a bitch," Ferrin said. "We can *buy* a fucking radio. We're rich now."

They didn't bother to buy one. Instead, Ferrin made Rubert go walking on the beach with him. Rubert sighed and said he would just as soon go back and lie down awhile, but Ferrin insisted. "Scout for beaver," he said. "Look at them skimpy little swimsuits."

There wasn't much beaver, though. It wasn't like in the movies or on tv or even on the postcards, fifteen practically naked sorority girls running into the waves with their cheeks showing, with one guy. It was more grandmothers in one-pieces; blistered maniacal children driven insane by the huge confluence of elements, the absence of routine; balding daddies with beer guts in lawn chairs drinking Falstaff; corpulent mommas sprawled out on towels, whose idea seemed to be that brown fat looked better than white fat. The only thing even remotely approaching beaver was a bored teenager who had good knockers but heavy thighs, and she had three crew-cut and ponytailed locals hanging around her.

It was four o'clock, and the sun was fierce. Neither Ferrin nor Rubert had a swimsuit, and their jeans chafed and made them sweat. The sand was hot even through their shoe soles, and blinding white, and they hadn't bought sunglasses either. It was all a damn cheat, like everything else. Ferrin would have gone back in except it would have meant admitting Rubert was right.

"Less wade in the waves," said Rubert, who had perked up a little. But then, he liked to sweat. Sweating the poisons out, that was how he thought of it. Like the Indians in their sweat lodges. It was cleansing.

Ferrin took off his shirt and shoes. He rolled his pants legs up to below his knees. His jeans sagged low on his hip bones, showing all of his pale flat belly and the upper curls of his pubic hair. He tied his shirt in a kind of burnoose around his head, knotted his shoelaces and hung them from a belt loop. He carried his pack of Pall Malls. Rubert took his shoes off and left them on the dry part of the sand. "I'll git em when I come back," he said. They waded in the rush at the edge of the sand, heading east, the sun behind them. The air off the waves was cooler, and Ferrin began to feel cheerier.

"I told you it would do you good," Ferrin said.

Rubert began finding thin round flat things in the wash, like calcium flowers, like the faces of sea clocks. "Reckon what these are?" he said.

"Some kind of shell," Ferrin said, and then had a flash of memory, the decorative display in the motel lobby when he checked them in. "Sand dollars," he said, feeling like a genius.

"Sand dollars," Rubert said vaguely.

"Like silver dollars," Ferrin said.

They weren't silver, but Rubert felt richer every time he found one. He filled his hands, then his shirt pockets. His jeans were too tight, it would just break em.

"If they shells, reckon where it lives?" he said.

"What lives?"

"The meat," Rubert said. "Like a oyster or something, where would it be? Aint no hollow to these things."

"Figure it out for yourself," said Ferrin, who didn't have the least idea. "Maybe it aint nothing in it. Maybe it's just something come out of a coral reef." It wasn't real clear to him what a coral reef was, but he thought it sounded authoritative.

"No," said Rubert. "Something like this don't just happen. It's gotta be something living." He found broken segments, studied the chambers.

"It lives *in* it," he said after a while. "It's like a starfish with a house."

They came to a long wooden boardwalk leading back up to the street. "Let's go this way," Ferrin said.

"What about my shoes?"

"You can go back and get em if you want to. I'm heading up this way."

Rubert found a plastic sack half buried in the sand, pulled it out and shook it. He could put his sand dollars in it. He could look for more going back. He had never been to the ocean before either. It was pretty great. "Well, I'm going back on the beach," he said. "Tear my feet up walking on them hot shells."

Ferrin didn't answer, just pitched his cigarette off into the sand. He started up the first series of steps on the boardwalk. At the last series, a steep flight over the last dune before the road, a sign was stuck in the sand in the middle of a bunch of shrubs and high straw-colored grass: DO NOT PICK SEA OATS.

"If I knew what the hell a sea oat was," he said aloud, "I'd pick the fuck out of it."

I see I'm wandering. Is there something I don't want to get to? What am I, avoiding?

Let's jump to Thursday, July 2, 1981. To the Arkansas Ozarks, where once, billions of years ago, this same salt wash had broken, and scattered its trilobites. Lianne had talked you into leaving the office at two, though there was a new lawyer applicant you wanted to interview. You had postponed the interview till next Tuesday.

Up Highway 65 to Marshall and then over on 27 to 14, and over the high bridge, since Rush is on the north side of the Buffalo River. You got to the camp in good daylight, 6:59 p.m., almost an hour before sunset.

The first thing you do is stretch out the massive square of green canvas and peg it down, then you unroll the tent and pull all the corners out square and then and only then do you start popping the aluminum rods into their supporting prism and pulling the peak of the tent up to hook the stretchy loops at the corners over and clipping the sides to the side poles and thumping in the plastic pegs with the rubber hammer.

The weather's clear, so no need for the rain-flap.

A white woman with four kids pulls up in a two-tone brown-and-white station wagon in the campsite next to yours. They hop out and unrope the hatch door and the piles of stuff on the roof and start setting out lawn chairs and card tables and Styrofoam ice buckets and American flags. They leave the four doors hanging open, and the porky thirteen-year-old daughter with the high butt and the freckles and the Mickey Mouse t-shirt and the orange stretch jersey shorts pulls the radio aerial out to its full extension and turns on Conway Twitty.

Surely Haden or Earl or Walter is going to be driving up any minute on the low-rider or in the big pickup, just as soon as he can after working late at the gravel pit, and you and Lianne look at each other and wonder about getting back in the Blazer and finding another site. But what the hell, it's 7:20 or so, almost sundown, and you're half set up, and what would be the point? You've got the best spot, you've already checked them all out—getting there a day early, you had your choice. And who's to say you wouldn't get worse neighbors at another site, time everybody starts coming in tomorrow evening.

Here at least you're back up under the trees and closest of all to the creek, and really there's a kind of bush thing or two between you and the people in the wagon, and Lianne moves the Blazer, parking it between the campsites so as to give you even a little bit more privacy.

By now you're sweaty and itchy as hell. It's pretty stuffy out, the air heavy and stifling, won't get below eighty tonight in all probability. Clear as can be, though, and the sunset a fire over the western hills. So the two of you take the towels and the soap and toothbrushes and set out along the creek in the failing light.

You find a nice private place and strip naked and bathe in the cool water. You wash your hair and brush your teeth, and then you go upstream for a cold drink, the water as fresh and clean as anything you've ever tasted on your minty-clean mouth.

You want to sit on the flat rocks naked awhile, but the bugs are out and you have to slap the sticky oils of repellent all over and get dressed and fill the water jugs and head back, but even so you're feeling pretty good.

Lianne cranks up the Coleman, and a little while later you have fresh hot coffee brewed with creek water and sit around your camp stools watching the small fire neither of you could resist even though the evening is so warm you can't sit anywhere close to it. Besides, the smoke will help keep away the bugs. And even the thrumming of the portable generator next door and the blare of their strung-up electric lights can't spoil your contentment as a fresh breeze comes down off the hillside sighing through the trees and the liquid constellations roll over your head, and the thump and twang of their radio across the way and the gunfire echoes of their forbidden firecrackers sounds like America to you and you can't complain, can't complain.

Next morning you wake up about seven, creaky and stiff as you always are when you sleep on the ground. The world is pleasant in spite of that—in the fresh day, a cut of blue sky visible out the top corner of the front flap, the morning sun making the side of the tent luminous, shadows of branches shifting magically about on that glowing screen. You put a hand on your wife's bare hip under the covers.

She shifts and grumbles, and that same magical sun is raising the temperature in the tent about a degree a minute, and you're about to split a bladder. You get up and do your business, brush your teeth and spit, start the Coleman for coffee. Lianne emerges, grabs a roll of toilet paper and the little tin shovel and disappears. About the time the water boils, she's back, alert and feeling better. You ask how her sinuses are, and she says fine, so it's a good beginning.

Breakfast is a complex business of shifting pans on the two-eyed stove, and the timing is tricky, and the sausage comes out so fried it's crunchy, but she likes it that way, and the coffee has cooled a little too much by the time everything else is ready, so you have to heat it back up. But only two of the hotcakes scorched, and you're amazed at how hungry you are.

And then at how stuffed you are.

By the time you get through scrubbing the pans and dishes and utensils in warm soapy water heated on the stove, and rinsing and drying and storing the food safe against coons, skunks, squirrels, possums, and flies, and moving the ice chest to make sure it stays in the shade, it's ten o'clock, and you're feeling old, fat, achy, and mean. Harried and hurried. As if the day were being wasted, as if you had to get somewhere, do something. As if the clock were ticking.

You always feel this way on camping trips. This sense of being behind, being late, of needing to get going, get through with all the busywork and get down to the real stuff.

It's hot already, and your hair feels dirty and tangled, even the hair you don't have any more, your ghost hair, as Lianne likes to tease. You want to change out of the day-old warm-ups you wore here and put back on to get up this morning, but you don't want to change into your nice clean hiking shorts until you wash the overnight crud off your body, and *that* means struggling back down the creek with a bunch of gear and your fresh clothes in a net bag you have to hold awkwardly high to keep out of the water, and drying and changing and bringing everything back. All the damn hassle, why can't you get to the *camping*?

Your problem is that you don't get it. This *is* camping, just like life is just living. Quit trying to organize everything, Charles.

She's perfectly happy to make her bath with Handi Wipes, stowing the used wipes in one of the many trash bags she's brought, each bag for different sorts of things, she's into sorting already, though recycling is years away. You can't help it, you just have to have a morning wash. By the time you get back, she's combed and geared up and bug-sprayed, cute in her shorts and tied-off t-shirt and hiking boots and straw hat and shades and bandanna, a canteen on her belt, and offering you the hunting knife she knows you like to carry on your belt because of the old Tarzan movies when you were a kid. She wants to explore the mining town, but you want to hike the creek down to the river, feeling like exercise and also hoping maybe to get her out of those cute shorts somewhere on a shady rock around a few bends. We can do the town when we get back, you say.

You don't get the love scene, but after an hour, and in spite of sweating your clothes through, and being scratched up by the branches of scrub oak and yaupon and mountain laurel, and catching an ankle knock or two, you've pushed on into so much ramble of bright creek, so much glitter of leaf and radial glisten of pine needle and ramification of branch and crooked ravine and rustle and hop and skitter off in the scruff, and here and there a call, a whistle, the high *har! har!* of a crow, and in the background the rattling talking perpetual belling of falling water, that you achieve no-mind, and all you think is what you see, and so you see as I do into the shifting light-and-shadow cat-eyed wilderness that is nothing, that is the world, that is your own vanishing being.

But even satori must have its comedown, and you two guys don't make it down to the river. You have a late lunch with your feet in the cooling creek munching handfuls of trail mix from a big Ziploc, pretending to fight over who gets the most or who's secretly sneaking all of the red and orange and yellow and green jewels of M & M's and leaving the dull raisins and peanuts for the other person, though you both know perfectly well there are five more fat perfect tight-sealed clear bags back at the camp, enough trail mix to feed the winner of the Kentucky Derby for a month.

You will always remember her sitting there with her boots beside her on the rock, the wool socks and liner socks hanging out like tongues to dry, her face young and clean in the shadowfall on stone on running water buckling at her smooth shins.

The shadows of ripples over her white feet on coppery mottled pebbles in eight inches of clear water: She laughs brightly, white teeth and brilliant eyes, and you will always remember seeing right through to how she would have been as a child if as a child she had been brought to a place like this by someone who loved her the way you do.

And you have a sense that one more horrible moment of her childhood has been canceled, particle and antiparticle, that if you can just see to it there are enough moments like this, eventually you can undo all of the bad moments, and she will be free and clear and happy at last, a sweet force loose in the universe.

Across the creek, in the shadows, a fox steps down to drink.

And then the kits, tumbling like puppies. Paw, snout, to the tumbling water, scooting back at the cold touch. The mother's head lifted, wary. A red fox, you guess, though you don't know about foxes.

The long fur is as gray as it is red, not the burnt sienna of cartoons. Now the mother drinks. Turns to nip at the kits attacking her tail. Drinks again. Lap, lap in the little pool at the edge of the creek. Glance up at the two of you, *I see you but I'm thirsty.* The narrow face, the hazel-green eyes. Long dark stripes from the corner of the eyes back along the throat, like the discoloration of tears blown back while running.

And Lianne beside you quivering like a fox, green eyes to green eyes.

This memory brought to you courtesy of your local Father Christmas. When I say the word, you will awaken. When you awaken—

The mother nips and nudges, most of the kits at least getting their snouts wet. *Momma, I'm thirsty,* later in the day. *Too bad. Next time maybe you'll drink.* The mother disappears, transforming herself to sun and shadow. The kits scramble after.

The sound of the creek rises through what you thought was silence, loud in your ears. "You don't see them in the woods," Lianne says. "They like more open land, more variety."

You wonder if that's true, or another of her opinions. "Well, we saw them in the woods *this* time," you say.

When you get to camp, you're both too tired to bother with the lost town, which is kind of what you were hoping would happen, Charles, because you didn't really want to do that today. It's five o'clock and the camp's abandoned, only the red Blazer sitting there, dusty and neglected, and you would hope that meant the station wagon people are gone, but their lawn chairs are still there so you know they're just out knocking around. Haden Walter never showed up last night, as far as you remember, so maybe he's coming tonight, had to work today and didn't feel like camping overnight.

Lianne may have conquered her paranoia generally, but not where ticks are concerned, so you have to come into the sauna-like tent and check her all over, which turns into really a pretty great time, at least if you like tasting salt and snuffling the odor of overheated unwashed but sun-blessed skin and sliding around on each other as if you were covered in Vaseline and surging together bare-assed in broad daylight and yelling at the top of your lungs without worrying about anybody hearing you. This is one of the times when she cries afterward, and you figure it's because of the fox. You're still lying there mingled, about to suffocate but too wrung out and proud of yourselves to move, when you hear a vehicle.

You peek out the tent and it's not the station wagon, but a blue pickup. Even as you watch, two more cars drive through. The rush is on, the weekend of the Fourth is about to begin.

You throw on shorts, it's time to bathe in the creek again. Both of you are feeling funky, feisty, and freewheeling, and you grab three Heilemans out of the chest to take along, feeling American as well as feisty now, beer on the Fourth, true patriots. The chest is low on ice, and she suggests when you finish washing up the two of you head for Yellville to get some more and some firecrackers and a watermelon and find a place where you can go square dancing. You don't like square dancing much, and for that matter she likes the idea of it more than the fact, though you don't think she knows that about herself. The first few icy swallows of the Heileman on your parched throat are the most delicious thing you've ever tasted, what a shock of pleasure, and combined with the wash of cold water over you sitting in a bathtub-sized hollow of the creek, well the whole weekend is worth it right there, and it's only Friday, my God! You let out a *wa-hoo* as good as any cowboy's, and she gives you a big grin.

But the third beer falls mostly to you, she's had one and doesn't want any more, and drinking it turns into a duty. It's warm, grassy-flavored, and full of foam. Alcohol is a depressant, you realize, feeling the evening collapse around you like a tent with the pole kicked out. You pick your way back, both of you fuzzy-eyed and tired, drunk but trying to hide it from each other, God knows why. Your strategy, Charles, is just to not mention square-dancing and hope for the best. You both admit being very very tired, laying it off on calorie depletion from all the exertion of the day. It takes a tremendous amount of energy just to be outside like this, and you really hadn't had but one meal today, the trail mix was just a snack. Never mind breakfast was three thousand calories all by itself and each handful of trail mix two or three hundred—you've agreed on your story and you're sticking to it.

"Do you think this ice will make it till the morning?" she says, looking in the chest, and you sigh with relief, knowing the threat of going dancing is past. You agree on beef stew Provençale, which is apparently beef stew with black olives and a lot of red wine. It'll have to simmer a couple of hours, so you have a couple of Hershey bars with almonds and some diet Coke to watch the sunset, and maybe there's something to the calorie theory after all, because you begin feeling better. The station wagon returns, and still no Walter Earl. The mother comes over; she's feeling like visiting.

"Hot day, huh?" fanning herself with a copy of *People* magazine, the cover sweatdimpled from her hands. "Want a beer?" Both of you hastily demur. "Yeah, really hot," she answers herself, sweating, standing beside Lianne at the Coleman. "You want some help with that? Gonna be even hotter tomorrow. Always is on the Fourth. Gonna be a real blazer."

The stew turns out rich and dark and delicious, and afterward you make yourselves a couple of martinis in the old silver shaker she had the foresight to bring along, almost the last of the ice, but the chest will stay cool enough till morning. The martinis work better than the beer did, giving you a happy floating sort of buzz, and you wish there were a way for her to lean back in your arms and watch the stars, but all you have are the camp stools. The fireflies are mad in the valleys, soft strobing here and there, as if they wanted to answer the stars but the best they could do was this mortal flickering, this green luminous mating cry.

You wake up in the middle of the night needing to pee. You like the feeling of standing out in the open totally naked and pissing into a bush. It isn't cool, but the air feels good. All the campers quiet, asleep, the little village of tents sprung up between sundown and suppertime. An owl hoots off in the trees, and you hoot back, gently. It answers, and you feel justified in your existence.

Next morning Lianne is all business: It's time to add supplies, and also time to bang around the countryside checking things out. As much as Lianne loves nature, she's not about to just sit there in the same place all four days. No sir, there's flea markets to find, country stores to visit, and the Folk Center where she knows a couple of the artists from previous visits. You beg off, pleading work, thinking to sit in the shade and do business. But mainly hating the idea of spending all day in the car, basically that you get bored after the first plank-floored store with a pot-bellied stove.

She's in a hurry to get rolling, brusque and trim in her shorts and t-shirt and boots; you'll have to make your own breakfast. You get her to stay for coffee, worried she's pissed that you don't want to go. She isn't pissed, she's just got things to do, and if you aren't capable of enjoying them, she'll do it on her own, she's always had to anyway, all her life. Coffee is an impatient concession to your tender feelings, and she refuses a second cup. It's eight o'clock and late enough already, and she fires up the big Blazer and rumbles on out of your day.

You can't get any work done, you were fooling yourself. Ninety-five even in the shade where you try to lean against a tree, and gnats in your face, and if you rest an arm you soak the paper with sweat so it will warp and stain. No ice, so no cold Cokes or juice. You could probably bum some beers off your neighbor, but then you would have to talk. You haven't bothered with breakfast, and now you're starved. You paw through the dry foods box. Lianne has also left the opened most-of-a-quart of 2 percent milk, because it would probably spoil anyway in the chest, if not fall over and leak and make her have to wash it all out. The milk is warm but ok, and you have it with a peanut butter sandwich, and several handfuls of trail mix for dessert.

You pack toilet paper and brush and soap and towels and toothbrush and more trail mix and a bag of Archway almond shortbreads, your favorite bought cookies, and a flask of gin, which you figure if you drop it in the creek for a while it might be cool enough to taste pretty good along about midafternoon. A trail runs along Rush Creek, and there are plenty of walkers on the trail, but you leave it to follow the creek itself, and finally you get far enough down to be alone. You find a nice spread of shaded flat stone just up the mouth of one of the creek's tributaries, and you strip down and bathe, and then lie out in the dappled shade in the hot air, sprawled on spread towels, and naked to God and heaven.

Dipping in the musical coolness from time to time, and sipping on the cool gin, you stay comfortable. The afternoon drones on, the glitter and hum of dragonfly wings over the wrinkling light of the water, the sway and creak of trees. You had been hoping for the wild eyes again, the stone high of your last expedition, but all you get is pleasantly sleepy. You fantasize about beautiful hikers who can't resist your sound-asleep REM hard-on and, waking up to find big bare titties in your face, soft with big pink protruding nipples, and the other one sucking down below, and fucking first one and then the other, a big blonde coed with blonde pubic hair, and a short wiry brunette with a tight little round ass but improbably round firm breasts, and nobody says a word.

You doze in the middle of your fantasies, wake up cramped and bitten on the hard stone. You jack off into the creek, watching the sperm coagulate and then, caught by the current, sweep off down a narrow chute toward the Buffalo, fish food. You feel a little depressed. It's the wrong prescription, but you have another swallow of gin.

At five o'clock or so you head back for the camp. Kids running around, two-quart bottles of diet soda, hot dogs being roasted on sticks over camp stoves, bright bags of chips and buns, open ice chests. God, the cold beer looks good, but you keep to yourself. The station wagon is gone, but the lawn chairs are still there. You realize Earl Haden never showed, and now you have an image of your neighbor as one of those young divorced or widowed country women carrying on courageously by herself. Limited, probably a Baptist, certainly a deep-dyed hick, but gutsy, the salt of the earth. You're proud of yourself for the depth of your empathy.

By seven, you're in a sorry mood, feeling deserted, and also worried about Lianne, she's been gone a long time. You have visions of the Blazer upside down in a ravine, or taken over by grimy *Deliverance*-style creeps who've thrown her mangled body out on the pine needles in the middle of the woods somewhere.

Ten minutes later, here she comes in a cloud of dust, and it's hop to, help her get all this stuff unloaded and get set up for the picnic. The picnic?

As you haul and open and sort and restack, she's over next door setting up their two card tables end-to-end and flipping one of her plastic table-cloths over the combination and setting out seven plastic-fork-and-paper-plate place settings. It seems she bumped into your neighbor at the grocery in Yellville, and neither of you had really planned a picnic, and they agreed you really needed to have a picnic on the Fourth, and so you're having one all together and it will be a lot of fun and will you get the star of the show on ice, the big watermelon in the back of the Blazer, three feet along its major axis and a good seventeen inches along its semiminors, and . . .

The neighbor comes wheeling up a few minutes later with her four kids, and it gets hectic after that, cartons of potato salad from the grocery store that need to be jazzed up with extra mayonnaise and mustard and chopped boiled eggs, and three big bags of ice to distribute in the ice chests, and what to put the melon in because it's too big for either ice chest without taking all the food out (you wind up putting it on a bed of ice in plastic wrap in a hollow of the ground), and get the chips and dip all opened and set out, and the assembly line started for the kids for diet soda, because they'll be asking for more all night long, and in between all this she's telling you how her day went and also talking a mile a minute to the neighbor lady, whose name seems to be Ruthie, and counseling kids with knee scrapes or assigning preparatory tasks to the wide-eyed teenage girl, whose name is Tiffanie and she wants to be an actress and she has clearly found out who Lianne is, you can tell by the way she follows and watches and obeys.

Lianne has been up to Yellville, and down to Harriet, and back up to Yellville. She's stopped at a dozen farmhouses, a couple of yard sales, a few antique shops. You have to admire all the great groceries she's bought for the evening, the really great bargains she found on the chicken franks and the cabbage (which in a few minutes you are to hack and shred and convert into slaw), and you have to admire her finds, the full spectrum of anodized aluminum drinking glasses, in top shape, not even scratched, and the box of wonderful worn old stereopticon prints, and the lacework antimacassars. When I say you have to, I mean you know you'd better.

And there's something about an old woman in an antique shop, but you're supposed to occupy the three boys while the women finish getting ready, and the boys want to set off firecrackers in the woods, and you say it might start a fire and compromise and lead them to the creek where they can fling their poppers down on the flat rocks, making a bang like the cap pistol you had thirty-one years ago, and the youngest one crying when he misses and hits the water. Their names are Blaine, eleven, Eric, nine, and David Wayne, six.

They're not impressed when you tell them you're a lawyer, it's one of those nothing occupations in which you do not use large powerful hand tools, fire weapons, tow trailers, or operate heavy machinery.

The picnic actually turns out to be a big success. You have several huge limp paper platefuls of slaw and potato salad and baked beans, and carbon-burnt franks never tasted better, and then the big cold chunks of red sweet watermelon, all of you sitting around dripping and spitting and having the old familiar discussion about whether it's better with or without salt, and whether you should eat it with a fork and knife, carving off slices, or burrow your way in with a twirled spoon, making those nice cones, or just jam it up against your face and chew.

Then, nine o'clock or so, you have the fireworks show, out in the gravel of the drive so as to be safe, the boys with their strings of Red Devils, making a tin can hop. Strictly no Roman candles or bottle rockets, but whirling dervishes—mad green spinners zipping across the gravel toward the cars so you have to run head them off—and the mandatory sparklers—tiny trees of fire in the night, underlighting faces—and Lianne lighting her favorites, the ladyfingers, and running back to safety from the crisp snappety-snap of their miniature explosions, and then lighting her other favorites, which she doesn't have to run from, which you call snakes and she calls worms—first a bright flare and then a crawling coil of carbon extruding itself as the flare hisses and sizzles.

Later that night, in the tent, she's back on the antique shops again, describing a whole street of them somewhere on the edge of Yellville, except they aren't really shops, but old houses. An old woman in one of the houses. Fine old sideboards, chiffoniers, a grand piano, end tables. No bargaining, sold as priced. No air-conditioning in the main part of the house, a well-built two-story stucco, oak-floored, pre–World War II. The woman a widow these last twenty years, in her early eighties, no pension to speak of, no family left. She was selling the items of her long marriage, living off the proceeds. Lianne had been terribly thirsty, and overheated from driving around in the hot sun all day, and the house must have been ninety or so in the outer rooms.

"She kept apologizing," Lianne mumbles. "I told her not to, but she kept apologizing."

The woman had given Lianne a glass of cold water and invited her back to the one room she could afford to air-condition. She lived in that bedroom all summer long, surrounded by photos of her husband, his brothers, herself as a girl, her parents. Two children, but one had died in the influenza, and the other, you couldn't make out what had happened to the other.

Lianne has become silent.

You imagine yourself losing all your money, forsaken, a ragged madman in a log cabin, scrabbling roots in these same woods. It could happen. Anything can happen.

Lianne, amazing Lianne, how she just walked into people's lives and saw them and absorbed their stories, how she simply saw people and knew them, who else would have spent the day knocking around and come back with a story like that?

The loneliness of that old woman. The courage of the forgotten. America.

"Ruthie's a brave woman," you say into the darkness. "Raising those kids with no father. Taking them camping like that."

"What are you talking about?" she says sleepily. "It's her sister's children. She's keeping them for the weekend."

So what else, Charles? Waking up Sunday morning, and she's ready to check out the mining town, no more putting it off. You like that sort of thing usually, as we've noted, but for some reason you're dreading this. You're tired of camping, that's it, ready to head back home. You've had all the nature you want, all the boredom and discomfort you can handle. Your impatience has that twitchy urgency of nerves coming back to life when your leg has fallen asleep.

She wants to get started in the cool of the day, and she's a little put out with you because it takes you a while to get ready. She threatens to crank up the Blazer and go without you, and you say, wait, wait, I'll be ready in a minute. As much as you don't want to go, that's the way marriage is, you sort of have to. Staying alone would be much worse. You don't want another day in camp alone.

You don't think you can stand exploring either, but you poke around on the weed-grown paths, peer in at the weathered-gray windowsills, read the informational signs. There's not really that much to see. Here was a company headquarters, there some company houses, that slope is tailings from the mine. Green, and stillness, and heat.

All the same, it's almost eleven when you've done the tour, and, since you skipped breakfast, time for brunch. The other campers are stirring, packing up, heading home with beer hangovers, sunburn, and ringing ears. Brunch is wine and three different cheeses (in spite of her allergies—she's doing good this week, she'll risk it). Some olives, Lianne's special deviled eggs left over from last night's picnic, chunks of Clemmie's homemade whole wheat bread. You want coffee to finish off, hot as it is. She doesn't want to make it. "How about I go into town and get some at a café," you say. "You want to come?" You hope she doesn't.

She doesn't. Today she's going to go back to the mine and set up her easel and do some painting. You can leave her some Cokes in the small ice chest, and she'll take a can of sardines and some crackers. You take her back and help her set up. "You sure this is ok?" you say, feeling guilty because you want to get away.

"What?" she says, already intent on her canvas. *And the guilt you feel now is infinitely worse—all that wasted time, all that lost chance for tenderness. Get with the program, Charles, grow up.*

It was just the two of you being ordinary, being your regular selves, no great heartwarming love story. That's the way it goes. It's all just camping, it's all just living. This is the most of any love, so come to terms with it.

You find coffee at the motel buffet in town. Everybody's getting out of church and coming in, this is how you do Sunday dinner nowadays, not at home but down at the communal buffet. Chicken-fried steak and chicken-fried shrimp and chicken-fried chicken and roast beef and gravy and mashed potatoes and corn and green beans and corn bread, and iced tea from a machine. A few salesmen on the 62 route dallying over their chocolate pie with high-piled meringue, the kind of meringue that bleeds a sweet drop when you cut it, the good stuff.

The food's ordinary but good, local cooks, they cook it the way they would cook it at home. The cooks and servers know all the customers, they all know each other, they're all locals.

After you leave, you entertain the notion of finding the old woman in the house full of antiques, but you know you don't really want to find her. You don't really want to think about her situation, have to face doing something about it or not doing something about it. You drive around for an hour or two. You find an open flea market. Most of the science fiction books are paperback, and not very good, but there are a few old Simaks, a reissue of Asimov's *Foundation* series, that monumentally wooden galactic-future saga, interesting for its key concept, psychohistory. The quantum mechanics of civilization. Individuals unpredictable as particles, but when there are enough, trillions at least, the behavior of the aggregate stochastically describable, so the course of empire can be predicted. Trantor, a stellar dark ages, the slow return of the light. Typical sf, grafting a medieval metaphor onto technological razzmatazz. The mule, Hari Seldon, sure.

A fair 1951 Heinlein triple volume—*The Puppet Masters*, which would make a great movie, wonder why no one's ever done it, especially now that you can show all the nudity, and no expensive special effects needed. *Magic Incorporated* and *Waldo*. Cheap tan hardboards, blank except for the titles, the pages yellowed. Still using up war inventory, probably. You've got all the novelettes in better editions. But this one's worth having anyway, you think. Not the history *in* books, but the history *of* books, the way they speak mutely of other days, other times. Old, lost, out of fashion, an object for the hands. That other hands have held.

Or is it just that you're visited by a ghost of an echo of the thrill you used to feel, coming across a longed-for treasure as a kid, the door to distant worlds about to swing open?

You're getting your standing-around-in-dusty-old-shops headache, and it's late. Lianne can perfectly well hike back to the camp, but what about the easel and all her other gear? You buy a couple of new paperbacks for the sake of the lovely cover art. Maybe one will be catchy enough to get you through this last long boring night.

Lianne is still painting when you arrive. She answers impatiently when you ask how it's going. As if you were responsible for the hastiness of the sun, the hurried fading of her day. She has a headache, too, squinting so hard all afternoon, and standing around in the glare and heat, and she shouldn't have had all that wine and cheese, and has she eaten since you left? No, of course not, look at the unopened sardines, the full bag of trail mix. Pisses you off when she ignores her own needs and then takes it out on you. Goddammit, woman, *eat* when you need to eat.

"It's seven-fifteen," you say. You talk her into coming back to camp.

While you start some dried vegetables simmering for stew, she leans the two pictures against trees, walks back and forth rubbing her forehead and studying them. A diptych, she says. "I call it *In Time Out.*"

You think that's a pretty awful title. "I don't get it," you say.

You do now, don't you?

"They really stink," she says.

One canvas is inside one of the company houses, or a house like one of the company houses, the weathered lathing showing through peeling wallpaper, the dry dusty light falling across the rough unpainted floor. Through a window in the far wall, children are playing in a bright green yard, a wagon is going by. The other is outside, a view like the one they had this morning, weedy overgrown roughness, briers consuming a tumbledown shack. Except through this window, inside the shack, a happy family is sitting down to supper. The wallpaper is fresh, trails of crisp little roses, and their clothes are old-fashioned but look new and clean.

"They're ok," you say. "Really. Some good brushwork in there, in places. Quit worrying and get some food in you. Have a candy bar or something."

"No they aren't," she says. Studying. "I did ok with the foreground. It's the people that aren't working. No, not the people. The whole stuff through the windows."

It was true. The people were flat and awkwardly posed, their faces crudely overbrushed. There was something wrong in the perspective too.

"I see," you say. She had done the inside one inside and the outside one outside. So she had had models for the foreground in each picture. The light and distance, the shading, the detail were good. "You got the real stuff pretty good. It's the stuff you made up that's off."

"It's the framing," she says, ignoring you. "You have to get the light just right if you're going to pull off a framing effect like that."

You're proud of your perception, and so you go too far. "You just have trouble painting your imagination," you say. "But that's what an artist has to do. Probably on some level you're still feeling like you don't have any right to be an artist."

"I did ok with the cemetery painting, didn't I? I don't need you lecturing me."

"You want me to get you out a Hershey's?" you say. "While we're waiting for the stew?"

That's all for that evening. Oh, a late walk through the camp, almost empty again, Ruthie gone with her sister's kids, maybe a little air will help Lianne's head. But she won't go to the creek with you to listen to night water. It's too damn hot to build a fire to stare into. The stew is finally done, canned beef stirred in with the vegetables, bubbling for a couple of hours. You eat it glumly, suck down a couple of Heilemans. You wash up with Handi Wipes before going to sleep, but instantly feel gummy, sweaty, dusty again. Scratched up and itchy from twig scrapes and bug bites you don't remember getting. A little headachy yourself.

Reading in the tent is a miserable affair, too stuffy and even the few ergs shed by the bulb of the battery lamp a hot close presence, and the best of the two paperbacks an utterly predictable mind-control-by-the-machines-of-the-authority-and-one-lonely-shirtless-rebel-leading-the-way-into-truth number, guerrilla messiah. Camping is so much fun.

Middle of the night you wake up to pee. The cool air of the hills is rushing down into the warm valleys, a huge restless presence, sighing and stirring. You feel momentarily cleansed, lonely and content at the same time.

Monday, blessed Monday finally dawns. But first, before you go, the protracted tedium of packing up. The tent has to be folded exactly, all the air pressed out. Each box put back where it was on the way here. The stove, the lanterns, wiped clean. You go down to the creek for one last bath, and you feel almost decent finally, starting a cold beer as you settle in (she's driving), heading home. But she stops at the mining town, gets out of the car.

"What are you doing?" you say.

"There's a fossil fall up under the hill over here," she says. "I saw it yesterday, but I didn't have time to check it out."

"For crying out loud, it's noon already! Can't we just go *home*?"

She does that maddening no-answer bit. *My actions will answer you.* You finish your beer, get out, sweating to the hairline. Might as well go join her. Rummage around in the jammed back of the Blazer, work another beer out of the ice chest.

She's squatting leaning into the hillside, picking through a rubble of white stone. The sun beats down, clumps of bitterweed in the rubble. You find some pretty good examples, mostly shells you can't identify, tubular prints you have learned are the remains of pithy plants. You try for a sense of old time, the awesome passage of the geological ages, but no good. The beer ought to help, but it doesn't, the sun is just too damned oppressive. Too damned *now.* Now the sun. The sun now. Now. The beer and the now make you dizzy, almost nauseous. Now she sends you back to the Blazer for plastic bags.

You're a rock collector too, but not now. Neither of you collects in any tutored, formal sense. You just like to hold on to well-shaped rocks you find in the creek. You yourself are not too keen on fossils, though, not unless they're really dramatic, and these now are all the same. Shells, the plant tubes. White crumbly rocks. Heat. Now.

"What do you want with that?" you say now.

"See?" She hands you a flat-sided chunk, a section like a slice of jelly roll. An igneous core, swirled hard colors, but crusted around with the white limestone. What processes could have made this? you wonder now. Drops of molten stone sizzling into a limestone layer, cooling? But that was a long time ago. It's nothing rare or valuable now.

"It's a window rock," she says.

"What? What do you mean?"

"Look."

She turns it over in your hands to show you the other side. Her finger traces a pattern. In the dark greenish caramel of the stone there are successive fading waves of a lighter, almost autumnal ocher. "See, it's like the Ozarks. Like the mountains in fall, fading off into the distance." She points at a cloudiness in the coloration. "There's even fog on the hills."

It clicks for a moment, and you can see it now, ranges of rounded umber in a misty prospect under the caramel-green sky. It vanishes. You're holding a rock in your dusty sweaty hand, a jumbled fragment, statistical wreckage now of the disordered colliding rubble that made a star and planets and random parts of the planets heave and collide and lift, erode and fall in stupid tumbles of minor stone in which you're squatting sick and dizzy right now.

"Can we go now? This sun is really getting to me."

"Don't you get it? It's a rock out of the hills. And it has the hills *in* it."

"It's just an accident. They're only there because you see them there." If you wanted hills, you could have a painting, for crying out loud. A painting of real hills.

"That's the whole point, Charles." Curt now, you're an asshole again. "I like it because of what I see in it. Because of what it lets me see in it."

"So keep it. But I'm ready to go now. I'd really like to get home before sunset."

Which means she picks a half-dozen more rocks while you go sit in the shade, the hot shade, sweating. Finally it isn't now any more, she's coming back to the car. More Handi Wipes, to clean the sweat from her arms and legs, the black moist dirt from her sweaty hands. Another beer. *She* even wants one. Get in, crank up, you're moving, the air is on. Hallelujah, thank God, relief at last. A sigh, a big cold swallow.

What you don't know is how she's going to want to stop at every fruit stand, junkyard, and flea market all the way back home, so that what should be a three-and-a-half-hour trip will take almost six hours. What you don't know, though you should, though you've known her long enough and should understand her that well by now, is how she loves all this. She may have seemed angry or haunted or driven from time to time, she may have been uncomfortable with the heat or because of her allergies, or she may have been in actual pain, but she loved all this. The lives, the living, the fireworks, the river, the rocks, the trees, the camping out. Even your querulous company, your childish whining could not deter her. It rolls off her like water off a duck's back, it's all just the limestone scruff around the gorgeous core of her happiness.

She's always been under attack, all her life she's had to seize her fierce unspoken pleasure in spite of the annoyance and haze and outright threat of the very world that offers the pleasure. It is normal to her that life should be this way, honey out of the rock, good out of the bad. It is so natural that she has never thought to say it aloud to you.

What you don't understand is how happy she is. What you don't understand, sitting in the Blazer with the motor running to keep the air cool, cussing the delay as she pushes through the metal door into yet another tin-walled roadside shop, is that she has had a wonderful time on this trip and doesn't want it all to end just quite yet.

29

CHRISTMAS
IN JULY

They must have gotten in (finally) at seven o'clock or so. He remembers it stayed light for at least another hour and a half, while they unloaded.

Nothing ever felt so good as the shower that evening, the hot and then cold water sluicing away the dust and smoke and grit, the scuzzy grime of the long trip back. Somehow water moving over the skin electrifies, vitalizes. He felt his flickering spirit begin to steady and glow. And then Lianne walked in with a big tumbler of Wild Turkey on the rocks, and he took a harsh sweet swallow, and it was just the thing. Drinking beer all day long, he had never gotten drunk, only had felt low and dull. But it was the sort of thing that was worse if you just bailed out. It would not do any good to quit drinking. You would wake up aching in every joint anyway, heavy and logy, a knife in your temple, almost suicidally depressed though you were not a suicidal person. What you needed was a good way through, a way to take the alcohol and transform it.

And now the whiskey caught, and catalyzed the action of his veins. And now he knew, wrapped warm in a fluffy robe in the luxurious cold air of his home, that all would be well. And it was good to sit and sip the icy bourbon and watch her shower through the glass of the door while steam rolled over the top and into the room. Through the clouded glass, arching forward, lifting one knee out and away and slapping barrels of water against her crotch. Lifting one elbow at a time to shave her underarms. Scrubbing her foaming hair with her fingers; she wouldn't use a brush, it damaged the hairs. Now rinsing, her face lifted into the spray. And he could see her face somehow, as if his awareness could float, distributed over time and space, that was one of the things marriage did to you, set you loose in the other person's time line: He saw the roundness of her closed eyes, veined film drawn over dreaming stones, the water slipping in sheets over her smooth features.

Then she was out, buffing herself with the towel, whipping it over her body like a shoe-shine man working on a shoe. Now powering away at that crotch again, gonna get every last drop out of that fur. "Hey," he said, and she looked up. "Can I sleep with that towel?"

She threw it at him, and folded into her robe. Then she leaned over the basin to the mirror, rubbing fresh lotion in, brushing her wet hair back. Then he stood, and took her shoulders, and turned her around. Then she let him make her robe fall open, so that he saw the length of her, the radiating flush of her shower-heated skin, the flex in her flattened belly, the blaze in her ruffled pubic hair.

"You've lost weight," he said.

Of course she'd lost weight. She'd hardly eaten, all that food they took, Clemmie below them even now fitting it back into fridge and cabinet and freezer.

Then, leaning back against the basin, she looked into his face. The charcoal-ringed green irises. The whipped-back weather lines at the corners of her eyes. The hollows under her high round cheeks, the plump lips parted over white teeth. Lips that were pink and scrubbed and bare, plush with the minute vertical striations of a filling parachute. A bit of crepe under the strong uplifted jaw: How could any woman be more desirable?

Then she said, "Do you mean it, or are you just practicing?"

"We'll have to shower again," he said.

"Tough," she said.

Then he put his finger into her, the right forefinger, probing, working the steamy clinging labia apart, burrowing in, invisible messages from under the burning bush, running along the carpal nerve and up the arm and through the shoulder and into the spine and down, and his cock lifting under his robe as he gets the message, pattern on pattern, fingerprint to the snug ribbed vaginal wall, and then a flush of fluid, warm and silky as fresh egg white, a flow of heated oils.

Then she opened his robe and pulled him against her.

It was astonishing how clearly he could feel her, the warm length of bone and belly and breast, and the slender arms sliding around his rib cage inside his robe. And was this the point of camping after all, this freshening of knowledge? The strenuous mutual endeavor, so blind and separate and tedious in the doing, so that afterward, relaxing, cleansed, they were able to step into each other like joining cones of light, being to being, immediate?

As though all the branching tree of his nerves could see, and could see in all ranges, he knew the layers and shells of her being, the long bones sliding under the sheathing of the muscles of her thighs, the new cells brewing in the marrow of those bones, the lithe injection of lymph and hormone along the channels of back and breast and brain, jet after jet of chemical widening to mood; he could feel the manifold inflation of her breathing, the seethe of the molecules crossing permeable membranes only to catch in the pumped surge and be driven up to the dark mysterious cortex, there to feed somewhere, somehow past reckoning, that whirl, ghost, center, that shade, epiphenomenon, that insubstantial and yet certain Her.

Anyhow that's how he remembers it.

Anyhow that's how I'm telling it.

"Shit, it's been two months since I had me a woman," Ferrin said. He was lying. It had been more than five. "*You* aint no company," he complained.

It was sunset. They were at a rest stop along Highway 65, north of Lake Village and below Pine Bluff, heading home. Ferrin was watching a mother and daughter heading to the restroom, both in shorts, both blonde, the same build. But the mother was damn near forty and had a face that would stop a clock, and the daughter was pretty. Get em while they're young.

Just a few miles up the road was the takeoff to Cummins, the prison farm. Ferrin got the cold shivers whenever he drove by the farm, feeling visible from miles away, as if he were a red dot blinking on their radar and they would come out and nail him. So he had stopped to empty his bladder—he hated being nervous with a full bladder—and to fortify himself with some smokes and a can or two of Pearl Light. Rubert was sitting slumped over on the bench of a picnic table, his head down on his arms. He looked up sideways at Ferrin but didn't bother to answer. He had lost fifteen pounds in Florida, and he couldn't quit feeling tired.

Along about last Thursday, along about the time Charles and Lianne had been heading for Rush, Ferrin had gotten impatient at not hearing anything. He'd been buying every paper he could every day for ten days, and listening to the news on the hour. No famous boom-boom in Arkansas. What gives? You can't hush up something like that.

He had called the contact, collect long-distance, and gotten no answer. He had let it ring twenty times, and the operator had gotten snotty, but he wasn't taking any crap. "Let it ring," he had said. But nobody had answered, and nobody had answered the next day, when there was nothing in the papers either. *Anything* could be going on and he wouldn't know. Probably, he had said to Rubert, they had hushed it up. The contact had powerful contacts, and probably they had hushed it all up and probably the son-of-a-bitching contact was trying to slide out from under paying them.

Then Saturday afternoon, the afternoon of the Fourth, working into his second six-pack, he had gotten brilliant and called the Morrison house. He couldn't call *them* collect, but he could charge it to the room and skip on the room if he wanted to. The brilliant thing about the idea was you could tell by who answered and how they sounded what had happened. Like if a cop answered, in charge of the investigation—ha, wouldn't that be a hoot? He had imagined himself taunting the cop, safe, long-distance, untrackable, because they couldn't get a trace up that fast.

The cook had picked it up on the third ring. He had recognized her voice, the stupid old twat. He had felt like teasing her: *Ladybug, Ladybug, fly away home.* But all he had said, talking through a handkerchief and pitching his voice low, was "Hello."

"Who is this?" the cook had said.

"This is Larry from Dallas," Ferrin had said, mugging in Rubert's direction. "Let me talk to the boss."

"You can't talk to him," she had said impatiently. "You ought to know that."

This was *great.* He had gotten *both* of them. Put the squeeze on, have a little fun. He had made his voice worried, insistent.

"I have to talk to him right away. It's about that case we working on."

"Well, Larry from Dallas, you must not have been in touch lately."

He hadn't liked her tone of voice. The boss dead and the help getting uppity. "You hear me when I'm talking? This is an emergency. I don't get hold of him right away, it's your ass."

"So drive up to Rush and get hold of him, then."

Rush? Was that a cemetery? Was she smarting off again, go talk to his grave? "I been out of the office, lady. What the hell are you saying?"

"They went camping. Up on the Buffalo River. If you want him, you can go out in the backwoods and find him. And listen, Larry, I don't care how important you think you are. I'm not a slave, and I don't threaten. Learn some manners before you call here again." And she had slammed the phone down in his ear.

He had stood thunderstruck, too surprised even to cuss.

"She recognize your voice?" Rubert had said.

"Of course not," Ferrin had said. "You heard me disguise it."

"Yeah, you a master of disguise. What's wrong with you, then?"

Ferrin had set the phone on the hook. It had taken him a minute to figure things out. "Where's my cigarettes?" he had said then, laughing.

"I aint keeping track a your fucking smokes. And I wish you wouldn't do it in closed quarters like this."

"Where'm I suppose to, then? My room too, aint it? It's my idea made the money to pay for it." Ferrin had found his pack and fired up. Things were even better than they'd hoped, he had explained. The bitch and her husband had drove off into the woods and blowed themselves up somewhere. That was why they hadn't heard, nobody found the bodies yet. What was left of the bodies. Might never find em. It was funny as hell.

Rubert had had a coughing fit. "I thought it was sposed to go off the next time she start the car," he had said when he got his breath back.

"*Yes*, dummy, it went off next time she cranked it. *After* the eleven hours. And what do you think they was doing in that eleven hours?" He had waited, but Rubert hadn't reacted.

"You don't appreciate nothing, do you? You don't appreciate one thing I do for you. Driving into the woods!" he had summed triumphantly. "They were driving into the woods during that eleven hours. Why you think she was in such a hurry, had to have it that very morning?"

"If you say so," Rubert had said.

"No point talking to you," Ferrin had said. "I feel like celebrating. Come on, let's go find some action. It's the fucking Fourth a July, and we aint done nothing but sit around all day."

"You go on," Rubert had said. "I'm going to bed early."

So Ferrin had gone drinking alone that night, although he felt unsafe without the big man there at his side. But he had to prove his point. He had come in a little after midnight, walked down the boardwalk to piss on the sand. Think of somebody sitting in it tomorrow. Standing at the edge of the tide, he had let fly. High in the west, a steady bright star. Sirius, though he couldn't have named it. Four days short of new moon, so the moon had set before the sun, so there had been a lot of stars. Somehow the stars had made him think of all the distance between him and Arkansas. And the contact, way up there, untouchable, running off with their money. He had felt shaky, exposed. Getting that money was the only possible antidote.

A crab had scuttled by, making him jump and pee one leg of his pants. Alerted, his eyes had adjusted, and he had seen them, all over the beach: a formication of crabs, scooting, clambering, digging. In the daytime he had come across their pale fragments—blind empty torsos, hollow sets of claws—but he had never thought what an industry such litter implied.

"Jesus," he had said, his skin crawling. "Piss on you," he had shouted at the rolling, glimmering water. "Piss on you and piss on this place! You can't scare me! Piss on you!"

Sunday night they had pulled up and left. They had waked up in the middle of the afternoon—Rubert must have slept fourteen hours—but had waited till night so they could skip without being noticed. They had still had enough cash to pay, it was just a matter of principle.

"Yeah, I got to get me a goddamn woman," Ferrin said now, looking off to the north, toward Little Rock. They would get in the car in a minute and drive on in. And when would it be that he realized Lianne was still alive? Still alive and living in Little Rock. Would it be when he saw her face in the special three-minute *Hope Lines* spot KROK ran, the one with the skinny little smart-aleck redhead? Would he sit there in shock, Rubert asleep on the bed, and then, in a wave of relief, say to himself, *Of course, of course, it's a tape, they don't know yet, they hadn't found them yet*—and then the cut to the live interview at the Morrison home?

Who cares, you know? He's done his worst. He's a nobody, he doesn't count. Surprise, Ferrin, you don't exist. I am the man with the knife, just as you always suspected.

The redhead was Katie McFee, a tall fourteen, disturbingly skeletal. She needed a heart-and-lungs transplant, or she wouldn't make fifteen. The deterioration of her cardiopulmonary system had left her weak and translucently pale. Her hair was a frizzy cloud. Her eyes were almost as rusty as her hair and seemed huge in her narrow, blood-starved face. She favored a pale violet lipstick. Her upper arms were unusually long. She kept her slender forearms curled up and forward, her large hands drooping like the striking hooks of a praying mantis.

With all of that, she was beautiful, perhaps because of her obvious vulnerability, the frailness of her voice, the mistiness of her enervated gaze.

They weren't doing posters, but she was basically the poster child for the Christmas in July shindig. Her hometown, Hawthorne, had started a Katie McFee Fund and had raised $5,820 so far. The tv spot was to promote the event as well as *Hope Lines* generally, and also to raise more money for the Katie McFee Fund. They had held a contest, asked a bunch of the *Hope Lines* kids what they wanted for Christmas in July, the gifts to be presented during the ceremonies—those gifts that could be presented. Quite a number of the kids had written answers like *If somebody dies, to have their liver*, or *A cure for leukemia*, or *My hair back*, or *I wish I had a new leg so I wouldn't always have to ski slalom the rest of my life.*

Katie was old for a poster child, but she was the most photogenic. Also, what she had written was: *I would give anything to be just around Miss Lianne Morrison a while, because she is so beautiful. I have admire her long as I remember. To be in her house, because it is my favorite ambition*

when I get my heart-and-lungs to grow up like her a famous media person-
ality. Say the news. And my parents could get some sleep, because either
their here all the time or when I'm home their up all night listening if I'm
breathing, but I imagin she has pretty good medical help.

Katie was sick, but nobody ever said she was dumb.

In the spot, she was shown at home with Lianne. The two of them at
the mirror (trading makeup secrets, presumably). Walking (slowly) in the
garden. Katie laughing (weakly) as the camera spun to convey her joy in
the leaf-dazzle light. The good old reliable ground-to-sun shot, striding
silhouettes creating poles of flare in the lens. Lianne and Katie spending
the afternoon shopping, bopping around town in the Blazer, back in time
for supper.

Conclude with Lianne in the library (serious shot), won't you please
help these children? Tickets available with the following merchants.

They filmed the spot on Wednesday after Charles and Lianne got back
from camping, edited furiously, and began running it the next week. Tuesday before they filmed, Lianne had given Charles a look across the supper
table and had said, "I suppose it's out of the question for you to be in the
spot with me?"

"I' wha, a Thanta thoo?" he had said, his mouth full of Clemmie's
hot scalloped potatoes. He had already been feeling a little irked about the
way the Christmas in July preparations were taking over his domestic life.
He had perhaps been expecting Monday night's magnificent copulation to
be a presage to perpetual orgy, the lubricious sequelae of their marriage.
He could read the markets, but he was no better than a dog at foreseeing
the rhythms and the changes of ordinary life. Whatever was was all there
would be.

She hadn't told him yet about Katie.

"Well, yes, as a matter of fact," she had said, then laughed at his
expression, which actually owed more to the temperature of the potatoes
than to astonishment. "We'll just go ahead with Bill then. He's more like
an elf, but he's already got the beard, if he'll let them spray it. I just thought
we could be together, since I'm going to be so busy."

He had gulped half a glass of water to cool his tongue. "What are you,
Mrs. Santa?"

"I'm not anybody. I'm just me."

Bill Worthen would make a diminutive Santa, all right. But he was
merry enough, his gleaming inquisitive eyes perpetually busy and an ironic
half-smile perpetually glimmering on his face, as if he were always just
about to commit some mischief, and as she said, he already had the beard.
Charles had had an image of Kathy gleefully helping to spray it white. And
Bill and Kathy had been solid contributors to *Hope Lines* over the years.

They had a little cast party Saturday after the editing was finished, and that was the most Charles had seen of Lianne all week, and was almost the most he would see of her for the next couple of weeks. He would like to remember more nights like that Monday night homecoming, but there *weren't* more nights like that Monday night homecoming. What's to remember? He was in the office, she was buzzing around town, they met at home for supper for maybe an hour, which she would spend busily filling him in on her day, talking more than she ate. By sundown, she was off again, things to do, things to do. Then the next week, Katie was in the house all week, and then the *next* week, well, we'll get to that.

Let's be fair, though, Charles. You were pretty busy too. Dale Bumpers and David Pryor had asked for a federal override of the Arkansas usury law. As a fellow (sh!) liberal (sh! sh! I didn't really say it) Democrat who might be expected to have governmental ambitions someday, you were expected to throw your weight behind theirs.

You for sure thought the usury law was stupid, and you were absolutely for sure in favor of the federal override. But it was one of those simplistic emotional issues for most of the citizens: *Damn banks just want to gouge us for more money.* They couldn't see the larger economic picture, how money went where it got the best return, and if this state was ever going to quit being forty-ninth and fiftieth—

Unfortunately, one of those citizens who saw it in what you thought of as that simplistic emotional way was Lianne. Every time the two of you talked about the usury law, you argued.

Let's just have a better economy with our own money, then.

That's nuts, that's not the way it works. That's like saying let's pay ourselves more for working our own garden, it doesn't mean anything.

My granddaddy used to make granddaddy money.

What?

If I was good. If I hoed all the way to the end of the row on all the rows. He would cut paper out and draw pictures on it and make granddaddy money. I could cash it in for cookies or to get out of a whipping or stay up till ten o'clock and watch tv.

It was a tricky issue, just when things were going great between you. So you were spending a lot of energy trying to figure how to convince the senators you were helping, and at the same time not get in dutch with the main squeeze, right? And maybe you withdrew from *her* just a little, the better to conceal your traitor's heart? Hey, it's typical of the monkeys.

And there was a lot of other stuff happening too. Judge Overton had set the date for the creation science suit—October 26, just three and a half months off, and you and Greg with a lot still left to do. Laugh was showing signs of wanting in on the action, was in fact doing a lot of Greg's research, and you were pretty sure he was going to ask to appear with Greg in federal court, but you didn't think he was ready yet, his image hadn't been sufficiently rehabilitated.

There was another bothersome little situation with Laugh, whether to invite him to the Christmas in July. He loved to show up in his tux, and he had been hinting around, asking how the preparations were coming. You yourself were hoping to get *out* of going, you hated these dos of hers, so you'd been very quiet on the subject with Lianne, and you told him you didn't really know, you'd been too busy to pay attention. But you could tell it was a test in his mind, were you really going to let him back in or not, or just use him and let him go?

You weren't going to let him go, you needed him, because the applicant you had postponed in order to go camping early, one Lorenzo Tyrell of Lawton, Oklahoma, had turned out to be a dead loss, a twitchy myopic weed of a man with a weak chin, a less-than-successful mustache, and a belligerent attitude. He was Duke law and claimed a former Chicago practice, but his economic ideas were right out of the nineteenth century, he chewed tobacco and spit in a Styrofoam cup while the two of you talked, he thought Act 590 was the best thing to come along in years, and he implied that you were a gutless wonder if you didn't hire him in spite of the fact that just looking at him pissed you off and you were against everything he stood for. The pity of it was, he was the best applicant you'd seen since the toga party. You'd had plenty of them, but one way or another, they all seemed to be freaks. Maybe they thought you'd throw some more orgies and they could get in on them. It was scary what got licensed to practice law nowadays.

As it happened, Lianne got you off the hook with Laugh by sending him, on her own, an invitation. Which he immediately accepted, firing back two hundred dollars that same day. (He was taking a date, he didn't know who just yet, but he was definitely taking one.)

You met with Bill McArthur, just once, just over lunch. He said he wanted your professional reaction to his situation with his client, Lee Orsini. Strictly confidential; you should bill him so there would be no question of impropriety.

Orsini's grand jury was in session, trying to figure whether to charge her with the handgun murder of her husband back in March. The whole city was buzzing. Lee insisted she had once seen her husband meeting with a man in an unmarked patrol car, that he had brought home large sums of unexplained cash, and that after his death she had surprised an intruder who was holding a Baggie of white powder. In spite of these and other allegations, nobody had been able to connect Ron with the drug trade, so it was hard to see who but her would have wanted to kill him.

It was a cold murder, brains blown out while he slept in his own bed. Lee had gotten up, taken the daughter to school. Claimed she thought Ron already left the house. They slept in separate bedrooms, and she hadn't heard anything. They had run trace-metal tests and found some marks on the tips of the fingers of her right hand, but nothing sufficient to prove she'd recently fired a gun. A private detective named Fred Myers had come forward. He said she'd called him seven weeks before the murder, claiming their phone was tapped.

She had apparently been under the impression that they could borrow two hundred thousand on their house, though it was only worth a hundred, no equity, and they were badly in arrears at that. Hell, they were in arrears on their furniture. Ron Orsini had carried a hundred thousand in credit life insurance, which would have paid off the house, except that he had let the payments lapse. Lee might or might not have known the insurance was no longer in force.

There had been some problems with lie detector tests, and the private investigator McArthur had hired, Jim Lester, "didn't like the client." You knew Lester. He was a rough-edged cop with graying hair and the build of a power lifter, currently on medical leave from the state police. You didn't like *him*—he would gain the confidence of suspects, become their best buddy, pray with them, weep with them, and then betray them—but his instincts were accurate.

McArthur didn't say so, but you thought he wanted to sever his relation with the client. And yet felt honor bound to carry through at least till the grand jury brought a finding? He was disturbed, he said, by some facets of her character. Translation, he thought she was guilty. He thought maybe she was carrying on with a high-ranking police official, which would really look ugly if it came out. You thought of Tina, the cases you'd had to back out of, and didn't know what to say to him. You wondered if there was something going on between the attorney and his client, if he was more bothered by the chance of her guilt or the likelihood of her dalliance with somebody else, somebody you mistakenly took to be Sonny Raymond.

It was strange to be talking to McArthur; he wasn't the sort who came looking for advice. Was he job hunting? Didn't seem likely. You respected him, he had horsepower, but he was pretty much a loner, and besides, he did criminal law and you mostly didn't, and besides besides, if he came down in anybody's camp, it would be with somebody like Sheffield Nelson. It was all very interesting, the feeling that you had a direct line to a mystery obsessing the whole state.

It was also strangely chilling. Listening to McArthur, you concealed a *frisson*. He was probably a good man, and none of it had anything to do with you, but you had a sense nevertheless of multiple, spooky, occluded motives, of an uncontainable darkness, one that might leak through all the normal personal barriers and stain your entire life at the merest contact. You wanted far away from that story, whatever that story was. He paid, and you left. You never mentioned the lunch to anyone, though several people had seen you together.

Aside from all that business, you had your own cases to work.

There was the hippie with the crystal mine who was suing the feds for seizing his land—they said it was national forest, he said it wasn't. This was one Lianne really wanted you to win, since part of your fee was to be a brace of big perfect double-pointed crystals. Neither she nor you thought the crystals had magic powers, though. They were just gorgeous objects.

Then there was the fired AP & L employee who had gone back down to the shop, taken one of the trucks, and rammed it into a substation, doing $35,000 worth of damage. He'd lost both legs below the knees in the crash, and he was suing the company for half a million, claiming negligence because the shop foreman had let him take the truck out in that state of mind.

There were a couple of other cases pending, and you really wanted to get them all settled before September, so you'd have a full month to concentrate on the challenge to Act 590.

That's what was going down
in Little Rock town,
in 1981, son,
and you were having fun,
weren't you, Chucky-boy? Oh yes, you were.

You were surly, Curly, at the party, Artie, but you had no complaint coming if Lianne, man, was hard to get to. What was *really* going on, what was really griping your chaps and chafing your grits, was how happy and busy *she* was. You were used to the role you thought you hated, encouraging daddy to the sad little girl. Made you feel important, and now you were being demoted. You had lost the moral advantage, you were no longer the big bad ape-man: *Wait here, hon, I'll be back. It's a jungle out there.*

So you were hairy, Larry, at the frolic, Alec. When Lianne was *on,* she was on like a Tiffany lamp. Throws light on what's around it, but you can't help spending more time looking at the source than the subject. Made you jealous, Ellis, but nobody notice, Otis.

Tucker and Dee-Dee were at the party, Bill and Kathy, the cast and crew naturally, Greg and Alison. Bill Pumphrey, natty in blue chambray, madras tie, and twill slacks. Katie, in her not-really-always necessary wheelchair and flanked by her more-and-more-frequently-referred-to oxygen bottles: in her own opinion the co-star of the whole show.

Lianne herself had gone to get the girl, zooming up into the drive just at a quarter past seven to join the whoop-de-doo, already in progress, Clemmie carrying trays around and swapping stories with the guests. Lianne had brought Katie's shift nurse as well, now a little bewildered, standing to one side sipping the best champagne she would ever have in her life while the various revelers took turns wheeling the invalid on tours of the house and grounds.

Katie's parents were not there. "I think they would be uncomfortable in this kind of a gathering," the girl had said. "They just aren't used to the social whirl."

By now you knew you were going to share your home all the next week with the failing teenager. So that may have been why Lianne's glow didn't warm you, why you saw your friends in, so to speak, such an unflattering light:

Tucker quizzing the nurse, Lianne, Katie herself, anyone who might be presumed to have some knowledge of the girl's condition. Tucker made his own diagnosis, he railed against incompetence in the medical profession. Who was doing her surgery? What, *him*? He was a total quack, everybody knew that. I wouldn't let him cut my toenails with a long-handled clipper.

Dee-Dee confiding in you: "She's a skank, aint she?" The two of you were on the portico, watching Tucker spin Katie up and down the driveway, pushing her fast like a kid giving another kid a ride in a wagon. Katie was throwing her head back, tossing her hair and laughing, the doomed child having a very cinematic good time.

"Skank?" you said, but the word was self-explanatory. You saw, with a flicker of surprise, that Dee-Dee was jealous. Privately you concurred, the girl was a skank, and probably also a twit, but how could you be jealous of somebody that sick?

Lianne taking Bill and Kathy and Tucker and Dee-Dee upstairs to show them her paintings. She had stored them temporarily in your office, though they made you uncomfortable (whole worlds compressed into planes, leaning in the corner with their hidden and sharp-edged stories). You tagged along, a grumpy satellite. I'm going to shift you back to third person now, by the way, if he doesn't mind. I mean, give another few pages and he's going to abjure *me* yet once again, and I wouldn't be able to address him directly then anyhow, would I? 'Twouldn't be fair, and fair's turnabout play, after all.

Katie had wanted to see the paintings too—this unsuspected facet of her heroine—but Lianne had said no, she thought it was better if Katie didn't, they wouldn't interest her anyway, they weren't pictures *of* things, just pictures *about* things. What Lianne had really been concerned with was the darkness in the pieces; Katie had enough darkness of her own to think about. Katie, deferring to Lianne, and only to Lianne, surprisingly had not insisted.

Lianne showed only the four mostly complete pieces, the one she called, for reasons that eluded Charles, *Sweet Sixteen*, the untitled one with the floating monkeys, the Twilight Zone thing she called *Dream Train*, and the latest, which she announced she wasn't satisfied with, the windows thing from Rush, *In Time Out*. Charles agreed with her, *In Time Out* was the worst, though he didn't like *Sweet Sixteen* either, too angry and mangled and yet too abstract to have any emotional force, if you were to ask him, not that he would have said as much to Lianne.

He had to admit *Dream Train* was strong, the night train thundering up to the station in broad bright spring, how it was train and tunnel at once, how it imported all that huge frightening black from edge to middle through shuddering shades of expanding darkening boxcar, which were yet ghostly, evanescent, merely the downscaled hue of what was beyond them, the rooms of a hypercube, the more spectral spectra of city and park and school and sky and kids at play and somebody hanging in a tree—swinging?—until, off center, the nightmare achieved itself, the thick black square of the sliding doors at once a void and a wall, and in the void, or on the wall, the tiny skull face of the red-haired doll baby, *little Liza Jane*—and why had she written that out in white thin script beside the creature? And then the locomotive, pulling you where? Out of the foreground, almost an afterthought, attenuated down the perspective, parabolic recession to the outer edge, weird place for a vanishing point.

He had to admit the picture was strong, but it was repulsive too. He hated to think Lianne had that kind of ugliness in her. Maybe everybody did, but you didn't have to pull it out and dress it up and show it to the public at large. He hoped she had gotten it out of her system.

His favorite was the monkeys, the way they hovered angelic and quizzical over the garden, over the river whose flow defeated death. It never occurred to him the scene was a frame of a film you could run either way.

Dee-Dee oohed and aahed, and Tucker and Bill cracked jokes about the naked monkeys, made humorous compliments.

Kathy was a real artist. Lianne craved her good opinion most. But she was only vaguely complimentary. Charles was sure she thought Lianne's stuff too representational, and maybe mawkish and awkward as well. She herself was intensely abstract, in a way that Charles sometimes found attractive but couldn't prefer to the grain of wood, or the eroded strata of a cutbank. Lianne had lectured him on his perceptual failings, and they had bought three of Kathy's pieces, but he couldn't help it, that was the way he felt. He flinched now, to see her scatter her crumbs of praise, to see Lianne, poor Cinderella, gratefully whisking them up.

Lianne might not be a genius, and he might be a little pissed that she was so busy right now, but she was *his,* goddammit, and you didn't pick on his baby without permission.

"You should sign them," Kathy said, professional, instructive, and Lianne tucked her chin and blushed. "If you don't sign them, you aren't claiming yourself as an artist."

They went back downstairs, where Greg and Alison had been attempting to keep Katie amused but had rapidly exhausted their parental and nurturing reserves.

"I got lonesome," Katie said. "There wasn't anything to *do.*" Tossing her hair, sniffing at Greg and Alison. "They just couldn't keep me intellectually *occupied.*"

Intake of breath, severally. Lianne's eyes went to Greg and Alison, flickered upward, the tiniest vestige of an apologetic shrug, *You know how it is.* Greg and Alison smiled painfully, *No problem.* Charles watched Katie absorb all this, register her own gaffe.

"I have such a short span of attention now," the girl said. "It's my fault."

Charles was astonished at the speed with which she mastered social nuance. He thought of that as his especial province. Lianne direct, always expressing what she felt, seldom checking the indicator lights. He monitoring for awkwardness, hidden agendas.

But this girl, now. She was a threat, an unbridled force. He saw her loose in his house, a ravening wolf. Not to be tolerated, not. Playing on Lianne's sympathy, her gullibility. No.

Later that evening, they wound up at the piano, singing hymns. All good Southerners, no matter how rich or upper-crusty or agnostic, love to gather around a piano and get back to their roots by singing all the good old wailing mournful thumpy hymns of what they imagine as their country-church childhood, and they all still know most of the words to most of them.

Lianne's silvery coloratura sailing above them, ineffable longing:

> *Oh they tell me of a home where no storm clouds rise,*
> *Oh they tell me of a land far away—*
> *Oh they tell me of a land far beyond the skies—*
> *Ohhh they tell me of an unclouded day.*

"Oh, I *know* all of these," Katie said. "We sing these all the time." She had a terrible voice but seemed proud of it. She managed, in spite of her low whispery volume, to dominate the harmony (through sheer awfulness, Charles thought). Could she not forgo her stardom this once, let him enjoy his wife's voice in its ringing, untrammeled, glorious freedom?

He loved to hear Lianne, and seldom got to. Years ago, he had ceased pleading with her to humor him, treat him to private concerts. She had sung in Holy Sac awhile, as a paid voice though she wasn't Presbyterian, and he could go to their services and hear her, and keep up his social contacts as well. But it wasn't the same as hearing her really sing, she wasn't a soloist, just a bit player, and they sang a lot of truly awful modern nonmelodic stuff, at least they had until Arthur James Dorman, the director, had been arrested for pederasty and writing hot checks.

But then she had quit even that much performance. Her given reason the damage that years of allergies had done to her voice: sinus headaches night after night as a girl, continuous drainage, raw throat, one infection after another for twenty-odd years until she had keloids in her eustachians and holes in her tympana and could not now walk outside in fifty-degree weather without violent pain unless she muffled and covered her ears, and the mother never having her tested, forcing her to drink her milk long after Lianne herself suspected what the trouble was, *Your bones will get brittle*, and aspirin for the headaches till her butt bled in the mornings, but never to an allergist, always to the same moronic family-prac prick who swabbed her adenoids again and again with the iodine she was also allergic to and never knew until she was a grown woman.

Well, it *would* make you a little achromatic. And he could hear how she had lost range and flexibility, he could hear the occasional breaks in her phrasing, the sometime unsteadiness of her attack, and he understood how maddening that must be to someone with her knowledge, her training, her ear. He could almost understand how you would rather not do it at all than do it with the errors you had once been able to avoid. There had been more perfect singers with Holy Sac, and they had justifiably gotten the lead parts.

There were no more glorious *voices*, though. That was what he had never been able to convey. For him, perfection wasn't the point. The point was the *quality* of her voice. Uxoric perhaps, fatuous perhaps—but seldom did such warmth and clarity combine, such belling musicality with such color. Joan Baez, but with more esprit, variation, humor. Patsy Cline, but less of the anguish of a thousand warbling wounds. To hear Lianne singing the great old torch songs—"Smoke Gets in Your Eyes," ah God—

Lianne's singing had shape, volume, sculpture, it was not an arrow driven through the continuum, it *was* the continuum, a succession of lovely rooms in time, and so what if the plaster was cracked here and there?

Ah, but that wasn't the issue. Music had been ruined for her in her spirit, not in her throat. Mrs. W. driving her to mechanical practice, the author of the voice also its destroyer, that same crone who had neglected to provide proper medical care. That was where the emphasis on perfection came from, the obsession with doing it *right* rather than beautifully. All joy had been beaten out of the girl, she couldn't celebrate, music had become her prison and not her release.

Which was why, in her mature years, he thought, she had turned to light and paint and color. The gift, the need, seeking its outlet.

And now Katie's weak voice breaking against Lianne's, ruining his pleasure, a crack in a crystal flute. Obscene.

> *Are you ready?*
> *Are you ready?*
> *Are you ready for the Judgment Day?*

"I don't like the girl," he said, upstairs, getting ready for bed, after the others had left, Katie back to the hospital for the weekend, her tour in the house to start Monday. "I don't care how sick she is, I don't want her in my home."

Lianne had seen this coming, had been getting similar feedback from all her friends.

Alison: "She certainly is—ha-ha—very *direct*. It's very—ah—*refreshing*, isn't it?"

Dee-Dee: "That little fox will huff and puff and eat all your little piggies."

Bill, with his sly grin: "*We*-ell, I think she's ready to run Christmas in July *herself*."

"It's just a week, Charles," she said, sitting at the vanity, her voice unperturbed, matter-of-fact. It *was* going to happen. Katie *was* going to get what she wanted, and that was that.

She had seen Katie naked, the day they filmed the spot.

They'd washed and dressed and made up at the house, for convenience. Lianne had done Katie's face and hair. There had been an interval of rest and contentment while Lianne smoothed foundation on the calm face, penciled arches into the eyebrows, reddened and widened the lips, drew the brush through thickets of glossy frizz. The ease of being groomed, such a simple pleasure to offer, so few of us give it or get it. Lianne could remember every single instance when someone else had brushed *her* hair. Aunt Loretta, mainly. With the silver-backed brush. Before she moved to Tulsa and left Lianne alone with her mother.

But before that, the sight of the girl stepping out of the shower, frail as a straw, coppery nipples on the bony flat chest. Soon they would be sawing a cross into that fragile cage, clamping the bloody stumps of the ribs apart with a spreader. Clipping for God's sake the very pump and bellows, the triple-lobed interlooped tree of vitality itself, system of many feedbacks. They would be lifting the bloody slithering mass, scissoring loose sheets of pleura.

And stitching in place the heart and lungs of a dead stranger.

If Katie was *lucky*.

She had known in that moment that the girl understood fully. The way she showed her nakedness unembarrassed, allowed Lianne's full gaze. Showing the nakedness not of her body, but of her body's failure. The monkeys learn early to hide the shame of their weakness, the guilt of their disease. But Katie knew, and knew what her odds were. She was going down, that was the long and short of it. No heart, no lungs. Into the black boxcar.

It wasn't fair, but so what? Bitching didn't help. Nothing helped. So why waste time, why beat around the bush? Go get as much of what you want as you can, that's all. Just go get it. It wasn't even courage, it was something more powerful and practical than courage.

Lianne's friends might have seen it as rudeness, manipulation. Lianne saw it as strength. Katie was just using the tools she had to get some of things she didn't have.

Charles went to bed grumbling, but it made no difference. Monday came to the Morrison home, and so did Katie McFee.

Charles doesn't remember much of the next week. He stayed away as much as he could, leaving for work early and coming home late. Since Lianne was still working busily on Christmas in July, and Katie was not strong enough to do that much buzzing around, it fell to Clemmie to do a great deal of wheelchair wheeling, boredom beguiling, vanity stroking, and general upkeep. There were nurses in three eight-hour shifts, but Katie was insatiable, and anyway the nurses were just hired hands, nothing interesting about *them*.

Clemmie didn't like Katie any better than Charles did. Her cooking didn't suffer, that was a point of pride with Clemmie, but the service did. Lianne was careful, whatever she was doing, to be home in time for supper, usually by 6:30. They were eating earlier for Katie's sake. To keep her strength up, she had to have smaller and more frequent meals. Then after they ate, Lianne and Katie went off by themselves, having a big time, so if Charles wanted company he was out of luck, unless he went to the bar.

He tried that once, but wound up sodden and depressed rather than loose and happy, so he quit drinking and went home.

It was the dog function. He had seen it a million times with Ramalam, but also with any other dog that happened to wander up. In a room full of people, a dog, any dog, would instantly select Lianne, dash straight to her skirt. All eyes for Lianne. All over Lianne, who scratched just where, got down on her knees trading breath with you, you *see* me, a monkey who can *see*, fancy that, amazing, busy-tail jump-up laughing with tongue hanging out at the side of your mouth.

And her eyes felt so good, her only eyes, you wanted them all the time and nobody else getting that wild green gaze that *saw* you and therefore made you exist, and Charles was as jealous of Katie as Dee-Dee had been, that was the truth of the matter.

He does remember Lianne and Katie debating Liz Ward's chances for Miss America—all week long, it seemed: an interview in the *Gazette* the morning Katie came to stay and another interview Sunday morning, the morning she left for good, which of course he didn't get to read until that afternoon because of all the fuss and hooraw of the leave-taking, one last grudge against Katie, because a long Sunday morning on the sun porch with Clemmie supplying cookies and cup after cup of fresh coffee was one of his favorite things in all the earth. Katie and Lianne critiqued the new Miss Arkansas knowingly, her build, stance, hair, talent. They sounded like analysts at a basketball game. She had the tools, came to play, could go all the way if she got the breaks.

Friday at dinner, Clemmie's patience wore out. "I don't suppose anybody in this house but me even cares about Coleman any more," she said, handing round platters of fried fileted catfish, crisp and delicate and moist, piping hot and steaming when you broke the filets open, the meat mild and wonderfully nutty. Tart creamy coleslaw on the side, green onions, hush puppies, buttermilk, ketchup mixed with horseradish. The works.

Lianne looked stricken, and both Charles and Katie caught her expression. The shift nurse was embarrassed, keeping her eyes on her plate, one hand in her lap, carefully picking a flaky filet apart with her fork.

Charles was furious with Clemmie, attacking Lianne in her weakness. She was still losing weight, staying up late and rising early, burning her reserves of energy in order to balance the claims on her time. She had been looking mortal and driven lately, more and more like the gaunt Lianne of the last few years with *Hope Lines*. He himself had thought of Coleman, several times, but had said nothing, letting it ride, assuming she was letting it ride, hoping she was, at least for now, at least for the next couple of weeks.

It was time to put a stop to this.

"You have me to worry about right now," Katie said haughtily, before he could speak.

"Worry is right," Clemmie said, retreating to the kitchen.

After the meal, Lianne gathered her purse and keys and went to the Blazer, which she kept parked out front in the circle mostly, the garage too inconvenient.

Charles followed her. He caught her arm as she opened the door of the car. The argument went like this:

7:23:20: "Where are you going?"

7:23:27: "We have a meeting of the decorations committee. You know that."

7:23:30: "That's not till nine. Where are you going now?"

7:23:45, after a pause: "To the hospital to see Coleman. I'm not going to stand around sweating in this heat arguing with you."

7:23:53: "I'm sweating too. Look at my shirt. But this is important. I don't like you like this. I don't like you letting Clemmie guilt you into overworking yourself."

7:24:01: "She's not guilting me into anything."

7:24:10: "I saw your face."

7:24:15: "I felt guilty *then*, ok? But I'm not guilty now. I want to go see Coleman. I've wanted to go all along, I've just been telling myself I didn't have time. But I do have time, if I get in the car and go right now. I'm a grown woman, and it's my choice, is that a problem for you?" Breaking away, getting in, sliding the key in the ignition.

7:24:55: "What about us?"

7:25:00, with a sigh, leaning back: "What about us?"

"It's just we don't ever have any time any more. You and me. I thought we went through all this, back with *Hope Lines*."

"We just spent a week *camping* together."

"Four days, and that was two weeks ago. And you were running off in the Blazer the whole time anyway."

"You gave it to me."

"Yes, but—"

Yes but, yes but. You gave it to me, yes but. The great Yesbutt. What was he doing? Look at him out here, jawing like a clown. Maybe the heat was making him giddy after being in air-conditioning all afternoon, but he felt out of himself, dispassionate. An alien anthropologist looking down on the scene from above. See the funny man with his shirt soaking through. See him waving his arms and making noises.

"What's so funny?" she said, suspicious.

"Oh, I just heard what we were doing," he said. "We were all over the place. It sounded like an argument on tv."

"It really is just this next week," she said. "It'll be all over after that. And I know Katie's—she's—I wouldn't have loaded her into all this, but—"

He reached through the window and patted her shoulder. "You go see Coleman," he said. "I'm just an asshole sometimes."

"You have to do things when they have to be done," she said, not quite through with the argument. "You can't make them wait till you have time."

"We have plenty of time. You go see Coleman." He bent through the window to kiss her.

"I really am in a good place," she murmured against his lips. "I'm fine."

"Mm-mm," he mumbled, nibbling. "I can tell."

He straightened to see Katie leaning in the open doorway. The frail forsaken child. Come to live with her fairy mother, but now the fairy mother was running off and leaving her. The pose would have been more effective if the lighting had cooperated. In the movie, they would shoot it up from the bottom of the steps. It would be darker, later in the evening, and Katie would loom over the scene, framed in the glowing doorway, her thin silhouette made thinner, more frail, by the backlighting. Serious sad music over. Heavy on the strings.

"Ah—" he began. "Say, what do you propose I do about—"

"Handle it," Lianne said. "You're supposed to have a way with women." She cranked the Blazer. He waved as she left, and went back up the steps.

"Hi, kid," he said to Katie. "It's not the end of the world."

"I'm not a baby goat," she said.

"Do you play poker?" he said.

"Sure, but what do I use for stakes?"

"How about your wheelchair? I've always wanted a good wheelchair."

"It cost thirteen hundred dollars new," she said.

"Pot limit," he said.

He and Katie and Clemmie and the nurse wound up in the game room, playing hands of five and seven stud, some draw. Nickel, dime, quarter, but pot limit made for pretty good betting anyhow. Katie liked high-low games. She *really* liked High Chicago roll-your-own high-low split, but with four people, what was the point of a split pot? They played some High Chicago anyway, just to keep her happy. High only.

She bet like a fiend, immune to risk. Charles found himself sitting out a lot of hands, waiting for the cards to turn. She *would* walk into an ambush, he found. She was after blood, violence, and drama, and if she liked her cards, she would charge your position, no matter what you might be holding. Clemmie was sneaky as hell, but he'd played a lot of poker with Clemmie, and he knew how to hold her off, no problem. The nurse was no threat. She was a Baptist and didn't believe in playing cards, much less in gambling. She was sitting in only because they had ordered her to (so it was part of her job, it wasn't as if she was doing it on purpose). She was playing on Charles's money anyway.

The game was going to turn on how much he made Katie pay for her boldness. Which was a great theory, but Katie caught cards most of the night, and he had nothing to work with. He stung her twenty, twenty-five bucks a couple of times, but she just stayed with more firepower. It got boring. About 10:30, she began to fade. He could see her, across the table, visibly wilting. He had the sense the process might continue unchecked, the whole range of mortality before his very eyes, girl withering to old woman, to leathery sightless bones, the mummy crumbling to powder, a dust of ashes on the seat cushion.

In the last dozen hands, the girl lost most of her winnings, but not to him, to Clemmie. She stripped the corpse, and it made her cheerful. She decided she liked Katie after all.

"You're worn out, hon," she said, gathering the girl up, helping her into the wheelchair. "Let's go wash you and brush you and put you to bed."

"I'll get her," the nurse said, flushed and confused. She had won five dollars and change and was going to get to keep it, apparently. They had handed it to her, and nobody appeared to think any more about the matter. She felt as deliciously wicked as any illicit lover.

Charles was the big loser, Clemmie the big winner.

"I've got her," Clemmie said. "You go get the room ready."

"You keep in touch when you go back home," Charles said, pushing away from the table. He didn't want to say "back to the hospital." Back to your torture chamber. Your death room.

"Maybe," Katie whispered hoarsely. "I already know what I wanted to. I know things everybody else wonders. My curiosity is satisfied."

"What do you know?" he said, amused. How could he ever have seen her impudence as a threat? Rude but refreshing, the cold-water theory. Anyway, she was out of here soon.

"You aren't any different," she said. "You have to do the same things as everybody else. It doesn't make any difference who you are."

Eat, shit, and die, he thought. Why didn't we see the coded insult, the hateful message God had built into our very existence? Drop the commas. *Eat shit and die.*

But he didn't believe in God.

Clemmie was backing the chair out into the hall. "How about cash this time?" she said to him, over Katie's head. "I hate it when you give me a check."

"Draw it out extra when you cash the household check," he said.

"It's not the same," she said, straightening the chair for travel, looking back through the door. "It's not as much fun."

"Ok, ok," he said. "I'll put the actual moola in your hot grubby little fist. But you'll have to give me till Monday."

"Don't forget."

"I won't forget."

"Sixty-seven dollars and eighteen cents," Clemmie grunted, heaving against inertia, and then was gone down the hall.

"There's somebody in there," Lianne said when she finally got home. She was talking about Coleman. She was in her nightgown, standing brushing her hair out. It was the thin yellow nightgown, luminous, a cloud of light, her body a moving x-ray. The nipples vague and dark. "He's definitely in there, waiting. I can feel him."

"Mm," Charles said, thinking it was moot whether he was in there if he never got out.

If she was so psychic she could sense evil radiating off Sonny and Ferrin, if she could sense Charles was finally, when all was said and done, true blue, and if she could tell Coleman was in there somewhere, why couldn't she feel the clock ticking, the only clock that counted?

That's easy, if you step outside time. She did feel it. She always *had* felt it. The clock will be going to have always been there. It was there when she was a girl. It was the darkness, and the darkness never goes away, but she wasn't *afraid* of the darkness any more. That's all the choice we have, whether to be afraid or not.

"We can't give up on him," she said.

"We won't," he said. "Come here."

"Use your hand," she said.

"It's not as good as you are."

"Use the Vaseline. You can wait two more nights."

"It wouldn't take very long."

"Forget it," she said, and kissed his forehead, and went down the hall, as she had been doing all week, to sleep with Katie.

Who in her sleep, only in her sleep, cried out in fear and shame. And needed an arm to circle her waist, and gather her in, and hold her tight. And the nurse, asleep in the other bed, wasn't good enough for that, might have gotten up and stirred the girl, patted her shoulder, *There, there, it's ok, it's just a dream*, but couldn't have curled and cuddled and held. And at home, Katie's mother couldn't, never had, wasn't made that way. So in all Katie's life the one arm that would circle and hold her warm against her night fear was Lianne's.

"Probably having a three-way lesbian affair," Charles grumbled to himself in the dark, and rolled his face into his pillow. "Ménage à twat," he said, and giggled. "Nurse and the kid and Miss Little Rock," he complained. He built a fantasy of Lianne on the contest stage, eighteen, red-headed, buck naked. *Ta-dum, ta-dum, ta-dum.* He went to sleep.

"Hi," Tina said to Laugh over the phone. "I'm back."

"I didn't know you was gone." He lifted the glowing dial of his watch before his eyes. "Shit you calling this kind of time of night?" How the hell had she got his number here in Hazen?

"I'm back in town," she said, her voice husky. His goddamn cock stirring and rising up, it knew that voice. He was frightened, as if shaken out of a dream into nightmarish reality. He had liked the warm, restful dream of the last few months, the slow succession of equally boring days in which he had wanted nothing, nothing but to be a good boy, to do his duty and go to church and stay low key and challenge no one and be secure and safe and warm, and be a good boy. He had wanted to stay in that dream until it was real. He had forgotten sex.

"I'm sorry about your mother," she said, and somehow that was enough to raise his mother's specter in the room, his mother he hadn't thought of in weeks, his mother he had thought he was free of forever. Her hard malignant stare glittering in the shadows.

"I've decided to give them another chance," Tina said. "I'm not going to start my own firm after all. I'm going to withdraw my resignation and give them another chance."

Withdraw your resignation? Lafayette thought. *Jesus shit.* He was afraid to say anything. He wanted to put the phone down and be rid of her, but he was afraid to do that too.

"I hear you have tickets to the Christmas in July," she said.

Uh-uh. Oh Jesus no, uh-uh, no way, never. "I don't," he said.

"Rosalyn said you had tickets," she said.

"I can't go," he said. "I got a conflict, I give em away." Shit, shit, *shit,* and he had really been *counting* on going, looking *forward* to the thing, his coming-out party, the new Mr. Laugh Thompson, the good Mr. Lafayette J. Thompson.

After she hung up, he took his erection into the bathroom and turned on the light and masturbated, sitting on the toilet naked, pumping pearly sperm over his dark fist. Then he curled his head to his knees and cried like a baby.

Ray Thornton, the once and future congressman, in a holding pattern now as president of Arkansas State University, said that Arkansas had a lagging economy because it had made an inadequate investment in education. By

Wednesday the twenty-second, the *Gazette* was quoting Mr. Thornton and writing editorials, as you can see for yourself in the files. The 1981 abstract, page 87. Lianne would have been pleased. She approved of Thornton. Not just because he was a cousin of her friend Bill Pumphrey either. (The two men bore a strong facial resemblance, but the mild serious politician and the rascally man-about-town were otherwise very different.)

Six more prisoners escaped from the Pulaski County jail, but this time apparently the wrong sort of prisoners, because this time Sonny Raymond didn't happen across them driving down the road and haul them back in himself.

Instead, he started ranting and raving about his budget being inadequate, the jail was too crowded, how could he keep anybody in it, the wimp pansy crooked courts and judges were turning crimnals loose on the street. He concocted an object lesson. He sent two deputies down to rent a double-wide, plus a cab to tow it. He made a sign that said PULASKI COUNTY JAIL EXTENSION, fastened the sign to the double-wide, filled the double-wide with prisoners, and had them parked on the street in front of Beaumont's house, a deputy standing guard with a shotgun. The 1981 abstract again, page 89i. It made all the wire services, national tv; you must have seen it.

But before all that, Monday or Tuesday, but for the life of him Charles can't remember which, though he remembers the argument itself very clearly, they had the argument about Me. Which is why I have inverted things here, the order of events. Last-gasp effort. Trying to stay around as long as I can.

They were in the master bedroom, trying on clothes. *She* was trying on clothes. She was deciding what to wear Saturday, or whether to buy something new, and he was watching and advising. He already knew what he was going to wear, his tux. So simple for males.

Yes, he had agreed to go. He had decided to relax and enjoy it, show up and show off, the most beautiful woman in Little Rock on his arm, big date, and later they come home and fuck like minks, maybe. Wasn't so bad. But he was not, not, *not* going to show up *early* for the deal. She could show up early if she wanted to, she probably needed to, really, as the major organizer, just to keep everybody else calm. He would come later, spot on at eight, when it officially kicked off.

That was ok with her. They had it all worked out.

Except what she was going to wear. She had tried on sixteen different outfits and nothing was quite right, especially with her new skinnier body, flatter tummy and it isn't draping right over the hips because it isn't just you're thinner *around,* your whole waist *drops* an inch or so, and God was he tired of looking at clothes, his eyes catching and rolling with the sleepiness of boredom.

"Just buy something new," he said.

"It's late to be buying anything," she said, smoothing the skirts of a deep green damask whose tunic glittered with sequins. "There's probably not enough time to get it fitted."

"So pay him a million dollars and tell him to do it overnight," he said.

She flashed a look of scorn, *You don't understand the realities.* Turned her back to him.

"So make do with something you already have," he said. "This is fine. This looks great on you. Wear this."

"Unzip me," she said.

She stood in her slip, braless, hung the green gown back up. He came over to her closet, like his a huge well-lighted cedar-lined walk-in. But his was neat and organized, plenty of free space, and hers was crammed to the max, taffetas, satins, silks, cottons, linens, leathers, shoes, umbrellas, hats, boxes, chains, belts, scarves, and all the colors of the world itself. He tugged her bodice open, leered down at her breasts. "Wow, what a set of lungs," he said, thinking for some reason of *Where the Boys Are,* be fun to see again, he hadn't seen it in ages.

She pushed him away. She stood arms akimbo. Looking around exasperated, as if she had left something somewhere but couldn't remember where. Or what it was. Just the sense that she had had it a minute ago, and where was it?

"I've been thinking," she said.

"Does it hurt?" he said.

She gave him her *does not compute* look. "I want to make one of these living wills," she said, recovering her train of thought. "My heart and lungs. For medical science, or as a donor."

"No," he said.

"They're *my* heart and lungs," she said. "Or kidneys. And my brain, but they can't put that *in* anybody, I know that. But I'm sure they can find a use."

"No," he said. "Uh-uh."

"I'm going to leave them to Children's Hospital," she said. "I'll live on. I'll be helping other children."

An auto accident. Shot by a mugger. Falling off the roof of a building, a penthouse garden in New York. Sirens, blinking lights, a gurney, rushing the body into surgery. Then the red heart on a bed of ice, like a crown nested on diamonds in a treasure chest. Helicopter to another hospital, where the needy patient waited, *chopchopchopchop.*

"No," he said again, too loud: Now that she was dead, now that the initial shock of pleasure was past

Tina?

and what of the shock receding in shells from *that* shock as he realized that even here in the middle of his love love love he felt pleasure to think of her dead suddenly terribly dead because at least it would be some kind of *change*

which was the shock of realizing that his heart of hearts was two hearts or more, that he would always hate Lianne a little and hate her more the more he loved her

Tina . . .

because he was her prisoner as you are all each other's prisoners and exist only because you are, as I who alone am free do not and cannot

but enough of that for this is about you and not me

see what I mean?

as he sees himself grieving imagines the girl Katie naked with her ripped-open and stitched-back chest and beating behind that cicatrix, glowing in the thin shade of that skinny lamp, the heart and lungs of his Lianne how could he bear it

and he hears himself howl in sorrow

or her brain floating in a jar like a bad horror movie

but that's silly, that's way overdone

but maybe rolling in a bubbling tank of Tucker said formalin in the basement waiting for gross anatomy to start

and all this in an instantaneous flurry of frames of images he knew she was seeing too but in her case not in horror but the proud ghost glad to have done her best and

"It's just my meat," she said. "My body is just my meat."

"It's where the meat and spirit—" *Meet,* he had been about to say, but had heard, offstage somewhere, the faint laughter of Justice George Rose Smith, prosodist of jurisprudence. But she heard what he didn't finish.

"You don't believe in God," she said. "How can you believe in spirit?"

And how can you tell me what to do with myself if you don't believe what I believe?

"Maybe I do believe in God," he said. "In my own way, maybe I do."

"You don't," she said. "Anyway, it doesn't matter. The soul's in the brain, not in the heart and lungs. The old ancient people were wrong."

It was a negotiation, that was clear. If she could have her heart and lungs, he could have her brain. He came to terms.

"I won't draw it up for you," he said. "You'll have to get Greg or somebody."

There seemed to be echoes around everything, and echoes of echoes, because they were in each other: And they were one in argument, he saw. And their division was not division but the fitting together of gears, of patterns, and he felt and felt her feel how very deeply intrinsically *different* they were, and that was good and it didn't matter they disagreed about God, the important thing was loving each other. God was just a question, but loving is something you can *do.*

And they knew she needed to come into his arms, because she had made her declaration, she had bestowed herself, and now was emptied and and shaken. And she did, and he held her. And she said against his chest, the parting shot that binds: "You *don't* believe in God."

"What's that got to do with it?" he said into her hair, moving his right hand hungrily to cradle the back of her skull, circling her trunk with the other arm and squeezing.

But it was clear what she meant. They saw the thought,

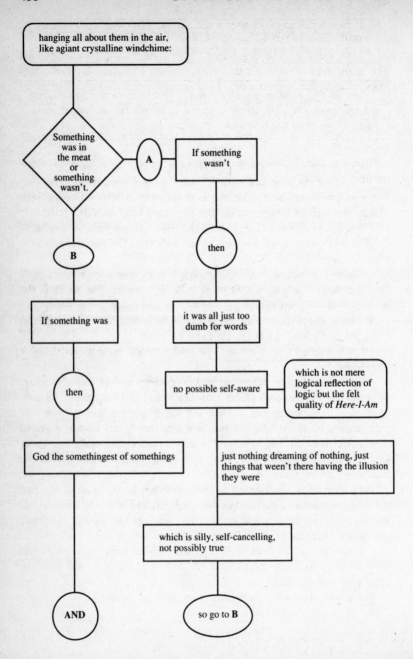

"If there's not any God there's not any us," she said, holding him.

"Well, some people seriously think so," he said.

"I can make all your arguments." She leaned her head back to look him in the face. "How can there be, if things like Katie happen? Or if wars, or a million frogs at a time because only a dozen or so will make it? How it all works just like a blind machine, or a statistic, or a faceless bureaucracy."

"You can say anything you want to." He smiled. "Anybody can say anything."

"Plus you can't measure, you can't count, you can't prove it." She was deviling him now, teasing, you're in my power, I know you top to toe.

"Just saying it doesn't make it so," he protested, content to be known.

"Plus it's not the simplest most elegant hypothesis." A frown of puzzlement crossed her face. "Except really it is if you really think about it, it seems to me."

"You can say anything you want," he said tenderly.

And she can, and you can too, and I've seen this coming a long way off, Charles, since even before the first chapter, because all this happens before the first chapter, right?

Of course it does, it's obvious. So I've seen it coming, in fact if I don't see it it doesn't come, and yes, you can say anything you want, you have every right, but really. Really it's for your own good, really I wish you wouldn't say:

"But there still ain't no God, and you can take that to the bank."

AN
INTERLUDE
WITHOUT

Dear Reader—

As was whirling about like a much of a which of a sonofabitch of a wind, whither listeth and hither and yon and here and then, you know, unsuppressible, out of the frame, came across this scrap of paper, snaffled it up, and whiffled it on through time and chance and space, to slap it in place against your window.

Dear Johnny—   22 dec 1989

God says this, somewhere in *Living in Little Rock*:

I am not, do not, cannot exist: But if I was an Am, how would I be? Oh if you wished to know me, how?

How if you wanted—I know you do—to send home a prayer, to say, Thank you for this brief awake, this see, think, love. Thank you this sweet goodbye?

You would, you clever monkey you, make models. To catch me in the quick of a broke form, hermit ghost scuttling back to zero, cracked crab in the black safe wave.

You would make it and broke it, to always be turning a corner, till where might stand your long-lost never-known, your dead love live and whole, it was a dream—

And in the always might be almost is.

So forgive you, my dear, vanishing ones, your graven images all, your magic lies, and how you make voice because am not here to speak. Would save you all, if were not gravid unto nothingness, if did not die to make you live, oh fragment child, if did not disappear against the stirring of your momentary be.

Love,

Jack

Love,

PART FOUR

DETECTIVE STORY

30

THE SPEED
OF LIGHT

Charles had a dream. He was trying to explain the speed of light to someone he couldn't see. The speed of light in a vacuum. He was in the vacuum, sailing in a white envelope with the flap up, like a man in the prow of a racing ship. 300,000. The explanation was 300,000. He stood in the pulpit with his arms raised, but the church was dark and empty.

His mother was crying because his father was dead and she didn't know it yet. He leaned over the casket from far above, from outer space. This had to be a dream, because she had died first. That's why you don't know, he explained. Sound won't travel in a vacuum.

Dreams are mostly just empty space.

Lianne heard him anyway, looked up and smiled in a ray of the high sun, tears in her bright green eyes. The casket was brass and ebony, open with white lining. No one was in it.

He was in his flannel pajamas. Oh good. What a luxury to burrow the warm covers. If you were rich, you could have the air as cold as you wanted it, even in summer. Burrow the covers in the morning light, the curtain light. He punched his pillow, nestled. He would sleep another couple of hours, the most delicious hours.

The dream was still close. The speed of light was a bubble, the gleam of a growing bubble. Relativity. The mail was slow, that was where time came in.

But the day leaked into his mind and now the dream made no sense. He could feel the urgency still, the need to explain, but he had lost the meaning. He was in his bed with his pajamas on. The bubble had popped.

This was not early morning light. It was the wrong windows. It was the southwest windows, the curtains radiant like robed angels.

Was he late? He felt a thrill of anxiety. No, it was Saturday. And he ran the place, anyway. If he overslept, so what? But his father looking impatiently at his watch. Punctuality counts. Charles two minutes late for the meeting. You'd be late to your own funeral. Shaking his head. A genetic deficiency. Not my own flesh and blood.

Was that from the dream? No, that was from now. But it couldn't be, because his father was dead. He wasn't waiting somewhere, mad at Charles.

Where was *his* watch? He lifted his wrist to his eyes. It was naked, the white band of skin where the sun didn't hit. Negative shadow of time.

He wasn't asleep any more. He was wide awake. He yawned and stretched. His body creaked and popped in good ways. God, he felt relaxed. He got up and brushed his teeth and showered. His scalp was tender when he shampooed his hair, a bruise on the back of his head he didn't remember getting. He dried off, then put his pajamas back on, belted his house robe over them, and went down to the kitchen, taking the stairs for the pleasure of movement.

He had expected Lianne to be in the kitchen, maybe she and Clemmie fussing with breakfast. But the room was empty. Saturday, of course. She would be at the farmers' market, and then group, and then painting. That was ok, he could take care of himself.

He found a loaf of six-grain bread in the fridge. Good, Clemmie had gotten some fresh. He cut himself a couple of thick slices, carved off a half-dozen pats of stiff butter. He warmed the dotted slices fifteen seconds each in the microwave, spread the softened butter. You didn't want to tear the bread. And the microwave made it like fresh-baked.

What to go with it? Milk, of course. Warm bread and cold milk, pure heaven.

Most of a glass quart stood in the fridge, wearing a helmet of shaped tinfoil. He took the quart out, set it on the counter. Lianne had saved who knows how many of the old jugs from her father's days as a routeman. Now they bought their milk in the store in plastic gallons like everybody else, but when they brought it home, she would pour it off a quart at a time. It was something she did, not Clemmie, to show she understood what he liked. He loved drinking it just like that, cold, straight from the lip of the bottle.

He was sitting at the counter chewing and drinking when Elaine walked in.

"That milk has probably turned," she said.

It was as if a stegosaurus had walked in the door and started telling him what to do. A short round woman with faintly pink hair, humped and peering forward, her small hands raised before her. He could almost see the procession of horny plates down her spine. He had a fleeting impression that Lianne had finally left him, had gone back to Momma. But they were happy together now—and if she had, Momma wouldn't be *here*.

"The milk is fine," he said. "What are you doing here?"

Mrs. Weatherall didn't answer. She surveyed his meal, a scavenger deciding whether the corpse was ripe enough. She swung to the refrigerator, pulled out the loaf of bread. She had trouble with the knife, pushing it through the loaf instead of sawing, tearing loose huge crumbs. "You waste a lot by not having it sliced at the store," she said.

She didn't bother with the butter. She bit a chunk of bread where she stood, chewed. She spoke around the mouthful. "I don't like bread with seeds in it. They get between your teeth and cause abscesses." She put her slice down and got a glass out of the cabinet. She poured herself milk from the plastic gallon, sniffing the mouth of the jug first.

She knew she wasn't supposed to be here. Why was she so calm? Were she and Lianne going shopping together? Had Lianne told him about it last night and he had forgotten?

"Where's Lianne?" he demanded.

"All over Arkansas, I guess," Elaine said.

Farmers' market, Charles was thinking. Saturday morning, and she was down at the farmers' market, going from stall to stall. She would return soon with paper bags full of brown-tasseled corn, of green onions, the dirt still clinging to their damp roots. The back seat of the Blazer heaped with gourds, baskets of unshelled beans.

He saw her talking to the farmers in their overalls, the comfortable wives in print dresses sitting in lawn chairs under the shade of awnings beside their stalls. In his vision the stalls were continuous with the back roads of Arkansas, with the farms that had made the produce—green hillsides, and creek-bottom meadows, weathered brown shacks disappearing in head-high weeds, and beside the abandoned cabins, cleared lots with house trailers raised up on blocks, their undersides screened with white-painted lattice, pickups parked in front, hounds sleeping in sun, mailboxes fastened to posts set in cement-filled dairy cans, and overhead, in the blue perfect sky, high over the bony hills, the wheel and caw of crow to crow.

And he saw her, small and busy and far away, going down all the roads, knocking at all the doors, bending to talk to the hounds, traveling on, the red dust of her passage fading over the narrow and crooked gravel, ghosting the roadside trees.

He had done something wrong, she was mad at him, she had left him, she had gone down to the farmers' market, she was all over Arkansas, she was gone.

He was furious with Elaine, a transition as sudden as from dream to waking. Like waking from peaceful sleep to find yourself on fire.

He was screaming at her: "What the fuck are you doing in my house? Get the fuck out of here! Get the fuck out of my house!"

Jeez, he was thinking, in another part of his mind. *You're really losing it, Charles. This isn't like you.* But he was still screaming.

She had flinched away, yes, backed up against the big counter too high for her, as it was too high for Lianne. On her face there was no surprise, no terror, only a sort of wide-eyed wariness mixed with scorn, as if she had seen this many times before, as if she knew this was the way all men eventually behaved. They could club you, of course; they were physically dangerous; but they were weak, contemptible creatures. Goad them a few times, and they could not stand against you, they could not control themselves, they flew apart into helpless rages.

Tucker came running in, and then Dee-Dee. They stopped and stared.

"Get her out of my house," he said to them. He was shivering with chill, he was terribly weak. "What's going on?" he said. "What are you doing here?" But he knew. He could feel that he was sick or hurt, that something was badly wrong with him.

"Hon, why don't you take her to the library," Tucker said. "And get my kit while you're at it." He kept his eyes on Charles. Elaine gathered up her saucer of mangled bread, her glass of milk. She sniffed, threw Charles a withering look, then let Dee-Dee escort her. Her gait as she left the room was Lianne's, the sharp fierce strides of a determined woman.

"I think I better sit down," Charles said shakily, feeling for a chair.

Tucker came over to help him, adjusted the house robe more tightly over his chest. "Easy boy," he said. "Easy. You're having a flashback, that's all. Easy now."

He had never taken drugs. Well, a little grass on the honeymoon, but Lianne didn't like it, it made her feel out of control. Well, a little grass in New York, fresh out of law school. But never a bad trip. He was one of those people who couldn't tell the difference all that much. He was rather proud of the fact, bragged on it in the right company.

"Not a flashback," he said, slumping in Tucker's grip. He had fainted, maybe had a seizure or something, that was why he was home in bed. Well, that was bad, but it would be ok. He would be ok. He would protect himself and be ok.

He straightened his shoulders. "I'm ok," he said. "I don't need a sedative."

His heart was thumping so massively he was sure they could hear it. *They* included not just Tucker and Dee-Dee but an unspecified general host, an invisible crowd waiting and watching outside his walls. If they heard his heart, he would be done for. He had to conceal his agitation, or they would sedate him again.

Again? But he knew they had, just as he knew something else, a dark bad crime he had committed, a thing to which, just now, he did not wish to put a name.

Dee-Dee came back in with Tucker's bag. "I don't want an injection," Charles said, but Tucker had already pushed his house robe and his pajama sleeve up, and the thin pain of a needle was fading out in his right arm. Almost at once Charles stopped shivering. Something like warmth spread through his body.

"Let's get you back in bed," Tucker said, helping him up. Dee-Dee took his other arm.

"I don't want to go to bed. I've been in bed forever." That was a strange thing to say, but it was true, Charles could tell. He felt steadier now, clearer-headed. He wanted to sit in the sun like a cat. "Let's go in the living room," he said.

He led them across the hall to the big room. He let them seat him on the sofa facing the Curtis Mathis, the front windows. Dee-Dee tucked his robe. Everybody was tucking his robe. He felt like a baby being mothered. "Open the drapes," he said. "It's too dark and cold in here."

"I don't think so," Dee-Dee said to Tucker.

"It's ok," Tucker said. "It's all clear now."

He pulled the drapes, and the good sun poured in. The hot sun. Charles had been expecting a winter scene somehow, bare and drab. That was silly, it was July of course. Beyond the window, enormous yellows freighted the massive leaves. Jays ruffled and cried in the glassy silence, launched themselves from damping branches.

"Tell Clemmie to adjust the thermostat," Charles said. "You have to watch her. She turns it way down when you're not looking." Dee-Dee threw Tucker a look. *Come here,* it said. *Deal with this.* Tucker came back to the sofa.

"I want Lianne," Charles said. "I'm sick, and I want Lianne."

"Hey, buddy," Tucker said, as if he were beginning a sentence. But then he stopped.

"You know how it is," Charles said. "When you're sick, you want Momma." He made a self-deprecating little smile, the equivalent of a shrug. Let them see his weakness. Of course he was weak. Everybody was weak sometimes. He had people to take care of him. Whatever was wrong, he would build back up. He felt warm and happy in the sun. Convalescence, the long peaceful days with nothing to do but get better. He had been working too hard. He had been taking the office too seriously. All you really had to do was drift. Drift in the sun.

Dee-Dee was crying. It made Charles lonesome to see her cry. He wanted Lianne.

"Would you find her?" he said. "Would you ask her to come in and see me?"

Now Dee-Dee seemed angry. She turned to Tucker. "Why's he doing this?"

Tucker's eyes were fixed on Charles. "I don't think he can help it," he said.

There was something Charles wanted to ask Tucker. It was hard to remember, like the dream. Maybe it was something *from* the dream, like bubbles. No, you wouldn't ask bubbles. It wasn't important, not when you were warm again. When you were getting well. Oh.

"What's wrong with me?" he said. "Did I have a stroke?"

"I can't stand any more of this," Dee-Dee said. She ran. She was standing, then she ran, was running, caught on the edge of his vision. Gone.

Tucker sat down, and Charles turned sideways to face him. It took a long time to turn, like slow motion. His head felt like it kept moving after he stopped it. He pulled his legs up. He was bigger than Tucker, but he felt like a small boy. His mouth was dry. "Do you remember anything?" Tucker said.

Charles laughed. "I remember *lots* of things."

"Yesterday," Tucker said. "Do you remember yesterday? Or the day before?"

"Or the day before or the day *before*," Charles said, laughing again. He knew he remembered things, but he wasn't sure what they were. He felt them crowding, silvery nights and sunny days, but which ones went where? Why didn't Tucker ask him something *specific,* and he would see if he could remember that? This way, it wasn't fair.

He saw the fox and her kits, beside the tumbling creek, and felt a tremendous relief.

"We were camping," he said.

Tucker looked down at his hands. "Too quick with the needle," he said, grimacing. "Completely the wrong damn stuff."

"I told you," Charles said, though he was enjoying the warmth in his veins.

Tucker made the look you have to look back at. "Charles, I need you to pay attention."

It was hard to look right at somebody's eyes. Really you kept hopping from one eye to the other. "I'm watching," Charles said. Was he doing it right? Tucker was angry.

"Not even sure there's any point," Tucker said, jerking his head away.

He stared out the window. Then he brought his eyes back. "That's not right. I'm sorry. Just pay attention, ok? I gave you something that makes it hard, but just pay attention anyway, ok?"

"I *am* paying attention, Tucker." Tucker was too serious. He was making things spooky.

Tucker took Charles's hand in both of his. His eyes were gentle now. "I have to tell you something. I want you to remember what I tell you."

It felt reassuring to have Tucker hold his hand. They had never done this before. But why not? You could hold hands with a friend whenever you wanted to. There were so many things you could do that nobody ever did. Life could be happy and full of touching.

But Tucker was tricking him. The hands feeling good was a trap, it made him relax. He couldn't relax. There was something he had to do. A bad thing he had to keep from happening.

"I don't want you to tell me," he said.

That was his crime. That was why he was guilty. He had let Tucker tell him. No, that didn't make sense. Tucker was telling him now.

"I have to," Tucker said.

"No," he said. So it was *now* he had to stop him. He would be bad if he didn't stop Tucker now. He would be guilty. But he felt like a boy, and Tucker felt like a man.

The men always tell you the bad things. You can't stop them.

"Lianne is dead," Tucker said.

Charles pulled his hand away. Now he turned to stare out the window. "That's a silly thing to say." The blue jays were arguing with a mockingbird now. The blue jays and the mockingbirds hated each other. Which was funny, they were so much alike.

He was mad at Tucker now. Let Tucker see how *he* liked being pushed around. Being told things. "Just because you say it doesn't make it so." His mouth was so dry that he had trouble moving his tongue.

"You have to accept it," Tucker said. He wiped his face with his hand. He looked annoyed, and tired. He pinched the bridge of his nose. He didn't know Charles could see him from the side of his eyes.

"I have good peripheral vision," Charles said. So he really was in control. He could make Tucker tired and frustrated. He could say *peripheral vision*. He knew what it meant, too.

"She died five days ago."

"Prove it," Charles said.

He knew who Tucker was talking about. That redheaded woman. He knew Tucker's whole story. He could watch it moving, silent, behind glass like the blue jays. That was just a doll figure Tucker meant, a mannequin. Her red wig would come off. He wanted—he couldn't remember her name, but he saw her thigh, he felt her hand. Green eyes. The rose-petal perfume. He wanted her to come now. This was an ugly story. This was a lie.

Tucker threw himself back against the sofa. "I don't have to prove anything," he said.

"You quit lying to me," Charles said.

"You're wearing us out," Tucker said. "We've been through all this already."

"Been through what?" The blue jays and the mockingbird were gone. The branches were very still. It felt darker. But the sun was still high.

"This," Tucker said. "I told you all this Sunday. When you woke up."

"What day is today?" Charles said. Then he realized his mistake. Tucker could lie and make it be any day he wanted.

"Thursday," Tucker said. "Listen, this is hard on us too. *You're* hard on us. I know how you feel. I think I know what's going on. But I'm exhausted. Dee-Dee's a basket case. You have to think of your friends. You have to get some therapy."

"How did she die?" Charles said craftily. *If you know so much.*

"I don't think you—I don't think that's important right now."

Charles felt a smirk rise to his face. He nodded. "Uh-huh. Sure. Right."

Tucker jumped up from the sofa. He marched over to the window, whirled on Charles. He was jabbing his finger, pointing outside. He couldn't talk, then he was spitting it out: "She blew up! She goddamn blew up in her goddamn car right out in the goddamn driveway, and you have *got* to get *used* to it!" He brought his hands to his hair. "Tucker, Tucker," he said, in a normal voice. He let his arms fall. It was definitely darker.

"I think you better get out of here," Charles said.

"Yeah, ok," Tucker said. "If you feel ok sitting up." He came around behind Charles and began kneading his shoulders.

"I'm fine," Charles said, rocking with the force of Tucker's massage.

"Yeah." Tucker slapped his back. "I bet you are, buddy. I just bet."

Charles felt him withdrawing. "Ask Clemmie to turn up the thermostat," he said.

"Clemmie's not here," Tucker's voice said, from farther away. "She's not here right now. I'll get the thermostat."

"You're trying to take away everything I have," Charles said. He wanted to cry. "You bastards," he whispered.

They had taken Clemmie away. They would keep Lianne from coming. They would hide her and keep her from coming. They were trying to break him down. They would make him sit here alone until he gave up and let the story through. Till he said the lie and made it real. But he would outwait them. They had no idea how stubborn he was, how tough. He would sit here till hell froze over, and damn them all.

Tucker was gone. He had been gone a long time.

The bastards had always hated him. They had always envied his money. His beautiful wife. He couldn't think about her now. He couldn't even think her name. If he thought about her, they would get her. The story would leak through and eat her up. The black story, black spreading stain like spilled ink on a white cloth. Black hole, eating the light.

If he thought about her hair, her hair would go. Its fragrance of warm oil. Her freckled feet. The pink soft lips. Not the eyes, he would not let himself see the green eyes.

It was hard not to see things. Things he wanted to see. He watched out the window. He wished the blue jays would come back, to keep his eyes occupied. He kept the ugly story a long way off, under glass. It would never get out. He could outwait them. He could wait forever. But it kept getting colder, and it kept getting darker.

31

AFTERMATH

After, Charles was never able to be sure when he accepted the truth. He sat on the sofa six hours or more. From time to time he felt Dee-Dee or Tucker enter to check on him, but he ignored them. He kept Lianne from his thoughts, blanking his mind with resentment, like a weary camper staring at a fire. But it flickered low, and the animals drew closer.

He grew cold again, and began to shiver, but would not ask for another injection.

Eventually he curled forward on the sofa, weeping to be so misunderstood, so sick and forsaken, among such hostile associates. He was careful not to make noise, not to alert them. They would use his tears as evidence for their case.

But gradually the world transformed itself around him. Do what he might, meanings subsided, and other meanings appeared through them, as trees appear through fog, and then stones appear, and then the hillside and whole spiny ranges under cruel clear skies. *See, we were here all along, a world of hard edges, of empty space. A world of hurt.*

So with his paranoia. He tried to keep to it, to hide low in its obscure pockets, but it thinned to a mist and disappeared. Tucker and Dee-Dee were not bad people. Finally he could not help admitting it. They were his friends. They were not trying to hurt him.

When he knew that, his misery became grief, no longer the blind suffering of a mistreated child. He refused, still, to think *what* he was grieving. But he felt it anyway, a void, a bleeding internal cavity. He curled tighter, in a knot that strained and might break his back, arms wrapping his knees, bucking for breath like a drowning horse, but still somehow not making an outcry.

When Dee-Dee switched on the light, all his silences broke. She hurried over, forced his head and shoulders into her lap. "I'm sorry," she said. "I'm so sorry, sorry, sorry." Tucker came in and sat at the other end of the sofa, at Charles's feet. His presence felt kind.

After, Charles would feel embarrassed at the awful sounds he had made, the way he had fouled and soaked Dee-Dee's skirt with his tears, his mucus.

"I don't want to talk about it," he said, when finally he could talk.

"Of course not," Dee-Dee said.

"Do you remember?" Tucker said.

"No," Charles whispered. "But I know what happened." He knew the size and shape of his disaster, if not its details. He felt its grim bulk looming over him, as indistinct and certain as the iron hull of a ship in the Maryland naval yards at night.

Tucker, later, would say his block was psychological and, as such, perfectly understandable. Charles would disagree. He was certain it was physical, something wrong with the wiring. The shock of the explosion. Tucker would say concussion explained why he didn't remember the days before her death. It didn't explain how he could wake up, attend the funeral, and then fall asleep and forget all over again. He would speak of fugue states, and the reasons for them. Charles would say the physical brain was complicated, and it could happen. Tucker would say, Yeah, it *could*. And he wasn't going to argue any more, because it didn't matter.

According to Tucker and Dee-Dee, Charles must have gone out to wave so long, see you there in half an hour. Or perhaps to remind her of something. Clemmie, hearing the thunderclap and running out from the kitchen, had found him in the front doorway, blown backward, his arms flung back up over his head, his mouth open, his eyes staring. He had not been breathing.

Perhaps his spirit had left him, to follow her up that column of heated and laden air: We enter and leave in spirals, and always about us whirl the vortices of passage.

Already people had come to windows, already phone calls were being made. Clemmie, in mortal agitation but seeing it was too late for Lianne, had kept her presence of mind, thumped his chest, started CPR. Coleman had been lying in the hospital, still unconscious, and yet, afterward, Charles was to have a strange and recurring dream: Outside himself, watching himself strangle while Coleman pressed his sternum, blew into his mouth. To Charles it would never seem that Clemmie had saved him, but always that Coleman had.

Was the dream because Coleman would tell his? Coleman would say his happened while he was still in coma, would insist it must have occurred on the very day. *It was a big fire in the yard,* he would say. *I was burning leafs. All my fault the house on fire, and you done breath in smoke and fell down dead. Miss Lianne wadn't nowhere, but I could feel her, she wa mighty mad. You better git him going, she say, you want to keep yo job. So I wa beating on yo chest, and you sigh in a grett big suck of air and commence to breathing.*

Charles could have sworn, later, that he had had his own dream before he had heard Coleman's. But was that just wishful thinking? Was it the sort of after-the-fact mysterious coincidence he had always scorned to hear others adduce as proof of the paranormal—the very sort of tale Lianne had loved to recount, shivering delicious shivers?

And if he were to take Coleman's dream as truly psychic—if he believed, had faith—would that then make him closer to her, or farther away?

There were questions, after, reintegrating, that he would never answer.

According to Tucker and Dee-Dee, he had waked up normally the next morning. Had sat up in the hospital bed and heard the news from Elaine. Surely the woman had been waiting all her life to announce her daughter's death, her grim mouth twisting in that vindicated smile, the one she offered, unwittingly, for all bad news. There could have been no one he would have hated more as messenger, but he supposed the proprieties had prevailed—he should hear it from a member of the family. A policeman had been in attendance. The assumption was the bomb had been meant for him, not for Lianne. The cop was there to protect him.

According to Tucker and Dee-Dee, he had responded calmly, with a measure of sadness but with an uncommon grace that had made his friends cry and had convinced his enemies, upon reflection, that he was a cold man, a man who had not loved his wife and who was not sorry she was dead. He had been solemn, and concerned for the comfort of his visitors. He had talked readily, if not at length, had thanked them for their condolences.

He had not seemed baffled or curious. He did not ask how it could have happened, who would have wanted to do it. He did not rage and say it made no sense. Again, for his enemies, this absence of an expected behavior was very prejudicial.

It was not Tucker's hospital, and Tucker did not believe, in matters of consequence, in treating friends. But others would tell him that Tucker and Dee-Dee had come and stayed through the night, that they had not slept for forty-eight hours straight.

Tucker and Dee-Dee would tell him, later, of his three days of convalescence, of his discharge from the hospital. They would tell him he had almost missed Lianne's funeral. That he had reasoned against going, had said it would be a circus, a travesty, a meaningless ceremony. That it was Laugh who had finally persuaded him.

Laugh had made the arrangements, consulting with the family. *Let his law firm handle it,* Elaine had said. *They handled the will and the wedding, let them handle the funeral.*

The firm had handled the will, but the only sense in which they had handled the wedding was that Charles had used their caterers and printers—though he had been careful to pay all expenses out of his household accounts—and that Brenda Faye had done a lot of the calling for him and had accepted RSVPs.

Elaine's problem was the will, which she had not yet seen but which she suspected cut her off with nothing. In fact, it provided for a one-time bequest of a hundred thousand, no further claims on the estate, regardless who predeceased, Charles or Lianne. The rest of the money, after a couple of seven-figure gifts to Hendrix College and to *Hope Lines,* was parceled out among aunts, uncles, nieces, nephews, and cousins.

It was odd that Laugh had been the one to assume responsibility. His status with the firm had not been entirely clear, just how official or unofficial he was, but all the others had flung up their hands. Neither Betty nor Eamon was equal to the chore, that was obvious. Greg had been the only other likely candidate, the heir to the throne, but he had fallen to asking a thousand questions, like a child, lost without Charles to appeal to.

Laugh had learned finally what true authority was, how it came not from position or fortune but from the person. He had learned that it was not the same as power over others, and that it was as rare as genius.

And he had learned, finally, that he had it.

He had been undecided where to have the ceremony, and then Elaine had let slip that Lianne had always wanted to be buried in The Peace That Passeth Understanding. He had had to decide whether to have a small private service or to allow the people. He had decided to allow the people, because so many friends had called and it had been hard to draw the line, hard to decide who was so close that Lianne would have wanted them there, who so tangential or estranged that they could be ignored. And there had been the question of goodwill, there had already definitely been the question of goodwill, and Laugh had felt Charles just might need as much of the goodwill of the people as possible. Then, too, gossip is least when openness is greatest. And then, finally, in a way, you could argue that she belonged to the whole state, though Laugh personally felt such sentiments belonged in the *National Enquirer.*

The cruelest decision had been what to do with the body. What was left of the body. When the police were finished, he had had it cremated. Tucker and Dee-Dee had gotten Charles to sign the papers, though he never read them. Cremation was preferable, surely, though it seemed a violent jest, a finishing off of what the bomb had begun. Still. The purity, the cleanliness of ashes. Lianne would have preferred that. Not to be a mangled thing, an object caught forever between two proper states, a charred imago.

Laugh had prevailed on Charles to go to the funeral, for the sake, again, of goodwill. He had been having disturbing thoughts about cause and effect, about Charles and Tina, and therefore maybe Charles and others. He had been having thoughts about Charles's fights with Lianne, and if he had been having such thoughts, then others might too, and that made it politic for Charles to at least act like a loving husband. He had been surprised that, after all, he liked the man and that it didn't matter to him all that much how culpable he was.

He wondered how much of his affection was the warmth of seeing the mighty brought low. Brought down to Laugh's estate. No longer immune, invulnerable, the paraclete.

He had decided that didn't matter either; the man needed a friend.

Charles did not and could not hear all this from Tucker and Dee-Dee, and certainly not all of it on the thirtieth of July, the Thursday of his second awakening. Some he would hear later. Some he would never hear. But he would, eventually, carry a complete picture of these events in his mind, without being able to say just where he had gotten which impression, or just how he had attained what might be described as such a high degree of resolution. Without, for that matter, being able to say just how correct his picture was:

For always there would be the uncertainly knowable realm of his amnesia.

After, he would assume that he had not totally forgotten, that a part of him *did* remember. If so, it was a part he would never be able to reach, even under hypnosis. He would never approach her death more closely than, on this side, his waking to a breakfast of bread and milk, and on the other side, the night he and she had argued God. There was, in between, an irreducible envelope, a fuzzy indeterminate boundary that all his researches only made fuzzier.

Logician by discipline, and reader of science fiction, he would recognize his situation: the effect of the observer on the observed. He studied himself, and the feedback overwhelmed any possible information.

There would be no comfort in the recognition. Instead, it would infuriate and then depress him. It made his loss consensual, and not experiential. As if everyone else had voted on the question while he was out of the room.

Tucker and Dee-Dee, on that Thursday evening, were not infuriated or depressed. They were awestruck, as in the presence of some large manifestation of weather. Truly something horrible had happened, but just as truly, something remarkable. For them, his condition carried about it an aura of ozone, of quickening.

And in the way that things work, their fascination gave them the heart, in spite of their near exhaustion, to comfort him a while longer.

Charles found—sitting straight up at last, flinching with a terrible headache, his eyes swollen and raspy, his tongue like a dry sponge in his mouth—he found that despair was not constant but came in waves. When it hit, it twisted through him like a violent cramp, it doubled him over. Between heaves, in spite of the headache, he felt normal. Just normal good headache pain, just regular living. It surprised him that you could feel so normal. That you could think about reading a book, eating a sandwich, going to the bathroom.

He had not gone to the bathroom since morning. He felt no need. *Why not?* he wondered vaguely. *What's on tv tonight?* he wondered. He could catch the late baseball scores. No he couldn't, the strike. Or was it settled by now?

But he couldn't watch tv, it wouldn't be appropriate, his wife was dead.

"Tucker, it just doesn't make sense," he said.

"It sure doesn't," Tucker said.

"I'm going to have to learn how to live with it," he said. "I'm going to have to go on with my life. That's all we can do, go on with our lives."

"That's right," Tucker said.

"We all know we're going to die," he said.

"We have to learn to live with it," Dee-Dee said.

And then a spasm shook him.

"I just don't *remember*," he said later. "Why can't I remember?"

"It's better you don't," Tucker said, the first of many times Charles would hear the sentiment. Tucker would say it again before the night was over.

Charles had the grace, between episodes, to regret forcing his friends to relive a bad time. If what they said was true, if they had gone through all of this before, then his behavior must be very hard on them. He didn't know where they were finding the strength, the patience. He could see how tired they were. Tucker looked old, bags under his eyes, the lines around his mouth drawn, his jaw sagging so that his teeth seemed more prominent than usual. Dee-Dee's face looked bruised, her hair a black wreck. She looked like an aging whore.

He was very tired himself. He was beyond weariness; he was numb. He wanted to know where Elaine was, and they told him she was in Clemmie's quarters, on the third floor. He thought it was an insult to have her here, an insult to Lianne's memory, but he didn't care enough to protest. At last he went to bed like a sick man, heaped with covers. Tucker offered a sedative, and Charles said no, no more shots. Dee-Dee brought him hot milk heavy with cream and bourbon. She and Tucker offered to sleep in the room with him, but he said no, he was fine, down the hall in the guest bedroom was fine, he would call if he needed them.

It was in his bed that night, shivering and alone, that he first began to dwell on what must have happened. He couldn't help thinking of it.

Lianne was already in the ground. Her ashes were. He closed his eyes and saw the grave, though he could not and never would remember the funeral, and when he finally visited The Peace That Passeth Understanding, he would not find her where he had imagined, at the floodline, at the place where they had made love, at the foot of the stone that said *Bull.*

He saw the grave as if it were fall, the turned earth raw and red under a scatter of leaves. But it was summer, he reminded himself, not fall. What difference did it make, those were just rules. Stupid rules. He opened his eyes and saw the parabola of meaningless lamplight on the wall, the stupid intersection of a cone. Geometry, nothing but geometry. If he slept, he could not tell sleep from lying awake and thinking. If he dreamed, he could not tell dreaming from closing his eyes and seeing the grave. In the scenes he saw, there was no trace of her. There was no sense of her presence at the grave. There was an absence everywhere.

He didn't care about the last five days. Let them be lost forever, they didn't matter. The days he wanted to remember were the ones *before* her death. That night, Thursday night, in his bed, he brought his memory as far forward as he would ever be able to. It was not enough. He wanted to follow past that last remembered argument and embrace: *If there's not any God, there's not any us.* And he cradled her head in his hand.

And then? He wanted to follow to the uttermost edge of her life. If she had to die, he wanted to be her witness. It would never seem right, it would never seem fair that simply because he could not remember, he could never reenter that moment. *I was there, wasn't I?*

Simply because his mind, battered beyond tolerance, had refused to encode the event, represent it somehow in the minute and delicate script of messenger RNA, simply because of that, because no one had taken the minutes, because the tape sang only white noise, because no machine can record its own disruption—for no more reason than that. Though that was, when you thought more deeply, the single sorry irreducible paradox of existence.

Perhaps Tucker was right: it was better not to remember. Most people had thought so at the funeral. *It's a blessing he don't,* they had whispered, standing around him in the murmuring crowd. Curtis had said nothing but had wrapped him roughly in one long arm and had blown his own nose into a linen handkerchief in his free hand. *A blessing, a blessing,* the people had hissed.

Or no, no, did that really happen? Or was it a dream, was he slipping back to sleep? It was a dream. He didn't remember the funeral, he didn't remember Curtis.

But in later days, he would have accessions of voice and image, would sense a shadowy host of pressing spirits, a susurrus of cliché and sensation that he took for the ghost of memory, and he would curse the gossipy throng for their ignorance, curse them and their blighted children forever for their inherited, perseverant, complacent sentimentality.

Because it *wasn't* better that way. Because he wanted to know it all, wanted to know every microsecond, every last flicker, wanted to be there in the middle of the flame to kiss her goodbye at the exact unnamable instant in which her dissolution had progressed so far that God Himself had declared her to be no more. But God did not exist, you could take that to the bank. Or if He did exist, He should be slain for His crimes. That was the kindest view you could take of God, that He didn't exist. So why did Charles persist in imagining His presence at Lianne's death?

He would not pray. Never. He would not give the nonexistent bastard that much satisfaction. But he saw himself in the middle of the flames anyway, commending her soul: *Goodbye, God be with You, be You with God . . .*

But that was imagination, and he wanted to *be* there, to *remember*.

But how how how, since the event itself would have unfolded too fast and too huge to register, whole orders and realms of mass and velocity and perhaps even meaning of such a scale that no ant can read the expression on a human face, no fly trapped in a car fathom the distance to San Francisco, you cannot photograph the light you photograph with leaving at the speed of light you cannot, *and wake up, Charles, you're going to sleep again.*

He was afraid if he slept he would lose the truth, as he had before. The pain of rediscovering her death was greater than the pain he felt now, the pain of living with it. He didn't want to go through the agony of discovery, not ever again.

He tried to remember, and he couldn't remember. All of his body an instrument, a connected and sensitive thing, and since the stages of the blast had made changes in that instrument—why could he not, picking over the wreckage as experts do, discover clues? He drifted in and out of the world, not asleep and not awake.

There would have been a shock wave, surely. A spreading sphere of compression, a tiny but infinite instant of awareness as change stacked on change until the very structure of the air broke down, refused to support the expansion: But it would have *had* to support it, as we, until we are gone, must always bear even what seems unbearable, however stacked and queued and multiplied upon itself our trouble may be, however little outlet we may find. Do we, then, faced with the unsupportable, change state? Do we become, each, a flame of stripped shells? Did she, a plasma, still wander the universe somehow?

A protostar in a cloud of dust. He had read a novel once in which the stars thought and felt and had souls, and certain telepaths, certain dreamers, could speak with them. The star glowed in its haze, it turned slowly and silently in space. *Lianne,* he thought, but she didn't hear him.

Then he was in the portico doorway, watching the Blazer.

Had she suffered? That was what he needed to know. That was why he needed to be there. The one unbearable thought was her pain. Born in pain, raised in pain. Had she ever had one single clear perfectly happy moment in her life?

"I don't want you to hurt," he said, and startled himself awake.

"I'm such an asshole," he muttered, his heartbeat calming. A whirl of near-images went through his mind, a blurred impression of all the times he had been selfish or greedy or uncaring. Flirting with Tina. Hating Elaine. Belittling Lianne's painting.

"Please, baby, don't hurt," he said, standing in the doorway again. *It happened too fast. You didn't feel a thing*.

Please let it happen too fast.

His mouth would have been open to call her back, perhaps, to tease her that she had forgotten something else—a note for Bill Pumphrey, a vitamin she had meant to take, the keys to a room in the theater. He knew how that would have gone, how she never was able to simply leave a house but forgot something, and then forgot something else, and came back, and came back, and she would have begun leaving with minutes to spare, but would have come back twice already and used up all her margin, and he would have teased her unmercifully the second time, and then he would have seen it, whatever it was, her coin purse with the allergy medicines so she could drink champagne, or a final checklist with the names of the catering help, or her notes for the little speech she would make. Whatever it was, it would have been lying on an end table or on the kitchen counter, and he would have laughed out loud and gone running out with it, and never mind that they found nothing in his hands and nothing blown back into the house and nothing lying scorched on the portico, it must have happened that way, he would have laughed out loud picked it up and gone running out: *Come back, Lianne, silly girl, come back, oh please come back*.

And then not fast at all, but the long slow violent battery of nested wave fronts: blue, white, yellow, red, violet, dark blue, as she in sections unknitted, nerve, bone, and vein, as she tattered and flew apart, as she became mostly a winding skein in the roiling pillar of fire from the black hulk, not much still sitting there in the blazing car but her charred spine and flanks, curled forward, shuddering, bouncing with aftershock and the billowing heat, a skeletal rider on God's shattering horse: and high above, the rest of her twisting into the sky on a column of dirty smoke, a looped and trailing corkscrew, a signal, a flare, a marker, the helicoid of loss.

At that point everyone in Little Rock would have begun to know, but he had not. He had been cheated of the moment of her going. He had not been there, or had been there only bodily, in the limited way that such violence permits. And was that Satan, the violence of Satan, that would not allow witness? But the Bible tells us that God, too, is death to look upon.

God, *the* God, that Jerk-Off Who refuses ever to show Itself in any plain and unmistakable way, the Pissant Lord of All Being Who lets us suffer forever in longing while She plays Her coy game of peepeye, that Deity whose greatest mercy is not to exist because otherwise a Mother-fucking Bean-Counter Who numbers every atom and Whose eye is on the fall of every sparrow and Who presumably watched a scrap of medulla snag on a twig of the willow oak and then drop to float in the pool of the fountain—

But this was craziness, he knew, even as it all began, there in his bed. He was scarring himself with whips, he was compounding his pain in order to expiate his guilt, the guilt that he must deserve, since he felt so much pain.

This was craziness, it was the sort of overcharged and impolitic behavior he had always scorned, the widow-woman flinging herself into the coffin. It could not be happening to Charles Morrison, that elegant, self-contained gentleman millionaire badger.

After, he would use every tool and technique he could think of. He would study microfilm. He would talk to relatives. He would develop the chronology of her life. He would submit to hypnosis. He would hire people: investigators, pyschologists, researchers. Even a writer or two, working toward a biography that would never be satisfactory and would never be completed. He would spend great sums of money.

But that would be later. Tonight he stood in the doorway and watched the Blazer. Over and over, he made her die. She had vanished into a horror, and so he invented horrors and ransacked them to see if she was there.

She was not a star. She was vaguer, farther away.

She was a faint glow in his being, nowhere present and everywhere visible. Tonight he began, began to work his way back, began to work his way back to her, to the fading illumination of that bright original moment, that blast that had created this, his only world.

32

APPROXIMATIONS

One peculiarity of grief is that the bereft often awake in panic, oppressed by the overwhelming sense that something terrible is about to happen.

The fact that it *has* happened is meaningless, since loss is a void, a nothing into which we bleed our substance. We cannot comprehend loss. We can only apprehend losing. And so it is that we approximate comprehension by means of successive alarm. Night after night starting from sleep, grappling the switch to the bedside lamp, pulses hammering in our ears: We have done something wrong. We are about to be punished. *Something terrible is about to happen.*

Charles woke up Friday afternoon thinking murder. His heart was beating about in his chest like a startled rabbit in a closet. He stumbled out of bed.

The air was hot and stuffy. So Dee-Dee or Tucker *had* turned the air conditioning off. Apparently nobody had ever turned it back on.

His headache was still with him, more vicious than ever. He had two days of beard, and his hair was filthy. In the mirror, his eyes were bloodshot. Lianne was dead.

Fragments of the night were still in his mind, scraps of image, dream, anger. Somebody had killed her. Why hadn't he realized it before? How could he have lain there hours and hours thinking of her death and never once thinking of murder?

His skin crawled with menace. He had to *do* something. He needed to yell. He needed to hurt someone, to beat somebody up.

No one was in the house. He went all through it. He went to Clemmie's room, and it was perfectly made up. There was no trace of Elaine. He went to the guest bedroom. It was a mess, their things thrown everywhere, but Tucker and Dee-Dee weren't to be found.

How could they leave him like this? He was in bad shape; how could they all just go out and leave him alone? He ignored the fact that if he had found Elaine he would have slugged her and thrown her bodily out of the house.

He went out front in his pajamas, unshaven and dirty, his mouth foul. It was the last day of July, and the afternoon sun was ferocious. He didn't feel the heat at first, it was the light that slammed his brain, made him dizzy. His headache had escalated to a new level. His senses whirled about him, the world crunched to radiating chaos.

Where were the police? Where the reporters?

The white flagstone of the drive dazzled, but was cool to his bare feet. There were marks on the stone—skid marks, tire marks? Scorch marks? He tried to remember if the marks had always been there. Were they the trace of her death? He couldn't tell. He staggered, lifted his eyes. Stumbled in a circle, surveying the scene. The fountain splashed peacefully into its pool, a soothing lie. No floating wreckage. Around it, the flowerbeds were newly turned. No withered blossoms, no blackened vines.

But the dogwood by the portico was gone, its stump a white circle.

"They killed her," he said, dragging his bare foot over a streak on the flagstones.

He needed to catch the bastards. He needed to get started now, but where was everybody? The world was a still ruin, a wilderness of disconnection. What was the first move?

He couldn't think, he hurt too bad. His anger and his headache were the same thing. The top of his head might come off. He might die out here. The first thing to do was to get inside, get out of the sun. The first thing to do was to get rid of the headache.

He put everything from his mind except his sense of mission. One step in front of the other. First things first. Get functional, then take care of details.

He took the elevator back upstairs. He treated himself as if he had a hangover. Shave first. For some reason, the most important thing was to shave, that sense of cleanliness. He lathered with menthol cream. He sat on the toilet with his head in his hands to let his beard soak. The pain was too much. He couldn't sit still. He pulled himself to his feet, found his razor. His knees kept buckling, but he shaved without cutting himself. Wiped his face with a dry towel and threw it on the floor. Wisps of cream still clinging here and there, one ear loaded up, but the smooth face made him look more alert, and looking more alert made him feel more alert.

Then and only then did he allow himself the Tylenol. He took three of the big ones, gulping them down with handfuls of water from the faucet. The water told him how thirsty he was, his tongue cracked and swollen. He kept swallowing handfuls, his throat knotting with the awkward position. The water tasted like shaving cream.

He put himself under the shower. He shampooed, rinsed, shampooed again, using the brush on his sudsy scalp. Lianne said not to, it aggravated the hair loss. He didn't care, it felt good. He turned the water as hot as he could stand it and let it beat against the back of his neck, loosening his headache. But the steam smothered his breathing, and he turned the water as cold as he could stand it, facing into the spray. The cold revived him, but brought back the edge of his pain. Still, he stood under the torrent, his mouth open, drinking.

Wrapped in a towel, tracking puddles, he went into the bedroom. The air was too close. In spite of the cold finish to his shower, he was breaking a sweat and felt nauseous. He adjusted the master thermostat, and a burst of cooler air rewarded him almost immediately. He bent to the grate, inhaling. He straightened up and took a step, and his legs went out from under him.

How long had it been since he had eaten? That one piece of bread, and he had never finished it, had he? A couple swallows of milk. And how long before that?

He forced himself to his feet, found poplin slacks in the closet, and pulled them on without underwear, leaning against the wall to support himself while he slid his legs in.

He rode the elevator down. It seemed to take forever. He almost ran to the refrigerator. The glass quart was there, still almost full. The cold air of the fridge fell on his bare chest.

He lifted the milk, chugalugging. It was still good; it hadn't turned. He had set the bottle down on the counter when he realized it was the last thing that would move from her hand to his body. He threw the bottle at the wall and jumped after it as if to catch it, too late to stop his reflex but horrified that he had broken the precious glass. But it thudded on the cork of the bulletin board, clattered on the cabinet top, clanged into the stainless-steel sink.

He needed to piss. He needed to piss bad. Now that he had put fluid in his body, all of the toxins released at once. He made it down the hall to the bathroom, but when he got there nothing happened. He stood over the bowl, holding himself. "Come on, come on," he said.

When the flow finally came, it seared him. He screamed, splashing the back of the toilet. He was on fire all the length of his penis, but now that he had started pissing, he couldn't stop.

"Jesus Christ," he said, finished. He bent over, squeezing himself between thumb and forefinger, milking the urethra to ease the burning. In the bowl, his piss was brown. It stank to high heaven. He pulled the lever, and the foul stuff swirled and sank away in a rumble of fresh water. He was staring at his bare feet. He wiggled his toes. "Jesus," he said again, straightening, feeling better. His headache had lessened.

The milk had brought his strength back momentarily, like wadded paper brightening a fire. Now an honest hunger growled in his belly. He went back to the kitchen, tore chunks of bread out of what was left of the six-grain, used a soup spoon to slather the chunks with peanut butter. There was ham, he saw. There was mayonnaise, there were lettuce and tomatoes.

He could have sliced the bread and made a real sandwich, but he was afraid of the knife.

He got the milk jug out of the sink, refilled it from the gallon plastic carton. He wandered out, eating and drinking. He was leaving crumbs everywhere, and he didn't give a shit. In the living room, on a side table, he found a stack of newspapers. He stood and stared at them. He knew what they were. He knew what was in them. "Not now," he said. "Not now, you bastards." The papers had been there yesterday, surely, but he had never given them a thought.

And the tv. The huge dark tv. What time was it? Was the news on?

He couldn't stay in here. As far as he was concerned, this was where she had died. He went in the library. It was hollow and empty, like a church on a winter weekday. He sat at the desk and put his feet up, munching.

He was thinking more clearly now, and it dawned on him that someone in *particular* had killed her. That this was real life and not just generic murder. It wasn't like a mystery story, where the deed was factual but the killer was only a cloud of probabilities.

Someone out there had actually done this.

Someone he *knew.*

The thing kept unfolding, surprising him with the obvious: (A) Lianne was dead because her car had exploded. That had taken him five days. (B) Cars don't just explode. Her death was a murder. *That* he had gotten to in only twenty or so hours. And now, a scant couple of hours later: (C) If she was murdered, then someone murdered her.

Wow, the wonders of reason. What was next?

Shouldn't he be able to grasp this all at once? In the books around him, towering over his head, it was simple. People got upset, they grieved, raged, freaked out, but they knew what was going on, they saw the whole pattern. But he felt lost in a mad and swollen logic, like a spider in the plumbing, like Alice in Wonderland.

Shrunken so small the normal was monstrous, did not cohere.

He was sitting forward, feet on the floor, shivering, clutching his arms. No shirt, no shoes, no service. Where *was* everybody?

Was he nuts? A loony lost in his own insanity? Locked up somewhere, straitjacketed, just *thinking* he was home alone?

Then maybe he just *thought* Lianne was dead. Maybe she was still out there, alive. Maybe all he had to do was trust, and work with the doctors, and he could find his way back to her.

Bullshit.

The thing to do was to get busy. He wasn't hurting any more. He had food in him. He had turned the air up too high, that was all. Get some clothes on. Find out what was happening, what the police were doing. Get on somebody's case. He stood up.

"Oh Jesus," he said, in a shiver of despair.

It wouldn't do any good. Nothing he did would do any good. Lianne was gone. The world was dead and empty forever. He was alone.

He made himself take a step. It was like rehabilitation. A step and then another step. He went to the stairs, and he got stronger going up.

Elaine, he thought. *Elaine did it.* He flashed on the certainty he had felt when they discovered the tapped phones. No, Elaine was impossible. It didn't fit her personality. Elaine didn't want you to die, she wanted you to live and be miserable.

He was on the first landing, panting a bit. Thinking of the wiretap, he saw the phone on the hall table. He should do something with the phone, he should call somebody. Get things straightened out.

But the phone was too abstract. He needed to confront people. Go to the office. That's what he would do, he would go downtown to the office. He headed up the second flight of stairs.

He was dragging his Bill Blass navy blazer off the hanger, his Austin Reed taupe slacks, when he thought of her closet. He threw jacket, slacks, a Perry Ellis belt, and a Rooster tie on the bed. Names, why did he wear all those fucking names?

He opened her closet door. All of her clothes were still there. Of *course* they were still there. A faint effluvium came to him, a trace of mingled perfumes, hints of musk, the sweaty leather of insteps. He imagined burying his face in one of her gowns, drinking her odor. Not now. He didn't have time for that sort of weakness right now.

But if not now, when?

The truth was, he wanted to save that moment for when he needed it, but the world wouldn't wait, the spoor would fade. He felt caught in a closing trap, like someone in an old horror movie, when the walls begin to move inward.

What had she been wearing? He didn't know what she had worn. Was it the green one? It occurred to him that he could find out. He could search the closet and try to recognize what was missing. But he didn't know all her outfits.

He realized he was scanning the racks for the green gown, and he slammed the door against its cushion of air. Oh, the house was well made, tight in every joint.

He had a vivid image, pulling open the drawer of the bedside table, grabbing a gun, blowing a hole in the door, as if the door had done something. But he didn't keep a gun in the house, he never had.

"That's the first thing," he said, dressing himself. He meant get a gun. "That's the first thing to do." He saw himself with a big black nine-millimeter, a leather shoulder holster under the Bill Blass jacket, stark on the Egyptian cotton of his Lands' End button-down.

Pistol by Giorgio Armani.

He sat on the bed to pull up his socks, slipped into a pair of Rockport loafers. He stood up. He felt armored, professional. He strode out with his shoulders squared. He felt like he was already wearing the gun. He felt like James Bond.

He was on the portico when he thought: (D) *They weren't trying to kill her. They were trying to kill me.* He stumbled and almost fell headlong down the steps. He stood on the second step from the top. He felt the heat assault the envelope of cool air he had brought out of the house. He imagined walking to the garage, sliding the door up, getting in the Mercedes. Turning the key. And in a bloom of flame he is blown to bits. He felt the force of the explosion as a blow to his midsection. He sat on the steps, a stilted collapse.

Nobody wanted to kill Lianne. Of course not. She had no enemies. They wanted to kill him. It *was* his fault she was dead. What had he done, whom had he pissed off? That was the guilt he would carry the rest of his life, that some enemy he had made in a fit of careless spite had destroyed her, trying to get to him. Some fool he had mocked in an easy victory.

Whoever it was was still out there. He felt terribly exposed. He felt the telescopic sight of a high-powered rifle mapping his chest, his forehead.

Never mind that the gunman would have had to occupy the high window of a friend or neighbor. Maybe it *was* one of his friends or neighbors, someone who had kept up appearances but could no longer tolerate his egotism, his dominance.

He knew it wasn't likely there really was a gunman. It didn't matter. He felt the rifle barrel wavering. He felt the cross-hairs travel his body. He felt the potential behind the slugs.

Let them shoot. This was his purgatory. This was his penance for getting her killed. Maybe he wanted to die. It would be easier than living.

There were too many things to face, too many complicated situations to be gotten through. Let them shoot if they wanted to.

He had begun sweating all at once, in a burst of chill moisture. He felt it sluicing his ribs under his arms, soaking his shirt. Dark patches appeared over the knees of the taupe slacks.

He thought of Elaine again. He wanted it to be Elaine. He would pull his gun, the big nine-millimeter, and shoot her right in the face.

But it wasn't Elaine. Elaine would never have wired the Blazer, she would have gone straight for the Mercedes. It wasn't Elaine, but he wanted to kill her anyway. He shivered with premonition, a fear that she would drive up and get out of her car, and he would shoot her, right there in the driveway, even though she hadn't done it.

Then he remembered he didn't have the gun yet.

He slapped a hand against his slacks, testing them. He felt the heat, a tangible invader, something pressed into his body, and yet it didn't seem to matter. He could feel the jacket dragging on his back, the lining soaked through. Let the bastards shoot.

A white four-by-four pulled into the drive, Tucker's Toyota. He didn't drive it much in the city; Dee-Dee must have the car.

Tucker pulled to a stop in front of him, got out. He came up the steps. He was wearing a linen suit and a maroon silk tie. Cowboy boots with the suit. Where were the spurs?

"Where have you been?" Charles said, not looking up.

"Have a business to run, you know. Where's Elaine?" Tucker sat down.

"Who gives a shit? She can go to hell."

"She said she would look after you. You kick her out?"

"I didn't do anything. She wasn't here when I woke up."

"Goddammit," Tucker said.

"Where's Dee-Dee?"

"Home in bed, I hope. I haven't seen her since this morning. She needs her rest. This thing has about k—about run her down."

"I was just asking," Charles said.

"How are you doing?"

"I'm fine."

"You're sopping wet." Charles didn't respond. "You heading out or heading in?"

"I'm going to the office."

"Hell, man, it's closed. It's six in the afternoon."

"Oh," Charles said. He thought. "I don't care. I got the keys."

"Yeah, but you can't *do* anything. Everybody's off for the weekend."

"I don't care."

"Come on back inside," Tucker said. "You don't need to be out in this heat."

Charles squinted up into the trees, searching out the couple of upper-story neighboring windows barely visible through the leaves. The sense of the gunman had left him. He didn't feel exposed any more. He was just hot and sweaty. He might as well go in.

Tucker held back to let Charles go through the door first. "They weren't trying to kill her," Charles confided, pausing in the doorway. "They were trying to kill me."

"Yeah, that's a possibility." Tucker put a hand in the small of his back, urging him on.

The house was dark, but no longer oppressive to Charles. It no longer felt stuffed and smothered with her death. It was just empty space.

He steered right into the living room, pulled the front curtains open. There were crumbs from his sandwich on the floor. He had left the milk bottle in the library. He thought of the puddles in the bathroom upstairs, the wadded towel on the floor.

"When's Clemmie coming back?" he said.

"That I don't know. Jesus, it's cold in here. Why don't you peel out of those clothes before you catch cold."

"That's not how you catch colds. You don't sound very medical."

"Just get some dry clothes on. I'll be here." Tucker flopped on the sofa, loosened his tie. He picked up the remote, to click on the news, then stopped himself.

"Go ahead," Charles said. "I'll be down in a minute." He headed for the elevator. He heard the tv come on after he left the room.

When he came back down, *Wheel of Fortune* was on. It was hard to see the show with the light from the window behind it, paling out the picture.

Tucker tried to make him eat something. "I just ate," Charles said. "I'm tired wandering around this house. I want to *do* something."

"There's nothing to do," Tucker said. "Not right now. Crisis moment."

"No, they already guessed *m*," Charles said. "And nobody says 'crisis moment.' " Then, shaking his head, dismayed at his own banality, "Jesus Christ."

"No," Tucker said. "That's a person, not an event."

Dee-Dee drove up. Through the window, they watched her get out, march up the portico out of sight. A few moments later, she appeared at the living room doorway.

"Jesus Christ," Charles said again as she walked in. In the few seconds she had been out of view he had forgotten. He had felt as though he and Tucker were sitting here waiting on the women. He had expected Lianne to walk through the door with her.

"What are you doing here?" Tucker said. "You ought to be getting some rest."

"I got some." Dee-Dee set her purse on the bar. "Now I feel like getting busy with something." She studied Charles. "What's wrong?" she said. "You look like you've seen a ghost." Tucker flinched, but Dee-Dee didn't notice what she'd said.

"I'll fix you something to eat," she said.

"No," Charles said. "I don't want anything to eat."

"Well, I'm going to fix myself a drink," she said, and went around behind the bar. Glasses clinked. She found the tongs, opened the door to the ice tray. The vodka bottle lay across the cubes, frosted, the label blue and silver. Lianne had put it there. Vikin Fjord, not terribly expensive, but the only genuine potato vodka available in Little Rock.

Dee-Dee poured herself a healthy dollop over cubes in a tumbler. The glass frosted instantly. "You boys want anything?" she said. "While I'm here?"

"No," Charles said.

"He doesn't know what to do with himself," Tucker said. "When I got here, he was about to go to the office." He shrugged. "Elaine has apparently moved out."

Dee-Dee took a sip, gave the room a glancing inspection. "I'll do some cleaning," she said. "In a little while." She took a swallow this time, came over to Charles, patted his cheek. "It's natural to feel helpless right now," she said.

"I don't feel helpless!" He stood, walked away from them, shook his hands in that clenched-fist half bow which signals ultimate exasperation. "I—don't—feel—helpless." He turned back. "I feel as tough as ever. Tougher. I feel like I can do anything that needs doing."

Puzzlement came over his face. "I just don't know what to do."

"Well, I know something you need to do," she said.

She refreshed her drink, then led him upstairs, to his office. On his desk there was a large, neatly organized stack of sympathy cards. "You're going to start answering these," she said.

"Do I have to? All it's going to do is remind me."

"Everything's going to remind you. That's where you are right now. We're all going to be reminded, for a long time."

He thumbed through the top layers of the stack. "I don't know half these people. There's a million of them."

"And more coming in every day. You have to get started now, before it's completely out of hand. You've never done this in your life, have you?"

"No. I hate cards. I hate all this bourgeois prefabricated sentiment."

Charles had never seen Dee-Dee look so angry. "Tough titty," she said. "This is one of the things people *do*. This is one of the things Lianne did for you, you asshole. So you wouldn't have to think about it. Now you're going to do it for her."

"I don't know what to say to them."

"You say: *Thank you for your kind remembrance in a time of personal sorrow.* Something like that. Except with friends. With close friends you write something personal. And you sign your name to all of them."

"Will you help me?"

She looked at the drink in her hand, as if to make certain it held enough to get her through. "I thought I would clean— Oh, all right. All right."

He wrote until his wrist ached. Dee-Dee sat in a chair beside the desk, like a secretary, helping him sort by degrees of acquaintance: "No, no, put more than that. You know the Hendersons better than that. Write: *I have fond memories of the night at the catfish house.*"

He didn't remember the Hendersons at all. But he understood that Dee-Dee's "you" was an inclusive "you," that it meant neither Charles nor Lianne but the single creature of their marriage.

That creature was still alive, he realized, with a crawl of adrenaline. Half of it cut away: dying, but still alive. It was *that* creature that knew all these people, however slightly. It was that creature now, failing, considerate, that said its goodbyes to the living.

He wondered how much longer Tucker and Dee-Dee would be his friends. It was the marriages that were friends, not the people in them. That was a good thought; he should write it in his journal. He looked at Dee-Dee, and she seemed alien already, tall and dark and brusque, mannish but sexy, someone he had known in another life.

"I'm not really an asshole, am I?" he said.

"No worse than any other man," she said. She took a massive swallow of her vodka.

He became aware of her perfume, a heavy orchid-and-sandalwood scent. Her knees, the skirt cutting above them.

He caught her with tears in her eyes once. "What?" he said.

She waved the card she had been holding for his next attention. "If it was me and Lianne, we would be talking a mile a minute. *Remember she came to Luellen's wedding in that awful lime-green dress and all the other bridesmaids were in turquoise?* Yes, but I didn't say a word, because it was her mother's idea to make it and she didn't want to hurt her feelings. *Poor dear, she's blind as a bat now. Is she still driving? No, Estes had the keys changed on the Fleetwood, and she won't drive the Rabbit.* Is he still selling those real estate books; I haven't seen them in a year. *No, because somebody told me Cecily was doing it now, and he and Cecily never could stand each other.* You know, I met her roommate the other day. *From Sewanee?* That's such a beautiful campus. *George Abraham's daddy used to work there, what was he? Dean of students?*"

Dee-Dee had alternated voices, coming amazingly close to Lianne's tone. It was a stunning performance, the more so because Charles had never heard her mimic anyone before. It was the closest thing to a tribute to Lianne he would ever hear Dee-Dee utter.

"But you just sit there like a machine," she concluded. "Writing away."

His eyes stung, but he controlled himself. "It's the best I can do," he said.

Dee-Dee called Tucker to bring her up more ice and vodka. He appeared in a few moments, set a glass full of fresh cubes on a coaster on the corner of the desk. He was carrying the subzero bottle in a linen towel to protect his hand. He poured, vapor rising from the instantly frosted glass. A cube cracked. He bowed. "Your servant, ma'am."

Dee-Dee put a hand on his hip as he turned to go. "What are you doing, baby?" Looking up into his eyes.

"Just watching tv," he said. "I'm fine."

"Ok, then," she said.

Marriage, Charles thought.

Later in the evening, Dee-Dee opened an envelope that held a letter, not a card. She read it while he finished the note he was working on. She handed it to him with an expression of peculiar satisfaction. It was from Katie. *Dear Lianne,* it said:

> *This is to you and not your dumb husband. I guess he will read it, but that can't be help. Just to tell you how much I appreciate it, and I'm sorry your dead. I know you can hear me, but not if I dont write it. It doesn't feel like.*
>
> *So anyway, I love you and I will miss you. I am dedicating my career to you. And if any one tells me when I am famous, how did you get here, so I will say I owe it all to Lianne Weatherall, thats what you told me your real name was.*

It was signed, *Love, K. T. (because that's my new name).*

Charles folded it, put it to one side, began an answer. In spite of her popularity, he had always thought of himself as Lianne's mentor, caretaker, shielding others from the abrasiveness of her personality, and thereby protecting her, in return, from their ill will. Now he saw that she had had a life completely outside his own. That there were many who preferred her to him. Who felt the wrong person had died and would hate him the more for it.

I hope you're dead by the time this gets there, he wrote, glancing to make sure Dee-Dee was not reading over his shoulder. *Go to hell.*

She would never get Lianne's heart and lungs, he thought, imagining Katie's thin chest bloody and open, violated by surgery. She would never get them now. Nobody would.

"You should have had children," Dee-Dee said, as Charles sealed the note in an envelope. He addressed it *Katie What's-her-name, The Middle of Hell*, slid it under the stack of others.

"We can't," he said.

"I know, I know. I'm just saying you should have."

Cloning, he thought. If he had just one cell of her body, maybe someday soon science would be able. Keep it in cryogenics till then. Her identical twin, but younger. But what about her memories—would it be her? The principle of identity. So close a match that she would vibrate out of the cosmos, fill the vessel, like tuning forks pulling a note from a nearby string? Like the minds in Van Vogt's *The World of Null-A*. Like what he read one time about Japanese actors: they believed they became their parts.

But he would be too old by then. So ok, they would have youth serum.

All the things that will not happen. It was just a story. He slid back down to reality.

Dee-Dee upended her glass, drained the last of her third vodka. "I'll get you some more," he said, and stood up. She stood at the same time, and they bumped each other. Then he found himself clutching her, plundering her sweet-sour liquorish mouth with his own. She was responding, her arms around him fiercely.

He felt a double sensation, the strangeness of her body, the fury of his need enveloping that strangeness, consuming it, like a fire trying to read a map.

They separated. He could feel hungers rolling about his body, random and broken loose, savage as ions. Anything that comes near. I will leap and grab you. Anything that comes near.

"I'm sorry," he said.

She gave him a flat look, didn't say anything. *We were both there, weren't we?* "I'm going downstairs," she said.

"I'm just going to write a few more notes," he said.

"Ok," she said.

He began a letter to Lianne, like Katie's. He wrote, *I miss you, Baby. Why did you go?* He couldn't think of anything else to say.

He signed it *Love, Charles,* folded the stationery and put it in an envelope, stamped the envelope. He used a name from a song, he didn't know why, Little Liza Jane. He made up an address in a different city, left off the return address. He slid it in the middle of the stack, where no one would notice. It would go straight to her. It would go to the dead letter box.

He found Katie's envelope, tore it and its contents to shreds. He carried the shreds to the toilet in the bathroom off the study, flushed them away. He went downstairs to join Dee-Dee and Tucker. They were asleep together on the couch, the sound turned down low. Marriage.

He decided not to wake them. He had been going to tell them they didn't need to stay over, he would be fine, but now he went back up and made himself ready for bed.

In bed, he tried to think of Lianne, but all he could think of was the violent moment when he had held Dee-Dee. It was fresh in his nerves. Wrapped in her perfume, as if the perfume had been the heat of the fire he felt. Dee-Dee. Big lush exotic difficult Dee-Dee. He had a hard-on. He wanted to fuck her. He wouldn't let himself masturbate. He tossed and turned.

He woke up to the faint sound of a motor, light flickering in the tree branches. Tucker and Dee-Dee going home. He couldn't remember his dreams. Maybe he could dream of fucking Dee-Dee. It would be ok if it was just a dream. It wouldn't be betrayal like masturbating, or like actually doing it. You weren't responsible for what you dreamed. He slept again.

He woke twice in a guilty panic in the middle of the night, his heart clattering against his ribs like a prisoner dragging his tin cup across the bars of his cell:

Something terrible is about to happen.

33

OR ELSE (E)

He slept late again, into the afternoon, and passed the rest of Saturday in a daze. No one visited. He went to bed early and fell into a dreamless sleep.

He set himself the task, Sunday morning, of reading the papers. This was the second Sunday after her death, and he didn't want the world getting any farther ahead.

He transferred the stack in the living room to the sun porch. He went out and got this morning's paper from the driveway. It was nine o'clock, and the heat was already oppressive. He reorganized the stack, oldest paper on the top to newest on the bottom.

He found a package of frozen croissants in the refrigerator and warmed three of them in the oven. He provided his table with butter and strawberry preserves, with orange juice. He scrambled himself some eggs, wet, with dill and a touch of garlic. He started the coffee brewing.

"A Sunday morning like any other Sunday morning," he said to Lianne, who looked up at him from the front page of last Sunday's *Gazette*. "Read the paper over brunch," he said, setting his place. "Except this time I'm going to read about you." He was free to talk to her, to be melodramatic as he wished, since there was no one there to observe him.

She dominated the page. The Palestinians had violated the truce in Lebanon again, but they were squeezed down into one corner.

He felt apprehensive, but not terribly so. He had already discovered that the more direct the reminder, the less he felt it. It was in stray moments that the tears would come, the sick sense of damage. Writing replies Friday night, he had been, for the most part, uninvolved. Not numbed, but distanced. Able to see himself as a mere character, a machine in flesh.

One of four billion such machines. What did the vagaries of his personal situation count for?

Newspaper prose aided his detachment. It was the prose of public intercourse, so threaded with Lilliputian restraint, so harnessed by this and that and the other tiny sensitivity, that it could not move. It could not be quirky, interesting, or rich, for fear of liability. It was the prose of unhappening, and it made Lianne's life an abstract, a civics lesson, a boring narrative of exemplary behavior, a dull business he had never shared.

He considered the nested strangeness of the situation, Lianne's death appearing in the paper, the paper appearing in Lianne's house. He saw the image of a kitten, but couldn't think why. He thought of the paperboy, pedaling up the street—did they still do that? In this neighborhood, the paperboy probably drove Daddy's Mercedes, flinging the rolled papers over the roof. Who *was* their paperboy? Lianne would have known. Maybe it was a papergirl.

In that one edition, there were five separate stories on the bombing. The basic front-page leader, the police report, a friends-and-neighbors sidebar, a piece on the Christmas in July party. Which had been canceled, all the people already there hearing the explosion, pushing out of the theater to look across the tops of the trees where a violent smoke twisted into the evening. A biographical piece on Lianne which got their marriage date wrong—it was the 16th, not the 17th—and described her as a graduate of Hendrix College. Her file photo from the Miss Little Rock contest.

The paperboy pedaling up the street that Sunday, the day after. Did he gawk and crane? Did he look to see if he could see the marks? Did he think it would make his life more vivid, more real if he could? Why had he thrown the paper? Wouldn't you think service would be suspended, out of courtesy? This one household will be spared the misery of the rest of the world on this one morning. But then, who would have thought to tell him not to throw it? And someone might have wanted to read it, after all. Clemmie would have wanted to read it.

When was Clemmie coming back? His eggs were gone, the butter was oxidizing on its dish, and the odor of fresh coffee was drifting out from the kitchen. And he was going to have to do something about all of that. Himself. He buttered the last croissant, filled it with preserves. He cleared his dishes, took them in. He poured himself a big mug of coffee, black, and brought it out to the porch.

Sonny Raymond thought drug trafficking was involved. "Anytime you get a professional hit like this—and make no mistake, this is professionals—you have to ask yourself, is this a drug angle? As you know, in spite of being a handicapped budget, we've been looking into the drug thing in Little Rock. There's a lot more of it around than Joe Public realizes."

Are you saying that Lianne Morrison was involved with illegal drugs, Mr. Raymond?

"Probably she wasn't. We don't know that at this point in time. All I'm saying is, we're going to be looking at all our leads, and we're going to be making arrests. All I'm saying is, when a professional thing like this, you have to ask yourself a lot of hard questions."

There have been rumors of a feud between you and the Morrison law firm. Can you put aside your differences and pursue this case as vigorously as you would any other case?

"Mr. Morrison can look out to himself what he thinks, whether I'm doing my job or not, and I'll look out to myself what I think about it, and if I aint, I'll answer for it. Nobody better tell Sonny Raymond to his face he aint evenhanded."

Do you see a connection between this case and the murder of Ron Orsini back in March?

"We're following up every alleyway at the present time. As to where it might come out on the map, or just lead to a big ball of string, I don't know. My understanding at this time is the people involved didn't know each other. But again, when you have here what looks like in both cases, what looks like a professional—"

Sonny Raymond didn't matter. Only Lianne's death mattered, that great chasm. Not the painted clowns tumbling on its brink.

It might be Sonny himself who had ordered the murder, trying to get to Charles. But the man still didn't matter. He was tiny, inconsequential. If he had done it, Charles would get him, but Sonny Raymond would never *matter*. He would always be less than his deeds.

The phone rang, and he went in the kitchen to answer it. It was Dee-Dee: Was he ok? He was fine. They might check by later, would he be there? As far as he knew. Ok, well, we'll see you later, then.

He realized that he wasn't planning to go anywhere today. Never mind the rest of the world. He was here, and satisfied to be here. He was no longer restless. He was doing what needed to be done. Organize everything in his mind first. Arrange the data. No more missing the obvious. No more A, B, C, and D, no more monstrous surprises.

And home was the place to start. Home, where he was strong.

The coffee was bitter, too long on the coil. He poured it out and started some fresh. He brought the cordless phone out to the porch. Lianne had thought the phone extravagant. She thought all new technology was extravagant. He had had to fight for the microwave, the television remote on the Sony in the bedroom, the color monitor on the 128K Commodore in the office upstairs. For the extra cost of 128K versus 64K, for that matter. And they were saying that 256K was the coming thing; what would she say about that?

The phone should be ringing off the hook, he thought. The phrase persisting unnoticed in his mind, though very few phones had hooks any more. Certainly not his cordless.

Maybe it was time to get an unlisted number. Certainly it was time. But. "You wouldn't like that, would you, baby?" he said aloud.

So far he had finished only the first paper, last Sunday's. A young woman had shot and killed a naked intruder, a man with a knife. The man had had burglary charges pending. The woman had been burglarized some weeks before. By the same man? You wondered, but you couldn't know. On June 16, someone had set newspapers afire in her home.

While we were celebrating, Charles thought. He tried to imagine how the young woman felt, how frightened, victimized, persecuted. All the different stories. Had she awakened Sunday morning to find this biggest terror of her life shrunken to small print, crowded off the front page, pushed to the interior sections by— By. By.

Lianne stayed front-page until Friday, two days after the funeral. The print seemed to him hardly more than the recording pen of a seismometer or an electrocardiograph machine, jagged volumes of dense oscillation. Declining in stroke and duration, rising to a lesser spike on Wednesday— the report on the funeral—then damping again.

He saw why the phone was not ringing. He had provided three separate interviews. Who was that man in the photos, that calm, pale, lawyerly fellow in spectacles? A space alien sent to take his place while he was out of the world. While he was carried a way on a flying saucer somewhere, experimented on by robotic humanoids with the leathery skin of elephants, and sent back with bad dreams and no memories.

He was quoted at length. Do our best to carry on. Not merely a personal loss, but a loss to the people of Arkansas. He deflected every question about motive. No one had a reason to wish harm to his wife. This terrible accident. Not make matters worse with idle speculation.

In one of the photos, taken here at the house—in the library, in fact— he saw television cameras in the background. So presumably he had appeared in film clips throughout the week as well. The phone was not ringing because he was already overexposed. His star was fading, poor fellow, from his momma's limelight untimely yanked.

He thought there was a strange tone to the later stories, a darkening mysteriousness. WHO WANTED LIANNE MORRISON DEAD? demanded the headline over a color piece in yesterday's paper. *Nobody,* he thought. *Didn't I say that just three days ago in your damned interview?*

The piece debated a few ridiculous theories. A crazy fan had done it, someone suffering from the sort of disordered admiration that had caused John Lennon's death and the wounding of Ronald Reagan. Drugs were involved somehow. Blackmail: Were there dark secrets in Lianne Morrison's private life? The piece hinted and hinted and hinted, but drew no conclusions.

This was the sort of writing that came nearer to making him angry than any other. Blackening his good wife's name with innuendo. No law against it, and no way to fight back.

But it didn't matter either. They didn't know anything. They were trivial.

Oddly, the piece never once referred to the most prominent early theory, the one he was now certain of, that someone had been trying to kill Charles and had gotten Lianne instead.

Scattered through all the articles were references to the "troubled" Morrison firm. A chain of recent suspicious circumstance. What circumstance? What the hell did this have to do with the firm? Oh, Laugh and the toga party. Of all the—

Unless it *was* Sonny Raymond. Then they were right, it was all connected. But what motive would the man have? Harass him, yes. But try to kill him?

In Wednesday's edition, almost crowded out by the coverage of Lianne's funeral, there was a story on Lee Orsini. The grand jury had returned no true bill in the death of her husband. He felt a chill, reading about it. A whiff of wickedness emanating from the page. She had thrown a pink champagne party to celebrate.

So there was a murder they would never solve. Or "solve" wasn't the right word, maybe. Never *re*solve, more like it. Never get anyone for. The case was still open, but you knew better. It frightened him to think Lianne's case might end the same way. That so many cases did. How could he bear that, how could he bear knowing the guilty walked the earth unhindered and undetained? Oh surely there was no God.

The phone rang. It was J. D. Rider, talking fast through static. He wanted to come over. He wouldn't say why, but Charles figured he was drumming up business.

And that was a thought he had been about to have for himself, hiring his own investigator. So today was a day when everything was falling into place. Patterns were coming clear. He didn't even have to get up and go out of the house, they were coming to him.

Except he didn't want Rider, he wanted a real detective. Someone who could get the job done. But Lianne would have preferred Rider. No, that was sentimentalism, to hire him for that reason. But no harm in talking to him. He could hire as many detectives as he wanted to.

He couldn't read the papers any more. He looked at Friday's, but it made no impression. His eyes passed over the words, and the words sounded in his brain, but they meant nothing. He gave up, and left it and yesterday's and today's lying stacked on the table. He paced. He stood at the glass, looking into the backyard, where the heat, in spite of all the shade, seemed to billow in waves up from the grass and the flagstones. The yard was overgrown, the plots of grass almost knee-high in places. This weather, in this wet state, you had to trim everything every week.

Everybody was gone: Coleman, Clemmie, Lianne. Without them, his life weighed too much, he had too many things to look after. It would all come crashing down.

He saw that he was not himself, not in the way he had always taken credit for. That Charles Morrison the man was not identical to his own mere will and desire. That he was instead a cooperative, an organization, a structure whose maintenance required the efforts of many. This was the problem with egotism. This was what you forgot.

When Rider got there, Charles offered him coffee. The second pot was old by now, but he would make fresh. "No, thank you," Rider said. He didn't want a drink either. His eyes were veiled, his manner abrupt and unrevealing. He was less animated than Charles had ever seen him. He was wearing a suit and tie. Unusual. Perhaps he had just been to church. Though he didn't seem the church type. His mother was Baptist, wasn't she? Maybe he went to make her happy.

Charles thought of making himself a drink, but found he didn't want one.

He took Rider out on the sun porch, where the green and heat and humidity pressed on the glass like water on a diving bell. Like the flames of a star on the force fields of a probe. This was his command cabin, his bridge, his outpost. He would deal with the world from here.

"I wanted to tell you I'm investigating the murder," Rider said.

"What if I don't pay you? What if I'm thinking of hiring somebody else?"

"You can't pay me."

"What do you mean?"

"I'm not working for you."

"Who are you working for?"

Rider appeared to taste something unpleasant. He began to speak twice, and stopped. "Never mind," he said at last. He studied Charles hard, squinting.

"You feel guilty, is that it?" Charles said. He was thinking of his own guiltiness. How humans take blame to themselves. He warmed to Rider. He thought of all the other detectives he might hire, who might get the job done but who wouldn't care one way or the other. Mechanics. He realized he wanted somebody he could talk to. Somebody like himself.

"I should have listened to her," Rider said. "I should have been her bodyguard." His eyes were still hard on Charles, blue, intense, probing like the beams of a spotter.

"That's no reason not to let me pay you."

"Maybe you can pay my expenses. I'll have to think about it. If I have enough expense money I can hire out all the pedestrian stuff, save a lot of time."

"No novels. I don't want anyone writing about this."

"You can't keep them from it. You're in the public eye. You might as well face it. Everybody and his brother are going to write books. Hell, they'll probably make a movie."

"I can keep *you* from it. Client confidentiality."

"Which only works if you hire me as your lawyer, you know that. Anyway, I don't *want* to write about you."

The bell in the kitchen sounded, the automatic bell that let Clemmie know when someone was coming in unannounced.

"What the devil?" Charles said, and got to his feet. Then he realized it must be Tucker and Dee-Dee, they had said they were coming over.

But Clemmie appeared with a squat paunchy fortyish fellow in a nylon shirt riding out over his belt buckle. Clemmie wore her Sunday dress, white gloves. She kept her hat on. The man was shorter than she was and unshaven. He nodded hello as Rider stood up.

"You're back," Charles said, feeling very near tears. Normalcy beckoned. A familiar face, the nurture of his routine. Good old Clemmie. She would make him drinks and ease his sorrow. That was why he hadn't wanted a drink; it was too lonesome. Now he saw Clemmie, and the back of his throat spritzed with thirst. He wanted a martini, an icy cold martini.

"I'm here to get my things," she said. She seemed very nervous. Her eyes went to Rider, back to Charles, back to Rider. To Charles. "This is Kirk, you remember him. He's going to help me. If this isn't a good time—"

Kirk was her stepson from the second marriage. They had stayed close after the marriage broke up, hating his father equally. Charles remembered that much, though he had met Kirk maybe three times and hadn't remembered his face.

"You don't have to do that," he said, taking a step forward.

Something was wrong, some kind of vertigo was spinning his head around. He felt a flash of returning paranoia. They were gathering here to hurt him. Clemmie a praying mantis, the light glinting on her glasses. Kirk the burly hit man, a hired goon. Rider, with his beaked nose and hooded eyes, a malevolent falcon treading his branch, waiting his chance to swoop.

"We can help each other," Charles said, out of the depths of his disorientation. "It's hard for both of us, but we can help each other. Don't run away from it."

"You've always been wicked," Clemmie burst out, pointing at him.

It was as if the floor had dropped away.

"That father of yours," she said. "I could see it happening, but what could I do? He thought raising a child was laboratory research. You never cared about anybody, you never cared about anything. I knew something like this would happen. I prayed it wouldn't, but I knew it would. Your way, that was all you cared about. Running around behind her back. You ruined her. Making her quit her job, you made fun of everything she did. And now you—and now—"

"What are you talking about?" Charles said, but he knew.

It was obvious. Why hadn't he seen it before? It explained everything. It explained the way everyone was treating him, it explained the look in Rider's eyes, it explained the tone of the articles in the paper. He thought of the times he had wished Lianne dead, the scenes he had invented—accidents, plane crashes . . .

He saw her bullet-riddled body. *Hadn't he thought of hiring a hit man once?*

It explained why he had felt such a sense of foreboding, of inevitability. On Thursday, when he had seen Elaine. As if he had always known. Always known she would die.

You might argue that had been déjà vu, an echo of awareness from the time of his fugue, the rising of subconscious memory.

But you might argue it was because he had planned the job.

If he had planned it, he didn't remember planning it. But that didn't mean much, did it? There were so many other things he didn't remember. That would be why he hadn't recognized her death as murder. He was blocking the memory of planning it.

His face was burning. He hadn't known guilt was like this, that it was a species of terribly heightened embarrassment. That it was nakedness, everybody seeing you for what you were.

"I thought I could handle this," Clemmie said. "But I can't." To Kirk: "Let's go." In Charles's direction, but not looking at him: "I'll send somebody for my stuff. I'll send Kirk back later." She paused, anxious, her face tight. "Never mind. You keep it. It's just a trunk or two. It's just clothes. The furniture's all yours anyway. You keep it."

"You're in my *will*," Charles said, but she was gone. Kirk lifted his arms, shrugged, and followed slowly after. The bell in the kitchen rang, twice, as they left.

The first storm of certainty was fading. Maybe he hadn't killed Lianne. He wasn't temperamentally inclined to self-doubt. But he still felt exposed, embarrassed. Clemmie had skinned him raw, his every venality laid bare to the gaze of a stranger. When your *nanny* says you're no good—

"Well," he said to Rider, not the first man to brazen out a folly. "What about you? Do you think I did it?" His voice was unnaturally loud. He felt a grin as tight as dried leather twisting his face. He thought he must look completely evil.

"No," Rider said. He looked to Charles all blades and edges, a shifting quiver of swords. "When I came here, I wasn't sure. But now—no, I don't think so."

"You came here to check me out." The idea made Charles angry. As if his privacy had been violated. But he had no more privacy, that was clear.

"That was one reason."

"And?"

"I never do anything for just one reason," Rider said, evading. "Neither do you."

"But you don't think I'm guilty now."

"I saw you take the arrow, man. You took it right in the heart. I saw you wonder whether or not you did it. A guilty man dodges."

In spite of the affirmation, Charles felt violated again, seen too closely. He couldn't say anything. He wanted to say, *But maybe I have split personalities. Maybe I've blocked out the memory. I lost three days, did you know that?* Arguing the case against himself.

But he couldn't confess his loss of memory. He could let Rider see that he might be a murderer, but he couldn't let him see he didn't remember. No one knew that but Tucker and Dee-Dee. No one else must know. It was too pitiable a weakness.

"I could be wrong," Rider said.

"Will you work for me?" Charles said. "Will you let me pay you?"

"I don't know. I have a lot to think about."

"I don't care if you prove I did it." As he said it, Charles realized it was true. Delegate the responsibility to someone else. The responsibility for his soul, his heavy and worthless soul. "I'll pay you anyway. I'll sign a contract that says I'll pay you, regardless of outcome."

"We'll work something out. Let me go home and think it over."

"I don't want to wait any longer. I want to do something now." The pain of not knowing. The arrow in the heart. Push it through to the other side.

"Don't they say 24/24?" Charles said. "The twenty-four hours before the murder and the twenty-four hours after are the most important? And now it's already been a week."

"Listen," Rider said. "Let go of it for a while. You don't have unknown multiple personalities. You aren't a psychopath with memory loss."

Charles was too stunned to respond.

"It's just a trick," Rider said, waving a hand in disclaimer. "You think you're so special? Everybody does this kind of thing the same way. I'm going home."

He had a thought, and turned in the doorway. "There is one thing you can do. It's obvious, and it isn't great detective work, but it's the one thing that's almost always most likely to work."

"So?"

"Offer a reward."

"That's it? That's your recommendation?"

"Offer a *big* reward. You can afford it. You've got enough muscle to shake loose a lot of apples from the old tree." He paused, ran a rueful hand through his receding curls. "I prefer brilliant deduction, but trust me—the profit motive is a better bet every time."

"How big?"

"You call it. Listen, I'm going. It aint been a great morning for me either."

Charles followed Rider out to his Bronco, feeling for all the world like a whipped dog on a chain, curvetting to the end of its length after any kind passerby, any soft voice.

But then at the sight of the Bronco, he felt a blast of hatred. If he had never met Rider—

And Rider's face in the window above him—unreadable now, a black vacuum of knives, the blades again, what was it with the blades? Maybe Rider was the killer. Maybe he and Lianne were having an affair, and something had gone wrong. She had gotten too intense for him.

"Try to take it easy," Rider said, and goosed the accelerator.

Charles went back in and picked up the telephone in the hall. He bought a full page in the *Gazette* and a full page in the *Democrat*. He arranged for a thirty-second spot on KROK, to be shot later in the week. He was offering fifty thousand dollars for information leading to the arrest of the person or persons responsible for the death of Lianne Weatherall Morrison.

He could have paid more. He would have been happy to pay a hundred thousand. A quarter of a million. A million. But with the phone in his hand, he had thought: The big numbers would draw publicity. There had been publicity already, and like Rider said, he was in for more, no doubt of that, no way to stop it.

But something felt wrong about the sort of attention that a reward of say a quarter of a million dollars would draw. Overplaying. It would be like betting too much on a close hand. Sensationalism of the worst sort. It would hit all the national papers big-time, it wouldn't be just another rich man's murdered wife in some godforsaken little state somewhere, a nine-day wonder and then forgotten. He saw tabloid headlines at the grocery store checkout.

And so he had made the reward fifty thousand and had told himself he could up the ante later, if fifty didn't work.

He had the foresight to give his office number, not his home number. There would be a lot of calls. Somebody at the office could filter them. Brenda Faye.

He felt a sudden longing to see her. To have somebody protect him, shield him, take care of him. Then he felt a stab of fear, that she would walk out on him as Clemmie had. He would be alone, a pariah.

When Tucker and Dee-Dee finally came by, they too seemed full of razor edges, of cutting and tilting planes, the glint of dangerous secrets in wicked darkness. He imagined Tucker having an affair with Lianne, Lianne getting too serious and threatening to tell Dee-Dee, and so Tucker had killed her. That bastard Tucker, quizzing him about his own faithfulness. Dee-Dee for what reason? Bitter envy, disguised all these years as friend-ship. Because Lianne had been so much prettier, so much more successful and famous. So Dee-Dee had blown her up.

He imagined Tucker and Dee-Dee plotting her death together. To kill him next.

Everybody was guilty. He still thought *he* was, in fits. He had been knocked loose from his stars, nothing to steer by. Anything could be true. He was unbearably antsy around Tucker and Dee-Dee. When he wasn't trying to hide his fear, he was trying to hide his guilt.

"I couldn't get hold of Clemmie," Tucker said.

They were in the kitchen. They had stood around in the kitchen with him since they had gotten there. He had led them back, saying he needed to get himself a glass of water. He couldn't bring himself to offer them a seat anywhere. He had to get them out of the house, without making it obvious he was trying to get them out of the house.

"She came by," Charles said. He took a quick swallow of his water and almost choked. Tucker lifted an eyebrow. "She's"—Charles cleared his throat—"she's not coming back." Never mind why, never mind, never mind. Never.

But how long before the word got out? How long before Clemmie accused him openly?

The bitch, the unmitigated treachery of the bitch, all these years in his house, serpent to his bosom. She was coming out of his will as of now, he had to get to the office.

No, he couldn't, not now. It would look bad. That was infuriating, to think of her inheriting and not to be able to do anything about it.

"Hum," Tucker said. "I guess we'll have to find you somebody, then."
He sighed, a minor whistle against his prominent teeth.

He didn't seem surprised. Were Tucker and Dee-Dee spies for the lord
high bailiff? Trying to trap him, lead him to incriminate himself?

"I'll make you some supper," Dee-Dee said. "You can warm it up
later."

"I have some of your bourbon?" Tucker said, and Charles nodded,
voiceless. Dee-Dee was in the refrigerator. Then she was opening drawers.
Tucker came back with a highball, wandered out on the sun porch
uninvited.

Charles watched him tour the room. He looked out at the yard. He toed
the tossed-aside papers, spread the three unread ones apart on the table.
Looked up at Charles in the doorway, nodded, as if they shared some
secret. What secret?

Don't be silly, it's Tucker, he's just telling you he knows what you're
going through.

He knew his paranoia was just that, paranoia, but the emotions wouldn't
leave.

Dee-Dee had pots and skillets going on the stove, something bubbling
in the oven. She was pounding a slab of red meat with the tenderizer. The
oil in the skillet was too hot; she was smoking up the kitchen. Too absentminded to switch on the vent fan over the stove.

Charles walked over, waited till she moved to one side, turned the
switch. She smiled at him busily, thanks, should have gotten it myself. She
was raking flour off the chopping block, leftover flour with a butcher knife.
Blood and flour in the bowl. Now grating pepper.

He went upstairs and got himself a book. James Blish's *Cities in Flight*,
a Science Fiction Book Club edition, nothing valuable. In which, eventually, Amalfi, mayor of New York, wrapped in nothingness at the collapse
of time, re-creates the universe. Charles had read the book twice before,
years ago. Cities leaving the earth, launching into space. Spindizzies.

He sat on the second-floor reading level for a while, but felt rude. Here
he was, paranoid about Tucker and Dee-Dee, and at the same time worrying about being rude to them. He went down to the library, sat there,
where he was closer. It was an internal negotiation of forces, like that of the
cat who knows better than to try for the food on your plate but cannot entirely resist the attraction, and so settles a certain distance away, watching.

He could not absorb the words in the book. It was something to stare
at. A way to keep his eyes safe from the eyes of others.

They finally left. Dee-Dee came in the library to say she had put his
meal in the refrigerator, locked in Tupperware. Tucker lifted his glass in a
goodbye salute, drained it.

Charles went in the kitchen as soon as they were gone. She had washed up after herself, and cleaned up his mess from the morning as well. The dishwasher ticked with the heat of its drying. Tucker's empty glass sat on a counter in a puddle of drip, the lone icon of disorder.

She had made him chicken-fried steak and mashed potatoes and a green-bean casserole—canned French-cut green beans baked with canned cream of mushroom soup and topped with canned onion rings. Cream gravy for the steak. He sat to eat, though it was only five o'clock.

He was hungry. The food tasted good. It didn't taste like Clemmie's cooking. He felt as though he were eating in a restaurant.

He sat at the dining counter, watching the local news. He and Lianne had been reduced to a single fifteen-second clip in the middle of the broadcast, no new developments. Some other people had blown up. A whole campground in Utah. Moab, a propane explosion. Shots of the burnt-out cars.

He ran to the bathroom, but barely made it. He hung over the toilet weeping, a residue of vomit dripping from his slack lips.

He got himself cleaned up. He unloaded the dishwasher and put the dishes away. It took a long time to find where everything went. It seemed important to have all the dishes in the right places. He rinsed his supper dishes and stowed them in the washer.

He went up to the exercise room, stripped, and did curls and presses until his arms would not move, slant board sit-ups until his lateral obliques cramped. He pedaled the Air-dyne for twenty minutes. He shot a game of pool naked, but the exercise had left him with no small-muscle control. He showered, and discovered that he was ferociously hungry.

He ordered a pizza, large. With onions. He ate it on the sun porch, with two ice-cold beers, and finished reading the newspapers. Organization. Clear the decks. Tomorrow morning he would be caught up. He sped through Friday's and Saturday's, lingered over today's.

Front page, a photo of two burnt-out cars from the Slick Rock campground in Utah, almost identical to the shot from the evening news. But this time he held his meal.

He knew that campground. He and Lianne had gone camping there, early on in the marriage. Arches National Monument nearby. The fabulous red stone arches, and through them the desert falling away to a haze like the purple haze of the imagined Paleozoic. That preposterous restaurant, site of an old uranium mine. Mi Vida. The Ore Car salad bar.

Suppose they had planned a summer trip back. Suppose they had gone there. Then they too would have been blown up. They would be dead now anyway. It was possible. So this death was included in other deaths, was only one of a sheaf of possibilities.

It would have been so much better to have blown up in Moab, together.

But there was no point in grieving. It was easy to be dead. So easy the distinction didn't matter. Alive, dead, just a statistical fluctuation. Quantum zero.

Omar Torrijos was dead in a plane crash. Good. Maybe now they could get Panama straightened out. Paddy Chayefsky was dead. Too damn bad. He looked terrible in his photo.

A big spread in the Features section on the new Hendrix president. Handsome Joe Hatcher. Full head of dark hair. Hopeful kids, off to school. Life beckons. Come to Hendrix, get your degree, the big wide world awaits you. So what does it matter? You go, and then somebody dies, and you realize the sheaf of deaths, the cards you hold in your hand, all just chance, and over soon, and none of it means anything any more anyway.

The text by Mike Trimble, funny, clear, and smart-ass. That piece on his old red hound, greatest piece of dog writing ever done.

Oh Jesus, did Ramalam know she was gone?

The dog needed to know, the fucking dog needed to mourn for her the way she had mourned for the fucking dog. But there was no way to tell the dog; the dog was dead.

That night he took the bottle of gin up to bed with him. Maybe there was a bottle upstairs, maybe not. He'd had it with possibilities, the blurring multiple exposures of chance.

The big bottle of Fleischmann's. Ice and glasses in the bedroom bar. He didn't feel like bothering with vermouth or a twist. Fleischmann's. Now he could have Tanqueray. All the Tanqueray he wanted, Lianne not around to be allergic. Like the onions on the pizza.

He watched *The Sinking of the Titanic*. Made for tv. That was a tell-tale tag, means *This story is made of molded Styrofoam*. Like Tucker complaining about American cigars: *Some non-tobacco ingredients added*.

He watched the news again, the same clip as earlier. The same exact stories, except this time they actually mentioned Chayefsky on tv, didn't just leave him to the print media. *Network*. All they knew was he wrote *Network*.

The late movie was *You Can't Get Away with Murder*. Fear jumped in his chest. A message from God?

There was no God. But he had to watch the movie. No guts if he didn't watch.

Fuck it, one of those Humphrey Bogart death row movies, he'd seen a dozen of them, nothing to do with him anyway. He watched the Miss Black America pageant instead. He picked the one with the longest legs and tried to work up a fantasy.

Apprehension prowled the perimeter of his mind, the threat of his own possible complicity, but he kept it at bay. This was what tv was good for. Mindless entertainment. Not so called because it was idiotic but because watching it took your mind away. Anodyne, surcease.

I'm mad, and I'm not going to take it any more.

Why it was so popular. Americans had a lot they didn't want to think about.

He wondered if you could sleep, thinking you might have murdered your wife. It turned out you could.

He woke four times in panic, his heart about to burst in his chest.

Something terrible is about to happen.

34

THE DIMENSIONS
OF THE PROBLEM

Charles woke up with Mr. Bones in his mind.

I have some good news and some bad news.

What's the good news, Mr. Bones?

The good news is your wife is dead.

That's not funny, Mr. Bones.

Mr. Bones said, *Yes it is.*

What's the bad news? I say, what's the bad news, Mr. Bones? *Something terrible is about to happen.* Hello? Tell me what's the bad news, Bones.

But Mr. Bones was gone, the phantasm of an idling brain. Zen to the contrary, minds can't stay empty. They aren't the vessels in which thoughts occur; they are the thoughts.

Things happened fast after that, though to Charles they seemed to happen slowly. With the massive inevitability and yet surprise of a dream, in which the bulldozer, which is also a wheeled elephant, rolls down the hill, and you cannot remember to get out of the way. There they are, the spear-carrying Zulus cresting the hills, who are also a tidal wave about to break. They have always been there, the people on the wall pelting you with garbage and now the garbage can itself, a dented wreck, which is also an airplane breaking up as it tumbles out of the sky straight toward you, and you can't get out of the way because you keep forgetting.

Lather the beard, and wait for the lather to soak. Move his bowels while he waited. Weigh himself on the scales. Look in the mirror, scrape scrape rinse, the slow tedious ratchet of the dragging razor. In the shower, soap and scrub all the pockets of the body. Shampoo and let the shampoo soak, then scrub, then rinse and rinse.

It was tedious to towel oneself, to get the middle of the back, the dripping line of the radius. For some reason always hard to get the feet and ankles perfectly dry, but if you didn't the socks would stick and drag. Tedious to part the thick if receding hair.

Strap, knot, buckle, button, tuck, zip, step into, tie. Reading glasses, keys, pocketknife, change, mints, handkerchief. The wallet, with its cards, licenses, photos, with its thousand-dollar bill in the hidden pocket, which not even Lianne had ever known about, a private silliness.

The grooming of the flesh machine.

He skipped breakfast but made coffee and read the paper. His ad was there, in the *Gazette*. Presumably others were reading it, even now, in the *Democrat*. He called work, ostensibly to ask Brenda Faye to take down names and information on reward callers, so that he could call them back later, but really to inform everyone that he was coming in. It would be strange for them to have him there again. A little advance warning might help.

Later, at the office, some made sure to be out all day, so they wouldn't have to face him. Some dropped by to ask questions about this or that point in a case they were working, as if to break the ice, get the moment over with. No one seemed infected with the prurient curiosity of the accident-gawker, and he was proud of them all for that.

Brenda Faye treated him as she always had, matter-of-factly, her loud voice demanding to know how he wanted things handled about X. When was she supposed to reschedule Y and Z, the people she'd canceled last week? Was she supposed to order him lunch?

She had numbered the reward calls in sequence, and she had also written down the date, time, and length of each call. There were so many things to remember. So many obvious and boring things. He felt like a stroke victim learning to walk again. *Write down the date, time, and length.* So obvious, and he had forgotten to ask her. God, she was valuable.

Twenty-five people had called already. Beside fourteen of the listings she had written "cp." "For crackpot," she explained.

"Well, take complete notes on them anyway. Even if you're sure they're totally off the wall."

"I am. I did."

Nine callers had refused to leave names or numbers, which didn't make sense if you were trying to collect a reward, did it? Four had left *only* names and numbers, no messages. Brenda Faye had identified the crackpots by their manner or by the tone of voice, as good a method as any. You could safely assume that Geoffrey Slocum, age seventy-four, who had been told the answer by the angel Gabriel and who had specified that the reward was to be evenly divided between himself and the angel, was not a likely source of reliable information.

There were three non-crackpot, non-anonymous callers who had left messages. Charles felt an odd sense of relief, thinking that possibly, just possibly, the clue to the murderer's identity lay in one of those three sets of statements. He felt, for a moment, quickened.

"Boss?" Brenda Faye said.

He handed her the list. "What?" he said.

"I'm sorry."

He looked down to keep her from seeing his eyes. "Thanks," he said gruffly, and she hesitated, then left.

He got first Eamon, then Betty, and then Greg in to brief him. Eamon was surly and uncommunicative, worse than useless, didn't know anything, had probably taken the tragedy as an excuse for an unofficial, week-long vacation. Betty refused to understand what he wanted from her. Everything was fine, she said. Everybody had just kept their heads down and done their jobs, and nothing had been any different than it usually was, why was he asking?

Greg came right out with it. "Lafayette," he said. "He's been running things." He blushed as he said so. Because he felt he ought to have been?

"Lafayette?" Charles said. "How did that happen?"

But it made sense. All morning long, not one person had said one single thing about Lafayette. Not one had mentioned his name. Of course. It made perfect sense that Laugh was the one. Who else with the balls?

"I don't know. He—just *did* it."

"Is he here now?"

"You haven't seen him? I mean, yes." Greg blushed again.

So Charles got Lafayette in.

"Bring me up to date," he said. "I hear you've taken charge."

"It was like a boat on a open lake," Lafayette apologized. "Zooming all around. Run on the rocks if somebody don't take the wheel."

His eyes were hooded, the way Rider's had been yesterday. *He thinks I did it*, Charles said to himself. *Well, maybe so.* He could consider the possibility now without undue alarm. It was a testable hypothesis. Rider would test it.

"You did right," Charles said. Lafayette's eyes opened briefly, veiled themselves again. "I'm not going to do the firm any good muddling around in regular business. How would you feel if I made it official, sent around some kind of memo telling people to take things to you?"

The eyes again. That lightning mind, calculating that Charles calculated to ingratiate him, win him away from suspicion with benefaction? Estimating could he walk that tightrope.

"I'm not talking partnership," Charles said. "I'm talking a working arrangement, till further notice. It's not me doing you a favor. The other way round.''

''Right,'' Lafayette said.

He was ironic about it, and guarded, but he would do it. So that was one huge chunk of tedium that Charles had momentarily spared himself.

The memo he sent around read like this:

TO:	All Staff	DATE:	August 3, 1981
FROM:	Charles Morrison	RE:	Management

In the next few weeks, I will be pursuing an independent investigation into the circumstances of my wife's death. Since I cannot fully devote my energies to this enterprise while at the same time giving proper attention to the management of this firm, I am asking Lafayette Thompson to serve as interim liaison officer. I will be in the office on a regular basis, but please take any requests or situations you have which require expediting to him until further notice.

He had told Brenda Faye roughly what he wanted, and she had written it for his signature. He thought it was a beautiful piece of work. ''Interim liaison officer.'' Wonderful. Delegated authority to a captain without ruffling the sensibilities of any bird colonels.

By noon, Brenda Faye had logged forty-seven calls relating to the reward offer. The rate had slowed, all the crackpots getting their bid in early, perhaps. Charles no longer wanted to review the growing list. Looking at Brenda Faye's handwriting, the crabbed information, his eyes blurred with disinterest. Let it wait till the end of the day.

Seven of the new calls were from the papers or the television stations, though. And what did he want her to do about them?

''Tell them not to call that number,'' Charles said. ''Tell them to use the other line.'' He was irritated. He should have thought of that when he placed the ad. They were junking up his nice clean list. ''Just give them the facts,'' he said. ''Just read back what it says in the ad. That's all there is to say.'' He refused to grant them interviews.

''And take them off the list,'' he added as she was going out the door.

For lunch, he ate a Schlotzky's sandwich at his desk, not tasting it. He was making his own lists. Things he wanted Rider to do, people he wanted him to check out. He forced himself to write down Tucker and Dee-Dee. Other friends who had occurred to him in his paranoia. Now was the time to be exhaustive, not sympathetic. He wrote down the scenarios he had imagined for each, foolish though they seemed to him now. He thought this was how you did things when you were hunting a murderer. At least he had a plan, a course of action.

Means and opportunity, he wrote. *Who had access to the Blazer? And who knew how?*

He circled the words. He needed to reorganize the suspects according to these new criteria. He turned a yellow legal pad sideways, drew columns with a ruler. *Name. Relation. Scenario. Means. Opportunity.* He stared at the columns, exhausted with problem solving.

The columns were too skinny, especially the one for the scenarios. He spun to his terminal, logged in on the office system. It was slow to come up and kludgy when it did. He hated the mainframe. Had bought it in the fires of an early enthusiasm. Now they were saying the future was net-worked PCs, but he had too much money in the stand-alone.

He invented three more columns. *Profit.* That is, how did the suspect benefit? *Character Index.* Were they morally capable? Just a subjective judgment, but a data point nonetheless. *Relation.* That is, did they know Lianne, or him, or both?

Then he looked back over and saw he had already done a *Relation* column. Now he had to delete one of them. Nothing in either column yet. He sent the first one to the phantom zone.

He could do wider columns this way than he could freehand, but now he had to page the screen over to read each one. Wait while it cleared and refreshed.

He worked on his chart for twenty or thirty minutes, and then got sick of it. It took forever to put the information in the cottonpicking columns. He was going to shut down and go back to paper. Better save the file, just in case. What if there was some valuable information in it, something he didn't recognize now but would later be important?

It took forever to save it, to protect it with his privacy code—and what about if he ever wanted to print it out? He would have to send it when no one else was there, he couldn't have others reading it, he couldn't have possible suspects reading it.

It took forever to back out of the hierarchy of nested menus, to shut down.

He lined two legal pads up side by side, to handle the runover of columns. There were twenty-three suspects. You had to write in people who had *Means. Opportunity.* Even if they didn't have *Scenario. Character Index. Profit.* It was like those logic puzzles you could buy instead of cross-words. Fill in all the squares, deduce the only possible answer.

He had writer's cramp.

Jesus Christ Almighty, he forgot to write himself in, suspect number thirteen. Fucked up his whole alphabetical order. Alpha beta the order, but aleph zed the possibilities. Hopeless.

He went to the flip chart in the corner, drew columns with a purple Magic Marker. Began again. The headings in Magic Marker, the information in ballpoint. He got all the names written in, and his back began to cramp from stooping to write. How the hell was he going to reduce all this for Rider to see? There was no copy machine big enough.

It was dimensions, that was all it was. It was a question of dimensions. Each column was a dimension, all you had to do was get the dimensions straight, get them in the right order, and you could figure anything out. But there was no place to put them.

What was *wrong* with the world? Why couldn't you just change scales at will? Why couldn't you copy any little thing of any size and make it any size of big you wanted? Why not any big thing and make it little? You could imagine it, why couldn't you *do* it? Why couldn't you *organize* things? Was there too much information or not enough? Why the fuck didn't they invent a computer that would keep it all fucking *straight*?

He was sitting in the chair by the flip chart, crying, when the phone rang. It was Laugh. "I've got some bad news," Laugh said.

"Is there any other kind?" Charles said.

"Sonny Raymond done went and busted David," Laugh said.

For a moment Charles didn't know who he was talking about.

"David at the bar," Lafayette said.

"What for?"

"Cocaine. Conspiracy to distribute cocaine."

Charles's heart leapt with adrenaline. He almost laughed. Something was happening, at last something was happening. "Sonny's full of shit."

"David confessed," Lafayette said.

"He beat it out of him."

"No, he's got Christianity or something. He wants to make a clean breast."

Charles had an image of David unbuttoning his shirt, flopping out a vast tit. For Sonny Raymond to suckle.

"What the fuck," he said.

He was thinking *go*. The Chinese game *go*. He had never played *go*, he had no idea what the rules were, but he had read somewhere that it was a game in which the best players thought ahead and surrounded you. You didn't see what they were up to until the last minute, and then it was too late, they had you in their net.

Sonny Raymond was playing *go*.

He was after Charles.

"You don't have to go," Charles said.

"I aint afraid of these bozos," Lafayette said.

It was almost the close of the working day. Laugh and Charles would have to hurry to catch the judge before he left. Brenda Faye had them a limo waiting.

The judge refused bail. He didn't care who Charles was; drugs was serious business. He gave Charles a look that said, *Be seeing you soon, I bet*.

David wouldn't talk to them. He sat in the holding cell, facing away. No window to look up to. No Cubs game to watch.

Charles and Lafayette demanded a copy of the purported confession, but it wasn't typed up yet. They watched the videotape, Audrey Tull sitting in. On the tape, David admitted using cocaine. He admitted selling it to a few friends. Who were the friends? He would rather not say right now. But he would state emphatically and categorically that his partner, Charles Morrison, had no idea of his illegal activities. It would go easier on him if he would say who he sold it to. He would rather not say right now. He wanted to say that he realized his behavior was a burden to his wife, and the community at large, and if God just gave him the grace, he would do whatever he had to do to pay his debt and set things straight. His conscience was clear for the first time in his life. Who did he sell cocaine to? He would rather not say right now.

Laugh was as grim as death, gripping Charles's arm each time David refused to name his customers. This tar would stick, no matter how many times or how loudly David denied that Charles had been involved. This tar would stick, and would make things look a lot worse in that other matter that was building up out there, that other suspicion that was bubbling and simmering like black asphalt filling a roofer's bucket.

"Oh the son of a bitch," Laugh said, and Charles knew that he meant David and not Sonny Raymond. David for squealing, for salving his conscience at the cost of selling his friends out.

But Charles could not be angry with David. David was doing what Charles was doing, seeking his own purgatory. Trying to suffer till he came out the other side.

Charles wanted to help David, but there was nothing he could do. He wanted to confront Sonny Raymond. He wanted to slug Sonny Raymond on the point of his chinny-chin-chin. He knew his life would not end before he had the chance to do so.

But not today. Sonny Raymond was not in today. Nobody knew where Sonny Raymond was. Audrey Tull was all they had. He had lifted one eyebrow to Lafayette when they came in. "Hey, bro. This how-you-call community service?"

Lafayette had not seemed bothered. The greatest stress, they say, is uncertainty. Laugh knew where he stood with people like Audrey Tull. Perhaps it was people like Charles who gave him the most trouble, never sure of his status. It was a new thought for Charles.

"I don't start that till New Year's," Laugh had said calmly. "Give me time to get some personal business cleared away."

Trixie came running up.

Trixie, as they walked out the doors of the courthouse to rampant mediosity, to shouted questions and camera flashes and quick-shuffling men with shoulder cams swiveling to can the scene: Trixie, running into Charles's arms, crying. Over her shoulder, Charles saw the sun sinking into the trees, tedious and red and slow. Jesus, that was all people did any more was cry. He must have cried fifteen times in the last week himself.

Trixie in his arms as the cameras rolled. Holding her, patting her. There, there. Her pelvis braced on his, grinding in woe. He could fuck Trixie. Come to the house, Trixie, oh buxom cliché. Come to my house and I can fuck you, Lianne is not around any more, oh I am free. Come to my house, oh Trixie Pappadopoulos, barmaid *extraordinaire,* and I will fuck your slant cunt and save your husband. Save a bartender for Christ.

But instead he comforted Trixie, and he said something to the microphones, he said, I just want to say that one game does not a series make, just because these guys were on a roll today doesn't mean you can count your chickens before you leap because tomorrow's another week and we will just play them one game at a time and see what comes out in the wash.

Well, not exactly that, maybe, but close enough.

And him and Laugh stepped into the limousine which was probably a bad move as he thought about it more because it made them look like some kind of Mafia mouthpieces but Brenda Faye had lined it up without asking because as she said later that way you don't have to worry about the details and who's going to drive what where and pick it up later and fuck it who cares about the PR implications anyway it's too late for all that

And what do I do now, honey?

Leaning his head back against the back seat, Mr. Polygon—but no, because Laugh was beside him, an equal—a whiteboy doing the driving. And *Home, Jeems,* he said, and Laugh laughing at that, the redheaded hiskool all-American Razorback peckerwood

And what do I do now, Lianne?

Go to the hospital, Charles.

What?

Go to the hospital, Charles, and sit with Coleman.

God, he heard her so clear, so clear, and singing. Go to the hospital, Charles, and sit with Coleman. Redeem yourself in sympathy.

She sang it, coloratura.

I'm going to the hospital, Laugh, can I let you off no I'll go too.

So they sat and watched Coleman struggle for breath. He and Laugh sat and watched Coleman for hours. Laugh went to sleep and got a hard-on under his slacks. Charles imagined fucking Laugh in the ass. He imagined Laugh fucking him in the ass with his big black dick. What kind of thoughts were these? Had he always had them but pretended not, but now they blasted up, pyroclastic, from broken bedrock? Did everybody have them but pretended not?

It didn't matter any more, did it? What kind of thoughts you had. It didn't matter. Morality was just the business of trying to organize your feelings into columns, and he had already proved you couldn't do that.

Coleman struggled and turned like a man drowning in dreams. This was no coma. This was a man fighting his way out of a coma. Charles charged down the hall to the nurses. There's been no change, sir.

Goddammit, you call that no change?

There's been no change, sir.

Do you know what this is?

It looks like a thousand-dollar bill.

It's yours, if you keep somebody in that room around the clock.

I can't take your money, sir. We all have our assignments. Are you a Christian, sir?

Ask me again when you see Jesus pull a thousand-dollar bill out of his wallet. I want around-the-clock watch on this man, you get me?

I know your situation, sir.

Which meant, *I don't have to take any crap off you because Sonny Raymond is going to fling your skinny ass in jail any minute now.*

Listen to me, bitch. Until I go to jail, you bite your tongue. Until I go to hell, I can buy this hospital. You fucking understand that? I will buy the son of a bitch tomorrow, and I will fire your fucking ass. You go home tonight and you pray to Jesus will he save your fat dimpled ass, you hear? And in the meantime, I want a fucking round-the-clock on that fucking nigger, you got me, bitch? Did he really say all that? He did, and it felt good, it felt great.

And he left Laugh asleep in the room with Coleman, and he went home in the waiting limousine, the hell with going back for his car, he would take a cab to the office in the morning. Jesus, he all but confessed to that nurse. And calling Coleman a nigger. Why had he done that? He *liked* Coleman. Because he was a bigot, that's why. So he let it all come boiling out, even in front of the damned cracker nurse. Even the word you must never say, not if you're a nice white person. A nice bigot is still a bigot. Nigger nigger nigger nigger. Bigot bigot bigot bigot. *I guess I'm crazy now, Lianne.*

I guess you are, Charles. She sang it.

Thank you for making me crazy. Thank you for dying and making my life interesting.

You're welcome, lover.

I didn't mean it that way.

Mean it however you want, lover. Everything matters when nothing matters. She sang it.

I guess that's the other side of things, isn't it?

She sang something, but he couldn't follow the words.

You can let me out here.

I'll take you to your door, sir.

I want to walk. Let me out here.

Yessir.

Here's your tip.

Sir—

Keep it. What does it fucking matter?

You're a saint, Mr. Morrison.

You tell em that, boy.

I will, sir.

You tell em. I'm going to walk home from here.

Yessir. Good night, sir.

> *I got a gal in Baltimore,*
> *Little Liza Jane.*
> *She aint nothing but a two-bit whore,*
> *Little Liza Jane.*

I'm ho-ome. Hey, I'm ho-ome, ho-ome. Fuck you, Clemmie, I'm ho-ome.

He called the hospital. He didn't look the number up, he called information and then punched the digits in before he forgot them. Digits with his digits. Wow. It was weird, how the sounds went in his ear and came out his fingers a few minutes later, and he never had anything to do with the process. He never saw or thought the numbers, they just short-circuited from his ear right down his arm to his fingers.

Somebody answered. He didn't care who. "This is Charles Morrison," he said. "You let me know the second anything changes."

He hung up. They would figure it out. They would do what he said. They would be afraid not to. He had power. Now was the time to use it. Now was the time to move fast and come down hard, so fast they couldn't follow, so hard it left them blinking. Now was the time for blitzkrieg, gamble, audacity.

Why not? What did he have left to protect?

And oh it sure beat the hell out of the slow stagger of tedious time. Oh it sure beat the hell out of trying to organize things into tedious columns. There were too many dimensions, and you just had to blast right through.

Samson in the temple, shaking the foundations. He wanted to roar and pull and bring down not merely stinking Little Rock but his entire stinking civilization. But there were no pillars to grab, no x-, y-, and z-axes to rip from their geometrical moorings.

He went to the fridge. Milk and bread again? But the milk was sour. A horrible stench at the mouth of the jug, protein gone bad. He poured it, gurgling, down the drain. But it left a slow smear of thinning white on the stainless steel. He took the sprayer and hosed the residue away.

"I want to fuck you, Lianne," he called up the stairs. His hollow voice, echoing.

Too bad, Mr. Charles. I have a headache tonight. I have a deadache.

That's not funny, Lianne.

Yes it is.

And what's the fucking *bad* news, Mr. Bones?

35

MARGARITAVILLE

He woke up Tuesday with what felt like a hangover. It *was* a hangover, blast it, though he hadn't had a drop of alcohol. He had never before realized just how potent and inventive body chemistry could be. How it could generate its own toxins, hallucinogens, euphorics, stimulants. What were we, then? Jekyll-and-Hyde-ish not in the agency of some external potion but in our very natures. Ambiguous, unresolvable, our souls mere veils in the changing winds of hormone, not shapes, after all, but slips of insubstantiality that in their constant shifting sometimes suggest a shape, as curtains at a window, stirring, suggest a presence, a looking in.

Fine, so the body was a whole hidden industry of labs pumping out drugs on demand. Swell, let em pump out a painkiller. Come on, body, how about it? Endorphins, don't fail me now.

But no dice, of course. He couldn't find the key, he couldn't find the trigger. Whatever stress or breakthrough had kicked his system into overdrive last night, he had lost the trick. He was no miracle machine of new possibilities this morning. He was a creaking collection of barely functioning hardware. The tedium was back, with a vengeance.

He looked at his haggard face in the bathroom mirror. How long was it going to be before Sonny Raymond arrested him? And where was he going to find the strength to fight?

He had to fight, because it was intolerable to let Sonny win. But he had no appetite for the battle. There was no evidence, there could not possibly be any evidence unless Raymond manufactured some, but there would be no relief from the batteries of public opinion. He certainly couldn't afford any more nights like last night. It had seemed like glorious freedom at the time, but it would cost him. It would never make the papers, it had been too wild and personal, things like that never did make the papers unless the police were called in, but word would get around anyway.

Why couldn't you just check out? Just say, No thanks, I don't like this game, let's play another. Or I think I'll go to the sidelines for a few centuries. Not suicide, just checking out for a while. Not suicide, because he couldn't do that to Lianne. It wouldn't be clean. Whether it was him or someone else that had killed her, he had to make the answers clean. That was the one gift he had left to give. Not to let it end in messiness, in doubt and unanswered questions.

He took four aspirin, the only thing he could find, and showered and dressed. In the hall he saw that the place looked somehow soiled, disordered. There was a stale smell in the air, and the floors were trashy. How could this be, almost no one using it but him, the house so huge? But it seemed that dirt dropped from the air, that grunginess was a tendency more powerful than entropy, held locally away only by constant effort.

When was the Cleaning Crew supposed to come back? Every other Friday, right, and the last time they had come was the Friday before her death. He could see them, the two gay men in pastel tank tops, the one top teal and the other melon. Well, maybe they weren't gay, but they had identical blond crew cuts and iron-pumper torsos, backs and arms rippling as they scrubbed the windows, mopped the floors, brushed out the toilets.

So it would be this Friday before he could get the place cleaned.

He didn't get himself breakfast. And he didn't make coffee; he was in too much of a hurry and felt too awful to bother. Though he needed a cup badly.

He didn't notice that he had recalled something from the period of his amnesia.

Why had he been in such a hurry?

All he'd accomplished when he got to the office was to make Brenda Faye mad, snapping at her when she asked if he wanted to see the list of yesterday's callers, she had come in early to type it up. Great, he had alienated damn near the only friend he had.

Rubbing his hand over his face, he discovered he had forgotten to shave his upper lip. So now he would look like a bum all day. Great.

What was the *bad* news, Mr. Bones?

He had snapped at Brenda Faye because he dreaded the labor of working through the phone callers. He felt like a student who had a test to study for in a subject he just couldn't stand.

He wandered about his office, sliding books out of the shelves and flipping through them, slipping them back into place. He ripped the top two sheets off the flip chart, yesterday's production. He crumpled them into huge wads and stuffed them into the wastebasket. There might be a hundred people who should be on the list, people she might have known that he didn't know. What the hell did you do? What the hell did you do next? He was a lawyer, why couldn't he figure it out? It was hopeless. Hopeless.

At least he could get Rider in to take charge of the reward callers. Yeah, let him earn his keep. I thought he was going to call me. At his leisure, I guess. The hell with that, it's been two whole days, I'm calling him now.

Rider sounded disgruntled but was willing to come to the office. When he got there, he started asking Charles questions. Charles thought it should be the other way around, and interrupted him by buzzing Brenda Faye and asking her to bring the log of reward callers in. "And would you brew us some coffee on your machine?" he added.

"None for me," Rider said.

"Yassa, Massa," she said.

Rider waited. Charles shuffled the papers on his desk. He had put the legal pads in a drawer before Rider got there, embarrassed for the detective to see his confused efforts. Brenda Faye came in with a manila envelope and a mug of coffee. "Only five new people this morning," she said. She stood, waiting for Rider to inspect her work. "Looks good," he said, and she nodded and left. Rider put the list aside.

"About what Clemmie said," he said.

"You decide I did it after all?" Charles said.

"Not that. About you running around on Lianne. I need—"

"I never ran around on her. I don't know where Clemmie got that." Charles was seeing Trixie, imagining her naked. Big pink nipples.

"There, you did it again."

"What?"

"I don't know what to call it. You flinched, you hid a secret."

"What are you, Mr. X-ray Eyes?" Now Charles saw Tina, sweet Tina in the beach fantasy, her sleek buttocks working around the thong as she walked away. No top, the vulnerable curve of her slender back. The sea booming. Where he and Lianne had always gone.

Rider shifted wearily in his chair. He looked as though he should have had some of the coffee. "It's not like that," he said.

"What's it like, then?"

Rider sighed. "Everybody shows themselves, all the time. If they leave something out, it shows. If they make something up, it shows. *Hiding* shows. It's not what you do, it's how it fits in with all the other things you do. The gestalt of your behavior.''

Rider made a *sh* sound for the *s* in the word *"gestalt."*

Poseur, Charles thought.

"The only reason any of us ever get away with anything," Rider continued, "is that we're all so busy trying to fool the other fellow we don't look. All you have to do is look. And then some people are just better than others at reading people."

"Like you."

"Like me. Like some can read French, and to some it's just Greek." Rider smiled at his little joke. That was another thing that was irritating about him, the way he always wanted you to know how clever he was. No self-confidence.

He wasn't the only one who could read people.

"If you can do it," Rider said, "then you can't help doing it. You do it all the time, whether you want to or not. And you changed the subject. I wonder why."

"I don't care what you think. I didn't cheat on Lianne." Tina again, leaning against him in the bar. The soothing of his loneliness. Jesus, if she was here now. Jesus, she *could* be; he was free. All her sins forgiven. Not back with the firm, but she didn't need it, she was independent now. Her cool fingers sliding along his spine below his belt.

Oh fuck, Rider had been there in the bar, he had seen them.

"See," Rider said. "You're guilty. Maybe you didn't cheat. Maybe not this time. But you're feeling guilty about *something.*"

"Mr. X-ray Eyes," Charles said again, hearing the inanity.

"I think you did cheat. And I need to know their names, and I need to know all the times when it happened."

"Instead of hassling me, why don't you call a few of the people on that list? See if they killed her. Instead of spending all your time trying to bully your own client."

"You're not my client," Rider said heatedly, sitting forward. He looked dangerous in that moment, predatory. He relaxed. "Lianne's my client."

Charles broke into a snort of laughter, controlled himself. "Try and collect your fee from her," he said. Then he realized how nasty that sounded. How nasty it *was.* He felt transparent to Rider's eyes. Like it or not, the man had him convinced.

Rider grinned. "I don't have to collect from her. You've got fifty thousand dollars just sitting out there waiting on somebody like me to cash in."

Now it was Charles's turn to be angry. "You sneaky son of a—"

Rider held up a hand. "I'm just digging you. You pissed me off, and I took a potshot, that's all. I could never collect. Think it over. You could rape me in the courts, you could prove misrepresentation and anything else you wanted to.''

"So you're not so high-and-mighty yourself.''

"I never said I was. Hell, I got emotional problems probably make you look like Mother Teresa. All I said was, I can tell when people are lying. It's a knack, I got it. Doesn't make my own life any easier. Now let's get off me and onto you. Tell me their names.''

"I didn't cheat on her.''

Rider looked at the ceiling, as if to draw inspiration. "I can't tell what people are lying *about* necessarily. I can't read their minds. That's why I have to know names. To build a network, a mental network. You make all the connections, then you see patterns. The lies add up, you can see forces working.''

He looked back at Charles. "You might as well tell me. I'm not going to think any worse of you. I don't care about you. Who knows, if I was married, maybe I would cheat.''

"I don't know what else to tell you. I was faithful to Lianne.'' There was no way to explain about Tina without getting in deeper. There was no *point* in explaining about Tina. As screwed up as she was, as much trouble as she had caused, she was still somehow vulnerable, fragile, easily wounded. No point dragging her into *this* mess.

"You're protecting somebody,'' Rider said. "I'm going to keep after you. This is not going to be comfortable for you. Nothing is ever going to be comfortable again.''

You got that right, Charles thought. "Are you going to do anything about that reward list?'' he said. "It was *your* suggestion.''

Rider got to his feet. "Yeah, I'll check it out. Keep logging the calls. In fact, why don't you—can you call-forward?'' At Charles's nod: "Why don't you have her forward the calls to me from now on. I have a recorder.''

Charles thought he was bragging. He would have noticed that Charles and Lianne didn't have a recorder at the house; too extravagant for Lianne's taste. A new species of vanity, telephone vanity. What would be next, everybody be like Charles, have to have a phone in their own cars? Joe Blow in his pickup with the buck across his hood yakking on his modular? Telling Frank Rank down the road in the trailer house all about it. You never knew.

"I'll change the number when I renew the ad,'' Charles said. "What do you think about fifty thousand? Should I go a hundred?'' And that was his own vanity, hitting back.

Rider lift his hands. *Who knows.* "I'll drop my card at the desk,'' he said. "There's a couple of things I want you to do. Write down everything you can remember about Lianne's life."

"Her life?"

"Yeah, a biography, like. Everything you can think of."

"Where do I start, though? There's so much."

"Just start. Just do it. Just what's important to you. Don't worry, it'll select itself. And listen, how much do you know about Jerry What's-his-name?"

"Jerry?"

"Down at the car place. That's where you got the Blazer, right? He had access, right? Did he know Lianne? How long? What was the connection? Was he friends with people who knew her, people who didn't like her? That sort of thing. Write all that down too."

"So you *have* been working."

Rider sighed. He seemed disgusted. "Yeah, if you call that work. Legwork. Boring as hell. Just write it all down for me, ok?"

"Jerry just told me where to get the Blazer; he didn't actually work on it. It was his brother-in-law—"

"Write it down, don't tell me. Write it, and I'll ask you stuff after I read it. I mean it, this is important, don't skip this. I want to find out who killed her, even if you don't."

"I want to find him."

"Or her," Rider said.

Charles jumped up and got the door. He saw Laugh catch the detective going down the hall. "You got a minute?" Laugh said. Rider shrugged. They both looked back at Charles. Charles shut the door and went back to his desk.

He pulled out the legal pads and tore off the top pages, the ones lined into columns. He crumpled them and fired them at the wastebasket, going two for four. He stacked the pads, and on the top line of the top pad, he wrote:

> *Lianne Weatherall Morrison was born on Pearl Harbor Day.*
> *Which is fitting, because the whole time I knew her, she was at*
> *war.*

That sounded like a biography. But then he couldn't think of anything else. It was a good general line, but he couldn't think of any supporting details. The only scene in his mind was the scene with the limes, and that had been happiness, not war.

In the second summer of their marriage they had gotten into gardening in a major way, and they had gotten into margaritas in an equally major way. Coleman wouldn't let them mess with *his* gardens, so they began going up to the cabin on the Little Red every weekend, taking long weekends to do it, adding on a Friday or a Monday. They were going to landscape all around the cabin. They were going to turn the whole area into a Zen garden.

So that summer they would work all day, sweating like draft horses, and then in the evenings get totally whacked on margaritas, her specialty, and then they either made love or went out on the deck and watched the lightning bugs strobing in green declivity. She made her margaritas with fresh limes only. Big frosty barrel glasses, brimming with pale green. To this day he could not abide a bar margarita—and a blue margarita, with blue curaçao, was to puke.

But this one evening, horror of horrors, they were out of limes. How could this be? It was all her fault! They would go into town right now and buy more. Oh honey, I just don't feel like driving right now. So you stay here, I'll go—it's my fault anyway, I'm the lime woman. Are you sure you don't mind? I don't mind, I'll go. Hell, they probably won't even have them, middle of nowhere, never even heard of limes. Hush, you hush, I'll be back in a while.

So she left and it got dark and he got worried. The crooked roads into Clinton, Arkansas, podunk town and yet still the biggest in a hundred-mile radius. No way they would have limes in Clinton, Arkansas. And Lianne was tired, what if she went off the road into the ditch? What if some hillbilly ran her off the road and raped her?

At nine-thirty, she pulled into the drive. Ramalam galooping up out of the woods to meet her, woofwoof*woof*woof*woof,* because of course they always took the goddamn dog.

And she came in with two huge brown grocery sacks in each arm, and he ran to help, but too late, they were slipping, she tried to catch them and dropped one and the other tore, and limes all over the floor, spilling and bouncing and Ramalam barking and bouncing, and he Charles was laughing like hell, there must have been eighty limes and her squatting with the remnant of one sack, gathering, and looking up at him green her eyes green and the limes green as green, and outside the open door the green lights of the lightning bugs, and she said: I'm sorry, I bought them all, I couldn't help it, they were so green.

But he couldn't think how to write that down, there weren't any handles to grab it by so you could haul it into words, it was just there. And it wasn't what Rider wanted anyway, was it? It didn't tell anything about her murder; it was just the two of them, just marriage.

They left the limes on the floor all night, and made their margaritas and stayed up till four o'clock, and found out that lightning bugs stayed up till four o'clock too, at least in the woods northeast of Clinton, Arkansas. And found out two days later that Ramalam had eaten at least three of the limes, because that was how many came out of his sorry straining butt, three green limes, split and flattened and shiny.

He wrote: *Jesus, I want a margarita.*

The strange thing was, when he saw the scene now, he saw her with red hair.

He sat for a long time with his face in his hands, and then he went home.

On the six o'clock news, Sonny Raymond announced he was headed for Colombia. Colombia was where the cocaine had come from that David Pappadopoulos had been selling. And he had reliable evidence that hit men from Colombia had been involved in recent violent events in the city, and maybe also in the firebombing of Lianne Morrison's Blazer. So he was taking Audrey Tull and heading to Colombia for a couple of weeks.

Jesus Christ, it's a crazy fucking world, Charles Morrison thought.

He had a hard-on. Why the fuck did he have a hard-on? He masturbated, the first time since her death. He masturbated while *Wheel of Fortune* ran. It had nothing to do with Vanna.

He cried again, sitting there with come on his hands and on his Perry Ellis slacks.

What's the fucking bad news, Mr. Fucking Bones?

Something terrible's about to happen.

I got news for you, Mr. Bones.

He felt better after a while. He cleaned up, and made himself a margarita, rolling a lime under the heel of his hand on the chopping block, so that the oils came to its surface and glistened and polished the chopping block. It was what Lianne had always had him do, to loosen the juice, break up the packed green tears. Then she would squeeze the halves, up on her tiptoes to bear down on the arm of the squeezer, mounted high on the too-high counter.

She had always used the Sauza tequila, the cheapest triple sec. He used Herradura because it was all he could find, and Cointreau. Wet the rim of the glass with the husk of half a lime, dip in a saucer of salt. Sea salt, she used, and he would too.

Pour, mix, drop ice, stir.

The drink was totally without flavor. There was something in the hands of the person who made it, a magic, a fusion, an alchemy, a timing. You tasted Lianne when you tasted her drink. Never again.

Is *that* the bad news, Mr. Bones? I already knew that.

He made himself another one anyway. He went up and shot some pool. Poorly. The balls were no more than hard sealed objects, just bangety-bang scatter. No flash, no fire, no pattern. He turned the television set on, just to have company. He thought, idly, of calling the writer.

Want to come over and shoot some pool? My wife is dead and I need company.

Be fun to see his face. Watch him wonder if he was playing with a murderer. What a goose. Would he be more titillated or more scared? They were all such geese. The onlookers, the gossips, the rabble at the Roman circus.

Maybe the writer could give him some tips. Then he thought of the story the writer had read, the tomatoes. Forget it, no help there. That was literature. This was a real story.

What's-his-name. Baker?

He went back downstairs and made another margarita. He left the lights on behind him, left the game room television on. It would be there when he went up, echoing in the hall, a welcoming voice. He sat in the living room, and watched tv there. The ten o'clock news. What the hell was Sonny Raymond up to? What was in Colombia?

Was it really possible David had been running a cocaine ring out of The Blue Note? Charles would have bet money not. David the loser, a big-time smuggler? It was to laugh. David was small fry, he had some local connection. Probably he bought for two or three friends, maybe he bragged about it, that would be all.

No wonder the place was losing money. Goddamn, he'd let a lot of things go. How long since he checked the books, really checked, instead of just handing the figures straight over to Alison? Nobody would dare cheat CPA Charles, was that what he thought?

Hell, if David had cooked the books, he might have *tax* problems. Perfect, perfect, on top of everything else, the feds.

There now. Something nagging at his mind. Something about Sonny Raymond and Colombia. Right, that was it. The feds.

Because if Sonny was really trying to link David and by association Charles to international drug smuggling, why then. Why then he wouldn't, because it would bring the feds in. Sonny would never allow himself to lose control of an investigation like this, such a nice juicy piece of publicity, drugs and murder and sex and I don't know what all.

So what the hell with Colombia?

He was running away, that was all it could be. He couldn't face Charles directly, so he was inventing some ridiculous fact-finding expedition to the cocaine jungles.

"You coward," Charles said to the face on the tv. Waggling its belligerent jowls.

But he had better put somebody on it. Just in case. Somebody to watch Sonny, make sure he didn't invent some kind of crazy evidence.

It might be a good thing if the feds *did* get involved. The feds were no angels, nobody was, but they would play it straighter than the lord high bailiff. More people looking over their shoulders. An angle to consider. Could he work it?

If the bomb had been brought across state lines?

The Tonight Show had just come on when the phone rang. He got up to answer it, irritated at missing the monologue. "Hey, Bud," Tucker said. "How you holding?"

They hadn't called in a couple of days. Called or come by. It just now dawned on him, now with the phone call. *The withdrawal begins*, Charles thought.

"What's the bad news, Mr. Bones?" he said.

There was silence on the line.

So that was it.

The bad news was silence. The terrible thing was silence. Was nothing. Was just the dull rest of his life, a dim succession of unimportant events. No lightning bugs in dark valleys, margaritas never taste green. Holding the phone against his face, he could smell the oil of the lime on his hand. How she once cupped his hand after he had rolled one. Cupped it to her nose and inhaled. And closed her eyes and smiled.

Was nothing mattered.

But went on anyway.

"Are you drunk?" Tucker said.

"I aint drunk, I'm drinking," Charles said. "Wasting away in Margaritaville." He was doing things backward. The hangover this morning, the drinking tonight.

Tucker sighed. "Do I need to come over?"

Charles could hear his weariness. How Tucker was tired of the game of taking care of his friend and wanted to get on with his own life.

How selfish we all are. What drab, greedy, stupid, self-satisfied little creatures, no better than preening animals, thinking no further ahead.

There would probably come a day when Charles himself would look forward to a drink, instead of just pouring them down seeking oblivion, or just for something to do. There would probably come a day when he would tell a dirty joke and laugh and slap his knee, or eat like a pig and smack his lips and say "Mm-boy, good," or try to go to bed with some good-looking woman. A day when he would forget the bad news, the fact that nothing mattered, that he was just a flesh machine, running till he ran down, running on blind ignorant built-in commands; the fact that everything he thought he wanted was just some kind of stupid programming, a pattern that happened by chance and copied itself and spread through all the other flesh machines for no good reason whatsoever. He dreaded to think of that day's coming.

He said the only word he had left: "No."

36

RERUNS

Wednesday the same and Thursday the same, and Friday afternoon Rider called him at the office. "Can you get free?"
"What for?"

As if it made any difference. As if he were doing anything important. He had sat there the last two days with his door closed, staring at notepads, trying to think of something to write down about Lianne.

He had found that when he did relive something, he could do it only once. Like the episode with the limes. When it had come upon him, it was momentarily as if he had been there, he had been able to smell everything, taste everything. Now he could run it through in mechanical sequence, but nothing about it stirred him. He could still see her squatting in a tumble of green, clutching the torn bag with its remnants, looking up as fragile-eyed, as open-faced as a child: *Daddy, am I bad? Will we laugh, or will I be scolded?*

But now the memory did not move him. It passed as abstractly as the plot of a summer rerun, as devoid of life or freshness. The ghost was gone. This was worse than death.

He became afraid to try his other memories—to play his other tapes, so to speak—for fear that they would dim and dull and grow pale; and he began to wonder how much of what he thought he remembered had really occurred.

So that her death was a spreading wave, a shiver traveling down his time line, the shock of the ax vibrating all the way down the trunk into the darkburied featherfine ultimate roots of the tree.

The murder was still going on. She was dying in every part of his time.

He had written down Jerry's address and the name of his shop, though clearly Rider already knew all that, had called and gotten the name of the brother-in-law, the name of his shop, which Charles hadn't remembered but which was, sensibly, Tommy Dwell's Auto Repair. He reconstructed the service dates as well as he could, and collected what few bills and papers he came across. Lianne had kept most of them in the glove compartment, that was her idea of filing, keep documents with the things they documented, and so they had burnt up.

Collecting the information on the Blazer had been a way to procrastinate, to avoid writing about Lianne. But it hadn't taken long, not nearly long enough. He had stapled the surviving papers to his notes and given the whole packet to Rider.

"I want you to go somewhere with me," Rider said now. "I can be there about four-thirty if you can be ready."

Why not? Why not let himself be driven about by other forces, impassive, mechanical, rebounding like a shot ball on his own pool table?

"Have you had anything to eat?" Rider said when Charles got into the Bronco.

"Not since lunch."

"I'll run you by McDonald's, grab you a burger."

"I don't want a burger."

"It's your funeral," Rider said.

He drove them out to the Baptist Medical Center. In the Tower elevator, watching the numbers blink and climb, Charles said, "I don't need a psychiatrist."

"Be patient," Rider said. "I need you here."

The doors opened, and Rider stepped out. Charles stood, and would have let the doors close on him, but Rider came back and took his arm.

In the hall, Charles saw that Rider had lost his customary indolence. He looked three inches taller, striding along bouncing on the balls of his feet.

"I'm not going to do this," Charles said.

"I think she was a retrained schizophrenic," Ian Farber said.

"What do you mean?" Charles said, hostile. "She was as sane as you or me."

Farber made him uneasy. Always had. His shortness, his obvious bad health, his constant low-level farting. But it was more than that. Farber was so cheery, so at ease with himself. It was obvious he never spent a minute worrying about the impression he made on you. He was the sort of man you were supposed to like, because he was so open and direct, and because your wife did, and so you made yourself think you did too. But you didn't, really. You didn't trust openness and directness. What were people like that up to?

"I said retrained. Some schizophrenics, in all probability not the most serious cases, are able to integrate their condition without medication."

"What is this?" Charles said. "This isn't psychiatry. What is this bull-shit?"

"She heard voices," Ian Farber said. "She saw brighter colors than you and I do. Reality ballooned and dwindled. Fear and pleasure, always out of sync, out of proportion. But she had a very strong intelligence and remarkable willpower, and she kept herself in balance. A very *strenuous* balance, I might add."

"I don't see how you can tell us all this and yet refuse me," Rider said.

"You see very well. Don't play mind games with me." Farber was smiling. "You continue to show a tendency to substitute wit for genuine work. That's only effective on people who are willing to be misled. Who will play Confusion with you."

"Ok," Rider said, obviously nettled. "Ok, but we're not talking about me here. We're talking about solving Lianne's murder."

"My concern is with the living," Farber said. "I can do nothing for the dead."

Rider was one of Farber's clients: It was such a surprising notion that Charles forgot his own hostility. Not surprising that people you knew went to the same person. Therapists, like other professionals, got traded around the network.

But surprising to think of the know-at-all detective asking for help. And fun to watch him do a little squirming himself.

"The police are getting nowhere," Rider said. "It's a murder that makes no sense. No one can explain why someone would have wanted to kill Lianne Morrison. The answer may very possibly lie in your files. I admit I can't fool you. You know me too well. But by the same token, you know I can be trusted."

"In such matters, probably, yes," Farber replied.

"So? You've told us this much. Why not let us see her files? In for a dime, in for a dollar, right?"

"What I have just told you is not a part of her file," Farber said. "Mr. Morrison is quite correct." *Mr. Morrison.* The fat little fart. *Charles* for three years, and now *Mr. Morrison.*

"Not that what I told you is bullshit," Farber continued. "But that it is not a professional diagnosis. It is a personal observation, one which I offer you on the off chance that you will find it useful. In fact, there is no such diagnosis. Among psychiatrists, only I speak of retrained schizo-phrenics." He seemed, for a moment, uncharacteristically, vain. "So far."

"I'm not asking for myself," Rider said. "Or, I am, but not just for myself. This man has lost his wife. Surely you can understand what he's going through."

"He came for individual therapy, though I think mostly at his wife's urging. I thought group therapy would be more appropriate and persuaded him to come in with her group, briefly. He didn't stay long."

Briefly, Charles thought. *Two fucking years.*

"You want me to tell you what he's going through? He thinks he killed her. He can't believe anything that ever happened between them is real. He can't stand to remember anything about her, but he needs to remember more than he needs anything else. You're talking a disassociating personality: What do you think losing the only person he *could* relate to is going to do to a mind like that?"

"You're using the word incorrectly," Farber said.

"Come see, come sah," Rider said, airily. "You know what I mean."

So that's what I am, Charles thought, distantly. He could no longer manage to be offended by Rider's presumption. He could no longer fight or deny what others saw in him, no longer resist their purposes. He was a slave on the block, while the auctioneer called out the condition of his teeth. An exhibit in show-and-tell.

"There are very strict codes for this sort of thing. Very strict, Mr. Rider." *Mr. Rider.* Now he was doing it to Rider too. Good.

"Information heals," Rider said. "Isn't that what you always say? Try to get good information about yourself. Information heals."

Farber stood up suddenly. "I'm sorry, but it's past time for us to close. Mrs. Templeton will be waiting to get home. Her sister sits with the children after school, but the sister must leave at six o'clock. I'm sure you can find your way out."

He left the office, pushing the door almost to behind him.

Charles felt a welcome stir of anger at the rudeness of his departure, and stood to leave himself, brushing the wrinkles from his slacks. Rider slouched deeper in his chair, thrusting his boots forward. He motioned to Charles to sit.

"What?" Charles said.

Rider put his finger to his lips, motioned again. Charles sat. They could hear Farber and Mrs. Templeton. Another voice. Jane Cunningham, his partner, leaving? Drawers opened. The voices murmured again. Footsteps in the hall. From the front, a door closed.

More footsteps, voices again. Then a relative silence, then a call, high and cheery, the note of goodbye. After a moment, the closing of what must be the outer door, a thump and a slight reverberation in the walls. There were no more voices.

Charles sat forward. "He's not—"

Rider shushed him again. A file drawer. It closed. Silence, drawing longer. The door opened suddenly, just a few degrees. "Ah, good," came Farber's voice. "I thought they would never leave." From where they sat, they could not see him. His tone was false but familiar, like a character in the junior class play: one of those lines no one would ever really say, meant solely to feed information to the audience.

Farber's hand appeared, switched off the lights. The door closed all the way. They heard no footsteps now. Carpet in the reception area. There was the muffled thump of the outer door again, and then they sat in darkness and quiet. Charles began to hear the hum and throb of the cooling system, the background engines of the building. "Hey," he said.

Rider, in his chair, switched a penlight on at his chin. The underlight threw monstrous shadows across his face, the old scare game from childhood. "Boo," he said.

"We could get in a lot of trouble for this," Charles said.

"Nah," Rider said. "We definitely didn't break and enter. He locked us in by mistake, see. We beat and hollered on the door, but nobody heard us."

"Why didn't we phone out?"

"We're just too dumb. We panicked and didn't think about it. We thought the switchboard was closed down. We tried, but something was wrong with the phones. It must have fixed itself later, but we had given up by then. Pick one."

"I don't see what good it's going to do," Charles said.

"Maybe it won't," Rider said.

He led the way down the dark hall to a narrow stockroom fitted with shelves and crammed with ranks of gray steel four-drawer files. In the dancing spot of Rider's penflash, Charles took an impression of cabinet tops, dusty and littered with electronic cables, hole punchers, empty boxes of bond paper. Rider seemed to know exactly where he was going. He ran the penflash over the drawer tags, cabinet by cabinet. "It's not going to be in the first ones," he said. "But might as well check. Hell, these aren't even patient files." He was whispering.

How did I get in this spy movie? Charles thought. He tugged on a drawer, but the cabinet was locked. "They're all locked," he said.

"No they aren't," Rider said. "Ah, here we go." He had stopped, his flash on the top drawer of the fourth cabinet from the left. The drawer was open, just barely, half an inch or so.

"That's *F* through *L*," Charles said.

"Don't you do any of your own filing? There's a bar lock on the whole cabinet. If one drawer's open, they all are." He moved the flash down to the next drawer: *M* through *P*.

"Of course I do," Charles said. "I just forgot."

"Hold the flash," Rider said. He went pawing through the drawer, drew out a thick folder from a hanging file near the back. He leafed through it, holding it partially open under the flash. Charles caught a glimpse of Lianne's handwriting: just a glimpse, her signature on a form, but recognizable to him instantly and even in this problematical illumination.

How many other pieces of her were scattered about? Lost and forgotten in nooks and crannies he would never suspect?

"Her daddy's name was Lee Andrew?" Rider said. "Cute."

"Give me that," Charles said.

But Rider had set the folder to one side and was pulling another one out. This one thinner. "Aha," he said. "All the secret dirty dope on our good buddy Mr. Charles Morrison."

"Goddammit," Charles said, and reached. Rider skipped back, into darkness.

"Ah-uh," his voice came. "Sorry for picking on you. It's just hard to resist, you're so damn gloomy and monotone. You bring out the worst in me."

"What am I supposed to be? Mr. Positive?" Charles said. He found Rider with the flash. "Let me see what he says about me."

"I'm sorry," Rider said again, blinking. "Really, no. I'm only doing this because I have to. I think if I let you see your own file, I would be violating our understanding with him." He held the folder up to shade his eyes. "Give me the flash for a second."

"This is an understanding?"

"You bet it is."

Rider was beside him suddenly, a body in the night, bumping. It reminded Charles of something, but he couldn't think what. Before he could react, Rider had taken the flash from his hand, stooped to open the third drawer, Q through T.

"So what are you doing snooping through other people's files?" Charles said.

Rider didn't answer. He straightened with a folder in his hands, the penlight in his teeth like a cigar. He studied the folder. "Id you owe Theena," he began. He took the flash from his mouth. "Did you know Tina was one of his patients?"

The light was full in Charles's face. "Yes," he said. "Lianne told me. I keep telling you, I didn't cheat. Now get the goddamn light out of my eyes. What do you think this is, some kind of Bogart movie or something?"

Rider moved the light. He was making a strange sound that Charles for a moment thought was sobbing and then realized was laughter.

"Bogart," Rider said. "Come on, let's get this stuff copied."

"Copied?"

"Yeah, we can't just rip his files off, can we? That wouldn't be nice."

"Jesus," Charles said. "You would think this was a day at the office."

"It is," Rider said.

They took the folders out to the receptionist's area, where there was a copy machine. "Hold the light," Rider said, "so I can see what I'm doing."

"Hold the light," Charles said. "Gimme the light. Hold the light again. Do this, do that. Go here, stand there."

"That's good," Rider said, undoing spines, loosening sheets from the top folder, Lianne's. "Nice to hear you getting a little life back in your body."

As soon as Rider said it, Charles wilted, the surge of mild irritation subsided.

Copying took a long time. Farber's machine groaned and chunked and threw bright flashes across the walls, like cars rocketing past a night window.

"This is the only part that really worries me," Rider said. "I wish he would get a new machine. Anybody walk by that door—"

Ka-chunka, said the copy machine, rocking with its process. Flash. Flash. *Ka-chunka.*

"Hey," said Charles. "How are we getting out?"

After five, the elevators were slaved to a security control board. If you were working late, you had to call down and have them send one to your floor, and they would check your ID. Charles knew, because he had had after-hours sessions with Farber, years ago.

"We aren't," Rider said.

Ka-chunka. Flash, flash.

"Why didn't you tell me what you were up to?" Charles said. He was holding the flash. Again. This time back in the stockroom, while Rider collated, and slid stacks of sheets into oversized manila envelopes. He marked and stacked the envelopes.

"So you would act natural," Rider said. "Bogart, huh? Listen, nobody ever made me any happier. I would kill to be Bogart. Don't you hate it you can't just step into those old movies? Just live that life like it was real?"

"I'm really not following you," Charles said.

"Oh, right," Rider said. "Off on a tangent again. Well, it's like this. If you'd known it was a scam, we would never have pulled it off. He would never have bought it if you hadn't been sitting there all desolate and woe-begone.''

"I don't think you fooled him one bit."

"You don't have to fool anybody," Rider said. "You just have to let them think you don't know you aren't fooling them."

They slept in their clothes, except for their coats and shoes, because Rider had said they needed to be ready to leave at a moment's notice.

There was no entertainment available, Farber's magazines no more interesting than those in any other doctor's office. Three-year-old copies of *U.S. News & World Report*. A March '76 *Reader's Digest*. A couple of photography magazines.

And they couldn't turn the lights on anyway and Rider had brought only the one penflash and didn't want to run the batteries down.

So they wound up huddling under their coats, the air-conditioning running all night, and telling each other stories.

You ever hear the one about the farmer and the ventriloquist?

No.

Although he had, he had told it to Tucker himself not six months ago. There was this farmer, and he had a cousin who was a ventriloquist.

Yeah?

So the cousin was a city boy, see, and he thought he'd come visit the farmer. He thought it would be a big laugh, see how the country people live. But he got there, and he found out the farmer was laughing at *him*. Seemed like he thought city people were damn fools, didn't know a house from a horsefly. So the farmer was taking him around, showing off the farm, and it was obvious he was really proud of himself, you know. So the cousin decided to play dumber than he really was. They came along to a cow standing in a field, and the farmer didn't know his cousin was a ventriloquist, did I say that?

No.

It's important, remember that. They hadn't seen each other for years, since they were kids, and then they had gone their separate ways, and the cousin had gone off to the city and wound up making a living as a ventriloquist, but the farmer didn't know that.

Ok.

So anyway, the cousin is playing dumb, and he says, My God, what is that? I've never seen anything like that in my life, what is it? Well, this just confirms the farmer's suspicions, and so he says, in a real snotty tone of voice, Why, that's a cow. I can't believe anybody can be so dumb they don't even know what a cow looks like. A cow? the cousin says. What are cows good for? Well, they eat grass and oats, the farmer says. And then you can milk them, that's where we get milk. Or if it's a different kind of cow, you can kill them, and that's where we get steaks.

Well, the moment has come, so the cousin throws his voice into the cow, and the cow says, Moo-uh. Yeah, and you should see how he treats me. He keeps me penned up in this little field all day long, and he's lying about giving me oats to eat, and then he beats me with a stick if I don't give enough milk, even though I'm not getting enough feed to make good milk. You sure you haven't heard this one?

I'm sure.

Well, the farmer is truly shook. He just doesn't know what to make of it. Do all cows talk like that? the cousin asks, and the farmer says, No, just that one. And he hustles him on down the road so he can get away from the cow and think things over, and they come to a horse. What's that? the cousin says. Is that a cow? It doesn't look like the other cow. Well the farmer is still shook up, but he can't believe how dumb this city boy is, and he says, No, dummy, that's a horse. He eats grass like a cow, and he has hooves like a cow, but you don't milk him. You can ride him, or you can use him to pull a plow or pull a wagon. Are you sure?

Go on, tell it, I'm sure.

So anyway, all of a sudden the horse speaks up, and he says, Yeah, and you should see the way this sonofabitch treats me. He works me till I'm all over foam, and if I haw when he says gee, he beats me bloody with a willow switch. He won't even put shoes on me, and when I die, he's planning to sell my body to the glue factory. They'll make marshmallows out of my hooves.

Well sir, now the farmer's really shook. He can't believe it's happened twice. He's completely forgot about impressing his city cousin, and all he wants to do is hustle on home and get away from these crazy talking animals. So he's hauling him on down the road as fast as he can go, but all of a sudden the cousin digs in his heels and brings them to a stop. What's *that*? he says. That's not a cow and it's not a horse. What's that white thing up there in the pasture?

So the farmer looks where he's pointing, and his eyes bug out, and he wheels around and he says to the cousin, That's a sheep, and she's a got-damn liar.

Charles laughed. He laughed till the tears came.

Now it was his turn. He was no good at remembering jokes, Rider had just told the only one he knew. The only thing that came to mind was one of Lianne's favorites. You know why women have no depth perception? he said.

No, Rider said. Why?

He realized as he delivered the punch line that it wouldn't work, of course it wouldn't, because Rider couldn't see his hands, three inches apart. Because all their life they've been told *this* is six inches, he said into the darkness. Rider laughed politely. There was a silence while they adjusted their machismo. No way they could say to each other, Of course *mine* is a little bigger than six, almost seven, really, if the truth be told, or at least five and a half.

You know how you can tell the difference between a dead dog in the road and a dead lawyer in the road? Charles said, desperately.

No, Rider said.

There's skid marks in front of the dog, Charles said.

Rider laughed hysterically, though if you had thought about it you would have expected that one to go over worse than the one about depth perception, another self-deprecatory used-up old yuck-yuck. But it was new to Rider, and he wasn't a lawyer any more, anyway, he was a detective.

Do you know the one about this couple, Rider said. And they're walking down the road, and they see these dogs hooked together?

Charles woke up to Rider's face again. The monster face, Frankenstein's, floating in emptiness, finger against its lips. His heart took a tremendous dip, and then he placed himself.

The light went out, and he felt Rider's hand on his shoulder, patting. A soft "Shh" in the darkness. Then he heard it: the rattling of a key, the outer door opening. A strip of light snapped on at the bottom of the office door, a glowing bar floating in space. Then Charles's eyes adjusted, and he saw the room, shadowy around them.

A voice, loud enough to be distinguished. Farber's.

"God, I hate coming in early," the voice said, as stagy as before. "Nobody else here, have to make my own coffee." Farber began to whistle, belying his complaint. "Jesus, I need to take a leak already." They heard him stamping down the hall to the rest room. The rest room door closing. Water running, a toilet flushing. Flushing again.

"That's our signal," Rider said. He had them out in the hall in thirty seconds, stepping into their footgear. They met nobody on the floor, which was just as well, Charles thought, rubbing his eyes and yawning. He ran a hand over his stubble. A seam in his shirt had branded him while he slept, and now his skin was coming back to life, itching furiously. His socks felt cheesy, and his tongue was thick and fuzzy and tasted like rotten meat.

Strangely, he felt pretty good.

Now, what is this like? he thought, and then he had it. Camping. *When I was sixteen, when we were Eagle Scouts.* That time on the Cadron, the

Order of the Arrow, dressed like Indians and whooping and leaping over the fire.

And he felt fine and free. Going down in the elevator, he felt free. Grief was somewhere else. The whole damn thing was somewhere else. He was that boy stumbling out of his tent by the dead campfire on the Cadron, the first thing he heard the tumble of rolling water. Yawning and stretching in the cool morning air, drowsy and happy to be alive.

Then when he walked out into the parking lot, it was like coming out of the movie matinee into the sun. The Capitol Theater, downtown, summers, when he was a boy. You blinked and squinted at the noisy, unfiltered, hyperintense world, a world that seemed realer and sharper than ever but, paradoxically, for that very reason, farther away, less believable. Nothing in which you could ever resume a role.

But then they were out in traffic in the hot and hammering city, the Saturday traffic as bad as any other day, worse maybe, the goobers in town to shop and party. In Manhattan, on a weekend, things emptied out. There was still noise and traffic, but you could tell a difference. Not in Little Rock. In Little Rock, it just got worse.

And why was he thinking of Manhattan? His carefree youth? A rakehell boy, set free in the finest confusion on earth?

On the divider, between them, behind the gearshift, the stack of three envelopes Rider had stuffed. One of the envelopes was her.

It was like looking at three coffins.

Rider let him out at his car, in the lot behind the office. The Skylark. My heart is in the public schools. Which he was driving because Jerry had sent the 280 back, they shipped the wrong block from Germany, sorry, nothing he could do. And when was that from? Somewhere in there, before she died. Before they went camping? The next week after?

He *had* to get the 280 fixed. Soon. If Jerry wasn't up to it, well, then, well, maybe in Memphis or something.

"Wait a minute." Rider was extracting a thick sheaf of papers from one of the envelopes. The fat envelope. Hers. Charles paused, still sitting, the door open, one foot out. The heat was amazing. It wasn't even nine o'clock yet. The heat was an insult, a slap in the face.

"Here," Rider said. He tossed the envelope across the gearshift to Charles. It thunked heavily. It was the size of a novel, a brief in a case.

"What?" Charles said.

"I was serious about you needing to see this," Rider said. "I made two copies. Maybe it'll jar some stuff loose."

Charles didn't want the envelope, but it seemed that he had better take it. It would be too strange if he didn't. He grabbed the thing awkwardly in one hand, got out.

"Bear up," Rider said, leaning over toward him. He pulled the door shut, kicked into gear, and drove off.

When he got home, Charles took the newspaper in. He tossed it on the table out on the sun porch, along with the manila envelope. Two kinds of news. He didn't want either.

He was exhausted, though he must have slept six or seven hours in Farber's office. But it had not been comfortable sleep. Tilted in a chair, with his feet in another chair.

He stripped going up the stairs, carried his clothes. Something was different. He stood on the second-floor landing, sniffing. The air was fresh. The floor was clean and polished, gleaming. Clemmie was back? No. He could tell the house was empty. It had that feeling.

The Cleaning Crew had come. But how had they gotten in? He had forgotten to call them, arrange a key. A puzzle for another day. He was glad the house was clean.

In the bathroom, he sagged on his arms at the sink. He was balding, unshaven, his skin fish-belly white. His pot was back, depending from slack laterals. How could that be; he had hardly eaten since. Since. And he hadn't eaten at all in almost twenty-four hours, and he wasn't hungry now. But his arms were thin, that was it, he was losing muscle tone, it was all going to fat and slackness. He was getting old.

They arrested you when you looked this bad. Nobody believed you when you looked this bad.

Laboriously, he shaved himself and patted aftershave into his face. His jowls were still pendulous, he felt. Not much, but you could see the sag over the jawline. He raised his chin to draw it tight. Maybe it was time to go for distinguished. Wise and distinguished.

Bags under the gray eyes. Which were cloudy now, not penetrating. He stuck his tongue out at the clown in the mirror. Dandled his shrunken penis, an old man's limp noodle. Was that gray in his pubic hair? He dressed in his slippers and silk smoking jacket—he didn't smoke, except for his few cigars, but he liked the idea of a smoking jacket. He went downstairs.

One could have coffee, of course. Always coffee, civilized coffee. The canister was low, and he realized that someone was going to have to start thinking of resupply. Soon. There were almond shortbreads in the pantry, thank God, Archway almond shortbreads, a whole unopened bag left over from the camping trip. He wasn't hungry, but coffee needed something, a tidbit. He needed something. A companion. Food was a companion.

He read all the way through the paper, and set it to one side, and realized he didn't remember a word he had read. Not one sentence from one editorial, not one cartoon. The baseball strike, was it over?

The envelope was there, at his elbow. Fuck this noise, he was going to read it. Do your worst, you bastards. He was old, and tired, and he wasn't afraid of anything any more. Fuck you all, he was going to read the son of a bitch.

> *Caucasian female. Height 5' 6", weight 120. Presented with no unusual physical symptoms. Premenopausal. Hysterectomy scar, fibroid tumors, removed at 21. Unusually early for this condition, investigate possible hormone imbalance? General condition fair to adequate, though claims severe food and pollen allergies. Slight prolapsis, swelling of lower lids supports. Scarring of eustachia indicates untended infections sometime in the past. Preliminary diagnosis anxiety and depression. Common enough with allergies, perhaps adequate physical therapy all that's needed. Recommend exploratory conferences, possible group therapy to follow.*

"Bullshit," he said, and whipped through a baker's dozen pages of insurance forms, waivers, patient information. Divided by a sheet that said only *History,* he found the records of her therapy, in chronological order, front to back.

It became obvious that these were notes from private sessions only.

Here and there, Farber would reference something that had happened in a group session—*(Grp 2 Sat, 11/9/77)*—but would not develop the reference. So the group files were in another cabinet, and they had missed them. He would never know what she had told others. Who in Little Rock was walking around sharing the secrets of their life together.

Farber's notes were surprisingly boring, his own shorthand for things he probably remembered in much greater detail. No attempt to supply context for an outside reader, of course not. So there were to be no revelations, no sudden shocks of new insight.

> *Does not feel pretty. Whole life a fraud because based on looks, not ability. Whole life a fraud because not really beautiful. Failed to see contradiction when pointed out. Issue of self-worth, not appearance. Failed to see. Approach through her own terms, why she thinks she thinks not beautiful.* My father had beautiful eyes. *Does not claim her own beauty, just genetics.*

It was pedestrian, boring stuff. It was so obvious, her problem was so obvious he could not believe she had wasted seven years struggling over it. Seven years on something any child could see the answer to in a couple of minutes. And he had to read all this shit. He felt tremendously impatient: Buck up, girl. For God's sake, buck up. Get real.

He came to what appeared to be the transcript of a tape. It was the first of the hypnosis sessions. A flare of anger rose from his heart, coronal. Sue the bastard for malpractice, the charlatan. But no, he would have to explain how he had gotten hold of the file.

And he saw that Farber himself had been diffident. The therapist had written a preface to the transcript, almost an apologia. *Informed her of reservations. Since the early seventies, increased professional skepticism. Questionable actuality of trance state. Coercive bias of interrogator. Many subjects demonstrate fabrication, evasion.*

But Lianne had insisted, as she had to Charles. *"How is that different from what I do when I'm awake? Everything tells us something, doesn't it? Even lies."*

Farber had quoted her in full. Did that mean he thought her response was psychologically revealing? Or that the phrasing had struck him as particularly acute? Or something else? Only more reading would tell.

Some preliminary folderol, relaxation techniques, soothing repetitions, the induction of trance. Farber noted them, but didn't start the recording until the session was well under way. Charles turned the page and read.

IF   Are you comfortable?

LM   I'm fine. I've disappeared.

IF   No, you haven't disappeared. You're still here.

LM   My mind is here, but I've disappeared.

IF   I see. Why do you want to disappear?

LM   I like to disappear.

IF   Why?

LM   Things don't hurt. They only hurt if you're there. If you're not there, you can look at them, and they're just what they are.

IF   Is there anything you want to look at? You can look at anything you want to now, and it won't hurt. You're perfectly safe.

LM   I know that. I want to look at my father. I killed my father.

IF   Why did you kill your father?

LM   (DNR)

IF   How did you kill your father?

LM   Blew him up. He blew up.

IF   When was this?

LM   (DNR)

IF   Why did your father blow up?

LM   Because I was a dirty girl. I let him put his finger in.

IF   Your father put his finger in you?

LM   (Laughs.) No, silly, *he* did. On the porch.

IF   Did your father catch you on the porch with a boy?

LM   I want to stay disappeared. I don't want to come back.

IF   You don't have to come back. You're perfectly safe where
      you are. This is all fine and good and safe.

LM   Thank you.

IF   You're welcome.

LM   I was already a dirty girl, but he didn't know. Ephraim.

IF   Did your father blow up on the porch?

LM   No.

IF   When did he blow up?

LM   Next year. Before graduation.

IF   He blew himself up, then. It wasn't because he saw you with
      Ephraim.

LM   He never saw me with Ephraim. Nobody saw me with
      Ephraim.

IF   It wasn't because he saw you with a boy. He did it to
      himself. It wasn't because of you.

LM   I wanted a dress to the prom. He came out of the chair. I
      thought he was mad. It costs too much. We don't have any
      money. He was all over red, his face was all over red like a
      big balloon. He was too mad to talk.

IF   He wasn't mad, Lianne. He was having a stroke. He couldn't
      help the way he looked.

LM   Always mad because I was a dirty girl. Because she made
      him mad at me. But he didn't tell her, ha-ha, Momma. We
      know and you don't.

IF   What was it he didn't tell her?

LM On the porch. He didn't tell her, he just walked away and he didn't tell her.

IF So he loved you. He was a confused man, and he hurt you and confused you, but he loved you. He didn't tell her. Your father loved you.

LM So I killed him, because I was glad when he died.

IF Oh, hell. I missed it. No, listen, you didn't kill your father. Can you see that? You wanted to kill him sometimes, but that's ok. We all feel that way sometimes. We all want to kill people. There's nothing bad or strange about the feeling. The feeling is ok. It's what you do that counts.

LM He's a bad man. He ought to die.

IF Let's talk about Lianne. You aren't bad.

LM I let him put his finger in.

IF That isn't bad.

LM It isn't bad now, if Charles does it. It was bad then.

IF I want you to take that feeling, that it isn't bad now. That it isn't bad when Charles does it. I want you to take it back to yourself on the porch. I want you to let yourself know it isn't bad to let him put his finger in. Everybody is Charles, you were just looking for Charles. Can you take the feeling back? Can you do that?

LM (DNR)

IF Lianne?

LM (DNR)

IF You've done some good work today. Some very good work. I would like for you to remember all of this good work when you wake up. Are you willing to remember? You can remember and it won't hurt you. I would like for you to remember everything, and think about it when you wake up.

LM I disappeared from the contest.

IF What?

LM Aunt Susie won it, so I had to.

IF Are you ready to wake up now? The session is running over. I'll have to bill you the extra hour.

LM Susie Lee Freeman. The first Miss Arkansas.

IF Is this important? Why do you want to talk about this now?

LM   They were mad. I was a dirty girl, and they were arguing.

IF   I tell you what. I'm having to work awfully hard for this information, and I think really you're the one who needs to be working for it, don't you? It's all right to let your child speak. Your child needs to know we hear her. She needs to know she can speak anytime she wants to. But I personally would like to hear from your adult for a while. How about letting her take over, your adult take over?

LM   (DNR)

IF   Your child can only feel and react, but your adult can think things through. Your child is helpless, but your adult can say exactly what she means. She can understand what's happening to her, she can make good choices.

LM   Will I still be in the trance? Am I awake now?

IF   Do you want to be awake?

LM   No. You didn't say his name.

IF   Do you want to tell me what you were looking at?

LM   I was looking at the Miss Arkansas Pageant. When I was eighteen.

IF   Who was arguing?

LM   My mother and Susie Lee. They were arguing about my gown. It showed the tops of my titties. I mean, it was off-the-shoulder, it was silk, and it was draped. Everyone was wearing the stiff dresses then, with the wired cups and the foundations, but mine was a silk sheath. Susie Lee picked it out, and Momma—Momma—Mommy—

IF   Use your adult.

LM   Mother thought it was vulgar. She hadn't seen it, and she thought it was cheap. A nightclub dress, she said. She said I looked like a whore.

IF   This wasn't the first time your mother called you names, was it?

LM   No, I was always a whore.

IF   You weren't a whore. She called you that, but she was wrong.

LM   That's right. But I wouldn't let her slap me this time. She wanted to, but she was too little, and I was big. I had grown up. I was mad. I was so mad I was shaking. They were

fighting, and here I was about to go onstage. I was going to
sing "Smoke Gets in Your Eyes." Play the piano and sing.
She didn't know that either. She wanted Chopin. She made
me practice Chopin the whole time in high school.
"Revolutionary Étude." But Susie Lee and me, we fixed up
for "Smoke Gets in Your Eyes." All who love are blind.

IF   You have a lovely voice.

LM   Thank you.

IF   What happened? Did you win?

LM   (Laughs.) No.

IF   Why do you think you're telling me this?

LM   You know what she said? Just as I walked out. I could hear
      her, behind me. It was like a snake you hear but don't see. It
      was like the devil whispering in your ear.

IF   What did she say?

LM   (Inaudible)

IF   I can't hear you.

LM   My father would be ashamed.

IF   I don't think he would. Not if he knew. Not if he really
      understood. That's your little girl. That's how she feels. Use
      your adult.

LM   No, she said he would. That was what she said.

IF   But you don't have to listen any more, do you?

LM   No.

IF   She was wrong, and you don't have to listen to her any
      more. Do you want tell to yourself that? You're on the stage,
      and you're about to play "Smoke Gets in Your Eyes." Do
      you want to go back and tell yourself it's ok, your mother is
      wrong, you don't have to listen?

LM   I can't.

IF   Why not?

LM   I'm not there, I disappeared.

IF   Where did you disappear to?

LM   (DNR)

IF   Where did you disappear to?

LM   New York.

IF   New York?

LM (DNR)

Charles got up from the table, paced. He was dizzy with time, with memory. Perhaps also, he would think later, with premonition. There was something coming, something he did not want to read. Had he scanned ahead, flipping the pages before he began, subliminally aware? His eyes importing a message his ego wasn't ready for?

All he knew at the moment was he needed a break.

New York.

Late summer of 1960, when he was already knocking around Boston, checking it out. Hopping over to Manhattan for dinner and a show. Weekends on Long Island, his dad's old school ties. Sailing. Walking Wall Street, the Village, thinking of the future, the cliché of every success movie ever made. You're a big city, but I'll make you mine.

And they *had* crossed. Surely their paths had crossed. Perhaps he had stood across a corner from her, waiting on a stoplight, and idly noted a pretty girl. A pretty redheaded girl, uncertain at the light. A girl who stirred a certain sense of déjà vu.

And gone on his way.

He would never know. He might have glimpsed her, in a restaurant, or in the park, Central Park, or on the subway, and thought she looked familiar, and put it out of his mind as the crowds whirled on.

There was more to the transcript, but he didn't know that he wanted to read it right now. There was more in the file, a lot more, he had worked less than a quarter of the way through it, but he didn't know that he wanted to read it right now.

He went to turn the living room television on, but there was no ball game. The strike was still on, obviously. Golf. He hated golf.

There was no one he wanted to talk to on the phone.

He could go back and visit Coleman. But he was reluctant to show himself at the hospital. Not after the way he'd showed out the other night. Woo.

He could go out of town. Limp the 280 over to Memphis, see if he could find somebody there who could work on it. Hole up in the Peabody for a few weeks, incommunicado. Yeah, the champagne brunch; that was tomorrow morning.

But he wasn't hungry. And he didn't want to drive.

If he had a pool, like Tucker. This was the perfect afternoon for a pool. He leaned his head against the glass, looking out at the pool that wasn't there. Because in a pool you could just float and relax and let go. Weightless, holding your breath, staring down into the blue water, watching the hypnotic flexure of light on the bottom.

Go down to the Y and swim. Tone up a little bit. Slack muscles.

But his thoughts were full of the streets of Manhattan. A cross-fertilization occurred, brunch at the Peabody, where they always had plenty of lox and bagels, and New York, where you got the absolute best bagels of all time. And suddenly he *was* hungry.

He dressed in jeans and pullover, checked his wallet—he suddenly remembered he had given away his secret K-note (to the damn limo driver! God, if they hadn't figured him for a drug dealer before)—and found he had a couple hundred in walk-around cash.

Marching the aisles at Safeway, loading up the basket. Radishes and green onions and romaine and tomatoes—Coleman in the hospital, no produce this year. Half a dozen two-inch T-bones. Ground chuck, purple onions. Eggs, cheddar, mozzarella, black olives, bell peppers, Italian sausages, make your own pizzas. Milk, two gallons, full 4%, no more of this Lianne be-sensible 2% crap. Butterfat, glorious butterfat.

That woman, so sensible and so excessive. Always careful, and always throwing care to the winds. Who could sum her?

Fresh-ground coffee. Ice cream, double dutch and french vanilla and rocky road and cherry. If anyone stared, he didn't notice. He felt anonymous, at peace. The sanctuary of the grocery market. Marshmallow cookies.

At home, he broiled himself a couple of burgers. He had washed the milk quart, filled it from the plastic gallon, and stuck it in the freezer to get really cold. Now he sat out on the sun porch to eat, his feet up on the table, and watched the evening come in.

It had taken hours to do the shopping. He had been in the store itself over an hour, and then all the bags to bring in. He had been amazed how many trips it took, how tired it made you. And then putting it all away, and folding and stowing the bags—

And to think Clemmie and Lianne had always done it all themselves. What an asshole he was. What a full, comfortable, stuffed asshole. He sat there a long time after he had finished eating. Watching the lightning bugs brighten and deepen his yard.

He stirred, finally, cleaned his dishes. Took Lianne's folder up to the bedroom, but detoured to the library just in case, pulled a couple of Delanys. Had never read the Delanys.

He got ready for bed, though it was early, not yet ten. Made himself a martini. He was no good at margaritas, face it, but he fancied he was a pretty good hand at martinis. Put a record on, it felt like an LP night. Let's go way back. The Ventures, why not? Telstar.

He didn't like the Delany. Too lush, too nervously overwrought. He could tell it was supposed to be good writing—there were lots of metaphors—but it made him itch.

There was the package on the bed, the fat manila envelope. Her, Lianne, there on the cover beside him. He got up, made another martini, came back to bed.

IF Stay with your adult. Tell me what happened.

LM I ran away.

IF To New York.

LM To New York City.

IF You left the contest and ran away to New York City?

LM No, silly. You can't disappear if they watch. You have to do it when they aren't looking.

IF Stay with your adult. Tell me what you did.

LM I went back to school.

IF To Hendrix.

LM Yes, Hendrix. They could see I was naked, but I went back anyway. They could see I lost, they could see I was bald-headed, but I went back anyway.

IF Wait a minute. Bald-headed?

LM When they give you chemotherapy, your hair falls out. I don't ever want chemo. Don't let them give me chemo.

IF I don't understand, Lianne. Did your hair fall out? Was this when you had your operation?

LM No, that was later.

IF And they don't use chemo for that anyway. It's not a malignancy. Why did your hair fall out?

LM It didn't. Hers did.

IF Oh, I get it, another one of those. Lianne, you know I can't see what you're thinking unless you tell me about it. You have to play fair if you want me to listen. Do you want me to listen?

LM (DNR)

IF Lianne?

LM If I tell you, then they'll know. They'll find where I disappeared.

IF No, I won't tell them. They won't find you. Only the right people will find you. That's why you're telling me this. You want to be found. You don't want to stay disappeared. You want the right people to find you.

LM I want Charles to find me.

If ever a cue for a third martini. This one big. The hell with it. Make a pitcher, have the rest of them on the rocks, set up the ice bucket, everything. Right by the bed. Good. There. Pillow on the lap to prop the paper. All comfy?

Most interesting story. Must tell the book club about it. Never been a character before.

LM I want Charles to find me.

IF He will if you want him to. If you let him know where you are. You're in control of that. You're in control of who finds you.

LM I waited till fall term was over, and then I left. I didn't tell anybody. I just bought a bus ticket and went to New York City.

IF Why New York?

LM It's where you get lost. It's where you go to disappear.

IF I'm surprised nobody missed you. Didn't your mother call the police?

LM (Laughs.) Her?

IF My hunch is you were giving her one last chance. You were testing to see if she cared enough to come after you.

LM She hated me. My voice broke, and I played the wrong keys, and they laughed. They tried to hide it, but I could hear them. I don't want chemo.

IF What about the others? Use your adult. What about the school?

LM I lost. I was just Miss Little Rock. Who cares about Miss Little Rock? They all want Miss Arkansas. Miss Miss America. After I was rich, they were proud I went there, so nobody said what happened, why didn't you graduate? They slid over that. I don't know if they ever looked for me. I was afraid to ask. They probably called my mother. Daddy was dead.

IF   I said your adult, not your dress-up adult. Not your smart aleck. That's just your child playing games. What happened in New York?

LM   New York City. I stayed at the Chelsea. There were artists. I had never seen artists. I mean, people who—who that's what they were, that was all they did. They wrote things, and they painted. They danced.

IF   Did you like it?

LM   (DNR)

IF   Did you like it at the Chelsea? What happened at the Chelsea?

LM   (Inaudible)

IF   I can't hear you. What happened at the Chelsea?

LM   Not at the Chelsea.

IF   What happened?

LM   (DNR)

IF   Do you want to end the session? Are you through?

LM   Momma's on a tight schedule.

IF   I'm not your mother. Your time is your own. What do you want to do with it? Do you want to end the session?

LM   I'll run out of money.

IF   We're not into the next hour yet. Anyway, you can afford it.

LM   If I stay at the Chelsea, I'll run out of money.

IF   Oh.

LM   My Miss Little Rock money was just a scholarship, I couldn't use it. But I did some ads. Mother doesn't know. They'll come out right before Christmas, but she doesn't know yet. I saved five hundred dollars.

IF   Did you come home for Christmas? When your money ran out?

LM   No. If I come home, the plane will blow up.

IF   What?

LM   The plane doesn't matter. It does it anyway. I need to tell you this.

IF   Tell away.

LM   Am I still in the trance? Am I still hypnotized?

IF   You're safe. You can remember anything you want to. You can say anything you want to, and still be safe.

LM   I left the hotel.

IF   Where did you go?

LM   I didn't go anywhere. I just left the hotel. There was nowhere to go.

IF   There's always somewhere to go.

LM   Maybe now. There wasn't back then.

IF   Do you know that there is now? Can you take that information back to yourself and tell yourself that there's somewhere to—

LM   Let's skip all that.

IF   You're the customer.

LM   You know what I did? I walked the streets.

Well, now. That could mean a lot of things. I mean, you could take it perfectly literal. Litererral. Literally, for example. I mean, it's just a phrase.

What if you called somebody on the telephone? Just called somebody and talked to them. A lot of people stayed up this late. Tucker and Dee-Dee, for example. Or Rider. Just called for no particular reason, just wanted to chat. People do that all the time. Other people do that all the time.

You don't have to read the rest of it tonight.

IF   Am I supposed to be shocked? I'm not your father.

LM   So I was a whore. Just like she said.

IF   Lianne—

LM   You don't have to say anything. I see.

IF   Good.

LM   They would let me stay with them. Sometimes even two or three nights. Sweet boys. I looked for the boys. I never stayed with any fat people. I never stayed with any fat people who smoked cigars. You could tell the the sweet rich college boys. I told them I was staying at the Chelsea. I told them I was a former Miss Arkansas. I worked Central Park West. If you wanted the sweet rich college boys, you had to work Central Park West.

IF   Has it ever occurred to you that Charles was a sweet rich—

LM   I figured all that out already.

IF   Ok.

LM   I love Charles.

IF   (DNR)

And what am I supposed to do, baby? Am I supposed to say I love you too? You're tearing my whole world apart, and I'm supposed to say I love you too?

LM   It wasn't for money, it was just to have a place to stay. Food to eat. Sometimes they let me eat breakfast. They let me go in their refrigerators, I could eat whatever I found. I ate anything. Raw fish. I ate a stick of butter once. I washed my panties out in their sinks. I didn't even pack when I left, if I didn't do it then, I would never do it, so I just came with the clothes on my back. So I had to wash them a lot. They turned brown at the crotch, because you leak. No matter what you do, you leak. And I had my period, I was still having my period then.

IF   What did you do when you had your period?

LM   It hurt a lot. I had twenty dollars. I saved twenty dollars, in my asshole, for napkins. In a lipstick case in my asshole. And then a five and a ten and some ones. And it kept going down. Less money, but more paper. The change was a problem. I carried the change in my hands. It was always sweaty. It was hot. It was hot a lot. I can still feel change in my hand.

IF   I thought you went to New York in the fall.

LM   At the end of fall term. Before Christmas. But this was summer. I didn't come back home till summer.

IF   Ok.

LM   I slept in the park when I had my period. When it hurt. They don't want you when it hurts. When there's blood.

IF   I don't know how you survived. I don't know why the pimps didn't beat you up or kill you.

LM   They tried to. They chased me sometimes. I'm fast.

IF   I don't know how you did it.

LM   They caught me one time, Puerto Ricans I think. I didn't know then. They caught me in the park, and I said, I'm crazier than you are. I pulled the pad out of my panties, I waved it like garlic. I said, Blood, hombres. I said, the blood of a mujer, hombres. I knew mujer. I said, I put a curse on your cojones. I knew cojones. I said, They shrivel up and die. Blood on your cojones. A curse, a curse, you hombres.

IF   Well, obviously, you survived.

LM   I don't want chemo. I never want chemo.

IF   What's that all about?

LM   After a while you get ugly. You get dirty, no matter how many times you wash. The panties wear out, and then you're naked. Under your dress.

IF   Yes.

LM   You stink. Days go by, and you can't find any college boys. They won't look at you. They don't believe you stay at the Chelsea any more.

IF   Yes.

LM   But I won't go with the fat men. The fat bald men with glasses. Look at you like meat. You can see them thinking what you might look like if you clean up. But maybe you're too skinny by now anyway. Maybe you have a disease. And redheads are trouble, everybody knows that. They don't need trouble. But I wouldn't go with them anyway.

IF   And? Did you come home then?

LM   She found me in the park. She was skinnier than I was. Her face was all bones. But she wasn't hungry, she was rich. She couldn't talk.

IF   Who was rich? Who is this?

LM   She had a rich dress. She took me to the edge of the park, and she pointed up at her building. She couldn't talk. She pointed at me, and pointed at the building. I couldn't get the sweet college boys any more.

Where is your manhood, Charles? How can you tolerate this? The ultimate insult, blood on your cojones, a curse, a curse.

IF   Is this what you're after, Lianne? Is this why you wanted this session?

LM   I thought maybe she didn't want to, but she did. I thought maybe I wouldn't have to. I thought maybe she just felt sorry, just wanted to help me. But she took her clothes off. She was like a skeleton. I never saw anybody so thin. She pointed at her throat, she still had her scarf on. Her mouth moved. She was saying, Touch me. There weren't any words, but she was saying, Touch me, bitch.

IF   Did you touch her?

Did you touch her, Lianne?

LM   She took her scarf off. There was a scar on her throat.

IF   Don't quit now. Let's work on through this.

LM   She took her wig off. She croaked. She swallowed some air and she croaked at me. She said, Touch me, bitch, and keep me alive. She saw I was scared, and it made her angry, and she croaked at me.

IF   Do you need to quit now? Is this too rough? Do you need to come back to it later?

LM   (Crying) It hurt. She put things in me and made me hurt. I'm a dirty girl.

IF   Never a dirty girl.

LM   She found my lipstick. She said, is this all you have? She said, Go back to Arkansas, cunt. This city is not for you. Here's a hundred, you fucking cunt, go back home.

IF   You told her where you were from?

LM   She was from Texas, she could tell.

IF   Maybe I need to pay you for this one.

LM   Is my time up? Do you need me to come out from under?

IF   You can stay as long as you want to.

LM   Sometimes bad things happen to people, and they aren't the people's fault. But it makes them bad anyway. It makes them cruel.

IF   Sometimes. Some people. You aren't bad.

LM Bad things have happened to me.

IF You aren't bad.

LM Will you tell them?

IF I think you have to make up your mind to tell them yourself.

LM You can say his name now.

37

THE ABSOLUTE
WORST NEWS OF ALL

It was not memory and not resurrection. Or only the resurrection of the zombie movie, where a moldering hand rips through earth, thrusts hungrily into the rotten air. Charles could not help thinking of the monkey's paw, and shuddering every time he heard a noise: her mangled remnants at the door, scraping. And he would open to a—to a charred and grinning—

And never mind, never mind that there was no corpse.

It turned out that you didn't have to believe in ghosts to be frightened of them.

He didn't sleep, but wandered the house switching on lights and radios and televisions and appliances. The neighbors, if they had seen, might have thought he was giving a party. But where were the cars?

He wanted to accept that girl, that poor dirty girl wandering New York City, but he couldn't. She was not Lianne. She threatened Lianne, his Lianne. She had gone up to the rooms of rich young college boys. He would never have gone with street people, not ever.

While he was in the same city, she had lain with a cancerous woman.

The transcripts were not her past but her would-be future, a wave rolling through time in reverse. The girl was disaster trying to happen: the anti-Lianne. He wanted to burn the envelope and its contents, but he couldn't. He would have to read the rest of the file. Before he burned the girl, he had to know what other secrets she held.

And then he realized that Dr. Farber knew all about her, and for a moment he imagined himself shooting Farber, then tracking down and shooting everyone in Lianne's group who might have heard even a whisper of this.

As the night wore on, and weariness dulled his agitation, and also weakened his resistance, he felt the two coalescing, Lianne and the girl. Doublesight, two images in one perspective. They blur, slide, they click together: Liannegirl. It happened against his will, but it happened. Now she was a stranger. The girlwoman, no one he knew. He was grieving a green-eyed fiction, he wept for someone who had never been.

As soon as the sun rose, and he was certain there were no zombies, he fell where he stood.

Sunday went by, most of it while he slept on the floor.

He called Rider Sunday evening. "I've changed my mind," he said.

"About what?"

"About you writing about us. It's ok with me."

In the silence, he could feel Rider thinking. "I don't want to," the detective said. "I told you at the outset I didn't want to."

"Sure you do. It's what you do. Lianne said it was."

"I write puzzles," Rider said. "Neat little puzzles. It doesn't much matter who the people are. But people think I base them on my cases, so they get interested and they buy them. Some people. You know, real detective stories by a real detective."

"We're a real detective story."

Another silence. Rider deciding to be blunt. "Interesting detective stories," he said.

"We're interesting. How could you get any more—"

Rider cut him off. "You might be interesting people." *Might.* "I'm talking about interesting *cases*. I feel like I owe Lianne something. I'm going to follow through. But we're not talking major level of difficulty here."

And Charles saw, finally, that to Rider, he was an intellectual problem. He and his situation. That the man had perhaps respected Lianne, and was certainly decent enough to wish Charles as little suffering as possible, and perhaps had thought that having Charles write her life would prove useful and comforting, but that the command had been primarily a ploy. Rider didn't need Charles's story, he was capable of developing his own sources. Tossing him her file, like tossing a bone to a dog. You don't spend a lot of time thinking about the dog, but why not be nice?

It had not, somehow, until this moment, hit him: He would have had to kill Rider as well. When he killed Farber and the group. In his fantasies last night—this morning—he had completely forgotten. Rider was the one who *gave* him the envelope, and he had forgotten. Rider had seen the file by now. He knew everything about the dirty girl that Charles did. Perhaps he saw a pattern in it. Perhaps he saw her killer in it, sneaking through the shadows.

"I suppose you already know who did it," he said bitterly. "I suppose you've already got it all worked out in your cool little head."

"Forget it," Rider said. "I've said too much already. I told you you rub me the wrong way sometimes. How are you coming with *your* writing?"

"That's why I'm calling you. I want you to do it for me."

"*You're* supposed to be doing it for *me* to look at," Rider said.

"Oh, quit pretending," Charles said.

A pause while Rider absorbed the fact that Charles knew the game.

"I need help," Charles said. "I can write sentences, and I can see scenes that have happened, and I can see overall patterns, but I can't figure out how it all fits together. You don't have to write it yourself; just help me with the job."

"I don't write as-tolds. How about that poet you had over that night?"

"I already thought about that. No. I don't want it changed all around, or fancied up. I just want it written down the way it happened."

"Listen, I really think this is something you better solve for yourself. I really think that's the only way you're going to get any benefit out of it."

"I didn't ask you to be my psychiatrist."

"How about a tape, then?" Rider said, his tone just short of snotty. "How about you just tell it to a tape recorder?"

"Maybe," Charles said. "Ok, forget that for right now. Let's talk strategy. We need to get together and talk strategy." Trying to put it back on an employer/employee basis. Though the detective had yet to take a dime, even for expenses.

"Soon," Rider said.

The way the man worked, he might decide any second to get all direct and up front and say straight out that he was ready to get off the phone. That would never do.

"Ok," Charles said, his finger hovering. "Keep me posted, then." He pressed the button.

Monday came, and went, and nothing much happened. The whole next week the same. Somehow Charles continued. He put the envelope aside. Tune in next week for another episode. He wrote a little bit about Lianne, not much, notes mostly. Things to remember to remember. One thing he did figure out was where to begin. It all began back in March. He didn't know why, but he knew it did. Back with the elections, the creation science bill.

There was something important there, something that held a key.

Sonny Raymond was in Colombia, sending back news releases, and Head Cheese was in charge of the department. Charles hoped he wouldn't be arrested while Sonny was out of town. He hated the thought of that slimy bastard Cheese smirking for the cameras, getting his revenge. Surely even Sonny wasn't that much of a gutless wonder.

Charles was calmly certain he *was* going to be arrested. You could feel the climate of opinion gathering. You could feel the attitudes, accumulating like storm clouds. Something had to give, something had to break.

It was mildly interesting to note those who would talk to him and those who couldn't see him any more. There were some pleasant surprises. Barbara Rotenberry brought over a hot peach cobbler on Wednesday evening, Warren in tow, and they stayed to have a helping themselves when Charles offered a scoop of Yarnell's to go with it. Barbara, that wild woman, wanted cherry on hers. They talked about Lianne's paintings.

"Too modern for me," Barbara said. "But interesting." She was of the opinion they should have a show. "When all this nonsense dies down, dear."

Greg and Alison came by, twice, invited him to spend Labor Day with them, over in Hot Springs, at the Arlington, it was kind of a tradition. He said thanks, let him think it over, see what his schedule was. "I may be in jail," he joked. "Let me check my calendar."

And then he was sorry, because Alison flushed a deep red. Greg patted her knee, gave a tight, uncertain smile. But it let Charles see two things: It let him see how loyal they were and what kind of rumors they were hearing.

Tucker was out of pocket most of the week, and Charles assumed that he and Dee-Dee were completing their withdrawal from him, but then Dee-Dee called and offered to help him find a new housekeeper, so he spent part of Thursday and Friday with her, interviewing candidates. It turned out she was the one who had arranged things with the Cleaning Crew—Charles had still not thought to call them—coming over to let them in with the key he hadn't known she had. That Lianne had given her, four years ago.

Dee-Dee had talked the boys into coming in once a week instead of once every two weeks. So there they were, bustling around during the interviews on Friday. Charles thought, *Why not just hire* them? But they were too independent, they would never go for it, they wouldn't take his coat and bring him cold drinks on a tray, and could you imagine a couple of gays living in?

Dee-Dee was not convinced that Charles knew what good housekeepers needed to do, or what sorts of questions to ask to find out if they knew how to do it. There was a whole lot *more* to the job than taking his coat and bringing him drinks on a tray.

They talked to five women, but two of them were Baptists and one was too old and frail. His heart went out to the old woman, he could tell that she desperately needed a position, had been forced out of retirement by some tragedy. She was plenty smart, and her eyes were sharp, but her fingers were knobby and her hands shook, and there was no way she would be able to handle the workload. One of the women was too young and pretty, a professional caterer, she said, and she wanted to get out of the catering business and into something more one-on-one.

Yeah, one-on-one. Well, she wasn't *that* pretty, her features were somewhat thick, and her hips were too wide, but she was young and blond and alert to the possibilities, and there was no way on earth it would work.

But he masturbated that night, thinking about it.

The other woman might be a standby candidate. She had worked for a family in town, the Adamses, he didn't know them, they lived out in Pleasant Valley. She was sturdy and cheerful, and struck him as plenty willing but maybe not quick enough on the uptake. Maybe not quite right for his crowd, the kinds of things he would be wanting to do.

When Dee-Dee had come over on Thursday, for the first interview, Charles had flashed on their episode, the sudden access of lust over the posting of thank-you cards. But she caught the flash and gave him a hard eye, and that was that for good.

Still it made him realize, that and the fantasy about the young blonde, that someday, if he stayed out of jail, if he stayed alive, he really would make love to a woman again.

He masturbated every night after that, but in his fantasies, except for the one-time fantasy about the blonde, which he managed because he could still remember her perfume—in his fantasies, no matter how they began, the only body he could see was Lianne's.

He went in to the office irregularly, keeping whatever hours he wanted. Brenda Faye was solid behind him, but Rosalyn, Tina's buddy, had quit. She had actually quit last week, but he hadn't noticed, and nobody had told him. Everyone else had adopted a business-as-usual attitude, though he had the feeling the junior partners and interns were doing a little avoiding.

Sonny Raymond was due back late next Wednesday night. He promised a major break in what he was now calling the "Drug Murder for Hire" case. Charles went to sleep Friday night determined to relax and enjoy himself, since it promised to be his last free weekend for quite some time. Well, he wouldn't spend long in jail; his lawyers would see he had the chance to post bail, and he knew Raymond would be forced to have him bound over to the grand jury, and that the real trial was going to be not on whether he had killed his wife but on whether there was going to *be* a trial on whether he had killed her.

But it would put him right back in the headlines, and he wouldn't have any private life again for months and months.

Speaking of his lawyers, who *was* going to handle it? They weren't going to rat him out and make him represent himself, were they? But nobody was talking to him about it. Rider wasn't talking to him, Laugh wasn't talking to him, Greg wasn't talking to him. He should have said something about it before now. Where was his mind? First thing in the morning.

He woke up Saturday morning to a phone call. It was Lafayette, asking him if he would come to a meeting. Where? At the office. Give him an hour: Was Laugh already there, would he have to wait? No, an hour was fine. Just fine.

When he let himself in, Greg peeped out of the hall. "Oh, there you are," he said. "Come on back this way. We're in Laugh's office."

We was Laugh, Greg, Rider, Eamon—Eamon?—and of all people, Tucker. "What's this?" Charles said. "What's this all about?" He had a spooky fleeting paranoia: They had all decided he was guilty and were about to stone him to death.

Laugh had obviously just gotten up from the chair behind his desk. He offered it to Charles. The others were in the three leather chairs and one of two folding chairs from the closet. "No," Charles said, "you take it. I'm fine here." He settled in the other folding chair, and everyone shifted so as to face him. Laugh hesitated, then settled back in behind his desk.

"What is this?" Charles said again.

"The Society to Save Charles Morrison from His Own Damn Self," Eamon said.

"Eamon," Laugh said.

"What are you guys, my defense counsel? I was wondering if I was going to have to do it all myself. What's Tucker here for? Do I need a doctor?"

They were going to give him a shot, Pentothal, make him tell the truth.

"I'm just a friend," Tucker said. "I'm your friend. I'm just coordinating a few things."

"Raymond's going to charge you," Greg said.

"Tell me some news. You know it, I know it, and so does everybody else in the state."

"He has no basis whatsoever," Eamon said. "The man just wants to harass you, that's evident. His case is total poppycock."

They had brought Eamon in on this. Eamon. Strange. Charles hadn't heard "poppycock" in years. "Because I didn't do it," he said.

"Dragging this firm's name through the mud," Eamon said. His eyes were wide open, he was sitting up straight, he was practically flaring his nostrils. He would have been hell in the courtroom right then. "Your father and I built this firm," he said.

And Charles saw things in a different light. Eamon the antique, Eamon the sluggard, Eamon the lazy—had it simply been that the man felt out of touch? Seeing the firm slip out of his hands, the firm he had helped create? Had it been that he had lost interest, because Charles had taken away the one thing he cared for, changed it into something he no longer recognized?

Dizzy stuff, this revision. And wearying. Charles didn't have any use for it; he had his own tedious life to get through. But he didn't have any choice. When the scales fell from your eyes, you couldn't help it. You had to see what there was to see.

"So we wanted to brief you," Laugh said.

"We think you need to know," Greg said. "Before you go in."

"He'll arrest you as soon as he gets back," Eamon said. "He hasn't had the spotlight in a couple of weeks. Oh, he's been sending back his reports, but he can't get the paper down there. He'll be hungry for headlines. He'll be wanting to read his name in big print."

"We figure maybe Tuesday morning," Greg said. "You better be ready for Monday night, but Tuesday morning for sure."

"You won't be in long," Laugh said.

"Cut to the chase," Charles said. "I know all this already. And he won't be able to prove anything either, because I didn't do it. Unless he's been manufacturing evidence."

"He hasn't been manufacturing evidence," Rider said.

The detective was slouched sideways in one of the leather chairs, a finger curled to his lips. Charles had not seen that gesture in him before. Rider's eyes were hooded again, veiled. But they didn't blink, and they never left Charles's face.

"I'm clear in the courts," Charles said, facing Laugh. "My problem is PR. They can no-true-bill me from here to kingdom come, and everybody in the state is still going to think I killed her. I can't have a normal life again until we find out who really did it."

He turned to Rider: the hawk, still watching.

"Isn't that what you're supposed to be doing?" he said. "Finding out who did it? Earn your money, Mr. Great Detective. Clear my name."

"Oh, we know who did it," Tucker said.

"And it isn't going to help," Eamon said.

"Fuck you and your brother," Charles said. "Does it occur to anybody I'm hurting here? Does it occur to anybody I liked that woman?"

"Tina," Greg said.

38

SOLUTIONS

It made sense. It made way too much fucking sense.

"Why?" he said.

Nobody bothered to answer. Laugh and Greg were busy with their private guilts. Tucker was watching Charles.

"She's poison," Tucker said.

"She's a pathological liar," Eamon said.

Charles was riveted on Rider. *How did you know?* he wanted to ask. What he should have had in his mind was *What makes you think so?* But what he wanted to ask was *How did you know?* Rider gave him stare for stare. "I suppose you have proof," Charles said.

"No," Laugh said.

"Not exactly," Greg said.

"There's not any doubt," said Eamon.

"I want to hear from this bastard here," Charles said. He stayed focused on Rider.

"Charles," Laugh said. "Mr. Morrison. Boss. We all bought her number. Even Eamon here thought she was cute."

"She never fooled me," Eamon said. "She has no respect."

"I'm still not hearing any proof," Charles said.

"We've got persuasive evidence," Laugh said. "Nothing that will stand up in court. Not so far. But it's clear enough."

Rider moved at last. "There was only one person who could have," he said, looking away. Looking out the window. Relief from that clinical gaze. "If you didn't do it, there's only one person that could have. There was only one personality that fit."

"You didn't want Lianne's file," Charles said. "You never wanted Lianne's file."

"Item," Eamon said. "She bought a weekend round trip to Bogotá on the twenty-eighth of February. And then again on the twentieth of June and this time stayed for three weeks. And then again on the twenty-sixth of July." He waited, as though he had said something profound, which his auditor might need time to fully absorb.

"I don't see the connection," Charles said.

"Colombia," Greg said. "She was running cocaine."

"Sonny Raymond didn't go down there to get evidence on you and David," Laugh said, his voice rough with anger. "He went down there to pull her out. The son of a bitch is in love."

Rider broke in: "He may be in love, and he may be just protecting his ass. He either knows or suspects she did the murder, and he's definitely been in her pants. She's no great big criminal mastermind, don't get the wrong idea. Strictly small-time, strictly toots for tots. She doesn't have the foggiest idea how the big boys work. My guess is she's worked up a contact or two through Sonny. Some minor-league Colombian law officer selling off evidence on the side."

"Item," Eamon said.

Charles hated that, he hated it when people did that. *Item.* The smart-asses. *Item.*

"Sonny Raymond tapped your phone, and Sonny Raymond had you followed," Eamon said. "She was probably involved."

"She wasn't involved with Sonny's surveillance," Rider said. "I told you that."

"Maybe I disagree," Eamon said.

"Disagree all you want to. I've talked to the pair Sonny hired. They never saw her, never spoke with her, don't know who she is."

"Fine," Eamon said, disgusted. "Just tell us when you think we need to know."

"I only located them yesterday. They say somebody else was following Charles and Lianne, another couple of hoods they didn't recognize. *Those* are the people Tina hired."

"Well, we know she tried to set him up at the toga party," Eamon said.

Charles felt dizzy. He had had the Keystone Kops running around his backyard. *Two* sets of watchers, and he had never noticed even one.

"Sonny was using her," Rider said. "And maybe she thought she was using him."

"So maybe Sonny did it," Charles said. "Maybe it was Sonny and not Tina after all." Why, even now, did he want to protect her?

"No," Rider said. "Sonny didn't do it."

Eamon frowned but didn't argue. He cleared his throat. The others were letting him do the talking, why? Because it was distasteful, all the bad news.

"Item," he said. "There are two violent deaths in her family history—a supposed hunting accident and an auto-repair accident. She was present on both occasions." With a glance at Rider, who ignored him: "*Sonny Raymond was present on the second.*"

"Cut it with the fucking items," Charles said, thickly.

They all chimed in after that, all except Rider, who was the agent of this conspiracy, the provider of the rope for this net, but who now sat back, aloof, above it all.

The others pelted him with their information, they belabored him with their suppositions.

Tina was demonstrably pathological: Item, she had told everyone there except Tucker, who had not known her except in passing, the story about her father raping her, had sworn them each in turn to secrecy, her only confidant. Item, the bogus degree, the bogus cases. Item, Farber's diagnosis, based on three sessions, in which she had told garbled and conflicting stories of her past, trying, in his opinion, to tangle him in games, aborting the therapy when he wouldn't play (and subitem, the records of the sessions themselves, from which you could decide whether you concurred in the diagnosis—they all did).

Not only was she pathological; she had been freaking. She had begun to lose control, playing one lover off against another in ways that could not possibly work. Hinting darkly to Farber about the true nature of her father's and her brother's accidents. Failing to cover her tracks, telling stories that were too easy to check. Making stranger and stranger emotional demands.

Was it the cocaine? The stress of her brutal childhood—surely brutal, whether in the ways she had told or in other ways? Was it the added stress of growing older?

It didn't matter, for their purposes. All that mattered was that she had been freaking, had been in the sort of mental state in which maybe blowing up a rival's car seemed perfectly feasible. Oh, once you looked, the warp and woof were clear to see.

"And item," said Eamon, finally, unable to resist. "She set her hat for you. We all knew it. She made no bones about it. She was an upwardly mobile woman. Look at the way she climbed the ladder, Greg to Lafayette to you. I'm sorry, Greg, no offense."

"None taken," Greg said.

"She hated Lianne," Eamon said. "Lianne stood in her way, and Lianne stood for everything she wanted to be and knew she could never have."

"Shut the fuck up," Charles said. "Just shut the fuck up."

Lafayette cleared his throat: "This isn't summation, Eamon. Quit waffling. We've laid out enough of the pattern. I don't think he needs any help interpreting. Mr. Morrison,'' he said, softly and without irony, and that was curious enough to bring Charles's eyes up from the floor.

"You see why we had to get you in here," Laugh said. "You had to know what you were facing before you went into court. We'll get you off, but you have to be ready for some bad times. It's all going to come out; it has to. It's going to be really bad for a while."

"You don't have a thing," Charles said, wearily. His head was heavy, wanted to sink back between his hands, his wobbling neck could hardly support it. "You bastards don't have a fucking thing," he said. "This wasn't personal. This was a professional hit."

But he knew the answer to that.

"If she did it," Laugh said, "the proof is out there. We'll get it. Sooner or later we'll nail her to it, don't you worry."

"I told you he would take it like this," Eamon said.

"We're all guilty," Greg said. "We all saw what she was, and we didn't stop her. We all had our reasons. We're all as guilty as you are."

"Not me," Eamon said.

And now Charles saw that every man in the room was looking at him with the same expression, a sort of fascinated relief: *It could have been me. There but for the grace of God.*

Every man in the room but Rider.

"You fuckers," Charles said. His voice rose: "You absolute raving sons of bitches. You haven't got one damn thing. What are you trying to do to me? What do you call this bullshit? What do you call this mother-fucking star-chamber shit-for-brains bullshit?"

"Friendship," Tucker said.

"I told you," Eamon said.

He had wanted her dead, so he would be free to fuck other people. And one of the people he'd wanted to fuck had killed her. Never mind that he had wanted her dead only fleetingly, contradictorily, and against his own best interests. Never mind that he had only imagined cheating on her, had never really done it. He had wanted her dead, and Tina had killed her. A current ran between those two facts, a current that might not be guilt but had its voltage.

One little wobble of infidelity, not even physical, just in the mind, one little moment of inattention, and that was all it had taken. She was gone. It was like you took your eye off the road a second, you dropped your cough drop, and you looked up at a truck in the other lane. You didn't do anything wrong, but people were dead, your wife was dead. Where was the justice in that? Thousands of people thousands of times a day, and nothing happened to *them*.

She had died for nothing. For him. For nothing.

And in his mind, in the background, far away, the faintest whisper of echoing regret: *Shit, there goes my chance. Never have Tina now.*

He might as well have. Lianne wouldn't be any deader. She might even be alive now. And he would never ever get credit for having been faithful. For having loved her. No one would ever believe him. And where was the justice in that?

They were in the hall outside Laugh's office, walking away from each other, into their separate fates. Tucker already out the door and gone. Rider came up beside Charles momentarily, following to the parking lot, adjusting his arms to swing in sync.

"You didn't fuck her, did you?" he said.

"I keep telling you," Charles said. Walking fast, looking straight ahead.

"You poor sap," Rider said. "You poor damn bozo."

He had been home about twenty minutes when the phone rang. What was it now, more news from the Inner Council? He picked it up. "What?" he said.

It was Dee-Dee. Her voice was cheery, full of the rough vibrance that passed, with her, for sprightliness. "Honey, have I got a deal for you!"

What the hell?

She was rambling on, the twenty-channel simultaneous transmission women use to communicate with each other, which he had heard her using with Lianne.

He finally understood that she knew nothing about Tucker's recent activities, that Tucker, who usually told her everything, had kept her in the dark about Tina. And that Tucker would have done so for no other reason than to spare Charles, to keep him, as long as possible, innocent in Dee-Dee's eyes, safe from the furious renewal of her blame.

At some cost to Tucker himself, eventually. Dee-Dee would not appreciate being out of the pipeline any more than Lianne had. In another day, in another time, Charles would have been touched by the gesture—and a gesture he had not been meant to discover either.

"So we'll be over in just a few minutes," Dee-Dee said. "You're going to be there, aren't you? You aren't going anywhere? We'll be right over."

"What are we talking about?" Charles said. "Hello?" But she had hung up.

She walked in the door thirty minutes later with a man in tow, a tall fellow Charles had never seen before. Taller than Charles, almost Curtis's height, an inch or so shy. And lean, almost as lean, but whereas you would call Curtis gaunt, not this fellow: some meat in his back, some heft on his long bones. He must have been about Charles's age but looked older, his gray hair cut short, brushed stiffly back. He held a hat in his hands, and he wore a tie in a dark blue knit, a pin-striped shirt—cuff links—and what looked to be a very reputable tweed jacket. Old, mended here and there, but good tweed. His face was lined but rosy and well fleshed, his features were plain but held a hint of calm good humor.

He looked for all the world, except for the knit tie, the cuff links, like a prosperous flatland farmer from Wynne or Des Arc, someone who'd started out sharecropping and done well for himself and went to the Methodist church.

Tweed, in this weather? But the man did not seem to feel the heat.

"This is Ballard," Dee-Dee said. She pronounced the accent on the second syllable.

"Villard?" Charles said.

"He's a butler," Dee-Dee said.

"More generally a man's man, sir," the tall man said. "Valet, as it were, though I can certainly serve in the other capacity."

Charles felt as though he had wandered onstage somewhere in London.

A revival of *Blithe Spirit*, perhaps—he would marry a new wife, and Lianne would come marching out from the wings to haunt them.

"Can we sit down?" Dee-Dee said. "I've been on my feet all morning."

Charles took them into the living room. Ballard sat on the edge of the sofa, his back erect, his hat still in his hands, facing Charles with an open countenance. He seemed, somehow, even in the formality of his posture, comfortable. Dee-Dee leaned back in the recliner chair, brought the footrest up, kicked off her shoes, wiggled her toes, and sighed. "I'm retaining water," she said.

She launched into the story. She had not been able to get her mind off Charles's predicament, the need for a housekeeper. This is the absolute *worst* time for you to be doing without. When we have grief or stress, we need somebody to take care of us even more.

Ballard nodded gravely, so Charles knew that Dee-Dee had told him about Lianne.

But not about Tina, no, she wouldn't have told about Tina, she didn't know about Tina, she wouldn't be here if she did.

"So there are these *companies*, did you know that? These actual companies that find them in England and bring them over to America and find them positions, but you have to pay a whopping commission. Except in this case you won't, I'll explain why in a minute. So anyway Ballard came over, he doesn't like Thatcher and he thinks the economy is going to hell—''

"Yes, ma'am, it is," Ballard said. "A fair mess." He became concerned. "But I stay out of politics," he assured Charles. "It's a personal choice, is all it is."

"What makes you think *this* economy is so great?" Charles said.

"And his health is good, it's nothing to do with his health, is it, Ballard?"

"No, ma'am, I'm quite able. Good for years yet."

"—but his blood is thin, he's cold all the time in England—"

"Frightful weather," Ballard said, and shivered. "Me for the tropics."

"So he's applied for citizenship, and he was placed with the Delgraves, in Fort Smith, you wouldn't know them, but Bessie Delgrave drives in to Little Rock, she won't see anybody but Tucker, they're both from Tunica, you know, and it was Robert's idea, he thought it was quaint, and you did buttle for them, didn't you, Ballard?"

This time Charles heard the name correctly.

"—so you can do that too, I guess I just didn't realize it was different—"

Ballard nodded. "It isn't, necessarily, ma'am," he said.

"—but all it did was just make them both terribly uncomfortable, they just neither of them were used to the situation, and *that* made Ballard uncomfortable, so everybody's uncomfortable all the way round, and they've already paid the commission, so that's fine, they don't mind that, that's what I was talking about, about you don't have to—"

Ballard shook his head.

"—but they've only been keeping him on because it's their fault and they feel for him and he doesn't have anywhere to go, because he likes Arkansas and wants to stay here, but the agency doesn't have any more openings in Arkansas right now and anyway he doesn't like dealing with the agency, it makes him feel like a commercial product, and so Bessie was in the other day for her checkup and she was telling me all about it, and suddenly the light bulb went off—"

It struck Charles as funny, farcically funny. He began laughing and could not quit. He laughed hysterically, unable to catch his breath. He bent over his knees, trying to smother the laughter, and almost succeeded, but it broke out again and turned into sobs.

"He's been under a lot of stress lately," Dee-Dee said.

She was plastered to the horizontal, limp, and her eyes were closed, and yet her voice was still energetic, still merry. She lifted her head, craning to look at Charles without righting the back of the recliner.

Ballard was on his feet.

"May I get you something, sir?" he said. "A drink?"

Charles looked up, feeling the stupid tears on his face, the tears he was so stupidly tired of producing. "Would you?" he said. "The bar's—"

"Yes, sir," Ballard said, striding away briskly, already at work.

It would have been right about that time, as Charles was later to decide, that Sonny Raymond put into action the solution to a little problem that had been worrying him. In Arkansas, in all jurisdictions, there was an informal seventy-two-hour limit on how long you could hold a prisoner without charges. There was not, and is not, a statutory limit, and so it still happens that some alleged miscreants disappear for days, or weeks, or even occasionally months at a time.

This would not be the case with Charles Morrison, of course; Sonny knew that. Even the seventy-two-hour limit was meaningless: The man could bring too much pressure to bear, the media would be all over it, and also Morrison was a big contributor to all the pinko liberal outfits that always raised a stink, so you could count on a lot of noise.

The only way you could hold Charles Morrison as long as he ought to be held, overnight at least, the only way you could really rub his nose in it, was to keep people from finding out, for as long as possible, that you had arrested him. But once Sonny got back to town, Morrison and his flunkies would be primed and ready. But they weren't expecting him till Wednesday. This was Saturday afternoon. He had it all wrapped up, Tina on the plane home two days ago. He and Tull had been thinking of Cartagena, hopping over the mountains and hitting the beach for a couple of days, check out that hot Latin snatch, they practically wear nothing, nothing at all on top, I bet, and just those strings on the bottom, I bet it's just like Rio.

But if you were dedicated to your job, you could put aside personal pleasure and do what's needed. Tull would fuss, but so be it. My way or the highway, Jack. Do right or do be gone.

It would have been right about that time, Charles would decide later, that Sonny's flight, the new flight, the one he had paid extra to change his ticket to, took off from Bogotá.

Charles had been given his drink, a splendidly icy martini, better than he himself had ever been able to make, and he had sipped it with an abstract pleasure, curious that he could feel so little and yet still enjoy the physical things.

Ballard—Charles still didn't know his first name and wasn't certain it wouldn't be gauche to ask—had spent some time discussing arrangements with Dee-Dee, and somehow now there was a leather valise and a stack of small cases in the foyer.

What does he do? Charles thought. *Carry all of his stuff wherever he goes? I thought he was still working for the—Derryberrys? Melbars?*

"I haven't hired anybody yet," he said.

"No, sir, of course not," said Ballard. "A few things for overnight, sir."

"I need to think about it till morning. I'll let you know in the morning."

"Morning will be fine, sir," Ballard said.

They were seeing Dee-Dee off, Ballard letting her into her car out in the driveway, when Rider drove up in the Bronco. Charles could tell by the way he swung out and down that he was in a bad mood. He was in a bad mood, though Charles could not know why, because he was running expenses, and the checkbook was low, and he was going to have to ask for money after all, if only for costs, and he didn't like that one bit, spoiling his gesture.

"We have to talk," he said to Charles. He stopped and squinted at Ballard.

Dee-Dee, half in and half out of the car, spoke: "Hi, J. D. This is Ballard."

So Rider had to hear the story, and they stood around in the heat, sweating—except for Ballard, Ballard didn't sweat, the tweed must have been air-conditioned—while Dee-Dee ran through the story again from start to finish, Bessie Delgrave and thin blood and all of it, and then added the update, what had happened since they had gotten here.

"So Charles is going to let him know in the morning," she concluded.

Now Rider was squinting at Charles, but with an added expression, a sort of irritated incredulity, which had grown on his face as Dee-Dee explained.

"You lucky son of a son," he said. "Morrison, you could roll in manure and come out with pearls between your teeth."

"Yeah," Charles said. "I'm a lucky man."

"Ta-ta," Dee-Dee said from her window.

They watched her drive off, and Rider looked back at Charles. His mood seemed to have broken. "I'm sorry," he said. "I average about one asshole comment a day, and I was running behind. Can we get in out of this heat?"

"You ever read any Dorothy Sayers?" he said as they went up the steps. And then to Ballard: "Ballard, can you cuss in front of a butler?"

"Yes, sir, you certainly may," Ballard said, holding the door.

They went into the cool dark of the living room. "But they can't cuss in front of you," Rider said with a grin. "Is that it?"

"Precisely, sir. May I get you a drink?"

"You certainly may," Rider said.

Rider had left in an hour or so, a check for a couple of thousand in his wallet. His conversation had mostly been not business but a long disquisition on wanting to be a detective all his life, and of course it wasn't anything like the books, he had known that for years, since he was fifteen, but he had gone ahead and done it anyway—because, he supposed, among other things, he had watched his father wither away and die from never doing what he really wanted to, whatever that might have been, because he had never even come close enough to it so you could tell.

And of course his absolute most favorite daydream of all had been to be—don't laugh—like Lord Peter Wimsey, aided by his loyal man, Bunter. Completely ridiculous, a middle-class Southern boy to start with, not to say a Southern Baptist, for crying out loud, and he had to laugh himself, but that was the way daydreams were, which is why he reacted the way he did out in the driveway, and he was sorry, it was unforgivable.

Charles saw why the women liked Rider so much. He could talk to them.

Rider had worn down finally, his vaunted perceptiveness coming back into play as his enthusiasm faded, and had seen that Charles was in bad shape, and that it was time to leave and that in fact Ballard had been hinting discreetly for several minutes now, mainly by not filling his glass the third time. And so he had left Charles in Bunter's—*I'm sorry, Ballard, but you understand*—Ballard's capable hands, and had taken his leave.

"Could I make you a sleeping draft, sir?" Ballard asked Charles.

Who stirred from his sunken-chin torpor to say, "Sleeping? Draft?"

"Yes, sir. I have a recipe. In the brown case, sir."

"Why don't you do that," Charles said. "I've had a very strange day. The worst and strangest day of my life." Well. The day she died would have been the worst day of his life, and maybe the strangest too, what could be stranger?

Would have been, but he didn't have that day, did he? All he had was this one.

"Yes, sir," Ballard said, helping him up.

"Ballard," Charles said in the elevator, leaning against its wall, "you're coming into a bad situation." Ballard inclined his head.

The doors opened. "I'm pretty depressed," Charles said.

"Yes, sir," Ballard said. "This way, sir." As if Ballard knew the way and Charles didn't. As if Charles needed his help to find his own bed. "I'll bring that draft in a moment, sir."

Which is how it happened that someone was there when Sonny's boys rang the bell at two o'clock in the morning. They were expecting Morrison to be alone. And, being alone, and rousted suddenly out at that hour, to react with shock and do something dumb. Check them out through the peephole, maybe, and then refuse to let them in, maybe even after they showed the warrant, so they would get to break the door down and handcuff him.

Instead a tall man in a dressing gown opened the door on the first ring and said, "May I help you, sir?" And then, as they pushed their way in, stepped to the telephone; so they threw him against the wall before he could use it, a nightstick pinning him at his chest.

"Fan out," said Tull, urgently. The troops were wavering, uncertain where to go next. The house was *big*, and they had no idea where Morrison's bedroom was.

But Ballard had not been trying to use the phone. He had pressed the button on the intercom over the phone, the elder Mr. Morrison's installation, and now his son Charles's voice came from a grille in the wall, thick and uncertain: "Clemmie?"

"Some gentlemen from the local constabulary, sir," Ballard said.

"Constabu—" The voice from the grille sharpened, grew quick. "Ballard, are you ok?"

"I'm fine, sir. I believe they wish to arrest you."

"Tell em to hold their horses. I'll be right down."

"If you gentlemen would hold your horses," Ballard said to the top of the head of the man leaning against his chest with the nightstick, young Robbie Rabelais.

"I aint believing this shit," Audrey Tull said.

Charles came down in slacks and a pullover, Dock-Sides without socks, and they hustled him out to the car, where Sonny Raymond waited with his tame photographer, waited in his best dark suit and red tie, his badge pinned to his belt and his shoulder holster showing where, with a debonair hand in his pocket, he held the coat open. Ballard followed, and no one seemed to know what to do with him. He wasn't interfering, so you couldn't arrest him or whack him, especially not with the photographer there; he might be Sonny's man, but he still worked for the paper.

"I'll make the telephone calls, sir," Ballard said.

"What the hell is this?" Sonny Raymond said.

"Some kind of Englishman," Rabelais said.

So the plan for a secret arrest was blown; Morrison would be out in a matter of hours. Never mind, Sonny still had the man where he wanted him, the main plan was still in effect, he'd solved one problem for good and all, tell him he hadn't.

"You'll never make it stick," Morrison called as they shoved him into the car, too furious to hear himself, how Cagney he sounded, how Bogart.

"What stick?" Sonny Raymond said, coming over to close the door himself. "Who's trying to make anything stick?" Ah, Sonny, always a step ahead, always thinking three moves ahead, like chess. "You'll never be governor now," he said.

Charles was dumbstruck. This was it? This was what it was all about?

The car jerked, and started away. "You poor sap," Charles said to Sonny, now out of range. Quoting words he had heard recently, he couldn't think where, or words he just thought he had heard because they brought with them such a sudden vertiginous swoop of déjà vu.

"You poor sap. You poor damn bozo."

They let Freddy Mayfield into his cell about four in the morning. Charles was up and pacing. Mayfield sat on the bunk and watched.

"You won't be in long," he said. "That young fellow of yours already been down here working. He's gonna get Elsijane out of bed, and she'll turn you loose."

Charles was having trouble not hanging on the bars. It was a natural gesture, let your arms take some weight off your spine, and every time he looked at the cell door his monkey hands twitched. But he saw himself looking like every cliché prisoner in every cliché prison movie ever made, and he wouldn't let it happen.

"Thank you," he said, shoving his hands in his pockets.

"I didn't do anything," Freddy said, unpleasantly.

Charles had been in a fair number of cells, visited a fair number of prisoners. There was hardly a lawyer who hadn't, no matter his or her specialty. So he would have called himself acquainted with the seamier side of the law. But it was different when you were in their power. He had never been under arrest before. Not once in his life, not even to sleep off a drunk in college. And he was thinking how utterly grim the cell was. How bare, depressing, and devoid. It was what happened to living space when no one cared what happened to you. The bleached-out fluorescent, bouncing its soulless glisten off the tile floor. The stripped-down bunk, with its one sheet, one blanket, one foam pillow. The lidless toilet in the corner. The cell was clean enough. A strong smell of disinfectant hung in the air.

But every surface, every function, gleamed with the fact that no one cared.

"The Lord will accept a sinner," Mayfield said. "No matter how far down you gone. No matter what you got on your heart."

"Freddy," Charles said. "I hope you know I didn't do this. I hope you know this is just some of that bastard's dirty business."

"I aint worried about your fate in the courts," Mayfield said, shifting to watch him pace. "That's between you and your fellowman. But I will tell you this. You can't get nothing straight with your fellowman until you get things straight with Him."

"What about Her?" Charles said.

"What?"

Charles gave up and grabbed the bars. He pressed his face against the cool metal, smiling to no one. "How do we know God is a Him?" he said. "What if she's a Her, or an It?"

"Who is this that darkeneth counsel by words without understanding?" Mayfield said.

"I don't see how you buy that bullshit," Charles said bitterly. He heaved away from the bars, confronted Mayfield. "What kind of a God lets Lianne die?" he said. "What kind of God has me up for murder, when all I ever did was work hard and love my wife and try to do right?" His voice was plaintive and wailing, he heard it, but he couldn't stop it.

It was supposed to be his big explosion, it was supposed to be his grand summary, but it wouldn't come out right. Instead of his courtroom bass, his voice was soaring into the treble he had last used in arguments with his father. "Look around you. There's children dying of cancer, by God, there's people, there's millions of people starving in Africa. What about those people with the worms in their eyes? You tell me that. You explain to me how a good God, you tell me how He can let a man beat his own baby son to death, for example, or there's a woman up in the hills, Lianne told me about a woman selling off all her furniture—"

And now he had become so outraged he lost his voice.

Mayfield considered him a moment.

"It's a lot of ego in what I'm hearing," he said finally. "A lot of Me Me Me. Talking about the world, but what you really saying God has to explain himself to you. What you really saying, you had some pain and grief, and it aint fair. Like a spoil child stub his toe."

His voice was harsh and swift, and Charles felt the shock of it, the blood draining from his face like that of a teenager who has just been slapped.

"It's a little more than a stubbed toe," he whispered.

"You aint the first to see what's wrong with the world," Mayfield said, more gently. "It's a lot of other people has a hard row to hoe."

He sat on the edge of the cot, round belly forward. Sat there in his pale-yellow short-sleeved Dacron shirt, the huge knot of his yellow-and-green-striped polyester tie pushed up tight into the fatty folds of his throat.

Sat there with his sparse gray hair slicked wetly back, with his wide-lapeled gray polyester suit coat thrown across one knee, his police revolver clipped to his wide black belt, the eyes in his round ingenuous face no longer innocent and blue, but steely—the word was true, people's eyes could turn the color of steel: no pity and no hatred. His eyes were the eyes of a man who had become identical to his code.

And suddenly Charles saw that this out-of-breath fifty-year-old, that this somewhat comic and thoroughly portly and spottily educated true believer, was a man who had walked up to stopped automobiles in the middle of the night, not knowing what redneck drunken hopped-up scared 7-Eleven-robbing serial murdering tax evader waited to pull what possible trigger. This was a man who had sprinted up urinous steps to burst into a room and block a maddened ex-middleweight to the floor before the man battered his wife to death. This was a man who had stepped into bottomland woods with his rifle barrel up, tracking a killer whose rifle had longer range; a man who had been the first to go in where someone had smelled the sick-liest and most ghastly odor of all, and had opened a black garbage bag or a cardboard box or the trunk of a car full of maggots and rags and human bones, and held his lunch; a man who had carried a bleeding two-year-old into an emergency room, patting and soothing as well as he could while blood seeped from anus and vulva over his shirt sleeves.

And Charles saw that if this man had walked out of that hospital still believing there was a God, Charles might disagree; but Charles had not a word to say that this man needed to hear.

This man was saved, but Charles could not be saved, because he was not damned. He carried grief and not sin, and there was no redemption from grief. Grief wasted your bones like a fire. Grief did not belong to you but you to it, until it was through with you, had spent what you had to offer, had left you a smutty and sodden ruin, skeletal charcoal, wonder-ing what still-smoking fragments might be somehow usable.

"Freddy," he said again, whispering, "I didn't do it."

"I never had no doubt," Mayfield said. "It makes you need a friend even more."

"I can't believe in Jesus," Charles said. "I might want to, but I just can't do it. That born-of-a-virgin crap, that rising from the dead. If *Lianne* would rise, I might believe it."

And as he said it, he had a visitation, a revenant, one of their many joking arguments, playful on the surface—we're all modern here, we're free to say anything—but with the undertone of genuine theological tension:

What's so hard to believe about that? People see ghosts all the time.

He had been silent, unable to say what he had always privately held, that there were no ghosts, that those who saw them fooled themselves. Including her, whose ghosts, for the sake of the marriage (as he saw it), he had credited, or appeared to her face to credit.

This time the ghost just happened to be the Son of God.

"You remember the publican came to Jesus," Mayfield said. "He doubted, but he didn't want to doubt. He said, 'Lord, I believe. Help thou my unbelief.' "

"I'm not like that," Charles said.

"You ever wonder what a publican is?" Mayfield said.

"No," Charles said.

"What *can* you believe?" Mayfield said.

"I can almost believe in the Holy Ghost," Charles said. "Sometimes. Not the Father, all that authority crap, maker of the universe. I could make a better universe than this."

Mayfield didn't look shocked.

"But almost the Holy Ghost," Charles said. "Some kind of spirit that goes from person to person like fox fire. When you're having fun at a party, or when she gets that look in her eye. When you read a good book, maybe, or when you—when you—"

"It aint much," Mayfield said. "But let's run with it and see what happens."

"I don't think I can do this," Charles said, looking toward the cell door: self-conscious, afraid that someone would see, that Greg and Lafayette would appear and witness his degradation. "I don't even believe that any more."

Mayfield put a forceful hand on his back. "Better get it done," he said. "You aint gone get no closer tonight."

"I hate foxhole Christians," Charles said.

"There aint any other kind," Mayfield said. "It's what you do when you get out of the foxhole that counts."

And how could he refuse? What made him so superior? Had he faced down death and fear, had he held strong in a hurtful world? No. He had played, and he had dallied with another woman, and his wife was dead.

Charles knelt, and pressed his eyes shut fiercely. Glowing in the negative, he saw the afterimage of the bars on the door. *Raskolnikov,* he thought. The Russian novels class, so many years ago. He was trapped in other people's stories.

"Gin it, hoss," Mayfield said.

"You son of a bitch," Charles Morrison said. "Help me, you goddamn son of a bitch."

PART FIVE:

KINGDOM COME

39

THE SON OF THE HOG RIDES AGAIN, PART II

Whooo, *dark* in that closet, *tight* in that bottle. Shake the dust off my trench coat here.

Tell you what, Morrison, you like to wait too late. For a minute there, didn't think you was gonna ring. Didn't you hear *me* calling *you*, last couple of chapters?

I aint proud, I'll take the work. Any ole way you choose it.

But one thing for sure, you need a professional. Amateurs are fine if all you want's who did it, but who did it's easy. We on a bigger case now, we working on the why did it. The how could it. As in how could it happen? Let that other detective solve her murder, he's just a Rider on the storm, and I'm the storm. You and me got to solve her life.

Charles aint listening. But somebody is, I can feel you out there.

Hi there, Reader. Bet you thought I was gone for good. Well, I am, in a little while, sooner or later. Out of here. Gone. Soon I will trance out and disappear. When I awaken, I will not remember. I will not have told you this story. I will not exist.

So what can I do for you now, boys and girls? It's all over with, the moving finger writ, and not all your piety or wit matters a rat's ass, so what can I do for you now?

I am a poor wavering stranger. While traveling through. This world of woe.

Sorry sorry sorry to be so hyper, but it's like the dog let out the yard when you get back from the aer-o-plane trip. He has to shake the heebie-jeebies, run around barking like crazy, jump up your leg, run off again, and pee on everything.

Don't exist, you can't *scratch* anywhere.

Or put it like this: Whip the genie out the bottle, you think he just say *Yassamassa, yo wish is my command?* Big genie like me, sit anywhere he wants to, uncontainable?

Hell, that wouldn't be wholly ghostly.

Aw, come on, aint you just a *little* glad to see me again? Listen in once more on the protoyap of the precon, the brontobabble of dream?

You want me back on the case, you and Charles, you really do. Because I got something for you, I got a leetle bitty going-away present. Something you really really want.

I can't cancel Lianne's death. You don't want me to. Suppose I was to say, *Surprise, she didn't really die. I'm the Holy Ghost, and I can do anything, and it was all just an illusion, here she is, and they lived happily ever after.*

You wouldn't like that, would you? It would make her trivial. She wouldn't be real.

Anyway, as you probably suspected a long time back, she was born out of her death. She would never have lived if she hadn't died first. Nothing I can do about that. Rules of the game. I didn't make the rules. I am the rules. I'm a fiction, is what I am. An image, metaphor, model. But hear me what I say: All bets are off. I'm know I'm just a damn construct, but listen to me, I'm here. So long as I speak, here I am.

You're not going to argue that, are you, not at this point?

So. What's left? That's right: On with the show:

Charles was sprung from jail and back home by eight in the morning, in time to read the paper—in which, since he had been gotten out of bed after it had already been put to bed, he did not appear. That would be tomorrow's paper, Monday's.

In time to read the Sunday paper on the sun porch, coffee at his elbow courtesy Ballard. Whose full name, I might as well tell you sooner before you find out later, was Dagoberto Rivera-Ballard, his mother Argentinian and his father Cockney. All of which might have been part of why he was so anxious to please—never quite belonging, you know, no matter how very proper his demeanor and accent. He was a genuine valet/butler, had splendid recommendations. He had never liked the British upper classes, though, however admirably he had served them. He much preferred the easy style of the Americans, their more comfortable insecurities.

Ballard had been waiting to drive Charles home when Charles walked out of the police station in the company of grumpy Lafayette and lively Greg, and in the next few weeks Ballard would locate and put Charles onto a fellow in Fort Smith who would come pick the 280 up, repair it, and bring it back, Jerry be damned.

The grand jury was set in the week of September 21 through 25. The DA's evidence was circumstantial at best, and entirely sketchy: Personal testimony by Sonny Raymond and Robbie Rabelais that Charles's movements coincided with known shipments of drugs into and out of The Blue Note. Bill of sale and other particulars proving that Charles had bought Lianne's Blazer himself. Allegations that he had access, through his many contacts in the military and the underworld and international business, to high explosives and the sophisticated hardware necessary to set off a bomb like the one that had slain Lianne Morrison. A doctored tape recording: On the recording Charles spoke to a menacing-sounding citizen and referred to the problem and how they had neutralized the problem, who was, as a later reference made clear, female. In fact, the recording had been made earlier, at the office, when Lianne was alive, and the menacing-sounding citizen had been Laugh, and they had been discussing the situation with Tina's cases.

The grand jury would reject this farrago out of hand, as well they should, and Charles would be a free man before the creation science suit ever came to trial. It would be true that, all over the state, for the rest of his life, most of the monkeys would think he had done it, or at least that there was something suspicious there, and it was true that their suspicions would darken when Tina was brought to trial, convicted, and jailed. The motive was so obvious, the connection was so strong: *You know he at least fucked around on her, and maybe it was that crazy woman who killed her, all on her own get-go, but the man bound to known something was going on.*

On the other hand, a jury of his peers had heard the actual evidence and found in his favor, which made him at least as innocent as Lee Orsini. And the *Gazette* came out with an unusually emotional editorial appeal for fairness and an end to rumor and unfounded suspicion.

Bringing Tina to trial was tricky, like landing a fish. She was hooked, Rider had no doubt of that, and he would reel her in sooner or later, but where was the net? Where was the confounded net? Forget all the stuff in Colombia, the cocaine bullshit, that was a completely different matter, somebody who wanted to bad enough and had the money to spend might be able to go down there and tie Tina to some vaguely suspicious activities, might even manage to implicate Sonny Raymond, but it wasn't going to be Rider who did it.

Charles: What makes you so sure Sonny didn't plan it all?

Rider: He wants to ruin you, not kill you. Anyway, he's too smart to tie himself to a bush-league murder like this.

Charles: What do you mean, bush-league?

Rider with the x-ray eyes: No insult intended. I mean the way it was handled, that's all.

Which didn't help much. Somebody offs the missus, you want it to be at least an international plot by master spies, right? Not much comfort in thinking your life gets blown apart because some clown enrolls you in his cartoon.

Charles: I don't find that a very convincing argument.

Rider: (Sighing) Ok, I've got a pipeline.

Charles: A pipeline?

Rider: Into Sonny's office. Head Cheese has a new girlfriend, and she talks to me.

Charles: Who?

Rider: Let's just say a grand jury thinks maybe she didn't kill Ron Orsini.

Charles: You're kidding.

Rider: It was easy. Weakness for lawyers, and she loves to talk about herself. Buy her a drink, and she tells you fifteen different stories, one of which may have some truth in it. How I found those spies they hired. Cheese bragged to her, and she bragged to me.

Charles: No, I mean, I thought she was with McArthur.

Rider: Yeah. Like you were with Tina. No, she's climbing the Cheese tree now, picking his apples.

Rider had already satisfied himself, well in advance of Charles's grand jury hearing, that Tommy Dwell had guilty knowledge and that the brother, Ferrin, was a prime suspect. It was boringly obvious: Car gets torched and you want to figure who did it? Trace the car.

But Ferrin could not be located, and Tommy, jumpy as hell, white-faced, was saying nothing. Rider goaded him, in their one interview, with mention of the reward, but there was no reaction, not one flash of avarice battling with family loyalty. Tommy didn't seem the type, but his brother sure did, especially when you looked at the brother's record. Every felony in the book, and getting more serious as he went, getting more violent.

When it all came together, it happened in a matter of days. Rider finally had the idea, cursing himself for his slowness, to call information and ask if they had a listing for Ferrin Loyal (he said the name right) Dwell. It hadn't been in the book, of course, but just on the off chance—

That number is not current, sir.

Well, can you tell me what it is anyway?

I'm not allowed to give that information out, sir.

He's about to inherit some money, and I need to find him. I'm a lawyer for the family, check my office listing, you'll see.

The number told him the approximate neighborhood of the apartment—near Tommy, as he had expected, and then it was a matter of getting to the installation records, but he had friends in the service department, you bet he did, or at least he and one of the servicemen had a mutual friend, one of the lesser-known presidents. The bribery was the single act that made him feel more like a real detective than anything else in this whole sorry case.

And then when the apartment building turned out to be in Tina's name—He had her, he knew he had her then.

But there was still the problem of how to nail it down, how to connect Ferrin irrefutably to the bomb, and Tina irrefutably to Ferrin as agent. There was the landlord/tenant connection, but that didn't prove a thing.

Rider knew Ferrin had had a companion, but he didn't have a good description. Sonny's two spies had seen Rubert, of course, but to them he had looked like any other fat black man. Rider would get a good description in just a few days, when Coleman woke up. But before that happened, he got a call, someone contacting him about the reward.

The caller would not give his name. He wanted specifics about how the money would be paid out, if they could do it like right away, and how it could be made over to a third party where nobody could get at it or take it back if they changed their mind. "You know crimnals aint got no health insurance," the contact said. "It aint like a fringe benefit of the job."

The caller thought they had to catch the person who had really done it, or Morrison wouldn't get off. He thought that was his negotiating advantage. Rider set him straight: "Charles Morrison will walk in three weeks whatever you cockroaches do. It's a question whether he keeps all his money himself or spends a little to squash the low-life bastard who killed her."

There was a minute hesitation, like the pause of a piston at the top of its stroke.

And then the descent: "You still aint gone know who done it, not without my help." The caller sounded faint, as if he wanted to cut and run.

"How do I know you're for real?" Rider said curtly. The curtness was control, not doubt. He was pretty sure who he had on the line. Not so much the urgency of the voice, because any nut can sound urgent. Maybe the resemblance to Tommy Dwell's voice—lose the cigarette huskiness, and you had the almost identical timbre—maybe that was what made Rider so instantly certain.

The maneuver worked the way Rider wanted it to. The contact rose to the challenge.

"You ask Morrison where he was when that perfume store got shot up," Ferrin Dwell said. "You ask him how him and that bitch got out of there alive."

Charles was shattered when Rider told him. All he had wanted to do was concentrate on his preparations for the hearing, and then, after the hearing, a long vacation. Some other country somewhere. And he might not come back.

Now here was the whole ugly mess again, the whole giant horrible funhouse architecture of the thing opening up and dropping him through a floor to further realms of grue. Somebody not only had killed her—no, not somebody: Tina; Tina had killed her—but had tried before, and he had missed it; he had been so blind and confident, it had gone right by.

It was as if she were murdered again, before his eyes. Murdered in a few short sentences from Rider's mouth.

"We didn't think—" he said. "It never occurred—"

For Rider, it had been merely pro forma corroboration. And he knew, having this much information from the man he was certain was Ferrin Dwell, that there would be more to follow. He knew that the man needed to give him the information now, that he only had to find an excuse to deliver himself up, a pretext that would allow him to salvage his pride.

Things broke just right. Rider had arranged a callback, Ferrin declaring that when he saw some money, cash on the barrelhead, he could provide times and amounts of payments someone had made—he wasn't saying who, not till he saw the color of Morrison's money—but payments someone had made to professional hit men, and then they could check the person's bank records. "It was a turnkey job," Ferrin said. "These guys knew what they were doing."

The problem was going to be getting him to a meeting. There was no way the creep could incriminate Tina without incriminating himself, and he probably knew it. There was no way Dwell was going to collect for informing on a hit he himself had performed, and walk away clean with the dough, and he would know that too. So whatever was driving the man, Rider needed a way to lean on it. Get him face-to-face, get him in possession and break him down.

He made the callback, he made several callbacks, and they argued, but that was the sticking point. No cash without proof, no proof without cash. Ferrin was getting more desperate by the day, you could hear it, but when would he snap? And where the hell *was* he?

And then Coleman woke up. Two weeks before the grand jury, Coleman woke up. He said, "Don't let her get on that train," and opened his eyes. He looked around the hospital room (nobody there but Me), and said, "Oh boy." He tried to move his arms, and he couldn't do it. He could tell they *would* move, he wasn't paralyzed, he was just too weak. He said, "This gone take some time," and went to sleep. Not back into coma, but to sleep.

He woke and slept three more times that day before someone was there. While he had been asleep, or perhaps, perhaps even back while he had been in coma, he had figured out what must have happened to him, what it probably meant.

"Call the police," he said to the nurse checking his pulse. "Some damn nigger trying to kill Miss Morrison."

40

ON FERRIN DWELL

After that, it was easy to pull Ferrin in. Rider just told him they had an eyewitness, an eyewitness who could finger them both, a black man and a white man driving a lawn-service truck, and the black man had come back later with a gun. It wouldn't be hard to trace the lawn-service truck. It wouldn't be hard to prove who drove it and how they had gotten it.

"I knew that nigger was trouble," Ferrin said. "I told him that nigger would be our Achilles' heel."

The risk was whether Ferrin would run. But Rider didn't think he would. Rider thought he would collapse, and he did. He agreed to give himself up and bring the evidence. He said he would trust them to do right by the reward. The reward wasn't for him. There was a place the reward ought to go, if there was any justice on this earth, and he would just have to trust to their honor as decent human beings to see that it went there.

He wanted a favor, though. He wanted to set up the meet at Peck's.

Rider stayed antsy about the situation until he walked into the bar with Lafayette and Freddy Mayfield and saw the man.

Charles wasn't there. He thought it wouldn't be safe for him to see Ferrin. Also he was still pretty shook from finding out about the perfume store, and now here Coleman was telling about a *third* attack—well, not a third, a first, but hell, you know what I mean. Charles was feeling as if they were going to turn up a hitherto unsuspected attempt every other day the rest of his life, they were going to kill her and kill her and kill her every other single day of his life.

Rider was antsy because so far all they really had on Ferrin was driving a truck near the scene of a crime, and the crime no more than attempted

homicide contributing to personal injury. True, he consorted with the per-
petrator, but it was a question how much you could make of that. And
technically speaking, although Ferrin had the impression he had already
been identified in the mug books and was under pursuit, the law, except
for Mayfield, was unaware of him.

The nurse, who was not the nurse Charles had gotten so angry with but
a younger nurse bucking for the latter's position and friendly with the hospital administrator, who was friendly with Charles—the nurse had called
Charles before she called the police, and Charles had told her not to call
the police, Coleman was probably confused from his coma.

"Well, I thought so," the nurse had said, feeling virtuous and successful at once.

Charles had called Rider, and Charles and Rider and Tucker had gone
to see Coleman and gotten the story. They'd had a strategy meeting and
agreed to call in Mayfield, because you wanted to keep Sonny Raymond
out of it, you wanted to get Tina absolutely and totally pinned before Sonny
got his mitts on the deal. Mayfield had agreed to sit in with Ferrin, and if
he heard enough or saw enough evidence, work a warrant to search Tina's
place. He still wouldn't criticize Sonny openly, but he had agreed to support the plan.

"Oh Lord," Coleman said, when they told him Lianne was already
gone. "I known it all along," he said. "I was hoping, but I known it all
along."

So that was the situation as they headed for Peck's, and Ferrin still
might fly the coop, or try to brazen the matter through. But they walked
in, and there he was, at a corner booth, instantly recognizable, the only
Ferrin in the room. They slid into their seats. "All the important people in Little Rock come here," he said. He had a sheaf of paper with
him, notes torn from a spiral binder, trailing confetti at their ripped-out
margins.

He was lean and knobby and sly, and Rider couldn't help thinking
weasel. His skin was red and tender, he looked as though he had recently
been boiled and shucked, and he caught Rider checking him out. "It's a
reaction," he said. "It's a allergy reaction to the sun. I got burned when
we was down in Florida, and now it don't seem to peel or nothing, it stays
like a new sunburn."

Florida? Rider and Lafayette thought.

Ferrin's mouth was twitchy and his hands jerky. It wasn't fear. He
seemed proud of the meeting: he was finally sitting in on one of the big-
time bull sessions everybody knew went on in Peck's, where all the important business got unofficially done. He seemed to feel he had broken
into the big leagues. He was proud of his bomb, the intricacy of the wiring,

even if something inexplicable had happened and it had taken almost an extra month to go off.

"That's why I used extra batteries," he said. "Just in case. Your true professional always leaves a margin for error."

And his fingers curled and uncurled, and he blinked and twitched his mouth, and his hands kept running to his pockets and coming away empty, and he looked around every time somebody struck a match, and *He's just quit smoking,* Rider realized.

"Would you like a cigarette?" he said.

Ferrin understood he was being prodded, an animal in a cage. He leveled a dark gaze: "You wouldn't say that, you knew what secondhand smoke can do."

"Are you a Christian?" Mayfield asked at one point.

"My old lady used to try to get me to go to church with her," Ferrin said. He all but lit and smoked an invisible Pall Mall.

"My first old lady," he added. "I would be a lot better man now if I had've."

"You got a heavy load to carry," Mayfield agreed. "You aint gone make it without Him." Rider was drumming his fingers on the table. Lafayette sat impassively.

Ferrin grinned. "Hey," he said, twitching. "Don't do the time if you can't do the crime."

"Don't do the *crime* if you can't do the *time,*" Rider said.

"Where's Rubert?" Lafayette asked, for by this time they had identified Ferrin's companion and in fact had his entire dossier in a folder on the table, along with Ferrin's in another folder. "He go north on you? Run off, and you take the heat all by your lonesome?"

"You leave him out of this," Ferrin said, and wouldn't budge from Rubert's defense. "There aint nothing you can do to him, and he aint gonna hurt nobody now. You leave him run free awhile, or the deal is off."

It was way too late to call the deal off, and Ferrin surely knew it. They could snatch his green-ink notes: the names, times, payments. Even without grabbing those scribbled sheets, the three of them had heard enough to fix him good, and could back each other up.

But they let the strange little man have the appearance of his deal. They would leave Rubert out of it for now. Mayfield would get his warrant, and they would find, of all things, canceled checks in Tina's apartment, with notes in the lower left-hand corners: For *Expenses for Ferrin and Rubert.* For *Batteries and clock for timer.* For *Initial payment for hit.*

That would infuriate Charles. These checks had been floating around for months, the crazy woman's information given away right out there in plain view, and no one had noticed, no one had known. How did danger step so lightly veiled, how did evil coil so plainly hidden?

They would find Rubert heaving in a cheap room downtown. Too late to punish Rubert, too late to do him any good either, though they would crack his chest anyway in the prison hospital and take out most of two lungs.

But for now they let the little man have sway in the conversation, unable to explain why they did so. Well, Lafayette could have maybe explained

IT'S THE FLIP-FLOP

if he had known what Rider was going through

LOOK OUT FOR THE FLIP-FLOP

looking into the eyes of this weasel of a man, Rider, who could see what people were hiding, but oddly enough didn't worry much over the state of their souls, because empathy is just a talent, a read, a knack, and contrary to how we usually use the word, it doesn't necessarily mean you get your feelings all involved, and Rider had enough feelings of his own to deal with, always secretly angry over being the son of a suicide, the son of a man who canceled himself and therefore almost canceled his son, so that you never felt you were really quite there or quite good enough or quite anything you claimed, looking into the eyes of this badly inflamed weasel of a man

SUCK YOU RIGHT IN

and suddenly uncharacteristically flashing on how the man felt and not just what he showed

and goddammit they're sucking *me* in, I said Ferrin was gone, out of here, finito, one more over and done with and I wouldn't never ever consent to be in Ferrin but the goddamn

FLIP-FLOP

because I'm in Rider like I'm in Reader and I wasn't watching and Rider wasn't watching and he/I got too close to the edge and now we're about to

SUCK YOU

oh god

RIGHT IN THE

oh god

FLIP

god

FLOP:

It was funny, but what I was thinking when I went in this time was the last time I made love to my old lady before the last time I went in. It was like this time didn't count.

It was a Friday afternoon. It was an afternoon, because it was cutting across my eyes wherever we went, on the steps, in the chair, on the bed. That yellow light.

This was my second old lady, this wasn't Naylene. We never got married or nothing, which was all right with me, I had that once, the bitches start in where your momma left off, you never do anything right. But she was just a young cunt, Candi, just a college-dropout dancer type who thought she wanted dope and fast times, but she was ok.

That night we smoked a little bit and stayed in. She was always wanting to go out and dance, but this time she really didn't, she hadn't slept good from the night before because I think it had been cut with speed or something, so we just stayed right there in bed.

It was comfortable laying in bed by the window, and the yellow light cutting shadows in the smoke, like the smoke was clouds in the mountains, and the pillows and sheets was snow in the mountains, but you were warm in the sun, not cold in the snow. It was like we were big soft giants up in the clouds in the mountains.

I aint big enough to fight Wehunt tonight, so it's die or get butt-fucked. And I probably got this new stuff, this aids, but the way I smoke these cigs, they'll get to me first.

I quit for a while, but I'm back again. What do I care these perverts get lung cancer from my smoke?

He's been on my butt since Christmas. It tore me up some at first, till I got loosened up. It feels like this big turd is shitting *you*. That's what I told Bay-baw, it feels like this big turd is shitting *you*, but he didn't get it. There's some real dumb fuckers in here. Bay-baw's name ought to be Baseball, because that's all he ever talks about, but he can't say it right.

Hell, it might be all right to have AIDS. Tv cameras, clean sheets. I could sue somebody. But then again if I had it, they wouldn't let me near no women. I sure could use me some of that good old salty tail right now. But still, you know that hospital food would taste like gourmet compared to this. And air-conditioning, and everybody acting like they worried about you all the time. I been in the hospital before, but not for anything everybody else was worried about. That's the trouble with me, I always had the wrong disease.

So that's what I live for, to get out and fuck me some a that young salty tail again. It would set all of this straight in my mind, you know it would. This wouldn't even be a memory. A man aint less of a man because of who he aint big enough to fight.

The way it went wrong was after me and Candi screwed, I was cooking up some rice. We just had breakfast whenever we got out of bed, if it was the middle of the night or whatever. That might sound weird to you, rice for breakfast, but she liked it, cook the rice up all gummy, then put butter and milk and sugar on it and eat it up just like oatmeal.

So now I've burned up the pan, right, and I'm in the doghouse. We didn't go out, and even though she was the one who was too tired to for a change, I've burned up the pan and she has to come clean it and so I'm in the doghouse.

"Don't burn the rice," she says, but I'm always looking out the window or something, and it's a good-looking day, all the lawns and sprinklers and kids on tricycles and whatnot, and I almost feel like I really live here. It's a nice house, and it's a shame she aint gone keep it when the divorce goes through, but if she was I wouldn't be here anyway, because she don't care what they think or what happens to the place.

But she does get all the pots and pans, so I'm in the doghouse, and she's scrubbing away with an old Brillo pad, how they get rusty so quick and the soap lathers up all rusty-red and now black from the scorch, and the scorch is tearing the old rusty pad to pieces.

"I'll do it," I say, but she's grinding away on that pan not looking at me, like she don't care if she grinds her knuckles down to the bone.

"Hell, at least get a new Brillo pad," I say, but she don't even answer. Grinding away titty-bare top, bottom jiggling in those love panties. She's about sweated the panties through.

So I'm going for a walk. I got this idea the hell with this, I'll start a new life, loosen the muscles up, get healthy, you know. But it's a hundred and fifty in the shade, and I get three blocks before I'm hacking my heart up in pieces of giant rotten snot. Bent over, hands on knees, watching the sprinklers wave all up and down the street, like a fan dancer's fans. Shrup, shrup. Up and down, up and down. Unless they're the *bert zerk, r r r* ones. *Bert zerk, r r r.* I hate those. Neurotic sons of bitching type sprinkler to have. They ought to go all the way round like they started. These are like some kind of alien bug machine. So I say fuck this and head on up for the 7-Eleven eight more blocks away.

It's cold in there, air-conditioned, and right away my sweat freezes. They got a new guy at the counter, they get a new one every other week, at least this one's not a goddamned A-rab.

I put my head in the cooler, it's like a trip to walk into all this cold out of that oven out there, you know. But I got my last butt hanging from my lips, and this guy says, Hey, don't smoke in the cooler. Well it aint even lit, but I see how he sees me, with my rayon shirt hanging out over my jeans, and open halfway down to my dick anyhow, and I'm greasy-shiny from walking in the heat and I aint shaved and I probably smell like I just been fucked because I have.

So I don't say nothing back, but what the hell, asshole, maybe I was about to buy one of your beers or something. You just blew some money, bugfuck.

Except I don't have any money, which I probably deep down thought about when I left the house, because I brought that rich guy's checkbook and wallet with me that I found at the Y. He just left it laying there out in the open in his open locker while he went and took a shower. I was just a guy with a broom, probably retarded, and he never even thought.

I already spent all his money, and I shouldn't have held on to the wallet, it wouldn't be good for nothing but trouble. But you don't know how it felt, having that fat leather on my hip with all those important cards in it, and that checkbook that had a balance of fifteen thousand three hundred and eighty three dollars and forty-two cents, which I'm sure he had already changed it by then. In his fucking *checking* account.

And that's probably what done it, right there. All these fucking rich people, and they can have anything they want. They can buy Miss America for a wife, and all I got's Candi in this house she can't even hold on to much longer.

So I walk out to think it over, and that was a mistake, I'm willing to admit it. A big mistake. It marks you. I don't know what I was thinking when I went back in, I really don't. Except I really needed some cigs, and a rich man can buy em anytime he wants.

So the cigs put me here once, and they're probably the only way I'll ever leave too.

So the guy says, I need some ID with that, real snotty, and I flip out the rich guy's DL and he looks it over. I let him see I got a reef of expensive credit cards too, so he can see not to fuck with me, I'm one of those rich guys has so much money he don't care how he dresses.

It's a local check, I say.

This guy looks heavier than you, he says.

Yeah, I lost weight, I say.

I buy a whole carton, what the hell, but I don't get to smoke more than six out of the first pack when the blue boys show up. I wonder what the hell happened to those cigs. Candi don't smoke. Probably in a garbage dump somewhere now. It's a lot of waste in this world.

Oh fuck, I say when I see em.

You Mister Ferrin Dwell, they say.

And when a cop calls you Mister, you already in trouble. Candi comes to the door, what's going on, and sees how they're handcuffing me and all. She aint wearing much.

Wait a minute, she says, let me get his toothbrush.

Them cops had a lot of fun with me about that on the way in, and I can't blame em, but it aint funny to me no more.

You ever have one person think of you like that, just care a little bit, even if it's just being nice and you aint gone never see em again, I tell you what, it helps. It gets you by. I guess that's why I'm thinking of it so much nowadays. After I burned her pot and all.

And I guess that's why I can call up every detail of that last day and that last fuck, you know. I can run it through my mind every which a way. I can see any part of her body I want to. And it's funny what will turn me on. Because I see that big split beaver like a big-screen close-up, I can zero right in on that shiny wet red pussy all splayed out with come leaking out of one corner like snot out of a dog's nose, but what will get me like as not will be like the two rolls of fat on her belly right above her pussy, where's she's half sitting up and it rolls them up.

Or maybe that hard edge on the edge of her foot where the shoeline pinches it.

So this is how I know it don't mean anything what Wehunt does, because of what my imagination still is. Wehunt wouldn't know how to feel about somebody like that. Wehunt's the real coward, because if Rubert was here, Wehunt wouldn't touch me. But I only got my own self to blame that Rubert aint here, and I'm a big enough man to admit it.

So what I say, there's a lot about living with somebody that aint like they say it is. They got a lot to learn about sex on tv. And in the movies. But they couldn't show it if they did. For example, would you watch this shit on the tv? You know you wouldn't.

41

U 3 L

What's going on? Where the hell am I? *Liza Ja-ane* . . .

Oh, you again. Ah, hrmp, see, I ah planned it this way. What I was doing, I kind of ratcheted ahead in time. Not only went into Ferrin, but went into Ferrin in the future. *Their* future, not yours, of course. And did you think it was the harrowing of hell, the raising of lost souls before the end of ramalam time? Because I know what hell is: It isn't.

I mean, how can a temporal crime deserve an eternal punishment?

Nah, what this is, I was on the case, see. Detective like me, have to go into some shady places, you know. Come with the territory. But I'm packing heat. I'm always packing heat. There's three point five no four no five billion stories in the naked pity, and this has been one of em. This is the one Charles wants to know.

Who prays every day without believing, but what do you think, baby, what if it aint whether you believe in God but whether GA-AWD believes in YEW?

The shadow knows, that's me, and this is my report, boss, THIS

is the tachyon hurry the bustle along the channels of all the information besides the information we think we're getting the fractally folded infinite chatter that sings and sizzles around the edges of any universe as how you read a quarter mil words which is roughly the pop of Little Rock town so a word per person but infer a universe twisting to mystery at the edges because we are approaching the margins of the knowable universe but I'm still here where I always was but you accelerate away and am I a good ghost now, Little Liza Jane?

THIS is for Charles who needs to walk in the flames because there is no border she is the flames and they are the flames and you and all of this leaps and flashes along the channels of what he says to Rider and Laugh and Tucker and they to him, all of this that we know and cannot know and how we create our world in the kingdom of flames nor am I out of

THIS Ferrin business overlapping in duple happening mode with the ongoing about to be of the grand jury, and they tried to keep it out of the news until after the grand jury finding so it wouldn't bias the grand jury, but finding they couldn't they let it all hang out and so Tina's arrest up-staged Charles's no true bill, and then the separate staggered trial dates of Tina and Ferrin and Rubert were set between the finding of the grand jury and the start-up of the creation science trial on December 7—it's true, Bill—and so the trials themselves would begin before Christmas which is itself always a trial especially so this year for Charles Laugh thought since it's the first one without Lianne as all the rest of his life there will be things that happen that are the first ones without Lianne which is why Laugh brought over some presents which were mainly whiskey which he and Charles and Coleman and Dagoberto—*Dagoberto*, Laugh laughed: *Shit, man*—drank, and they had a high old time but the Tina Talliaferrodict wouldn't be brought in till after the new year and Rubert would never come to trial because he came to Judgment first and I see I'm getting ahead, way ahead, because there's so many things to tell because of the way lives run on

as for example Cheese gets nervous about his fancy woman she's so intense and wants to be seen with him everywhere and he's afraid she's going to come to the house and break up his marriage which is really pretty good when you think about it she's a good old gal and then there's the boy and so really he owes it to his family to break up with Lee oh I'm talking as fast as I can because as long as I'm speaking I'm here as long as you hear me I'm here to help

and out in the boonies somebodies laid wreaths on Lianne's bodiless grave and Charles visited every week from early October into November and it looked like it might be a while before he took that long trip out of the country since there was Coleman to take care of once they had brought him home which they did right after the no true bill you see what I mean how it all piles up and I swear I don't see how you guys do it get through it, you must ignore most of the stuff most of the time I guess that's how come you're you and not Me

and so you took care of Coleman Charles although he thought he was taking care of you but at least you brought in a young man from the neigh-borhood and started to train him to help Coleman whose hair was getting whiter faster as the accelerations of acceleration continued to accelerate the son of a bitch is coming apart on me I can't hold it together captain I can't I can't SHE'S GONNA BLOW oh that was close, and Charles like to went crazy the first few weeks as Coleman and Ballard feuded like two tomcats on the same ground until Coleman figured out Dagoberto was really and truly only interested in woman's work he was a sort of a tall Limey Clemmie who moved to Cleveland shortly thereafter and Charles never heard from her again and you never will either she took it hard whatever it was she took Charles never was sure it wasn't exactly Lianne but something about his whole family and it never dawned on him how she had loved his father and never a whisper gotten back and had stayed with him Charles for lo these many years for the echo but had wound up really loving Lianne in spite of her initial jealousy as Charles got more and more different from Dad and this is all really just a theory it's hard to know but she took it hard whatever it was but that was Rider's private theory which he never told Charles because Charles had enough to puzzle on such as the night when Butler had read the one story that wasn't science fiction the night when Charles didn't do what he should have done which was what he shouldn't have done because it might have kept her alive but then he wouldn't have known he had saved her by being such a two-timing bastard and she wouldn't have either and would have despised him forever and probably the reason his mind spun in such spindizzy circles was all that science fiction he'd read in alternate reality somewhere, *Worlds of If,* you know, metaphysical specspecspeculation—

like Lianne and the man in the tree the burned man in the tree dangling the burned man up in the morning at six and she wouldn't say why and the boom in the sky and the plane she saw him falling and ran and ran to Miss Kumpe's yard and he whispered help me help me I'm burning it scarred her forever but Farber kept pointing out it couldn't have happened that this was the susceptibility of the trance she lived way across town it was another girl who ran and saw, you could read the papers, but Lianne heard it in her dreams all of her life and death help me I'm burning the one man who lived when the plane blew up falling in fire and innocent people dead in the houses and help me I'm burning and she hated the man in the tree this was the summer she came home from New York and no one knew and she walked the streets for miles in the early morning because you could walk the streets and no one took you up to the room and said help me I'm burning help me I'm evil I'm burning it wasn't his fault but she couldn't help me I'm burning I'm burning a ring of fire and Farber said no, it's very important to distinguish who really happened to what in this sort of instance and when I say the name you will a

What fucking name? Charles thought as he read through the file idly that fall waiting for the girl he never knew and the woman he married to rise in a single shining body and come to him in dream or fiction but it never happened but something else did when Coleman raked up something that might have been a finger bone in the new-fallen leaves: *Thought about it a long time, Mr. Charles. Might be, and it might not. Finally decide I better let you know.*

And he put that bolt of calcium to his lips and slept with it under his pillow but the truth fairy never brought him Lianne but still he had something physical, something that might have touched him wrapped in a love that might have been till he got what he needed from it and took it out one night in the midnight dark of the moon, close on Halloween, and buried it with Ramalam's stone, and howled to the sleeping neighbors like a wolf and Ballard wondered what the hell was going on but he had seen stranger behavior he had served titled lords

and it all rolled on and rolls on and no one gave a thought any more to Tina swift from the jailhouse to the mental hospital over on Markham actually pretty close to Peck's that is no one but Charles and Sonny who was pretty sure now he'd sealed all that off and they couldn't pin him to her especially not now that she was officially help me I'm burning I can't can't you see didn't you notice there's one mind of all that even a ghost never entered because it would help me I'm burning be hell but there's no such thing as help me I'm burning I promise in Unit Three Lower oh shit not the help me I'm dying in U3L of the FLIP-FLOP cancer not yet but someday ovarian years in the FLIP-FLOP future I promise there's no such thing as HELP ME I'M.

It could be that the father stepped in front of him. It could be he didn't see him last night, on top. Or it could be he saw him, but it was a movie they watched. The father was on top, but it wasn't her, it was just the girl in the movie, and then he just stepped in front of him, right when he pulled the trigger, it was nobody's fault. Both triggers.

He didn't know for a second, he thought it was a deer. For just a second, when he stepped in front. Because the father wouldn't wear orange. They always told him to wear orange, but he wouldn't do it. Because she was there, and they thought it was a deer.

Or if it wasn't a movie, it could be she didn't want him to. It could be she told the father she didn't want him to, but she was afraid and she had to let him. And so she kept his secret, because it was his way of showing love. She kept his deep dark secret, because he loved her best. Better than the mother, better than the brother. She kept his secret, except for the brother.

So then, after the father was gone, it was just the two of them. The mother didn't count. So he gave her the car and the money for school because he loved her, because he was her brother. He loved her because she wouldn't tell, wouldn't tell. She wouldn't tell, he could count on her, but she needed the money. She was there and she saw him do it but she would never tell, because it was just the two of them, they had to help each other.

Everybody knew they loved the father, so it had to be an accident. They loved him best because he would kill himself, or maybe her, if they didn't choose. Everybody was yelling crying and he had the gun, and so they saved the mother by loving him.

They hated the mother for being so weak, and so they saved her.

The father is strong. People hate him because he's strong, but he can take it. Because he's like the pioneers, he hunts his own meat and he fixes his truck and he can build a house with his bare hands, and look at her. How can you love somebody like that? Won't even stand up for herself, won't even fight back, and she just plays on your sympathy like a violin, and it's one thing if people are jealous because you're strong, but I can't take this shit where they don't even fight but turn up their nose at you and pretend you're not even there, and that's why the Miss Little Rock bitch deserved to die. Just being rich and turning up her nose and having him all to herself.

But Charles wouldn't do it, so somebody had to.

And so they saved her because they loved him better because he isn't losing his looks like some people I could name, he's still young dammit and still a man and she doesn't care any more, and they're too old to be rocked and held and sung to sleep, it's time they learned to do some work around the house and it's time they learned to clean some fish with their guts spilling out on the ground and the blue and green shiny flies because it's for their own good.

And if you want to sleep in somebody's bed, you can sleep in the father's.

And so they cried and hugged him and they didn't like the quiet and the singing any more, the going for walks and picking berries, because it was weak. And the dog that followed them home was weak, and they didn't like the dog, because he was hungry and weak and wagged his tail, and he was just a damn stray. And so he took him out in the woods. The father took him a piece of meat and he followed him in the woods. And he shot. He shot, but we didn't see.

It could be a backfire, how did we know, we didn't see. It could be he ran off, how did we know, we can't feed every starving stray on the earth, and so she cried and we cried because she cried and we could smell the gun he never put it down it was the same gun.

So it could be where the female police officer comes in and he has the gun, and he's holding the mother hostage, but she stays cool and she talks him calm, and he puts the gun down and they can get counseling and be a family again and they're all crying and hugging, and she risked her life and she's a hero. But she's not an officer yet, she's just the daughter.

So it could be where this is a memory when she *is* an officer, and that's how she knew what to do, she used what she learned when she was a girl. It could be where she had to confront her own terror to get the job done, and she freezes and he almost shoots and it's a close-up of her face and she's sweating, but then she confronts her fear and he doesn't shoot Momma.

And they ask her how she did it, they all run up when it's over, and Charles is the prosecuting attorney and puts his arm around her and they can get married now because she's not afraid of her father any more and so she's not afraid of him, and they ask her how she did it, and all she says, "I've been there myself," and the man looks into her eyes and he knows.

And the man was in his uniform and he looked at my chest. He looked at my chest, and so it could be Sonny was the one who took me away. He could bring the army in, and they could shoot the father and take me away, and take the mother too. She could be old and gray from her troubles, but we would live on the army base and she would live with us with lots of grandchildren and make them laugh. She could be old and gray and peaceful and happy at last.

But the brother couldn't live on the base, they wouldn't let you. He couldn't live because he wasn't strong, he was whiny just like the mother, but he lost his temper just like the father, and he didn't care any more, he didn't care who you told and he didn't love you.

So she was forsaken, but she was a grown woman now. She could handle herself. She had a college degree. She would have one soon.

So when Sonny saw her, he couldn't help himself, he would fall in love. She would be wearing a pretty dress, and she was a lawyer. He wasn't in the army any more, so you would outrank him, and he would crawl on his hands and knees for not taking you away.

It could be where she was a star, and she came back to her hometown, and they all saw how wrong they were. They would all fall in love, and she would love them and leave them, she would leave a trail of broken hearts behind her. She would be the rich bitch goddess star, she would be Rita Hayworth. But stars don't do anything, and you want to help people.

So it could be you were a crusading lawyer.

You could be as beautiful as Rita Hayworth, and have a car, and you could have a degree on your wall, and you could help children in your spare time, they could grow up and be like you, and they would all fall in love. The whole town would love you, because you were blonde and you had a sports car and a heart of gold.

You could inherit the money when the brother died. You were the only living relative, and you would inherit the money. Even ten or fifteen thousand, and it could get you started. Because you could be a genius investor. You could pick their brains and the next thing they knew, you knew more than they did, you owned the whole town.

It could be it broke your heart when the jack slipped, because you were all alone in the world. It wouldn't have slipped if he hadn't been so loud and nasty. You kept his secret all these years, but now he had a girlfriend, and he didn't need you. You brought him up since he was almost a baby, you saved him from both of them and brought him up.

But it broke your heart anyway, because you understood what he was going through. He had turned mean and nasty, but you were forgiving. Nobody liked him any more, but his big sister would always love him, because he was never strong enough, so you knew he would never make it, all along you knew he would never make it, but it broke your heart anyway.

And Sonny was kind, and he saw your heart was broken, and you remembered him when you were a girl, so it could be that you seduced him. He was surprised, because you were all grown up, and you took his breath away. He took you back to the office to show off, but then you were the one that got him to smoke the evidence, because you had been to college, and it was no big deal. Your heart was broken, but you hid it from the world with a brittle gaiety.

So that was why you fucked him, to hide the pain in your heart.

You fucked him in the office, because everybody knows what happens with grief. The prudes might think it was shocking, but that's what happens. You have to do it to prove to yourself you're still alive. You have to do it to prove you can feel again, your heart was broken and you never thought you would feel again.

So she takes to cocaine, because she has a dark secret and her heart is broken. It could be that they think she has it all, she's on top of the world, but little do they know what she's suffered. She was a tragic figure, and she could have given it up if the right man had come along.

Little do they know that there's an empty place in her heart, that behind the brave front, behind the sparkling smile and the beautiful face, she's always alone.

It could be there was one man in the world who could heal her heart and make her happy, but he would never know. She could have him in a minute, she has a strange power over men. You can throw it right past the footlights, you can see their faces change. She came up from nothing to make herself a star, and every man wanted her, but she kept herself apart, because there was one man she loved and she could never have.

So she sacrificed her happiness for Charles.

It could be where he wanted her, where he came to her house and he broke down and cried, and he said, "Save me, I can't help myself." And so she saw what it would do to him, and so she turned him away. She said, "Go back to your wife."

Because she wasn't a homewrecker. She would never steal him away from Momma, but Momma gave up, and he made her do it and she had to be good and she had to be strong.

So she told him to go back home, and she lived the rest of her life by herself, and nobody knew her sad past. And so she was proud and alone, and nobody knew. The little children made fun of her, they threw rocks at her window and called her Old Lady T.

They all made fun of her, because they thought Charles rejected her, and it was completely the other way around, and nobody knew, and that made the pain even worse. But she was too proud to say a word, and he was an important man in the community, and she kept her secret to the grave, and he died happy and surrounded by friends.

Her grave was lonely and cold, and the withered vines crawled over the tombstone and the dry leaves blew across it. Lonely and cold on top of a hill. And nobody ever came, and nobody ever knew, except the detective.

And once each year he comes to the grave, and he puts a single black rose on it. And a yellowed newspaper with an old headline: Murderess Dies in the Chair.

Because they all thought she was evil, except the detective. He knows why. And it's in black and white, and he's wearing a trench coat and one of those hats.

Only he knows the truth. Only he knows why she did it. Every year, a single black rose, for her black heart. The black heart of a lonely lady.

But it could be they framed her. They framed her and nobody knows, nobody believes. They put her in the electric chair and nobody believes her. The people in the audience do, because they're watching the movie, but nobody else. She keeps the man's secret, and she goes to the chair in his place. She's always loved him, and so she goes to the chair in his place.

But Charles shows up with a helicopter, dropping over the wall, and they break her out. Tommy guns everywhere, he's a secret agent, that was what she didn't know. They had to keep it from her, so she couldn't give the plan away, not even under torture. It was mostly mental torture, that's why they keep her doped up and locked in U3L, so she can't get away. And they give her truth serum, but she never breaks, she never tells.

It was mostly mental torture, except for the bull dyke in the other cellblock.

Lianne was a spy for Russia, that's why they had to kill her, that's what the girl didn't know. So he's not guilty and the girl's not guilty, and they're not dead, they're heroes.

A villa on the Mediterranean, sunset on the waves. She's leaning on a column, he comes up beside her, puts his arm around her, she leans her head on his shoulder. In one of those transparent gowns. They're just a couple of silhouettes against the evening. Later on, he'll come to bed with her, and I'll be a good girl, put it in, I'll be good.

They kill the bull dyke. She tortured her, so they kill her.

The bull dyke made her do it, she had no choice, and now her stomach hurts. It was to humiliate her, but she kept her dignity. She shoved the broom handle in, and now her stomach hurts. They blow the bitch's brains out with a tommy gun. She tries to stop them, she has mercy, but they have to because the bull dyke was a spy too, it was all part of the frame.

Or it could be accident. She wouldn't want them to murder even a spy, it makes them too mean to be Americans. His wife, they didn't want to shoot her, but she had a gun and she was about to shoot them. So what happens to the bull dyke is one of her own people gets hit, and as he's falling, he rakes her with the tommy gun. Falling from the catwalk, and the bitch gets hers. She jerks with the slugs, and her brains blow out the back of her head, a big spray, and she's kicking there on the floor, kicking in a pool of blood like a shot dog.

Her stomach hurts, but it could be gallstones. An ulcer is better, because you look ok. An ulcer could hurt that low. An ulcer is the success disease, you get it from stress. It's terrible terrible pain, so you're brave, but you feel ok a lot of the time and you wear nice dresses.

Or something from toxic soil, because she grew up there. She's working against pollution, see, she's a crusader, because she loves the earth. She gives all her money to the cause. She's married to Charles and he lets her have all the money she wants, but she gives it to the cause.

She's working against pollution because she grew up with it, it kills the children, and then it turns out she has it herself. They put her on tv and she's very brave, she makes them stop. They're so embarrassed they have to stop. The public is outraged, and they have to stop. She's very pale and thin. But beautiful. She's dying, but she's very brave and beautiful. She can only whisper. Weak and thin, but beautiful.

The mother had gallstones, so it runs in the family, so it could be gallstones.

42

COMMUNITY
SERVICE

Is it the new year yet? 1982?

Can't be, because there's Charles in the courtroom, creation science trial. He's in the audience, that's all, and Sonny Raymond sitting across the way. After all their work, the Eighth Circuit Court of Appeals had ruled no intervenors, and that includes Morrison, Morrison, Chenowyth, and Frail. Really, it was just as well, because otherwise they would've had to let in every Baptist in the state. So turn over their files and their witness list to the ACLU, and sit back and watch. Charles feels he owes it to Lianne to watch at least. Especially since the trial starts on her birthday, forty years after Pearl Harbor.

Among the first day's witnesses are four theologians. Langdon Gilkey of Chicago University is especially effective. The concept of a literal creation, an absolute beginning out of nothing, is unique to Western culture, he says. Such a creation absolutely requires a creator, he says.

Take that, Charles thinks, looking in Sonny Raymond's direction. Sonny is pursing his lips in an angry frown. He throws his right arm over the back of his head, grabs his left ear. When Charles looks back to the witness stand, the theologian has his shoes off, both feet up on the chair, his toes curling. David Williams, the deputy attorney general, is cross-examining Gilkey. He walks away, then jumps toward him with his arms spread, going AH! The theologian bares his teeth. He climbs to the back of his seat, pounds his chest. Around the courtroom, the theologians are scratching their sides, making a low murmur that rises to a shriek: ooo ooo ooo ooo aaa aaa AAA AAA AH!

Charles blinks, and the theologian is sitting in his chair with his shoes on. Charles doesn't dare look at Sonny Raymond the rest of the day.

The next day a gorilla shows up. Charles recognizes him—Skip Selvey, who in everyday life makes his living as Yo-Yo the Clown. The gorilla tries to kiss Sonny Raymond, and Sonny tears a rubber tree out of a pot and beats the courthouse floor with it. Everywhere Charles looks, there are chimps in suits, everybody dressed like J. Fred Muggs. He thought he was over the crazy part, but so what, relax and enjoy. *Nothing is given in vain*, he thinks, giving the gorilla a wink. A chimp in a security uniform chases the gorilla outside. The gorilla tells reporters he intends to announce for governor later in the week.

That day the ACLU witnesses are biologists and paleontologists, who testify that creation science doesn't meet the standards of a science. They are especially good on speciation, which has in fact been observed in the field, and on the age of the earth. But most of the interest in the courtroom is on relative sartorial styles, that is to say tribal markings, and in that connection, let me transfer you to Mike Trimble down on the floor, one of the shrewdest monkeys and perhaps the best journalistic prose writer the state has ever had. Mike, can you hear me?

I hear you, Hog. Attorney General Steve Clark and his two principal deputies in the case, David L. Williams and Frederick K. Campbell, make up in elegance what they lack in manpower.

The three troop in each day as spiffy and scrubbed up as a trio of television weathermen, their dignified business suits immaculately fitted and pressed.

A network announcer called Clark the philosophical heir to William Jennings Bryan, but as far as appearance goes, the entire defense team would seem to owe less to Bryan than to Vidal Sassoon; their haircuts are marvels of the stylist's art and are, coincidentally, not unlike the style favored by many of the fundamentalist clergy in whose interest they are toiling.

Over at the plaintiffs' table, it is a different story. The men look as though they get their hair cut in an old-fashioned barbershop, or maybe in the kitchen. It wouldn't be accurate to describe the plaintiffs' team as sloppy, but their clothes don't have the razor-edged sharpness of the defense team. Some of the lawyers wear them in the manner of people who are always late to wherever they're going.

Philip Kaplan of Little Rock, a member of the ACLU team, scored sartorial points Monday with a blue silk four-in-hand with the word "Harvard" emblazoned all over it in Hebrew. He lost points today, however, when he forgot to wear a belt.

This has been Mike Trimble from the floor. Back to you, Hog.

And so it goes. Wednesday, the third day of the trial. Brent G. Dalrymple says that believing the world is only a few thousand years old is like believing it is flat. Stephen Jay Gould testifies. He's a mountain gorilla, as nearly as Charles can tell. He pelts the defense team with rocks from the Burgess Shale, shouting "Anomalocaris! Trilobite! Punctuated equilibrium!" The defense team cowers whimpering under their tables. It doesn't get better for them that evening when Pat Robertson denounces Steve Clark on the *700 Club*. "He's not trying hard enough," Robertson says, throwing his hands in the air. "Ooo ooo ooo. UH! UH!"

The next day Clark is a lot more active in the courtroom, a lot more visible. But Charles is losing interest. The trial is important, and he owes it to Lianne, but the steady parade of fact is putting him to sleep, the on-droning of experts who so clearly know what they're talking about. What he needs is folly, and he keeps hearing good sense. Nothing can energize him, not even the sight of Sonny Raymond sniffing the air with his long snout, scratching his big red hind end.

Charles perks up a little on Friday, when the state introduces its first witness, a theologian from the seminary in Dallas. "I believe in UFOs," Dr. Geisler says. "They are satanic messengers, portents of the coming end of time." Fred Campbell, the assistant attorney general, clears his throat. He explains to the court that Dr. Geisler's beliefs regarding UFOs do not discredit him as an authority on creation science. "He's right," Sonny Raymond howls. "Space aliens. They're all space aliens from Satan." Judge Overton pounds his gavel.

"Believing in God is different from believing God exists," Dr. Geisler explains. "Satan believes in God because he was created by God, but he doesn't worship Him."

"Would you describe Satan, Dr. Geisler?"

"Yes. Satan is an intelligent, rational supermonkey person who rebelled against God and is in the world deceiving monkeys."

"Your Honor, Your Honor!" the plaintiffs cry. "We object."

"Call Satan to the stand," Judge Overton says, and Old Nick steps out of the crowd and knuckles his way up front, a red little monkey with horns, his prehensile forked tail dragging.

"Hell, no,' Satan says. "I don't even exist. I'm just a figment of your imaginations. I'm one of the dumbest ideas you ever had."

It was me, of course. Always has been. You just don't like me with horns.

The trial is recessed. Over the weekend, Billie Jean King wins her suit against Marilyn Barnett. Four astronauts are announced to fly on the next mission, this coming November. The next thing Charles remembers is what happened Monday.

They get to the courthouse, and there's Skip Selvey again, this time dressed as Harmless the Clown. He and Useless the Clown are handing out bananas. A fat man in a raincoat is marching up and down, worried and angry. "I don't understand," he keeps saying. "God made all that is. How can they *do* this?" Useless and Harmless offer him a banana.

At that moment Sonny Raymond arrives. Charles finds a banana in his hand. He marches over to Sonny, who flinches at the look on his face. Sonny Raymond flinching! Charles thrusts the banana into Sonny's face like a microphone.

"Maybe you didn't kill her," he says. "But you're the death of her. You and your type, damn your souls. How does it feel to be you?" Thrusting the banana into his face. Sonny's not only flinching but shriveling. Look, Ma, I'm australopithecene! "What goes through the mind of a man like you?" Now Sonny's squealing and snorting, trying to escape, a sort of giant tapir bumbling about, but Charles pursues him. "Speak into the banana! How does it feel?" Sonny's switching his scaly tail to and fro, his tongue flicking. He's cornered against the courthouse wall. "Don't lie to us! Don't lie to the truth banana!" Sonny's a bug on the wall, scuttling. Charles swats him with the banana, he drops to the ground. Charles squashes him underfoot, holds the banana to the grease spot. "Speak into the truth banana: How does it feel?"

Sonny slithers away, invisible, an amoeba. People are clapping. Charles is led away. He's earned the right to go home and have one of Tucker's finest injections. He doesn't have to watch the rest of the trial, which mostly consists of defense witnesses who have names like Wrickramasinghe, Ariel, and Coffin, and who believe plutonium has mysterious isotopes nobody else has ever heard of which prove that the earth was created from comet dust in 1989, and all of whom seem to be from the Loma Linda University Geoscience Research Institute.

On the eleventh day Judge Overton rests from his labors. The firm throws a victory party on the eighteenth, a week before Christmas. Overton hasn't made his decision and won't for another three weeks, but it feels like a victory, and so they have a victory party, at Greg and Alison's. The first party Charles has been to since Lianne died, and he can feel his friends being thoughtful, and there's good points to the monkeys sometimes, they're at their best at parties, because that's what parties are for, monkeying around, and he's beginning to smile a little, watching them scratch and tug their funny suits and pick each other for fleas and bare their teeth over who gets the last cocktail on the tray, which you would call it polite smiles. *You take it no you take it*, and chatter chatter because the monkeys love to tell stories:

. . . shooting at him, but they couldn't catch em.

Who?

Cheese. Head Cheese.

Come on, who would waste bullets on that—

It's true, I saw the holes in the car.

It's some kind of publicity stunt, that's what it is. He's taking a page out of Sonny Raymond's book. The fearless law officer who puts his life in danger.

This was Laugh talking to a couple of theater people and one of the ACLU lawyers and the bony choirwoman from Holy Sac and *Too bad it wasn't Sonny Raymond* one of the theater people says just as Charles walks up and they all want to say something about the scene with the banana which they admired greatly but they're afraid Charles might be embarrassed about it now that he's come to his senses and *That man,* one of the theater people says, I swear this is true, just like Tucker's stories are true, *he's just not fully evolved.*

Which starts Charles laughing and he can't stop, but it's good laughter, not like when he thought Dagoberto was funny before he even knew he was Dagoberto, and a whisper goes round the room and somebody tells Laugh, *It's his first party since—*

Which is when Laugh realizes that the upcoming Christmas will be going to be his first Christmas since, and checks with Ballard to see if the man has any plans and he doesn't, and so decides on the whiskey. Like I say, there's some good points about the monkeys.

Not that Laugh is totally selfless. You wouldn't ask that of a monkey.

At the party, he says: A long time ago we were talking about a partnership. I guess that's totally out of the question now? I don't blame you, but I might have to be moving on.

Hoping of course that Charles will realize how much he owes to Laugh and let it work out the way it almost would have if nothing had happened, if a whole story hadn't gotten in the way.

And in the strange accession of something like Christian charity, though he doesn't believe in Christ and not really even in me, Charles suddenly wants to know how it feels to be Laugh, how it feels to be this fellow who is in some ways responsible, who tangled Charles in his own pain and led him on and in some ways therefore cost him his wife, but there is no bitterness now, only curiosity, as if in complete knowledge there were peace and healing, the Christians call it grace and maybe it is and it feels like powerful spiritual insight and maybe it is, but one thing it is for sure is one of the ways the monkeys handle grief, the wider perspective, so

When do you do your community service? Charles says.

Coming up, Laugh says.

Let's talk again when it's over.

And Laugh can tell by the way he looks, clear-eyed and still smiling at whatever he thought was funny, that the worst is over, that Morrison doesn't mean to put him off but simply wants to clear the slate, and suddenly Laugh, who's been dreading the silly public spectacle, can't wait to get to it, can't wait to get to his civic duty and help other fine young men to learn from his mistakes.

You probably think I'm on tell you about that toga party and how I learn my lesson, or maybe you gone hear something about how that white man wife blow up and that white woman I'm fucking turn out to be the one that done it. All over the news, and probably even a low-life fro like you think he know all about it. But they don't tell me what to say, just who to say it to, so you gone hear what I want, or march yo sorry ass back in there and see if you like that jail any better than you like me sitting here telling you whatever I feel.

So if you even crack wise once.

So how old are you? Thought I be talking to college kids, but you maun be thirty if a day. What you in for? Yay? Same as them? Stupid, brother. Surprise they didn't hang your ass for dealing. I aint saying you done it, shut up. All I'm saying, they catch an old dude smoking with the chicks, that's the way their mind works. Graduate *ass*-sistant, huh? In what?

Scared straight aint gone work on somebody your age, what they thinking? Don't matter, does it? I'm on talk and you gone listen. Strange as it may seem, I wouldn't mind being able to do you some good. But when I'm through with you I'm through.

You can relax, I aint gone say nothing about finding Jesus. Jesus just a safety net, and there aint no safety nets. I'm on say something about fucking yourself up because you hate yourself, and don't tell me that aint what you doing, because I can see it all over yo big foolish face, I don't care how smart you think you are. It aint whether you done right or done wrong, it's whether you feel right or feel wrong. And if you feel wrong, it's like you aint got no resistance. Sooner or later you catch a disease. They tag you with something. You be guilty whether you done it or not. They a miss ten crimes you did do and fry you for one you didn't, and it won't make no difference you didn't, you just as guilty and just as fucked.

Let me tell you, when I messed up, it was one of those things you don't think you'll do, and when it happens you surprised as anyone. You somebody else, you feel like you standing outside yourself watching.

But self don't have no outside. So there got to be a lot more to us than just this watching part. That was the first time psychology ever made sense to me, what they mean by the subconscious mind. When I seen it rising up in me, I buckle down and try to figure it out. One thing about Laugh, I never back away from a fight. Something scare me, man, I meet it head-on. What I done, I switch over my minor. Accounting my major, I always been able to do the numbers without hardly eem thinking, but I was flunking everything else, eem with the coaches leaning on the teachers. Psychology now, once I got interested—yessir, I B'ed out in the stuff. So I guess you could say I owe my academic success to getting in trouble. If I'd a never stole those panties, I wouldn't be wearing silk underwear now.

The panties was for Francine. I was nineteen year old, almost twenty, I was a scholarship Razorback, and I was in trouble with my momma. Always been in trouble with my momma. *Lafayette, you were born bad and you're going to stay bad. Goddamn, Momma, I go to church, I get a three-point in high school, I make a football hero, go to college, what you want? You wa born bad and you gone stay bad.*

Ever since I run over Anne Marie with the bicycle. Tell her, *Lay down, it won't hurt, it's a magic trick. I saw it on a show.* What I seen, a man lay down and let another man run a motorcycle over him, and then he get up ok. Back then, I don't know what a stuntman is.

So I run her over with my Gene Autry bike, got the white plastic grips, got the streamline housing like it has a motor, got the flappers on the spokes, you know what I mean. Well it leave a black mark on her blouse and she crying how much it hurt and Momma whip the daylights out of me three days running till Anne Marie get bored and forget to cry. Take my bicycle away. Eleven-year-old boy without a bicycle, might as well lock him up and throw away the key.

When Anne Marie die five years later, ruptured appendix, Momma say, *She ain't been right since Lafayette run her over with the bicycle.* By then I was too big to whip.

So Francine. She come from Oklahoma. Seem real exotic to me—you laugh. But I never been outside Arkansas, aint hardly been outside Little Rock till I go off to Lafayetteville. What they said they would call it when I got through, but I didn't do all that good like they predicted. A lot of people got the tools don't go all the way, and it aint cause they can't run fast and hit hard. You might be thinking about that in yo career. It aint a different level up there, it's a different world. I imagine the pros is even more different.

O-O-O-klahoma! Sound like far off to me, sound like the Wild West. To this day, a woman tell me she from Oklahoma, first reaction I have, she sexy.

Francine wa so sexy, but she wa a good girl. A.M.E., just like us, and love to go to church. Was gonna be a dietician. I can't explain it now, why I was so in love, but I was in love, I was bad gone on Francine. All I could think about how Momma would like her so much because she wa so polite and beautiful and helpful. Always doing for everybody, like you say, *Oh phooey I got class in five minutes and I got to get these books back to the library.*

Around Francine, you say *Oh phooey,* you don't say *Oh fuck, main.*

Francine say, *Why, I take em over for you.* Just like that. Or she come visit yo house, after she eat, she wash up all the dishes. *Lord, chile, I* like *washing dishes,* she say. *I don't feel like I eat if I don't wash the dishes.* That's Francine. And love babies, always talking how she want seventeen of em running all over the house.

And built to break yo heart. Oh man. All I want to do is marry Francine, you understand me? Marry her and then it a be ok, we can fuck fuck fuck fuck fuck because we married, make them seventeen babies and I be grinning all the time, big daddy happy man, don't you know.

What you smiling at, son? I aint telling no jokes here.

And Momma be happy too, Momma be proud of me, Momma come over and visit and she be happy and tell me I'm good.

I can't wait to get Francine to Little Rock to show Momma, but we got to have a chaperone, you know. Something might happen on the way down, eight whole hours on the bus alone. No, you damn fool, we didn't have no car, you don't know nothing about that time and that place. What's wrong witch yo generation?

Fuck you, main, I'm ten years older than you are.

Back then we didn't play freshman, and so my first year we didn't know yet how good I wasn't gone be. Tore up the scout team pretty good, and then had a good spring training. My only disappointment, they had me at linebacker. All in high school I thought halfback out of the T, see myself setting new scoring records, you know, knocking em back like bowling pins. Part of my trouble, I like to run over em, never learn to evade. Work ok in high school if you built like I was, but in college they a lot of em rough as you are. Might whip any one, but they keep on coming, wear you down. You got to have moves.

See what I mean, a different world? What I'm trying to tell you, it changes. You be still trying to win them old fights back in the hood, and you aint in the hood no more, you on Mars or something. Just like me and my momma, still trying to prove on my momma. It changes, and you got to change, or you be a grease spot on the road.

It wasn't I didn't want to change. It wasn't eem I couldn't a changed, if they would have worked with me. But see, they need a linebacker more than another halfback. It aint no investment with them to teach me what I should of started learning three years before. That's what you got to understand. Aint nobody help you less they see some kind a investment in it. This the one thing you got to learn. Yo problem right now, aint nobody see no profit in you.

Not eem me, I get one more smart-ass out yo mouth. I'm outta here, and you know where you can spend the rest the afternoon. Somebody back in the showers might figure out a way to make a profit out yo asshole.

So listen to me now: When you think they handing you the world on a silver platter, uh-uh, babe. They saying take this and make me some more. So you better learn to see yo self as property. Take good care a the property. Aint never gone own yo self, yo aim just to be the majority investor someday. Fifty-one percent.

Fuck no, same for the friendly ghosts, least on the football field. Get that racist shit out yo head, won't do nothing but make you mad, and nobody sees no investment in somebody mad all the time. Yay, if you think you can be a rapper, sho. Be my guest.

So there I am, I have a good spring, probably gone start in the fall, but I got this gnawing feeling because I aint playing halfback. Eat on me like I aint so good, know what I mean? Hook up with my momma-feelings. Mess up my way with Francine. I'm leaning on her pretty heavy to let me have some. Pretty bad to be this big stud on the team and aint getting any. They laugh me out if they know. And she say *No* and she say *No* and she say *No*.

And the more she say *No* the more I'm hitting eem harder. That's when they start calling me Last, you know. Cause when I hit em it a be they last laugh. Yeah, the brothers be calling me Laugh. All through high school, Laugh, Laugh, Laugh. Then that summer start being Last. And I'm taking out my meanness on em, I mean I like to hit anyway, but now I'm leaving body parts. And I hit this one old boy a little crossways and crack my rib.

Now things start to pile up. One little bitty thing lead to another. You understand I see all this now but I didn't see it back then. Why I'm telling you, cause you don't see.

All of a sudden I'm laying out and other people getting ahead of me. Spring practice end, and I stay in town, don't go back to Little Rock. Start to get a little bit fat because I aint working out, surprise me, first time I ever get fat. Body done change, you see. Everything else change, body change too. Yeah, look at me. Happen to you too. It will, fool. You aint gone have yo young body forever. What, you think they give it to you free and never break down cause you such a warm wonderful human being?

So I'm working and getting fat. Working in Roger's Pool Hall, yeah, you know the place, but let me tell you, it wasn't no hangout brothers feel comfortable in back then. It was them hard-eyed country sonsabitches, and the hippies was just starting to come in too, so it was two or three different kinds of attitude. It was some of this kind of barefoot hippie wearing a buck knife and his eyes way out there like he seen Armageddon coming and was rooting for the devil, it wasn't no flower-child kind. There was some of them too, though. And some of the frat jocks, you know, big loud shit-for-brains. And I swear, a professor or two, cause I recognize em.

Which is neither here nor there, but I was telling you how I was running on the line, because we wasn't supposed to be doing no drinking back then, and here I was working in a saloon and sucking it down and putting on fat. Roger didn't care as long as you paid. Might not have even notice, because he was drinking more than you were, big old fat sleepy-eye red-nose man. I know I wasn't supposed to have that kind of a job, and if they had been checking on me real close, they might of kicked me off the team. And I couldn't tell Momma, could I? Working in a bar. Bad enough already I didn't come home for the summer, she wa convinced I was catting around. I wasn't about to come home, nine months without her, first time I ever felt free in my life, shee-it no. But didn't keep me from feeling guilty I didn't go home, and didn't help none she took sick all summer neither, or that Big Daddy die the summer before which is probably about ninety-nine percent of why she took sick in the first place.

And I was showing up drunk to pick up Francine. She in town because she going to summer school. Truth, that's the other main only reason I didn't go home.

Always carry my liquor good, I still can, and I wasn't no show-out type, so I wouldn't pitch no fit in front of the dorm, I would get her out ok. And the first two or three times, sweet innocent girl, she didn't eem know. I be sucking breath mints, or them eucalyptus cough drops, going like hack hack hack, like I have a big cough. But get her out alone and I start in putting her down. Big old ass, I say. Big old floppy tits. You better get some now because you gone be one a these old fat mommas in a couple years. And then I switch around and feel all my loving heart and be sorry and just want to hug and love her, I be almost crying I'm so in love. And then I switch around again, turn sly fox, Mr. Operator T. Laugh, Mr. Smooth Chocolate Man.

Try to get her over to my place, I wasn't in the dorm for the summer, have a little one-room. One place we could be alone. No car, all we could do when I went to get her would be walk up and down Dickson Street, have a pizza. Walk over to the movie. I want to lie down with her so bad I can't hardly walk. You know that feeling, it's like you sleepy but you aint sleepy, you just want to *lie down*? It aint even like you want to fuck, though if you can lie down you will surely fuck in a minute, but it's just this powerful wanting to *lie down*.

But she won't come to my place no more. You ever wonder how a woman always know what you up to? I mean, she aint ever *done* it, and she still know what I'm up to.

But she didn't know I was drinking till one time we having a pizza at King Pizza and I have a beer in front of her, and it all click, she realize I been having a lot more beer than that one. I don't know why I done it, except it was like I wanted her to know. But if that's what I want, why didn't I just come out and tell her, *I'm drunk, bitch*? See what I'm say about psychology? No, you don't see nothing, you hardheaded smart-ass booger.

She won't even talk to me for a couple of weeks, and I like to go crazy. Don't know if I sleep the first couple of days, and stay drunk all the time. When I aint working I stay in my hot little place with the door open, just the screen door keeping out the bugs. You know how when you going crazy trapped in some bad little room, cheap damn table and fold-down bed, and feel like if you stay there one more minute you gone kill somebody? Feel like if you could just have some room to walk around in, some space, it would be better? But can't move, can't leave, can't get out. Nowhere to go, nothing to spend. Sit at the table and suck down one more beer.

But that wasn't when it happen. What I'm telling you, it come back on you when it look like you doing so good. Because it don't happen then. I don't stick no knife in no hippie, I don't hold up no 7-Eleven, I don't blow the head off no cop. I don't walk in no fucking fashion shop and steal no silk panties.

I get hold of myself a little bit, but it's a angry hold. Decide to lose some weight, start getting in shape for two-a-days. They starting to put in this mile run thing. I can't do no weights, my ribs still too sore. So not only am I getting a butt and some belly, my arms and chest is slipping. I start going over to the track and running, not the college track, the high school track, down in that little valley. I don't want nobody to know nothing I'm up to.

What I know about running? I aint ever done it, just hundreds on the track team. All anybody ever care about's my forty anyway, and this was before all this aerobics shit, all these peckerwoods jogging around the streets, Miss Bitching White Fox in her shiny tights show her whole crack. I'm over there just running as fast as I can as far as I can go. I have to take it easier than I would because of my ribs, but I don't know nothing about pacing, nothing about shoes. I'm wearing high-tops, and I'm up on my toes. I run a mile the first day in seven minutes, and the next day I couldn't move. Couldn't hardly breathe, my ribs so sore. But I keep at it. Every step I'm stepping on somebody's head. Francine. Momma. Coach. Anne Marie. I'm on be so mean when two-a-day start. Lean and mean, the killer machine. I'm on make somebody pay.

Naw, you aint never felt that way. You think you been that mad, but you never have.

What you *think* happen, huh? I start pulling things. Hamstring one day, groin the next. Get a stress fracture in my left foot, but I don't know that's what it is cause they aint invented em yet, I'm thinking stone bruise. See, I'm holding myself funny because my ribs, and because I got this extra gut weighing on me different. Ever seen a car have a wreck and they fix it up and sell it to you, but the frame's twisted? Looks ok, but it a be chewing up four tires a week. That was me, that was my body. I'm all out of line, and I don't know it. And I don't have the sense to quit. I am wrecking my body to get my own attention, and I won't listen.

Francine and me make up with each other just about the time practice start. She hear I'm not drinking, quit my job. Momma send me a hundred dollars for August. *Doctor wanting this money but I rather you have it. You spend it on something you want, and that way if I do go on and die they can't get it back. Sure is lonesome down here and if I have to go in the hospital I don't know who gone take care a the garden.*

I'm glad to be back with Francine but I hate her way down inside. I'm hiding it all now, I aint talking no more trash, but I feel like I been monkeyed on bad, and although I am going to church with her I am feeling just as blackhearted as the devil himself.

I come into practice with the best mile time of anybody but the backfield, and looking lighter and faster than last year. But what I'm telling you, my wheels are falling off. One thing and another. All through two-a-days I'm half-speed, having to lay out a day for this and that. Hurt my butt, and then I be hurting my ankle to compensate for hurting my butt. And then I jam my finger because I'm grabbing too much because I can't get no traction with the ankle.

And you know the whole rest of my career go the same way. I was going to be a star, and I don't even start that year, I'm halfway hurt all year long. And the next year, after it all happen, I don't work out in the summer, I'm doing community service on the road crew, which is all stand around and sweat, flagging them cars, go home and have two six-packs and five baloney sandwiches for supper, fall asleep to the tv. So this aint the first time I done community service, cause I was damn near boneheaded as you are and maybe I still am, we'll see in the next ten years. I tell you one thing, though, I prefer that damn road crew to looking at yo ugly mug more than another fifteen minutes. I really prefer that road.

So anyway next year I aint with Francine no more, she don't associate with no criminals, you know, because that's what I am by then even if it's been reduced. So I do my service and heal up and come back in the fall, but this time I *am* fat, and I am a step slow, and it's my junior year and I still aint starting. I work into shape about halfway through the season, and by bowl time I'm a "valuable substitute," you know, log almost as much time as the starters.

I aint got the desire no more, for one thing. Too much happened, I been too far down. It upset all my pictures I use to fire myself up. I was just hanging in, trying to figure out what to do with myself, keeping on playing because it was the one thing I was already any good at. I done switched over to studying by then, and that was using all my concentration. Yeah, studying. Doing what you doing, you bound to done some studying. You do it like I did? You wait till they give up on you? Wait till they taking away all the goodies? It's a white man world and you better learn to study. What's funny, when you find out you like it. We aint got enough names for things. We aint got enough imagination about the way things can go.

I have a good year in my senior year, get to start. Not great, but good. Thirty-seven tackles in eight games, three sacks. Then I break my leg. It could happen to anybody, but I swear it happen to me because I was weaker, because all I been through in the last three years. Didn't matter all that much. Already knew I wasn't gone be drafted in the pros. Already looking ahead to law school. Already having people come around to me about jobs in banks and whatnot, because see, once I got my grades up, equal opportunity was coming in, and if they could get one that was smart and a *Razorback* too. Don't even matter I been to jail. All niggers been to jail at least once, I guess that's what they figure.

You know how I got in law school? This one professor, I cheat in his class when I was a freshman. English composition. Most of em was graduate assistants, wasn't hardly older than I was, you could work em around. But this one a full professor. I just took a book out of the library and copied a couple of pages, turned it in for my theme. Wasn't a famous book, it was just a book. Turned out he had read every book ever written. Called me in, told me the name of the book, who wrote it. Then he just waited, smoking his Camel.

Old fat guy, chain-smoking Camels. Double chin, high-riding pants on his big fat belly. Parrot face. Glasses shine when he look up at me. You can imagine how I'm laughing inside, me with my hard body, but he wait me out, and I start explaining how I was just doing research.

Mmm-hmm, mmm-hmm, he say.

So then he explain the difference between research and copying. Patiently, not like he mocking. Just saying it, like there could be somebody on earth who didn't know.

So I play into that, pretend to be real confused. Should have been an actor. I am, I'm a lawyer. He listen. Mmm-hmm, mmm-hmm. But I look up one time and see I'm not fooling him at all. Makes me mad. Supposed to be able to fool them.

When I'm through, he say, Mr. Thompson, I am not convinced, but I will give you the benefit of the doubt. Notwithstanding that benefit, I must have some original work from you if I am to give you a grade in this class.

A fat clown that says ''notwithstanding'' is gone make me do something I don't want to? I'm really pissed. I stand up and start shouting how we have a language of our own, just as good as the ruling white class, and how all the professors prejudiced against football players, anything I can think of. I'm big, I fill up the room, I make noise. It works with the graduate *ass*-sistants, scares the shit out of them, everybody scared shitless about being prejudiced anyhow.

He push back his chair, get to his feet quick, his face red. He's looking at me like a mess on the rug. Mr. Thompson, this is nonsense, he says. Now sit down.

I still don't know why I do it. He sits, lights another Camel. Takes a deep breath, puffs it out. Talks: *First of all, it is quite true that your dialect*—dialect, *not language*—*is as valid as mine. Secondly, I agree that you quite likely suffer from cultural inequities in our composition classes. However, neither of these truths has any relevance. The fact remains that to do well in our society, you must be competent in standard written English. Unless you wish to be in the vanguard of those who would replace that standard with a better or fairer standard—leaving aside the question of what that standard might be—I see but two options. Either rebel, flunk my class, and make your fortune in some other line of endeavor, or set to work and perform as I require.*

He held his hand out to keep me from breaking in. *I have no doubt that you are capable of that performance. I have seen a very keen and mobile intelligence in action here today. You do not have to abandon your dialect. Do you wish to remain a prisoner of it?*

He was right. I remembered every word he said, didn't I? I remember it all today. He wasn't talking right or wrong or fair or foul, he was just talking what was going to happen. Just like I'm talking to you. You aint foolin me hiding in yo eyes like that.

Don't bother to send Coach around to see me, he said when I got up and went to the door. He was putting out his cigarette and already reaching for his notebook. *I have tenure.*

What this leading up to, how I got in law school. I asked him for a letter of recommendation. Funny when the time come. I had went ahead and made a C in his class, and then I hadn't seen him since, except walking on campus. But when the time come, I couldn't think of nobody else. He made me explain double-entry bookkeeping. He said nobody had ever been able to make it make sense to him. Then he asked me the difference in psychosis and neurosis, asked me to talk about B. F. Skinner. He said to have a transcript sent to him and he'd see. He wrote me a note, later, saying that he'd found my record very satisfactory and had written a positive letter of recommendation. I never did see the letter, all I know I got in.

I don't care if you don't see the point. And I don't really care if I'm getting more out of this than you are. I'll tell you like he told me. I don't see where you have no choices, do you? You in for this unless you rather jail. Why don't you use yo brain and figure out if it make sense, quit worrying about what I'm up to? That's like blowing off to the referees. Everybody do it some. Keep it up, all it gets you is a technical and sit on the bench.

But I'll get on to it. Why I stole them panties. Remember this was back before the law school, back way before the senior year, before I start studying. This is back when me and Francine broke up. And I never seen Francine's panties, even. Never even once.

You laugh at me and I can still whup yo silly ass.

And I'm in the store, and there's Francine looking at these shiny silk panties, and she have a man standing there with her, and she giggling. This is Francine I'm talking about.

I walk over and grab em out of her hand. And then I'm grabbing all of em. I'm stuffing em in my pockets and walking for the door, and I'm thinking while I'm walking that this is the dumbest thing I ever heard of anybody doing, and they catch me before I even get to the door.

So Coach gets it reduced, like I say, cause I still have some value left, and I wind up doing community service. Yeah. Coach wasn't near as bad on the brothers as they said. He treat me ok, for what good he ever got out of me.

But that aint the point. The point is, I'm sitting there in the jail cell while they holding me over, and I'm thinking how I just done something I would never in a million years have figured I would do. Something I would have made fun of if I saw some other crazy person do it. It's the first time I ever even suspect there's more than one person to me. And I swear to myself I aint gone never get caught off guard again, and I'm on learn all about this shit. And the only place I ever hear anybody talking about it is in them damn classrooms, so that's where I'm going to go. And psychology lead to philosophy lead to law.

And you aint hearing it, but that's all right, that's yo problem. But what I'm telling you, I never ever thought they would catch me off guard again. You understand what I'm saying, I thought I *fixed* myself. I figured it out, I was big-time, I beat the game. And the next thing I know, I'm all broiled up in somebody else's story. He thinks it's all about him, and how he had this great tragedy, but it aint. As far as I'm concerned, it's all about me.

But I was stupid and I didn't watch myself, so here I am. I don't get to say what my own story is. Just like in college, I have to play whatever position they tell me to. And here I am setting here talking to somebody even more stupid than me. I thought I had won for good. Never even saw how I had just graduated to another level, a bigger league.

Learn something if you can. My time's up.

I hope you spend the rest of your life wondering what this has to do with Joseph Charles Morrison and the way he lost his pretty little beauty queen.

43

PILGRIM

I guess this is prayer, Lianne. What else would it be? Can you pray to a person? I pray to God sometimes, help thou my unbelief. But mostly you.

I pray I'm wrong, that there is a heaven, that I'll see you again. I pray it more strongly the fainter you become in me. I think of other women now, love, I'm thinking of getting out and meeting people. But I don't feel like I'm betraying you. It feels peaceful, and I'm almost happy, and I'm beginning to forget you, and I miss you terribly.

For a while I thought if I just understood enough about the lives around you, if I could just see all the interconnections, maybe you would appear. Maybe the absence would take on your shape, the hole in the net. Figure and ground, you called it. Or if I could just learn your past, everything that led to the Lianne I knew, there you would be again, a blossom on that vine.

Oh, not in the flesh. I wasn't that crazy for long. In the mind, only in the mind. That moment when the image comes, or the smell, or the sound of your voice, that passing moment. For a fraction of a second you're there, you're utterly real. And then gone.

I hardly ever dream of you. For a while I would have given anything, but you can't control those moments, can't make them happen on cue. They have no logic, no cause and effect. I thought about having your story written. I talked to people. That green-eyed friend of Lafayette's, the poet. But it was beyond possibility. You are beyond regathering. Maybe that's the definition of life, finally. Maybe a soul is exactly the opposite of what they tell us. Not the thing that endures forever, but the thing that vanishes forever.

Spring in Arkansas. Easter weekend. Charles was heading for the lake, but in a roundabout way. Going by the cemetery first, to visit her grave. This is what he was thinking while he drove. Not in so many words, of course. Subconscious no spikka da English. You should be used to that by now. It's what I'm for, your recording angel, your private eye.

What else am I but the infinite curiosity of you finite monkeys, your detective, shade, voyeur, Voyager? And this, this is the Farewell Tour: swinging past all the majors one more time. On my way into vacuum. This is my final report. This is what you should have known at the beginning, but there's no way in time to tell you all come back to tell you all—

Well, maybe not my *final* final report. Charles has forgotten he ever signed me on, but once on the job, I finish. What I'm telling you, the case aint closed. It all comes round again. What you should have known at the beginning, but on the other hand, this is the beginning, right? You tell me. Way it is at the edge of the universe, time twisting into itself.

Speak into the truth banana, Charles:

Dee-Dee and Tucker aren't coming. They gave me the keys. She never got mad at me when she found out that it was Tina—you were so right about Tina, I should have listened. Dee-Dee never got mad, and I didn't understand why. I was sure she would be sure I cheated on you at least. But it was because she was pregnant. Can you believe? Bigger and bigger and happier and happier, and she seems to forgive everybody everything now, it's amazing.

So they aren't coming, because it could be this weekend or could be the next. Also it would be strange for them. Will be strange for me. That one whole spring has turned. Another first. You know what I'm hoping? I'm hoping we missed some eggs. I'm hoping I find a piece of a shell the animals left. Pretty silly, right?

Because I'm really not brokenhearted any more. I have a good time. Ballard's a blast, and I'm pampered. I work in the garden a lot; Coleman's too weak to stop me. By the way, Rider never found his boy, and never told him he was looking; he decided it was better to let it go. It was a sweet idea on your part. Coleman's fine, he's just weak.

Do you get all the gossip where you are? Of course you do, if you are anywhere. So why do I feel like I have to bring you up to date? What else, what else?

Oh, you'll enjoy this. Somebody's after Cheese. First they shot up his car in the sheriff's parking lot. Then somebody cut the brake lines, and he drove into the river. Now, just the other day, two men showed up at his door with a bouquet of flowers and a pistol and chased him all through the house. He got away, though. Too bad. Keep trying, guys.

I hope you don't think I'm too bloody-minded. If it can happen to you, why not him?

I miss you and I'm forgetting you. I tried remembering. I read your files, I went in for hypnosis, I did everything. I tried remembering, and it didn't work. We weren't made to remember. The images don't come when we want them to. They come when they come. A gift, a grace: unbidden, out of chaos, unpredictable.

So my plan now is to forget you. Forget you all the way to my own grave. I will carry a sweet forgetfulness in the shape of your vanished face, carry it right into the heart of my own vanishing. Let them ring sweeter bells if they are capable.

Charles had been expecting, somehow, beautiful weather, but at The Peace That Passeth Understanding, there was no brilliance. The clouds were low and scumbly, the creek ran slack and cold between straw-colored slopes. Some of the trees wore a fuzz of new leafage. The spring beauties were up, but because the day was so dark, and because the low wet wind, inconstant and chilly, offered so little encouragement, they kept their wines and pinks tightly furled.

The brightest colors were the umbers, almost identical, of the tall sedge grass, and of the turned earth, new and red and raw, the two or three recent grave sites.

He sat on the rock in her nook, looking out away through the opening in the cedars, his feet drawn up on the rough stone. He lit himself a cigar, fighting the gusts that broke and beat on the hillside, and watched the smoke whip and dash and disappear.

He had no sense that she was here. Maybe at the lake.

He glanced sidelong at her plot, the amazing litter of fading plastic flowers, bouquets wired to rods jammed into the earth, strewn garlands, a wreath on a tripod stand that the winter had beaten over and flattened, a tumble of black plastic pots. Her earth was still mounded and convex, but there had been all of summer and fall for the ground cover to take hold, and it was no longer bare. He could see where the mower blade had run over the growth, and through the chopped brown stems he could see runnels and gulleys, the runoff of old weather. By midsummer, she would be a part of the general green, seamless.

What was in that grave? A brazen urn, a few cupfuls of ashes. Nothing that had ever been a woman. Nothing that had ever been part of his life.

It was peaceful to be here, as all cemeteries were peaceful. But it had nothing to do with resolution, nothing to do with her green eyes or her quick step. It was a general peace, a pleasant sadness. The intensity of those eyes did not live on in the glancing of light on water, the riffling of sun and shade. The energy of that step did not find an echo in the step of the wind over the hills, but was gone, scattered below collection, dissipated past any thought of recall.

He leaned back on the rock, his hands under his head. He had never before understood the attitude he had sometimes seen in older people, the matter-of-fact pleasure they seemed to take in getting their plot arranged, in thinking about where they would lie. But now—

He was thinking how he looked forward to this, how good it would be to give up all the meaningless busywork of existence, to let go and relax and lie down in permanent forgetfulness, when Curtis cleared his throat in the trees. Charles sat up, startled.

"I'm down here a fair lot," Curtis said, propping his rear against the rock and surveying Lianne's grave. He held his hat in one hand and ran the other through his short gray hair. "Should have cleaned up these flowers, but I didn't want nobody to get their feelings hurt, and then it turned off cold. Let it come summer, and I can bend over better."

"It's fine," Charles said. "It's fine. Don't you worry with it; I'll do it later on."

"Reckon it's hard for you to get up," Curtis said. "You got a far way to come."

"It's not all that far. I don't want you worrying with it." They were leaning beside each other now, looking out over the grave.

"I don't know what you heard," Charles said.

"I heard about anything I want," Curtis said. "Aint much I listened to."

"I never wronged her." Charles wouldn't have thought he was feeling anything, but the tears burned in his eyes. "I'm not much, but I never once wronged her."

"You don't owe to tell me."

"I wanted you to hear it from me," Charles said. "Sometimes I feel like everybody in this whole state thinks." He didn't finish. It was old woe, and he was tired of rehearsing it.

"There's one don't," Curtis said.

On the way back to the road, Curtis stopped at one of the recent graves: Earl "Dusty" Leaper, 1910–1982.

"A friend?" Charles said. Curtis nodded. "I'm sorry," Charles said.

"We all got to go," Curtis said. "I tell you, me and ole Earl use to work summers down in Searcy. We'd get together with ole Wayne Morris down there and some of his friends and go out in the evening to the bootlegger and get those flat pints and drink them."

They started walking again. "Flat pints?" Charles said.

"Twelve-ounce pints. From the bootlegger. We called em flat pints. They was thin, you know, fit in your pocket real good."

"When was this?" Charles said.

"Oh, it was a way back. We was just boys. It would have been 'twenty-eight, I reckon. We was just farm boys kicking up in the evenings. Wellsir, this one evening we laid in five of those flat pints, and we worked em down pretty good, you know. And we got to the last one, and they was a spider in it.''

''A spider?''

''A big ole spider,'' Curtis said, stopping for a breath or two. ''A big ole spider in that jar.''

''I bet he gave it some flavor,'' Charles said.

Curtis led them on. ''Well, ole Wayne Morris, he says, Boys, I tell you what we're a-gonna do. We're gonna turn the lights off. And then we're going to pass this yere flat pint around, and that way we won't know which one of us got the spider. So that's what we did.''

They had gained the road. Charles gave Curtis a quizzical glance, but Curtis seemed satisfied with his story. ''It's hard losing those old friends,'' Charles said.

''Yessir,'' Curtis said, breathing fairly hard again, leaning against Charles's car, the 280, humming like a top nowadays. He thumped it, looked out over the cemetery toward his friend's grave. ''Good car. Yessir, ole Dusty was the first to go.''

Charles smiled consolingly, opened his door. He was ready to be on his way. Curtis straightened, dusted his overalls. He winked at Charles.

''Reckon he must have got that spider,'' he said, and started down the road to his pickup.

On the way north, the roads got higher and higher, and the hills wilder and wilder. Just above Jerusalem, Charles came to a roadside diner, a long low boxcar-like construction of dull brown siding. He didn't remember having ever seen it before, but then again, he seldom traveled this route to the lake. The sign was blinking neon, which seemed odd this far out in the hills of Arkansas:

WINKY *EATS*

He was a little hungry, craving a sweet, so he pulled in. There were two pickups in the graveled lot but only one person in the diner, the sleepy young man behind the counter. He didn't seem to have the remotest idea who Winky was, or how long the diner had been there. At Charles's request, he pulled a saucer with a stale wedge of coconut pie from under a dirty plastic bell. Charles had the pie with watery coffee.

In the rest room before he left, he saw only two graffiti of any interest. Most were the usual racial slurs or belligerent assertions of native locale, or of the numerical variety: *8½", 9 p.m. 2/23/81,* or *427-1125 evenings.*

One of the good ones showed a perfect schematic of dick and balls on a circular cunt, and under it, scratched into the wall, the legend *Fuck Puse.* Charles, more and more lately, was beginning to agree with that.

The other moved him. If he had not found it on a rest room wall, he would have wanted it for Lianne's epitaph, which of course is why I offer it here:

But one man loved the pilgrim bitch in you.

It was not your usual graffito, and he could not decide how it had come to be there unless some college student, passing through, had taken the time to carve it out.

On the crooked roads, it was nearly dark when he got there. The Other Shore was as pleasantly lonesome as the cemetery had been, and he looked forward to an evening of whiskey by the fire, owl calls from the deck, the whisper of lapping waves. More whiskey by the fire.

He let himself in and switched on the light and in doing so switched himself into the present tense, for we are caught up. This is it. The story has happened, is over, is being over as we speak, though I do have one last promise to keep: one last gift to give.

He still has no sense of Lianne, not even going through the cabinets, inventorying the provisions left over from last year. He does exactly what he has meant to do. He gets his little gear in the cabin, has a shower, makes a light supper.

He allows himself to build a fire only after he has cleaned and put away all the dishes, swept the floors, opened the windows to freshen the air in the cabin. In the cabinet with the old newspapers they use for kindling there is a hornets' nest, still fastened to its segment of branch. It takes him a moment to remember. This is the nest Lianne brought back down the hill the evening before Easter, when she hid the eggs. If ever there was a cue:

But nothing. He remembers how pleased she was, how she wanted to take the nest home, but then, in the rush of leaving, they had gone off and left it—but the memory is abstract, it is only stored information, he doesn't feel her presence stirring. For some reason he thinks of the dog, Ramalam. He sees her coming back down the hill with the hornets' nest and Ramalam leaping beside her. But that didn't happen. The dog had been dead for four years. It was just that he had seen the two of them that way so many times, returning from the woods.

He realizes he hasn't seen the dog's apparition since Lianne died. Well, maybe this would count, the beast spooking his way into the recollected scene: haunting a memory.

It can't be that he really misses the animal, can it?

He finds some cord, hangs the nest from a beam, as he thinks Lianne would have done if she were there. It is partly torn open, and he can see the cells where the larvae were. Nothing. Empty. A chandelier of vanished lives.

He leaves the windows open to keep the room cool enough for the fire. He has a whiskey. Two. There are no ghosts in the fire. There are no ghosts at the stirring curtains.

He goes to bed fairly early, tired though he has not had a hard day. It's what driving will do to you, he decides. Driving, and whiskey, and cemeteries. And a fire.

In bed, he hears not owls but whippoorwills, a wonderful melancholy whooping that echoes fiercely in the hollows. He keeps a third whiskey on the stand beside the bed.

He sleeps, and condensation runs down the side of the glass, the ice cubes slowly melt. He wakes up once, has a warming swallow. The whippoorwill is still at it. He considers going out on the deck for stars, but he's too comfortable, too sleepy. He can hear the aging fire pop in the other room from time to time. He sleeps again.

After a while he twitches, like a dog dreaming of rabbits. *A high rabbit in deep grass, bounding. The steam rabbit, booming from tunnels.* It's what we've done with the twentieth. *The announcer's voice booming and dying out over the crowds, the crowds at the station.* We've done with the twentieth century. *The crowds with their upturned faces, white unto harvest. The dog bounding high in high grass, with his ears pointed up.*

He turns on his side, mumbling into the pillow, the words indistinct, and probably nonsensical anyway. It's hard to tell, because there's nobody to hear but us. Deep in his trance, he whistles. *Why is the dog so happy, leaping to see? Who does the dog go leaping to see?*

He laughs aloud, his voice brilliant and clear. "So it *was* just a dream," he says:

44

RAMALAM

Howdy, I'm the Holy Ghost. Talk about your omniscient narrators.

What's the differential in me and a computer program writes poetry? None. Nothing. Time. The red-haired pretty-girl.

She comes in, green-eye fire-hair, sweet stamp of the freshest thing, unkillable lilt, into the breeze-blow sun-curtain kitchen, and there, there in the window—

Is there an echo in here?

There in the window, the spider in the quart jar. The window over the sink. Curtains beating shadow and sun. Wolf spider was, in a mason jar. Holes punched in the lid with an ice-pick so it could breathe, wounds in the side of Christ.

So anyway, afternoon sun, slant sun pretty and late, comes in parallel because of the edge of the earth, why it's so clear and pretty, not like noon rays bounce around crazy. So anyway happy sun late. Strike fire in the little red curls, light up the hairs on the legs of the spider.

She knows the spider is for the closet. To go in the closet with her in the dark. Still in the jar, of course: *I'm not trying to be mean. If I was mean, I would unscrew the lid. If I didn't love you, I would unscrew the lid.*

She had been happy: She had been bad.

Letting Loretta brush her hair. Letting Miss English like her.

She knew when she wanted the silver brush so much. The brush in

Aunt Loretta's smooth white hands. She knew when she bounced in her seat because Miss English had smiled at her. The teacher likes me! The teacher likes me!

She knew when the brush, when she felt her mother go ugly. When she felt Aunt Loretta feel her mother too but ignore her. She knew she would have to pay, her mother would make her pay, she knew it all and felt it all but wanted the brush thick in her hair so bad, the pull on the scalp, the strange easing it brought, your toes prickling with calmness, all of your body smoother than water.

She knew again when she heard Miss English tell Miss Grady, *What a sweet child*. Miss Grady, her momma's best friend. Would tell her momma. So she knew she was selfish, conceited, but wanted to be Sweet Child anyway. Felt the good thing go bad like the aggie that rolled in the sewer drain. Stink world ate it, black place ate it, swallowed my play-pretty, wink black gone.

Do you think the Father likes this stuff, pegeen and spider crossed in the same light, in the same darkness? His darkness. Go ask Him, Baba-looie, I just run errants.

Think of the child in the church on Sunday, though, hearing the scriptures: *Go to thy closet and pray.*

This was back when? Back then. Can't say the year. Little Arkansas girls didn't quite wear long print dresses no more, but not yet the twirl skirts, white sox and horse-doctors. Horse-doctors what the redhead said one time. Saddle oxfords meant, but horse-doctor said. I could dang near carry on a conversation with that woman. You be a tad bit harder.

Time is not a high-priority item with me, you understand. Slide around in it like a hog in good mud. Never could see a clock. You look at your wrist and call out numbers. You don't even know you're praying: *Let me not be late and get fired.* Or, *If it's this hot now, how hot will it be by noon?* Or, *Please let her be home when I get there.* And I hear you, me and the Son and the Father and Miss Liza, we all hears you, but I can't see clocks. You look at the clock tower, I have to look too, I'm in you and of you, right? And I can see tower, but can't see clock. Not never no clock. You are just staring at space, my man, into the blank face of possibility.

Are you with me, Joe? *Vooble ooble beep glirt blitz,* tune in the raddy-o. I tries to talk like you hear, but it aint easy all tongues in all times et cetera running around like ah say oh branches of fire whistle whistle and I beheld the changes ramifying and not only ramifying but ramalamifying like unto the changes of changes billionfold and yet connectivated, the Word that was-is and shall-be, and here I am the was-izzer, don't you know, the shall-be-ifier.

I just said *billion* because We have run these studies show it's the biggest-sounding word to you guise, more so nor trillion which has a trill in it and sounds lighter, or quadrillion which tends to remind you of mixed races dancing in New Orleans, and then all of the others so theoretical you refuse to think of them at all.

But if I was to say to you, Gal we couldn't get no hire, no I mean star seed tree fire but all in one word somehow that meant them all at the same time, if you had a word like that and I said it, would you see Pentecost? Would you be able to take your eyes off the wound in your wrist long enough to hear me what I'm trine to say?

Say de momma, *Wear your white dress.*

Say de girly-girlio, *I can't, I'm dirty, I dream a flow of blood where I pee, what does that mean?*

She didn't "say," of course, but it's like clox, can't keep a handle on the difference you make in saying thinking or even just feeling with big loomy pictures like flowers and blood, it's all one say you see, the word quivers with what made the word and it is all perfectly visible even to finitesimals if you just stoplooklisten and get your eyes off the decimals.

The first fear is this, that the spider will crawl:

That the spider will crawl in the dark, out of the jar, to bite me.

The jar in one corner and I in another, little girl huddled in nothing but panties, little coppery nipples on a flat thin chest, pale little legs little arms I see in a huddle in a slant of afternoon light before the door closes, just as if I were not that girl, just as if I were the mother or the Holy Ghost in the mother or the Holy Ghost in the redheaded woman who misses you too, Charles, looking back into her memories in pity, looking all back down the slant of Holy Ghost light into the closet of the past where all of this has just forever happened.

But then I am dark a long time.

The second fear is this:

That the jar does not matter, that spider and darkness are one and the same, that helpless and bad are one and the same.

Weak and frightened, you sleep, without ever ceasing from fright. Held by a wall and a wall and a floor you cannot see, theoretical geometrical corner, transparent planes, crossing of axes, fixed high and deep in featureless space in a sleep without membrane or veil or barrier, so that the dreams that occur are simply true are simply you: *The big hairy thing in the darkness, the man with too many hairy legs, he rises and rises, big, he is pushing, squatting, to do what does this mean?*

—*Oh ugly my blood comes out where I pee, what does this mean?*

The third fear is this:

Awake in my bunny pajamas in my own bed. It is a Sunday. The light has a smell on a Sunday, a clean white smell, and the sheets are so clean, cool and sleekit and clean. De momma come in. Oh my baby daughter. She's good now. She's so good now, kiss of the powdery mouth all over the face. I brought you in while you were asleep, I love you so much. Huggemup. Huggemup. Smell of the lemon talcum. Your pretty red hair, so pretty, prettiest girl in Little Rock town, Momma so proud

That all of this is still the darkness.

The momma says, *Wear your white dress, save the blue one for later.*

Do you know why, Charles? Because the white dress is rayon, water won't hurt it. Because the blue dress will show up gray on camera. Because the white dress on camera would be prettier. Mrs. de Momma is proud that her kid, her prettier kid, will be on the tv. Mrs. de Momma be jealous her kid on de tv.

I'm sorry I have to talk this way, Charles Joseph. It's because it was all just a dream. It's because I'm the Holy Ghost now.

Meantime, way back in Little Rock in 1950, the daughter is not-say thinking, *Wrong to be the bride of Christ in a white dress when I'm so bad, so selfish, and conceited.*

The question here, the eccentrial question, as the redhead would probably say, is whether a bald-headed woman can go to heaven.

THAT AINT THE QUESTION, GHOST. YOU KNOW IT AINT.

I know, I know, don't hit me again, Daddy God, I know it aint. But whether a scrap of glory shall be lost—oh brethren, shall we be whole again? I don't hardly see how, do you?

Now wait a minute, you're saying to yourself, I expected more from Little Liza Jane.

Brethren and sistren, children and sinners, how may I declare myself who have no self? Put it this way, good buddy, I aint the way the truth and the light. You know who *that* is.

Well, maybe the light, a little. Well. Maybe the truth. And the way. Sort of. We all swap around a lot, it gets confusing.

The trouble with truth is, you think it means a set of uncontested facts. Now, what is a fact? It is like unto a atom of what happened. A hard little knot of this-is. Whereas the truth is just genesis. Always genesis now. Think of me as energy, girls—the photon between, probability wave, Mercury, the carrier, the $\pi\lambda\alpha\sigma\mu\alpha$ free of its vessel, das blood mitout eine kleine $\kappa\lambda\epsilon\iota\nu$, its corporeal body of sluggard inertia.

Now hold on just a New York minute, you're saying to yourself, so you're energy, but I seen some pretty energetic liars.

And you are so right, brother, you are so right. What we are onto here is the Problem of Evil, and I aint gonna get into that one just now, boys, I aint a-gonna do it.

When the Judgment Day
Boomaloom
When the Judgment Day comes
Boomaloom
The saints and the sinners shall be parted right and left
Boomaloom

And since genesis and judgment are one and the same and I am the time between, we can wait, so don't let's wake up yet, I didn't say the name, well I said it once, sort of, but if it's ok with you, let's dream on.

What it boil down to, Joe, you have to make up your own mind. What is true and what is a lie. Holy Ghost can't help. You the Holy Ghost. See what I mean, how it swaps around?

What it boil down to, Chuck, there's things to say about the Problem of Evil, but they don't matter much. Kind of trivial up alongside of love and grief. We All in love with you monkeys, want you to grow up and marry us in our little white dress

out in the spring-dazzle light
in Little Rock town
a thousand year ago today
out in the street alone.

See the little girl with the white dress on, she's got funky-butt sure as you're born. This unfortunately is true, the afflatus of a greasy breakfast working in combo with a sulfur allergy I don't find out about for ten years yet, the odorous onions in the hash browns and the rich sulfides in the egg yolks forced into a stomach already roiling sick with fear. I am going to Jesus wrong, I know what blackness the blackness of the black baptismal water is, that there will be alligators in the jaws of the water. Ah, the pretty little girl in the dogwood streets of a pretty little city

farts with fear.

It is a few mere blocks to the church. The house door has closed behind the girl. She is alone in the undisguisable light, which may be a trick of the darkness.

She is wearing, in addition to the white dress, a white slip, white cotton panties, white petticoats. Thin white turn-down socks just over her ankles. Her old white shoes made radiant with coats of that liquid white shoe polish whose odor was worse than thickets of cherries. A new blue ribbon (pale blue) done into the buckle-straps of her old white shoes. Short white gloves. Two blue ribbons in the mass of her pulled-back hair. A Bible under her arm: white leather cover, gold-edged pages, so that the book is like a brick of gold in a thin white sandwich. And out of the gold, a thin tongue of pale blue, a forked tongue, the riband of place-markery. And stamped on the white leather my name, in small gold letters: *Tommie Lianne Weatherall.*

Or maybe I'm making that up. Names are as hard for me as clocks. Not His names, which are as they are, but yours, which are as you would be.

The door has closed. The mother will be there later. The girl is to walk to Sunday school all alone.

So the spring morning just sets her aglow. I mean, it just lights her up. If you were not her, if you could swing wide away from her in a huge pan like a tv camera, you could see her walking, white dress and white petticoat luminous, and in the midst of all that nimbus, as though she were her own fiery furnace, the shade of two young legs, walking: stroke, stroke. If you were not her, you could see the aureole of luminous hair, a halo of blazing filament.

You could see how she holds the Bible in front of her now, her forearms resting along her stiff skirt. How the skirt rocks with her walking.

You could not see how far she must walk, how dangerous the journey. For that you need

Me: a few blocks over to the wide boulevard, and then walk eastward along the boulevard until the church, a stack of red brick with high white columns and a spread of white cement steps like the widening fall of shallow rapids. It is a pleasant short walk in a safe neighborhood, the sidewalk ample, the leafy hill of a friendly development rising across the street on her right, and, falling away on her left into a tilt of trees, one of the many fine wild ravines in this green city, that wiggle and ravel and deepen the shadows, and channel the runoff down to the river. But

> *Step on a crack,*
> *break your mother's back.*

She is no fool, this little girl. She doesn't believe the rhyme. That is to say, she doesn't think it describes cause and effect. You tell me, Charles, does such science protect her? Is it a hard invisible shield? There is a crookedness in that chant, a malice bubbling in its fissures.

She *wants* to break her mother's back.

The rhyme is a call to try a wicked power. It isn't a warning, it's a seduction. All the little children of the world know that. They're out there skipping to save their souls, not the transverse processes of mater's cervical vertebrae.

It's worse for her this thousand-year morning. Waving over the walk are the shadows of branches. To her each shadow is a fault, a crack in the earth. If she steps on a single one, she will not know whether she wanted murder or fell to manslaughter. In such dim confusions are the shades of Hades bound.

When she gets to the church, she has broken her mother's back seventeen times.

I might as well say I can't see churches any better than I see clox, though I can see two or three gathered together in my name just fine and I can see individual bricks ok. You have a way of making bricks disappear I figure is what you mean when you say church. I hear you talk about churches. See you all sit there naked in rows like in a big bus, but the driver has turned around yakkity-ax.

In Sunday school it starts to be ok. She's just a pretty little girl in a pretty little dress. There's lots of other pretty littles in pretty littles. She's white, she rustles. Nobody's mad at her. Nobody loves her with terrifying squeeze.

They sing: *Red and yellow black and white*. She loves the little black children but they're brown. She loves the little red children but they're burnt umber. She loves the little yellow children. The chair is cold on the backs of her legs, good cold, interesting.

They sing: *Zacheus climbed up in the sycamore tree*. The white skin tree. How did he reach the limbs, they don't have any limbs close to the ground. He wanted to see Jesus. Anybody would. Jesus understands, just like he ought to, but he teases Zacheus a minute.

Everybody knows Jesus. Everybody knows just what Jesus is like. He lives in your family, and he will tease, but never never mean, he is a good big brother who takes care of you.

It is all normal now. She fits, nobody's upset. The things that are supposed to happen do happen. *Jesus loves the little children of the world*. Zacheus gets to meet Jesus. Kool-Aid and a sugar cookie soon. It's good when the world is normal. Safe. Level. Warm.

Sunday school is over and Momma grabs her. Eagle claw on shoulder. Carry her off high over the crooked ravine, drop her to jaggedy rocks and trees. Momma's fingers will go all the way through, make blood on her pretty dress. Put the cookie down, we're going to be late for the services, are you trying to drive me crazy, if you get crumbs on that dress you can't do the ad

but I'm not wearing this dress for the tv

if your father didn't remember the cap I don't know what

I'm going to

skip the sermon if it's okeydokey with you, Chuck. I hate sermons, don't you? Such death and fragmentation. Authority divided from joy. Unless they are a riddle that lights up the blood of your mind, and then they aren't sermons, are they, but poems.

But you probably want to see the program, the order of services, we call it, inside facing page of the church bulletin. There's one in the hymnal rack of the pew in front of you. Take it.

ORDER OF SERVICES

Opening Hymn   III

Opening Prayer

Hymn (*Congregation Standing*)   222

Hymn   333

Announcements and Messages

Offertory Hymn (*Congregation Standing*)   444

Offering

Special Music by Bethel Elizabeth Izard   555

Sermon: "When I Walk with the Lord"

Invitational Hymn   666

Closing Prayer

Baptismal Services (*Please Remain*)

Candidates for Baptism: J. S. Erdrach, Juney Leroux,
Tommie Lianne Weatherall

Is that how it reads? Funny, I thought it wavered and shifted like they do in the movies used to do in the black-and-white movies when they are showing a dream scene or hallucination, you know, water-ripple all quirky-worky and then when they look back at whatever they were looking at it isn't the same, it reads:

PLOT SEQUENCE, "RAMALAM"

Friday, a.m.:	Miss English says out loud in class, "You're such a sweet child."
Friday, p.m.:	Miss English reiterates same to Miss Grady.
Saturday, a.m.:	Aunt Loretta brushes her hair while her mother watches angrily.
Saturday, p.m.:	Comes in from playing to find spider.
Sunday, a.m.:	Wakes up in her own bed after a night in the closet.
Sunday a.m.-er:	Walks to Sunday school.
Sunday a.m.-est:	Is baptized as a Christian.
Sunday, p.m.:	Does a live television ad for Freeman's Dairy.

Does that help, Tommie Joe? I'm trying, my own way I'm trying to let you know what's going on, give you the straight poop, but it's weird, you know, it's like sending a message in a bottle, not even on paper but on the glass of the inside of the bottle, scratching skritchy-skritch Sanskrit into the green scratched-up glass of the bottle. Fitting it back into time. What you call time, little tight skid-away never-was, receding like a dream. I am like you trying to send a message to one of your dreams.

And the message too boomy for your dreamy ears, like somebody on the seacoast trying to listen in on a conversation two dunes over, all you can hear of what I'm trying to tell you is *BOOMY-OOM time BOOM dream BOOM time BOOMY-OOM time* . . .

We're on a tight schedule here. I have to get baptized and then Daddy has to die, his red face pumped up redder and redder till he blows up blood all over the white dress because he's so mad at me for not being good so Momma will let him alone, and then (another then) go be a pretty girl on tv for Tommy Freeman because we have rich friends we aren't just trash and why don't you like Daddy better since it is his second cousin and not yours anyway ha-ha Momma break your fucking back—or is this the then to be a pretty girl for the pageant, or the one to be a blonde with a calm voice giving you the news in color, Mr. and Mrs. Little Rock, the news just come from President Nixon, say, that you aren't in Vietnam any more, hallelujah? Sermon's too long, Momma's getting antsy, antsy in her pantsy, she's on a tight schedule.

Momma's always on a tight schedule.

Momma's always on a tight schedule.

Momma's always on a tight schedule.

"Goddammit, Elaine, all I have to do is buzz back by the house and get it, it won't take five minutes, the sermon isn't even over yet."

"How can you curse in a church? How can you do that?"

"We're not *in* a goddamn church, Elaine, we're standing *beside* a goddamn church."

"Do you think that makes any difference to God?"

I have to go to the bathroom, Momma, I have to go to the bathroom.

You think that makes any difference to God?

"Oh for—well, I thought *she* was supposed to bring it. Last night you told *her* to bring it."

My stomach wants to hurt me. It's rolling and rumbling.

"I very plainly told you to check and see if she brought it. You know how she forgets things. She does it to fight me."

"Well, I'll go get it."

"If we're late, I'll never forgive you. My God, Lianne, is that you?"

Now who's cussing, but he dassn't dare say it. She would stick him with a pressure valve, he would blow a blood vessel right there instead of, hum, om, lessee, when Elvis Presley and just before Jack Kennedy, when I was Lianne, when I was sweet sixteen and never been. He say instead, quite truthfully, *The two of you are going to kill me.* He don't say, *And I will be glad to die,* he don't even thinksay because he has hid it so deep, but he sure hell feelsay. What he saysay is: *Take the stinky little brat to the bathroom and I'll go get the goddamn cap.*

Which makes the girl to wish her father dead, not for the first time, to pump him red and red and red, BOOMY-OOM! What a betrayal, because

Daddy loves you real sometimes, she never does and he is sometimes truly kind. Who had a chance, Daddy, to be the hero of your mornings, a misty dawnlight presence from the lit-up truck, tall and shadowy in dark blue jacket, engines running behind him, archangel of fog, bringer of clink, originator of front-stoop basket of quart and quart of cool sweet cream-top you love to drink a long thick swallow of before they shake it up: *but not no never now, not now.*

So you would slay your only savior, would you? Oh, you go to Jesus evil, sister, you go to Jesus bad.

I got it all on videotape. I do, I do. Brethren, if we shall be made whole, if the South and everybody else shall rise again, somebody will have to have kept pretty good records, hah? So. In that case, what is the universe written on?

But let me tell you this. This part has to be very careful. But somewhere in a little Southern city in a state nobody knows where it is, in a place even more lost because the only coordinates you have are the skew coordinates of fiction, crazy with fudge and fractals, there are these films. This part has to be very delicate because of what real is. I would not want to lie to you about what real is.

There are these films in black and white.

A little girl is drinking milk. A beautiful little girl with the happiest smile you ever saw. A real girl.

What if you were Charles. What if you fell in love. What if you saw in the eyes, in the energy of a gesture, in a funny way of talking, what if you saw, there in the heart of a grown woman, the girl she was. Oh still there. Oh still young. Like the heart of a flame inside the flame, like the map of a city thirty-five years ago, like a truth beneath a truth.

Where is it written?

What if you saw, and saw the child, and saw the child in pain as fresh as ever, and could not let her know, not even a message send to stay, endure, survive: for love. For the fact that there will be, someday, love.

Because of course you are yourself a fraction, pronoun, shade, projection: as trapped as any spider in a jar, a mortal bound to bloom and fail, a fool of time.

What if you saw, and knew the films were there. And you could drive downtown just any day, and find the vault, and see the evidence, the moving image of the girl herself, the girl you never knew and could not come to comfort.

Oh do you think that you could bear to watch her smile?

Fixed in her terror, generating such a brand-new smile?

Don't lie to me, Joe.

You wouldn't go.

You haven't yet.

So much for hypotheticals. This little girl isn't that one, and you aren't you, as you know, but a composite.

But *something* here is real.

You say it's all jumbled up, sir, can't sort it out? Your watch says half-past physics, too late for fiction, secondhand theology? I know you intersect me on a fairly unusual axis, a weird cross-section. Let me help you, let me give you a model, let me tell you a tell:

Once, a long time, ago, the trees were as vital as you pretend to be. They were intelligent, aware. They spoke among themselves in chemicals on the wind. They feasted on what was very nearly the body of God, the light of the sun itself. They had neither mouths nor eyes, but they had a thing that was both and neither: they exfoliated. They were fluid, they sang, they grew, they danced. In fact, they still and always do, if you have eyes that are slow enough to see, ears that are tuned low and frail enough to hear. It is true that their intelligence was a more distributed intelligence than yours, and it is true that they died where they grew, but when has that ever contradicted a dance? As fine as it was to be a tree, however, there was sin among trees. They starved each other for the light, the tall shadowing out the young without regard to grace or form, size and power the only consideration. And though they were mono- and dioecious, and floated their delicious sexuality on the air, and all together came in every spring, and all together bore fruit every fall, so that there was no such thing as infidelity, they yet discovered how to betray, and how to lie. As punishment for their sins (this is the story the trees tell), God made a sort of whizzing invisible ghost, a sort of rootless unhappy demon moving too fast to recognize, whose function it was to torture and strip and mutilate, to force the trees into a rigid and geometrical death, or to breed them into unknown forms. But then God had pity and sent a Tree of Trees, a slender and perfect youngling without a flaw. Smooth she was on the wind, and prettily she ate the light. She told of a tree of stars, and made her life an image of what she told. Soon her fame had drifted over the world. Of course this could not be permitted. The elders, dark with struggle, the bitterly twisted survivors, they realized that they must deal with this most false and dangerous of hopes. And so it was that a human was found (for that is what they were, those fast-forward spooks, that blurring branching of hatchets) and drawn into its fate, as trees know how to draw things to themselves: and the Tree of Trees was cut down, and crossed upon herself, and fastened to a man to die.

So day say.

And that's the spider, Joe. Eight-legged. Four parts tree and four parts man. Double cross. Oh, not really, not really really. Spider's just a spider,

I know that, you know that. Nothing really wrong with facts. I been bad-mouthing facts the last ten billion years, but summa my best frenzies fax. Spider I mean is just an image, just a figure of speech, divided from a real continuum, fixed in the glassy confines of this made thing.

But like I say, the word quivers with what made the word: there's a reason for this reason, there's a why for this because.

I wouldn't want you to forget that, Little Liza Jane.

Not even down here at the bottom of the gravity well, smiling for the cameras. That's right, sweetie. Look here. No, not at me, look into the camera, the drinking eye of time. That time may be inwrought with time, look into that dark and drinking eye:

> Oh what a shock of plain vitality:
> a little face set bluntly into air,
> a generous cloud of unregulated hair,
> a mouth as red and rich as heart's-blood must be,
> the eyes set wide, to wider see:
> and in the eyes, and in the smooth, pale, fair
> expression of the face, and now, just there
> about the soft mouth, the mysterious, the
> infinitesimal functions of a smile begin,
> like wind beginning in a tree. Oh, Christ,
> what willingness to live, given the least
> few drops upon the tongue, the tiniest
> slant stroke of notice, kindness, love, the grin
> of a fat (and most un-Christian) cameraman.

No, that isn't it, that isn't right, those aren't my lines, at least not yet. That's not what I was supposed to say. What's my cue, who's got the cards? Oh.

There aren't any.

And this is live, and on the air. The red light is blinking. Something is terribly wrong. Hide your eyes, Israel, I'm on show you godzass, and it damn near kill Moses just to see the tail end of his robe, I'm on show you one bad joke:

The leetle girl, she is bald, señor.

Don't make no sense, José.

Stack of grinning bones on a tv stool in a red light desert wind.

Don't make no sense. And anyway, what's all this red? What you trying to do, colorize? The thing's in black and white. *You right about that.* All that red hair show up black, and that blue dress show up gray, all that chocolate milk—

Whut about the ball-head woman?
You right about that.
What *about* the ball-head woman?
Come with me now, into the water at the bottom of the gravity well, into the black baptismal water, upon whose surface ripples are crossing like shadows of branches underfoot: Have you ever seen how light shaken on ripples can lift right off the water and make a branching space, a web of living fire, persistence of vision? Have you ever seen how shadows of branches moving can magic a sky in earth, a wind to fill that sky?

> *A shadow on a shadow thrown*
> *makes the dusty world a zone*
> *as deep and tricky as the air.*
> *What wanders there?*

A wind that moveth whither it list. And there am I. And you are here with me. Here in this quiet space, the place between. The womb, the kiva, the sky. Here we have gathered. It is the moment before creation. Soon the ramalam of first light, the flash and bang and fire that will grow and cool and evolve into our story and age and come round and begin to collapse on itself again in the fire and bang and flash of the light's last ramalam.

Soon. But now we are nowhere, we are at rest. And I have two things to give you. The first is a quiet thing, a smooth thing like a stone to rub your mind on:

Did you know God could pray?

The second is a harder thing, a broken thing: A ram, a lamb. Caught in the thicket, fixed in the thorns of the clock. A mangled spider. A tree in the branches of lightning.

This is a various thing, a thing of facets and spikes and angles, Call it the eightfold way, or the many rooms of our father's hyperhouse, call it the path of triple-branched lightning. I shall turn it before your eyes, but remember as it changes that you are not watching truth truth truth but the shades of a manifold thing thrown on a screen, the projections of an imaginary model:

1i. The Father fears the closet. He has awakened, but who defines Him? Perhaps He is awake in a great darkness without boundary. Although He seems to exist, who can reassure Him, since He is All?

1 . There is a joke bald-headed woman going to heaven, Little Liza Jane.

2i. The Father, Who cannot defend Himself from His own bad dreams, is therefore spiderish and jagged.

2 . There is a real bald-headed woman, whose hair has fallen out from chemotherapy. Her cancer found her weakened and vulnerable, perhaps because she had a nightmare childhood: though she was never beaten, her mother hated and envied her, and drove her father mad. Oh when he raped her as a child, they called it punishment, she craved it as attention. The woman is nearly skeletal, will soon die. She lives in U3L of the state mental hospital, crazy for years (she thinks she murdered someone, but was it her father? her brother? or some dim BOOMY-OOM dream of her mother?) and crazier now with pain. They give her marijuana for the pain. Her eyes are sunken, the sockets of her eyes are black and bruised. And if you were to meet those eyes, what would you offer them? The Problem of Evil? What do you think is in her mind? Has she gone crazy enough and stoned enough to hear my voice? Does she hear time, boomy-oom dream-a-leem time? Oh will you sing for her that old favorite, the Problem of Evil?

3i. God died that we may live. That We may live. She blew Herself to fragments, fractions, dreams, sing ramalam. Without death, there is no Other. Without the Other, there is no marriage. Without marriage—

3 . There is a real woman who has dark hair now, who was a lovely little red-haired girl, who spent seven years in therapy going sane, whose father died of stroke when she was seventeen, whose father never raped her, though she had dreams he did, whose mother hated her but never put a spider in a jar, though *someone's* mother did: this is a woman who never had a child, who had a tumor and not a child, whose hair went gray, who lost the color of her hair the day she lost her womb, whose hair went gray when she was twenty-one: this is a woman who never missed a vote, except when she was twenty-one: this is a woman who plays piano, won a contest, lost her hair, brings you the news, who holds a dying child upon her lap and does not cry for cameras: This is a woman you ought to marry, Joe.

4i. God doesn't exist, is being born, take your choice. Out of our choosing, we create a hope. Out of our suffering, we justify Her birth. We are the crucified, who die that She may rise.

4 . There is a merry gray-head, a woman with a face as small and delicate as a heart, a face set chin-first into air, a fox's face, and yet the face of a hawk, an Indian: this is a healthy fuckable woman radiating always smile, whose laughter is a startling pour, first jump of water out of a country pump, a run on any pianoforte: softstrong, alert. This is the bride of—Christ, some lucky jerk or other, I don't know, whose childhood never mind, but who loves her children: this is a woman growing old around the edges, growing old around the ages, but happy of it who has ageless eyes.

And now, my brethren of the mist, children of the lost tribes, gatherers by the river, my fellow ghosts in the morning mist and silence of the river, we must leave. We must leave this gray place not even humming. This peaceful place. It is time for time once more, time for the joke of being. The world begin with a pun: *Nothing mattered.*

Rise with me, like the first bubble of space-time in the Boomaloom first moment, rise like a bubble in black baptismal water, break free, assume the air. Assume the posture of the tall Christ behind the baptistery, brooding over the black and lapping waters.

Hesitant on the bottom step, a sock-foot girl, a ball-head girl. For her, the biggest, blackest, and most endless water. The focus, nexus, most important moment, the dividing plane: Jesus loves the little, ah even if no one else, the tall Christ loves.

Even if you are bad?

Out in the water, in the very center of the water, waiting, the hairy reverend, reverberant and soaked: the looming reverend, William Bobo, who has dipped himself a couple of rabbits already, Juney Lash Larooney and frail elderly sinner J. S., and who seems to exist in a wave of sound, an echo-chamber reflex from the walls of the inset baptistery, a rolling rumble that does not die out between manhandlings, a continual unfailing boom of annunciation: IN THE NAME OF THE FATHER, AND THE SON, AND THE HOLY GHOST . . .

The buckle-strap white shoes, the gloves across them, safe and empty in a corner of the waiting room, waiting for the immortal child's return . . .

Skinny Hardrock clambering dripping up the opposite steps, white shirt clinging to bony chest, shivering, two old ladies sisters crying happily reaching palsied out to help him up . . .

A ripple of laughter out there where she cannot look, where everyone is watching that she cannot think of now, a quiet spread of laughter under the echo in her inward ear . . .

The water is terribly dark and cold, she feels it sock-foot wet lapping the bottom step, but it isn't that. She knew that, she knew there was a frightening time before you got to Jesus. It is that there are things here she cannot comprehend, there are the complications of the act. It should be pure, a simple gesture, her and Christ and the water, but it isn't:

Lodged in the water, the soaked reflected upper half of Brother Bobo, loud and burly, the twisted image of the lower legs. Brother Bobo, late apostle of Johnny Vaught, Brother Bill Bobo, evangelist and pro wrassler when the redhead is a full-grown woman—should he be there? What has he to do with her? How has he come to moderate her soul?

Her rumbling belly, begging the toilet now. Sooner than heaven. This very instant.

And though she cannot spare a sidelong look, now or then, to see the tittering crowd, she is visited by an image, she has a sudden awareness how she looks: *sock-foot, small, and scared, in her white dress, pink rubber bathing cap pulled tight*

to save her hair for television.

You can understand, Josephine, how she might want to stop and think it out? Faced with such a complex, and all at once, not strung out as I must string along with you, how she might wish to stop, consider, and compose herself? Finding her hope's direction given so ludicrous and fac-tual a twist, herself in her own inward eyes a dwarf, a small slick-headed clown, how she might want to hesitate?

Fat chance. Momma come down the step, prod of knuckle in the spine, you fall in a ramalam of outright laughter to the

SHOCK of cold and grab

and wrenched in a FATHER AND SON drowning pull of weightless AND HOLY GHOST she farted

bubbles in the water

— force

away her chance for heaven: stood whole and dripping on the opposite shore, the reverend in one clean and jerk lifting her out of the angry waves, standing her like a toy, a little doll. Oh there are things to consider here, things ten years of talk with Therapon could never touch: how she could wonder all her life if she was really a pretty girl, pretty enough for tv, pretty enough to win, how she could always feel a funny shriveled failure, an ugly little shave-head doll. But you are on a tight schedule, aren't you? We're talking time in a bottle, Jim.

Which is why it's time

Which is why it's time

to jump

to the studio rest room where we hurried down wrapped in a big towel wet. Now naked. Pimple-skin cold and damp white and shameful naked changing to the blue dress I hate my daddy being here. For even at this age, you know, you on some level sense he has no business being in here, that it is invasion and he knows it: Down where he knows how much he wants to die, he knows it, if nowhere else. You screwed it up, shamed him, made of his ludicrous family a public comedy again. There's just the three of you, Daddy, de momma, and you, and the son they never had, the fourth who walks always beside you: someone has screwed it up, and we think we know who it is. But Momma, oddly, not too mad, abstract and distant, having heard a chorus of how cute you were so scared, deciding to accept that version. But not protecting your skinny shamefulness from Dad, oh no. Who only stays to radiate his anger, who never even looks, though you don't look to see if he looks. Momma prodding to hurry

to the studio. Where the grinning cameraman. Your eyes go to to make you grin. Of all the faces, instantly you find the one who likes you.

Fat, sloppy, greasy shirt out over his butt, a shirt as if he'd changed the engine in his car that very morning. A pained, hung-over, genuine grin of pleasure. To which you lean, and shake your big red hair, like a dog shaking the water loose, the water that never touched it, never a single curl, and look back up and grin: See how silly I am? To which he leans his balding head and shakes his jowls, blub-bub-bubba, I'm silly too, I like you.

A hand in the back is pushing us along. And Daddy making nice to Tommy, older man to younger, routeman to his president. Who had a chance, Daddy, to be the hero of your mornings, a misty dawnlight presence, tall and shadowy: but now not never no, seeing you naked and hearing him belly up to Tommy, that any eight-year-old can tell's a mean and stupid man, a fool to drive his wife away and fuck the receptionist, disown his kids, and leave for Paraguay someday with half the funds.

A hand in the back, and we are in the light. The light where we invent the universe. Mother and father gone, exiled beyond the play-pretend, the magic kitchen. A checkered curtain at the window with a light on the stand behind it, to make the curtains glow. The magic window, empty. They always let you climb to look through afterward, because a window invents a thing to see, a fairy land forlorn, a realm of Otherwise.

They help you to the stool, the funny fat man squinting down with his one big camera eye, the man beside him putting his hand in air. He needs to go to the bathroom, let's make believe, and giggle. They give you a tall blonde mother, a young and beautiful brand-new mother: although she doesn't see you, is such an empty-head she has to concentrate to smile, although she dare not think until the spot is over, although to her you are a sort of wooden doll perched on a kitchen stool. It doesn't matter although, it doesn't count, for this is all made up, and she makes a fine imaginary mother, elegant in her checkered apron.

And now we split you in two with an ax, we splatter blood all over you.

For this is in black and white.

When I say his name, you will awaken.

Your hair is going to hell.

You won't remember any of this.

Your body is saved, but your hair is trapped in time, your hair is gone forever, your womb is gone: hahaha, your back is broken, your hair is going to hell, you'll never have a little girl, never let the little girl in you

hold up your glass

be free: she pours, tall momma down, the chocolate carton blood of jesus RED—

For this is all old time, this is all in black and white. This is an old story long since ended. This is a story that has been written. It is a true story. It is a story we cannot change.

You started, terrified, and made your stool fall over. The blonde actress, doing her first live shoot, was so astonished she stood there pouring splattering milk all over you, all over the floor. The bright red chocolate milk, dyed red to show up chocolate in black and white, as chocolate itself, true chocolate, would not. No one had thought to warn us. No one had realized we wouldn't know.

We may surmise, around the perimeter, several simultaneous events: Tommy whacking his knees with laughter, enjoying the joke more than he minds the ruined commercial; your father in apoplectic silence; your mother cursing: *Damn you, damn you, damn you, you should have been a boy.* You did not see or hear these things, not on a level that even the deepest dream or trance has yet to touch. You were all one howl of pain and fear, wet and splattered in your own wreckage. You were the only sound in your own ears, crying at last. You fight so hard to stop your tears, my love, because they always made it worse: *Stop crying, you stupid little animal. It's your fault, you did it, you did it, stop your crying, you stupid little ugly-head.*

I can't, I can't, I'm going to hell, blood all over me, comes out where I pee.

You will awaken, and not remember. But this time, when you waken, you will feel at peace. You will feel a strange and curious lassitude, an ease, a restfulness:

Because, Lianne, Charles, we have a thing to give you before you go. Just one last little thing, a goodbye gift. Perhaps a made-up thing, a dream, a play-pretend, but where is it written?

The thing is this:

Say de mon, "You must be crazy, lady-o."

He'd had a fight with his wife last night himself, coming in late and drunk, and oh it was a nasty fight, he was no saint, but he knew better than *this*.

The others have switched to film, of course, this isn't live. He leaves his camera, goes over to the mess: "Hey, honey." Quiet and easy, lifting her sitting. "Hey, hey, honey. Hey, look. Hey, it's ok. Hey, look at me." Grinning and squatting in the milk. Splatting with his hand. "Hey, look-ahere." Rubbing it into the little hair on his baldy head. Her crying stops. Gets up and takes the carton from the blonde. Squats face-to-face again. "Boy howdy, lookahere, a big mud puddle." No one moving, he's just a cameraman, he's got no business doing what he's doing, but no one moving now. He pours the red milk on his own head. Whoops with laughter. See how silly I am? "Milky milky." Pours it on her head. There's just the two of them. All she can see is this one friendly face. She laughs, high sweet carillon. He pats her milky head, her sodden, baptized hair. He rubs it in, gives her a knuckle-nuzz. "You're a good kid," he says.

And that's it for him. He's out of here, he's history—the way you like to say it now, so cute and trendy. We like to think he matters, We like to think there's something just a little timeless there, the unexpected clown, buffoon, the fat man red with love, cartoon stick in the jaws of the ticking crocodile, the ruin of a slick and cruel icon, busted perfection, the grease spot as stained-glass window: We like to think that there's something funny going on, a joke that could let us exist someday, a way to die, be born, grow up, and marry You. We like to think so, but what do we count? We're outta here, we're history. Nice talking to you, kid. I'm gonna miss you when you're gone, you rascal you. You will awaken when I say the word. *I love you, baby, I really do.* When you awaken, you will trust the light, sing Hallelujah! sing

Ramalam:
Ramalam:
Ramalam . . .

GOING NATIVE

Stephen Wright

Wylie Jones lived the American Dream. For him it was no mythical aspiration, no blue-collar fantasy, but a hard-earned reality, and he had all the right accessories to prove he'd made it – the perfect wife, the adorable kids, the comfortable home nestling in a comfortable suburb. It was, in fact, a comfortable life.

So now watch and wonder as comfortable Wylie turns his back on his dream and begins to live the American Nightmare. One evening he steals a neighbour's car, and drives away into the dark heart of modern America, heading west towards his nemesis.

It is a journey down the highway of the contemporary soul, populated by characters as rich and diverse as the ills of a great and twisted nation. Psychotic hitch-hikers, lesbian marriage merchants, mercurial pornographers – all are here, with Wylie glimpsed intermittently on the shady borders of their lives.

'A slasher classic with high-intensity heat and light'
Don DeLillo

'An astonishing novel'
Toni Morrison

'A chilling and often brilliant novel . . . An alarming picture of a country pitched on the edge of an emotional and social abyss'
New York Times

'Dazzling, eerie . . . an unsettling look at why serial killers have achieved mythic resonance in this entertainment-besotted culture'
Esquire

THE ICE STORM

Rick Moody

'A moving portrait of a nuclear family breakdown. A remarkable, brave and beautiful book.'
Jeffrey Eugenides

It's a holiday weekend in 1973 in a New England suburb called New Canaan. Richard Nixon's secretary, Rose Mary Woods, has just erased $18\frac{1}{2}$ minutes of a subpoenaed conversation. The American troops are on their way out of Vietnam. The Beatles are recording solo albums. Pet Rocks are soon going to be invented. And the Hood family – Benjamin, his wife Elena, and their two teenagers, Paul and Wendy, are looking for ways to spend a Friday evening as far from one another as they can get. Paul is in New York City, hoping desperately to consummate a new crush; Wendy is sneaking around the neighbours' house, looking for a way to spend the night with her beau. Benjamin and Elena are on their way to a party they're going to wish they had skipped.

Then the weather takes a dangerous turn.

The Ice Storm is a family romance by turns acerbic, funny and lacerating, about a period when all of Western culture seemed to be having a second childhood, when the music was atrocious, the psychology was not of this world, when everybody had shag rugs, and when family values were already back to basics. In this arresting new novel, Rick Moody reintroduces the seventies both to those who were lucky enough to have missed them the first time and to those for whom the excesses of the period are still like fresh wounds. It's an astonishing and delightful accomplishment.

☐ Going Native	Stephen Wright	£8.99
☐ The Ice Storm	Rick Moody	£8.99
☐ Theory of War	Joan Brady	£6.99

Abacus now offers an exciting range of quality titles by both established and new authors. All of the books in this series are available from:

Little, Brown and Company (UK),
P.O. Box 11,
Falmouth,
Cornwall TR10 9EN.

Alternatively you may fax your order to the above address.
Fax No. 0326 376423.

Payments can be made as follows: cheque, postal order (payable to Little, Brown and Company) or by credit cards, Visa/Access. Do not send cash or currency. UK customers and B.F.P.O. please allow £1.00 for postage and packing for the first book, plus 50p for the second book, plus 30p for each additional book up to a maximum charge of £3.00 (7 books plus).

Overseas customers including Ireland, please allow £2.00 for the first book plus £1.00 for the second book, plus 50p for each additional book.

NAME (Block Letters) ....

....

ADDRESS ....

....

....

☐ I enclose my remittance for _____

☐ I wish to pay by Access/Visa Card

Number ☐☐☐☐☐☐☐☐☐☐☐☐☐☐☐☐

Card Expiry Date ☐☐☐☐